D1095035

THE HARVARD CLASSICS

Registered Edition

◈

Don Quixote and Sancho Panza
From the painting by Gustave Doré

THE HARVARD CLASSICS
EDITED BY CHARLES W. ELIOT, LL.D.

The First Part of
the Delightful History of the
Most Ingenious Knight

Don Quixote of the Mancha

By Miguel de Cervantes

TRANSLATED BY THOMAS SHELTON

W*ith* I*ntroductions and* N*otes*

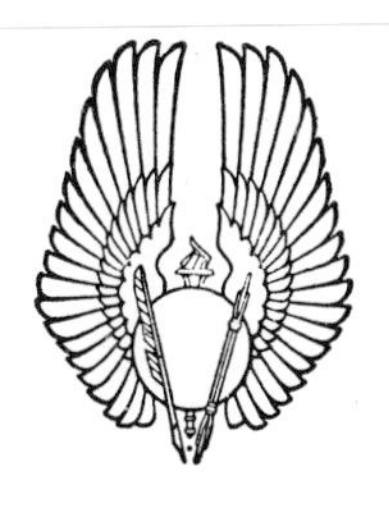

P. F. Collier & Son Corporation
NEW YORK

62nd Printing, 1969

Manufactured in U. S. A.

CONTENTS

THE FOURTH BOOK

INTRODUCTORY NOTE

Miguel de Cervantes Saavedra was born at Alcalá de Hènares in Spain in 1547, of a noble Castilian family. Nothing is certainly known of his education, but by the age of twenty-three we find him serving in the army as a private soldier. He was maimed for life at the battle of Lepanto, shared in a number of other engagements, and was taken captive by the Moors on his way home in 1575. After five years of slavery he was ransomed; and two or three years later he returned to Spain, and betook himself to the profession of letters. From youth he had practised the writing of verse, and now he turned to the production of plays; but, failing of financial success, he obtained an employment in the Government offices, which he held till 1597, when he was imprisoned for a shortage in his accounts due to the dishonesty of an associate. The imprisonment on this occasion lasted only till the end of the year, and, after a period of obscurity, he issued, in 1605, his masterpiece, "Don Quixote." Its success was great and immediate, and its reputation soon spread beyond Spain. Translations of parts into French appeared; and in 1611 Thomas Shelton, an Englishman otherwise unknown, put forth the present version, in style and vitality, if not in accuracy, acknowledged the most fortunate of English renderings.

The present volume contains the whole of the first part of the novel, which is complete in itself. The second part, issued in 1615, the year before his death, is of the nature of a sequel, and is generally regarded as inferior.

In writing his great novel, Cervantes set out to parody the romances of chivalry, the chief of which will be found in the description of Don Quixote's library in the sixth chapter of the first book. But, as in the somewhat parallel case of Fielding and "Joseph Andrews," the hero got the better of his creator's purpose, and the work passed far beyond the limits of a mere burlesque. Yet the original purpose was accomplished. The literature of Knight Errantry, which Church and State had sought without success to check, was crushed by Cervantes with this single blow.

But the importance of this greatest of novels is not merely, or mainly, that it put an end to an extravagant and outworn form of fiction. Loose in structure and uneven in workmanship, it remains unsurpassed as a masterpiece of droll humor, as a picture of Spanish life, as a gallery of immortal portraits. It has in the highest degree the mark of all great art, the successful combination of the particular and the universal: it is true to the life of the country and age of its production, and true also to general human nature everywhere and always. With reference to the fiction of the Middle Ages, it is a triumphant satire; with reference to modern novels, it is the first and the most widely enjoyed. In its author's words: "It is so conspicuous and void of difficulty that children may handle him, youths may read him, men may understand him, and old men may celebrate him."

THE AUTHOR'S PREFACE TO THE READER

THOU mayst believe me, gentle reader, without swearing, that I could willingly desire this book (as a child of my understanding) to be the most beautiful, gallant, and discreet that might possibly be imagined; but I could not transgress the order of nature, wherein everything begets his like, which being so, what could my sterile and ill-tilled wit engender but the history of a dry-toasted and humorous son, full of various thoughts and conceits never before imagined of any other; much like one who was engendered within some noisome prison, where all discommodities have taken possession, and all doleful noises made their habitation, seeing that rest, pleasant places, amenity of the fields, the cheerfulness of clear sky, the murmuring noise of the crystal fountains, and the quiet repose of the spirit are great helps for the most barren Muses to show themselves fruitful, and to bring into the world such births as may enrich it with admiration and delight? It ofttimes befalls that a father hath a child both by birth evil-favoured and quite devoid of all perfection, and yet the love that he bears him is such as it casts a mask over his eyes, which hinders his discerning of the faults and simplicities thereof, and makes him rather deem them discretions and beauty, and so tells them to his friends for witty jests and conceits. But I, though in show a father, yet in truth but a step-father to Don Quixote, will not be borne away by the violent current of the modern custom nowadays, and therefore entreat thee, with the tears almost in mine eyes, as many others are wont to do, most dear reader, to pardon and dissemble the faults which thou shalt discern in this my son; for thou art neither his kinsman nor friend, and thou hast thy soul in thy body, and thy free-will therein as absolute as the best, and thou art in thine own house, wherein thou art as absolute a lord as the king is of his subsidies, and thou knowest well the common proverb, that 'under my cloak a fig for the king,' all which doth exempt thee and makes thee free from all respect and obligation; and so thou mayst boldly say of this history whatsoever thou shalt think good, without fear either to be controlled for the evil or rewarded for the good that thou shalt speak thereof

I would very fain have presented it unto thee pure and naked, without the ornament of a preface, or the rabblement and catalogue of the wonted sonnets, epigrams, poems, elegies, etc., which are wont to be put at the beginning of books. For I dare say unto thee that, although it cost me some pains to compose it, yet in no respect did it equalise that which I took to make this preface which thou dost now read. I took, oftentimes, my pen in my hand to write it, and as often set it down again, as not knowing what I should write; and being once in a muse, with my paper before me, my pen in mine ear, mine elbow on the table, and mine hand on my cheek, imagining what I might write, there entered a friend of mine unexpectedly, who was a very discreet and pleasantly-witted man, who, seeing me so pensative, demanded of me the reason of my musing; and, not concealing it from him, said that I bethought myself on my preface I was to make to Don Quixote's history, which did so much trouble me as I neither meant to make any at all, nor publish the history of the acts of so noble a knight. 'For how can I choose,' quoth I, 'but be much confounded at that which the old legislator (the vulgar) will say, when it sees that, after the end of so many years as are spent since I first slept in the bosom of oblivion, I come out loaden with my grey hairs, and bring with me a book as dry as a kex, void of invention, barren of good phrase, poor of conceits, and altogether empty both of learning and eloquence; without quotations on the margents, or annotations in the end of the book, wherewith I see other books are still adorned, be they never so idle, fabulous, and profane; so full of sentences of Aristotle and Plato, and the other crew of the philosophers, as admires the readers, and makes them believe that these authors are very learned and eloquent? And after, when they cite Plutarch or Cicero, what can they say, but that they are the sayings of St. Thomas, or other doctors of the Church; observing herein so ingenious a method as in one line they will paint you an enamoured gull, and in the other will lay you down a little seeming devout sermon, so that it is a great pleasure and delight to read or hear it? All which things must be wanting in my book, for neither have I anything to cite on the margent, or note in the end, and much less do I know what authors I follow, to put them at the beginning, as the custom is, by the letter of the A B C, beginning with Aristotle, and ending in Xenophon, or in Zoilus or Zeuxis, although the one was a railer and the other a painter. So likewise shall my book want sonnets at the beginning, at least such sonnets whose authors be dukes, marquises, earls, bishops, ladies, or famous poets; although, if I would demand them of two or three artificers of mine acquaintance, I know they would make me some such as those of the most renowned in Spain would in no wise be able to equal or compare with them.

'Finally, good sir, and my very dear friend,' quoth I, 'I do resolve that Sir Don Quixote remain entombed among the old records of the Mancha, until Heaven ordain some one to adorn him with the many graces that are yet wanting; for I find myself wholly unable to remedy them, through mine insufficiency and little learning, and also because I am naturally lazy and unwilling to go searching for authors to say that which I can say well enough without them. And hence proceeded the perplexity and ecstasy wherein you found me plunged.'

My friend hearing that, and striking himself on the forehead, after a long and loud laughter, said: 'In good faith, friend, I have now at last delivered myself of a long and intricate error, wherewith I was possessed all the time of our acquaintance; for hitherto I accounted thee ever to be discreet and prudent in all thy actions, but now I see plainly that thou art as far from that I took thee to be as heaven is from the earth. How is it possible that things of so small moment, and so easy to be redressed, can have force to suspend and swallow up so ripe a wit as yours hath seemed to be, and so fitted to break up and trample over the greatest difficulties that can be propounded? This proceeds not, in good sooth, from defect of will, but from superfluity of sloth and penury of discourse. Wilt thou see whether that I say be true or no? Listen, then, attentively awhile, and thou shalt perceive how, in the twinkling of an eye, I will confound all the difficulties and supply all the wants which do suspend and affright thee from publishing to the world the history of thy famous Don Quixote, the light and mirror of all knighthood-errant.'

'Say, I pray thee,' quoth I, hearing what he had said, 'after what manner dost thou think to replenish the vacuity of my fear, and reduce the chaos of my confusion to any clearness and light?'

And he replied: 'The first thing whereat thou stoppedst—of sonnets, epigrams, eclogues, etc., (which are wanting for the beginning, and ought to be written by grave and noble persons)—may be remedied, if thou thyself wilt but take a little pains to compass them, and thou mayst after name them as thou pleasest, and father them on Prester John of the Indians or the Emperor of Trapisonde, whom, I know, were held to be famous poets; and suppose they were not, but that some pedants and presumptuous fellows would backbite thee, and murmur against this truth, thou needest not weigh them two straws; for, although they could prove it to be an untruth, yet cannot they cut off thy hand for it.

'As touching citations in the margent, and authors out of whom thou mayst collect sentences and sayings to insert in thy history, there is nothing else to be done but to bob into it some Latin sentences that thou knowest already by rote, or mayst get easily with a little labour; as, for example, when thou treatest of liberty and thraldom, thou mayst cite that, "Non bene pro toto libertas venditur auro"; and presently quote Horace, or he whosoever else that said it, on the margent. If thou shouldest speak of the power of death, have presently recourse to that of "Pallida mors aequo pulsat pede pauperum tabernas, regumque turres." If of the instability of friends, thou hast at hand Cato freely offering his distichon, "Donec eris foelix multos numerabis amicos; Tempora si fuerint nubila, solus eris." If of riches, "Quantum quisque sua nummorum servat in arca, tantum habet et fidei." If of love, "Hei mihi quod nullis amor est medicabilis herbis!" And so, with these Latin authorities and other suchlike, they will at least account thee a good grammarian, and the being of such an one is of no little honour and profit in this our age. As touching the addition of annotations in the end of thy book, thou mayst boldly observe this course: If thou namest any giant in thy book, procure that it be the Giant Goliah; and with this alone (which almost will cost thee nothing), thou hast gotten a fair annotation; for thou mayst say, "The Giant Golias or Goliat was a Philistine, whom the shepherd David slew with the blow of a stone in the Vale of Terebintho, as is recounted in the Book of Kings, in the chapter wherein thou shalt find it written."

'After all this, to show that thou art learned in human letters, and a cosmographer, take some occasion to make mention of the River Tagus, and thou shalt presently find thyself stored with another notable notation, saying, "The River Tagus was so called of a King of Spain; it takes its beginning from such a place, and dies in the ocean seas, kissing first the walls of the famous City of Lisbon, and some are of opinion that the sands thereof are of gold, etc." If thou wilt treat of thieves, I will recite the history of Cacus to thee, for I know it by memory; if of whores or courtezans, there thou hast the Bishop of Mondonnedo, who will lend thee Lamia, Layda, and Flora, whose annotation will gain thee no small credit; if of cruel persons, Ovid will tender Medea; if of enchanters or witches, Homer hath Calypso, and Virgil Circe; if of valorous captains, Julius Cæsar shall lend himself in his Commentaries to thee, and Plutarch shall give thee a thousand Alexanders. If thou dost treat of love, and hast but two ounces of the Tuscan language, thou shalt encounter with Lion the Hebrew, who will replenish thy vessels with store in that kind; but, if thou wilt not travel for it into strange countries, thou hast here at home in thy house *Fonseca of the Love of God,* wherein is deciphered all that either thou or the most ingenious capacity can desire to learn of that subject. In conclusion, there is nothing else to be done, but that thou only endeavour to name those names, or to touch those histories, in thine own, which I have here related, and leave the adding of annotations and citations unto me; for I do promise thee that I will both fill up the margent, and also spend four or five sheets of advantage at the end of the book.

'Now let us come to the citation of authors, which other books have, and thine wanteth; the remedy hereof is very easy; for thou needst do nought else but seek out a book that doth quote them all from the letter A until Z, as thou saidst thyself but even now, and thou shalt set that very same alphabet to thine own book; for, although the little necessity that thou hadst to use their assistance in thy work will presently convict thee of falsehood, it makes no matter, and perhaps there may not a few be found so simple as to believe that thou hast holp thyself in the narration of thy most simple and sincere history with all their authorities. And, though that large catalogue of authors do serve to none other purpose, yet will it, at least, give some authority to the book, at the first blush; and the rather, because none will be so mad as to stand to examine whether thou dost follow them or no, seeing they can gain nothing by the matter. Yet, if I do not err in the consideration of so weighty an affair, this book of thine needs none of all these things, forasmuch as it is only an invective against books of knighthood, a subject whereof Aristotle never dreamed, St. Basil said nothing, Cicero never heard any word; nor do the punctualities of truth, nor observations of astrology, fall within the sphere of such fabulous jestings; nor do geometrical dimensions impart it anything, nor the confutation of arguments usurped by rhetoric; nor ought it to preach unto any the mixture of holy matters with profane (a motley wherewith no Christian well should be attired), only it hath need to help itself with imitation; for, by how much the more it shall excel therein, by so much the more will the work be esteemed. And, since that thy labour doth aim at no more than to diminish the authority and acceptance that books of chivalry have in the world, and among the vulgar, there is no reason why thou shouldest go begging of sentences from philosophers, fables from poets, orations from rhetoricians, or miracles from the saints, but only endeavour to deliver with significant, plain, honest, and well-ordered words, thy jovial and cheerful discourse, expressing as near as thou mayst possibly thy intention, making thy conceits clear, and not intricate or dark; and labour also that the melancholy man, by the reading thereof, may be urged to laughter, the pleasant disposition increased, the simple not cloyed; and that the judicious may admire thy invention, the grave not despise it, the prudent applaud it. In conclusion, let thy project be to overthrow the ill-compiled *machina* and bulk of those knightly books, abhorred by many, but applauded by more; for, if thou bring this to pass, thou hast not achieved a small matter.'

I listened with very great attention to my friend's speech; and his reasons are so firmly imprinted in my mind, as, without making any reply unto them, I approved them all for good, and framed my preface of them, wherein, sweet reader, thou mayst perceive my friend's discretion, my happiness to meet with so good a counsellor at such a pinch, and thine own ease in finding so plainly and sincerely related *The History of the famous Don Quixote of the Mancha,* of whom it is the common opinion of all the inhabitants bordering on the field of Montiel that he was the most chaste, enamoured, and valiant knight that hath been seen, read, or heard of these many ages. I will not endear the benefit and service I have done thee, by making thee acquainted with so noble and honourable a knight, but only do desire that thou gratify me for the notice of the famous Sancho Panza, his squire, in whom, in mine opinion, are deciphered all the squire-like graces dispersed throughout the vain rout of knightly books. And herewithal, I bid thee farewell, and do not forget me.

Vale.

CERTAIN SONNETS

WRITTEN BY KNIGHTS-ERRANT, LADIES, SQUIRES, AND HORSES, IN THE PRAISE OF DON QUIXOTE, HIS DAME, HIS SQUIRE AND STEED

Amadis of Gaule, in Praise of Don Quixote.

Thou that my doleful life didst imitate,
When, absent and disdained, it befell,
Devoid of joy, I a repentant state
Did lead, and on the Poor Rock's top did dwell;
Thou, that the streams so often from thine eyes
Didst suck of scalding tears' disgustful brine;
And, without pewter, copper, plate likewise,
Wast on the bare earth oft constrain'd to dine,—
Live of one thing secure eternally,
That whilst bright Phoebus shall his horses spur
Through the fourth sphere's dilated monarchy,
Thy name shall be renowned, near and fur;
And as, 'mongst countries, thine is best alone,
So shall thine author peers on earth have none.

Don Belianis of Greece to Don Quixote of the Mancha.

I tore, I hackt, abolish'd, said and did,
More than knight-errant else on earth hath done:
I, dexterous, valiant, and so stout beside,
Have thousand wrongs reveng'd, millions undone.
I have done acts that my fame eternise,
In love I courteous and so peerless was:
Giants, as if but dwarfs, I did despise;
And yet no time of love-plaints I let pass.
I have held fortune prostrate at my feet,
And by my wit seiz'd on Occasion's top,
Whose wandering steps I led where I thought meet;
And though beyond the moon my soaring hope
Did crown my hap with all felicity,
Yet, great Quixote, do I still envy thee.

The Knight of the Sun, Alphebo, to Don Quixote.

My sword could not at all compare with thine,
Spanish Alphebo! full of courtesy;
Nor thine arm's valour can be match'd by mine,
Though I was fear'd where days both spring and die.
Empires I scorn'd, and the vast monarchy
Of th' Orient ruddy (offer'd me in vain),
I left, that I the sovereign face might see
Of my Aurora, fair Claridiane,
Whom, as by miracle, I surely lov'd:
So banish'd by disgrace, even very hell
Quak'd at mine arm, that did his fury tame.
But thou, illustrious Goth, Quixote! hast prov'd
Thy valour, for Dulcinea's sake, so well
As both on earth have gain'd eternal fame.

Orlando Furioso, Peer of France, to Don Quixote of the Mancha.

Though thou art not a peer, thou hast no peer,
Who mightst among ten thousand peers be one;
Nor shalt thou never any peer have here,
Who, ever-conquering, vanquish'd was of none.
Quixote, I'm Orlando! that, cast away
For fair Angelica, cross'd remotest seas,
And did such trophies on Fame's altar lay
As pass oblivion's reach many degrees.
Nor can I be thy peer; for peerlessness
Is to thy prowess due and great renown,
Although I lost, as well as thou, my wit;
Yet mine thou may'st be, if thy good success
Make thee the proud Moor tame, [achieve] that crown,
Us equals in disgrace and loving fit.

Solis Dan to Don Quixote of the Mancha.

Maugre the ravings that are set abroach,
And rumble up and down thy troubled brain,
Yet none thine acts, Don Quixote, can reproach,
Or thy proceedings tax as vile or vain.
Thy feats shall be thy fairest ornament
(Seeing wrongs t'undo thou goest thus about),
Although with blows a thousand time y-shent
Thou wert well-nigh, yea, even by the miscreant rout.
And if thy fair Dulcinea shall wrong
By misregard thy fairer expectation,

And to thy cares will lend no listening ear,
Then let this comfort all thy woes outwear,—
That Sancho fail'd in broker's occupation:
He, foolish; cruel, she; thou, without tongue.

The Princess Oriana of Great Britain to Lady Dulcinea del Toboso.

Happy those which, for more commodity
And ease, Dulcinea fair! could bring to pass
That Greenwich, where Toboso is, might be,
And London chang'd where thy knight's village was.
Happy she that might body and soul adorn
With thy rich livery and thy high desire;
And see thy happy knight, by honour borne,
In cruel combat, broaching out his ire.
But happiest she that might so cleanly 'scape
From Amadis as thou hast whilom done
From thy well-manner'd knight, courteous Quixote!
O! were I she, I'd envy no one's hap,
And had been merry when I most did moan,
And ta'en my pleasure without paying shot.

Gandaline, Amadis of Gaule's Squire, to Sancho Panza, Don Quixote's Squire.

Hail, famous man! whom fortune hath so blist,
When first, in squire-like trade, it thee did place,
As thou didst soft and sweetly pass disgrace
Ere thou thereof the threatening danger wist.
The shovel or sickle little do resist
The wandering exercise; for now's in grace
Plain squire-like dealing, which doth quite deface
His pride that would the Moor bore with his fist.
Thine ass I jointly envy, and thy name,
And eke thy wallet I do emulate,
An argument of thy great providence.
Hail once again! who, 'cause so good a man,
Thy worths our Spanish Ovid does relate,
And lovely chants them with all reverence.

A Dialogue between Babieca, Horse to the Cid, a Famous Conqueror of Spain; and Rozinante, Don Quixote's Courser.

Ba. How haps it, Rozinante, thou art so lean?
Ro. Because I travel still. and never eat:

Ba. Thy want of barley and straw, what does it mean?
Ro. That of my lord, a bit I cannot get.
Ba. Away, sir jade! you are ill-mannered,
Whose ass's tongue your lord does thus abase.
Ro. If you did see how he's enamoured,
You would conclude that he's the greater ass.
Ba. Is love a folly?—*Ro.* Sure it is no wit.
Ba. Thou art a metaphysician.—*Ro.* For want of meat.
Ba. Complain upon the squire.—*Ro.* What profits it?
Or how shall I my woful plaints repeat?
Since, though the world imputes slowness to me,
Yet greater jades my lord and Sancho be.

THE DELIGHTFUL HISTORY

OF THE MOST INGENIOUS KNIGHT

DON QUIXOTE OF THE MANCHA

THE FIRST PART

THE FIRST BOOK

CHAPTER I

Wherein Is Rehearsed the Calling and Exercise of the Renowned Gentleman, Don Quixote of the Mancha

THERE lived not long since, in a certain village of the Mancha, the name whereof I purposely omit, a gentleman of their calling that use to pile up in their halls old lances, halberds, morions, and such other armours and weapons. He was, besides, master of an ancient target, a lean stallion, and a swift greyhound. His pot consisted daily of somewhat more beef than mutton: a gallimaufry each night, collops and eggs on Saturdays, lentils on Fridays, and now and then a lean pigeon on Sundays, did consume three parts of his rents; the rest and remnant thereof was spent on a jerkin of fine puce, a pair of velvet hose, with pantofles of the same for the holy-days, and one suit of the finest vesture; for therewithal he honoured and set out his person on the workdays. He had in his house a woman-servant of about forty years old, and a niece not yet twenty, and a man that served him both in field and at home, and could saddle his horse, and likewise manage a pruning-hook. The master himself was about fifty years old, of a strong complexion, dry flesh, and a withered face. He was an early riser, and a great friend of hunting. Some affirm that his surname was Quixada, or Quesada (for in this there is some variance among the authors that write his life), although it may be gathered, by very probable conjectures, that he was called Quixana. Yet all this concerns our historical relation but little: let it then suffice, that in the narration thereof we will not vary a jot from the truth.

You shall therefore wit, that this gentleman above named, the spurts that he was idle (which was the longer part of the year), did apply himself wholly to the reading of books of knighthood, and that with such gusts and delights, as he almost wholly neglected the exercise of hunting; yea, and the very administration of his household affairs. And his curiosity and folly came to that pass, that he made away many acres of arable land to buy him books of that kind, and therefore he brought to his house as many as ever he could get of that subject. And among them all, none pleased him better than those which famous Felician of Silva composed. For the smoothness of his prose, with now and then some intricate sentence meddled, seemed to him peerless; and principally when he did read the courtings, or letters of challenge, that knights sent to ladies, or one to another; where, in many places, he found written: 'The reason of the unreasonableness which against my reason is wrought, doth so weaken my reason, as with all reason I do justly complain on your beauty.' And also when he read: 'The high heavens, which with your divinity do fortify you divinely with the stars, and make you deserveress of the deserts which your greatness deserves,' etc. With these and other such passages the poor gentleman grew distracted, and was breaking his brains day and night, to understand and unbowel their sense, an endless labour; for even Aristotle himself would not understand them, though he were again resuscitated only for that purpose. He did not like so much the unproportionate blows that Don Belianis gave and took in fight; for, as he imagined, were the surgeons never so cunning that cured them, yet was it impossible but that the patient his face and all his body must remain full of scars and tokens. Yet did he praise, notwithstanding, in the author of that history, the conclusion of his book, with the promise of the Endless Adventure; and many times he himself had a desire to take pen and finish it exactly, as it is there promised; and would doubtless have performed it, and that certes with happy success, if other more urgent and continual thoughts had not disturbed him.

Many times did he fall at variance with the curate of his village (who was a learned man, graduated in Ciguenca) touching who was the better knight, Palmerin of England, or Amadis de Gaul. But Master Nicholas, the barber of the same town, would affirm that none of both arrived in worth to the Knight of the Sun; and if any one knight might paragon with him, it was infallibly Don Galaor, Amadis de Gaul's brother, whose nature might fitly be accommodated to anything; for he was not so coy and whining a knight as his brother, and that in matters of valour he did not bate him an ace.

In resolution, he plunged himself so deeply in his reading of these books, as he spent many times in the lecture of them whole days and nights; and in the end, through his little sleep and much reading, he dried up his brains in such sort as he lost wholly his judgment. His fantasy was filled with those things that he read, of enchantments, quarrels, battles, challenges, wounds, wooings, loves, tempests, and other impossible follies. And these toys did so firmly possess his imagination with an infallible opinion that all that *machina* of dreamed inventions which he read was true, as he accounted no history in the world to be so certain and sincere as they were. He was wont to say, that the Cid Ruy Diaz was a very good knight, but not to be compared to the Knight of the Burning Sword, which, with one thwart blow, cut asunder two fierce and mighty giants. He agreed better with Bernardo del Carpio, because he slew the enchanted Roland in Roncesvalles. He likewise liked of the shift Hercules used when he smothered Anteon, the son of the earth, between his arms. He praised the giant Morgant marvellously, because, though he was of that monstrous progeny, who are commonly all of them proud and rude, yet he was affable and courteous. But he agreed best of all with Reinauld of Mount Alban; and most of all then, when he saw him sally out of his castle to rob as many as ever he could meet; and when, moreover, he robbed the idol of Mahomet, made all of gold, as his history recounts, and would be content to give his old woman, yea, and his niece also, for a good opportunity on the traitor Galalon, that he might lamb-skin and trample him into powder.

Finally, his wit being wholly extinguished, he fell into one of the strangest conceits that ever madman stumbled on in this world; to wit, it seemed unto him very requisite and behooveful, as well for the augmentation of his honour as also for the benefit of the commonwealth, that he himself should become a knight-errant, and go throughout the world, with his horse and armour, to seek adventures, and practise in person all that he had read was used by knights of yore; revenging of all kinds of injuries, and offering himself to occasions and dangers, which, being once happily achieved, might gain him eternal renown. The poor soul did already figure himself crowned, through the valour of his arm, at least Emperor of Trapisonda; and led thus by these soothing thoughts, and borne away with the exceeding delight he found in them, he hastened all that he might, to effect his urging desires.

And first of all he caused certain old rusty arms to be scoured, that belonged to his great-grandfather, and lay many ages neglected and forgotten in a by-corner of his house; he trimmed and dressed them the best he might, and then perceived a great defect they had; for they wanted a helmet, and had only a plain morion; but he by his industry supplied that want, and framed, with certain papers pasted together, a beaver for his morion. True it is, that to make trial whether his pasted beaver was strong enough, and might abide the adventure of a blow, he out with his sword and gave it a blow or two, and with the very first did quite undo his whole week's labour. The facility wherewithal it was dissolved liked him nothing; wherefore, to assure himself better the next time from the like danger, he made it anew, placing certain iron bars within it, in so artificial a manner, as he rested at once satisfied, both with his invention, and also the solidity of the work; and without making a second trial, he deputed and held it in estimation of a most excellent beaver. Then did he presently visit his horse, who (though he had more quarters than pence in a sixpence, through leanness, and more faults than Gonella's), having nothing on him but skin and bone; yet he thought that neither Alexander's Bucephalus, nor the Cid his horse Balieca, were in any respect equal to him. He spent four days devising him a name; for (as he reasoned to himself) it was not fit that so famous a knight's horse, and chiefly being so good a beast, should want a known name; and therefore he endeavoured to give him such a one as should both declare what sometime he had been, before he pertained to a knight-errant, and also what at present he was; for it stood greatly with reason, seeing his lord and master changed his estate and vocation, that he should alter likewise his denomination, and get a new one, that were famous and altisonant, as became the new order and exercise which he now professed; and therefore, after many other names which he framed, blotted out, rejected, added, undid, and turned again to frame in his memory and imagination, he finally concluded to name him Rozinante, a name in his opinion lofty, full, and significant of what he had been when he was a plain jade, before he was exalted to his new dignity; being, as he thought, the best carriage beast of the world. The name being thus given to his horse, and so to his mind, he resolved to give himself a name also; and in that thought he laboured other eight days; and, in conclusion, called himself Don Quixote; whence (as is said) the authors of this most true history deduce, that he was undoubtedly named Quixada, and not Quesada, as others would have it. And remembering that the valorous Amadis was not satisfied only with the dry name of Amadis, but added thereunto the name of his kingdom and country, to render his own more redoubted, terming himself Amadis de Gaul; so he, like a good knight, would add to his own that also of his province, and call himself Don Quixote of the Mancha, wherewith it appeared that he very lively declared his lineage and country, which he did honour, by taking it for his surname.

His armour being scoured, his morion transformed into a helmet, his horse named, and himself confirmed with a new name also, he forthwith bethought himself, that now he wanted nothing but a lady on whom he might bestow his service and affection; for the knight-errant that is loveless resembles a tree that wants leaves and fruit, or a body without a soul: and therefore he was wont to say, 'If I should for my sins, or by good hap, encounter there abroad with some giant (as knights-errant do ordinarily), and that I should overthrow him with one blow to the ground, or cut him with a stroke in two halves, or finally overcome, and make him yield to me, would it not be very expedient to have some lady to whom I might present him? And that he, entering in her presence, do kneel before my sweet lady, and say unto her, with an humble and submissive voice, "Madam, I am the giant Caraculiambro, lord of the island called Malindrania, whom the never-too-much-praised knight, Don Quixote de la Mancha, hath overcome in single combat; and hath commanded to present myself to your greatness, that it may please your highness to dispose of me according unto your liking!"' Oh, how glad was our knight when he had made this discourse to himself, but chiefly when he had found out one whom he might call his lady! For, as it is imagined, there dwelt in the next village unto his manor, a young handsome wench, with whom he was sometime in love, although, as is understood, she never knew or took notice thereof. She was called Aldonsa Lorenzo, and her he thought fittest to entitle with the name of Lady of his thoughts, and searching a name for her that should not vary much from her own, and yet should draw and aveer somewhat to that of a princess or great lady, he called her Dulcinea del Toboso (for there she was born), a name in his conceit harmonious, strange, and significant, like to all the others that he had given to his things.

CHAPTER II

Of the First Sally That Don Quixote Made to Seek Adventures

THINGS being thus ordered, he would defer the execution of his designs no longer, being spurred on the more vehemently by the want which he esteemed his delays wrought in the world, according to the wrongs that he resolved to right, the harms he meant to redress, the excesses he would amend, the abuses that he would better, and the debts he would satisfy. And therefore, without acquainting any living creature with his intentions, he, unseen of any, upon a certain morning, somewhat before the day (being one of the warmest of July), armed himself cap-a-pie, mounted on Rozinante, laced on his ill-contrived helmet, embraced his target, took his lance, and by a postern door of his base-court issued out to the field, marvellous jocund and content to see with what facility he had commenced his good desires. But scarce had he sallied to the fields, when he was suddenly assaulted by a terrible thought, and such a one as did well-nigh overthrow his former good purposes; which was, he remembered he was not yet dubbed knight, and therefore, by the laws of knighthood, neither could nor ought to combat with any knight: and though he were one, yet ought he to wear white armour like a new knight, without any device in his shield until he did win it by force of arms.

These thoughts did make him stagger in his purposes; but his follies prevailing more than any other reason, he purposed to cause himself to be knighted by the first he met, to the imitation of many others that did the same, as he had read in the books which distracted him. As touching white armour, he resolved, with the first opportunity, to scour his own so well, that they should rest whiter than ermines. And thus he pacified his mind and prosecuted his journey, without choosing any other way than that which his horse pleased, believing that therein consisted the vigour of knightly adventures. Our burnished adventurer, travelling thus onward, did parley with himself in this manner: 'Who doubts, in the ensuing ages, when the true history of my famous acts shall come to light, but that the wise man who shall write it, will begin it, when he comes to declare this my first sally so early in the morning, after this manner?—"Scarce had the ruddy Apollo spread over the face of the vast and spacious earth the golden twists of his beautiful hairs, and scarce had the little enamelled birds with their naked tongues saluted with sweet and mellifluous harmony the arrival of rosy Aurora, when, abandoning her jealous husband's soft couch, she shows herself to mortal wights through the gates and windows of the Manchegall horizon; when the famous knight, Don Quixote of the Mancha, abandoning the slothful plumes, did mount upon his renowned horse Rozinante, and began to travel through the ancient and known fields of Montiel"' (as indeed he did). And following still on with his discourse, he said: 'Oh, happy the age, and fortunate the time, wherein my famous feats shall be revealed, feats worthy to be graven in brass, carved in marble, and delivered with most curious art in tables, for a future instruction and memory. And, thou wise enchanter, whosoever thou beest, whom it shall concern to be the chronicler of this strange history, I desire thee not to forget my good horse Rozinante, mine eternal and inseparable companion in all my journeys and courses.' And then, as if he were verily enamoured, he said: 'O Princess Dulcinea! lady of this captive heart! much wrong hast thou done me by dismissing me, and reproaching me with the rigorous decree and commandment, not to appear before thy beauty. I pray thee, sweet lady, deign to remember thee of this poor subjected heart, that for thy love suffers so many tortures!' And with these words he inserted a thousand other ravings, all after the same manner that his books taught him, imitating as near as he could their very phrase and language, and did ride therewithal so slow a pace, and the sun did mount so swiftly, and with so great heat, as it was sufficient to melt his brains, if he had had any left.

He travelled almost all that day without encountering anything worthy the recital, which made him to fret for anger; for he desired to encounter presently some one upon whom he might make trial of his invincible strength. Some authors write that his first adventure was that of the Lapicean straits; others, that of the Windmills: but what I could only find out in this affair, and which I have found written in the annals of the Mancha, is that he travelled all that day long, and at night both he and his horse were tired, and marvellously pressed by hunger; and, looking about him on every side to see whether he could discover any castle or sheepfold wherein he might retire himself for that night, and remedy his wants, he perceived an inn near unto the highway wherein he travelled, which was as welcome a sight to him as if he had seen a star that did address him to the porch, if not to the palace, of his redemption. Then, spurring his horse, he hied all he might towards it, and arrived much about nightfall. There stood by chance at the inn door two young women, adventurers likewise, which travelled toward Seville with certain carriers, and did by chance take up their lodging in that inn the same evening; and, forasmuch as our knight-errant esteemed all which he thought, saw, or imagined, was done or did really pass in the very same form as he had read the like in his books, forthwith, as soon as he espied the vent, he feigned to himself that it was a castle with four turrets, whereof the pinnacles were of glistening silver, without omitting the drawbridge, deep fosse, and other adherents belonging to the like places. And approaching by little and little to the vent, when he drew near to it, checking Rozinante with the bridle, he rested a while to see whether any dwarf would mount on the battlements to give warning with the sound of a trumpet how some knight did approach the castle; but seeing they stayed so long, and also, that Rozinante kept a coil to go to his stable, he went to the inn door, and there beheld the two loose baggages that stood at it, whom he presently supposed to be two beautiful damsels or lovely ladies, that did solace themselves before the castle gates. And in this space it befel by chance, that a certain swineherd, as he gathered together his hogs, blew the horn whereat they are wont to come together; and instantly Don Quixote imagined it was what he desired, to wit, some dwarf who gave notice of his arrival; and therefore, with marvellous satisfaction of mind he approached to the inn and ladies; who beholding one armed in that manner to draw so near, with his lance and target they made much haste, being greatly affrighted, to get to their lodging. But Don Quixote perceiving their fear by their flight, lifting up his pasted beaver, and discovering his withered and dusty countenance, did accost them with gentle demeanour and grave words in this manner: 'Let not your ladyships flee, nor fear any outrage; for to the order of knighthood which I do profess, it toucheth nor appertaineth not to wrong anybody, and least of all such worthy damsels as your presence denote you to be.' The wenches looked on him very earnestly, and did search with their eyes for the visage, which his ill-fashioned beaver did conceal; but when they heard themselves termed damsels, a thing so far from their profession, they could not contain their laughter, which was so loud, as Don Quixote waxed ashamed thereat; and therefore said to them: 'Modesty is a comely ornament of the beautiful, and the excessive laughter that springs from a light occasion must be reputed great folly. But I do not object this unto you to make you the more ashamed, or that you should take it in ill part; for my desire is none other than to do you all the honour and service I may.' This he spake unto them in such uncouth words as they could not understand him, which was an occasion, joined with his own uncomeliness, to increase their laughter and his wrath, which would have passed the bounds of reason, if the innkeeper had not come out at the instant, being a man who, by reason of his exceeding fatness, must needs have been of a very peaceable condition; who, beholding that counterfeit figure, all armed in so unsuitable armour as were his bridle, lance, target, and corslet, was very near to have kept the damsels company in the pleasant shows of his merriment, but fearing in effect the *machina* and bulk contrived of so various furnitures, he determined to speak him fairly; and therefore began to him in this manner: 'If your worship, sir knight, do seek for lodging, you may chalk yourself a bed for there is none in this inn, wherein you shall find all other things in abundance.' Don Quixote, noting the lowliness of the constable of that fortress (for such the inn and innkeeper seemed unto him), answered, 'Anything, sir constable, may serve me; for mine arms are mine ornaments, and battles mine ease, etc.' The host thought he had called him a castellano or constable, because he esteemed him to be one of the sincere and honest men of Castile, whereas he was indeed an Andalusian, and of the commark of St. Lucars, no less thievish than Cacus, nor less malicious and crafty than a student or page; and therefore he answered him thus: 'If that be so, your bed must be hard rocks, and your sleep a perpetual watching; and being such, you may boldly alight, and shall find certainly here occasion and opportunity to hold you waking this twelvemonth more, for one night.' And, saying so, laid hold on Don Quixote's stirrup, who did forthwith alight, though it was with great difficulty and pain (as one that had not eaten all the day one crumb), and then he requested his host to have special care of his horse, saying, he was one of the best pieces that ever ate bread. The innkeeper viewed and reviewed him, to whom he did not seem half so good as Don Quixote valued him, and, setting him up in the stable, he turned to see what his guest would command, who was a-disarming by both the damsels (which were by this time reconciled to him), who, though they had taken off his breastplate and back parts, yet knew they not how, nor could anywise undo his gorget, nor take off his counterfeit beaver, which he had fastened on with green ribbons; and by reason the knots were so intricate, it was requisite they should be cut, whereunto he would not in anywise agree; and therefore remained all the night with his helmet on, and was the strangest and pleasantest figure thereby that one might behold. And as he was a-disarming (imagining those light wenches that helped him to be certain principal ladies and dames of that castle), he said unto them, with a very good grace: 'Never was any knight so well attended on and served by ladies as was Don Quixote: when he departed from his village, damsels attended on him, and princesses on his horse. O Rozinante!—for, ladies, that is the name of my horse, and Don Quixote de la Mancha is mine own. For although I meant at the first not to have discovered myself, until the acts done in your service and benefit should manifest me; yet the necessity of accommodating to our present purpose the old romance of Sir Launcelot, hath been an occasion that you should know my name before the right season. But the time will come wherein your ladyships may command me, and I obey, and then the valour of mine arm shall discover the desire I have to do you service.'

The wenches being unaccustomed to hear so rhetorical terms, answered never a word to him, but only demanded whether he would eat anything. 'That I would,' replied Don Quixote, 'forasmuch as I think the taking of a little meat would be very behooveful for me.' It chanced by hap to be on Friday, and therefore there was no other meat in the inn than a few pieces of a fish called in

Castile *abadexo,* in Andalusia *bacallao,* and in some places *curadillo,* and in others *truchuela,* and is but poor-john.

They demanded of him, therefore, whether he would eat thereof, giving it the name, used in that place, of truchuela, or little trout; for there was no other fish in all the inn to present unto him but such. 'Why, then,' quoth Don Quixote, 'bring it in; for if there be many little trouts they may serve me instead of a great one; it being all one to me, to be paid my money (if I were to receive any) in eight single reals, or to be paid the same in one real of eight. And, moreover, those little trouts are perhaps like unto veal, which is much more delicate flesh than beef; or the kid, which is better than the goat; but be it what it list, let it be brought in presently; for the labour and weight of arms cannot be well borne without the well-supplying of the guts.' Then was there straight laid a table at the inn door, that he mought take the air; and the host brought him a portion of evil-watered and worse-boiled poor-john, and a loaf as black and hoary as his harness. But the only sport was to behold him eat; for by reason his helmet was on, and his beaver lifted, he could put nothing into his mouth himself if others did not help him to find the way, and therefore one of those ladies served his turn in that; but it was altogether impossible to give him drink after that manner, and would have remained so for ever, if the innkeeper had not bored a cane, and setting the one end in his mouth, poured down the wine at the other: all which he suffered most patiently, because he would not break the ribbons of his helmet. And as he sat at supper, there arrived by chance a sowgelder, who, as soon as he came to the inn, did sound four or five times a whistle of canes, the which did confirm Don Quixote that he was in some famous castle, where he was served with music; and that the poor-john was trouts; the bread of the finest flour; the whores, ladies; and the innkeeper, constable of that castle; wherefore he accounted his resolution and departure from his own house very well employed. But that which did most afflict him was, that he was not yet dubbed knight, forasmuch as he was fully persuaded that he could not lawfully enterprise, or follow any adventure, until he received the order of knighthood.

CHAPTER III

Wherein Is Recounted the Pleasant Manner Observed in the Knighting of Don Quixote

AND being thus tossed in mind, he made a short, beggarly supper; which being finished, he called for his host, and, shutting the stable door very fast, he laid himself down upon his knees in it before him, saying, 'I will never rise from the place where I am, valorous knight, until your courtesy shall grant unto me a boon that I mean to demand of you, the which will redound unto your renown, and also to the profit of all human kind.' The innkeeper seeing his guest at his feet, and hearing him speak those words, remained confounded beholding him, not knowing what he might do or say, and did study and labour to make him arise; but all was in vain, until he must have promised unto him that he would grant him any gift that he sought at his hands. 'I did never expect less,' replied Don Quixote, 'from your magnificence, my lord; and therefore I say unto you, that the boon which I demand of you, and that hath been granted unto me by your liberality, is, that to-morrow, in the morning, you will dub me knight, and this night I will watch mine armour in the chapel of your castle, and in the morning, as I have said, the rest of my desires shall be accomplished, that I may go in due manner throughout the four parts of the world, to seek adventures, to the benefit of the needy, as is the duty of knighthood, and of knights-errant, as I am; whose desires are wholly inclined and dedicated to such achievements.' The host, who, as we noted before, was a great giber, and had before gathered some arguments of the defect of wit in his guest, did wholly now persuade himself that his suspicions were true, when he heard him speak in that manner; and that he might have an occasion of laughter, he resolved to feed his humour that night; and therefore answered him, that he had very great reason in that which he desired and sought, and that such projects were proper and natural to knights of the garb and worth he seemed to be of; and that he himself likewise, in his youthful years, had followed that honourable exercise, going through divers parts of the world to seek adventures, without either omitting the dangers of Malaga, the Isles of Riaran, the compass of Seville, the quicksilver house of Segovia, the olive field of Valencia, the circuit of Granada, the wharf of St. Lucar, the Potro or Cowlt of Cordova, and the little taverns of Toledo; and many other places, wherein he practised the dexterity of his hands; doing many wrongs, soliciting many widows, undoing certain maidens, and deceiving many pupils, and finally making himself known and famous in all the tribunals and courts almost of all Spain; and that at last he had retired himself to that his castle, where he was sustained with his own and other men's goods, entertaining in it all knights-errant, of whatsoever quality and condition they were, only for the great affection he bore towards them, and to the end they might divide with him part of their winnings in recompense of his goodwill. He added besides, that there was no chapel in his castle wherein he might watch his arms, for he had broken it down, to build it up anew; but, notwithstanding, he knew very well that in a case of necessity they might lawfully be watched in any other place, and therefore he might watch them that night in the base-court of the castle; for in the morning, an it pleased God, the ceremonies requisite should be done in such sort as he should remain a dubbed knight, in so good fashion as in all the world he could not be bettered. He demanded of Don Quixote whether he had any money; who answered that he had not a blank, for he had never read in any history of knights-errant that any one of them ever carried any money. To this his host replied, that he was deceived; for, admit that histories made no mention thereof, because the authors of them deemed it not necessary to express a thing so manifest and needful to be carried as was money and clean shirts, it was not therefore to be credited that they had none; and therefore he should hold, for most certain and manifest, that all the knights-errant, with the story of whose acts so many books are replenished and heaped, had their purses well lined for that which might befall, and did moreover carry with them a little casket of ointments and salves, to cure the wounds which they received, for they had not the commodity of a surgeon to cure them, every time that they fought abroad in the fields and deserts, if they had not by chance some wise enchanter to their friend, who would presently succour them, bringing unto them, in some cloud, through the air, some damsel or dwarf, with a vial of water of so great virtue, as tasting one drop thereof, they remained as whole of their sores and wounds as if they had never received any. But when they had not that benefit, the knights of times past held it for a very commendable and secure course that their squires should be provided of money and other necessary things, as lint and ointments for to cure themselves; and when it befel that the like knights had no squires to attend upon them (which happened but very seldom), then would they themselves carry all this provision behind them on their horses, in some slight and subtle wallets, which could scarce be perceived as a thing of very great consequence; for, if it were not upon such an occasion, the carriage of wallets was not very tolerable among knights-errant. And in this respect he did advise him, seeing he might yet command him, as one that, by receiving the order of knighthood at his hands, should very shortly become his godchild, that he should not travel from thenceforward without money and other the preventions he had then given unto him; and he should perceive himself how behooveful they would prove unto him when he least expected it.

Don Quixote promised to accomplish all that he had counselled him to do, with all punctuality; and so order was forthwith given how he should watch his arms in a great yard that lay near unto one side of the inn. Wherefore Don Quixote gathered all his arms together, laid them on a cistern that stood near unto a well; and, buckling on his target, he laid hold on his lance, and walked up and down before the cistern very demurely, and when he began to walk, the night likewise began to lock up the splendour of the day. The innkeeper, in the mean season, recounted to all the rest that lodged in the inn the folly of his guest, the watching of his arms, and the knighthood which he expected to receive. They all admired very much at so strange a kind of folly, and went out to behold him from afar off, and saw that sometimes he pranced to and fro with a quiet gesture; other times, leaning upon his lance, he looked upon his armour, without beholding any other thing save his arms for a good space.

The night being shut up at last wholly, but with such clearness of the moon as it might well compare with his brightness that lent her her splendour, everything which our new knight did was easily perceived by all the beholders. In this season one of the carriers that lodged in the inn resolved to water his mules, and for that purpose it was necessary to remove Don Quixote's armour that lay on the cistern; who, seeing him approach, said unto him, with a loud voice, 'O thou, whosoever thou beest, bold knight! that comest to touch the armour of the most valorous adventurer that ever girded sword, look well what thou dost, and touch them not, if thou meanest not to leave thy life in payment of thy presumption.' The carrier made no account of those words (but it were better he had, for it would have redounded to his benefit), but rather, laying hold on the leatherings, threw the armour a pretty way off from him, which being perceived by Don Quixote, he lifted up his eyes towards heaven, and addressing his thoughts (as it seemed) to his Lady Dulcinea, he said, 'Assist me, dear lady, in this first dangerous scorn and adventure offered to this breast, that is enthralled to thee, and let not thy favour and protection fail me in this my first trance!' And, uttering these and other such words, he let slip his target, and, lifting up his lance with bold hands, he paid the carrier so round a knock therewithal on the pate, as he overthrew him to the ground in so evil taking, as, if he had seconded it with another, he should not have needed any surgeon to cure him. This done, he gathered up his armour again, and laying them where they had been before, he walked after up and down by them, with as much quietness as he did at the first.

But very soon after, another carrier, without knowing what had happened (for his companion lay yet in a trance on the ground), came also to give his mules water, and coming to take away the arms, that he might free the cistern of encumbrances, and take water the easier—Don Quixote saying nothing nor imploring favour of his mistress or any other, let slip again his target, and, lifting his lance, without breaking of it in pieces, made more than three of the second carrier's noddle; for he broke it in four places. All the people of the inn, and amongst them the host likewise, repaired at this time to the noise; which Don Quixote perceiving, embracing his target, and laying hand on his sword, he said: 'O lady of all beauty! courage and vigour of my weakened heart! it is now high time that thou do convert the eyes of thy greatness to this thy captive knight, who doth expect so marvellous great an adventure.' Saying thus, he recovered, as he thought, so great courage, that if all the carriers of the world had assailed him, he would not go one step backward. The wounded men's fellows, seeing them so evil dight, from afar off began to rain stones on Don Quixote, who did defend himself the best he might with his target, and durst not depart from the cistern, lest he should seem to abandon his arms. The innkeeper cried to them to let him alone; for he had already informed them that he was mad, and so such a one would escape scot-free although he had slain them all. Don Quixote likewise cried out louder, terming them all disloyal men and traitors, and that the lord of the castle was a treacherous and bad knight, seeing that he consented that knights-errant should be so basely used; and that, if he had not yet received the order of knighthood, he would make him understand his treason: 'But of you base and rascally kennel,' quoth he, 'I make no reckoning at all. Throw at me, approach, draw near, and do me all the hurt you may, for you shall ere long perceive the reward you shall carry for this your madness and outrage.' Which words he spoke with so great spirit and boldness, as he struck a terrible fear into all those that assaulted him; and therefore, moved both by it, and the innkeeper's persuasions, they left off throwing stones at him, and he permitted them to carry away the wounded men, and returned to the guard of his arms with as great quietness and gravity as he did at the beginning.

The innkeeper did not like very much these tricks of his guest, and therefore he determined to abbreviate, and give him the unfortunate order of knighthood forthwith, before some other disaster befel. And with this resolution coming unto him, he excused himself of the insolences those base fellows had used to him, without his privity or consent; but their rashness, as he said, remained well chastised. He added how he had already told unto him, that there was no chapel in his castle, and that for what yet rested unperfected of their intention, it was not necessary, because the chief point of remaining knighted consisted chiefly in blows of the neck and shoulders, as he had read in the ceremonial book of the order, and that that might be given in the very midst of the fields; and that he had already accomplished the obligation of watching his arms, which with only two hours' watch might be fulfilled; how much more after having watched four, as he had done. All this Don Quixote believed, and therefore answered, that he was most ready to obey him, and requested him to conclude with all the brevity possible; for if he saw himself knighted, and were once again assaulted, he meant not to leave one person alive in all the castle, except those which the constable should command, whom he would spare for his sake.

The constable being thus advertised, and fearful that he would put this his deliberation in execution, brought out a book presently, wherein he was wont to write down the accounts of the straw and barley which he delivered from time to time to such carriers as lodged in his inn, for their beasts; and, with a butt of a candle, which a boy held lighted in his hand before him, accompanied by the two damsels above mentioned, he came to Don Quixote, whom he commanded to kneel upon his knees, and, reading in his manual (as it seemed, some devout orison), he held up his hand in the midst of the lecture, and gave him a good blow on the neck, and after that gave him another trim thwack over the shoulders with his own sword, always murmuring something between the teeth, as if he prayed. This being done, he commanded one of the ladies to gird on his sword, which she did with a singular good grace and dexterity, which was much, the matter being of itself so ridiculous, as it wanted but little to make a man burst with laughter at every passage of the ceremonies; but the prowess which they had already beheld in the new knight did limit and contain their delight. At the girding on of his sword, the good lady said, 'God make you a fortunate knight, and give you good success in all your debates!' Don Quixote demanded then how she was called, that he might thenceforward know to whom he was so much obliged for the favour received. And she answered, with great buxomness, that she was named Tolosa, and was a butcher's daughter of Toledo, that dwelt in Sancho Benega's

Street, and that she would ever honour him as her lord. Don Quixote replied, requesting her, for his sake, to call herself from thenceforth the Lady Tolosa, which she promised him to perform. The other lady buckled on his spur, with whom he had the very like conference, and, asking her name, she told him she was called Molinera, and was daughter to an honest miller of Antequera. Her likewise our knight entreated to call herself the Lady Molinera, proffering her new services and favours. The new and never-seen-before ceremonies being thus speedily finished, as it seemed, with a gallop, Don Quixote could not rest until he was mounted on horseback, that he might go to seek adventures; wherefore, causing Rozinante to be instantly saddled, he leaped on him, and embracing his host, he said unto him such strange things, gratifying the favour he had done him in dubbing him knight, as it is impossible to hit upon the manner of recounting them right. The innkeeper, that he might be quickly rid of him, did answer his words with others no less rhetorical, but was in his speech somewhat briefer; and, without demanding of him anything for his lodging, he suffered him to depart in a fortunate hour.

CHAPTER IV

Of That Which Befel to Our Knight after He Had Departed from the Inn

AURORA began to display her beauties about the time that Don Quixote issued out of the inn, so content, lively, and jocund to behold himself knighted, as his very horse-girths were ready to burst for joy. But calling to memory the counsels that his host had given him, touching the most needful implements that he was ever to carry about him, of money and clean shirts, he determined to return to his house, and to provide himself of them, and also of a squire; making account to entertain a certain labourer, his neighbour, who was poor and had children, but yet one very fit for this purpose and squirely function belonging to knighthood. With this determination he turned Rozinante towards the way of his own village, who, knowing in a manner his will, began to trot on with so good a pace as he seemed not to touch the ground. He had not travelled far, when he thought that he heard certain weak and delicate cries, like to those of one that complained, to issue out from the thickest of a wood that stood on the right hand. And scarce had he heard them when he said: 'I render infinite thanks to Heaven for the favour it doth me, by proffering me so soon occasion wherein I may accomplish the duty of my profession, and gather the fruits of my good desires. These plaints doubtlessly be of some distressed man or woman, who needeth my favour and aid.' Then, turning the reins, he guided Rozinante towards the place from whence he thought the complaints sallied; and within a few paces after he had entered into the thicket, he saw a mare tied unto an holm oak, and to another was tied a young youth, all naked from the middle upward, of about the age of fifteen years, and was he that cried so pitifully: and not without cause; for a certain countryman of comely personage did whip him with a girdle, and accompanied every blow with a reprehension and counsel; for he said,

'The tongue must peace, and the eyes be wary.' And the boy answered, 'I will never do it again, good master; for the passion of God, I will never do it again. And I promise to have more care of your things from henceforth.'

But Don Quixote, viewing all that passed, said, with an angry voice, 'Discourteous knight, it is very uncomely to see thee deal thus with one that cannot defend himself. Mount, therefore, on horseback, and take thy lance' (for the farmer had also a lance leaning to the very same tree whereunto his mare was tied), 'for I will make thee know that it is the use of cowards to do that which thou dost.' The other, beholding such an antic to hover over him, all laden with arms, and brandishing of his lance towards his face, made full account that he should be slain, and therefore he answered, with very mild and submissive words, saying, 'Sir knight, the boy which I chastise is mine own servant, and keepeth for me a flock of sheep in this commark; who is grown so negligent, as he loseth one of them every other day, and because I correct him for his carelessness and knavery, he says I do it through covetousness and pinching, as meaning to defraud him of his wages; but, before God, and in conscience, he belies me.' 'What! the lie in my presence, rascally clown?' quoth Don Quixote. 'By the sun that shines on us, I am about to run thee through and through with my lance, base carle! Pay him instantly, without more replying; or else, by that God which doth manage our sublunar affairs, I will conclude thee and annihilate thee in a moment! Loose him forthwith!' The countryman, hanging down of his head, made no reply, but loosed his servant; of whom Don Quixote demanded how much did his master owe unto him. He said, nine months' hire, at seven reals a month. Don Quixote made then the account, and found that all amounted to sixty-one reals, and therefore commanded the farmer to pay the money presently, if he meant not to die for it. The fearful countryman answered, that by the trance wherein he was then, and by the oath he had made (which was none at all, for he swore not), that he owed not so much; for there should be deducted out of the account three pairs of shoes he had given unto him, and a real for twice letting him blood, being sick. 'All is well,' quoth Don Quixote; 'but let the price of the shoes and letting blood go for the blows which thou hast given him without any desert; for if he have broken the leather of those shoes thou hast bestowed on him, thou hast likewise torn the skin of his body; and if the barber took away his blood, being sick, thou hast taken it out, he being in health; so as in that respect he owes thee nothing.' 'The damage is, sir knight,' replied the boy's master, 'that I have no money here about me. Let Andrew come with me to my house, and I will pay him his wages, one real upon another.' 'I go with him!' quoth the boy; 'evil befall me then! No, sir, I never meant it; for as soon as ever he were alone, he would flay me like St. Bartholomew.' 'He will not dare to do it,' quoth Don Quixote; 'for my command is sufficient to make him respect me, and so that he will swear to me to observe it, by the order of knighthood which he hath received, I will set him free, and assure thee of the payment.' 'Good sir,' quoth the youth, 'mark well what you say; for this man, my master, is no knight, nor did ever receive any order of knighthood, for he is John Haldudo, the rich man, a dweller of Quintinar.' 'That makes no matter,' quoth Don Quixote; 'for there may be knights of the Haldudos; and what is more, every one is son of his works.' 'That's true,' quoth Andrew; 'but of what works can this my master be son, seeing he denies me my wages, and my sweat and labour?' 'I do not deny thy wages, friend Andrew,' quoth his master; 'do me but the pleasure to come with me, and I swear, by all the orders of knighthood that are in the world, to pay thee as I have said, one real upon another—yea, and those also perfumed.' 'For the perfuming, I thank thee,' quoth Don Quixote; 'give it him in reals, and with that I will rest satisfied; and see that thou fulfillest it as thou hast sworn: if not, I swear again to thee, by the same oath, to return and search thee, and chastise thee, and I will find thee out, though thou shouldst hide thyself better than a lizard; and if thou desirest to note who commands thee this, that thou mayst remain more firmly obliged to accomplish it, know that I am the valorous Don Quixote of the Mancha, the righter of wrongs and undoer of injuries; and so farewell, and do not forget what thou hast promised and sworn, on pain of the pains already pronounced.' And, saying these words, he spurred Rozinante, and in short space was got far off from them. The countryman pursued him with his eye, and, perceiving that he was past the wood, and quite out of sight, he returned to his man Andrew, and said to him, 'Come to me, child, for I will pay thee what I owe thee, as that righter of wrongs hath left me commanded.' 'That I swear,' quoth Andrew; 'and you shall deal discreetly in fulfilling that good knight's commandment, who I pray God may live a thousand years; for, seeing he is so valorous and so just a judge, I swear by Rocque, that if you pay me not, he shall return and execute what he promised.' 'I also do swear the same,' quoth the farmer; 'but in respect of the great affection I bear unto thee, I will augment the debt, to increase the payment.' And, catching the youth by the arm, he tied him again to the oak, where he gave him so many blows as he left him for dead. 'Call now, Master Andrew,' quoth he, 'for the righter of wrongs, and thou shalt see that he cannot undo this, although I believe it is not yet ended to be done; for I have yet a desire to flay thee alive, as thou didst thyself fear.' Notwithstanding all these threats, he untied him at last, and gave him leave to go seek out his judge, to the end he might execute the sentence pronounced. Andrew departed somewhat discontent, swearing to search for the valorous Don Quixote of the Mancha, and recount unto him, word for word, all that had passed, and that he should pay the abuse with usury; but, for all his threats, he departed weeping, and his master remained behind laughing: and in this manner the valorous Don Quixote redressed that wrong.

Who, glad above measure for his success, accounting himself to have given a most noble beginning to his feats of arms, did travel towards his village, with very great satisfaction of himself, and said, in a low tone, these words following: 'Well mayst thou call thyself happy above all other women of the earth, O above all beauties, beautiful Dulcinea of Toboso! since thy good fortune was such, to hold subject and prostrate to thy will and desire so valiant and renowned a knight as is, and ever shall be, Don Quixote of the Mancha, who, as all the world knows, received the order of knighthood but yesterday, and hath destroyed to-day the greatest outrage and wrong that want of reason could form, or cruelty commit. To-day did he take away the whip out of that pitiless enemy's hand, which did so cruelly scourge without occasion the delicate infant.'

In this discourse he came to a way that divided itself into four, and presently these thwarting cross-ways represented themselves to his imagination, which ofttimes held knights-errant in suspense which way they should take; and, that he might imitate them, he stood still a while, and, after he had bethought himself well, he let slip the reins to Rozinante, subjecting his will to that of his horse, who presently pursued his first design, which was to return home unto his own stable: and having travelled some two miles, Don Quixote discovered a great troop of people, who, as it was after known, were certain merchants of Toledo, that rode towards Murcia to buy silks. They were six in number, and came with their quitasoles, or shadows of the sun, four serving-men on horseback, and three lackeys. Scarce had Don Quixote perceived them, when he straight imagined them to be a new adventure. And because he would imitate as much as was possible the passages which he read in his books, he represented this to himself to be just such an adventure as he purposed to achieve. And so, with comely gesture and hardiness, settling himself well in the stirrups, he set his lance into his rest, and embraced his target, and, placing himself in the midst of the way, he stood awaiting when those knights-errant should arrive; for now he judged and took them for such. And when they were so near as they might hear and see him, he lifted up his voice, and said: 'Let all the world stand and pass no further, if all the world will not confess that there is not in all the world a more beautiful damsel than the Empress of the Mancha, the peerless Dulcinea of Toboso!' The merchants stayed at these words to behold the marvellous and ridiculous shape of him that spake them, and, by his fashion and them joined did incontinently gather his folly and distraction, and, notwithstanding, would leisurely behold to what tended that confession which he exacted of them; and therefore one of them, who was somewhat given to gibing, and was withal very discreet, said unto him, 'Sir knight, we do not know that good lady of whom you speak; show her therefore to us, and if she be so beautiful as you affirm, we will willingly, and without any compulsion, confess the truth which you now demand of us.' 'If I did show her to you,' replied Don Quixote, 'what mastery were it then for you to acknowledge a truth so notorious? The consequence of mine affairs consists in this, that, without beholding her, you do believe, confess, affirm, swear, and defend it; which if you refuse to perform, I challenge you all to battle, proud and unreasonable folk; and, whether you come one by one (as the order of knighthood requires), or all at once, as is the custom and dishonourable practice of men of your brood, here will I expect and await you all, trusting in the reason which I have on my side.' 'Sir knight,' replied the merchant, 'I request you, in all these princes' names, as many as we be here, that to the end we may not burden our consciences, confessing a thing which we never beheld nor heard, and, chiefly, being so prejudicial to the empresses and queens of the kingdoms of Alcaria and Estremadura, you will please to show us some portraiture of that lady, although it be no bigger than a grain of wheat, for by one thread we may judge of the whole clew; and we will with this favour rest secure and satisfied, and you likewise remain content and apaid. And I do believe, moreover, that we are already so inclined to your side, that although her picture showed her to be blind of the one eye, and at the other that she ran fire and brimstone, yet would we, notwithstanding, to please you, say in her favour all that you listed.' 'There drops not, base scoundrels,' quoth Don Quixote, all inflamed with choler,—'there drops not, I say, from her that which thou sayst, but amber and civet among bombase; and she is not blind of an eye, or crook-backed, but is straighter than a spindle of Guadarama. But all of you together shall pay for the great blasphemy thou hast spoken against so immense a beauty as is that of my mistress.' And, saying so, he abased his lance against him that had answered, with such fury and anger, as, if good fortune had not so ordained it that Rozinante should stumble and fall in the midst of the career, it had gone very ill with the bold merchant. Rozinante fell, in fine, and his master reeled over a good piece of the field; and though he attempted to rise, yet was he never able, he was so encumbered by his lance, target, spurs, helmet, and his weighty old armour. And in the meanwhile that he strove to arise, and could not, he cried: 'Fly not, cowardly folk! abide, base people, abide! for I lie not here through mine own fault, but through the defect of my horse.'

One of the lackeys that came in the company, and seemed to be a man of none of the best intentions, hearing the poor overthrown knight speak such insolent words, could not forbear them without returning him an answer on his ribs; and with that intention approaching to him, he took his lance, and, after he had broken it in pieces, he gave Don Quixote so many blows with one of them, that, in despite of his armour, he threshed him like a sheaf of wheat. His masters cried to him, commanding him not to beat him so much, but that he should leave him; but all would not serve, for the youth was angry, and would not leave off the play, until he had avoided the rest of his choler. And therefore, running for the other pieces of the broken lance, he broke them all on the miserable fallen knight; who, for all the tempest of blows that rained on him, did never shut his mouth, but threatened heaven and earth, and those murderers; for such they seemed to him. The lackey tired himself at last, and the merchants followed on their way, carrying with them occasion enough of talk of the poor belaboured knight; who, when he saw himself alone, turned again to make trial whether he might arise; but if he could not do it when he was whole and sound, how was it possible he being so bruised and almost destroyed? And yet he accounted himself very happy, persuading himself that his disgrace was proper and incident to knights-errant, and did attribute all to the fault of his horse, and could in no wise get up, all his body was so bruised and laden with blows.

CHAPTER V

Wherein Is Prosecuted the Former Narration of Our Knight's Misfortunes

BUT seeing, in effect, that he could not stir himself, he resolved to have recourse to his ordinary remedy, which was to think on some passage of his histories; and in the instant his folly presented to his memory that of Valdovinos and the Marquis of Mantua, then when Carloto had left him wounded on the mountain: a history known by children, not hidden to young men, much celebrated, yea, and believed by many old men; and is yet for all that no more authentical than are Mahomet's miracles. This history, as it seemed to him, was most fit for the trance wherein he was; and therefore he began, with signs of great pain, to tumble up and down, and pronounce, with a languishing breath, the same that they feign the wounded knight to have said in the wood:

> "Where art thou, lady dear! that griev'st not at my smart?
> Or thou dost it not know, or thou disloyal art."

And after this manner he did prosecute the old song, until these verses that say: 'O noble Marquis of Mantua, my carnal lord and uncle!' And it befel by chance, that at the very same time there passed by the place where he lay a man of his own village, who was his neighbour, and returned after having carried a load of wheat to the mill; who beholding a man stretched on the ground, he came over to him, and demanded what he was, and what was it that caused him to complain so dolefully. Don Quixote did verily believe that it was his uncle, the Marquis of Mantua, and so gave him no other answer, but only followed on in the repetition of his old romance, wherein he gave him account of his misfortune, and of the love the emperor's son bore to his spouse all in the very same manner that the ballad recounts it. The labourer remained much astonished, hearing those follies. And, taking off his visor, which with the lackey's blows was broken all to pieces, he wiped his face that was full of dust, and scarce had he done it when he knew him; to whom he said: 'Master Quixada' (for so he was probably called when he had his wits, before he left the state of a staid yeoman to become a wandering knight), 'who hath used you after this manner?' But he continued his romance, answering out of it to every question that was put to him; which the good man perceiving, disarmed him the best he could, to see whether he had any wound; but he could see no blood, or any token on him of hurt. Afterward he endeavoured to raise him from the ground, which he did at the last with much ado, and mounted him on his ass, as a beast of easiest carriage. He gathered then together all his arms, and left not behind so much as the splinters of the lance, and tied them altogether upon Rozinante, whom he took by the bridle, and the ass by his halter, and led them both in that equipage fair and easily towards his village, being very pensative to hear the follies that Don Quixote spoke. And Don Quixote was no less melancholy, who was so beaten and bruised as he could very hardly hold himself upon the ass; and ever and anon he breathed forth such grievous sighs, as he seemed to fix them in heaven; which moved his neighbour to entreat him again to declare unto him the cause of his grief. And it seems none other but that the very devil himself did call to his memory histories accommodated to his successes; for in that instant, wholly forgetting Valdovinos, he remembered the Moor Abindarraez, then, when the constable of Antequera, Roderick Narvaez, had taken him, and carried him prisoner to his castle. So that, when his neighbour turned again to ask of him how he did, and what ailed him, he answered the very same words and speech that captive Abindarraez said to Narvaez, just as he had read them in *Diana* of Montemayor, where the history is written; applying it so properly to his purpose, that the labourer grew almost mad for anger to hear that *machina* of follies, by which he collected that his neighbour was distracted; and therefore he hied as fast as possible he could to the village, that so he might free himself from the vexation that Don Quixote's idle and prolix discourse gave unto him. At the end whereof the knight said: 'Don Roderick of Narvaez, you shall understand that this beautiful Xarifa, of whom I spoke, is now the fair Dulcinea of

Toboso; for whom I have done, I do, and will do, such famous acts of knighthood as ever have been, are, and shall be seen in all the world.' To this his neighbour answered: 'Do not you perceive, sir, (sinner that I am!) how I am neither Don Roderick de Narvaez nor the Marquis of Mantua, but Peter Alonso, your neighbour? nor are you Valdovinos nor Abindarraez, but the honest gentleman, Master Quixada.' 'I know very well who I am,' quoth Don Quixote; 'and also I know that I may not only be those whom I have named, but also all the twelve Peers of France, yea, and the nine Worthies; since mine acts shall surpass all those that ever they did together, or every one of them apart.'

With these and such other discourses, they arrived at last at their village about sunset: but the labourer awaited until it waxed somewhat dark, because folk should not view the knight so simply mounted. And when he saw his time he entered into the town, and went to Don Quixote's house, which he found full of confusion. There was the curate and the barber of the village, both of them Don Quixote's great friends; to whom the old woman of the house said, in a lamentable manner: 'What do you think, Master Licentiate Pero Perez' (for so the curate was called), 'of my master's misfortune? These six days neither he nor his horse have appeared, nor the target, lance, or armour. Unfortunate woman that I am! I do suspect, and I am as sure it is true as that I shall die, how those accursed books of knighthood, which he hath, and is wont to read ordinarily, have turned his judgment; for now I remember that I have heard him say oftentimes, speaking to himself, that he would become a knight-errant, and go seek adventures throughout the world. Let such books be recommended to Satan and Barabbas, which have destroyed in this sort the most delicate understanding of all the Mancha.' His niece affirmed the same, and did add: 'Moreover, you shall understand, good Master Nicholas' (for so hight the barber), 'that it many times befel my uncle to continue the lecture of those unhappy books of disventures two days and two nights together, at the end of which, throwing the book away from him, he would lay hand on his sword, and would fall a-slashing of the walls; and when he were wearied, he would say that he had slain four giants as great as four towers, and the sweat that dropped down, through the labour he took, he would say was blood that gushed out of those wounds which he had received in the conflict, and then would he quaff off a great pot full of cold water, and straight he did become whole and quiet; saying that water was a most precious drink, which the wise man Esquife, a great enchanter or sorcerer, and his friend, had brought unto him. But I am in the fault of all this, who never advertised you both of mine uncle's raving, to the end you might have redressed it ere it came to these terms, and burnt all those excommunicated books; for he had many that deserved the fire as much as if they were heretical.' 'That do I likewise affirm,' quoth Master Curate; 'and, in sooth, to-morrow shall not pass over us without making a public process against them, and condemn them to be burnt in the fire, that they may not minister occasion again to such as may read them, to do that which I fear my good friend hath done.'

The labourer and Don Quixote stood hearing all that which was said, and then he perfectly understood the disease of his neighbour, and therefore he began to cry aloud: 'Open the doors to Lord Valdovinos and to the Lord Marquis of Mantua, who comes very sore wounded and hurt, and to the Lord Moor, Abindarraez, whom the valorous Roderick of Narvaez, Constable of Antequera, brings as his prisoner!' All the household ran out, hearing these cries; and, some knowing their friend, the others their master and uncle, who had not yet alighted from the ass, because he was not able, they ran to embrace him; but he forbade them, saying, 'Stand still and touch me not, for I return very sore wounded and hurt, through default of my horse: carry me to my bed, and, if it be possible, send for the wise Urganda, that she may cure and look to my hurt.' 'See, in an ill hour,' quoth the old woman straightway, 'if my heart did not very well foretell me on which foot my master halted. Come up in good time, for we shall know how to cure you well enough without sending for that Urganda you have mentioned. Accursed, say I once again, and a hundred times accursed, may those books of knighthood be, which have brought you to such estate!' With that they bore him up to his bed, and searching for his wounds, could not find any; and then he said all was but bruising, by reason of a great fall he had with his horse Rozinante, as he fought with ten giants, the most unmeasurable and boldest that might be found in a great part of the earth. 'Hearken,' quoth the curate, 'we have also giants in the dance; by mine honesty, I will burn them all before to-morrow at night.' Then did they ask a thousand questions of Don Quixote; but he would answer to none of them, and only requested them to give him some meat, and suffer him to sleep, seeing rest was most behooveful for him. All which was done; and the curate informed himself at large of the labouring man, in what sort he had found Don Quixote, which he recounted to him, and also the follies he said, both at his finding and bringing to town; which did kindle more earnestly the licentiate's desire to do what he had resolved the next day; which was to call his friend the barber, Master Nicholas, with whom he came to Don Quixote's house.

CHAPTER VI

Of the Pleasant and Curious Search Made by the Curate and the Barber of Don Quixote's Library

WHO slept yet soundly. The curate sought for the keys of the library, the only authors of his harm, which the gentleman's niece gave unto him very willingly. All of them entered into it, and among the rest the old woman; wherein they found more than a hundred great volumes, and those very well bound, besides the small ones. And as soon as the old woman had seen them, she departed very hastily out of the chamber, and eftsoons returned with as great speed, with a holy-water pot and a sprinkler in her hand, and said: 'Hold, master licentiate, and sprinkle this chamber all about, lest there should lurk in it some one enchanter of the many which these books contain, and cry quittance with us for the penalties we mean to inflict on these books, by banishing them out of this world.' The simplicity of the good old woman caused the licentiate to laugh: who commanded the barber to fetch him down the books from their shelves, one by one, that he might peruse their arguments; for it might happen some to be found which in no sort deserved to be chastised with fire. 'No,' replied the niece, 'no; you ought not to pardon any of them, seeing they have all been offenders: it is better you throw them all into the base-court, and there make a pile of them, and then set them a-fire; if not, they may be carried into the yard, and there make a bonfire of them, and the smoke will offend nobody.' The old woman said as much, both of them thirsted so much for the death of these innocents; but the curate would not condescend thereto until he had first read the titles, at the least, of every book.

The first that Master Nicholas put into his hands was that of *Amadis of Gaul;* which the curate perusing a while: 'This comes not to me first of all others without some mystery; for, as I have heard told, this is the first book of knighthood that ever was printed in Spain, and all the others have had their beginning and original from this; and therefore methinks that we must condemn him to the fire, without all remission, as the dogmatiser and head of so bad a sect.' 'Not, so, fie!' quoth the barber; 'for I have heard that it is the very best contrived book of all those of that kind; and therefore he is to be pardoned, as the only complete one of his profession.' 'That is true,' replied the curate, 'and for that reason we do give him his life for this time. Let us see that other which lies next unto him.' 'It is,' quoth the barber, '*The Adventures of Splandian,* Amadis of Gaul's lawfully begotten son.' 'Yet, on mine honesty,' replied the curate, 'his father's goodness shall nothing avail him. Take this book, old mistress, and open the window, throw it down into the yard, and let it lay the foundation of our heap for the fire we mean to make.' She did what was commanded with great alacrity, and so the good *Splandian* fled into the yard, to expect with all patience the fire which he was threatened to abide. 'Forward,' quoth the curate. 'This that comes now,' said the barber, 'is *Amadis of Greece;* and, as I conjecture, all those that lie on this side are of the same lineage of Amadis.' 'Then let them go all to the yard,' quoth the curate, 'in exchange of burning *Queen Pintiquinestra,* and the shepherd *Darinel* with his eclogues, and the subtle and intricate discourses of the author, which are able to entangle the father that engendered me, if he went in form of a knight-errant.' 'I am of the same opinion,' quoth the barber. 'And I also,' said the niece. 'Then, since it is so,' quoth the old wife, 'let them come, and to the yard with them all.' They were rendered all up unto her, which were many in number: wherefore, to save a labour of going up and down the stairs, she threw them out at the window.

'What bundle is that?' quoth the curate. 'This is,' answered Master Nicholas, '*Don Olivante of Laura.*' 'The author of that book,' quoth the curate, 'composed likewise *The Garden of Flowers,* and, in good sooth, I can scarce resolve which of the two works is truest, or, to speak better, is less lying; only this much I can determine, that this must go to the yard, being a book foolish and arrogant.' 'This that follows is *Florismarte of Hircania,*' quoth the barber. 'Is Lord Florismarte there?' then replied the curate; 'then, by mine honesty, he shall briefly make his arrest in the yard, in despite of his wonderful birth and famous adventures; for the drouth and harshness of his style deserves no greater favour. To the yard with him, and this other, good masters.' 'With a very good will,' quoth old Mumpsimus; and straightway did execute his commandment with no small gladness. 'This is *Sir Platyr,*' quoth the barber. 'It is an ancient book,' replied the curate, 'wherein I find nothing meriting pardon; let him, without any reply, keep company with the rest.' Forthwith it was done. Then was another book opened, and they saw the title thereof to be *The Knight of the Cross.* 'For the holy title which this book beareth,' quoth the curate, 'his ignorance might be pardoned; but it is a common saying, "The devil lurks behind the cross"; wherefore let it go the fire.' The barber, taking another book, said, 'This is *The Mirror of Knighthood.*' 'I know his worship well,' quoth the curate. 'There goes among those books, I see, the *Lord Raynold of Montalban,* with his friends and companions, all of them greater thieves than Cacus, and the twelve peers of France, with the historiographer Turpin. I am, in truth, about to condemn them only to exile, forasmuch as they contain some part of the famous poet, Matthew Boyardo, his invention: out of which the Christian poet, Lodovic Ariosto, did likewise weave his work, which, if I can find among these, and that he speaks not his own native tongue, I'll use him with no respect; but if he talk in his own language, I will put him, for honour's sake, on my head.' 'If that be so,' quoth the barber, 'I have him at home in the Italian, but cannot understand him.' 'Neither were it good you should understand him,' replied the curate; 'and here we would willingly have excused the good captain that translated it into Spanish, from that labour, or bringing it into Spain, if it had pleased himself; for he hath deprived it of much natural worth in the translation: a fault incident to all those that presume to translate verses out of one language into another; for, though they employ all their industry and wit therein, they can never arrive to the height of that primitive conceit which they bring with them in their first birth. I say, therefore, that this book, and all the others that may be found in this library to treat of French affairs, be cast and deposited in some dry vault, until we may determine, with more deliberation, what we should do with them: always excepting *Bernardo del Carpio,* which must be there amongst the rest, and another called *Roncesvalles;* for these two, coming to my hands, shall be rendered up to those of the old guardian, and from hers into the fire's, without any remission.' All which was confirmed by the barber, who did ratify his sentence, holding it for good and discreet, because he knew the curate to be so virtuous a man, and so great a friend of the truth, as he would say nothing contrary to it for all the goods of the world.

And then, opening another book, he saw it was *Palmerin de Oliva,* near unto which stood another, entitled *Palmerin of England;* which the licentiate perceiving, said, 'Let *Oliva* be presently rent in pieces, and burned in such sort that even the very ashes thereof may not be found; and let *Palmerin of England* be preserved, as a thing rarely delectable; and let such another box as that which Alexander found among Darius' spoils, and deputed to keep Homer's works, be made for it; for, gossip, this book hath sufficient authority for two reasons; the first, because of itself it is very good, and excellently contrived; the other, forasmuch as the report runs, that a certain discreet king of Portugal was the author thereof. All the adventures of the Castle of Miraguarda are excellent and artificial; the discourses very clear and courtly, observing evermore a decorum in him that speaks, with great propriety and conceit; therefore I say, Master Nicholas, if you think good, this and *Amadis de Gaul* may be preserved from the fire, and let all the rest, without further search or regard, perish.' 'In the devil's name, do not so, gentle gossip,' replied the barber; 'for this which I hold now in my hand is the famous *Don Belianis.*' 'What! he?' quoth the curate; 'the second, third, and fourth part thereof have great need of some rhubarb to purge his excessive choler, and we must, moreover, take out of him all that of the Castle of Fame, and other impertinences of more consequence. Therefore, we give them a *terminus ultramarinus,* and as they shall be corrected, so will we use mercy or justice towards them; and in the mean space, gossip, you may keep them at your house, but permit no man to read them.' 'I am pleased,' quoth the barber; and, being unwilling to tire himself any more by reading of titles, he bade the old woman to take all the great volumes and throw them into the yard. The words were not spoken to a mome or deaf person, but to one that had more desire to burn them than to weave a piece of linen, were it never so great and fine; and therefore, taking eight of them together, she threw them all out of the window, and returning the second time, thinking to carry away a great many at once, one of them fell at the barber's feet, who, desirous to know the title, saw that it was *The History of the famous Knight Tirante the White*. 'Good God!' quoth the curate, with a loud voice, 'is *Tirante the White* here? Give me it, gossip; for I make account to find in it a treasure of delight, and a copious mine of pastime. Here is Don Quireleison of Montalban, a valiant knight; and his brother Thomas of Montalban, and the Knight Fonseca, and the combat which the valiant Detriante fought with Alano, and the witty conceits of the damsel Plazerdemivida, with the love and guiles of the widow Reposada, and of the empress enamoured on her squire Ipolito. I say unto you, gossip, that this book is, for the style, one of the best of the world: in it knights do eat, and drink, and sleep, and die in their beds naturally, and make their testaments before their death; with many other things which all other books of this subject do want; yet, notwithstanding, if I might be judge, the author thereof deserved, because he purposely penned and wrote so many follies, to be sent to the galleys for all the days of his life. Carry it home and read it, and you shall see all that I have said thereof to be true.' 'I believe it very well,' quoth the barber; 'but what shall we do with these little books that remain?' 'These, as I take,' said the curate, 'are not books of knighthood, but of poetry.' And, opening one, he perceived it was the *Diana* of Montemayor; and, believing that all the rest were of that stamp, he said: 'These deserve not to be burned with the rest, for they have not, nor can do, so much hurt as books of knighthood, being all of them works full of understanding and conceits, and do not prejudice any other.' 'Oh, good sir,' quoth Don Quixote his niece, 'your reverence shall likewise do well to have them also burnt, lest that mine uncle, after he be cured of his knightly disease, may fall, by reading of these, in a humour of becoming a shepherd, and so wander through the woods and fields, singing of roundelays, and playing on a crowd; and what is more dangerous than to become a poet? which is, as some say, an incurable and infectious disease.' 'This maiden says true,' quoth the curate; 'and it will not be amiss to remove this stumbling-block and occasion out of our friend's way; and since we begin with the *Diana* of Montemayor, I am of opinion that it be not burned, but only that all that which treats of the wise Felicia, and of the enchanted water, be taken away, and also all the longer verses, and let him remain with his prose, and the honour of being the best of that kind.' 'This that follows,' quoth the barber, 'is the *Diana,* called the second, written by him of Salamanca; and this other is of the same name, whose author is Gil Polo.' 'Let that of Salamanca,' answered master parson, 'augment the number of the condemned in the yard, and that of Gil Polo be kept as charily as if it were Apollo his own work; and go forward speedily, good gossip, for it grows late. 'This book,' quoth the barber, opening of another, 'is *The Twelve Books of the Fortunes of Love,* written by Anthony Lofraso, the Sardinian poet.' 'By the holy orders which I have received,' quoth the curate, 'since Apollo was Apollo, and the muses muses, and poets poets, was never written so delightful and extravagant a work as this; and that, in his way and vein, it is the only one of all the books that have ever issued of that kind to view the light of the world, and he that hath not read it may make account that he hath never read matter of delight. Give it to me, gossip, for I do prize more the finding of it than I would the gift of a cassock of the best satin of Florence.' And so, with great joy, he laid it aside. And the barber prosecuted, saying, 'These that follow be *The Shepherd of Iberia, The Nymphs of Enares,* and *The Reclaiming of the Jealousies.*' 'Then there's no more to be done but to deliver them up to the secular arm of the old wife, and do not demand the reason, for that were never to make an end.' 'This that comes is *The Shepherd of Filida.*' 'That is not a shepherd,' quoth the curate, 'but a very complete courtier; let it be reserved as a precious jewel.' 'This great one that follows is,' said the barber, 'entitled *The Treasure of Divers Poems.*' 'If they had not been so many,' replied the curate, 'they would have been more esteemed. It is necessary that this book be carded and purged of certain base things that lurk among his high conceits. Let him be kept, both because the author is my very great friend, and in regard of other more heroical and lofty works he hath written.' 'This is,' said the barber, 'the *Ditty Book* of Lopez Maldonado.' 'The author of that work is likewise my great friend,' replied the parson; 'and his lines, pronounced by himself, do ravish the hearers, and such is the sweetness of his voice when he sings them, as it doth enchant the ear. He is somewhat prolix in his eclogues, but that which is good is never superfluous; let him be kept among the choicest. But what book is that which lies next unto him?' 'The *Galatea* of Michael Cervantes,' quoth the barber. 'That Cervantes,' said the curate, 'is my old acquaintance this many a year, and I know he is more practised in misfortunes than in verses. His book hath some good invention in it; he intends and propounds somewhat, but concludes nothing; therefore we must expect the second part, which he hath promised; perhaps his amendment may obtain him a general remission, which until now is denied him; and whilst we expect the sight of his second work, keep this part closely imprisoned in your lodging.' 'I am very well content to do so, good gossip,' said the barber; 'and here there come three together: the *Auracana* of Don Alonso de Ercilla, the *Austriada* of John Ruffo, one of the magistrates of Cordova, and the *Monserrato* of Christopher de Virnes, a Valencian poet.' 'All these three books,' quoth the curate, 'are the best that are written in heroical verse in the Castilian tongue, and may compare with the most famous of Italy; reserve them as the richest pawns that Spain enjoyeth of poetry.' The curate with this grew weary to see so many books, and so he would have all the rest burned at all adventures. But the barber, ere the sentence was given, had opened, by chance, one entitled *The Tears of Angelica*. 'I would have shed those tears myself,' said the curate, 'if I had wittingly caused such a book to be burned; for the author thereof was one of the most famous poets of the world, not only of Spain, and was most happy in the translation of certain fables of Ovid.'

CHAPTER VII

Of the Second Departure Which Our Good Knight, Don Quixote, Made from His House to Seek Adventures

WHILE they were thus busied, Don Quixote began to cry aloud, saying, 'Here, here, valorous knights! Here it is needful that you show the force of your valiant arms; for the courtiers begin to bear away the best of the tourney.' The folk repairing to this rumour and noise, was an occasion that any further speech and visitation of the books was omitted; and therefore it is to be suspected, that the *Carolea* and *Lion of Spain,* with the *Acts of the Emperor Charles the Fifth,* written by Don Louis de Avila, were burned, without being ever seen or heard; and perhaps if the curate had seen them, they should not have passed under so rigorous a sentence. When they all arrived to Don Quixote his chamber, he was risen already out of his bed, and continued still his outcries, cutting and slashing on every side, being so broadly awake as if he never had slept. Wherefore, taking him in their arms, they returned him by main force into his bed, and, after he was somewhat quiet and settled, he said, turning himself to the curate, 'In good sooth, Lord Archbishop Turpin, it is a great dishonour to us that are called the twelve Peers, to permit the knights of the court to bear thus away the glory of the tourney without more ado, seeing that we the adventurers have gained the prize thereof the three foremost days.' 'Hold your peace, good gossip,' quoth the curate, 'for fortune may be pleased to change the success, and what is lost to-day may be won again to-morrow. Look you to your health for the present; for you seem at least to be very much tired, if besides you be not sore wounded.' 'Wounded! no,' quoth Don Quixote; 'but doubtless I am somewhat bruised, for that bastard, Don Rowland, hath beaten me to powder with the stock of an oak-tree; and all for envy, because he sees that I only dare oppose myself to his valour. But let me be never again called Raynold of Montealban if he pay not dearly for it, as soon as I rise from this bed, in despite of all his enchantment. But, I pray you, call for my breakfast, for I know it will do me much good, and leave the revenge of this wrong to my charge.' Presently meat was brought; and after he had eaten he fell asleep, and they remained astonished at his wonderful madness. That night the old woman burned all the books that she found in the house and yard; and some there were burnt that deserved, for their worthiness, to be kept up in everlasting treasuries, if their fortunes and the laziness of the searchers had permitted it. And so the proverb was verified in them, 'that the just pays sometimes for the sinners.' One of the remedies which the curate and the barber prescribed for that present, to help their friend's disease, was that they should change his chamber, and dam up his study, to the end that, when he arose, he might not find them; for, perhaps, by removing the cause, they might also take away the effects: and, moreover, they bade them to say that a certain enchanter had carried them away, study and all; which device was presently put in practice. And, within two days after, Don Quixote got up, and the first thing he did was to go and visit his books; and seeing he could not find the chamber in the same place where he had left it, he went up and down to find it. Sometimes he came to the place where the door stood, and felt it with his hands, and then would turn his eyes up and down here and there to seek it, without speaking a word. But at last, after deliberation, he asked of the old woman the way to his books. She, as one well schooled before what she should answer, said, 'What study, or what nothing, is this you look for? There is now no more study nor books in this house; for the very devil himself carried all away with him.' 'It was not the devil,' said his niece, 'but an enchanter, that came here one night upon a cloud, the day after you departed from hence; and, alighting down from a serpent upon which he rode, he entered into the study, and what he did therein I know not; and within a while after he fled out at the roof of the house, and left all the house full of smoke; and when we accorded to see what he had done, we could neither see book nor study: only this much the old woman and I do remember very well, that the naughty old man, at his departure, said, with a loud voice, that he, for hidden enmity that he bore to the lord of those books, had done all the harm to the house that they might perceive when he were departed, and added that he was named the wise Muniaton. 'Frestron, you would have said,' quoth Don Quixote. 'I know not,' quoth the old woman, 'whether he hight Frestron or Friton, but well I wot that his name ended with "ton."' 'That is true,' quoth Don Quixote; 'and he is a very wise enchanter, and my great adversary, and looks on me with a sinister eye; for he knows, by his art and science, that I shall in time fight a single combat with a knight, his very great friend, and overcome him in battle, without being able to be by him assisted, and therefore he labours to do me all the hurt he may; and I have sent him word, that he strives in vain to divert or shun that which is by Heaven already decreed.' 'Who doubts of that?' quoth his niece. 'But I pray you, good uncle, say, what need have you to thrust yourself into these difficulties and brabbles? Were it not better to rest you quietly in your own house, than to wander through the world, searching bread of blasted corn, without once considering how many there go to seek for wool that return again shorn themselves?' 'Oh, niece,' quoth Don Quixote, 'how ill dost thou understand the matter! Before I permit myself to be shorn, I will pill and pluck away the beards of as many as shall dare or imagine to touch but a hair only of me.' To these words the women would make no reply, because they saw his choler increase.

Fifteen days he remained quietly at home, without giving any argument of seconding his former vanities; in which time passed many pleasant encounters between him and his two gossips, the curate and barber, upon that point which he defended, to wit, that the world needed nothing so much as knights-errant, and that the erratical knighthood ought to be again renewed therein. Master parson would contradict him sometimes, and other times yield unto that he urged; for had they not observed that manner of proceeding, it were impossible to bring him to any conformity. In this space Don Quixote dealt with a certain labourer, his neighbour, an honest man (if the title of honesty may be given to the poor), but one of a very shallow wit; in resolution, he said so much to him, and persuaded him so earnestly, and made him so large promises, as the poor fellow determined to go away with him, and serve him as his squire. Don Quixote, among many other things, bade him to dispose himself willingly to depart with him; for now and then such an adventure might present itself, that, in as short space as one would take up a couple of straws, an island might be won, and he be left as governor thereof. With these and such like promises, Sancho Panza (for so he was called) left his wife and children, and agreed to be his squire. Afterward, Don Quixote began to cast plots how to come by some money; which he achieved by selling one thing, pawning another, and turning all upside down. At last he got a pretty sum, and, accommodating himself with a buckler which he had borrowed of a friend, and patching up his broken beaver again as well as he could, he advertised his squire Sancho of the day and hour wherein he meant to depart, that he might likewise furnish himself with that which he thought needful; but above all things he charged him to provide himself of a wallet; which he promised to perform, and said that he meant also to carry a very good ass, which he had of his own, because he was not wont to travel much a-foot. In that of the ass Don Quixote stood a while pensive, calling to mind whether ever he had read that any knight-errant carried his squire assishly mounted; but he could not remember any authority for it; yet, notwithstanding, he resolved that he might bring his beast, with intention to accommodate him more honourably, when occasion were offered, by dismounting the first discourteous knight they met, from his horse, and giving it to his squire; he also furnished himself with shirts, and as many other things as he might, according unto the innkeeper's advice. All which being finished, Sancho Panza, without bidding his wife and children farewell, or Don Quixote his niece and old servant, they both departed one night out of the village, unknown to any person living; and they travelled so far that night, as they were sure in the morning not to be found, although they were pursued. Sancho Panza rode on his beast like a patriarch, with his wallet and bottle, and a marvellous longing to see himself governor of the island which his master had promised unto him.

Don Quixote took by chance the very same course and way that he had done in his first voyage through the field of Montiel, wherein he travelled then with less vexation than the first; for, by reason it was early, and the sunbeams striking not directly down, but athwart, the heat did not trouble them much. And Sancho Panza, seeing the opportunity good, said to his master, 'I pray you, have care, good sir knight, that you forget not that government of the island which you have promised me, for I shall be able to govern it were it never so great.' To which Don Quixote replied: 'You must understand, friend Sancho Panza, that it was a custom very much used by ancient knights-errant, to make their squires governors of the islands and kingdoms that they conquered; and I am resolved that so good a custom shall never be abolished by me, but rather I will pass and exceed them therein; for they sometimes, and as I take it, did, for the greater part, expect until their squires waxed aged; and after they were cloyed with service, and had suffered many bad days and worse nights, then did they bestow upon them some title of an earl, or at least of a marquis, of some valley or province, of more or less account. But if thou livest, and I withal, it may happen that I may conquer such a kingdom within six days, that hath other kingdoms adherent to it, which would fall out as just as it were cast in a mould for thy purpose, whom I would crown presently king of one of them. And do not account this to be any great matter; for things and chances do happen to such knights-adventurers as I am, by so unexpected and wonderful ways and means, as I might give thee very easily a great deal more than I have promised.' 'After that manner,' said Sancho Panza, 'if I were a king, through some miracle of those which you say, then should Joan Gutierez, my wife, become a queen, and my children princes!' 'Who doubts of that?' said Don Quixote. 'That do I,' replied Sancho Panza; 'for I am fully persuaded, that although God would rain kingdoms down upon the earth, none of them would sit well on Mary Gutierez her head; for, sir, you must understand that she's not worth a dodkin for a queen. To be a countess would agree with her better; and yet, I pray God that she be able to discharge that calling.' 'Commend thou the matter to God,' quoth Don Quixote, 'that He may give her that which is most convenient for her. But do not thou abase thy mind so much as to content thyself with less than at the least to be a viceroy.' 'I will not, good sir,' quoth Sancho, 'especially seeing I have so worthy a lord and master as yourself, who knows how to give me all that may turn to my benefit, and that I shall be able to discharge in good sort.'

CHAPTER VIII

Of the Good Success Don Quixote Had, in the Dreadful and Never-imagined Adventure of the Windmills, with Other Accidents Worthy to Be Recorded

AS they discoursed, they discovered some thirty or forty windmills, that are in that field; and as soon as Don Quixote espied them, he said to his squire, 'Fortune doth address our affairs better than we ourselves could desire; for behold there, friend Sancho Panza, how there appears thirty or forty monstrous giants, with whom I mean to fight, and deprive them all of their lives, with whose spoils we will begin to be rich; for this is a good war, and a great service unto God, to take away so bad a seed from the face of the earth.' 'What giants?' quoth Sancho Panza. 'Those that thou seest there,' quoth his lord, 'with the long arms; and some there are of that race whose arms are almost two leagues long.' 'I pray you understand,' quoth Sancho Panza, 'that those which appear there are no giants, but windmills; and that which seems in them to be arms, are their sails, that, swung about by the wind, do also make the mill go.' 'It seems well,' quoth Don Quixote, 'that thou art not yet acquainted with matter of adventures. They are giants; and, if thou beest afraid, go aside and pray, whilst I enter into cruel and unequal battle with them.' And, saying so, he spurred his horse Rozinante, without taking heed to his squire Sancho's cries, advertising him how they were doubtless windmills that he did assault, and no giants; but he went so fully persuaded that they were giants as he neither heard his squire's outcries, nor did discern what they were, although he drew very near to them, but rather said, as loud as he could, 'Fly not, ye cowards and vile creatures! for it is only one knight that assaults you.'

With this the wind increased, and the mill sails began to turn about; which Don Quixote espying, said, 'Although thou movest more arms than the giant Briareus thou shalt stoop to me.' And, after saying this, and commending himself most devoutly to his Lady Dulcinea, desiring her to succor him in that trance, covering himself well with his buckler, and setting his lance on his rest, he spurred on Rozinante, and encountered with the first mill that was before him, and, striking his lance into the sail, the wind swung it about with such fury, that it broke his lance into shivers, carrying him and his horse after it, and finally tumbled him a good way off from it on the field in evil plight. Sancho Panza repaired presently to succor him as fast as his ass could drive; and when he arrived, he found him not able to stir, he had gotten such a crush with Rozinante. 'Good God!' quoth Sancho, 'did I not foretell unto you that you should look well what you did, for they were none other than windmills? nor could any think otherwise, unless he had also windmills in his brains.' 'Peace, Sancho,' quoth Don Quixote; 'for matters of war are more subject than any other thing to continual change; how much more, seeing I do verily persuade myself, that the wise Frestron, who robbed my study and books, hath transformed these giants into mills, to deprive me of the glory of the victory, such is the enmity he bears towards me. But yet, in fine, all his bad arts shall but little prevail against the goodness of my sword.' 'God grant it as he may!' said Sancho Panza, and then helped him to arise; and presently he mounted on Rozinante, who was half shoulder-pitched by rough encounter; and, discoursing upon that adventure, they followed on the way which guided towards the passage or gate of Lapice; for there, as Don Quixote avouched, it was not possible but to find many adventures, because it was a thoroughfare much frequented; and yet he affirmed that he went very much grieved, because he wanted a lance; and, telling it to his squire, he said, 'I remember how I have read that a certain Spanish knight, called Diego Peres of Vargas, having broken his sword in a battle, tore off a great branch or stock from an oak-tree, and did such marvels with it that day, and battered so many Moors, as he remained with the surname of Machuca, which signifies a stump, and as well he as all his progeny were ever after that day called Vargas and Machuca. I tell thee this, because I mean to tear another branch, such, or as good as that at least, from the first oak we shall encounter, and I mean to achieve such adventures therewithal, as thou wilt account thyself fortunate for having merited to behold them, and be a witness of things almost incredible.' 'In God's name!' quoth Sancho, 'I do believe every word you said. But, I pray you, sit right in your saddle; for you ride sideling, which proceeds, as I suppose, of the bruising you got by your fall.' 'Thou sayst true,' quoth Don Quixote; 'and if I do not complain of the grief, the reason is, because knights-errant use not to complain of any wound, although their guts did issue out thereof.' 'If it be so,' quoth Sancho, 'I know not what to say; but God knows that I would be glad to hear you to complain when anything grieves you. Of myself I dare affirm, that I must complain of the least grief that I have, if it be not likewise meant that the squires of knights-errant must not complain of any harm.' Don Quixote could not refrain laughter, hearing the simplicity of his squire; and after showed unto him that he might lawfully complain, both when he pleased, and as much as he listed with desire, or without it; for he had never yet read anything to the contrary in the order of knighthood. Then Sancho said unto him that it was dinner-time. To whom he answered, that he needed no repast; but if he had will to eat, he might begin when he pleased. Sancho, having obtained his license, did accommodate himself on his ass's back the best he might. Taking out of his wallet some belly-munition, he rode after his master, travelling and eating at once, and that with great leisure; and ever and anon he lifted up his bottle with such pleasure as the best-fed victualler of Malaga might envy his state; and whilst he rode, multiplying of quaffs in that manner, he never remembered any of the promises his master had made him, nor did he hold the fetch of adventures to be a labour, but rather a great recreation and ease, were they never so dangerous. In conclusion, they passed over that night under certain trees, from one of which Don Quixote tore a withered branch, which might serve him in some sort for a lance; and therefore he set thereon the iron of his own, which he had reserved when it was broken.

All that night Don Quixote slept not one wink, but thought upon his Lady Dulcinea, that he might conform himself to what he had read in his books of adventures, when knights passed over many nights without sleep in forests and fields, only entertained by the memory of their mistresses. But Sancho spent not his time so vainly;

for, having his stomach well stuffed, and that not with succory water, he carried smoothly away the whole night in one sleep; and if his master had not called him up, neither the sunbeams which struck on his visage, nor the melody of the birds, which were many, and did cheerfully welcome the approach of the new day, could have been able to awake him. At his arising he gave one assay to the bottle, which he found to be somewhat more weak than it was the night before, whereat his heart was somewhat grieved; for he mistrusted that they took not a course to remedy that defect so soon as he wished. Nor could Don Quixote break his fast, who, as we have said, meant only to sustain himself with pleasant remembrances.

Then did they return to their commenced way towards the port of Lapice, which they discovered about three of the clock in the afternoon. 'Here,' said Don Quixote, as soon as he kenned it, 'may we, friend Sancho, thrust our hands up to the very elbows in that which is called adventures. But observe well this caveat which I shall give thee, that, although thou seest me in the greatest dangers of the world, thou must not set hand to thy sword in my defence, if thou dost not see that those which assault me be base and vile vulgar people; for in such a case thou mayst assist me. Marry, if they be knights, thou mayst not do so in anywise, nor is it permitted, by the laws of arms, that thou mayst help me, until thou beest likewise dubbed knight thyself.' 'I do assure you, sir,' quoth Sancho, 'that herein you shall be most punctually obeyed; and therefore chiefly in respect that I am of mine own nature a quiet and peaceable man, and a mortal enemy of thrusting myself into stirs or quarrels; yet it is true that, touching the defence of mine own person, I will not be altogether so observant of those laws, seeing that both divine and human allow every man to defend himself from any one that would wrong him.' 'I say no less,' answered Don Quixote; 'but in this of aiding me against any knight, thou must set bounds to thy natural impulses.' 'I say I will do so,' quoth Sancho; 'and I will observe this commandment as punctually as that of keeping holy the Sabbath day.'

Whilst thus they reasoned, there appeared in the way two monks of St. Benet's order, mounted on two dromedaries; for the mules whereon they rode were but little less. They wore masks with spectacles in them, to keep away the dust from their faces; and each of them besides bore their umbrills. After them came a coach, and four or five a-horseback accompanying it, and two lackeys that ran hard by it. There came therein, as it was after known, a certain Biscaine lady, which travelled towards Seville, where her husband sojourned at the present, and was going to the Indies with an honorable charge. The monks rode not with her, although they travelled the same way. Scarce had Don Quixote perceived them, when he said to his squire, 'Either I am deceived, or else this will prove the most famous adventure that ever hath been seen; for these two great black bulks, which appear there, are, questionless, enchanters, that steal, or carry away perforce, some princess in that coach; and therefore I must, with all my power, undo that wrong.' 'This will be worse than the adventure of the windmills,' quoth Sancho. 'Do not you see, sir, that those are friars of St. Benet's order? and the coach can be none other than of some travellers. Therefore, listen to mine advice, and see well what you do, lest the devil deceive you.' 'I have said already to thee, Sancho, that thou art very ignorant in matter of adventures. What I say is true, as now thou shalt see.' And, saying so, he spurred on his horse, and placed himself just in the midst of the way by which the friars came; and when they approached so near as he supposed they might hear him, he said, with a loud voice, 'Devilish and wicked people! leave presently those high princesses which you violently carry away with you in that coach; or, if you will not, prepare yourselves to receive sudden death, as a just punishment of your bad works.' The friars held their horses, and were amazed both at the shape and words of Don Quixote; to whom they answered: 'Sir knight, we are neither devilish nor wicked, but religious men of St. Benet's order, that travel about our affairs; and we know not whether or no there come any princesses forced in this coach.' 'With me fair words take no effect,' quoth Don Quixote; 'for I know you very well, treacherous knaves!' And then, without expecting their reply, he set spurs to Rozinante, and, laying his lance on the thigh, charged the first friar with such fury and rage, that if he had not suffered himself willingly to fall off his mule, he would not only have overthrown him against his will, but likewise have slain. or at least wounded him very ill with the blow. The second religious man, seeing how ill his companion was used, made no words; but, setting spurs to that castle his mule, did fly away through the field, as swift as the wind itself. Sancho Panza, seeing the monk overthrown, dismounted very speedily off his ass, and ran over to him, and would have ransacked his habits. In this arrived the monks' two lackeys, and demanded of him why he thus despoiled the friar. Sancho replied that it was his due, by the law of arms, as lawful spoils gained in battle by his lord, Don Quixote. The lackeys, which understood not the jest, nor knew not what words of battle or spoils meant, seeing that Don Quixote was now out of the way, speaking with those that came in the coach, set both at once upon Sancho, and left him not a hair in his beard but they plucked, and did so trample him under their feet, as they left him stretched on the ground without either breath or feeling. The monk, cutting off all delays, mounted again on horseback, all affrighted, having scarce any drop of blood left in his face through fear; and, being once up, he spurred after his fellow, who expected him a good way off, staying to see the success of that assault; and, being unwilling to attend the end of that strange adventure, they did prosecute their journey, blessing and crossing themselves as if the devil did pursue them.

Don Quixote, as is rehearsed, was in this season speaking to the lady of the coach, to whom he said: 'Your beauty, dear lady, may dispose from henceforth of your person as best ye liketh; for the pride of your robbers lies now prostrated on the ground, by this my invincible arm. And because you may not be troubled to know your deliverer his name, know that I am called Don Quixote de la Mancha, a knight-errant and adventurer, and captive to the peerless and beautiful Lady Dulcinea of Toboso. And, in reward of the benefit which you have received at my hands, I demand nothing else but that you return to Toboso, and there present yourselves, in my name, before my lady, and recount unto her what I have done to obtain your liberty.' To all these words which Don Quixote said, a certain Biscaine squire, that accompanied the coach, gave ear; who, seeing that Don Quixote suffered not the coach to pass onward, but said that it must presently turn back to Toboso, he drew near to him, and, laying hold on his lance, he said, in his bad Spanish and worse

Basquish: 'Get thee away, knight, in an ill hour. By the God that created me, if thou leave not the coach, I will kill thee, as sure as I am a Biscaine.' Don Quixote, understanding him, did answer, with great staidness: 'If thou were a knight, as thou art not, I would by this have punished thy folly and presumption, caitiff creature!' The Biscaine replied, with great fury: 'Not I a gentleman! I swear God thou liest, as well as I am a Christian. If thou cast away thy lance, and draw thy sword, thou shalt see the water as soon as thou shalt carry away the cat: a Biscaine by land, and a gentleman by sea, a gentleman in spite of the devil; and thou liest, if other things thou sayst!' '"Straight thou shalt see that," said Agrages,' replied Don Quixote; and, throwing his lance to the ground, he out with his sword, and took his buckler, and set on the Biscaine, with resolution to kill him. The Biscaine, seeing him approach in that manner, although he desired to alight off his mule, which was not to be trusted, being one of those naughty ones which are wont to be hired, yet had he no leisure to do any other thing than to draw out his sword; but it befel him happily to be near to the coach, out of which he snatched a cushion, that served him for a shield; and presently the one made upon the other like mortal enemies. Those that were present laboured all that they might, but in vain, to compound the matter between them; for the Biscaine swore, in his bad language, that if they hindered him from ending the battle, he would put his lady, and all the rest that dared to disturb him, to the sword.

The lady, astonished and fearful of that which she beheld, commanded the coachman to go a little out of the way, and sat aloof, beholding the rigorous conflict; in the progress whereof the Biscaine gave Don Quixote over the target a mighty blow on one of the shoulders, where, if it had not found resistance in his armour, it would doubtlessly have cleft him down to the girdle. Don Quixote, feeling the weight of that unmeasurable blow, cried, with a loud voice, saying, 'O Dulcinea! lady of my soul! the flower of all beauty! succor this thy knight, who to set forth thy worth, finds himself in this dangerous trance!' The saying of these words, the gripping fast of his sword, the covering of himself well with his buckler, and the assailing of the Biscaine, was done all in one instant, resolving to venture all the success of the battle on that one only blow. The

Biscaine, who perceived him come in that manner, perceived, by his doughtiness, his intention, and resolved to do the like; and therefore expected him very well, covered with his cushion, not being able to manage his mule as he wished from one part to another, who was not able to go a step, it was so wearied, as a beast never before used to the like toys. Don Quixote, as we have said, came against the wary Biscaine with his sword lifted aloft, with full resolution to part him in two; and all the beholders stood, with great fear suspended, to see the success of those monstrous blows wherewithal they threatened one another. And the lady of the coach, with her gentlewomen, made a thousand vows and offerings to all the devout places of Spain, to the end that God might deliver the squire and themselves out of that great danger wherein they were.

But it is to be deplored how, in this very point and term, the author of this history leaves his battle depending, excusing himself that he could find no more written of the acts of Don Quixote than those which he hath already recounted. True it is, that the second writer of this work would not believe that so curious a history was drowned in the jaws of oblivion, or that the wits of the Mancha were so little curious as not to reserve among their treasures or records some papers treating of this famous knight; and therefore, encouraged by this presumption, he did not despair to find the end of this pleasant history; which, Heaven being propitious to him, he got at last, after the manner that shall be recounted in the Second Part.

THE SECOND BOOK

CHAPTER I

Wherein Is Related the Events of the Fearful Battle Which the Gallant Biscaine Fought with Don Quixote

WE left the valorous Biscaine and the famous Don Quixote, in the First Part, with their swords lifted up and naked, in terms to discharge one upon another two furious cleavers, and such, as if they had lighted rightly, would cut and divide them both from the top to the toe, and open them like a pomegranate; and in that so doubtful a taking the delightful history stopped and remained dismembered, the author thereof leaving us no notice where we might find the rest of the narration. This grieved me not a little, but wholly turned the pleasure I took in reading the beginning thereof into disgust, thinking how small commodity was offered to find out so much as in my opinion wanted of this so delectable a tale. It seemed unto me almost impossible, and contrary to all good order, that so good a knight should want some wise man that would undertake his wonderful prowess and feats of chivalry: a thing that none of those knights-errant ever wanted, of whom people speak; for each of them had one or two wise men, of purpose, that did not only write their acts, but also depainted their very least thoughts and toys, were they never so hidden. And surely so good a knight could not be so unfortunate as to want that wherewith Platyr and others his like abounded; and therefore could not induce myself to believe that so gallant a history might remain maimed and lame, and did rather cast the fault upon the malice of the time, who is a consumer and devourer of all things, which had either hidden or consumed it. Methought, on the other side, seeing that among his books were found some modern works, such as the *Undeceiving of Jealousy,* and the *Nymphs and Shepherds of Henares,* that also his own history must have been new; and if that it were not written, yet was the memory of him fresh among the dwellers of his own village and the other villages adjoining. This imagination held me suspended, and desirous to learn really and truly all the life and miracles of our famous Spaniard, Don Quixote of the Mancha, the light and mirror of all Manchical chivalry, being the first who, in this our age and time, so full of calamities, did undergo the travels and exercise of arms-errant; and undid wrongs, succored widows, protected damsels that rode up and down with their whips and palfreys, and with all their virginity on their backs, from hill to hill and dale to dale; for, if it happened not that some lewd miscreant, or some clown with a hatchet and long hair, or some monstrous giant, did force them, damsels there were in times past that at the end of fourscore years old, all which time they never slept one day under a roof, went as entire and pure maidens to their graves as the very mother that bore them. Therefore I say, that as well for this as for many other good respects, our gallant Don Quixote is worthy of continual and memorable praises; nor can the like be justly denied to myself, for the labour and diligence which I used to find out the end of this grateful history, although I know very well that, if Heaven, chance, and fortune had not assisted me, the world had been deprived of the delight and pastime that they may take for almost two hours together, who shall with attention read it. The manner, therefore, of finding it was this:

Being one day walking in the exchange of Toledo, a certain boy by chance would have sold divers old quires and scrolls of books to a squire that walked up and down in that place, and I, being addicted to read such scrolls, though I found them torn in the streets, borne away by this my natural inclination, took one of the quires in my hand, and perceived it to be written in Arabical characters, and seeing that, although I knew the letters, yet could I not read the substance, I looked about to view whether I could perceive any Moor turned Spaniard thereabouts, that could read them; nor was it very difficult to find there such an interpreter; for, if I had searched one of another better and more ancient language, that place would easily afford him. In fine, my good fortune presented one to me; to whom telling my desire, and setting the book in his hand, he opened it, and, having read a little therein, began to laugh.

I demanded of him why he laughed; and he answered, at that marginal note which the book had. I bade him to expound it to me, and with that took him a little aside; and he, continuing still his laughter, said: 'There is written there, on this margin, these words: "This Dulcinea of Toboso, so many times spoken of in this history, had the best hand for powdering of porks of any woman in all the Mancha."' When I heard it make mention of Dulcinea of Toboso, I rested amazed and suspended, and imagined forthwith that those quires contained the history of Don Quixote. With this conceit I hastened him to read the beginning, which he did, and, translating the Arabical into Spanish in a trice, he said that it begun thus: '*The History of Don Quixote of the Mancha,* written by Cid Hamete Benengeli, an Arabical historiographer.' Much discretion was requisite to dissemble the content of mind I conceived when I heard the title of the book, and preventing the squire, I bought all the boy's scrolls and papers for a real; and were he of discretion, or knew my desire, he might have promised himself easily, and also have borne away with him, more than six reals for his merchandise. I departed after with the Moor to the cloister of the great church, and I requested him to turn me all the Arabical sheets that treated of Don Quixote into Spanish, without adding or taking away anything from them, and I would pay him what he listed for his pains. He demanded fifty pounds of raisins and three bushels of wheat, and promised to translate them speedily, well, and faithfully. But I, to hasten the matter more, lest I should lose such an unexpected and welcome treasure, brought him to my house, where he translated all the work in less than a month and a half, even in the manner that it is here recounted.

There was painted, in the first quire, very naturally, the battle betwixt Don Quixote and the Biscaine; even in the same manner that the history relateth it, with their swords lifted aloft, the one covered with his buckler, the other with the cushion; and the Biscaine's mule was delivered so naturally as a man might perceive it was hired, although he stood farther off than the shot of a cross-bow. The Biscaine had a title written under his feet that said, 'Don Sancho de Azpetia,' for so belike he was called; and at Rozinante his feet there was another, that said 'Don Quixote.' Rozinante was marvellous well portraited; so long and lank, so thin and lean, so like one labouring with an incurable consumption, as he did show very clearly with what consideration and propriety he had given unto him the name Rozinante. By him stood Sancho Panza, holding his ass by the halter; at whose feet was another scroll, saying, 'Sancho Zancas,' and I think the reason thereof was, that, as his picture showed, he had a great belly, a short stature, and thick legs; and therefore, I judge, he was called Panza, or Zanca; for both these names were written of him indifferently in the history. There were other little things in it worthy noting; but all of them are of no great importance, nor anything necessary for the true relation of the history; for none is ill, if it be true. And if any objection be made against the truth of this, it can be none other than that the author was a Moor; and it is a known propriety of that nation to be lying: yet, in respect that they hate us so mortally, it is to be conjectured that in this history there is rather want and concealment of our knight's worthy acts than any superfluity; which I imagine the rather, because I find in the progress thereof, many times, that when he might and ought to have advanced his pen in our knight's praises, he doth, as it were of purpose, pass them over in silence; which was very ill done, seeing that historiographers ought and should be very precise, true, and unpassionate; and that neither profit nor fear, rancour nor affection, should make them to tread awry from the truth, whose mother is history, the emulatress of time, the treasury of actions, the witness of things past, the advertiser of things to come. In this history I know a man may find all that he can desire in the most pleasing manner; and if they want anything to be desired, I am of opinion that it is through the fault of that ungracious knave that translated it, rather than through any defect in the subject. Finally, the Second Part thereof (according to the translation) began in this manner:

The trenchant swords of the two valorous and enraged combatants being lifted aloft, it seemed that they threatened heaven, the earth, and the depths, such was their hardiness and courage. And the first that discharged his blow was the Biscaine, which fell with such force and fury, as if the sword had not turned a little in the way, that only blow had been sufficient to set an end to the rigorous contention, and all other the adventures of our knight. But his good fortune, which reserved him for greater affairs, did wrest his adversary's sword awry in such sort, as though he struck him on the left shoulder, yet did it no more harm than disarm all that side, carrying away with it a great part of his beaver, with the half of his ear; all which fell to the ground with a dreadful ruin, leaving him in very ill case for a good time. Good God! who is he that can well describe, at this present, the fury that entered in the heart of our Manchegan, seeing himself used in that manner. Let us say no more, but that it was such that, stretching himself again in the stirrups, and gripping his sword fast in both his hands, he discharged such a terrible blow on the Biscaine, hitting him right upon the cushion, and by it on the head, that the strength and thickness thereof so little availed him, that, as if a whole mountain had fallen upon him, the blood gushed out of his mouth, nose, and ears, all at once, and he tottered so on his mule, that every step he took he was ready to fall off, as he would indeed if he had not taken him by the neck; yet, nevertheless, he lost the stirrups, and, losing his grip of the mule, it being likewise frighted by that terrible blow, ran away as fast as it could about the fields, and within two or three winches overthrew him to the ground. All which Don Quixote stood beholding with great quietness; and as soon as he saw him fall, he leaped off his horse, and ran over to him very speedily; and, setting the point of his sword on his eyes, he bade him yield himself, or else he would cut off his head. The Biscaine was so amazed as he could not speak a word; and it had succeeded very ill with him, considering Don Quixote's fury, if the ladies of the coach, which until then had beheld the conflict with great anguish, had not come where he was, and earnestly besought him to do them the favour to pardon their squire's life. Don Quixote answered, with a great loftiness and gravity: 'Truly, fair ladies, I am well apaid to grant you your request, but it must be with this agreement and condition, that this knight shall promise me to go to Toboso, and present himself, in my name, to the peerless Lady Dulcinea, to the end she may dispose of him as she pleaseth.' The timorous and comfortless lady, without considering what Don Quixote demanded, or asking what Dulcinea was, promised that her squire should accomplish all that he pleased to command. 'Why, then,' quoth Don Quixote, 'trusting to your promise, I'll do him no more harm, although he hath well deserved it at my hands.'

CHAPTER II

Of That Which after Befel Don Quixote When He Had Left the Ladies

BY this Sancho Panza had gotten up, though somewhat abused by the friars' lackeys, and stood attentively beholding his lord's combat, and prayed to God with all his heart, that it would please Him to give him the victory; and that he might therein win some island, whereof he might make him governor, as he had promised. And, seeing the controversy ended at last, and that his lord remounted upon Rozinante, he came to hold him the stirrup, and cast himself on his knees before him ere he got up, and, taking him by the hand, he kissed it, saying, 'I desire that it will please you, good my lord Don Quixote, to bestow upon me the government of that island which in this terrible battle you have won; for though it were never so great, yet do I find myself able enough to govern it, as well as any other whatsoever that ever governed island in this world.' To this demand Don Quixote answered: 'Thou must note, friend Sancho, that this adventure, and others of this kind, are not adventures of islands, but of thwartings and highways, wherein nothing else is gained but a broken pate, or the loss of an ear. Have patience a while; for adventures will be offered whereby thou shalt not only be made a governor, but also a greater man.' Sancho rendered him many thanks, and, kissing his hand again, and the skirt of his habergeon, he did help him to get up on Rozinante, and he leapt on his ass, and followed his lord, who, with a swift pace, without taking leave or speaking to those of the coach, entered into a wood that was hard at hand. Sancho followed him as fast as his beast could trot; but Rozinante went off so swiftly, as he, perceiving he was like to be left behind, was forced to call aloud to his master that he would stay for him, which Don Quixote did, by checking Rozinante with the bridle, until his wearied squire did arrive; who, as soon as he came, said unto him, 'Methinks, sir, that it will not be amiss to retire ourselves to some church; for, according as that man is ill dight with whom you fought, I certainly persuade myself that they will give notice of the fact to the holy brotherhood, and they will seek to apprehend us, which if they do, in good faith, before we can get out of their claws, I fear me we shall sweat for it.' 'Peace!' quoth Don Quixote; 'where hast thou ever read or seen that knight-errant that hath been brought before the judge, though he committed never so many homicides and slaughters?' 'I know nothing of omicills,' quoth Sancho, 'nor have I cared in my life for any; but well I wot that it concerns the Holy Brotherhood to deal with such as fight in the fields, and in that other I will not intermeddle.' 'Then be not afraid, friend,' quoth Don Quixote; 'for I will deliver thee out of the hands of the Chaldeans, how much more out of those of the brotherhood. But tell me, in very good earnest, whether thou didst ever see a more valorous knight than I am throughout the face of the earth? Didst thou ever read in histories of any other that hath, or ever had, more courage in assailing, more breath in persevering, more dexterity in offending, or more art in overthrowing, than I?' 'The truth is,' quoth Sancho, 'that I have never read any history; for I can neither read nor write: but that which I dare wager is, that I never in my life served a bolder master than you are; and I pray God that we pay not for this boldness there where I have said. That which I request you is, that you will cure yourself; for you lose much blood by that ear, and here I have lint and a little *unguentum album* in my wallet.' 'All this might be excused,' quoth Don Quixote, 'if I had remembered to make a vialful of the Balsam of Fierebras; for, with one drop of it, we might spare both time, and want well all those other medicines.' 'What vial, and what balsam, is that?' said Sancho Panza. 'It is,' answered Don Quixote, 'a balsam whereof I have the recipe in memory, which one possessing he needs not fear death, nor ought he to think that he may be killed by any wound; and therefore, after I have made it, and given it unto thee, thou hast nothing else to do, but when thou shalt see that in any battle I be cloven in twain (as many times it happens), thou shalt take fair and softly that part of my body that is fallen to the ground, and put it up again, with great subtlety, on the part that rests in the saddle, before the blood congeal, having evermore great care that thou place it just and equally; then presently after thou shalt give me two draughts of that balsam of which I have spoken, and thou shalt see me straight become sounder than an apple.' 'If that be true,' quoth Sancho, 'I do presently here renounce the government of the island you promised, and will demand nothing else in recompense of my services of you, but only the recipe of this precious liquor; for I am certain that an ounce thereof will be worth two reals in any place, and when I have it I should need nothing else to gain my living easily and honestly. But let me know, is it costly in making?' 'With less than three reals,' quoth Don Quixote, 'a man may make three gallons of it. But I mean to teach thee greater secrets than this, and do thee greater favours also. And now, let me cure myself; for mine ear grieves me more than I would wish.' Sancho then took out of his wallet his lint and ointment to cure his master. But when Don Quixote saw that the visor of his helmet was broken, he was ready to run mad; and, setting his hand to his sword, and lifting up his eyes to heaven, he said: 'I vow to the Creator of all things, and to the four gospels where they are largest written, to lead such another life as the great Marquis of Mantua did, when he swore to revenge the death of his nephew Valdovinos: which was, not to eat on table-cloth, nor sport with his wife, and other things, which, although I do not now remember, I give them here for expressed, until I take complete revenge on him that hath done me this outrage.'

Sancho, hearing this, said: 'You must note, Sir Don Quixote, that if the knight had accomplished that which you ordained, to go and present himself before my Lady Dulcinea of Toboso, then hath he fully satisfied his debt, and deserves no new punishment, except he commit a new fault.' 'Thou hast spoken well, and hit the mark right,' said Don Quixote; 'and therefore I disannul the oath, in that of taking any new revenge on him; but I make it, and confirm it again, that I will lead the life I have said until I take another helmet like, or as good as this, perforce from some knight. And do not think, Sancho, that I make this resolution lightly, or, as they say, with the smoke of straws, for I have an author whom I may very well imitate herein; for the very like, in every respect, passed about Mambrino's helmet, which cost Sacriphante so dearly.' 'I would have you resign those kind of oaths to the devil,' quoth Sancho; 'for they will hurt your health, and prejudice your conscience. If not, tell me now, I beseech you, if we shall not these many days encounter with any that wears a helmet, what shall we do? Will you accomplish the oath in despite of all the inconveniences and discommodities that ensue thereof? to wit, to sleep in your clothes, nor to sleep in any dwelling, and a thousand other penitences, which the oath of the mad old man, the Marquis of Mantua, contained, which you mean to ratify now? Do not you consider that armed men travel not in any of these ways, but carriers and waggoners, who not only carry no helmets, but also, for the most part, never heard speak of them in their lives?' 'Thou dost deceive thyself saying so,' replied Don Quixote; 'for we shall not haunt these ways two hours before we shall see more armed knights than were at the siege of Albraca, to conquer Angelica the fair.'

'Well, then, let it be so,' quoth Sancho; 'and I pray God it befall us well, whom I devoutly beseech that the time may come of gaining that island which costs me so dear, and after let me die presently, and I care not.' 'I have already said to thee, Sancho,' quoth his lord, 'that thou shouldst not trouble thyself in any wise about this affair; for if an island were wanting, we have then the kingdom of Denmark, or that of Sobradisa, which will come as fit for thy purpose as a ring to thy finger; and principally thou art to rejoice because they are on the continent. But, omitting this till his own time, see whether thou hast anything in thy wallet, and let us eat it, that afterward we may go search out some castle wherein we may lodge this night, and make the balsam which I have told thee; for I vow to God that this ear grieves me marvellously.' 'I have here an onion,' replied the squire, 'a piece of cheese, and a few crusts of bread; but such gross meats are not befitting so noble a knight as you are.' 'How ill dost thou understand it!' answered Don Quixote. 'I let thee to understand, Sancho, that it is an honour for knights-errant not to eat once in a month's space; and if by chance they should eat, to eat only of that which is next at hand; and this thou mightest certainly conceive, hadst thou read so many books as I have done; for though I passed over many, yet did I never find recorded in any that knights-errant did ever eat, but by mere chance and adventure, or in some costly banquets that were made for them, and all the other days they passed over with herbs and roots: and though it is to be understood that they could not live without meat, and supplying the other needs of nature, because they were in effect men as we are, it is likewise to be understood, that spending the greater part of their lives in forests and deserts, and that, too, without a cook, that their most ordinary meats were but coarse and rustical, such as thou dost now offer unto me. So that, friend Sancho, let not that trouble thee which is my pleasure, nor go not thou about to make a new world, or to hoist knight-errantry off her hinges.' 'Pardon me, good sir,' quoth Sancho; 'for, by reason I can neither read nor write, as I have said once before, I have not fallen rightly in the rules and laws of knighthood; and from henceforth my wallet shall be well furnished with all kinds of dry fruits for you, because you are a knight; and for myself, seeing I am none, I will provide fowls and other things, that are of more substance.' 'I say not, Sancho,' quoth Don Quixote, 'that it is a forcible law to knights-errant not to eat any other things than such fruits, but that their most ordinary sustenance could be none other than those, and some herbs they found up and down the fields, which they knew very well, and so do I also.' 'It is a virtue,' quoth Sancho, 'to know those herbs; for, as I imagine, that knowledge will some day stand us in stead.' And, saying so, he took out the provision he had, which they both ate together with good conformity. But, being desirous to search out a place where they might lodge that night, they did much shorten their poor dinner, and, mounting anon a-horseback, they made as much haste as they could to find out some dwellings before the night did fall; but the sun and their hopes did fail them at once, they being near the cabins of certain goatherds; and therefore they concluded to take up their lodging there for that night: for, though Sancho's grief was great to lie out of a village, yet Don Quixote's joy exceeded it far, considering he must sleep under open heaven; because he made account, as oft as this befel him, that he did a worthy act, which did facilitate and ratify the practice of his chivalry.

CHAPTER III

Of That Which Passed Between Don Quixote and Certain Goatherds

HE was entertained very cheerfully by the goatherds; and Sancho, having set up Rozinante and his ass as well as he could, he presently repaired to the smell of certain pieces of goat-flesh, that stood boiling in a kettle over the fire; and although he thought, in that very moment, to try whether they were in season to be translated out of the kettle into the stomach, he did omit it, because he saw the herds take them off the fire, and, spreading certain sheepskins, which they had for that purpose, on the ground, lay in a trice their rustical table, and invited the master and man, with very cheerful mind, to come and take part of that which they had. There sat down round about the skins six of them, which were all that dwelt in that fold; having first (using some coarse compliments) placed Don Quixote upon a trough, turning the bottom up. Don Quixote sat down, and Sancho stood to serve the cup, which was made of horn. His master, seeing him afoot, said, 'Sancho, to the end thou mayst perceive the good included in wandering knighthood, and also in what possibility they are which exercised themselves in any ministry thereof, to arrive briefly to honour and reputation in the world, my will is, that thou dost sit here by my side, and in company with this good people, and that thou beest one and the very selfsame thing with me, who am thy master and natural lord; that thou eat in my dish and drink in the same cup wherein I drink; for the same may be said of chivalry that is of love, to wit, that it makes all things equal.' 'I yield you great thanks,' quoth Sancho; 'yet dare I avouch unto you, that so I had therewithal to eat well, I could eat it as well, or better, standing and alone, than if I sat by an emperor. And besides, if I must say the truth, methinks that which I eat in a corner, without ceremonies, curiosity, or respect of any, though it were but bread and an onion, smacks a great deal better than turkey-cocks at other tables, where I must chew my meat leisurely, drink but little, wipe my hands often, must not neese nor cough though I have a desire, or be like to choke, nor do other things that solitude and liberty bring with them. So that, good sir, I would have you convert these honours that you would bestow upon me, in respect that I am an adherent to chivalry (as I am, being your squire), into things more essential and profitable for me than these; and though I remain as thankful for them as if they were received, yet do I here renounce, from this time until the world's end.' 'For all that, thou shalt sit; for the humble shall be exalted.' And so, taking him by the arm, he forced him to sit down near himself.

The goatherds did not understand that gibberish of squires and knights-errant, and therefore did nothing else but eat and hold their peace, and look on their guests, that tossed in with their fists whole slices, with good grace and stomachs. The course of flesh being ended, they served in on the rugs a great quantity of shelled acorns, and half a cheese, harder than if it were made of rough-casting. The horn stood not the while idle; for it went round about so often, now full, now empty, much like a conduit of Noria; and in a trice it emptied one of the two wine-bags that lay there in the public view. After that Don Quixote had satisfied his appetite well, he took up a handful of acorns, and, beholding them earnestly, he began to discourse in this manner: 'Happy time, and fortunate ages were those, whereon our ancestors bestowed the title of golden! not because gold (so much prized in this our iron age) was gotten in that happy time without any labours, but because those which lived in that time knew not these two words, 'thine' and 'mine'; in that holy age all things were in common. No man needed, for his ordinary sustenance, to do ought else than lift up his hand, and take it from the strong oak, which did liberally invite them to gather his sweet and savoury fruit. The clear fountains and running rivers did offer them these savoury and transparent waters in magnificent abundance. In the clefts of rocks and hollow trees did the careful and discreet bees erect their commonwealth, offering to every hand, without interest, the fertile crop of their sweetest travails. The lofty cork-trees did dismiss of themselves, without any other art than that of their native liberality, their broad and light rinds; where withal houses were at first covered, being sustained by rustical stakes, to none other end but for to keep back the inclemencies of the air. All then was peace, all amity, and all concord. As yet the ploughshare presumed not, with rude encounter, to open and search the compassionate bowels of our first mother; for she, without compulsion, offered up, through all the parts of her fertile and spacious bosom, all that which might satisfy, sustain, and delight those children which it then had. Yea, it was then that the simple and beautiful young shepherdesses went from valley to valley and hill to hill, with their hair sometimes plaited, sometimes dishevelled, without other apparel than that which was requisite to cover comely that which modesty wills, and ever would have, concealed. Then were of no request the attires and ornaments which are now used by those that esteem the purple of Tyre and the so-many-ways-martyrised silk so much, but only certain green leaves of burdocks and ivy intertexed and woven together; wherewithal, perhaps, they went as gorgeously and comely decked as now our court dames, with all their rare and outlandish inventions that idleness and curiosity hath found out. Then were the amorous conceits of the mind simply and sincerely delivered, and embellished in the very form and manner that she had conceived them, without any artificial contexture of words to endear them. Fraud, deceit, or malice had not then meddled themselves with plainness and truth. Justice was then in her proper terms, favour daring not to trouble or confound her, or the respect of profit, which do now persecute, blemish, and disturb her so much. The law of corruption, or taking bribes, had not yet possessed the understanding of the judge; for then was neither judge, nor person to be judged. Maidens and honesty wandered then, I say, where they listed, alone, signiorising, secure that no stranger liberty, or lascivious intent could prejudice it, or their own native desire or will any way endamage it. But now, in these our detestable times, no damsel is safe, although she be hid and shut up in another new labyrinth, like that of Crete; for even there itself the amorous plague would enter, either by some cranny, or by the air, or by the continual urgings of cursed care, to infect her; for whose protection and security was first instituted, by success of times, the order of knighthood, to defend damsels, protect widows, and assist orphans and distressed wights. Of this order am I, friends goatherds, whom I do heartily thank for the good entertainment which you do give unto me and my squire; for although that every one living is obliged, by the law of nature, to favour knights-errant, yet notwithstanding, knowing that you knew not this obligation, and yet did receive and make much of me, it stands with all reason that I do render you thanks with all my heart!'

Our knight made this long oration (which might have been well excused), because the acorns that were given unto him called to his mind the golden world, and therefore the humour took him to make the goatherds that unprofitable discourse; who heard him, all amazed and suspended, with very great attention all the while. Sancho likewise held his peace, eating acorns, and in the meanwhile visited very often the second wine-bag, which, because it might be fresh, was hanged upon a cork-tree. Don Quixote had spent more time in his speech than in his supper; at the end whereof one of the goatherds said, 'To the end that you may more assuredly know, sir knight-errant, that we do entertain you with prompt and ready will, we will likewise make you some pastime by hearing one of our companions sing, who is a herd of good understanding, and very amorous withal, and can besides read and write, and play so well on a rebec, that there is nothing to be desired.' Scarce had the goatherd ended his speech, when the sound of the rebec touched his ear; and within a while after he arrived that played on it, being a youth of some twenty years old, and one of a very good grace and countenance. His fellows demanded if he had supped; and, answering that he had, he which did offer the courtesy, said, 'Then, Anthony, thou mayst do us a pleasure by singing a little, that this gentleman our guest may see that we enjoy, amidst these groves and woods, those that know what music is. We have told him already thy good qualities, and therefore we desire that thou show them, to verify our words; and therefore I desire thee, by thy life, that thou wilt sit and sing the ditty which thy uncle the prebendary made of thy love, and was so well liked of in our village.' 'I am content,' quoth the youth; and, without further entreaty, sitting down on the trunk of a lopped oak, he tuned his rebec, and after a while began, with a singular good grace, to sing in this manner:

'I know, Olalia, thou dost me adore!
Though yet to me the same thou hast not said;
Nor shown it once by one poor glance or more,
Since love is soonest by such tongues bewray'd.

'Yet, 'cause I ever held thee to be wise,
It me assures thou bearest me good will;
And he is not unfortunate that sees
How his affections are not taken ill.

'Yet for all this, Olalia, 'tis true!
I, by observance, gather to my woe;
Thy mind is framed of brass, by art undue,
And flint thy bosom is, though it seem snow.

'And yet, amidst thy rigour's winter-face,
And other shifts, thou usest to delay me,
Sometimes hope, peeping out, doth promise grace;
But, woe is me! I fear 'tis to betray me.

'Sweetest! once in the balance of thy mind,
Poise with just weights my faith, which never yet
Diminish'd, though disfavour it did find;
Nor can increase more, though thou favoured'st it.

'If love be courteous (as some men say),
By thy humanity, I must collect
My hopes, hows'ever thou dost use delay,
Shall reap, at last, the good I do expect.

'If many services be of esteem
Or power to render a hard heart benign,
Such things I did for thee, as made me deem
I have the match gain'd, and thou shalt be mine.

'For, if at any time thou hast ta'en heed,
Thou more than once might'st view how I was clad
To honour thee on Mondays, with the weed
Which, worn on Sundays, got me credit had.

'For love and brav'ry still themselves consort,
Because they both shoot ever at one end;
Which made me, when I did to thee resort,
Still to be neat and fine I did contend.

'Here I omit the dances I have done,
And musics I have at thy window given;
When thou didst at cock-crow listen alone,
And seem'dst, hearing my voice, to be in heaven.

'I do not, eke, the praises here recount
Which of thy beauty I so oft have said;
Which, though they all were true, were likewise wont
To make thee envious me for spite upbraid.

'When to Teresa, she of Berrocal,
I, of thy worth, discourse did sometime shape:
"Good God!" quoth she, "you seem an angel's thrall,
And yet, for idol, you adore an ape.

' "She to her bugles thanks may give, and chains,
False hair, and other shifts that she doth use
To mend her beauty, with a thousand pains
And guiles, which might love's very self abuse."

'Wroth at her words, I gave her straight the lie,
Which did her and her cousin so offend,
As me to fight he challenged presently,
And well thou know'st of our debate the end.

'I mean not thee to purchase at a clap,
Nor to that end do I thy favour sue;
Thereby thine honour either to entrap,
Or thee persuade to take courses undue.

'The Church hath bands which do so surely hold,
As no silk string for strength comes to them near;
To thrust thy neck once in the yoke be bold,
And see if I, to follow thee, will fear.

'If thou wilt not, here solemnly I vow,
By holiest saint, enwrapt in precious shrine,
Never to leave those hills where I dwell now,
If 't be not to become a Capucine.'

Here the goatherd ended his ditty, and although Don Quixote entreated him to sing somewhat else, yet would not Sancho Panza consent to it; who was at that time better disposed to sleep than to hear music; and therefore said to his master, 'You had better provide yourself of a place wherein to sleep this night than to hear music; for the labour that these good men endure all the day long doth not permit that they likewise spend the night in singing.' 'I understand thee well enough, Sancho,' answered Don Quixote; 'nor did I think less, but that thy manifold visitations of the wine-bottle would rather desire to be recompensed with sleep than with music.' 'The wine liked us all well,' quoth Sancho. 'I do not deny it,' replied Don Quixote; 'but go thou and lay thee down where thou pleasest, for it becomes much more men of my profession to watch than to sleep. Yet, notwithstanding, it will not be amiss to lay somewhat again to mine ear, for it grieves me very much.' One of the goatherds, beholding the hurt, bade him be of good cheer, for he would apply a remedy that should cure it easily. And, taking some rosemary-leaves of many that grew thereabouts, he hewed them, and after mixed a little salt among them; and, applying this medicine to the ear, he bound it up well with a cloth, assuring him that he needed to use no other medicine; as it proved after, in effect.

CHAPTER IV

Of That Which One of the Goatherds Recounted to Those That Were with Don Quixote

ABOUT this time arrived another youth, one of those that brought them provision from the village, who said, 'Companions, do not you know what passeth in the village?' 'How can we know it, being absent?' says another of them. 'Then, wit,' quoth the youth, 'that the famous shepherd and student, Chrysostom, died this morning, and they murmur that he died for love of that devilish lass Marcela, William the Rich his daughter, she that goes up and down these plains and hills among us, in the habit of a shepherdess.' 'Dost thou mean Marcela?' quoth one of them. 'Even her, I say,' answered the other; 'and the jest is, that he hath commanded, in his testament, that he be buried in the fields, as if he were a Moor; and that it be at the foot of the rock, where the fountain stands off the cork-tree; for that, according to fame, and as they say he himself affirmed, was the place wherein he viewed her first. And he hath likewise commanded such other things to be done, as the ancienter sort of the village do not allow, nor think fit to be performed; for they seem to be ceremonies of the Gentiles. To all which objections, his great friend, Ambrosio the student, who likewise apparelled himself like a shepherd at once with him, answers, that all shall be accomplished, without omission of anything, as Chrysostom hath ordained; and all the village is in an aproar about this affair; and yet it is said that what Ambrosio and all the other shepherds his friends do pretend, shall in fine be done; and to-morrow morning they will come to the place I have named, to bury him with great pomp. And as I suppose it will be a thing worthy the seeing, at leastwise I will not omit to go and behold it although I were sure that I could not return the same day to the village.' 'We will all do the same,' quoth the goatherds, 'and will draw lots who shall tarry here to keep all our herds.' 'Thou sayst well, Peter,' quoth one of them, 'although that labour may be excused; for I mean to stay behind for you all, which you must not attribute to any virtue, or little curiosity in me, but rather to the fork that pricked my foot the other day, and makes me unable to travel from hence.' 'We do thank thee, notwithstanding,' quoth Peter, 'for thy good-will.' And Don Quixote, who heard all their discourse, entreated Peter to tell him who that dead man was, and what the shepherdess of whom they spoke.

Peter made answer, that what he knew of the affair was, 'that the dead person was a rich gentleman of a certain village seated among those mountains, who had studied many years in Salamanca, and after returned home to his house, with the opinion to be a very wise and learned man; but principally it was reported of him, that he was skilful in astronomy, and all that which passed above in heaven, in the sun and the moon, for he would tell us most punctually the clipse of the sun and the moon.' 'Friend,' quoth Don Quixote, 'the darkening of these two great luminaries is called an eclipse, not a clipse.' But Peter, stopping not at those trifles, did prosecute his history, saying, 'He did also prognosticate when the year would be abundant or estile.' 'Thou wouldst say sterile,' quoth Don Quixote. 'Sterile or estile,' said Peter, 'all is one for my purpose. And I say that, by his words, his father and his other friends, that gave credit to him, became very rich; for they did all that he counselled them: who would say unto them, Sow barley this year, and no wheat; in this, you may sow peas, and no barley; the next year will be good for oil; the three ensuing, you shall not gather a drop.' 'That science is called astrology,' quoth Don Quixote. 'I know not how it is called,' replied Peter; 'but I know well he knew all this, and much more.

'Finally, a few months after he came from Salamanca, he appeared one day apparelled like a shepherd, with his flock, and leather coat, having laid aside the long habits that he wore, being a scholar; and jointly with him came also a great friend of his and fellow-student, called Ambrosio, apparelled like a shepherd. I did almost forget to tell how Chrysostom, the dead man, was a great maker of verses; insomuch that he made the carols of Christmas Day at night, and the plays for Corpus Christi Day, which the youths of our village did represent, and all of them affirmed that they were most excellent. When those of the village saw the two scholars so suddenly clad like shepherds, they were amazed, and could not guess the cause that moved them to make so wonderful a change. And about this time Chrysostom's father died, and he remained possessed of a great deal of goods, as well moveable as immoveable; and no little quantity of cattle, great and small, and also a great sum of money; of all which the young man remained a dissolute lord. And truly he deserved it all; for he was a good fellow, charitable, and a friend of good folk, and he had a face like a blessing. It came at last to be understood, that the cause of changing his habit was none other than for to go up and down through these deserts after the shepherdess Marcela, whom our herd named before; of whom the poor dead Chrysostom was become enamoured. And I will tell you now, because it is fit you should know it, what this wanton lass is; perhaps, and I think without perhaps, you have not heard the like thing in all the days of your life, although you had lived more years than Sarna.' 'Say Sarra,' quoth Don Quixote, being not able any longer to hear him to change one word for another.

'The Sarna, or Scab,' quoth Peter, 'lives long enough too. And if you go thus, sir, interrupting my tale at every pace, we shall not be able to end it in a year.' 'Pardon me, friend,' quoth Don Quixote; 'for I speak to thee by reason there was such difference between Sarna and Sarra. But thou dost answer well; for the Sarna or Scab lives longer than Sarra. And therefore prosecute thy history; for I will not interrupt thee any more.' 'I say, then, dear sir of my soul,' quoth the goatherd, 'that there was, in our village, a farmer that was yet richer than Chrysostom's father, who was called William, to whom fortune gave, in the end of his great riches, a daughter called Marcela, of whose birth her mother died, who was the best woman that dwelt in all this circuit. Methinks I do now see her quick before me, with that face which had on the one side the sun and on the other side the moon; and above all, she was a thrifty housewife, and a great friend to the poor; for which I believe that her soul is this very hour enjoying of the gods in the other world. For grief of the loss of so good a wife, her husband William likewise died, leaving his daughter Marcela, young and rich, in the custody of his uncle, who was a priest, and curate of our village. The child grew with such beauty as it made us remember that of her mother, which was very great; and yet, notwithstanding, they judged that the daughter's would surpass hers, as indeed it did; for when she arrived to the age of fourteen or fifteen years old, no man beheld her that did not bless God for making her so fair, and most men remained enamoured and cast away for her love. Her uncle kept her with very great care and closeness; and yet, nevertheless, the fame of her great beauty did spread itself in such sort that, as well for it as for her great riches, her uncle was not only requested by those of our village, but also was prayed, solicited, and importuned by all those that dwelt many leagues about, and that by the very best of them, to give her to them in marriage. But he (who is a good Christian, every inch of him), although he desired to marry her presently, as soon as she was of age, yet would he not do it without her goodwill, without ever respecting the gain and profit he might make by the possession of her goods whilst he desired her marriage. And, in good sooth, this was spoken of, to the good priest his commendation, in more than one meeting of the people of our village; for I would have you to wit, sir errant, that in these little villages they talk of all things, and make account, as I do, that the priest must have been too good who could oblige his parishioners to speak so well of him, and especially in the villages.' 'Thou hast reason,' quoth Don Quixote; 'and therefore follow on, for the history is very pleasant, and thou, good Peter, dost recount it with a very good grace.' 'I pray God,' said Peter, 'that I never want our Herd's; for it is that which makes to the purpose. And in the rest you shall understand, that although her uncle propounded, and told to his niece the quality of every wooer of the many that desired her for wife, and entreated her to marry and choose at her pleasure, yet would she never answer other but that she would not marry as then, and that, in respect of her over green years, she did not find herself able enough yet to bear the burden of marriage. With these just excuses which she seemed to give, her uncle left off importuning of her, and did expect until she were further entered into years, and that she might know how to choose one that might like her; for he was wont to say, and that very well, that parents were not to place or bestow their children where they bore no liking. But, see here! when we least imagined it, the coy Marcela appeared one morning to become a shepherdess; and neither her uncle, nor all those of the village which dissuaded her from it, could work any effect, but she would needs go to the fields, and keep her own sheep with the other young lasses of the town. And she coming thus in public, when her beauty was seen without hindrance, I cannot possibly tell unto you how many rich youths, as well gentlemen as farmers, have taken on them the habit of Chrysostom, and follow, wooing of her, up and down those fields; one of which, as is said already, was our dead man, of whom it is said, that learning to love her, he had at last made her his idol. Nor is it to be thought that because Marcela set herself in that liberty, and so loose a life, and of so little or no keeping, that therefore she hath given the least token or shadow of dishonesty or negligence. Nay, rather, such is the watchfulness wherewithal she looks to her honour, that among so many as serve and solicit her, not one hath praised or can justly vaunt himself to have received, at her hands, the least hope that may be to obtain his desires; for, although she did not fly or shun the company and conversation of shepherds, and doth use them courteously and friendly, whensoever any one of them begin to discover their intention, be it ever so just and holy, as that of matrimony, she casts them away from her, as with a sling.

'And with this manner of proceeding she does more harm in this country than if the plague had entered into it by her means; for her affability and beauty doth draw to it the hearts of those which do serve and love her, but her disdain and resolution do conduct them to terms of desperation. And so they know not what to say unto her, but to call her with a loud voice cruel and ungrateful, with other titles like unto this, which do clearly manifest the nature of her condition; and, sir, if you stayed here but a few days, you should hear these mountains resound with the lamentations of those wretches that follow her. There is a certain place not far off, wherein are about two dozen of beech-trees, and there is not any one of them in whose rind is not engraven Marcela's name, and over some names graven also a crown in the same tree, as if her lover would plainly denote that Marcela bears it away, and deserves the garland of all human beauty. Here sighs one shepherd, there another complains; in another place are heard amorous ditties; here, in another, doleful and despairing laments. Some one there is that passeth over all the whole hours of the night at the foot of an oak or rock, and, without folding once his weeping eyes, swallowed and transported by his thoughts, the sun finds him there in the morning; and some other there is, who, without giving way or truce to his sighs, doth, amidst the fervour of the most fastidious heat of the summer, stretched upon the burning sand, breathe his pitiful complaints to heaven. And of this, and of him, and of those, and these, the beautiful Marcela doth indifferently and quietly triumph. All we that know her do wait to see wherein this her loftiness will finish, or who shall be so happy as to gain dominion over so terrible a condition, and enjoy so peerless a beauty. And because all that I have recounted is so notorious a truth, it makes me more easily believe that our companion hath told, that is said of the occasion of Chrysostom's death; and therefore I do counsel you, sir, that you do not omit to be present to-morrow at his burial, which will be worthy the seeing; for Chrysostom hath many friends, and the place wherein he commanded himself to be buried is not half a league from hence.' 'I do mean to be there,' said Don Quixote; 'and do render thee many thanks for the delight thou hast given me by the relation of so pleasant a history.' 'Oh,' quoth the goatherd, 'I do not yet know the half of the adventures succeeded to Marcela's lovers; but peradventure we may meet some shepherd on the way to-morrow that will tell them unto us. And for the present you will do well to go take your rest under some roof, for the air might hurt your wound, although the medicine be such that I have applied to it that any contrary accidents need not much to be feared.' Sancho Panza, being wholly out of patience with the goatherd's long discourse, did solicit, for his part, his master so effectually as he brought him at last into Peter's cabin, to take his rest for that night; whereinto, after he had entered, he bestowed the remnant of the night in remembrances of his Lady Dulcinea, in imitation of Marcela's lovers. Sancho Panza did lay himself down between Rozinante and his ass, and slept it out, not like a disfavoured lover, but like a man stamped and bruised with tramplings.

CHAPTER V

Wherein is Finished the History of the Shepherdess Marcela, with Other Accidents

BUT scarce had the day begun to discover itself by the oriental windows, when five of the six goatherds arising, went to awake Don Quixote, and demanded of him whether he yet intended to go to Chrysostom's burial, and that they would accompany him. Don Quixote, that desired nothing more, got up, and commanded Sancho to saddle and empannel in a trice; which he did with great expedition, and with the like they all presently began their journey. And they had not yet gone a quarter of a league, when, at the crossing of a pathway, they saw six shepherds coming towards them, apparelled with black skins, and crowned with garlands of cypress and bitter *enula campana.* Every one of them carried in his hand a thick truncheon of elm. There came likewise with them two gentlemen a-horseback, very well furnished for the way, with other three lackeys that attended on them. And, as soon as they encountered, they saluted one another courteously, and demanded whither they travelled; and knowing that they all went towards the place of the burial, they began their journey together. One of the horsemen, speaking to his companion, said, 'I think, Mr. Vivaldo, we shall account the time well employed that we shall stay to see this so famous an entertainment; for it cannot choose but be famous, according to the wonderful things these shepherds have recounted unto us, as well of the dead shepherd as also of the murdering shepherdess.' 'It seems so to me likewise,' quoth Vivaldo; 'and I say, I would not only stay one day, but a whole week, rather than miss to behold it.' Don Quixote demanded of them what they had heard of Marcela and Chrysostom. The traveller answered that they had encountered that morning with those shepherds, and that, by reason they had seen them apparelled in that mournful attire, they demanded of them the occasion thereof, and one of them rehearsed it, recounting the strangeness and beauty of a certain shepherdess called Marcela, and the amorous pursuits of her by many, with the death of that Chrysostom to whose burial they rode. Finally, he told all that again to him that Peter had told the night before.

This discourse thus ended, another began, and was, that he who was called Vivaldo demanded of Don Quixote the occasion that moved him to travel thus armed through so peaceable a country. To whom Don Quixote answered: 'The profession of my exercise doth not license or permit me to do other. Good days, cockering, and ease were invented for soft courtiers; but travels, unrest, and arms were only invented and made for those which the world terms knights-errant, of which number I myself (although unworthy) am one, and the least of all.' Scarce had they heard him say this, when they all held him to be wood. And, to find out the truth better, Vivaldo did ask him again what meant the word knights-errant. 'Have you not read, then,' quoth Don Quixote, 'the histories and annals of England, wherein are treated the famous acts of King Arthur, whom we continually call, in our Castilian romance, King Artus? of whom it is an ancient and common tradition, in the kingdom of Great Britain, that he never died, but that he was turned, by art of enchantment, into a crow; and that, in process of time, he shall return again to reign, and recover his sceptre and kingdom; for which reason it cannot be proved that, ever since that time until this, any Englishman hath killed a crow. In this good king's time was first instituted the famous order of knighthood of the Knights of the Round Table, and the love that is there recounted did in every respect pass as it is laid down between Sir Launcelot du Lake and Queen Genever, the honourable Lady Quintaniona being a dealer, and privy thereto; whence sprung that so famous a ditty, and so celebrated here in Spain, of, "Never was knight of ladies so well served as Launcelot when that he in Britain arrived," etc., with that progress so sweet and delightful of his amorous and valiant acts; and from that time forward, the order of knight went from hand to hand, dilating and spreading itself through many and sundry parts of the world; and in it were, famous and renowned for their feats of arms, the valiant Amadis of Gaul, with all his progeny until the fifth generation; and the valorous Felixmarte of Hircania, and the never-duly-praised Tirante the White, together with Sir Bevis of Hampton, Sir Guy of Warwick, Sir Eglemore, with divers others of that nation and age; and almost in our days we saw, and communed, and heard of the invincible and valiant knight, Don Belianis of Greece. This, then, good sirs, is to be a knight-errant; and that which I have said is the order of chivalry: wherein, as I have already said, I, although a sinner, have made profession, and the same do I profess that those knights professed whom I have above mentioned; and therefore I travel through these solitudes and deserts, seeking adventures, with full resolution to offer mine own arm and person to the most dangerous that fortune shall present, in the aid of weak and needy persons.'

By these reasons of Don Quixote's the travellers perfectly perceived that he was none of the wisest; and knew the kind of folly wherewithal he was crossed, whereat those remained wonderfully admired, that by the relation of the others came to understand it.

And Vivaldo, who was very discreet, and likewise of a pleasant disposition, to the end they might pass over the rest of the way without heaviness unto the rock of the burial, which the shepherds said was near at hand, he resolved to give him further occasion to pass onward with his follies, and therefore said unto him, 'Methinks, sir knight, that you have professed one of the most austere professions in the world; and I do constantly hold that even that of the Charterhouse monks is not near so strait.' 'It may be as strait as our profession,' quoth Don Quixote, 'but that it should be so necessary for the world, I am within the breadth of two fingers to call it in doubt; for, if we would speak a truth, the soldier that puts in execution his captain's command doth no less than the very captain that commands him. Hence I infer, that religious men do with all peace and quietness seek of Heaven the good of the earth; but soldiers and we knights do put in execution that which they demand, defending it with the valour of our arms and files of our swords; not under any roof, but under the wide heavens, made, as it were, in summer a mark to the insupportable sunbeams, and in winter to the rage of withering frosts. So that we are the ministers of God on earth, and the armies wherewith He executeth His justice; and as the affairs of war, and things thereunto pertaining, cannot be put in execution without sweat, labour, and travail, it follows that those which profess warfare take, questionless, greater pain than those which, in quiet, peace, and rest, do pray unto God that He will favour and assist those that need it. I mean not therefore to affirm, nor doth it once pass through my thought, that the state of a knight-errant is as perfect as that of a retired religious man, but only would infer, through that which I myself suffer, that it is doubtlessly more laborious, more battered, hungry, thirsty, miserable, torn, and lousy. For the knights-errant of times past did, without all doubt, suffer much woe and misery in the discourse of their life; and if some of them ascended at last to empires, won by the force of their arms, in good faith, it cost them a great part of their sweat and blood; and if those which mounted to so high a degree had wanted those enchanters and wise men that assisted them, they would have remained much defrauded of their desires, and greatly deceived of their hopes.' 'I am of the same opinion,' replied the traveller; 'but one thing among many others hath seemed to me very ill in knights-errant, which is, when they perceive themselves in any occasion to begin any great and dangerous adventure, in which appears manifest peril of losing their lives, they never, in the instant of attempting it, remember to commend themselves to God, as every Christian is bound to do in like dangers, but rather do it to their ladies, with so great desire and devotion as if they were their gods—a thing which, in my opinion, smells of Gentilism.' 'Sir,' quoth Don Quixote, 'they can do no less in any wise, and the knight-errant which did any other would digress much from his duty; for now it is a received use and custom of errant chivalry, that the knight adventurous who, attempting of any great feat of arms, shall have his lady in place, do mildly and amorously turn his eyes towards her, as it were by them demanding that she do favour and protect him in that ambiguous trance which he undertakes; and, moreover, if none do hear him, he is bound to say certain words between his teeth, by which he shall, with all his heart, commend himself to her: and of this we have innumerable examples in histories. Nor is it therefore to be understood that they do omit to commend themselves to God; for they have time and leisure enough to do it in the progress of the work.'

'For all that,' replied the traveller, 'there remains in me yet one scruple which is, that oftentimes, as I have read, some speech begins between two knights-errant, and from one word to another their choler begins to be inflamed, and they to turn their horses, and to take up a good piece of the field, and, without any more ado, to run as fast as ever they can drive to encounter again, and, in the midst of their race, do commend themselves to their dames; and that which commonly ensues of this encountering is, that one of them falls down, thrown over the crupper of his horse, passed through and through by his enemy's lance; and it befalls the other that, if he had not caught fast of his horse's mane, he had likewise fallen; and I here cannot perceive how he that is slain had any leisure to commend himself unto God in the discourse of this so accelerate and hasty a work. Methinks it were better that those words which he spent in his race on his lady were bestowed as they ought, and as every Christian is bound to bestow them; and the rather, because I conjecture that all knights-errant have not ladies to whom they may commend themselves, for all of them are not amorous.'

'That cannot be,' answered Don Quixote; 'I say it cannot be that there's any knight-errant without a lady; for it is as proper and essential to such to be enamoured as to heaven to have stars: and I dare warrant that no history hath yet been seen wherein is found a knight-errant without love; for, by the very reason that he were found without them, he would be convinced to be no legitimate knight, but a bastard; and that he entered into the fortress of chivalry, not by the gate, but by leaping over the staccado like a robber and a thief.'

'Yet, notwithstanding,' replied the other, 'I have read (if I do not forget myself) that Don Galaor, brother to the valorous Amadis de Gaul, had never any certain mistress to whom he might commend himself; and yet, for all that, he was nothing less accounted of, and was a most valiant and famous knight.' To that objection our Don Quixote answered: 'One swallow makes not a summer. How much more that I know, that the knight whom you allege was secretly very much enamoured; besides that, that his inclination of loving all ladies well, which he thought were fair, was a natural inclination, which he could not govern so well; but it is, in conclusion, sufficiently verified, that yet he had one lady whom he crowned queen of his will, to whom he did also commend himself very often and secretly; for he did not a little glory to be so secret in his loves.'

'Then, sir, if it be of the essence of all knights-errant to be in love,' quoth the traveller, 'then may it likewise be presumed that you are also enamoured, seeing that it is annexed to the profession? And if you do not prize yourself to be as secret as Don Galaor, I do entreat you, as earnestly as I may, in all this company's name and mine own, that it will please you to tell us the name, country, quality, and beauty of your lady; for I am sure she would account herself happy to think that all the world doth know she is beloved and served by so worthy a knight as is yourself.' Here Don Quixote, breathing forth a deep sigh, said: 'I cannot affirm whether my sweet enemy delight or no that the world know how much she is beloved, or that I serve her. Only I dare avouch (answering to that which you so courteously demanded) that her name is Dulcinea, her country Toboso, a village of Mancha. Her calling must be at least of a princess, seeing she is my queen and lady; her beauty sovereign, for in her are verified and give glorious lustre to all those impossible and chimerical attributes of beauty that poets give to their mistresses, that her hairs are gold, her forehead the Elysian fields, her brows the arcs of heaven, her eyes suns, her cheeks roses, her lips coral, her teeth pearls, her neck alabaster, her bosom marble, ivory her hands, and her whiteness snow; and the parts which modesty conceals from human sight, such as I think and understand that the discreet consideration may prize, but never be able to equalize them.' 'Her lineage, progeny, we desire to know likewise,' quoth Vivaldo. To which Don Quixote answered: 'She is not of the ancient Roman Curcios, Cayos, or Scipios; nor of the modern Colonnas, or Ursinos; nor of the Moncadas or Requesenes of Catalonia; and much less of the Rebelias and Villanovas of Valencia; Palafoxes, Nucas, Rocabertis, Corelias, Alagones, Urreas, Fozes, and Gurreas of Aragon; Cerdas, Manriquez, Mendoças, and Guzmanes of Castile; Lancasters, Palias, and Meneses of Portugal; but she is of those of Toboso of the Mancha; a lineage which, though it be modern, is such as may give a generous beginning to the most noble families of ensuing ages. And let none contradict me in this, if it be not with those conditions that Cerbino put at the foot of Orlando's armour, to wit:

> "Let none from hence presume these arms to move,
> But he that with Orlando dares his force to prove."'

'Although my lineage be of the Cachopines of Laredo,' replied the traveller, 'yet dare I not to compare it with that of Toboso in the Mancha; although, to speak sincerely, I never heard any mention of that lineage you say until now.' 'What!' quoth Don Quixote, 'is it possible that you never heard of it till now?'

All the company travelled, giving marvellous attention to the reasons of those two; and even the very goatherds and shepherds began to perceive the great want of judgment that was in Don Quixote: only Sancho Panza did verily believe that all his master's words were most true, as one that knew what he was from the very time of his birth; but that wherein his belief staggered somewhat, was of the beautiful Dulcinea of Toboso; for he had never heard speak in his life before of such a name or princess, although he had dwelt so many years hard by Toboso.

And as they travelled in these discourses, they beheld descending, betwixt the cleft of two lofty mountains, to the number of twenty shepherds, all apparelled in skins of black wool and crowned with garlands, which, as they perceived afterward, were all of yew and cypress. Six of them carried a bier, covered with many sorts of flowers and boughs; which one of the goatherds espying, he said, 'Those that come there are they which bring Chrysostom's body, and the foot of that mountain is the place where he hath commanded them to bury him.' These words were occasion to make them haste to arrive in time, which they did just about the instant that the others had laid down the corpse on the ground. And four of them, with sharp pickaxes, did dig the grave at the side of a hard rock. The one and the others saluted themselves very courteously; and then Don Quixote, and such as came with him, began to behold the bier, wherein they saw laid a dead body, all covered with flowers, and apparelled like a shepherd of some thirty years old; and his dead countenance showed that he was very beautiful, and an able-bodied man. He had, placed round about him in the bier, certain books and many papers, some open and some shut, and altogether, as well those that beheld this as they which made the grave, and all the others that were present, kept a marvellous silence, until one of them which carried the dead man said to another: 'See well, Ambrosio, whether this be the place that Chrysostom meant, seeing that thou wouldst have all so punctually observed which he commanded in his testament.' 'This is it,' answered Ambrosio; 'for many times my unfortunate friend recounted to me in it the history of his mishaps. Even there he told me that he had seen that cruel enemy of mankind first; and there it was where he first broke his affections too, as honest as they were amorous; and there was the last time wherein Marcela did end to resolve, and began to disdain him, in such sort as she set end to the tragedy of his miserable life; and here, in memory of so many misfortunes, he commanded himself to be committed to the bowels of eternal oblivion.' And, turning himself to Don Quixote and to the other travellers, he said, 'This body, sirs, which you do now behold with pitiful eyes, was the treasury of a soul wherein heaven had hoarded up an infinite part of his treasures. This is the body of Chrysostom, who was peerless in wit, without fellow for courtesy, rare for comeliness, a phoenix for friendship, magnificent without measure, grave without presumption, pleasant without offence; and finally, the first in all that which is good, and second to none in all unfortunate mischances. He loved well, and was hated; he adored, and was disdained; he prayed to one no less savage than a beast; he importuned a heart as hard as marble, he pursued the wind, he cried to deserts, he served ingratitude, and he obtained for reward the spoils of death in the midst of the career of his life: to which a shepherdess hath given end whom he laboured to eternize, to the end she might ever live in the memories of men, as those papers which you see there might very well prove, had he not commanded me to sacrifice them to the fire as soon as his body was rendered to the earth.'

'If you did so,' quoth Vivaldo, 'you would use greater rigour and cruelty towards them than their very lord, nor is it discreet or justly done that his will be accomplished who commands anything repugnant to reason; nor should Augustus Caesar himself have gained the reputation of wisdom, if he had permitted that to be put in execution which the divine Mantuan had by his will ordained. So that, Senor Ambrosio, now that you commit your friend's body to the earth, do not therefore commit his labour to oblivion; for though he ordained it as one injured, yet are not you to accomplish it as one void of discretion; but rather cause, by giving life to these papers, that the cruelty of Marcela may live eternally, that it may serve as a document to those that shall breathe in ensuing ages how they may avoid and shun the like downfalls; for both myself, and all those that come here in my company, do already know the history of your enamoured and despairing friend, the occasion of his death, and what he commanded ere he deceased: out of which lamentable relation may be collected how great hath been the cruelty of Marcela, the love of Chrysostom, the faith of your affection, and the conclusion which those make which do rashly run through that way which indiscreet love doth present to their view. We understood yesternight of Chrysostom's death, and that he should be interred in this place, and therefore we omitted our intended journeys, both for curiosity and pity, and resolved to come and behold with our eyes that the relation whereof did so much grieve us in the hearing; and therefore we desire thee, discreet Ambrosio, both in reward of this our compassion, and also of the desire which springs in our breasts, to remedy this disaster, if it were possible; but chiefly I, for my part, request thee, that, omitting to burn these papers, thou wilt license me to take away some of them. And, saying so, without expecting the shepherd's answer, he stretched out his hand and took some of them that were next to him; which Ambrosio perceiving, said, 'I will consent, sir, for courtesy's sake, that you remain lord of those which you have seized upon; but to imagine that I would omit to burn these that rest were a very vain thought.' Vivaldo, who did long to see what the papers contained which he had gotten, did unfold presently one of them, which had this title, 'A Ditty of Despair.' Ambrosio overheard him, and said: 'That is the last paper which this unfortunate shepherd wrote; and because, sir, that you may see the terms to which his mishaps conducted him, I pray you to read it, but in such manner as you may be heard; for you shall have leisure enough to do it whilst the grave is a-digging.' 'I will do it with all my heart,' replied Vivaldo; and all those that were present having the like desire, they gathered about him, and he, reading it with a clear voice, pronounced it thus.

CHAPTER VI

Wherein Are Rehearsed the Despairing Verses of the Dead Shepherd. With Other Unexpected Accidents

The Canzone of Chrysostom.

I

Since cruel thou (I publish) dost desire,
From tongue to tongue, and the one to the other pole,
The efficacy of thy rigour sharp,
I'll hell constrain to assist my soul's desire,
And in my breast infuse a ton of dole.
Whereon my voice, as it is wont, may harp,
And labour, as I wish, at once to carp
And tell my sorrows and thy murdering deeds;
The dreadful voice and accents shall agree,
And, with them, meet for greater torture be
Lumps of my wretched bowels, which still bleeds.
Then listen, and lend once attentive ear,
Not well-consorted tunes, but howling to hear,
That from my bitter bosom's depth takes flight;
And by constrained raving borne away,
Issues forth from mine ease and thy despite.

II

The lion's roaring, and the dreadful howls
Of ravening wolf, and hissing terrible
Of squammy serpent; and the fearful bleat
Of some sad monster; of foretelling fowls,
The pie's crackling, and rumour horrible
Of the contending wind, as it doth beat
The sea; and implacable bellowing, yet
Of vanquish'd bull; and of the turtle sole
The feeling mourning, and the doleful song
Of the envious owl, with the dire plaints among
Of all the infernal squadron full of dole,
Sally with my lamenting soul around
All mixed with so strange, unusual sound,

As all the senses may confounded be;
For my fierce torment, a new way exact,
Wherein I may recount my misery.

III

The doleful echoes of so great confusion
Shall not resound o'er father Tagus' sands,
Nor touch the olive-wat'ring Betis' ears.
Of my dire pangs I'll only make effusion
'Mongst those steep rocks, and hollow bottom lands,
With mortified tongue, but living tears:
Sometimes, in hidden dales, where nought appears,
Or in unhaunted plains free from access;
Or where the sun could ne'er intrude a beam;
Amidst the venomous crew of beasts unclean,
Whose wants, with bounty, the free plains redress;
For, though among those vast and desert downs,
The hollow echo indistinctly sounds
Thy matchless rigour, and my cruel pain,
Yet, by the privilege of my niggard fates,
It will their force throughout the world proclaim.

IV

A disdain kills; and patience runs aground,
By a suspicion either false or true;
But jealousy, with greater rigour slays;
A prolix absence doth our life confound.
Against fear of oblivion to ensue,
Firm hope of best success gives little ease,
Inevitable death lurks in all these.
But I (O unseen miracle!) do still live,
Jealous, absent, disdain'd, and certain too
Of the suspicions that my life undo!
Drown'd in oblivion which my fire revives,
And amongst all those pains I never scope
Got, to behold the shadow once of hope:
Nor thus despaired would I it allow;
But 'cause I may more aggravate my moans,
To live ever without it, here I vow.

V

Can hope and fear, at once, in one consist?
Or is it reason that it should be so?
Seeing the cause more certain is of fear;

If before me dire jealousy exist,
Shall I deflect mine eyes? since it will show
Itself by a thousand wounds in my soul there.
Or, who will not the gates unto despair
Wide open set, after that he hath spy'd
Murd'ring disdain? and noted each suspicion
To seeming truth transform'd? O sour conversion!
Whilst verity by falsehood is belied!
O tyrant of love's state, fierce jealousy!
With cruel chains these hands together tie,
With stubborn cords couple them, rough disdain!
But woe is me, with bloody victory,
Your memory is, by my sufferance, slain!

VI

I die, in fine, and 'cause I'll not expect
In death or life for the least good success,
I obstinate will rest in fantasy,
And say he doth well, that doth death affect,
And eke the soul most liberty possess,
That is most thrall to love's old tyranny.
And will affirm mine ever enemy,
In her fair shrine, a fairer soul contains;
And her oblivion from my fault to spring,
And to excuse her wrongs will witness bring,
That love by her in peace his state maintains,
And with a hard knot, and this strange opinion
I will accelerate the wretched summon,
To which guided I am by her scorns rife,
And offer to the air body and soul,
Without hope or reward of future life.

VII

Thou that, by multiplying wrongs, doth show
The reason forcing me to use violence
Unto this loathsome life, grown to me hateful,
Since now by signs notorious thou mayst know,
From my heart's deepest wound, how willingly sense
Doth sacrifice me to thy scorns ungrateful.
If my deserts have seem'd to thee so bootful,
As thy fair eyes clear heav'n should be o'ercast,
And clouded at my death; yet do not so,
For I'll no recompense take for the woe:
By which, of my soul's spoils possess'd thou wast:

But rather, laughing at my funeral sad,
Show how mine end begins to make thee glad
But 'tis a folly to advise thee this,
For I know, in my death's acceleration,
Consists thy glory and thy chiefest bliss.

VIII

Let Tantalus from the profoundest deeps
Come, for it is high time now, with his thirst;
And Sisyphus, with his oppressing stone;
Let Tityus bring his raven that ne'er sleeps,
And Ixion make no stay with wheel accurs'd,
Nor the three sisters, ever lab'ring on.
And let them all at once their mortal moan
Translate into my breast, and lovely sound
(If it may be a debt due to despair),
And chant sad obsequies, with doleful air,
Over a corse unworthy of the ground.
And the three-faced infernal porter grim,
With thousand monsters and chimeras dim,
Relish the dolorous descant out amain;
For greater pomp than this I think not fit
That any dying lover should obtain.

IX

Despairing canzone, do not thou complain,
When thou my sad society shalt refrain;
But rather, since the cause whence thou didst spring,
By my misfortune, grows more fortunate,
Ev'n in the grave, thou must shun sorrowing.

Chrysostom's canzone liked wonderfully all the hearers, although the reader thereof affirmed that it was not conformable to the relation that he had received of Marcela's virtue and care of herself; for in it Chrysostom did complain of jealousies, suspicions, and absence, being all of them things that did prejudice Marcela's good fame. To this objection Ambrosio answered (as one that knew very well the most hidden secrets of his friend): 'You must understand, sir, to the end you may better satisfy your own doubt, that when the unfortunate shepherd wrote that canzone he was absent from Marcela, from whose presence he had wittingly withdrawn himself, to see if he could deface some part of his excessive passions, procured by absence; and as everything doth vex an absent lover, and every fear afflict him, so was Chrysostom likewise tormented by imagined jealousies and feared suspicions as much as if they were real and true. And with this remains the truth in her perfection and point of Marcela's virtue, who, excepting that she is cruel and somewhat arrogant and very disdainful, very envy itself neither ought, nor can, attaint her of the least defect.' 'You have reason,' quoth Vivaldo; and so, desiring to read another paper, he was interrupted by a marvellous vision (for such it seemed) that unexpectedly offered itself to their view; which was, that on the top of the rock wherein they made the grave, appeared the shepherdess Marcela, so fair that her beauty surpassed far the fame that was spread thereof. Such as had not beheld her before did look on her then with admiration and silence, and those which were wont to view her remained no less suspended than the others which never had seen her. But scarce had Ambrosio eyed her, when, with an ireful and disdaining mind, he spake these words: 'Comest thou by chance, O fierce basilisk of these mountains! to see whether the wounds of this wretch will yet bleed at thy presence? or dost thou come to insult and vaunt in the tragical feats of thy stern nature? or to behold from that height, like another merciless Nero, the fire of inflamed Rome? or arrogantly to trample this infortunate carcase, as the ingrateful daughter did her father Tarquin's? Tell us quickly why thou comest, or what thou dost most desire? For, seeing I know that Chrysostom's thoughts never disobeyed thee in life, I will likewise cause that all those his friends shall serve and reverence thee.'

'I come not here, good Ambrosio, to any of those ends thou sayst,' quoth Marcela; 'but only to turn for mine honour, and give the world to understand how little reason have all those which make me the author either of their own pains or of Chrysostom's death; and therefore I desire all you that be here present to lend attention unto me, for I mean not to spend much time or words to persuade to the discreet so manifest a truth. Heaven, as you say, hath made me beautiful, and that so much that my feature moves you to love almost whether you will or no; and for the affection you show unto me, you say, ay, and you affirm, that I ought to love you again. I know, by the natural instinct that Jove hath bestowed on me, that each fair thing is amiable; but I cannot conceive why, for the reason of being beloved, the party that is so beloved for her beauty should be bound to love her lover, although he be foul; and, seeing that foul things are worthy of hate, it is a bad argument to say, I love thee, because fair; and therefore thou must affect me, although uncomely. But set the case that the beauties occur equal on both sides, it follows not, therefore, that their desires should run one way; for all beauties do not enamour, for some do only delight the sight, and subject not the will; for if all beauties did enamour and subject together, men's wills would ever run confused and straying, without being able to make any election; for the beautiful subjects being infinite, the desires must also perforce be infinite. And, as I have heard, true love brooks no division, and must needs be voluntary, and not enforced; which being so, as I presume it is, why would you have me subject my will forcibly, without any other obligation than that, that you say you love me? If not, tell me, if Heaven had made me foul, as it hath made me beautiful, could I justly complain of you because you affected me not? How much more, seeing you ought to consider that I did not choose the beauty I have! for, such as it is, Heaven bestowed it gratis, without my demanding or electing it. And even as the viper deserves no blame for the poison she carries, although therewithal she kill, seeing it was bestowed on her by nature, so do I as little merit to be reprehended because beautiful; for beauty in an honest woman is like fire afar off, or a sharp-edged sword; for neither that burns nor this cuts any but such as come near them. Honour and virtue are the ornaments of the soul, without which the fairest body is not to be esteemed such; and if that honesty be one of the virtues that adorneth and beautifieth most the body and soul, why should she that is beloved, because fair, adventure the loss thereof, to answer his intention which only for his pleasure's sake labours that she may lose it, with all his force and industry? I was born free, and, because I might live freely, I made election of the solitude of the fields. The trees of these mountains are my companions, the clear water of these streams my mirrors. With the trees and waters I communicate my thoughts and beauty. I am a parted fire, and a sword laid aloof. Those whom I have enamoured with my sight, I have undeceived with my words. And if desires be sustained by hopes, I never having given any to Chrysostom, or to any other, it may well be said that he was rather slain by his own obstinacy than by my cruelty. And if I be charged that his thoughts were honest, and that I was therefore obliged to answer unto them, I say, that when in that very place where you make his sepulchre, he first broke his mind unto me, I told him that mine intention was to live in perpetual solitude, and that only the earth should gather the fruits of my solitariness and the spoils of my beauty; and if he would, after this my resolution, persist obstinately without all hope, and sail against the wind, what wonder is it that he should be drowned in the midst of the gulf of his rashness? If I had entertained him, then were I false; if I had pleased him, then should I do against my better purposes and projects. He strove, being persuaded to the contrary; he despaired, ere he was hated. See, then, if it be reason that I bear the blame of his torment. Let him complain who hath been deceived; let him despair to whom his promised hopes have failed; let him confess it whom I shall ever call; let him vaunt whom I shall admit: but let him not call me cruel or a homicide, whom I never promised, deceived, called, or admitted. Heaven hath not yet ordained that I should love by destiny; and to think that I would do it by election may be excused. And let this general caveat serve every one of those which solicit me for his particular benefit. And let it be known, that if any shall hereafter die for my love, that he dies not jealous or unfortunate; for whosoever loves not any, breeds not in reason jealousy in any, nor should any resolutions to any be accounted disdainings. He that calls me a savage and a basilisk, let him shun me as a hurtful and prejudicial thing; he that calls me ungrateful, let him not serve me; he that's strange, let him not know me; he that's cruel, let him not follow me: for this savage, this basilisk, this ingrate, this cruel and strange one, will neither seek, serve, know, or pursue any of them. For if Chrysostom's impatience and headlong desire slew him, why should mine honest proceeding and care be inculped therewithal? If I preserve mine integrity in the society of these trees, why would any desire me to lose it, seeing every one covets to have the like himself, to converse the better among men? I have, as you all know, riches enough of mine own, and therefore do not covet other men's. I have a free condition, and I do not please to subject me. Neither do I love or hate any. I do not deceive this man, or solicit that other; nor do I jest with one, and pass the time with another. The honest conversation of the pastoras of these villages and the care of my goats, do entertain me. My desires are limited by these mountains; and if they do issue from hence, it is to contemplate the beauty of heaven—steps wherewithal the soul travels toward her first dwelling.' And, ending here, without desiring to hear any answer, she turned her back and entered into the thickest part of the wood that was there at hand, leaving all those that were present marvellously admired at her beauty and discretion.

Some of the shepherds present, that were wounded by the powerful beams of her beautiful eyes, made proffer to pursue her, without reaping any profit out of her manifest resolution made there in their hearing; which Don Quixote noting, and thinking that the use of this chivalry did jump fitly with that occasion, by succouring distressed damsels, laying hand on the pommel of his sword, he said, in loud and intelligible words: 'Let no person, of whatsoever state or condition he be, presume to follow the fair Marcela, under pain of falling into my furious indignation. She hath shown, by clear and sufficient reasons, the little or no fault she had in Chrysostom's death, and how far she lives from meaning to condescend to the desires of any of her lovers; for which respect it is just that, instead of being pursued and persecuted, she be honoured and esteemed by all the good men of the world; for she shows in it, that it is only she alone that lives therein with honest intention.' Now, whether it was through Don Quixote's menaces, or whether because Ambrosio requested them to conclude with the obligation they owed to their good friend, none of the shepherds moved or departed from thence until, the grave being made and Chrysostom's papers burnt, they laid the body into it, with many tears of the beholders. They shut the sepulchre with a great stone, until a monument were wrought, which Ambrosio said he went to have made, with an epitaph to this sense:

'Here, of a loving swain,
The frozen carcase lies;
Who was a heard likewise,
And died through disdain.
Stern rigour hath him slain,
Of a coy fair ingrate,
By whom love doth dilate
Her tyranny amain.'

They presently strewed on the grave many flowers and boughs, and everyone condoling a while with his friend Ambrosio, did afterward bid him farewell, and departed. The like did Vivaldo and his companion: and Don Quixote, bidding his host and the travellers adieu, they requested him to come with them to Seville, because it was a place so fit for the finding of adventures, as in every street and corner thereof are offered more than in any other place whatsoever. Don Quixote rendered them thanks for their advice and the good-will they seemed to have to gratify him, and said he neither ought nor would go to Seville until he had freed all those mountains of thieves and robbers, whereof, as fame ran, they were full. The travellers perceiving his good intention, would not importune him more; but, bidding him again farewell, they departed, and followed on their journey; in which they wanted not matter of discourse, as well of the history of Marcela and Chrysostom as of the follies of Don Quixote, who determined to go in the search of the shepherdess Marcela, and offer unto her all that he was able to do in her service. But it befel him not as he thought, as shall be rehearsed in the discourse of this true history; giving end here to the Second Part.

THE THIRD BOOK

CHAPTER I

Wherein Is Rehearsed the Unfortunate Adventure Which Happened to Don Quixote, by Encountering With Certain Yanguesian Carriers

THE wise Cid Hamet Benengeli recounteth that, as soon as Don Quixote had taken leave of the goatherds, his hosts the night before, and of all those that were present at the burial of the shepherd Chrysostom, he and his squire did presently enter into the same wood into which they had seen the beautiful shepherdess Marcela enter before. And, having travelled in it about the space of two hours without finding of her, they arrived in fine to a pleasant meadow, enriched with abundance of flourishing grass, near unto which runs a delightful and refreshing stream, which did invite, yea, constrain them thereby to pass over the heat of the day, which did then begin to enter with great fervour and vehemency. Don Quixote and Sancho alighted, and, leaving the ass and Rozinante to the spaciousness of these plains to feed on the plenty of grass that was there, they ransacked their wallet, where, without any ceremony, the master and man did eat, with good accord and fellowship, what they found therein. Sancho had neglected to tie Rozinante, sure that he knew him to be so sober and little wanton as all the mares of the pasture of Cordova could not make him to think the least sinister thought. But fortune did ordain, or rather the devil, who sleeps not at all hours, that a troop of Gallician mares, belonging to certain Yanguesian carriers, did feed up and down in the same valley; which carriers are wont, with their beasts, to pass over the heats in places situated near unto grass and water, and that wherein Don Quixote happened to be was very fit for their purpose. It therefore befel that Rozinante took a certain desire to solace himself with the lady mares, and therefore, as soon as he had smelt them, abandoning his natural pace and custom, without taking leave of his master, he began a little swift trot, and went to communicate his necessities to them. But they, who, as it seemed, had more desire to feed than to solace them, entertained him with their heels and teeth in such sort as they broke all his girths, and left him in his naked hair, having overthrown the saddle. But that which surely grieved him most was, that the carriers, perceiving the violence that was offered by him to their mares, repaired presently to their succours, with clubs and truncheons, and did so belabour him as they fairly laid him along. Now, in this season, Don Quixote and Sancho (which beheld the bombasting of Rozinante) approached breathless; and Don Quixote said to Sancho, 'For as much as I can perceive, friend Sancho, these men are no knights, but base, rascally people of vile quality; I say it, because thou mayst help me to take due revenge for the outrage which they have done before our face to Rozinante.' 'What a devil' quoth Sancho, 'what revenge should we take, if these be more than twenty, and we but two, and peradventure but one and a half?' 'I am worth a hundred,' replied Don Quixote; and, without making any longer discourse, he set hand to his sword, and flew upon the Yanguesians; and Sancho Panza, moved by his lord's example, did the like; when, with the first blow, Don Quixote piercing a buff coat that one of them wore, wounded him grievously in the shoulder. The Yanguesians, seeing themselves so rudely handled by two men only, they being so many, ran to the stakes and truncheons of their carriage, and, hemming in their adversaries in the midst of them, they laid on them with admirable speed and vehemency. True it is, that at the second peal they struck Sancho down to the ground; and the like happened to Don Quixote, his dexterity and courage being nothing available in that trance, and, his fate so ordaining, he fell just at his courser's feet, who had not yet gotten up; by which we may ponder the fury wherewithal truncheons batter, being placed in wrathful and rustical fists. The carriers perceiving the evil they had committed, trussing up their loading with all possible speed, followed on their way, leaving both the adventures in a bad fashion, and a worse talent.

The first that came to himself was Sancho Panza, who, seeing his lord near unto him, said, with a weak and pitiful voice, 'Sir

Don Quixote! oh, sir Don Quixote!' 'What wouldst thou have, brother Sancho?' replied the knight, with the like effeminate and doleful tune. 'I would,' quoth Sancho, 'have of your worship a draught or two of the liquor of Feoblas, if you have any of it at hand; perhaps it is good to cure broken bones as well as it helps wounds.' 'What would we want, unhappy that I am!' replied Don Quixote, 'if I had it here; but I swear unto thee, Sancho Panza, by the faith of a knight-errant, that before two days pass (if fortune dispose not otherwise), I will have it in my power, or it shall hardly escape my hands.' 'I pray you,' quoth Sancho, 'within how many days, think you, shall we be able to stir our feet?' 'I can say of myself,' quoth the crushed knight, 'that I cannot set a certain term to the days of our recovery; but I am in the fault of all, for I should not have drawn my sword against men that are not knights as well as I am; and therefore I believe that the god of battles hath permitted that this punishment should be given unto me, in pain of transgressing the laws of knighthood. Wherefore, brother Sancho, it is requisite that thou beest advertised of that which I shall say unto thee now, for it importeth both our goods very much; and is, that when thou beholdest that the like rascally rabble do us any wrong, do not wait till I set hand to my sword against them, for I will not do it in any sort; but draw thou thine, and chastise them at thy pleasure; and if any knights shall come to their assistance and succour, I shall know then how to defend thee, and offend them with all my force; for thou hast by this perceived, by a thousand signs and experiences, how far the valour of this mine invincible arm extendeth itself':—so arrogant remained the poor knight, through the victory he had gotten of the hardy Biscaine. But this advice of his lord seemed not so good to Sancho Panza as that he would omit to answer unto him, saying, 'Sir, I am a peaceable, quiet, and sober man, and can dissemble any injury, for I have wife and children to maintain and bring up; wherefore, let this likewise be an advice to you (seeing it cannot be a commandment), that I will not set hand to my sword in any wise, be it against clown or knight; and that, from this time forward, I do pardon, before God, all the wrongs that they have done, or shall do unto me, whether they were, be, or shall be done by high or low person, rich or poor, gentleman or churl, without excepting any state or condition.' Which being heard by his lord, he said: 'I could wish to have breath enough that I might answer thee with a little more ease, or that the grief which I feel in this rib were assuaged ever so little, that I might, Panza, make thee understand the error wherein thou art. Come here, poor fool! if the gale of fortune, hitherto so contrary, do turn in our favour, swelling the sails of our desire in such sort as we may securely and without any hindrance arrive at the haven of any of those islands which I have promised unto thee, what would become of thee, if I, conquering it, did make thee lord thereof, seeing thou wouldst disable thyself, in respect thou art not a knight, nor desirest to be one, nor wouldst have valour or will to revenge thine injuries, or to defend thy lordship's? For thou must understand that, in the kingdoms and provinces newly conquered, the minds of the inhabitants are never so thoroughly appeased or wedded to the affection of their new lord, that it is not to be feared that they will work some novelty to alter things again, and turn, as men say, afresh to try fortune; and it is therefore requisite that the new possessor have understanding to govern, and valour to offend, and defend himself in any adventure whatsoever.' 'In this last that hath befallen us,' quoth Sancho, 'I would I had had that understanding and valour of which you speak; but I vow unto you, by the faith of a poor man, that I am now fitter for plaisters than discourses. I pray you try whether you can arise, and we will help Rozinante, although he deserves it not; for he was the principal cause of all these troubles. I would never have believed the like before of Rozinante, whom I ever held to be as chaste and peaceable a person as myself. In fine, they say well, that one must have a long time to come to the knowledge of bodies, and that there's nothing in this life secure. Who durst affirm that, after those mighty blows which you gave to that unfortunate knight-errant, would succeed so in post, and as it were in your pursuit, this so furious a tempest of staves, that hath discharged itself on our shoulders?' 'Thine, Sancho,' replied Don Quixote, 'are perhaps accustomed to bear the like showers, but mine, nursed between cottons and hollands, it is most evident that they must feel the grief of this disgrace. And were it not that I imagine (but why do I say imagine?) I know certainly that all these incommodities are annexed to the exercise of arms, I would here die for very wrath and displeasure.' To this the squire answered: 'Sir, seeing these disgraces are of the essence of knighthood, I pray you whether they succeed very often, or whether they have certain times limited wherein they befall? For methinks, within two adventures more, we shall wholly remain disenabled for the third, if the gods in mercy do not succour us.'

'Know, friend Sancho,' replied Don Quixote, 'that the life of knights-errant is subject to a thousand dangers and misfortunes; and it is also as well, in the next degree and power, to make them kings and emperors, as experience hath shown in sundry knights, of whose histories I have entire notice. And I could recount unto thee now (did the pain I suffer permit me) of some of them which have mounted to those high degrees which I have said, only by the valour of their arm; and the very same men found them, both before and after, in divers miseries and calamities. For the valorous Amadis of Gaul saw himself in the power of his mortal enemy, Arcalaus the enchanter, of whom the opinion runs infallible, that he gave unto him, being his prisoner, more than two hundred stripes with his horse-bridle, after he had tied him to a pillar in his base-court. And there is, moreover, a secret author of no little credit, who says, that the Cavalier del Febo, being taken in a gin, like unto a snatch, that slipped under his feet in a certain castle, after the fall found himself in a deep dungeon under the earth, bound hands and feet; and there they gave unto him a clyster of snow-water and sand, which brought him almost to the end of his life; and were it not that he was succoured in that great distress by a wise man, his very great friend, it had gone ill with the poor knight. So that I may very well pass among so many worthy persons; for the dangers and disgraces they suffered were greater than those which we do now endure. For, Sancho, I would have thee to understand, that these wounds which are given to one with those instruments that are in one's hand, by chance, do not disgrace a man. And it is written in the laws of single combat, in express terms, that if the shoemaker strike another with the last which he hath in his hand, although it be certainly of wood, yet cannot it be said that he who was striken had the bastinado. I say this, to the end thou mayst not think, although we remain bruised in this last conflict, that therefore we be disgraced; for the arms which those men bore, and wherewithal they laboured us, were none other than their pack-staves, and, as far as I can remember, never a one of them had a tuck, sword, or dagger.' 'They gave me no leisure,' answered Sancho, 'to look to them so nearly; for scarce had I laid hand on my truncheon, when they blessed my shoulders with their pins, in such sort as they wholly deprived me of my sight and the force of my feet together, striking me down on the place where I yet lie straught, and where the pain of the disgrace received by our cudgelling doth not so much pinch me as the grief of the blows, which shall remain as deeply imprinted in my memory as they do in my back.'

'For all this, thou shalt understand, brother Panza,' replied Don Quixote, 'that there is no remembrance which time will not end, nor grief which death will not consume.' 'What greater misfortune,' quoth Sancho, 'can there be than that which only expecteth time and death to end and consume it? If this our disgrace were of that kind which might be cured by a pair or two of plaisters, it would not be so evil; but I begin to perceive that all the salves of an hospital will not suffice to bring them to any good terms.' 'Leave off, Sancho, and gather strength out of weakness,' said Don Quixote, 'for so will I likewise do; and let us see how doth Rozinante, for methinks that the least part of this mishap hath not fallen to his lot.' 'You ought not to marvel at that,' quoth Sancho, 'seeing he is likewise a knight-errant; that whereat I wonder is that mine ass remains there without payment, where we are come away without ribs.' 'Fortune leaves always one door open in disasters,' quoth Don Quixote, 'whereby to remedy them. I say it, because that little beast may supply Rozinante's want, by carrying off me from hence unto some castle, wherein I may be cured of my wounds. Nor do I hold this kind of riding dishonourable; for I remember to have read that the good old Silenus, tutor of the merry god of laughter, when he entered into the city of the hundred gates, rode very fairly mounted on a goodly ass.' 'It is like,' quoth Sancho, 'that he rode, as you say, upon an ass; but there is great difference betwixt riding and being cast athwart upon one like a sack of rubbish.' To this Don Quixote answered: 'The wounds that are received in battle do rather give honour than deprive men of it; wherefore, friend Panza, do not reply any more unto me, but, as I have said, arise as well as thou canst, and lay me as thou pleaseth upon thy beast, and let us depart from hence before the night overtake us in these deserts.' 'Yet I have heard you say,' quoth Panza, 'that it was an ordinary custom of knights-errant to sleep in downs and deserts the most of the year, and that so to do they hold for very good hap.' 'That is,' said Don Quixote, 'when they have none other shift, or when they are in love; and this is so true as that there hath been a knight that hath dwelt on a rock, exposed to the sun and the shadow, and other annoyances of heaven, for the space of two years, without his lady's knowledge. And Amadis was one of that kind, when calling himself Beltenebros, he dwelt in the Poor Rock, nor do I know punctually eight years or eight months, for I do not remember the history well; let it suffice that there he dwelt doing of penance, for some disgust which I know not, that his lady, Oriana, did him. But, leaving that apart, Sancho, despatch and away before some other disgrace happen, like that of Rozinante, to the ass.'

'Even there lurks the devil,' quoth Sancho; and so, breathing thirty sobs and threescore sighs, and a hundred and twenty discontents and execrations against him that had brought him there, he arose, remaining bent in the midst of the way, like unto a Turkish bow, without being able to address himself; and, notwithstanding all this difficulty, he harnessed his ass (who had been also somewhat distracted by the overmuch liberty of that day), and after he hoisted up Rozinante, who, were he endowed with a tongue to complain, would certainly have borne his lord and Sancho company. In the end Sancho laid Don Quixote on the ass, and tied Rozinante unto him, and, leading the ass by the halter, travelled that way which he deemed might conduct him soonest toward the highway. And fortune, which guided his affairs from good to better, after he had travelled a little league, discovered it unto him, near unto which he saw an inn, which, in despite of him, and for Don Quixote's pleasure, must needs be a castle. Sancho contended that it was an inn, and his lord that it was not; and their controversy endured so long as they had leisure, before they could decide it, to arrive at the lodging; into which Sancho, without further verifying of the dispute, entered with all his loading.

CHAPTER II

Of That Which Happened Unto the Ingenuous Knight Within the Inn, Which He Supposed to Be a Castle

THE innkeeper, seeing Don Quixote laid overthwart upon the ass, demanded of Sancho what disease he had. Sancho answered that it was nothing but a fall down from a rock, and that his ribs were thereby somewhat bruised. This innkeeper had a wife, not of the condition that those of that trade are wont to be; for she was of a charitable nature, and would grieve at the calamities of her neighbours, and did therefore presently occur to cure Don Quixote, causing her daughter, a very comely young maiden, to assist her to cure her guest. There likewise served in the inn an Asturian wench, who was broad-faced, flat-pated, saddle-nosed, blind of one eye, and the other almost out; true it is, that the comeliness of her body supplied all the other defects. She was not seven palms long from her feet unto her head; and her shoulders, which did somewhat burden her, made her look oftener to the ground than she would willingly. This beautiful piece did assist the young maiden, and both of them made a very bad bed for Don Quixote in an old wide chamber, which gave manifest tokens of itself that it had sometimes served many years only to keep chopped straw for horses; in which was also lodged a carrier, whose bed was made a little way off from Don Quixote's, which, though it was made of canvas and coverings of his mules, was much better than the knight's, that only contained four boards roughly planed, placed on two unequal tressels; a flock-bed, which in the thinness seemed rather a quilt, full of pellets, and had not they shown that they were wool, through certain breaches made by antiquity on the tick, a man would by the hardness rather take them to be stones; a pair of sheets made of the skins of targets; a coverlet, whose threads if a man would number, he should not lose one only of the account.

In this ungracious bed did Don Quixote lie, and presently the hostess and her daughter anointed him all over, and Maritornes (for so the Asturian wench was called) did hold the candle. The hostess at the plaistering of him, perceiving him to be so bruised in sundry places, she said unto him that those signs rather seemed to proceed of blows than of a fall. 'They were not blows,' replied Sancho; 'but the rock had many sharp ends and knobs on it, whereof every one left behind it a token; and I desire you, good mistress,' quoth he, 'to leave some flax behind, and there shall not want one that needeth the use of them; for, I assure you, my back doth likewise ache.' 'If that be so,' quoth the hostess, 'it is likely that thou didst also fall.' 'I did not fall,' quoth Sancho Panza, 'but with the sudden affright that I took at my master's fall, my body doth so grieve me, as methinks I have been handsomely belaboured.' 'It may well happen as thou sayst,' quoth the hostess's daughter; 'for it hath befallen me sundry times to dream that I fell down from some high tower, and could never come to the ground; and when I awoke, I did find myself so troubled and broken, as if I had verily fallen.' 'There is the point, masters,' quoth Sancho Panza, 'that I, without dreaming at all, but being more awake than I am at this hour, found myself to have very few less tokens and marks than my lord Don Quixote hath.' 'How is this gentleman called?' quoth Maritornes the Asturian. 'Don Quixote of the Mancha,' replied Sancho Panza; 'and he is a knight-errant, and one of the best and strongest that have been seen in the world these many ages.' 'What is that, a knight-errant?' quoth the wench. 'Art thou so young in the world that thou knowest it not?' answered Sancho Panza. 'Know then, sister mine, that a knight-errant is a thing which, in two words, you see well cudgelled, and after becomes an emperor. To-day he is the most unfortunate creature of the world, and the most needy; and to-morrow he will have two or three crowns of kingdoms to bestow upon his squire.' 'If it be so,' quoth the hostess, 'why, then, hast not thou gotten at least an earldom, seeing thou art this good knight his squire?' 'It is yet too soon,' replied Sancho; 'for it is but a month since we began first to seek adventures, and we have not yet encountered any worthy of the name. And sometimes it befalls, that searching for one thing we encounter another. True it is that, if my lord Don Quixote recover of this wound or fall, and that I be not changed by it, I would not make an exchange of my hopes for the best title of Spain.' Don Quixote did very attentively listen unto all these discourses, and, sitting up in his bed as well as he could, taking his hostess by the hand, he said unto her: 'Believe me, beautiful lady, that you may count yourself fortunate for having harboured my person in this your castle, which is such, that if I do not praise it, it is because men say that proper praise stinks; but my squire will inform you what I am: only this I will say myself, that I will keep eternally written in my memory the service that you have done unto me, to be grateful unto you for it whilst I live. And I would it might please the highest heavens that love held me not so enthralled and subject to his laws as he doth, and to the eyes of that ungrateful fair whose name I secretly mutter, then should those of this beautiful damsel presently signiorise my liberty.' The hostess, her daughter, and the good Maritornes remained confounded, hearing the speech of our knight-errant, which they understood as well as if he had spoken Greek unto them; but yet they conceived that they were words of compliments and love, and as people unused to hear the like language, they beheld and admired him, and he seemed unto them a man of the other world; and so, returning him thanks, with tavernly phrase, for his large offers, they departed. And the Asturian Maritornes cured Sancho, who needed her help no less than his master.

The carrier and she had agreed to pass the night together, and she had given unto him her word that, when the guests were quiet and her master sleeping, she would come unto him and satisfy his desire, as much as he pleased. And it is said of this good wench, that she never passed the like promise but that she performed it, although it were given in the midst of a wood, and without any witness; for she presumed to be of gentle blood, and yet she held it no disgrace to serve in an inn; for she was wont to affirm that disgraces and misfortunes brought her to that state. The hard, narrow, niggard, and counterfeit bed whereon Don Quixote lay was the first of the four, and next unto it was his squire's, that only contained a mat and a coverlet, and rather seemed to be of shorn canvas than wool. After these two beds followed that of the carrier, made, as we have said, of the pannels and furniture of two of his best mules, although they were twelve all in number, fair, fat, and goodly beasts; for he was one of the richest carriers of Arevalo, as the author of this history affirmeth, who maketh particular mention of him, because he knew him very well, and besides, some men say that he was somewhat akin unto him; omitting that Cid Mahamet Benengeli was a very exact historiographer, and most curious in all things, as may be gathered very well, seeing that those which are related being so minute and trivial, he would not overslip them in silence.

By which those grave historiographers may take example, which recount unto us matters so short and succinctly as they do scarce arrive to our knowledge, leaving the most substantial part of the works drowned in the ink-horn, either through negligence, malice, or ignorance. Many good fortunes betide the author of *Tablante de Ricamonte,* and him that wrote the book wherein are rehearsed the acts of the Count Tomillas: Lord! with what preciseness do they describe every circumstance. To conclude, I say that, after the carrier had visited his mules, and given unto them their second refreshing, he stretched himself in his coverlets, and expected the coming of the most exquisite Maritornes. Sancho was also, by this, plaistered and laid down in his bed, and though he desired to sleep, yet would not the grief of his ribs permit him. And Don Quixote, with the pain of his sides, lay with both his eyes open, like a hare.

All the inn was drowned in silence, and there was no other light in it than that of a lamp, which hung lighting in the midst of the entry. This marvellous quietness, and the thoughts which always represented to our knight the memory of the successes which at every pace are recounted in books of knighthood (the principal authors of this mishap), called to his imagination one of the strangest follies that easily may be conjectured; which was, he imagined that he arrived to a famous castle (for, as we have said, all the inns wherein he lodged seemed unto him to be such), and that the innkeeper's daughter was the lord's daughter of the castle, who, overcome by his comeliness and valour, was enamoured of him, and had promised that she would come to solace with him for a good space, after her father and mother had gone to bed. And holding all this chimera and fiction, which he himself had built in his brain, for most firm and certain, he began to be vexed in mind, and to think on the dangerous trance, wherein his honesty was like to fall, and did firmly purpose in heart not to commit any disloyalty against his lady, Dulcinea of Toboso, although very Queen Genever, with her lady, Queintanonia, should come to solicit him. Whilst thus he lay thinking of these follies, the hour approached (that was unlucky for him) wherein the Asturian wench should come, who entered into the chamber in search of her carrier, in her smock, barefooted, and her hair trussed up in a coif of fustian, with soft and wary steps. But she was scarce come to the door when Don Quixote felt her, and, arising and sitting up in his bed, in despite of his plaisters and with great grief of his ribs, he stretched forth his arms to receive his beautiful damsel, the Asturian, who, crouching and silently, went groping with her hands to find out her sweet heart, and encountered Don Quixote's arms, who presently seized very strongly upon one of her wrists, and, drawing her towards him (she daring not to speak a word,) he caused her to sit upon his bed's side, and presently groped her smock, and although it was of the strongest canvas, he thought it was most subtle and fine holland. She wore on her wrists certain bracelets of glass, which he esteemed to be precious oriental pearls. Her hair which was almost as rough as a horse-tail, he held to be wires of the glisteringest gold of Arabia, whose brightness did obscure that of the sun; and her breath, which certainly smelled like to stale salt-fish reserved from over night, seemed unto him a most redolent, aromatical, and sweet smell. And finally, he painted her in his fantasy of the same very form and manner as he had read in his books of knighthood, of a certain princess which came to visit a knight who was grievously wounded, being overcome by his love, embellished with all the ornaments that here we have recounted; and the blindness of this poor gallant was such, as neither the touching, savour, or other things that accompanied the good damsel, could undeceive him, being such as were able to make any other, save a carrier, vomit up his bowels; but rather he made full account that he held the goddess of love between his arms, and, holding her still very fast, he began to court her, with a low and amorous voice. in this manner: 'I could wish to find myself in terms, most high and beautiful lady, to be able to recompense so great a favour as that which, with the presence of your matchless feature, you have shown unto me; but fortune (who is never weary of persecuting the good) hath pleased to lay me in this bed, wherein I lie so broken and bruised, that although I were desirous to satisfy your will, yet it is impossible; especially seeing to that impossibility may be added a greater, to wit, the promised faith which I have given to the unmatchable Dulcinea of Toboso, the only lady of my most hidden thoughts; for did not this let me, do not hold me to be so senseless and mad a knight as to overslip so fortunate an occasion as this which your bounty hath offered to me.'

Maritornes remained sweating, through anxiety, to see herself held so fast by Don Quixote, and, without either understanding or giving attention to his words, she laboured all that she could to free herself from him without speaking a word. The carrier, whose bad intention kept him still waking, did hear his lady from the time that she first entered into the room, and did attentively give ear to all Don Quixote's discourses; and, jealous that the Asturian should break promise with him for any other, he drew nearer unto Don Quixote's bed, and stood quiet to see whereunto those words which he could not understand tended; but viewing that the wench strove to depart, and Don Quixote laboured to withhold her, the jest seeming evil unto him, he up with his arm, and discharged so terrible a blow on the enamoured knight's jaws as he bathed all his mouth in blood; and, not content herewithal, he mounted upon the knight, and did tread on his ribs, and passed them all over with more than a trot.

The bed, which was somewhat weak, and not very firm of foundation, being unable to suffer the addition of the carrier, fell down to the ground with so great a noise as it waked the innkeeper; who, presently suspecting that it was one of Maritornes' conflicts, because she answered him not, having called her loudly, he forthwith arose, and, lighting of a lamp, he went towards the place where he heard the noise. The wench, perceiving that her master came, and that he was extreme choleric, did, all ashamed and troubled, run into Sancho Panza's bed, who slept all this while very soundly, and there crouched, and made herself as little as an egg.

Her master entered, crying, "Whore, where art thou? I dare warrant that these are some of thy doings?' By this Sancho awaked, and, feeling that bulk lying almost wholly upon him, he thought it was the nightmare, and began to lay with his fists here and there about him very swiftly, and among others wrought Maritornes I know not how many blows; who, grieved for the pain she endured there, casting all honesty aside, gave Sancho the exchange of his blows so trimly as she made him to awake in despite of his sluggishness. And, finding himself to be so abused of an uncouth person, whom he could not behold, he arose and caught hold of Maritornes as well as he could, and they both began the best fight and pleasantest skirmish in the world.

The carrier, perceiving by the light which the innkeeper brought in with him, the lamentable state of his mistress, abandoning Don Quixote, he instantly repaired to give her the succour that was requisite, which likewise the innkeeper did, but with another meaning; for he approached with intention to punish the wench, believing that she was infallibly the cause of all that harmony. And so, as men say, the cat to the rat, the rat to the cord, the cord to the post; so the carrier struck Sancho, Sancho the wench, she returned him again his liberality with interest, and the inn-keeper laid load upon his maid also; and all of them did mince it with such expedition, as there was no leisure at all allowed to any one of them for breathing. And the best of all was, that the innkeeper's lamp went out, and then, finding themselves in darkness, they belaboured one another so without compassion, and at once, as wheresoever the blow fell, it bruised the place pitifully.

There lodged by chance that night in the inn one of the squadron of these which are called of the old Holy Brotherhood of Toledo; he likewise hearing the wonderful noise of the fight, laid hand on his rod of office and the tin box of his titles, and entered into the chamber without light, saying, 'Stand still to the officer of justice and to the holy brotherhood.' And, saying so, the first whom he met was the poor battered Don Quixote, who lay overthrown in his bed, stretched, with his face upward, without any feeling; and taking hold of his beard, he cried out incessantly, 'Help the justice!' But, seeing that he whom he held fast bowed neither hand nor foot, he presently thought that he was dead, and that those battaillants that fought so eagerly in the room had slain him; wherefore he lifted his voice and cried out loudly, saying, 'Shut the inn-door, and see that none escape; for here they have killed a man!' This word astonished all the combatants so much, as every one left the battle in the very terms wherein this voice had overtaken them. The innkeeper retired himself to his chamber, the carrier to his coverlets, the wench to her couch; and only the unfortunate Don Quixote and Sancho were not able to move themselves from the place wherein they lay. The officer of the Holy Brotherhood in this space letting slip poor Don Quixote's beard, went out for light to search and apprehend the delinquents; but he could not find any, for the innkeeper had purposely quenched the lamp as he retired to his bed; wherefore the officer was constrained to repair to the chimney, where, with great difficulty, after he had spent a long while doing of it he at last lighted a candle.

CHAPTER III

Wherein Are Rehearsed the Innumerable Misfortunes Which Don Quixote and His Good Squire Sancho Suffered in the Inn, Which He, to His Harm, Thought to Be a Castle

BY this time Don Quixote was come to himself again out of his trance, and, with the like lamentable notes as that wherewithal he had called his squire the day before, when he was overthrown in the vale of the pack-staves, he called to him, saying, 'Friend Sancho, art thou asleep? sleepest thou, friend Sancho?' 'What! I asleep? I renounce myself,' quoth Sancho, full of grief and despite, 'if I think not all the devils in hell have been visiting of me here this night!' 'Thou mayst certainly believe it,' replied Don Quixote; 'for either I know very little, or else this castle is enchanted. For I let thee to wit—but thou must first swear to keep secret that which I mean to tell thee now, until after my death.' 'So I swear,' quoth Sancho. 'I say it,' quoth Don Quixote, 'because I cannot abide to take away anybody's honour.' 'Why,' quoth Sancho again, 'I swear that I will conceal it until after your worship's days; and I pray God that I may discover it to-morrow.' 'Have I wrought thee such harm, Sancho,' replied the knight, 'as thou wouldst desire to see me end so soon?' 'It is not for that, sir,' quoth Sancho; 'but because I cannot abide to keep things long, lest they should rot in my custody.' 'Let it be for what thou pleasest,' said Don Quixote; 'for I do trust greater matters than that to thy love and courtesy. And that I may rehearse it unto thee briefly, know that, a little while since, the lord of this castle's daughter came unto me, who is the most fair and beautiful damsel that can be found in a great part of the earth. What could I say unto thee of the ornaments of her person? what of her excellent wit? what of other secret things? which, that I may preserve the faith due unto my Lady Dulcinea of Toboso, I pass over in silence. I will only tell thee that Heaven, envious of the inestimable good that fortune had put in my hands;

or perhaps (and that is most probable) this castle, as I have said, is enchanted; just at the time when we were in most sweet and amorous speech, I being not able to see or know from whence it came, there arrived a hand, joined to the arm of some mighty giant, and gave me such a blow on the jaws as they remain all bathed in blood, and did after so thump and bruise me as I feel myself worse now than yesterday, when the carriers, through Rozinante's madness, did use us thou knowest how. By which I conjecture that the treasure of this damsel's beauty is kept by some enchanted Moor, and is not reserved for me.' 'Nor for me,' quoth Sancho; 'for I have been bombasted by more than four hundred Moors, which have hammered me in such sort as the bruising of the pack-staves was gilded bread and spice-cakes in comparison of it. But, sir, I pray you tell me, how can you call this a good and rare adventure, seeing we remain so pitifully used after it? And yet your harms may be accounted less, in respect you have held, as you said, that incomparable beauty between your arms. But I, what have I had other than the greatest blows that I shall ever have in my life? Unfortunate that I am, and the mother that bare me! that neither am an errant-knight, nor ever means to be any, and yet the greatest part of our mishaps still falls to my lot.' 'It seems that thou wast likewise beaten,' replied Don Quixote. 'Evil befal my lineage!' quoth Sancho; 'have not I told you I was?' 'Be not grieved, friend,' replied the knight; 'for I will now compound the precious balsam, which will cure us in the twinkling of an eye.'

The officer having by this time lighted his lamp, entered into the room to see him whom he accounted to be dead; and as soon as Sancho saw him, seeing him come in in his shirt, his head wrapped up in a kerchief, the lamp in his hand, having withal a very evil-favoured countenance, he demanded of his lord,—'Sir, is this by chance the enchanted Moor, that turns anew to torment us for somewhat that is yet unpunished?' 'He cannot be the Moor,' answered Don Quixote; 'for necromancers suffer not themselves to be seen by any.' 'If they suffer not themselves to be seen,' quoth Sancho, 'they suffer themselves at least to be felt; if not, let my shoulders bear witness.' 'So might mine also,' said Don Quixote; 'but, notwithstanding, this is no sufficient argument to prove him whom we see to be the enchanted Moor.' As thus they discoursed, the officer arrived, and, finding them to commune in so peaceable and quiet manner, he rested admired. Yet Don Quixote lay with his face upward as he had left him, and was not able to stir himself, he was so beaten and beplaistered. The officer approaching, demanded of him, 'Well, how dost thou, good fellow?' 'I would speak more mannerly,' quoth Don Quixote, 'if I were but such a one as thou art. Is it the custom of this country, you bottle-head! to talk after so rude a manner to knights-errant?' The other, impatient to see one of so vile presence use him with that bad language, could not endure it; but, lifting up the lamp, oil and all, gave Don Quixote such a blow on the pate with it as he broke his head in one or two places, and, leaving all in darkness behind him, departed presently out of the chamber. 'Without doubt,' quoth Sancho, seeing this accident, 'sir, that was the enchanted Moor; and I think he keepeth the treasure for others, and reserveth only for us fists and lamp-blows.' 'It is as thou sayst,' quoth Don Quixote; 'and therefore we are not to make account of these enchantments, or be wroth and angry at them; for, in respect that they are invisible and fantastical, we shall not find him on whom we may take revenge, though we labour ever so much to do it. Arise, therefore, Sancho, if thou beest able, and call to the constable of this fortress, and procure me some oil, wine, salt, and vinegar, that I make the wholesome balsam; for verily I believe that I do need it very much at this time, the blood runneth so fast out of the wound which the spirit gave me even now.' Sancho then got up, with grief enough of his bones, and went without light towards the innkeeper's, and encountered on the way the officer of the holy brotherhood, who stood harkening what did become of his enemy; to whom he said, 'Sir, whosoever thou beest, I desire thee, do us the favour and benefit to give me a little rosemary, oil, wine, and salt, to cure one of the best knights-errant that is in the earth, who lieth now in that bed, sorely wounded by the hands of an enchanted Moor that is in this inn.' When the officer heard him speak in that manner, he held him to be out of his wits; and because the dawning began, he opened the inn-door, and told unto the host that which Sancho demanded. The innkeeper presently provided all that he wanted, and Sancho carried it to his master, who held his head between both his hands, and complained much of the grief that the blow of his head caused, which did him no other hurt than to raise up two blisters somewhat great, and that which he supposed to be blood was only the humour which the anxiety and labour of mind he passed in this last dark adventure had made him to sweat.

In resolution, Don Quixote took his simples, of which he made a compound, mixing them all together, and then boiling of them a good while, until they came (as he thought) to their perfection. He asked for a vial wherein he might lay this precious liquor; but, the inn being unable to afford him any such, he resolved at last to put it into a tin oil-pot, which the host did freely give him, and forthwith he said over the pot eighty paternosters, and as many aves, salves, and creeds, and accompanied every word with a cross, in form of benediction; at all which ceremonies, Sancho, the innkeeper, and the officer of the holy brotherhood were present; for the carrier went very soberly to dress and make ready his mules.

The liquor being made, he himself would presently make experience of the virtue of that precious balsam, as he did imagine it to be, and so did drink a good draught of the overplus that could not enter into his pot, being a quart or thereabouts; and scarce had he done it when he began to vomit so extremely as he left nothing uncast up in his stomach; and, through the pain and agitation caused by his vomits, he fell into a very abundant and great sweat, and therefore commanded himself to be well covered, and left alone to take his ease. Which was done forthwith and he slept three hours, and then, awaking, found himself so wonderfully eased and free from all bruising and pain, as he doubted not but that he was thoroughly whole; and therefore did verily persuade himself that he had happened on the right manner of compounding the Balsam of Fierabras; and that, having that medicine, he might boldly from thenceforth undertake any ruins, battles, conflicts, or adventures, how dangerous soever.

Sancho Panza, who likewise attributed the sudden cure of his master to miracle, requested that it would please him to give him leave to sup up the remainder of the balsam which rested in the kettle, and was no small quantity; which Don Quixote granted;

and he, lifting up between both hands, did, with a good faith and better talent, quaff it off all, being little less than his master had drunk. The success, then, of the history is, that poor Sancho's stomach was not so delicate as his lord's, wherefore, before he could cast, he was tormented with so many cruel pangs, loathings, sweats, and dismays, as he did verily persuade himself that his last hour was come; and, perceiving himself to be so afflicted and troubled, he cursed the balsam, and the thief which had given it to him. Don Quixote, seeing of him in that pitiful taking, said: 'I believe, Sancho, all this evil befalleth thee because thou art not dubbed knight; for I persuade myself that this liquor cannot help any one that is not.' 'If your worship knew that,' quoth Sancho,—'evil befall me and all my lineage!—why did you therefore consent that I should taste it?'

In this time the drench had made his operation, and the poor squire did so swift and vehemently discharge himself by both channels, as neither his mat or canvas covering could serve after to any use. He sweat and sweat again, with such excessive swoonings, as not only himself, but likewise all the beholders, did verily deem that his life was ending. This storm and mishap endured about some two hours, after which he remained not cured as his master, but so weary and indisposed as he was not able to stand.

But Don Quixote, who, as we have said, felt himself eased and cured, would presently depart to seek adventures, it seeming unto him that all the time which he abode there was no other than a depriving both of the world and needful people of his favour and assistance; and more, through the security and confidence that he had in his balsam. And carried thus away by this desire, he himself saddled his horse Rozinante, and did empannel his squire's beast, whom he likewise helped to apparel himself and to mount upon his ass; and presently, getting a-horseback, he rode over to a corner of the inn, and laid hand on a javelin that was there, to make it serve him instead of a lance. All the people that were in the inn stood beholding him, which were above twenty in number.

The innkeeper's daughter did also look upon him, and he did never withdraw his eye from her, and would ever and anon breathe forth so doleful a sigh as if he had plucked it out of the bottom of his heart; which all the beholders took to proceed from the grief of his ribs, but especially such as had seen him plaistered the night before. And, being both mounted thus a-horseback, he called the innkeeper, and said unto him, with a grave and staid voice: 'Many and great are the favours, sir constable, which I have received in this your castle, and do remain most obliged to gratify you for them all the days of my life. And if I may pay or recompense them by revenging of you upon any proud miscreant that hath done you any wrongs, know that it is mine office to help the weak, to revenge the wronged, and to chastise traitors. Call therefore to memory, and if you find anything of this kind to commend to my correction, you need not but once to say it; for I do promise you, by the order of knighthood which I have received, to satisfy and apay you according to your own desire.'

The innkeeper answered him again, with like gravity and staidness, saying, 'Sir knight, I shall not need your assistance when any wrong is done to me; for I know very well myself how to take the revenge that I shall think good, when the injury is offered. That only which I require is, that you defray the charges whereat you have been here in the inn this night, as well for the straw and barley given to your two horses, as also for both your beds.' 'This, then, is an inn?' quoth Don Quixote. 'That it is, and an honourable one too,' replied the innkeeper. 'Then have I hitherto lived in an error,' quoth Don Quixote; 'for, in very good sooth, I took it till now to be a castle, and that no mean one neither. But since that it is no castle, but an inn, that which you may do for the present time is, to forgive me those expenses; for I cannot do aught against the custom of knights-errant; of all which I most certainly know (without ever having read until this present anything to the contrary) that they never paid for their lodging, or other thing, in any inn wheresoever they lay; for, by all law and right, any good entertainment that is given unto them is their due, in recompense of the insupportable travels they endure, seeking of adventures both day and night, in summer and winter, a-foot and a-horseback, with thirst and hunger, in heat and cold, being subject to all the distemperatures of heaven and all the discommodities of the earth.' 'All that concerns me nothing,' replied the innkeeper. 'Pay unto me my due, and leave these tales and knighthoods apart; for I care for nothing else but how I may come by mine own.' 'Thou art a mad and a bad host,' quoth Don Quixote. And, saying so, he spurred Rozinante, and, flourishing with his javelin, he issued out of the inn in despite of them all, and, without looking behind him to see once whether his squire followed, he rode a good way off from it.

The innkeeper, seeing he departed without satisfying him, came to Sancho Panza to get his money of him, who answered that, since his lord would not pay, he would likewise give nothing; for being, as he was, squire to a knight-errant, the very same rules and reason that exempted his master from payments in inns and taverns ought also to serve and be understood as well of him. The innkeeper grew wroth at these words, and threatened him that, if he did not pay him speedily, he would recover it in manner that would grieve him. Sancho replied, swearing by the order of knighthood which his lord had received, that he would not pay one denier, though it cost him his life; for the good and ancient customs of knights-errant should never, through his default, be infringed; nor should their squires which are yet to come into the world ever complain on him, or upbraid him for transgressing or breaking so just a duty. But his bad fortune ordained that there were at the very time in the same inn four clothiers of Segovia, and three point-makers of the stews of Cordova, and two neighbours of the market of Seville, all pleasant folk, well-minded, malicious, and playsome; all which, pricked and in a manner moved all at one time, and by the very same spirit, came near to Sancho, and, pulling him down off his ass, one of them ran in for the innkeeper's coverlet, and, casting him into it, they looked up, and, seeing the house was somewhat too low for their intended business, they determined to go into the base-court, which was overhead only limited by heaven; and then, Sancho being laid in the midst of the blanket, they began to toss him aloft and sport themselves with him, in the manner they were wont to use dogs at Shrovetide.

The outcries of the miserable betossed squire were so many and so loud as they arrived at last to his lord's hearing, who, standing awhile to listen attentively what it was, believed that some new adventure did approach, until he perceived at last that he which cried was his squire; wherefore, turning the reins, he made towards the inn with a loathsome gallop, and, finding it shut, he rode all about it to see whether he might enter into it. But scarce was he arrived at the walls of the base-court, which were not very high, when he perceived the foul play that was used toward his squire; for he saw him descend and ascend into the air again, with such grace and agility, that, did his choler permit, I certainly persuade myself, he would have burst for laughter. He assayed to mount the wall from his horse, but he was so bruised and broken as he could not do so much as alight from his back; wherefore, from his back, he used such reproachful and vile language to those which tossed Sancho, as it is impossible to lay them down in writing. And, notwithstanding all his scornful speech, yet did not they cease from their laughter and labour; nor the flying Sancho from his complaints, now and then meddled with threats, now and then with entreaties; but availed very little, nor could prevail, until they were constrained by weariness to give him over. Then did they bring him his ass again, and, helping him up upon it, they lapped him in his mantle; and the compassionate Maritornes, beholding him so afflicted and o'erlaboured, thought it needful to help him to a draught of water, and so brought it him from the well, because the water thereof was coolest. Sancho took the pot, and, laying it to his lips, he abstained from drinking by his lord's persuasion, who cried to him aloud, saying, 'Son Sancho, drink not water; drink it not, son; for it will kill thee. Behold, I have here with me the most holy balsam' (and showed him the oil-pot of the drenches he had compounded); 'for, with only two drops that thou drinkest, thou shalt, without all doubt, remain whole and sound.' At those words, Sancho, looking behind him, answered his master, with a louder voice: 'Have you forgotten so soon how that I am no knight, or do you desire that I vomit the remnant of the poor bowels that remain in me since yesternight? Keep your liquor for yourself, in the devil's name, and permit me to live in peace.' And the conclusion of this speech and his beginning to drink was done all in one instant; but, finding at the first draught that it was water, he would not taste it any more, but requested Maritornes that she would give him some wine, which she did straight with a very good will, and likewise paid for it out of her own purse; for in effect it is written of her, that though she followed that trade, yet had she some shadows and lineaments in her of Christianity. As soon as Sancho had drunken, he visited his ass's ribs with his heels twice or thrice; and, the inn being opened, he issued out of it, very glad that he had paid nothing, and gotten his desire, although it were to the cost of his ordinary sureties, to wit, his shoulders. Yet did the innkeeper remain possessed of his wallets, as a payment for that he owed him; but Sancho was so distracted when he departed as he never missed them. After he departed, the innkeeper thought to have shut up the inn-door again; but the gentlemen-tossers would not permit, being such folk that, if Don Quixote were verily one of the knights of the Round Table, yet would not they esteem him two chips.

CHAPTER IV

Wherein Are Rehearsed the Discourses Passed Between Sancho Panza and His Lord, Don Quixote, With Other Adventures Worthy the Recital

SANCHO arrived to his master all wan and dismayed, insomuch as he was scarce able to spur on his beast. When Don Quixote beheld him in that case, he said to him: 'Now do I wholly persuade myself, friend Sancho, that that castle or inn is doubtless enchanted; for those which made pastime with thee in so cruel manner, what else could they be but spirits, or people of another world? which I do the rather believe, because I saw that, whilst I stood at the barrier of the yard, beholding the acts of thy sad tragedy, I was not in any wise able either to mount it, or alight from Rozinante; for, as I say, I think they held me then enchanted. For I vow to thee, by mine honour, that if I could have either mounted or alighted, I would have taken such vengeance on those lewd and treacherous caitiffs as they should remember the jest for ever, though I had therefore adventured to transgress the laws of knighthood; which, as I have ofttimes said unto thee, permitteth not any knight to lay hands on one that is not knighted, if it be not in defence of his proper life and person, and that in case of great and urgent necessity.' 'So would I also have revenged myself,' quoth Sancho, 'if I might, were they knights or no knights; but I could not: and yet I do infallibly believe that those which took their pleasure with me were neither ghosts nor enchanted men, as you say, but men of flesh and bones as we are; and all of them, as I heard them called whilst they tossed me, had proper names, for one was termed Peter Martinez, and another Tenorio Herriander, and I heard also the innkeeper called John Palameque the deaf; so that, for your inability of not leaping over the barriers of the yard, or alighting off your horse, was only enchantments in you. Whereby I do clearly collect thus much, that these adventures which we go in search of will bring us at last to so many disventures as we shall not be able to know which is our right foot. And that which we might do best, according to my little understanding, were to return us again to our village, now that it is reaping-time, and look to our goods, omitting to leap thus, as they say, out of the frying-pan into the fire.'

'How little dost thou know, Sancho,' replied Don Quixote, 'what appertaineth to chivalry! Peace, and have patience, for a day will come wherein thou shalt see with thine own eyes how honourable it is to follow this exercise. If not, tell me what greater content may there be in this world, or what pleasure can equal that of winning a battle, and of triumphing over one's enemy? None, without doubt.' 'I think it be so,' quoth Sancho, 'although I do not know it; only this I know, that, since we became knights-errant, or that you are one (for there is no reason why I should count myself in so honourable a number), we never overcame any battle, if it was not that of the Biscaine, and you came even out of the very same with half your ear and beaver less; and ever after that time we have had nothing but cudgels and more cudgels, blows and more blows; I carrying with me besides, of overplus, the tossing in the blanket; and that, by reason it was done to me by enchanted persons, I cannot be revenged, and by consequence shall not know that true gust and delight that is taken by vanquishing mine enemy, whereof you spake even now.' 'That is it which grieves me, as it should thee also, Sancho,' quoth Don Quixote. 'But I will procure hereafter to get a sword made with such art, that whosoever shall wear it, no kind of enchantment shall hurt him; and perhaps fortune will present me the very same which belonged to Amadis, when he called himself "the knight of the burning sword," which was one of the best that ever knight had in this world; for besides the virtue that I told, it did also cut like a razor; and no armour, were it ever so strong or enchanted, could stand before it.' 'I am so fortunate,' quoth Sancho, 'that when this befel, and that you found such a sword, it would only serve and be beneficial, and stand in stead, such as are dubbed knights, as doth your balsam; whilst the poor squires are crammed full with sorrows.' 'Fear not that, Sancho,' quoth Don Quixote; 'for fortune will deal with thee more liberally than so.'

In these discourses Don Quixote and his squire rode; when Don Quixote, perceiving a great and thick dust to arise in the way wherein he travelled, turning to Sancho, said, 'This is, Sancho, the day wherein shall be manifest the good which fortune hath reserved for me. This is the day wherein the force of mine arm must be shown as much as in any other whatsoever; and in it I will do such feats as shall for ever remain recorded in the books of fame. Dost thou see, Sancho, the dust which ariseth there? Know that it is caused by a mighty army, and sundry and innumerable nations, which come marching there.' 'If that be so,' quoth Sancho, 'then must there be two armies; for on this other side is raised as great a dust.' Don Quixote turned back to behold it, and seeing it was so indeed, he was marvellous glad, thinking that they were doubtlessly two armies, which came to fight one with another in the midst of that spacious plain; for he had his fantasy ever replenished with these battles, enchantments, successes, ravings, loves, and challenges which are rehearsed in books of knighthood, and all that ever he spoke, thought, or did, was addressed and applied to the like things. And the dust which he had seen was raised by two great flocks of sheep, that came through the same field by two different ways, and could not be discerned, by reason of the dust, until they were very near. Don Quixote did affirm that they were two armies with so very good earnest as Sancho believed it, and demanded of him, 'Sir, what then shall we two do?' 'What shall we do,' quoth Don Quixote, 'but assist the needful and weaker side? For thou shalt know, Sancho, that he who comes towards us is the great emperor Alifamfaron, lord of the great island of Trapobana; the other, who marcheth at our back, is his enemy, the king of the Garamantes, Pentapolin of the naked arm, so called because he still entereth in battle with his right arm naked.' 'I pray you, good sir,' quoth Sancho, 'to tell me why these two princes hate one another so much?' 'They are enemies,' replied Don Quixote, 'because that this Alifamfaron is a furious pagan, and is enamoured of Pentapolin's daughter, who is a very beautiful and gracious princess, and, moreover, a Christian; and her father refuseth to give her to the pagan king, until first he abandon Mahomet's false sect, and become one of his religion.' 'By my beard,' quoth Sancho, 'Pentapolin hath reason, and I will help him all that I may.' 'By doing so,' quoth Don Quixote, 'thou performest thy duty; for it is not requisite that one be a knight to the end he may enter into such battles.' 'I do apprehend that myself,' quoth Sancho, 'very well; but where shall we leave this ass in the meantime, that we may be sure to find him again after the conflict? —for I think it is not the custom to enter into battle mounted on such a beast.' 'It is true,' quoth Don Quixote; 'that which thou mayst do is to leave him to his adventures, and care not whether he be lost or found; for we shall have so many horses, after coming out of this battle victors, that very Rozinante himself is in danger to be changed for another. But be attentive; for I mean to describe unto thee the principal knights of both the armies; and to the end thou mayst the better see and note all things, let us retire ourselves there to that little hillock, from whence both armies may easily be descried.'

They did so; and, standing on the top of a hill, from whence they might have seen both the flocks, which Don Quixote called an army, very well, if the clouds of dust had not hindered it and blinded their sight; yet, notwithstanding, our knight seeing in conceit that which he really did not see at all, began to say, with a loud voice,—

'That knight which thou seest there with the yellow armour, who bears in his shield a lion, crowned, crouching at a damsel's feet, is the valorous Laurcalio, lord of the silver bridge. The other, whose arms are powdered with flowers of gold, and bears in an azure field three crowns of silver, is the dreaded Micocolembo, great duke of Quirocia. The other, limbed like a giant, that standeth at his right hand, is the undaunted Brandabarbaray of Boliche, lord of the three Arabias, and comes armed with a serpent's skin, bearing for his shield, as is reported, one of the gates of the temple which Samson at his death overthrew to be revenged of his enemies. But turn thine eyes to this other side, and thou shalt see first of all, and in the front of this other army, the ever victor and never vanquished Timonel of Carcajona, prince of New Biscay, who comes armed with arms parted into blue, green, white, and yellow quarters, and bears in his shield, in a field of tawny, a cat of gold, with a letter that says Miau, which is the beginning of his lady's name, which is, as the report runs, the peerless Miaulina, daughter to Duke Alfeniquen of

Algarve. The other, that burdens and oppresseth the back of that mighty courser, whose armour is as white as snow, and also his shield without any device, is a new knight of France, called Pierres Papin, lord of the barony of Utrique. The other, that beats his horse's sides with his armed heels, and bears the arms of pure azure, is the mighty Duke of Nerbia Espartafilardo of the wood, who bears for his device a harrow, with a motto that says, "So trails my fortune." '

And thus he proceeded forward, naming many knights of the one and the other squadron, even as he had imagined them, and attributed to each one his arms, his colours, imprese, and mottoes, suddenly borne away by the imagination of his wonderful distraction; and, without stammering, he proceeded, saying,—

'This first squadron containeth folk of many nations: in it are those which taste the sweet waters of famous Xante; the mountainous men that tread the Masilical fields; those that do sift the most pure and rare gold of Arabia Felix; those that possessed the famous and delightful banks of clear Termodonte; those that let blood, many and sundry ways the golden Pactolus; the Numides, unstedfast in their promise; the Persians, famous for archers; the Parthes and Medes, that fight flying; the Arabs, inconstant in their dwellings; the Scythians, as cruel as white; the Ethiopians, of bored lips; and other infinite nations, whose faces I know and behold, although I have forgotten their denominations. In that other army come those that taste the crystalline streams of the olive-bearing Betis; those that dip and polish their faces with the liquor of the ever-rich and golden Tagus; those that possess the profitable fluent of divine Genil; those that trample the Tartesian fields, so abundant in pasture; those that recreate themselves in the Elysian fields of Xerez; the rich Manchegans, crowned with ruddy ears of corn; those apparelled with iron, the ancient relics of the Gothish blood; those that bathe themselves in Pesverga, renowned for the smoothness of his current; those that feed their flocks in the vast fields of the wreathing Guadiana, so celebrated for his hidden course; those that tremble through the cold of the bushy Pirens, and the lofty Apennines; finally, all those that Europe in itself containeth.'

Good God! how many provinces repeated he at that time! and how many nations did he name, giving to every one of them, with marvellous celerity and briefness, their proper attributes, being swallowed up and engulfed in those things which he had read in his lying books! Sancho Panza stood suspended at his speech, and spoke not a word, but only would now and then turn his head, to see whether he could mark those knights and giants which his lord had named; and, by reason he could not discover any, he said, 'Sir, I give to the devil any man, giant, or knight, of all those you said, that appeareth; at least, I cannot discern them. Perhaps all is but enchantment, like that of the ghosts of yesternight.' 'How sayst thou so?' quoth Don Quixote. 'Dost not thou hear the horses neigh, the trumpets sound, and the noise of the drums?' 'I hear nothing else,' said Sancho, 'but the great bleating of many sheep.' And so it was, indeed; for by this time the two flocks did approach them very near. 'The fear that thou conceivest, Sancho,' quoth Don Quixote, 'maketh thee that thou canst neither hear nor see aright; for one of the effects of fear is to trouble the senses, and make things appear otherwise than they are; and, seeing thou fearest so much, retire thyself out of the way; for I alone am sufficient to give the victory to that part which I shall assist.' And, having ended his speech, he set spurs to Rozinante, and, setting his lance in the rest, he flung down from the hillock like a thunderbolt. Sancho cried to him as loud as he could, saying, 'Return, good sir Don Quixote! for I vow unto God, that all those which you go to charge are but sheep and muttons; return, I say. Alas that ever I was born! what madness is this? Look; for there is neither giant nor knight, nor cats, nor arms, nor shields parted nor whole, nor pure azures nor devilish. What is it you do? wretch that I am!' For all this Don Quixote did not return, but rather rode, saying with a loud voice, 'On, on, knights! all you that serve and march under the banners of the valorous emperor Pentapolin of the naked arm; follow me, all of you, and you shall see how easily I will revenge him on his enemy, Alifamfaron of Trapobana.' And, saying so, he entered into the midst of the flock of sheep, and began to lance them with such courage and fury as if he did in good earnest encounter his mortal enemies.

The shepherds that came with the flock, cried to him to leave off; but, seeing their words took no effect, they unloosed their slings, and began to salute his pate with stones as great as one's fist. But Don

Quixote made no account of their stones, and did fling up and down among the sheep, saying, 'Where art thou, proud Alifamfaron? where art thou? Come to me; for I am but one knight alone, who desire to prove my force with thee man to man, and deprive thee of thy life, in pain of the wrong thou dost to the valiant Pentapolin, the Garamante.' At that instant a stone gave him such a blow on one of his sides, as did bury two of his ribs in his body. He beholding himself so ill dight, did presently believe that he was either slain or sorely wounded; and, remembering himself of his liquor, he took out his oil-pot, and set it to his mouth to drink; but ere he could take as much as he thought requisite to cure his hurts, there cometh another almond, which struck him so full upon the hand and oil-pot, as it broke it into pieces, and carried away with it besides three or four of his cheek teeth, and did moreover bruise very sorely two of his fingers. Such was the first and the second blow, as the poor knight was constrained to fall down off his horse. And the shepherds arriving, did verily believe they had slain him; and therefore, gathering their flock together with all speed, and carrying away their dead muttons, which were more than seven, they went away without verifying the matter any further.

Sancho remained all this while on the height, beholding his master's follies, pulling the hairs of his beard for very despair, and cursed the hour and the moment wherein he first knew him; but, seeing him overthrown to the earth, and the shepherds fled away, he came down to him, and found him in very bad taking, yet had he not quite lost the use of his senses; to whom he said, 'Did not I bid you, sir knight, return, and told you that you went not to invade an army of men, but a flock of sheep?' 'That thief, the wise man who is mine adversary,' quoth Don Quixote, 'can counterfeit and make men to seem such, or vanish away, as he pleaseth; for, Sancho, thou oughtest to know that it is a very easy thing for those kind of men to make us seem what they please, and this malign that persecuteth me, envying the glory which he saw I was like to acquire in this battle, hath converted the enemy's squadrons into sheep. And if thou wilt not believe me, Sancho, yet do one thing for my sake, that thou mayst remove thine error, and perceive the truth which I affirm: get up on thine ass, and follow them fair and softly aloof, and, thou shalt see that, as soon as they are parted any distance from hence, they will turn to their first form, and, leaving to be sheep, will become men, as right and straight as I painted them to thee at the first. But go not now, for I have need of thy help and assistance; draw nearer to me, and see how many cheek teeth and others I want, for methinks there is not one left in my mouth.' With that, Sancho approached so near that he laid almost his eyes on his master's mouth; and it was just at the time that the balsam had now wrought his effect in Don Quixote his stomach, and at the very season that Sancho went about to look into his mouth, he disgorged all that he had in his stomach, with as great violence as it had been shot out of a musket, just in his compassive squire's beard. 'O holy Mother Mary!' quoth Sancho, 'what is this that hath befallen me? The poor man is mortally wounded without doubt; for he vomiteth up blood at his mouth.' But, looking a little nearer to it, he perceived in the colour and smell that it was not blood, but the balsam of his master's oil-bottle; whereat he instantly took such a loathing, that his stomach likewise turned, and he vomited out his very bowels almost, all in his master's face. And so they both remained like pearls. Soon after, Sancho ran to his ass to take somewhat to clear himself, and to cure his lord, out of his wallet, which when he found wanting, he was ready to run out of his wits. There he began anew to curse himself, and made a firm resolution in mind that he would leave his master and turn to his country again, although he were sure both to lose his wages and the hope of government of the promised island.

By this Don Quixote arose, and, setting his left hand to his mouth, that the rest of his teeth might not fall out, he caught hold on the reins of Rozinante's bridle with the other, who had never stirred from his master (such was his loyalty and good nature), he went towards his squire, that leaned upon his ass, with his hand under his cheek, like one pensative and malcontent. And Don Quixote, seeing of him in that guise, with such signs of sadness, said unto him: 'Know Sancho, that one man is not more than another, if he do not more than another. All these storms that fall on us are arguments that the time will wax calm very soon, and that things will have better success hereafter; for it is not possible that either good or ill be durable. And hence we may collect that, our misfortunes having lasted so long, our fortune and weal must be likewise near; and therefore thou oughtest not thus to afflict thyself for the disgraces that befal me, seeing no part of them fall to thy lot.' 'How not?' quoth Sancho. 'Was he whom they tossed yesterday in the coverlet by fortune, any other man's son than my father's? and the wallet that I want to-day, with all my provision, was it any other's than mine own?' 'What! dost thou want thy wallet, Sancho?' quoth Don Quixote. 'Ay, that I do,' quoth he. 'In that manner,' replied Don Quixote, 'we have nothing left us to eat today.' 'That would be so,' quoth Sancho, 'if we could not find among these fields the herbs which I have heard you say you know, wherewithal such unlucky knights-errant as you are wont to supply like needs.' 'For all that,' quoth Don Quixote, 'I would rather have now a quarter of a loaf, or a cake, and two pilchard's heads, than all the herbs that Dioscorides describeth, although they came glossed by Doctor Laguna himself. But yet, for all that, get upon thy beast, Sancho the good, and follow me; for God, who is the provider for all creatures, will not fail us; and principally, seeing we do a work so greatly to His service as we do, seeing He doth not abandon the little flies of the air, nor the wormlings of the earth, nor the spawnlings of the water; and He is so merciful that He maketh His sun shine on the good and the evil, and rains on sinners and just men.' 'You were much fitter,' quoth Sancho, 'to be a preacher than a knight-errant.' 'Knights-errant knew, and ought to know, somewhat of all things,' quoth Don Quixote; 'for there hath been a knight-errant, in times past, who would make a sermon or discourse in the midst of a camp royal with as good grace as if he were graduated in the university of Paris; by which we may gather that the lance never dulled the pen, nor the pen the lance.' 'Well, then,' quoth Sancho, 'let it be as you have said, and let us depart hence, and procure to find a lodging for this night, where, I pray God, may be no coverlets, and tossers, nor spirits, nor enchanted Moors; for if there be, I'll bestow the flock and the hook on the devil.' 'Demand that of God, son Sancho,' quoth Don Quixote, 'and lead me where thou pleasest; for I will leave the election of our lodging to thy choice for this time. Yet, I pray thee, give me thy hand, and feel how many cheek teeth, or others,

I want in this right side of the upper jaw; for there I feel most pain.' Sancho put in his finger, and whilst he felt him, demanded, 'How many cheek teeth were you accustomed to have on this side?' 'Four,' quoth he, 'besides the hindermost; all of them very whole and sound.' 'See well what you say, sir,' quoth Sancho. 'I say four,' quoth Don Quixote, 'if they were not five; for I never in my life drew or lost any tooth, nor hath any fallen or been worm-eaten or marred by any rheum.' 'Well, then,' quoth Sancho, 'you have in this nether part but two cheek teeth and a half; and in the upper neither a half, nor any; for all there is as plain as the palm of my hand.' 'Unfortunate I!' quoth Don Quixote, hearing the sorrowful news that his squire told unto him, 'for I had rather lose one of my arms, so it were not that of my sword; for, Sancho, thou must wit, that a mouth without cheek teeth is like a mill without a millstone; and a tooth is much more to be esteemed than a diamond. But we which profess the rigorous laws of arms are subject to all these disasters; wherefore mount, gentle friend, and give the way; for I will follow thee what pace thou pleasest.' Sancho obeyed, and rode the way where he thought he might find lodging, without leaving the highway, which was there very much beaten. And, going thus by little and little (for Don Quixote his pain of his jaws did not suffer him rest, or make overmuch haste), Sancho, to entertain him and divert his thought by saying some things, began to aboard him in the form we mean to rehearse in the chapter ensuing.

CHAPTER V

Of the Discreet Discourse Passed Between Sancho and His Lord; with the Adventure Succeeding of a Dead Body; and Other Notable Occurrences

METHINKS, good sir, that all the mishaps that befel us these days past, are, without any doubt, punishment of the sin you committed against the order of knighthood, by not performing the oath you swore, not to eat bread on table-cloths, nor to sport with the queen, with all the rest which ensueth, and you vowed to accomplish, until you had won the helmet of Malandrino, or I know not how the Moor is called, for I have forgotten his name.' 'Thou sayst right, Sancho,' quoth Don Quixote; 'but, to tell the truth, indeed I did wholly forget it; and thou mayst likewise think certainly, that because thou didst not remember it to me in time, that of the coverlet was inflicted as a punishment on thee. But I will make amends; for we have also manners of reconciliation for all things in the order of knighthood.' 'Why, did I by chance swear anything?' quoth Sancho. 'It little imports,' quoth Don Quixote, 'that thou hast not sworn; let it suffice that I know thou art not very clear from the fault of an accessory; and therefore, at all adventures, it will not be ill to provide a remedy.' 'If it be so,' quoth Sancho, 'beware you do not forget this again, as you did that of the oath; for if you should, perhaps those spirits will take again a fancy to solace themselves with me, and peradventure with you yourself, if they see you obstinate.'

Being in these and other such discourses, the night overtook them in the way, before they could discover any lodgings, and that which was worst of all they were almost famished with hunger; for, by the loss of their wallets, they lost at once both their provision and warder-house; and, to accomplish wholly this disgrace, there succeeded a certain adventure, which certainly happened as we lay it down, without any addition in the world, and was this. The night did shut up with some darkness, yet notwithstanding they travelled on still, Sancho believing that, since that was the highway, there must be within a league or two, in all reason, some inn. Travelling therefore, as I have said, in a dark night, the squire being hungry, and the master having a good stomach, they saw coming towards them in the very way they travelled a great multitude of lights, resembling nothing so well as wandering stars. Sancho, beholding them, was struck into a wonderful amazement, and his lord was not much better. The one drew his ass's halter, the other held his horse, and both of them stood still, beholding attentively what that might be; and they perceived that the lights drew still nearer unto them, and the more they approached, they appeared the greater. At the sight Sancho did tremble, like one infected by the savour of quicksilver; and Don Quixote's hair stood up like bristles, who, animating himself a little, said: 'Sancho, this must be, questionless, a great and most dangerous adventure, wherein it is requisite that I show all my valour and strength.' 'Unfortunate I!' quoth Sancho; 'if by chance this adventure were of ghosts, as it seemeth to me that it is, where will there be ribs to suffer it?' 'Be they never so great ghosts,' said Don Quixote, 'I will not consent that they touch one hair of thy garments: for if they jested with thee the other time, it was because I could not leap over the walls of the yard; but now we are in plain field, where I may brandish my sword as I please.' 'And if they enchant and benumb you, as they did the other time,' quoth Sancho, 'what will it then avail us to be in open field or no?' 'For all that,' replied Don Quixote, 'I pray thee, Sancho, be of good courage; for experience shall show thee how great my valour is.' 'I will, and please God,' quoth Sancho. And so, departing somewhat out of the way, they began again to view earnestly what that of the travelling lights might be; and after a very little space they espied many white things, whose dreadful visions did in that very instant abate Sancho Panza his courage, and now began to chatter with his teeth like one that had the cold of a quartan; and when they did distinctly perceive what it was, then did his beating and chattering of teeth increase: for they discovered about some twenty, all covered with white, a-horseback, with tapers lighted in their hands; after which followed a litter covered over with black, and then ensued other six a-horseback, attired in mourning, and likewise their mules, even to the very ground; for they perceived that they were not horses by the quietness of their pace. The white folk rode murmuring somewhat among themselves, with a low and compassive voice; which strange vision, at such an hour, and in places not inhabited, was very sufficient to strike fear into Sancho's heart, and even in his master's, if it had been any other than Don Quixote; but Sancho tumbled here and there, being quite overthrown with terror. The contrary happened to his lord, to whom in that same hour his imagination represented unto him most lively, the adventure wherein he was to be such a one as he ofttimes had read in his books of chivalry; for it figured unto him that the litter was a bier, wherein was carried some grievously wounded or dead knight, whose revenge was only reserved for him. And, without making any other discourse, he set his lance in the rest, seated himself surely in his saddle, and put himself in the midst of the way by which the white folk must forcibly pass, with great spirit and courage. And when he saw them draw near, he said, with a loud voice, 'Stand, sir knight, whosoever you be, and render me account what you are, from whence you come, where you go, and what that is which you carry in that bier; for, according as you show, either you have done to others or others to you some injury; and it is convenient and needful that I know it, either to chastise you for the ill you have committed, or else to revenge you of the wrong which you have suffered.' 'We are in haste,' quoth one of the white men, 'and the inn is far off, and therefore cannot expect to give so full a relation as you request'; and with that, spurring his mule, passed forward. Don Quixote, highly disdaining at the answer, took him by the bridle, and held him, saying, 'Stay, proud knight, and be bettermannered another time, and give me account of that which I demanded; if not, I defy you all to mortal battle.' The mule whereon the white man rode was somewhat fearful and skittish; and, being taken thus rudely by the bridle, she took such a fright, that, rising up on her hinder legs, she unhorsed her rider. One of the lackeys that came with them, seeing him fallen, began to revile Don Quixote, who, being by this thoroughly enraged, without any more ado, putting his lance in the rest, ran upon one of the mourners, and threw him to the ground very sore wounded. And, turning upon the rest, it was a thing worthy the noting with what dexterity he did assault, break upon them, and put them all to flight; and it seemed none other but that Rozinante had gotten then wings, he bestirred himself so nimbly and courageously.

All those white men were fearful people, and unarmed, and therefore fled away from the skirmish in a trice, and began to traverse that field with their tapers burning, that they seemed to be maskers that used to run up and down in nights of Jove and recreation. The mourners likewise were so lapped up and muffled by their mourning weeds, as they could scarce stir them; so that Don Quixote did, without any danger of his person, give them all the bastinado, and caused them to forsake their rooms whether they would or no; for all of them did verily think that he was no man, but a devil of hell, that met them to take away the dead body which they carried in the litter. All this did Sancho behold, marvellously admiring at his master's boldness, which made him say to himself, 'My master is infallibly as strong and valiant as he said.'

There lay on the ground by him whom his mule had overthrown, a wax taper still burning, by whose light Don Quixote perceived him, and, coming over to him, he laid the point of his lance upon his face, saying, that he should render himself, or else he would slay him. To which the other answered: 'I am already rendered more than enough, seeing I cannot stir me out of the place, for one of my legs is broken. And if you be a Christian, I desire you not to kill me; for therein you would commit a great sacrilege, I being a licentiate, and have received the first orders.' 'Well, then,' quoth Don Quixote, 'what devil brought thee hither, being a Churchman?' 'Who, sir,' replied the overthrown, 'but my misfortune?' 'Yet doth a greater threaten thee,' said Don Quixote, 'if thou dost not satisfy me in all that which I first demanded of thee.' 'You shall easily be satisfied,' quoth the licentiate, 'and therefore you shall wit that, although first of all I said I was a licentiate, I am none but a bachelor, and am called Alonso Lopez, born at Alcovendas; and I came from the city of Baeza, with eleven other priests, which are those that fled away with the tapers. We travel towards Segovia, accompanying the dead body that lies in the litter, of a certain gentleman who died in

Baeza, and was there deposited for a while, and now, as I say, we carry his bones to his place of burial, which is Segovia, the place of his birth.' 'And who killed him?' quoth Don Quixote. 'God,' quoth the bachelor, 'with certain pestilential fevers that he took.' 'In that manner,' quoth Don Quixote, 'our Lord hath delivered me from the pains I would have taken to revenge his death, if any other had slain him. He having killed him that did, there is no other remedy but silence, and to lift up the shoulders; for the same I must myself have done, if He were likewise pleased to slay me. And I would have your reverence to understand that I am a knight of the Mancha, called Don Quixote; and mine office and exercise is, to go throughout the world righting of wrongs and undoing of injuries.' 'I cannot understand how that can be, of righting wrongs,' quoth the bachelor, 'seeing you have made me, who was right before, now very crooked by breaking of my leg, which can never be righted again as long as I live; and the injury which you have undone in me, is none other but to leave me so injured as I shall remain injured for ever. And it was very great disventure to have encountered with you that go about to seek adventures.' 'All things,' quoth Don Quixote, 'succeed not of one fashion. The hurt was, Master Bachelor Alonso Lopez, that you travelled thus by night covered with those surplices, with burning tapers, and covered with weeds of dole, so that you appeared most properly some bad thing, and of the other world; and so I could not omit to fulfil my duty by assaulting you, which I would have done although I verily knew you to be the satans themselves of hell; for, for such I judged and accounted you ever till now.'

'Then, since my bad fortune hath so disposed it,' quoth the bachelor, 'I desire you, good sir knight-errant (who hath given me so evil an errand) that you will help me to get up from under this mule, who holds still my leg betwixt the stirrup and saddle.' 'I would have stayed talking until tomorrow morning,' quoth Don Quixote, 'and why did you expect so long to declare your grief to me?' He presently called for Sancho Panza to come over; but he had little mind to do, for he was otherwise employed ransacking of a sumpter-mule, which those good folk brought with them, well furnished with belly-ware. Sancho made a bag of his cassock, and, catching all that he might or could contain, he laid it on his beast, and then presently after repaired to his master, and helped to deliver the good bachelor from the oppression of his mule; and, mounting him again on it, he gave him his taper; and Don Quixote bade him to follow his fellows, of whom he should desire pardon, in his name, for the wrong he had done them; for it lay not in his hands to have done the contrary. Sancho said to him also: 'If those gentlemen would by chance know who the valorous knight is that hath used them thus, you may say unto them that he is the famous Don Quixote of Mancha, otherwise called the Knight of the Ill-favoured Face.'

With this the bachelor departed, and Don Quixote demanded of Sancho what had moved him to call him the Knight of the Ill-favoured Face, more at that time than at any other. 'I will tell you that,' quoth Sancho: 'I stood beholding of you a pretty while by the taper light which that unlucky man carrieth, and truly you have one of the evil-favouredest countenances of late that ever I saw, which either proceedeth of your being tired after this battle, or else through the loss of your teeth.' 'That is not the reason,' said Don Quixote; 'but rather, it hath seemed fit to the wise man, to whose charge is left the writing of my history, that I take some appellative name, as all the other knights of yore have done; for one called himself the Knight of the Burning Sword; another that of the Unicorn; this, him of the Phoenix; the other, that of the Damsels; another, the Knight of the Griffin; and some other, the Knight of Death; and by these names and devices they were known throughout the compass of the earth. And so I say, that the wise man whom I mentioned set in thy mind and tongue the thought to call me the Knight of the Ill-favoured Face, as I mean to call myself from henceforth; and that the name may become me better, I will, upon the first occasion, cause to be painted in my shield a most ill-favoured countenance.' 'You need not,' quoth Sancho, 'spend so much time and money in having the like countenance painted; but that which you may more easily do is to discover your own and look directly on those that behold you; and I will warrant you, that without any more ado, or new painting in your shield, they will call you "him of the ill-favoured face." And let this be said in jest, that hunger and the want of your teeth have given you, as I have said, so ill-favoured a face, as you may well excuse all other heavy portraitures.' Don Quixote laughed at his squire's conceit, and yet, nevertheless, he purposed to call himself by that name as soon as ever he should have commodity to paint his shield and buckler.

And after a pause he said to Sancho: 'I believe I am excommunicated for having laid violent hands upon a consecrated thing, *"Juxta illud, siquis suadente diabolo,"* etc.; although I am certain I laid not my hands upon him, but only this javelin; and besides, I did not in any way suspect that I offended priests or Churchmen, which I do respect and honour as a Catholic and faithful Christian; but rather, that they were shadows and spirits of the other world. And if the worst happened, I remember well that which befel the Cid Ruy Diaz, when he broke that other king's ambassador's chair before the pope's holiness, for which he excommunicated him; and yet, for all that, the good Roderick Vivar behaved himself that day like an honourable and valiant knight.'

About this time the bachelor departed, as is said, without speaking a word, and Don Quixote would fain have seen whether the corpse that came in the litter was bones or no; but Sancho would not permit him, saying, 'Sir, you have finished this perilous adventure most with your safety of any one of those I have seen. This people, although overcome and scattered, might perhaps fall in the consideration that he who hath overcome them is but one person alone, and, growing ashamed thereof, would perhaps join and unite themselves, and turn upon us, and give us enough business to do. The ass is in good plight according to my desire, and the mountain at hand, and hunger oppresseth us; therefore, we have nothing else to do at this time but retire ourselves with a good pace, and, as it is said, "To the grave with the dead, and them that live to the bread."' And, pricking on his ass, he requested his master to follow him; who, seeing that Sancho spoke not without reason, he spurred after him without replying; and, having travelled a little way between two small mountains, they found a large and hidden valley, where they alighted; and Sancho lightening his beast, and lying both along upon the green grass, holpen by the sauce of hunger, they broke their fasts, dined, ate their beaver and supper all at one time; satisfying their appetites with more than one dish of cold meat, which the dead gentleman's chaplains (which knew how to make much of themselves) had brought for their provision. But here succeeded another discommodity, which Sancho accounted not as the least, and was, that they had no wine to drink; no, nor so much as a drop of water to rinse their mouths; and, being scorched with drought, Sancho, perceiving the field where they were full of thick and green grass, said that which shall ensue in the chapter following.

CHAPTER VI

Of a Wonderful Adventure, Achieved with Less Hazard Than Ever Any Other Knight Did Any, by the Valorous Don Quixote of the Mancha

'IT is not possible, my lord, but that these green herbs do argue that near unto this place must be some fountain or stream that watereth them, and therefore, I pray you, let us go a little farther, and we shall meet that which may mitigate the terrible thirst that afflicts us, which sets us, questionless, in more pain than did our hunger.' This counsel was allowed by Don Quixote; and therefore, leading Rozinante by the bridle, and Sancho his ass by the halter, after laying up the reversion of their supper, they set on through the plain, only guided by their guess, for the night was so dark as they could not see a jot. And scarce had they travelled two hundred paces, when they heard a great noise of water, as if it fell headlong from some great and steep rock. The noise did cheer them very much, and standing to hear from whence it sounded, they heard unawares another noise, which watered all the content they conceived before, specially in Sancho, who, as I have noted, was naturally very fearful and of little spirit. They heard, I say, certain blows struck with proportion, with a kind of rattling of irons and chains, which, accompanied by the furious sound of the water, might strike terror into any other heart but Don Quixote's.

The night, as we said, was dark, and they happened to enter in among certain tall and lofty trees, whose leaves, moved by a soft gale of wind, made a fearful and still noise; so that the solitude, situation, darkness, and the noise of the water, and trembling of the leaves concurring, did breed horror and affright; but specially seeing that the blows never ceased, the wind slept not, nor the morning approached, whereunto may be added, that they knew not the place where they were. But Don Quixote, accompanied with his valiant heart, leaped on Rozinante, and embracing his buckler, brandished his lance, and said: 'Friend Sancho, I would have thee know that I was born, by the disposition of Heaven, in this our age of iron, to resuscitate in it that of gold, or the golden world, as it is called. I am he for whom are reserved all dangerous, great, and valorous feats. I say again, that I am he which shall set up again those of the Round Table, the Twelve Peers of France, and the Nine Worthies. I am he who shall cause the acts to be forgotten of those Platires, Tablantes, Olivantes, and Tirantes, the Phebuses, Belianises, with all the crew of the famous knights-errant of times past, doing in this wherein I live, such great and wonderful feats of arms as shall obscure the bravest that ever they achieved. Thou notest well, faithful and loyal squire, the darkness of this night, the strange silence, the deaf and confused trembling of these trees, the dreadful noise of that water in whose search we come, which seems to throw itself headlong down from the steep mountains of the moon; the inceasable blows which do still wound our ears; all which together, and every one apart, are able to strike terror, fear, and amazement into the very mind of Mars; how much more in his that is not accustomed to the like chances and adventures? Yet all this which I have depainted to thee are inciters and rousers of my mind, which now causeth my heart almost to burst in my breast, with the desire it hath to try this adventure, how difficult soever it shows itself. Wherefore, tie my horse's girths a little straiter; and farewell! Here in this place thou mayst expect me three days and no more. And if I shall not return in that space, thou mayst go back to our village, and from thence (for my sake) to Toboso, where thou shalt say to my incomparable Lady Dulcinea, that her captive knight died by attempting things that might make him worthy to be called hers.'

When Sancho heard his lord speak these words, he began to weep, with the greatest compassion of the world, and say unto him, 'Sir, I see no reason why you should undertake this fearful adventure. It is now night, and nobody can perceive us; we may very well cross the way, and apart from ourselves danger, although we should therefore want drink these three days. And, seeing none behold us, there will be much less any one to take notice of our cowardice; the rather because I heard ofttimes the curate of our village, whom you know very well, preach, "that he which seeks the danger, perisheth therein"; so that it is not good to tempt God, undertaking such a huge affair, out of which you cannot escape but by miracle; and let those which Heaven hath already wrought for you suffice, in delivering you from being tossed in a coverlet, as I was, and bringing you away a victor, free and safe, from among so many enemies as accompanied the dead man. And when all this shall not move or soften your hard heart, let this move it, to think and certainly believe, that scarce shall you depart from this place, when through very fear I shall give up my soul to him that pleaseth to take it. I left my country, wife, and children to come and serve you, hoping thereby to be worth more, and not less; but, as covetousness breaks the sack, so hath it also torn my hopes, seeing when they were most pregnant and lively to obtain that unlucky and accursed island, which you promised me so often, I see that, in exchange and pay thereof, you mean to forsake me here in a desert, out of all frequentation. For God's sake, do not me such a wrong, my lord; and if you will not wholly desist from your purpose, yet defer it at least till the morning; for as my little skill that I learned when I was a shepherd, telleth me, the dawning is not three hours off; for the mouth of the fish is over the head, and maketh midnight in the line of the left arm.' 'How canst thou, Sancho,' quoth Don Quixote, 'see where is the line, or that mouth, or that tail of which you speakest, seeing the night is so dark that one star alone appeareth not?' 'That is true,' quoth Sancho; 'but fear hath eyes which can see things under the ground, and much more in the skies. And besides, we may gather, by good discourse, that the day is not far off.' 'Let it be as little off as it lists,' quoth Don Quixote, 'it shall never be recorded of me that either tears or prayers could ever dissuade me from performing the duty of a knight; and therefore, good Sancho, hold thy peace; for God, who hath inspired me to attempt this unseen and fearful adventure, will have an eye to my weal, and also to comfort thy sorrow. And that thou hast therefore to do is to make strait my girths, and remain here; for I will return here shortly, either alive or dead.'

Sancho, perceiving his lord's last resolution, and how little his tears, counsels, or prayers could avail, resolved to profit himself a little of his wit, and make him if he could to expect until day; and so, when he did fasten the girths, he softly, without being felt, tied his ass's halter to both Rozinante's legs so fast, that when Don Quixote thought to depart, he could not, for that his horse could not go a step, but leaping. Sancho, seeing the good success of his guile, said, 'Behold, sir, how Heaven, moved by my tears and prayers, hath ordained that Rozinante should not go a step; and if you will be still contending, and spurring, and striking him, you will do nothing but enrage fortune, and, as the proverb says, but "spurn against the prick."' Don Quixote grew wood at this, and yet the more he spurred him he was the less able to go; wherefore, without perceiving the cause of his horse's stay, he resolved at last to be quiet, and expect either till the morning or else till Rozinante would please to depart, believing verily that the impediment came of some other cause, and not from Sancho; and therefore said unto him, 'Since it is so, Sancho, that Rozinante cannot stir him, I am content to tarry till the dawning, although her tardiness cost me some tears.' 'You shall have no cause to weep,' replied Sancho; 'for I will entertain you telling you of histories until it be day, if you will not alight and take a nap upon these green herbs, as knights-errant are wont, that you may be the fresher and better able to-morrow to attempt that monstrous adventure which you expect.' 'What dost thou call alighting, or sleeping?' quoth Don Quixote. 'Am I peradventure one of those knights that repose in time of danger? Sleep thou, who wast born to sleep, or do what thou please; for I will do that which I shall see fittest for my pretence.' 'Good sir, be not angry,' quoth Sancho; 'for I did not speak with that intention.' And so, drawing near unto him, he set one of his hands on the pommel of the saddle, and the other hinder in such sort that he rested embracing his lord's left thigh, not daring to depart from thence the breadth of a finger, such was the fear he had of those blows, which all the while did sound without ceasing.

Then Don Quixote commanded him to tell some tale to pass away the time, as he had promised; and Sancho said he would, if the fear of that which he heard would suffer him. 'Yet,' quoth he, 'for all this I will encourage myself to tell you one, whereon, if I can hit aright, and that I be not interrupted, is the best history that ever you heard; and be you attentive, for now I begin. It was that it was, the good that shall befall be for us all, and the harm for him that searches it. And you must be advertised, good sir, that the beginning that ancient men gave to their tales was not of ordinary things, and it was a sentence of Cato, the Roman Conrozin, which says, "And the harm be for him that searches it," which is as fit for this place as a ring for a finger, to the end that you may be quiet, and not to go seek your own harm to any place, but that we turn us another way, for nobody compelleth us to follow this, where so many fears do surprise us.' 'Prosecute this tale, Sancho,' said Don Quixote, 'and leave the charge of the way we must go to me.' 'I say then,' quoth Sancho, 'that in a village of Estremadura there was a shepherd, I would say a goatherd; and as I say of my tale, this goatherd was called Lope Ruyz, and this Lope Ruyz was enamoured on a shepherdess who was called Torralva, the which shepherdess called Torralva was daughter to a rich herdman, and this rich herdman—' 'If thou tellest thy tale, Sancho, after that manner,' quoth Don Quixote, 'repeating everything twice that thou sayst, thou wilt not end it these two days: tell it succinctly, and like one of judgment, or else say nothing.' 'Of the very same fashion that I tell are all tales told in my country, and I know not how to tell it any other way, nor is it reason that you should ask of me to make new customs.' 'Tell it as thou pleasest,' quoth Don Quixote; 'for since fortune will not otherwise but that I must hear thee, go forward.' 'So that, my dear sir of my soul,' quoth Sancho, 'that, as I have said already, this shepherd was in love with Torralva the shepherdess, who was a round wench, scornful, and drew somewhat near to a man, for she had mochachoes; for methinks I see her now before my face.' 'Belike, then,' quoth Don Quixote, 'thou knewest her?' 'I did not know her,' quoth Sancho, 'but he that told me the tale said it was so certain and true, that I might, when I told it to any other, very well swear and affirm that I had seen it all myself. So that, days passing and days coming, the devil, who sleeps not, and that troubles all, wrought in such sort, as the love that the shepherd bore to the shepherdess turned into man-slaughter and ill-will; and the cause was, according to bad tongues, a certain quantity of little jealousies that she gave him, such as they passed the line, and came to the forbidden. And the shepherd did hate her so much afterward, that he was content to leave all that country, because he would not see her, and go where his eyes should never look upon her. Torralva, that saw herself disdained by Lope, did presently love him better than ever she did before.' 'That is a natural condition of women,' quoth Don Quixote, 'to disdain those that love them, and to affect those which hate them. Pass forward, Sancho.' 'It happened,' quoth Sancho, 'that the shepherd set his purpose in execution, and, gathering up his goats, he travelled through the fields of Estremadura, to pass into the kingdom of Portugal. Torralva, which knew it well, followed him afoot and bare-legged, afar off, with a pilgrim's staff in her hand, and a wallet hanging at her neck, where they say that she carried a piece of a looking-glass, and another of a comb, and I know not what little bottles of changes for her face. But let her carry what she carries, for I will not put myself now to verify that; only I'll say, that they say, that the shepherd arrived with his goats to pass over the river Guadiana, which in that season was swollen very much, and overflowed the banks; and at the side where he came there was neither boat nor bark, nor any to pass himself or his goats over the river; for which he was very much grieved, because he saw that Torralva came very near, and she would trouble him very much with her prayers and tears. But he went so long looking up and down, that he spied a fisher, who had so little a boat as it could only hold one man and a goat at once, and for all that he spake and agreed with him to pass himself and three hundred goats that he had over the river. The fisherman entered into the boat, and carried over one goat; he returned, and passed over another, and turned back again, and passed over another. Keep you, sir, good account of the goats that the fisherman ferries over; for if one only be forgotten, the tale will end, and it will not be possible to tell one word more of it. Follow on, then, and I say that the landing-place on the other side was very dirty and slippery, which made the fisherman spend much time coming to and fro; yet, for all that, he turned for another goat, and another, and another.'

'Make account,' quoth Don Quixote, that thou hast passed them all over; for otherwise thou wilt not make an end of passing them in a whole year's space.' 'How many,' said Sancho, 'are already passed over?' 'What a devil know I?' said Don Quixote. 'See there that which I said,' quoth Sancho, 'that you should keep good account. By Jove, the tale is ended, therefore; for there is no passing forward.' 'How can that be?' said Don Quixote. 'Is it so greatly of the essence of this history to know the goats that are passed so exactly and distinctly that if one of the number be missed thou canst not follow on with thy tale?' 'No, sir, in no sort,' said Sancho; 'for as soon as I demanded of you to tell me how many goats passed over, and that you answered me you knew not, in that very instant it went from me out of my memory all that was to be told, and in faith it was of great virtue and content.' 'So, then,' quoth Don Quixote, 'the tale is ended?' 'It is as certainly ended as is my mother,' quoth Sancho. 'Surely,' replied Don Quixote, 'thou hast recounted one of the rarest tales or histories that any one of the world could think upon, and that such a manner of telling or finishing a tale was never yet seen, or shall be seen again; although I never expected any other thing from thy good discourse. But I do not greatly marvel, for perhaps those senseless strokes have troubled thine understanding.' 'All that may be,' said Sancho; 'but I know, in the discourse of my tale, there is no more to be said, but that there it ends, where the error of counting the goats that were wafted over the river begins.' 'Let it end in a good hour where it lists,' answered Don Quixote, 'and let us try whether Rozinante can yet stir himself.' Then did he turn again to give him the spurs, and he to leap as he did at the first and rest anew, being unable to do other, he was so well shackled.

It happened about this time, that, either through the cold of the morning, or that Sancho had eaten at supper some lenitive meats, or that it was a thing natural (and that is most credible), he had a desire to do that which others could not do for him; but such was the fear that entered into his heart as he dared not depart from his lord the breadth of a straw, and to think to leave that which he had desired undone was also impossible; therefore, his resolution in that perplexed exigent (be it spoken with pardon) was this: he loosed his right hand, wherewithal he held fast the hinder part of the saddle, and therewithal very softly, and without any noise, he untied the cod-piece point wherewithal his breeches were only supported, which, that being let slip, did presently fall down about his legs like a pair of bolts; after this, lifting up his shirt the best he could, he exposed his buttocks to the air, which were not the least. This being done, which, as he thought, was the chiefest thing requisite to issue out of that terrible anguish and plunge, he was suddenly troubled with a greater, to wit, that he knew not how to disburden himself without making a noise; which to avoid, first he shut his teeth close, lifted up his shoulders, and gathered up his breath as much as he might; yet, notwithstanding all these diligences, he was so unfortunate, that he made a little noise at the end, much different from that which made him so fearful. Don Quixote heard it, and said, 'What noise is that, Sancho?' 'I know it not, sir,' quoth he; 'I think it be some new thing for adventures; or rather, disventures never begin with a little.' Then turned he once again to try his hap, and it succeeded so well that, without making any rumour or noise but that which he did at the first, he found himself free of the loading that troubled him so much.

But Don Quixote having the sense of smelling as perfect as that of his hearing, and Sancho stood so near, or rather joined to him, as the vapours did ascend upward, almost by a direct line, he could not excuse himself but that some of them must needs touch his nose. And scarce had they arrived, but that he occurred to the usual remedy, and stopped it very well between his fingers, and then said with a snaffling voice, 'Methinks, Sancho, that thou art much afraid.' 'I am indeed,' replied Sancho; 'but wherein, I pray you, do you perceive it now more than ever?' 'In that thou smellest now more than ever,' quoth Don Quixote, 'and that not of amber.' 'It may be so,' quoth Sancho; 'yet the fault is not mine, but yours, which bring me, at such unseasonable hours, through so desolate and fearful places.' 'I pray thee, friend, retire thyself two or three steps back,' quoth Don Quixote, holding his fingers still upon his nose, 'and from henceforth have more care of thy person, and of the respect thou owest to mine; for I see the overmuch familiarity that I use with thee hath engendered this contempt.' 'I dare wager,' quoth Sancho, 'that you think I have done somewhat with my person that I ought not.' 'Friend Sancho,' quoth Don Quixote, 'it is the worse to stir it thus.' And thus, in these and such like conversation, the master and the man passed over the night. And Sancho, seeing that the morning approach, he loosed Rozinante very warily, and tied up his hose. Rozinante, feeling himself (although he was not naturally very courageous), he seemed to rejoice, and began to beat the ground with his hoofs; for (by his leave) he could never yet curvet. Don Quixote, seeing that Rozinante could now stir, accounted it to be a good sign, and an encouragement of him to attempt that timorous adventure.

By this Aurora did display her purple mantle over the face of heaven, and everything appeared distinctly, which made Don Quixote perceive that he was among a number of tall chestnut-trees, which commonly make a great shadow. He heard likewise those incessable strokes, but could not espy the cause of them; wherefore, giving Rozinante presently the spur, and turning back again to Sancho, to bid him farewell, he commanded him to stay for him there three days at the longest, and that, if he returned not after that space, he should make full account that Jove was pleased he should end his days in that dangerous adventure. He repeated to him again the embassage and errand he should carry in his behalf to his Lady Dulcinea; and that, touching the reward of his services, he should not fear anything; for he had left his testament, made before he departed from his village, where he should find himself gratified touching all that which pertained to his hire, according to the rate of the time he had served; but if God would bring him off from that adventure safe and sound, and without danger, he might fully account to receive the promised island.

Here Sancho began anew to weep, hearing again the pitiful discourses of his good lord, and determined not to abandon him until the last trance and end of that affair; and out of these tears and honourable resolution of Sancho, the author of this history collects, that it is like he was well born, or at the very least an old Christian, whose grief did move his master a little, but not so much as he should show the least argument of weakness; but rather, dissembling it the best he could, he followed on his way towards the way of the water, and that where the strokes were heard. Sancho followed him afoot, leading, as he was wont, his ass by the halter, who was the inseparable fellow of his prosperous or adverse fortunes.

And having travelled a good space among these chestnut and shady trees, they came out into a little plain that stood at the foot of certain steep rocks, from whose tops did precipitate itself a great fall of water. There were at the foot of those rocks certain houses, so ill made as they rather seemed ruins of buildings than houses; from whence, as they perceived, did issue the fearful rumour and noise of the strokes, which yet continued.

Rozinante at this dreadful noise did start, and being made quiet by his lord, Don Quixote did by little and little draw near to the houses, recommending himself on the way most devoutly to his Lady Dulcinea, and also to Jove, desiring him that he would not forget him. Sancho never departed from his lord's side, and stretched out his neck and eyes as far as he might through Rozinante his legs, to see if he could perceive that which held him so fearful and suspended. And after they had travelled about a hundred paces more, at the doubling of a point of a mountain, they saw the very cause patent and open (for there could be none other) of that so hideous and fearful a noise that had kept them all the night so doubtful and affrighted, and was (O reader! if thou wilt not take it in bad part) six iron maces that fulled cloth, which, with their interchangeable blows, did form that marvellous noise.

When Don Quixote saw what it was, he waxed mute and all ashamed. Sancho beheld him, and saw that he hung his head on his breast with tokens that he was somewhat ashamed. Don Quixote looked also on his squire, and saw his cheeks swollen with laughter, giving withal evident signs that he was in danger to burst if he vented not that passion; whereat all Don Quixote's melancholy little prevailing, he could not, beholding Sancho, but laugh also himself. And when Sancho saw his master begin the play, he let slip the prisoner in such violent manner, to press his sides hardly with both his hands to save himself from bursting. Four times he ended, and other four he renewed his laughter, with as great impulse and force as at the first; whereat Don Quixote was wonderfully enraged, but chiefly hearing him say in gibing manner, 'I would have thee know, friend Sancho, that I was born, by the disposition of Heaven, in this our age of iron, to renew in it that of gold, or the golden world. I am he for whom are reserved all dangerous, great, and valorous feats.' And in this sort he went repeating all or the greatest part of the words Don Quixote had said the first time that they heard the timorous blows. Don Quixote perceiving that Sancho mocked him, grew so ashamed and angry withal, that, lifting up the end of his lance, he gave him two such blows on the back, as if he had received them on his pate, would have freed his master from paying him any wages, if it were not to his heirs. Sancho, seeing that he gained so ill earnest by his jests, fearing that his master should go onward with it, he said unto him, with very great submission, 'Pacify yourself, good sir; for, by Jove, I did but jest.' 'But why dost thou jest? I tell thee I do not jest,' quoth Don Quixote. 'Come here, master merry-man; thinkest thou that, as those are iron maces to full cloth, if they were some other dangerous adventure, that I have not shown resolution enough to undertake and finish it? Am I by chance obliged, being, as I am, a knight, to know and distinguish noises, and perceive which are of a fulling-mill, or no? And more it might (as it is true), that I never saw any before, as thou hast done, base villain that thou art! born and brought up among the like: if not, make thou that these six maces be converted into giants, and cast them in my beard one by one, or all together; and when I do not turn all their heels up, then mock me as much as thou pleasest.'

'No more, good sir,' quoth Sancho; 'for I confess I have been somewhat too laughsome. But tell me, I pray you, now that we are in peace, as God shall deliver you out of all adventures that may befall you, as whole and sound as He hath done out of this, hath the not great fear we were in been a good subject of laughter, and a thing worthy the telling?—at least I; for of you I am certain that you do not yet know what fear or terror is.' 'I do not deny,' quoth Don Quixote, 'but that which befel us is worthy of laughter; yet ought it not to be recounted, forasmuch as all persons are not so discreet as to know how to discern one thing from another, and set everything in his right point.' 'You know, at leastwise,' quoth Sancho, 'how to set your javelin in his point when, pointing at my pate, you hit me on the shoulders, thanks be to God, and to the diligence I put in going aside. But farewell it, for all will away in the bucking; and I have heard old folk say "that man loves thee well who makes thee to weep." And besides, great lords are wont, after a bad word which they say to one of their serving-men, to bestow on him presently a pair of hose. But I know not yet what they are wont to give them after blows, if it be not that knights-errant give, after the bastinado, islands, or kingdoms on the continent.' 'The die might run so favourably,' quoth Don Quixote, 'as all thou hast said might come to pass; and therefore pardon what is done, since thou art discreet, and knowest that a man's first motions are not in his hand. And be advertised of one thing from henceforward (to the end to abstain, and carry thyself more respectfully in thy over-much liberty of speech with me), that in as many books of chivalry as I have read, which are infinite, I never found that any squire spoke so much with his lord as thou dost with thine; which, in good sooth, I do attribute to thy great indiscretion and mine; thine, in respecting me so little; mine, in not making myself to be more regarded. Was not Gandalin, Amadis de Gaul's squire, earl of the Firm Island? And yet it is read of him, that he spoke to his lord with his cap in his hand, his head bowed, and his body bended (more Turcesco). What, then, shall we say of Gasabel, Don Galaor's squire, who was so silent, as to declare us the excellency thereof, his name is but once repeated in all that so great and authentic a history? Of all which my words, Sancho, thou must infer, that thou must make difference between the master and the man, the lord and his serving-man, the knight and his squire: so that from this day forward we must proceed with more respect, not letting the clew run so much; for after what way soever I grow angry with thee, it will be bad for the pitcher. The rewards and benefits that I have promised thee will come in their time; and if they do not, thy wages cannot be lost, as I have already said to thee.'

'You say very well,' quoth Sancho; 'but fain would I learn (in case that the time of rewards came not, and that I must of necessity trust to my wages) how much a knight-errant's squire did gain in times past? or if they did agree for months, or by days, as mason's men?' 'I do not think,' quoth Don Quixote, 'that they went by the hire, but only trusted to their lord's courtesy. And if I have assigned wages to thee in my sealed testament, which I left at home, it was to prevent the worst; because I know not yet what success chivalry may have in these our so miserable times, and I would not have my soul suffer in the other world for such a minuity as is thy wages; for thou must understand that in this world there is no state so dangerous as that of knights-errant.' 'That is most true,' replied Sancho, 'seeing the only sound of the maces of a fulling-mill could trouble and disquiet the heart of so valiant a knight as you are. But you may be sure that I will not hereafter once unfold my lips to jest at your doings, but only to honour you as my master and natural lord.' 'By doing so,' replied Don Quixote, 'thou shalt live on the face of the earth; for, next to our parents, we are bound to respect our masters as if they were our fathers.'

CHAPTER VII

Of the High Adventure and Rich Winning of the Helmet of Mambrino, with Other Successes Which Befel the Invincible Knight

IT began about this time to rain, and Sancho would fain have entered into the fulling-mills; but Don Quixote had conceived such hate against them for the jest recounted, as he would in no wise come near them; but, turning his way on the right hand, he fell into a highway, as much beaten as that wherein they rode the day before. Within a while after, Don Quixote espied one a-horseback, that bore on his head somewhat that glistered like gold; and scarce had he seen him, when he turned to Sancho, and said, 'Methinks, Sancho, that there's no proverb that is not true; for they are all sentences taken out of experience itself, which is the universal mother of sciences! and specially that proverb that says, "Where one door is shut, another is opened." I say this because, if fortune did shut yesternight the door that we searched, deceiving us in the adventure of the iron maces, it lays us now wide open the door that may address us to a better and more certain adventure, whereon, if I cannot make a good entry, the fall shall be mine, without being able to attribute it to the little knowledge of the fulling-maces, or the darkness of the night; which I affirm because, if I be not deceived, there comes one towards us that wears on his head the helmet of Mambrino, for which I made the oath.' 'See well what you say, sir, and better what you do,' quoth Sancho; 'for I would not wish that this were new maces, to batter us and our understanding.' 'The devil take thee for a man!' replied Don Quixote; 'what difference is there betwixt a helmet and fulling-maces?' 'I know not,' quoth Sancho; 'but if I could speak as much now as I was wont, perhaps I would give you such reasons as you yourself should see how much you are deceived in that you speak.' 'How may I be deceived in that I say, scrupulous traitor?' quoth Don Quixote. 'Tell me, seest thou not that knight which comes riding towards us on a dapple-grey horse, with a helmet of gold on his head?' 'That which I see and find out to be so,' answered Sancho, 'is none other than a man on a grey ass like mine own, and brings on his head somewhat that shines.' 'Why, that is Mambrino's helmet,' quoth Don Quixote. 'Stand aside, and leave me alone with him; thou shalt see how, without speech, to cut off delays, I will conclude this adventure, and remain with the helmet as mine own which I have so much desired.' 'I will have care to stand off; but I turn again to say, that I pray God that it be a purchase of gold, and not fulling-mills.' 'I have already said unto thee that thou do not make any more mention, no, not in thought, of those maces; for if thou dost,' said Don Quixote, 'I vow, I say no more, that I will batter thy soul.' Here Sancho, fearing lest his master would accomplish the vow which he had thrown out as round as a bowl, held his peace.

This, therefore, is the truth of the history of the helmet, horse, and knight, which Don Quixote saw. There was in that commark two villages, the one so little as it had neither shop nor barber, but the greater, that was near unto it, was furnished of one; and he therefore did serve the little village when they had any occasion, as now it befell that therein lay one sick, and must be let blood, and another that desired to trim his beard; for which purpose the barber came, bringing with him a brazen basin. And as he travelled, it by chance began to rain, and therefore clapped his basin on his head to save his hat from staining, because it belike was a new one; and the basin being clean scoured, glistered half a league off. He rode on a grey ass, as Sancho said, and that was the reason why Don Quixote took him to be a dapple-grey steed, a knight, and a helmet of gold; for he did, with all facility, apply everything which he saw to his raving chivalry and ill-errant thoughts. And when he saw that the poor knight drew near, without settling himself to commune with him, he inrested his javelin low on the thigh, and ran with all the force Rozinante might, thinking to strike him through and through; and, drawing near unto him, without stopping his horse, he cried, 'Defend thyself, caitiff! or else render unto me willingly that which is my due by all reason.'

The barber, who so without fearing or surmising any such thing, saw that fantasy and spirit came upon him, had no other remedy, to avoid the blow of the lance, but to fall off his ass to the ground; and scarce had he touched the earth, when rising up again as light as a deer, he ran away so swiftly through the plain as the wind could scarce overtake him, leaving behind him on the ground his basin; wherewithal Don Quixote rested content, and said that pagan which lost it was discreet, and did imitate the castor, who seeing himself hotly pursued by the hunters, which tears and cuts away that with his teeth for which he knows by natural instinct he is followed.

Then he commanded Sancho to take up the helmet; who, lifting it, said, 'The basin is a good one, by God, and is as well worth a real of eight as a marvedi.' And, giving it to his lord, he presently set it on his head, turning about every way to see whether he could get the beaver; and, seeing he could not find it, he said, 'The pagan for whom this famous helmet was first forged had doubtlessly a very great head; and that which grieves me principally is that this helmet wants the one half.'

When Sancho heard him call the basin a helmet, he could not contain his laughter; but presently remembering of his master's choler, he checked it in the midst. 'Why dost thou laugh, Sancho?' quoth Don Quixote. 'I laugh,' said he, 'to think on the great head the pagan owner of this helmet had; for it is for all the world like a barber's basin.' 'Know Sancho, that I imagine,' quoth Don Quixote, 'that this famous piece of this enchanted helmet did fall, by some strange accident, into some one's hands that knew not the worth thereof, and seeing it was of pure gold, without knowing what he did, I think he hath molten the half, to profit himself therewithal, and made of the other half this, which seems a barber's basin, as thou sayst: but be it what it list, to me who knows well what it is, his transmutation makes no matter; for I will dress it in the first town where I shall find a smith, as that which the God of Forges made for the God of War shall not surpass, no, nor come near it; and in the meanwhile I will wear it as I may, for something is better than nothing; and more, seeing it may very well defend me from the blow of a stone.' 'That's true,' quoth Sancho, 'if it be not thrown out of a sling, such as that of the battle of the two armies, when they blessed your worship's cheek teeth, and broke the bottle wherein you carried the most blessed drench which made me vomit up my guts.' 'I do not much care for the loss of it, Sancho,' quoth Don Quixote; 'for, as thou knowest, I have the recipe in memory.' 'So have I likewise,' quoth Sancho; 'but if ever I make it or taste it again in my life, I pray God that here may be mine end: how much more, I never mean to thrust myself into any occasion wherein I should have need of it; for I mean, with all my five senses, to keep myself from hurting any, or being hurt. Of being once again tossed in a coverlet, I say nothing; for such disgraces can hardly be prevented, and if they befall, there is no other remedy but patience, and to lift up the shoulders, keep in the breath, shut the eyes, and suffer ourselves to be borne where fortune and the coverlet pleaseth.'

'Thou art a bad Christian, Sancho,' quoth Don Quixote, hearing him say so; 'for thou never forgettest the injuries that are once done to thee: know that it is the duty of noble and generous minds not to make any account of toys. What leg hast thou brought away lame, what rib broken, or what head hurt, that thou canst not yet forget that jest? For the thing being well examined, it was none other than a jest or pastime; for if I did not take it to be such, I had returned by this to that place, and done more harm in thy revenge than that which the Greeks did for the rape of Helen: who, if she were in these times, or my Dulcinea in hers, she might be sure she should never have gained so much fame for beauty as she did.' And, saying so, he pierced the sky with a sigh. 'Then,' said Sancho, 'let it pass for a jest, since the revenge cannot pass in earnest; but I know well the quality both of the jest and earnest, and also that they shall never fall out of my memory, as they will never out of my shoulders. But, leaving this apart, what shall we do with this dapple-grey steed, that looks so like a grey ass, which that Martin left behind, whom you overthrew, who, according as he laid feet on the dust and made haste, he minds not to come back for him again; and, by my beard, the grey beast is a good one.' 'I am not accustomed,' quoth Don Quixote, 'to ransack and spoil those whom I overcome; nor is it the practice of chivalry to take their horses and let them go afoot, if that it befall [not] the victor to lose in the conflict his own; for in such a case it is lawful to take that of the vanquished as won in fair war. So that, Sancho, leave that horse, or ass, or what else thou pleasest to call it; for when his owner sees us departed, he will return again for it.' 'God knows,' quoth Sancho, 'whether it will be good or no for me to take him, or at least change for mine own, which, methinks, is not so good. Truly the laws of knighthood are strait, since they extend not themselves to license the exchange of one ass for another. And I would know whether they permit at least to exchange the one harness for another?' 'In that I am not very sure,' quoth Don Quixote; 'and as a case of doubt (until I be better informed), I say that thou exchange them, if by chance thy need be extreme.' 'So extreme,' quoth Sancho, 'that if they were for mine own very person, I could not need them more.' And presently, enabled by the license, he made *mutatio caparum,* and set forth his beast like a hundred holidays.

This being done, they broke their fast with the relics of the spoils they had made in the camp of sumpter-horse, and drank of the mills' streams, without once turning to look on them (so much they abhorred them for the marvellous terror they had strucken them in); and having by their repast cut away all choleric and melancholic humours, they followed on the way which Rozinante pleased to lead them, who was the depository of his master's will, and also of the ass's, who followed him always wheresoever he went, in good amity and company: for all this, they returned to the highway, wherein they travelled at random, without any certain deliberation which way to go. And as they thus travelled, Sancho said to his lord, 'Sir, will you give me leave to commune a little with you? for, since you have imposed upon me that sharp commandment of silence more than four things have rotted in my stomach; and one thing that I have now upon the tip of my tongue, I would not wish for anything that it should miscarry.' 'Say it,' quoth Don Quixote, 'and be brief in thy reasons; for none is delightful if it be prolix.' 'I say then,' quoth Sancho, 'that I have been these later days considering how little is gained by following these adventures that you do through these deserts and cross-ways, where, though you overcome and finish the most dangerous, yet no man sees or knows them, and so they shall remain in perpetual silence, both to your prejudice and that of the fame which they deserve. And therefore, methinks, it were better (still expecting your better judgment herein), that we went to serve some emperor or other great prince that maketh war, in whose service you might show the valour of your person, your marvellous force, and wonderful judgment; which being perceived by the lord whom we shall serve, he must perforce reward us, every one according to his deserts; and in such a place will not want one to record your noble acts for a perpetual memory. Of mine I say nothing, seeing they must not transgress the squire-like limits; although I dare avouch that, if any notice be taken in chivalry of the feats of squires, mine shall not fall away betwixt the lines.'

'Sancho, thou sayst not ill,' quoth Don Quixote; 'but before such a thing come to pass, it is requisite to spend some time up and down the world, as in probation, seeking of adventures, to the end that, by achieving some, a man may acquire such fame and renown, as when he goes to the court of any great monarch, he be there already known by his works; and that he shall scarcely be perceived to enter at the gates by the boys of that city, when they all will follow and environ him, crying out aloud, This is the Knight of the Sun, or the Serpent, or of some other device under which he hath achieved strange adventures. "This is he," will they say, "who overcame in single fight the huge giant Brocabruno of the invincible strength; he that disenchanted the great Sophy of Persia, of the large enchantment wherein he had lain almost nine hundred years." So that they will thus go proclaiming his acts from hand to hand; and presently the king of that kingdom, moved by the great bruit of the boys and other people, will stand at the windows of his palace to see what it is; and as soon as he shall eye the knight, knowing him by his arms, or by the imprese of his shield, he must necessarily say, "Up! go all of you, my knights, as many of you as are in court, forth, to receive the flower of chivalry, which comes there." At whose command they all will sally, and he himself will come down to the midst of the stairs, and will embrace him most straitly, and will give him the peace, kissing him on the cheek; and presently will carry him by the hand to the queen's chamber, where the knight shall find her accompanied by the princess her daughter, which must be one of the fairest and *debonaire* damsels that can be found throughout the vast compass of the earth. After this will presently and in a trice succeed, that she will cast her eye on the knight, and he on her, and each of them shall seem to the other no human creature, but an angel; and then, without knowing how, or how not, they shall remain captive and entangled in the inextricable amorous net, and with great care in their minds, because they know not how they shall speak to discover the anguish and feeling. From thence the king will carry him, without doubt, to some quarter of his palace richly hanged; where, having taken off his arms, they will bring him a rich mantle of scarlet, furred with ermines, to wear; and if he seemed well before, being armed, he shall now look as well, or better, out of them. The night being come, he shall sup with the king, queen, and princess, where he shall never take his eye off her, beholding unawares of those that stand present, and she will do the like with as much discretion; for, as I have said, she is a very discreet damsel. The tables shall be taken up; there shall enter, unexpectedly, in at the hall, an ill-favoured little dwarf, with a fair lady that comes behind the dwarf between two giants, with a certain adventure, wrought by a most ancient wise man, and that he who shall end it shall be held for the best knight of the world. Presently the king will command all those that are present to prove it, which they do, but none of them can finish it but only the new-come knight, to the great proof of his fame; whereat the princess will remain very glad, and will be very joyful, and well apaid, because she hath settled her thoughts in so high a place. And the best of it is, that this king, or prince, or what else he is, hath a very great war with another as mighty as he; and the knight his guest doth ask him (after he hath been in the court a few days) license to go and serve him in that war. The king will give it with a very good will, and the knight will kiss his hands courteously for the favour he doth him therein. And that night he will take leave of his lady, the princess, by some window of a garden that looks into her bedchamber, by the which he hath spoken to her ofttimes before,—being a great means and help thereto, a certain damsel which the princess trusts very much. He sighs, and she will fall in a swoon, and the damsel will bring water to bring her to herself again; she will be also full of care because the morning draws near, and she would not have them discovered by any, for her lady's honour. Finally, the princess will return to herself, and will give out her beautiful hands at the window to the knight, who will kiss them a thousand and a thousand times, and will bathe them all in tears. There it will remain agreed between them two the means that they will use to acquaint one another with their good or bad successes; and the princess will pray him to stay away as little time as he may; which he shall promise unto her, with many oaths and protestations. Then will he turn again to kiss her hands, and take his leave of her with such feeling, that there will want but little to end his life in the place. He goes from thence to his chamber, and casts himself upon his bed; but he shall not be able to sleep a nap for sorrow of his departure. He will after get up very early, and will go to take leave of the king, the queen, and princess. They tell him (having taken leave of the first two) that the princess is ill at ease, and that she cannot be visited: the knight thinks that it is for grief of his departure, and the which tidings lanceth him anew to the bottom of his heart, whereby he will be almost constrained to give manifest tokens of his grief. The damsel that is privy to their loves will be present, and must note all that passeth, and go after to tell it to her mistress, who receives her with tears, and says unto her, that one of the greatest afflictions she hath is, that she doth not know who is her knight, or whether he be of blood royal or no. Her damsel will assure her again, that so great bounty, beauty, and valour as is in her knight could not find place but in a great and royal subject. The careful princess will comfort herself with this hope, and labour to be cheerful, lest she should give occasion to her parents to suspect any sinister thing of her; and within two days again she will come out in public. By this the knight is departed: he fights in the war, and overcomes the king's enemy; he wins many cities, and triumphs for many battles; he returns to the court; he visits his lady, and speaks to her at the accustomed place; he agreeth with her to demand her of the king for his wife, in reward of his services; whereunto the king will not consent, because he knows not what he is; but for all this, either by carrying her away, or by some other manner, the princess becomes his wife, and he accounts himself therefore very fortunate, because it was after known that the same knight is son to a very valorous king, of I know not what country; for I believe it is not in all the map. The father dies, and the princess doth inherit the kingdom; and thus, in two words, our knight is become a king. Here in this place enters presently the commodity to reward his squire, and all those that helped him to ascend to so high an estate. He marries his squire with one of the princess's damsels, which shall doubtless be the very same that was acquainted with his love, who is some principal duke's daughter.'

'That's it I seek for,' quoth Sancho, 'and all will go right; therefore I will leave to that, for every whit of it which you said will happen to yourself, without missing a jot, calling yourself, the Knight of the Ill-favoured Face.' 'Never doubt it, Sancho,' quoth Don Quixote; 'for even in the very same manner, and by the same steps that I have recounted here, knights-errant do ascend, and have ascended, to be kings and emperors. This only is expedient, that we inquire what king among the Christians or heathens makes war and hath a fair daughter: but we shall have time enough to bethink that, since, as I have said, we must first acquire fame in other places, before we go to the court. Also I want another thing, that put case that we find a Christian or pagan king that hath wars and a fair daughter, and that I have gained incredible fame throughout the wide world, yet cannot I tell how I might find that I am descended from kings, or that I am at the least cousin-german removed of an emperor; for the king will not give me his daughter until this be first very well proved, though my works deserve it never so much; so that I fear to lose, through this defect, that which mine own hath merited so well. True it is that I am a gentleman of a known house of propriety and possession; and perhaps the wise man that shall write my history will so beautify my kindred and descent, that he will find me to be the fifth or sixth descent from a king. For thou must understand, Sancho, that there are two manners of lineages in the world: some that derive their pedigree from princes and monarchs, whom time hath by little and little diminished and consumed, and ended in a point like pyramids; others, that took their beginning from base people, and ascend from degree unto degree, until they become at last great lords. So that all the difference is, that some were that which they are not now, and others are that which they were not; and it might be that I am of those, and, after good examination, my beginning might be found to have been famous and glorious, wherewithal the king, my father-in-law, ought to be content, whosoever he were; and when he were not, yet shall the princess love me in such sort, that she shall, in despite of her father's teeth, admit me for her lord and spouse, although she knew me to be the son of a water-bearer. And if not, here in this place may quader well the carrying of her away perforce, and carrying of her where best I liked; for either time or death must needs end her father's displeasure.'

'Here comes well to pass that,' [said] Sancho, 'which some damned fellows are wont to say, "Seek not to get that with a good will which thou mayst take perforce"; although it were better said, "The leap of a shrub is more worth than good men's entreaties." I say it to this purpose, that if the king, your father-in-law, will not condescend to give unto you the princess, my mistress, then there's no more to be done, but, as you say, to steal her away and carry her to another place; but all the harm is that, in the meanwhile that composition is unmade, and you possess not quietly your kingdom, the poor squire may whistle for any benefit or pleasure you are able to do him, if it be not that the damsel of whom you spoke even now run away with her lady, and that he pass away his misfortunes now and then with her, until Heaven ordain some other thing; for I do think that his lord may give her unto him presently, if she please to be his lawful spouse.' 'There's none that can deprive thee of that,' quoth Don Quixote. 'Why, so that this may befall,' quoth Sancho, 'there's no more but to commend ourselves to God, and let fortune run where it may best address us.' 'God bring it so to pass,' quoth Don Quixote, 'as I desire, and thou hast need of, Sancho; and let him be a wretch that accounts himself one.' 'Let him be so,' quoth Sancho; 'for I am an old Christian, and to be an earl there is no more requisite.' 'Ay, and 'tis more than enough,' quoth Don Quixote, 'for that purpose; and though thou wert not, it made not much matter; for I, being a king, may give thee nobility, without either buying of it, or serving me with nothing; for, in creating thee an earl, lo! thereby thou art a gentleman. And, let men say what they please, they must, in good faith, call thee "right honourable," although it grieve them never so much.' 'And think you,' quoth Sancho, 'that I would not authorise my *litado?*' 'Thou must say *dictado,* or dignity,' quoth Don Quixote, 'and not *litado,* for that's a barbarous word.' 'Let it be so,' quoth Sancho Panza. 'I say that I would accommodate all very well; for I was once the warner of a confratriety, and the warner's gown became me so well that every one said I had a presence fit for the provost of the same: then how much more when I shall set on my shoulders the royal robe of a duke, or be apparelled with gold and pearls, after the custom of strange earls? I do verily believe that men will come a hundred leagues to see me.' 'Thou wilt seem very well,' quoth Don Quixote; 'but thou must shave that beard very often; for as thou hast it now, so bushy, knit, and unhandsome, if thou shavest it not with a razor at the least every other day, men will know that thou art as far from gentility as a musket can carry.' 'What more is there to be done,' quoth Sancho, 'than to take a barber and keep him hired in my house? yea, and if it be necessary, he shall ride after me, as if he were a master of horse to some nobleman.' 'How knowest thou,' quoth Don Quixote, 'that noblemen have their masters of horses riding after them?' 'Some few years ago I was a month in the court, and there I saw that a young little lord rode by for his pleasure; they said he was a great grandee; there followed him still a-horseback a certain man, turning every way that he went, so as he verily seemed to be his horse's tail. I then demanded the cause why that man did not ride by the other's side, but still did follow him so. They answered me that he was master of his horses, and that the grandees were accustomed to carry such men after them.' 'Thou sayst true,' quoth Don Quixote, 'and thou mayst carry thy barber in that manner after thee; for customs came not all together, nor were not invented at once; and thou mayst be the first earl that carried his barber after him: and I do assure thee that it is an office of more trust to trim a man's beard than to saddle a horse.' 'Let that of the barber rest to my charge,' quoth Sancho, 'and that of procuring to be a king, and of creating me an earl, to yours.' 'It shall be so,' quoth Don Quixote. And thus, lifting up his eyes, he saw that which shall be recounted in the chapter following.

CHAPTER VIII

Of the Liberty Don Quixote Gave to Many Wretches, Who Were A-Carrying Perforce to a Place They Desired Not

CID HAMET BENENGELI, an Arabic and Manchegan author, recounts, in this most grave, lofty, divine, sweet conceited history, that, after these discourses passed between Don Quixote and his squire Sancho Panza, which we have laid down in the last chapter, Don Quixote, lifting up his eyes, saw that there came in the very same way wherein they rode, about some twelve men in a company on foot, inserted like bead-stones in a great chain of iron, that was tied about their necks, and every one of them had manacles besides on their hands. There came to conduct them two on horseback and two others afoot: the horsemen had firelock pieces; those that came afoot, darts and swords. And as soon as Sancho saw them, he said: 'This is a chain of galley-slaves, people forced by the king to go to the galleys.' 'How! people forced?' demanded Don Quixote; 'is it possible that the king will force anybody?' 'I say not so,' answered Sancho, 'but that it is people which are condemned, for their offences, to serve the king in the galleys perforce.' 'In resolution,' replied Don Quixote, 'howsoever it be, this folk, although they be conducted, go perforce, and not willingly.' 'That's so,' quoth Sancho. 'Then, if that be so, here falls in justly the execution of my function, to wit, the dissolving of violences and outrages, and the succouring of the afflicted and needful.' 'I pray you, sir,' quoth Sancho, 'to consider that the justice, who represents the king himself, doth wrong or violence to nobody, but only doth chastise them for their committed crimes.'

By this the chain of slaves arrived, and Don Quixote, with very courteous terms, requested those that went in their guard, that they would please to inform him of the cause wherefore they carried that people away in that manner. One of the guardians a-horseback answered that they were slaves condemned by his majesty to the galleys, and there was no more to be said, neither ought he to desire any further knowledge. 'For all that,' replied Don Quixote, 'I would fain learn of every one of them in particular the cause of his disgrace.' And to this did add other such and so courteous words, to move them to tell him what he desired, as the other guardian a-horseback said, 'Although we carry here the register and testimony of the condemnations of every one of these wretches, yet this is no time to hold them here long, or take out the processes to read: draw you nearer, and demand it of themselves: for they may tell it an they please, and I know they will; for they are men that take delight both in acting and relating knaveries.'

With this license, which Don Quixote himself would have taken although they had not given it him, he came to the chain, and demanded of the first for what offence he went in so ill a guise. He answered that his offence was no other than for being in love; for which cause only he went in that manner. 'For that, and no more?' replied Don Quixote. 'Well, if enamoured folk be cast into the galleys, I might have been rowing there a good many days ago.' 'My love was not such as you conjecture,' quoth the slave; 'for mine was that I loved so much a basket well heaped with fine linen, as I did embrace it so straitly, that if the justice had not taken it away from me by force, I would not have forsaken it to this hour by my good-will. All was done *in flagrante;* there was no leisure to give me torment; the cause was concluded, my shoulders accommodated with a hundred, and, for a supplement, three prizes of garrupes, and the work was ended.' 'What are garrupes?' quoth Don Quixote. 'Garrupes are galleys,' replied the slave, who was a young man of some four-and-twenty years old, and said he was born in Piedrahita.

Don Quixote demanded of the second his cause of offence, who would answer nothing, he went so sad and melancholy. But the first answered for him, and said, 'Sir, this man goes for a canary-bird, I mean for a musician and singer.' 'Is it possible,' quoth Don Quixote, 'that musicians and singers are likewise sent to the galleys?' 'Yes, sir,' quoth the slave; 'for there's nothing worse than to sing in anguish.' 'Rather,' quoth Don Quixote, 'I have heard say that he which sings doth affright and chase away his harms.' 'Here it is quite contrary,' quoth the slave; 'for he that sings once weeps all his life after.' 'I do not understand it,' said Don Quixote. But one of the guardians said to him, 'Sir knight, to sing in anguish is said, among this people, *non sancta,* to confess upon the rack. They gave this poor wretch the torture, and he confessed his delight that he was a quartrezo, that is, a stealer of beasts; and because he hath confessed, he is likewise condemned to the galleys for six years, with an amen of two hundred blows, which he bears already with him on his shoulders. And he goes always thus sad and pensative, because the other thieves that remain behind, and also those which go here, do abuse, despise, and scorn him for confessing, and not having a courage to say Non; for, they say, a No hath as many letters as a Yea, and that a delinquent is very fortunate when his life or his death only depends of his own tongue, and not of witnesses or proofs: and, in mine opinion, they have very great reason.' 'I likewise think the same,' quoth Don Quixote.

And, passing to the third, he demanded that which he had done of the rest, who answered him out of hand, and that pleasantly: 'I go to the Lady Garrupes for five years, because I wanted ten ducats.' 'I will give twenty with all my heart to free thee from that misfortune,' quoth Don Quixote. 'That,' quoth the slave, 'would be like one that hath money in the midst of the gulf, and yet dies for hunger because he can get no meat to buy for it. I say this, because if I had those twenty ducats which your worship's liberality offers me, in due season I would have so anointed with them the notary's pen, and whetted my lawyer's wit so well, that I might to-day see myself in the midst of the market of Cocodover of Toledo, and not in this way trailed thus like a greyhound. But God is great; patience, and this is enough.'

Don Quixote went after to the fourth, who was a man of venerable presence, with a long white beard which reached to his bosom; who, hearing himself demanded the cause why he came there, began to weep, and answered not a word. But the fifth slave lent him a tongue, and said, 'This honest man goes to the galleys for four years, after he had walked the ordinary apparelled in pomp and a-horseback.' 'That is,' quoth Sancho Panza, 'as I take, after he was carried about to the shame and public view of the people.' 'You are in the right,' quoth the slave; 'and the crime for which he is condemned to this pain was, for being a broker of the ear, eye, and of all the body too; for in effect I mean that this gentleman goeth for a bawd, and likewise for having a little smack and entrance in witchcraft.' 'If that smack and insight in witchcraft were not added,' quoth Don Quixote, 'he merited not to go and row in the galleys for being a pure bawd, but rather deserved to govern and be their general; for the office of a bawd is not like every other ordinary office, but rather of great discretion, and most necessary in any commonwealth well governed, and should not be practised but by people well born; and ought, besides, to have a veedor and examinator of them, as are of all other trades, and a certain appointed number of men known, as are of the other brokers of the exchange. And in this manner many harms that are done might be excused, because this trade and office is practised by indiscreet people of little understanding; such as are women of little more or less; young pages and jesters of few years' standing, and of less experience, which in the most urgent occasions, and when they should contrive a thing artificially, the crumbs freeze in their mouths and fists, and they know not which is their right hand. Fain would I pass forward and give reasons why it is convenient to make choice of those which ought in the commonwealth to practise this so necessary an office; but the place and season is not fit for it; one day I will say it to those which may provide and remedy it: only I say now, that the assumpt or addition of a witch hath deprived me of the compassion I should otherwise have to see those grey hairs and venerable face in such distress for being a bawd: although I know very well that no sorcery in the world can move or force the will, as some ignorant persons think (for our will is a free power, and there's no herb or charm can constrain it); that which certain simple women or cozening companions make, are some mixtures and poisons, wherewithal they cause men run mad, and in the meanwhile persuade us that they have force to make one love well, being (as I have said) a thing most impossible to constrain the will.' 'That is true,' quoth the old man; 'and I protest, sir, that I am wholly innocent of the imputation of witchcraft. As for being a bawd, I could not deny it; but yet I never thought that I did ill therein; for all mine intention was, that all the world should disport them, and live together in concord and quietness, without griefs or quarrels. But this by good desire availed me but little to hinder my going there, from whence I have no hope ever to return, my years do so burden me, and also the stone, which lets me not rest an instant.' And, saying this, he turned again to his lamentations as at the first; and Sancho took such compassion on him, as, setting his hand into his bosom, he drew out a couple of shillings and gave it him as an alms.

From him Don Quixote passed to another, and demanded his fault; who answered with no less, but with much more pleasantness than the former: 'I go here because I have jested somewhat too much with two cousins-german of mine own, and with two other sisters, which were none of mine own; finally, I jested so much with them all, that thence resulted the increase of my kindred so intricately, as there is no casuist that can well resolve it. All was proved by me; I wanted favour, I had no money, and was in danger to lose my head; finally, I was condemned for six years to the galleys. I consented it, as a punishment of my fault; I am young, and let my life but hold out a while longer, and all will go well. And if you, sir knight, carry anything to succour us poor folk, God will reward you it in heaven, and we will have care here on earth to desire God, in our daily prayers for your life and health, that it be as long and as good as your countenance deserves.' He that said this went in the habit of a student, and one of the guard told him that he was a great talker and a very good Latinist.

After all these came a man of some thirty years old, of very comely personage, save only that when he looked he seemed to thrust the one eye into the other. He was differently tied from the rest, for he carried about his leg so long a chain, that it tired all the rest of his body; and he had besides two iron rings about his neck, the one of the chain, and the other of that kind which are called a 'keep-friend,' or the 'foot of a friend,' from whence descended two irons unto his middle, out of which did stick two manacles, wherein his hands were locked up with a great hanging lock, so as he could neither set his hands to his mouth, nor bend down his head towards his hands. Don Quixote demanded why he was so loaded with iron more than the rest. The guard answered, because he alone had committed more faults than all together, and was a more desperate knave; and that, although they carried him tied in that sort, yet went they not sure of him, but feared he would make an escape. 'What faults can he have so grievous,' quoth Don Quixote, 'since he hath only deserved to be sent to the galleys?' 'He goeth,' replied the guard, 'to them for ten years, which is equivalent to a civil death: never strive to know more, but that this man is the notorious Gines of Passamonte, who is otherwise called Ginesilio of Parapilla.' 'Master commissary,' quoth the slave, hearing him say so, 'go fair and softly, and run not thus dilating of names and surnames. I am called Gines, and not Ginesilio; and Passamonte is my surname, and not Parapilla, as you say; and let every one turn about him, and he shall not do little.' 'Speak with less swelling,' quoth the commissary, 'sir thief-of-more-than-the-mark, if you will not have me to make you hold your peace maugre your teeth.' 'It seems well,' quoth the slave, 'that a man is carried as pleaseth God; but one day somebody shall know whether I be called Ginesilio of Parapilla.' 'Why, do not they call thee so, cozener?' quoth the guard. 'They do,' said Gines; 'but I will make that they shall not call me so, or I will fleece them there where I mutter under my teeth. Sir knight, if you have anything to bestow on us, give it us now, and begone, in the name of God; for you do tire us with your too-curious search of knowing other men's lives: and if you would know mine, you shall understand that I am Gines of Passamonte, whose life is written' (showing his hand) 'by these two fingers.' 'He says true,' quoth the commissary; 'for he himself hath penned his own history so well as there is nothing more to be desired, and leaves the book pawned in the prison for two hundred reals.' 'And likewise means to redeem it,' quoth Gines, 'though it were in for as many ducats.'

'Is it so good a work?' said Don Quixote. 'It is so good,' replied Gines, 'that it quite puts down Lazarillo de Tormes, and as many others as are written or shall be written of that kind; for that which I dare affirm to you is, that it treats of true accidents, and those so delightful that no like invention can be compared to them.' 'And how is the book entitled?' quoth Don Quixote. 'It is called,' said he, '*The Life of Gines of Passamonte.*' 'And is it yet ended?' said the knight. 'How can it be finished,' replied he, 'my life being not yet ended, since all that is written is from the hour of my birth until that instant that I was sent this last time to the galleys?' 'Why, then, belike you were there once before?' quoth Don Quixote. 'To serve God and the king I have been in there another time four years, and I know already how the biscuit and provant agree with my stomach,' quoth Gines, 'nor doth it grieve me very much to return unto them; for there I shall have leisure to finish my book, and I have many things yet to say; and in the galleys of Spain there is more resting-time than is requisite for that business, although I shall not need much time to pen what is yet unwritten; for I can, if need were, say it all by rote.' 'Thou seemest to be ingenious,' quoth Don Quixote. 'And unfortunate withal,' quoth Gines; 'for mishaps do still persecute the best wits.' 'They persecute knaves,' quoth the commissary. 'I have already spoken to master commissary,' quoth Passamonte, 'to go fair and softly; for the lords did not give you that rod to the end you should abuse us wretches that go here, but rather to guide and carry us where his majesty hath commanded; if not, by the life of— 'Tis enough that perhaps one day may come to light the sports that were made in the inn; and let all the world peace and live well, and speak better; for this is now too great a digression.' The commissary held up his rod to strike Passamonte in answer of his threats; but Don Quixote put himself between them, and entreated him not to use him hardly, seeing it was not much that one who carried his hands so tied should have his tongue somewhat free; and then, turning himself towards the slaves, he said:

'I have gathered out of all that which you have said, dear brethren, that although they punish you for your faults, yet that the pains you go to suffer do not very well please you, and that you march toward them with a very ill will, and wholly constrained, and that perhaps the little courage this fellow had on the rack, the want of money that the other had, the small favour that a third enjoyed, and finally, the wretched sentence of the judge, and the not executing that justice that was on your sides, have been cause of your misery. All which doth present itself to my memory in such sort, as it persuadeth, yea, and enforceth me, to effect that for you for which Heaven sent me into the world, and made me profess that order of knighthood which I follow. and that vow which I made therein to favour and assist the needful, and those that are oppressed by others more potent. But, forasmuch as I know that it is one of the parts of prudence not to do that by foul means which may be accomplished by fair, I will entreat those gentlemen, your guardians and commissary, they will please to loose and let you depart peaceably; for there will not want others to serve the king in better occasions; for it seems to me a rigorous manner of proceeding to make slaves of them whom God and nature created free. How much more, good sirs of the guard,' added Don Quixote, 'seeing these poor men have never committed any offence against you? Let them answer for their sins in the other world: there is a God in heaven who is not negligent in punishing the evil nor rewarding the good; and it is no wise decent that honourable men should be the executioners of other men, seeing they cannot gain or lose much thereby. I demand this of you in this peaceable, quiet manner, to the end that, if you accomplish my request, I may have occasion to yield you thanks; and if you will not do it willingly, then shall this lance and this sword, guided by the invincible valour of mine arm, force you to it.'

'This is a pleasant doting,' answered the commissary, 'and an excellent jest wherewithal you have finished your large reasoning. Would you, good sir knight, have us leave unto you those the king forceth, as if we had authority to let them go, or you to command us to do it? Go on your way in a good hour, gentle sir, and settle the basin you bear on your head somewhat righter, and search not thus whether the cat hath three feet.' 'Thou art a cat, and a rat, and a knave!' quoth Don Quixote. And so, with word and deed at once, he assaulted him so suddenly as, without giving him leisure to defend himself, he struck him down to the earth very sore wounded with a blow of his lance; and as fortune would, this was he that had the firelock piece. The rest of the guard remained astonished at the unexpected accident; but at last returning to themselves, the horsemen set hand to their swords, and the footmen to their darts, and all of them set upon Don Quixote, who expected them very quietly. And doubtlessly he would have been in danger, if the slaves perceiving the occasion offered to be so fit to recover liberty, had not procured it by breaking the chain wherein they were linked.

The hurly-burly was such as the guards now began to run to hinder the slaves from untieing themselves, now to offend Don Quixote who assaulted them; so that they could do nothing available to keep their prisoners. Sancho, for his part, helped to loose Gines of Passamonte, who was the first that leaped free into the field without clog, and setting upon the overthrown commissary, he disarmed him of his sword and piece, and now aiming at the one and then at the other with it, without discharging, made all the guards to abandon the field, as well for fear of Passamonte's piece as also to shun the marvellous showers of stones that the slaves, now delivered, poured on them. Sancho grew marvellous sad at this success; for he suspected that those which fled away would go and give notice of the violence committed to the Holy Brotherhood, which would presently issue in troops to search the delinquents; and said as much to his lord, requesting him to depart presently from thence, and embosk himself in the mountain, which was very near. 'All is well,' quoth Don Quixote; 'I know now what is fit to be done.' And so, calling together all the slaves that were in a tumult, and had stripped the commissary naked, they came all about him to hear what he commanded; to whom he said:

'It is the part of people well born to gratify and acknowledge the benefits they receive, ingratitude being one of the sins that most offendeth the Highest. I say it, sirs, to this end, because you have, by manifest trial, seen that which you have received at my hand, in reward whereof I desire, and it is my will, that all of you, loaden with that chain from which I even now freed your necks, go presently to the city of Toboso, and there present yourselves before the Lady Dulcinea of Toboso, and recount unto her that her Knight of the Ill-favoured Face sends you there to remember his service to her; and relate unto her at large the manner of your freedom, all you that have had such noble fortune; and this being done, you may after go where you please.'

Gines de Passamonte answered for all the rest, saying, 'That which you demand, good sir, our releaser, is most impossible to be performed, by reason that we cannot go all together through these ways, but alone and divided, procuring each of us to hide himself in the bowels of the earth, to the end we may not be found by the

Holy Brotherhood, which will doubtlessly set out to search for us. That, therefore, which you may and ought to do in this exigent is, to change this service and homage of the Lady Dulcinea of Toboso into a certain number of ave-maries and creeds, which we will say for your intention; and this is a thing that may be accomplished by night or by day, running or resting, in peace or in war; but to think that we will return again to take up our chains, or set ourselves in the way of Toboso, is as hard as to make us believe that it is now night, it being yet scarce ten of the clock in the morning; and to demand such a thing of us is as likely as to seek for pears of the elm-tree.' 'I swear by such a one,' quoth Don Quixote, thoroughly enraged, 'sir son of a whore, Don Ginesilio of Parapilla, or howsoever you are called, that thou shalt go thyself alone, with thy tail between thy legs, and bear all the chain in thy neck.' Passamonte, who was by nature very choleric, knowing assuredly that Don Quixote was not very wise (seeing he had attempted such a desperate act as to seek to give them liberty), seeing himself thus abused, winked on his companions, and, going a little aside, they sent such a shower of stones on Don Quixote, as he had no leisure to cover himself with his buckler; and poor Rozinante made no more account of the spur than if his sides were made of brass. Sancho ran behind his ass, and by his means sheltered himself from the cloud and shower of stones that rained upon both. And Don Quixote could not cover himself so well, but that a number of stones struck him in the body with so great force as they overthrew him at last to the ground; and scarce was he fallen when the student leapt upon him and took the basin off his head, and gave him three or four blows with it on the shoulders, and after struck it so oft about the ground as he almost broke it in pieces. They took from him likewise a cassock which he wore upon his armour, and thought also to take away his stockings, but that they were hindered by his greaves. From Sancho they took away his cassock, and left him in his hair; and, dividing all the spoils of the battle among themselves, they departed every one by the way he pleased, troubled with greater care how to escape from the Holy Brotherhood which they feared, than to load themselves with the iron chain, and go and present themselves before the Lady Dulcinea of Toboso. The ass and

Rozinante, Sancho and Don Quixote, remained alone: the ass stood pensive, with his head hanging downwards, shaking now and then his ears, thinking that the storm of stones was not yet past, but that they still buzzed by his head; Rozinante lay overthrown by his master, who was likewise struck down by another blow of a stone; Sancho, in fear of the bullets of the Holy Brotherhood; and Don Quixote, most discontent to see himself so misused by those very same to whom he had done so much good.

CHAPTER IX

Of That Which Befel the Famous Don Quixote in Sierra Morena Which Was One of the Most Rare Adventures That in This or Any Other so Authentic a History Is Recounted

DON QUIXOTE, seeing himself in so ill plight, said to his squire, 'Sancho, I have heard say ofttimes, that to do good to men unthankful is to cast water into the sea. If I had believed what thou saidst to me, I might well have prevented all this grief; but now that is past, patience, and be wiser another time.' 'You will take warning as much by this,' quoth Sancho, 'as I am a Turk. But since you say that if you had believed me you had avoided this grief, believe me now, and you shall eschew a greater; for you must wit that no knighthood nor chivalry is of any authority with the Holy Brotherhood; for it cares not two farthings for all the knights-errant in the world; and know that, methinks, I hear their arrows buzz about mine ears already.' 'Sancho, thou art a natural coward,' quoth Don Quixote; 'but, because thou mayst not say that I am obstinate, and that I never follow thine advice, I will take thy counsel this time, and convey myself from that fury which now thou fearest so much: but it shall be on a condition—that thou never tell, alive nor dying, to any mortal creature, that I retired or withdrew myself out of this danger for fear, but only to satisfy thy requests; for if thou sayst any other thing thou shalt belie me most falsely, and even from this very time till that, and from thence until now, I give thee the lie herein; and I say thou liest, and shalt lie, as ofttimes as thou sayst or dost think the contrary. And do not reply to me, for in only thinking that I withdraw myself out of any peril, but principally this, which seems to carry with it some shadow of fear; I am about to remain and expect here alone, not only for the Holy Brotherhood, which thou namest and fearest, but also for the brethren of the Twelve Tribes, for the seven Maccabees, for Castor and Pollux, and for all the other brothers and brotherhoods in the world.' 'Sir,' answered Sancho, 'to retire is not to fly, and to expect is wisdom, when the danger exceedeth all hope; and it is the part of a wise man to keep himself safe to-day for to-morrow, and not to adventure himself wholly in one day. And know that, although I be but a rude clown, yet do I, for all that, understand somewhat of that which men call good government; and therefore do not repent yourself for following mine advice, but mount on Rozinante if you be able, if not I will help you, and come after me; for my mind gives me that we shall now have more use of legs than hands.'

Don Quixote leaped on his horse without replying a word, and Sancho guiding him on his ass, they both entered into that part of Sierra Morena that was near unto them. Sancho had a secret design to cross over it all, and issue at Viso or Almodovar del Campo, and in the meantime to hide themselves for some days among those craggy and intricate rocks, to the end they might not be found by the Holy Brotherhood, if it did make after them. And he was the more encouraged to do this, because he saw their provision, which he carried on his ass, had escaped safely out of the skirmish of the galley-slaves; a thing which he accounted to be a miracle, considering the diligence that the slaves had used to search and carry away all things with them. They arrived that night into the very midst and bowels of the mountain, and there Sancho thought it fittest to spend that night, yea, and some other few days also, at least as long as their victuals endured; and with this resolution they took up their lodging among a number of cork-trees that grew between two rocks. But fatal chance, which, according to the opinion of those that have not the light of faith, guideth, directeth, and compoundeth all as it liketh, ordained that that famous cozener and thief, Gines de Passamonte, who was before delivered out of chains by Don Quixote's force and folly, persuaded through fear he conceived of the Holy Brotherhood (whom he had just cause to fear), resolved to hide himself likewise in that mountain; and his fortune and fears led him just to the place where it had first addressed Don Quixote and his squire, just at such time as he might perceive them, and they both at that instant fallen asleep. And as evil men are evermore ungrateful, and that necessity forceth a man to attempt that which it urgeth, and likewise that the present redress prevents the expectation of a future, Gines, who was neither grateful nor gracious, resolved to steal away Sancho his ass, making no account of Rozinante, as a thing neither saleable nor pawnable. Sancho slept soundly, and so he stole his beast, and was before morning so far off from thence, as he feared not to be found.

Aurora sallied forth at last to refresh the earth, and affright Sancho with a most sorrowful accident, for he presently missed his ass; and so, seeing himself deprived of him, he began the most sad and doleful lamentation of the world, in such sort as he awaked Don Quixote with his outcries, who heard that he said thus: 'O child of my bowels, born in mine own house, the sport of my children, the comfort of my wife, and the envy of my neighbours, the ease of my burdens, and finally, the sustainer of half of my person! for, with six-and-twenty marvedis that I gained daily by thee, I did defray half of mine expenses!' Don Quixote, who heard the plaint, and knew also the cause, did comfort Sancho with the best words he could devise, and desired him to have patience, promising to give a letter of exchange, to the end that they of his house might deliver him three asses of five which he had left at home.

Sancho comforted himself again with this promise, and dried up his tears, moderated his sighs, and gave his lord thanks for so great a favour; and as they entered in farther among those mountains we cannot recount the joy of our knight, to whom those places seemed most accommodate to achieve the adventures he searched for. They reduced to his memory the marvellous accidents that had befallen knights-errant in like solitudes and deserts, and he rode so overwhelmed and transported by these thoughts as he remembered nothing else: nor Sancho had any other care (after he was out of fear to be taken) but how to fill his belly with some of the relics which yet remained of the clerical spoils; and so he followed his lord, taking now and then out of a basket (which Rozinante carried for want of the ass) some meat, lining therewithal his paunch; and, whilst he went thus employed, he would not have given a mite to encounter any other adventure, how honourable soever.

But whilst he was thus busied, he espied his master labouring to take up with the point of his javelin some bulk or other that lay on the ground, and went towards him to see whether he needed his help, just at the season that he lifted up a saddle-cushion and a portmanteau fast to it, which were half rotten, or rather wholly rotted, by the weather; yet they weighed so much that Sancho's assistance was requisite to take them up: and straight his lord commanded him to see what was in the wallet. Sancho obeyed with expedition, and although it was shut with a chain and hanging lock, yet by the parts which were torn he saw what was within, to wit, four fine holland shirts, and other linens both curious and clean, and moreover, a handkerchief, wherein was a good quantity of gold; which he perceiving, said, 'Blessed be Heaven, which hath once presented to us a beneficial adventure!'

And, searching for more, he found a tablet very costly bound. This Don Quixote took of him, commanding him to keep the gold with himself; for which rich favour Sancho did presently kiss his hands; and, after taking all the linen, he clapped it up in the bag of their victuals.

Don Quixote having noted all these things, said, 'Methinks, Sancho (and it cannot be possible any other), that some traveller having left his way, passed through this mountain, and being encountered by thieves, they slew him, and buried him in this secret place.' 'It cannot be so,' answered Sancho; 'for, if they were thieves, they would not have left this money behind them.' 'Thou sayst true,' quoth Don Quixote; 'and therefore I cannot conjecture what it might be: but stay a while, we will see whether there be anything written in these tablets by which we may vent and find out that which I desire.'

Then he opened it, and the first thing that he found written in it, as it were a first draft, but done with a very fair character, was a sonnet, which he read aloud, that Sancho might also hear it, and was this which ensues:

'Or Love of understanding quite is void:
  Or he abounds in cruelty, or my pain
The occasion equals not; for which I bide
  The torments dire he maketh me sustain.
But if Love be a god, I dare maintain
  He nought ignores; and reason aye decides

Gods should not cruel be: then who ordains
  This pain I worship, which my heart divides?
Filis! I err, if thou I say it is;
  For so great ill and good cannot consist.
Nor doth this wrack from Heaven befall, but yet
  That shortly I must die can no way miss.
For the evil whose cause is hardly well exprest,
  By miracle alone true cure may get.'

'Nothing can be learned by that verse,' quoth Sancho, 'if by that *hilo,* or thread, which is said there, you gather not where lies the rest of the clue.' 'What *hilo* is here?' quoth Don Quixote. 'Methought,' quoth Sancho, 'that you read *hilo* there.' 'I did not, but Fili,' said Don Quixote, 'which is, without doubt, the name of the lady on whom the author of this sonnet complains, who in good truth seems to be a reasonable good poet, or else I know but little of that art.'

'Why, then,' quoth Sancho, 'belike you do also understand poetry?' 'That I do, and more than thou thinkest,' quoth Don Quixote, 'as thou shalt see when thou shalt carry a letter from me to my Lady Dulcinea del Toboso, written in verse from the one end to the other; for I would thou shouldst know, Sancho, that all, or the greater number of knights-errant, in times past, were great versifiers and musicians; for these two qualities, or graces, as I may better term them, are annexed to amorous knights-adventurers. True it is that the verses of the ancient knights are not so adorned with words as they are rich in conceits.'

'I pray you, read more,' quoth Sancho; 'for perhaps you may find somewhat that may satisfy.' Then Don Quixote turned the leaf, and said, 'This is prose, and seems to be a letter.' 'What, sir, a missive letter?' quoth Sancho. 'No; but rather of love, according to the beginning,' quoth Don Quixote. 'I pray you, therefore,' quoth Sancho, 'read it loud enough; for I take great delight in these things of love.' 'I am content,' quoth Don Quixote: and, reading it loudly, as Sancho had requested, it said as ensueth:

'Thy false promise, and my certain misfortune, do carry me to such a place, as from thence thou shalt sooner receive news of my death than reasons of my just complaints. Thou hast disdained me, O ingrate! for one that hath more, but not for one that is worth more than I am; but if virtue were a treasure of estimation, I would not emulate other men's fortunes, nor weep thus for mine own misfortunes. That which thy beauty erected, thy works have overthrown; by it I deemed thee to be an angel, and by these I certainly know thee to be but a woman. Rest in peace, O causer of my war! and let Heaven work so that thy spouse's deceits remain still concealed, to the end thou mayst not repent what thou didst, and I be constrained to take revenge of that I desire not.'

Having read the letter, Don Quixote said: 'We can collect less by this than by the verses what the author is, other than that he is some disdained lover.' And so, passing over all the book, he found other verses and letters, of which he could read some, others not at all; but the sum of them all were accusations, plaints, and mistrusts, pleasures, griefs, favours, and disdains, some solemnised, others deplored. And whilst Don Quixote passed over the book, Sancho passed over the malet, without leaving a corner of it or the cushion unsearched, or a seam unripped, nor a lock of wool uncarded, to the end that nothing might remain behind for want of diligence, or carelessness—the found gold, which passed a hundred crowns, had stirred in him such a greediness to have more. And though he got no more than that which he found at the first, yet did he account his flights in the coverlet, his vomiting of the drench, the benedictions of the pack-staves, the blows of the carrier, the loss of his wallet, the robbing of his cassock, and all the hunger, thirst, and weariness that he had passed in the service of his good lord and master, for well employed; accounting himself to be more than well paid by the gifts received of the money they found. The Knight of the Ill-favoured Face was the while possessed with a marvellous desire to know who was the owner of the malet, conjecturing, by the sonnet and letter, the gold and linen, that the enamoured was some man of worth, whom the disdain and rigour of his lady had conducted to some desperate terms. But by reason that nobody appeared through that inhabitable and desert place by whom he might be informed, he thought on it no more, but only rode on, without choosing any other way than that which pleased Rozinante to travel (who took the plainest and easiest to pass through), having still an imagination that there could not want some strange adventure amidst that forest.

And as he rode on with this conceit, he saw a man on the top of a little mountain that stood just before his face, leap from rock to rock and tuff to tuff with wonderful dexterity; and, as he thought, he was naked; had a black and thick beard, the hairs many and confusedly mingled; his feet and legs bare; his thighs were covered with a pair of hose, which seemed to be of murrey velvet, but were so torn that they discovered his flesh in many places; his head was likewise bare: and although he passed by with the haste we have recounted, yet did the Knight of the Ill-favoured Face note all these particulars; and although he endeavoured, yet could not he follow him; for it was not in Rozinante's power, in that weak state wherein he was, to travel so swiftly among those rocks, chiefly being naturally very slow and phlegmatic.

Don Quixote, after espying him, did instantly imagine him to be the owner of the cushion and malet, and therefore resolved to go in his search, although he should spend a whole year therein among those mountains; and commanded Sancho to go about the one side of the mountain, and he would go the other. 'And,' quoth he, 'it may befall that, by using this diligence, we may encounter with that man which vanished so suddenly out of our sight.'

'I cannot do so,' quoth Sancho; 'for that, in parting one step from you, fear presently so assaults me with a thousand visions and affrightments; and let this serve you hereafter for a warning, to the end you may not henceforth part me the black of a nail from your presence.' 'It shall be so,' answered the Knight of the Ill-favoured Face; 'and I am very glad that thou dost thus build upon my valour, the which shall never fail thee, although thou didst want thy very soul: and, therefore, follow me by little and little, or as thou mayst, and make of thine eyes two lanterns; for we will give a turn about this little rock, and perhaps we may meet with this man whom we saw even now, who doubtlessly can be none other than the owner of our booty.'

To which Sancho replied: 'It were much better not to find him; for if we should meet him, and he were by chance the owner of this money, it is most evident that I must restore it to him; and therefore it is better, without using this unprofitable diligence, to let me possess it *bona fide,* until the true lord shall appear, by some way less curious and diligent; which, perhaps, may fall at such a time as it shall be all spent; and in that case I am free from all processes by privilege of the king.'

'Thou deceivest thyself, Sancho, therein,' quoth Don Quixote; 'for, seeing we are fallen already into suspicion of the owner, we are bound to search and restore it to him; and when we would not seek him out, yet the vehement presumption that we have of it hath made us possessors *mala fide,* and renders us as culpable as if he whom we surmise were verily the true lord. So that, friend Sancho, be not grieved to seek him, in respect of the grief whereof thou shalt free me if he be found.' And, saying so, spurred Rozinante; and Sancho followed after afoot, animated by the hope of the young asses his master had promised unto him. And having compassed a part of the mountain, they found a little stream, wherein lay dead, and half devoured by dogs and crows, a mule saddled and bridled, all which confirmed more in them the suspicion that he which fled away was owner of the mule and cushion. And as they looked on it, they heard a whistle much like unto that which shepherds use as they keep their flocks; and presently appeared at their left hand a great number of goats, after whom the goatherd that kept them, who was an aged man, followed on the top of the mountain. And Don Quixote cried to him, requesting him to come down to them; who answered them again as loudly, demanding of them who had brought them to those deserts, rarely trodden by any other than goats, wolves, or other savage beasts which frequented those mountains. Sancho answered him, that if he would descend where they were, they would give him account thereof.

With that the shepherd came down, and, arriving to the place where Don Quixote was, he said: 'I dare wager that you look on the hired mule which lies dead there in that bottom; well, in good faith, he hath lain in that very place these six months. Say, I pray you, have not you met in the way with the master thereof?' 'We have encountered nobody but a cushion and a little malet, which we found not very far off from hence.' 'I did likewise find the same,' replied the goatherd, 'but I would never take it up nor approach to it, fearful of some misdemeanour, or that I should be hereafter demanded for it as for a stealth; for the devil is crafty, and now and then something ariseth, even from under a man's feet, whereat he stumbles and falls, without knowing how or how not.'

'That is the very same I say,' quoth Sancho; 'for I likewise found it, but would not approach it the cast of a stone. There I have left it, and there it remains as it was; for I would not have a dog with a bell.' 'Tell me, good fellow,' quoth Don Quixote, 'dost thou know who is the owner of all these things?'

'That which I can say,' answered the goatherd, 'is that, about some six months past, little more or less, there arrived at a certain sheep-fold, some three leagues off, a young gentleman of comely personage and presence, mounted on that very mule which lies dead there, and with the same cushion and malet which you say you met but touched not. He demanded of us which was the most hidden and inaccessible part of the mountain. And we told him that this wherein we are now: and it is true; for if you did enter but half a league farther, perhaps you would not find the way out again so readily; and I do greatly marvel how you could find the way hither itself, for there is neither highway nor path that may address any to this place. I say, then, that the young man, as soon as he heard our answer, he turned the bridle, and travelled towards the place we showed to him, leaving us all with very great liking of his comeliness, and marvelled at his demand and speed, wherewith he departed and made towards the mountain; and after that time we did not see him a good many of days, until by chance one of our shepherds came by with our provision of victuals; to whom he drew near, without speaking a word, and spurned and beat him, well-favouredly, and after went to the ass which carried our victuals, and taking away all the bread and cheese that was there, he fled into the mountain with wonderful speed.

'When we heard of this, some of us goatherds, we went to search for him, and spent therein almost two days in the most solitary places of this mountain, and in the end found him lurking in the hollow part of a very tall and great corktree; who, as soon as he perceived us, came forth to meet us with great staidness. His apparel was all torn; his visage disfigured, and toasted with the sun in such manner as we could scarce know him, if it were not that his attire, although rent, by the notice we had of it, did give us to understand that he was the man for whom we sought. He saluted us courteously, and in brief and very good reasons, he said, that we ought not to marvel seeing him go in that manner, for that it behoved to do so, that he might accomplish a certain penance enjoined to him, for the many sins he had committed. We prayed him to tell us what he was; but we could never persuade him to do it. We requested him likewise, that whensoever he had any need of meat (without which he could not live) he should tell us where we might find him, and we would bring it to him with great love and diligence; and that if he also did not like of this motion, that he would at leastwise come and ask it, and not take it violently, as he had done before, from our shepherds. He thanked us very much for our offer, and entreated pardon of the assaults passed, and promised to ask it from thenceforward for God's sake, without giving annoyance to any one. And, touching his dwelling or place of abode, he said that he had none other than that where the night overtook him, and ended his discourse with so feeling laments, that we might well be accounted stones which heard him if therein we had not kept him company, considering the state wherein we had seen him first, and that wherein now he was; for, as I said, he was a very comely and gracious young man, and showed, by his courteous and orderly speech, that he was well born, and a court-like person; for, though we were all clowns such as did hear him, his gentility was such as could make itself known, even to rudeness itself. And being in the best of his discourse he stopped and grew silent, fixing his eyes on the ground a good while; wherein we likewise stood still suspended, expecting in what that distraction would end, with no little compassion to behold it; for we easily perceived that some accident of madness had surprised him, by his staring and beholding the earth so fixedly, without once moving the eyelid, and other times by the shutting of them, the biting of his lips, and bending of his brows. But very speedily after, he made us certain thereof himself; for, rising from the ground (whereon he had thrown himself a little before) with great fury, he set upon him that sat next unto him, with such courage and rage, that if we had not taken him away he would have slain him with blows and bites; and he did all this, saying, "O treacherous Fernando! here, here thou shalt pay me the injury that thou didst me; these hands shall rend out the heart, in which do harbour and are heaped all evils together, but principally fraud and deceit." And to these he added other words, all addressed to the dispraise of that Fernando, and to attach him of treason and untruth.

'We took from him at last, not without difficulty, our fellow; and he, without saying a word, departed from us, embushing himself presently among the bushes and brambles, leaving us wholly disabled to follow him in those rough and unhaunted places. By this we gathered that his madness comes to him at times, and that some one, called Fernando, had done some ill work of such weight, as the terms show, to which it hath brought him. All which hath after been yet confirmed as often (which were many times) as he came out to the fields, sometimes to demand meat of the shepherds, and other times to take it of them perforce; for when he is taken with this fit of madness, although the shepherds do offer him meat willingly, yet will not he receive, unless he take it with buffets; and when he is in his right sense, he asks it for God's sake, with courtesy and humanity, and renders many thanks, and that not without tears. And in very truth, sirs, I say unto you,' quoth the goatherd, 'that I and four others, whereof two are my men, other two my friends, resolved yesterday to search until we found him, and being found, either by force or fair means, we will carry him to the town of Almodovar, which is but eight leagues from hence, and there will we have him cured, if his disease may be holpen; or at least we shall learn what he is, when he turns to his wits, and whether he hath any friends to whom notice of his misfortune may be given. This is, sirs, all that I can say concerning that of which you demand of me; and you shall understand that the owner of those things which you saw in the way, is the very same whom you saw pass by you so naked and nimble';—for Don Quixote had told him by this, that he had seen that man go by, leaping among the rocks.

Don Quixote rested marvellously admired at the goatherd's tale; and, with greater desire to know who that unfortunate madman was, purposed with himself, as he had already resolved, to search him throughout the mountains, without leaving a corner or cave of it unsought until he had gotten him. But fortune disposed the matter better than he expected; for he appeared in that very instant in a cleft of a rock that answered to the place where they stood speaking; who came towards them, murmuring somewhat to himself, which could not be understood near at hand, and much less afar off. His apparel was such as we have delivered, only differing in this, as Don Quixote perceived when he drew nearer, that he wore on him, although torn, a leather jerkin, perfumed with amber; by which he thoroughly collected that the person which wore such attire was not of the least quality.

When the young man came to the place where they discoursed, he saluted them with a hoarse voice, but with great courtesy and Don Quixote returned him his greetings with no less compliment; and, alighting from Rozinante, he advanced to embrace him with very good carriage and countenance, and held him a good while straitly between his arms, as if he had known him of long time. The other, whom we may call the Unfortunate Knight of the Rock as well as Don Quixote the Knight of the Ill-favoured Face, after he had permitted himself to be embraced a while, did step a little off from our knight, and, laying his hands on his shoulders, began to behold him earnestly, as one desirous to call to mind whether he had ever seen him before; being, perhaps, no less admired to see Don Quixote's figure, proportion, and arms, than Don Quixote was to view him. In resolution, the first that spoke after the embracing was the ragged knight, and said what we will presently recount.

CHAPTER X

Wherein Is Prosecuted the Adventure of Sierra Morena

THE history affirms that great was the attention wherewithal Don Quixote listened to the Unfortunate Knight of the Rock, who began his speech on this manner: 'Truly, good sir, whatsoever you be (for I know you not), I do with all my heart gratify the signs of affection and courtesy which you have used towards me, and wish heartily that I were in terms to serve with more than my will the good-will you bear towards me, as your courteous entertainment denotes; but my fate is so niggardly as it affords me no other means to repay good works done to me, than only to lend me a good desire sometime to satisfy them.'

'So great is mine affection,' replied Don Quixote, 'to serve you, as I was fully resolved never to depart out of these mountains until I had found you, and known of yourself whether there might be any kind of remedy found for the grief that this your so unusual a kind of life argues doth possess your soul; and, if it were requisite, to search it out with all possible diligence; and when your disasters were known of those which clap their doors in the face of comfort, I intended in that case to bear a part in your lamentations, and plain it with the doleful note; for it is a consolation in affliction to have one that condoles in them. And, if this my good intention may merit any acceptance, or be gratified by any courtesy, let me entreat you, sir, by the excess thereof which I see accumulated in your bosom, and jointly I conjure you by that thing which you have, or do presently most affect, that you will please to disclose unto me who you are, and what the cause hath been that persuaded you to come to live and die in these deserts like a brute beast, seeing you live among such, so alienated from yourself, as both your attire and countenance demonstrate. And I do vow,' quoth Don Quixote, 'by the high order of chivalry which I, although unworthy and a sinner, have received, and by the profession of knights-errant, that if you do pleasure me herein, to assist you with as good earnest as my profession doth bind me, either by remedying your disaster, if it can be holpen, or else by assisting you to lament it, if it be so desperate.'

The Knight of the Rock, who heard him of the Ill-favoured Face speak in that manner, did nothing else for a great while but behold him again and again, and re-behold him from top to toe. And, after viewing him well, he said: 'If you have anything to eat, I pray you give it me for God's sake, and after I have eaten I will satisfy your demand thoroughly, to gratify the many courtesies and undeserved proffers you have made unto me.' Sancho, and the goatherd present, the one out of his wallet, the other out of his scrip, took some meat, and gave it to the Knight of the Rock, to allay his hunger; and he did eat so fast, like a distracted man, as he left no intermission between bit and bit, but clapt them up so swiftly, as he rather seemed to swallow than to chew them; and whilst he did eat, neither he nor any of the rest spake a word; and having ended his dinner, he made them signs to follow him, as at last they did, unto a little meadow seated hard by that place, at the fold of a mountain, where being arrived, he stretched himself on the grass, which the rest did likewise in his imitation, without speaking a word until that he, after settling himself in his place, began in this manner: 'If, sirs, you please to hear the exceeding greatness of my disasters briefly rehearsed, you must promise me that you will not interrupt the file of my doleful narration with either demand or other thing; for in the very instant that you shall do it, there also must remain that which I say depending.' These words of our ragged knight's called to Don Quixote's remembrance the tale which his squire had told unto him, where he erred in the account of his goats which had passed the river, for which that history remained suspended. But returning to our ragged man, he said: 'This prevention which now I give is to the end that I may compendiously pass over the discourse of my mishaps; for the revoking of them to remembrance only serves me to none other stead than to increase the old by adding of new misfortunes; and by how much the fewer your questions are, by so much the more speedily shall I have finished my pitiful discourse; and yet I mean not to omit the essential point of my woes untouched, that your desires may be herein sufficiently satisfied.' Don Quixote, in his own and his other companion's name, promised to perform his request; whereupon he began his relation on this manner:

'My name is Cardenio, the place of my birth one of the best cities in Andalusia, my lineage noble, my parents rich, and my misfortunes so great as I think my parents have ere this deplored and my kinsfolk condoled them, being very little able with their wealth to redress them; for the goods of fortune are but of small virtue to remedy the disasters of heaven. There dwelt in the same city a heaven, wherein love had placed all the glory that I could desire; so great is the beauty of Lucinda, a damsel as noble and rich as I, but more fortunate, and less constant than my honourable desires expected. I loved, honoured, and adored this Lucinda almost from my very infancy, and she affected me likewise, with all the integrity and good-will which with her so young years did accord. Our parents knew our mutual amity, for which they were nothing aggrieved, perceiving very well, that although we continued it, yet could it have none other end but that of matrimony: a thing which the equality of our blood and substance did of itself almost invite us to. Our age and affection increased in such sort, as it seemed fit for Lucinda's father, for certain good respects, to deny me the entrance of his house any longer, imitating in a manner therein Thisbe, so much solemnised by the poets, her parents; which hindrance served only to add flame to flame, and desire to desire; for, although it set silence to our tongues, yet would they not impose it to our pens, which are wont to express to whom it pleased, the most hidden secrecies of our souls, with more liberty than the tongue; for the presence of the beloved doth often distract, trouble, and strike dumb the boldest tongue and firmest resolution. O heavens! how many letters have I written unto her! What cheerful and honest answers have I received! How many ditties and amorous verses have I composed, wherein my soul declared and published her passions, declined her inflamed desires, entertained her remembrance, and recreated her will! In effect, perceiving myself to be forced, and that my soul consumed with a perpetual desire to behold her, I resolved to put my desires in execution, and finish in an instant that which I deemed most expedient for the better achieving of my desired and deserved reward; which was (as I did indeed), to demand her of her father for my lawful spouse.'

'To which he made answer, that he did gratify the good-will which I showed by honouring him, and desire to honour myself with pawns that were his; but, seeing my father yet lived, the motion of that matter properly most concerned him: for, if it were not done with his good liking and pleasure, Lucinda was not a woman to be taken or given by stealth. I rendered him thanks for his good-will, his words seeming unto me very reasonable, as that my father should agree unto them as soon as I should explain the matter; and therefore departed presently to acquaint him with my desires: who, at the time which I entered into a chamber wherein he was, stood with a letter open in his hand; and, espying me, ere I could break my mind unto him, gave it me, saying, "By that letter, Cardenio, you may gather the desire that Duke Ricardo bears to do you any pleasure or favour."

'This Duke Ricardo, as I think you know, sirs, already, is a grandee of Spain, whose dukedom is seated in the best part of all Andalusia. I took the letter and read it, which appeared so urgent, as I myself accounted it would be ill done if my father did not accomplish the contents thereof, which were indeed, that he should presently address me to his court, to the end I might be companion (and not servant) to his eldest son; and that he would incharge himself with the advancing of me to such preferments as might be answerable unto the value and estimation he made of my person. I passed over the whole letter, and was strucken dumb at the reading thereof, but chiefly hearing my father to say, "Cardenio, thou must depart within two days, to accomplish the duke's desire, and omit not to render Almighty God thanks, which doth thus open the way by which thou mayst attain in fine to that which I know thou dost merit." And to these words added certain others of fatherly counsel and direction. The term of my departure arrived, and I spoke to my Lucinda on a certain night, and recounted unto her all that passed, and likewise to her father, entreating them to overslip a few days, and defer the bestowing of his daughter elsewhere, until I went to understand Duke Ricardo his will; which he promised me, and she confirmed it, with a thousand oaths and promises.

'Finally, I came to Duke Ricardo's court, and was so friendly received and entertained by him, as even then very envy began to exercise her accustomed function, being forthwith emulated by the ancient servitors, persuading themselves that the tokens the duke showed to do me favours could not but turn to their prejudice. But he that rejoiced most at mine arrival was a second son of the duke's, called Fernando, who was young, gallant, very comely, liberal, and amorous; who, within a while after my coming, held me so dearly as every one wondered thereat; and although the elder loved me well, and did me favour, yet was it in no respect comparable to that wherewithal Don Fernando loved and treated me. It therefore befel that, as there is no secrecy amongst friends so great but they will communicate it the one to the other, and the familiarity which I had with Don Fernando was now past the limits of favour and turned into dearest amity, he revealed unto me all his thoughts, but chiefly one of his love, which did not a little molest him; for he was enamoured on a farmer's daughter, that was his father's vassal, whose parents were marvellous rich, and she herself so beautiful, wary, discreet, and honest, as never a one that knew her could absolutely determine wherein or in which of all her perfections she did most excel, or was most accomplished. And those good parts of the beautiful country maid reduced Don Fernando his desires to such an exigent, as he resolved, that he might the better gain her good-will and conquer her integrity, to pass her a promise of marriage; for otherwise he should labour to effect that which was impossible, and but strive against the stream. I, as one bound thereunto by our friendship, did thwart and dissuade him from his purpose with the best reasons and most efficacious words I might; and, seeing all could not prevail, I determined to acquaint the Duke Ricardo his father wherewithal. But Don Fernando, being very crafty and discreet, suspected and feared as much, because he considered that, in the law of a faithful servant, I was bound not to conceal a thing that would turn so much to the prejudice of the duke, my lord; and therefore, both to divert and deceive me at once, [he said] that he could find no means so good to deface the remembrance of that beauty out of his mind, which held his heart in such subjection, than to absent himself for certain months; and he would likewise have that absence to be this, that both of us should depart together, and come to my father's house, under pretence (as he would inform the duke) that he went to see and cheapen certain great horses that were in the city wherein I was born, a place of breeding the best horses in the world.

'Scarce had I heard him say this, when (borne away by the natural propension each one hath to his country, and my love joined) although his designment had not been so good, yet would I have ratified it, as one of the most expedient that could be imagined, because I saw occasion and opportunity so fairly offered, to return and see again my Lucinda; and therefore, set on by this thought and desire, I approved his opinion, and did quicken his purpose, persuading him to prosecute it with all possible speed; for absence would in the end work her effect in despite of the most forcible and urgent thoughts. And when he said this to me, he had already, under the title of a husband (as it was afterward known), reaped the fruits of his longing desires from his beautiful country maid, and did only await an opportunity to reveal it without his own detriment, fearful of the duke his father's indignation when he should understand his error.

'It afterwards happened that, as love in young men is not for the most part love, but lust, the which (as [that which] it ever proposeth to itself as his last end and period is delight) so soon as it obtaineth the same, it likewise decayeth and maketh forcibly to retire that which was termed love; for it cannot transgress the limits which Nature hath assigned it, which boundings or measures Nature hath in no wise allotted to true and sincere affection,—I would say that, as soon as Don Fernando had enjoyed his country lass, his desires weakened, and his importunities waxed cold; and if at the first he feigned an excuse to absent himself, that he might with more facility compass them, he did now in very good earnest procure to depart, to the end he might not put them in execution. The duke gave him licence to depart, and commanded me to accompany him. We came to my city, where my father entertained him according to his calling. I saw Lucinda, and then again were revived (although, indeed, they were neither dead nor mortified) my desires, and I acquainted Don Fernando (alas! to my total ruin) with them, because I thought it was not lawful, by the law of amity, to keep anything concealed from him. There I dilated to him on the beauty, wit, and discretion of Lucinda, in so ample a manner as my praise stirred in him a desire to view a damsel so greatly adorned, and enriched with so rare endowments. And this his desire I (through my misfortune) satisfied, showing her unto him by the light of a candle, at a window where we two were wont to parley together; where he beheld her to be such as was sufficient to blot out of his memory all the beauties which ever he had viewed before. He stood mute, beside himself, and ravished; and, moreover, rested so greatly enamoured, as you may perceive in the discourse of this my doleful narration. And, to inflame his desires the more (a thing which I fearfully avoided, and only discovered to Heaven), fortune so disposed that he found after me one of her letters, wherein she requested that I would demand her of her father for wife, which was so discreet, honest, and amorously penned, as he said, after reading it, that in Lucinda alone were included all the graces of beauty and understanding jointly, which were divided and separate in all the other women of the world.

'Yet, in good sooth, I will here confess the truth, that although I saw clearly how deservedly Lucinda was thus extolled by Don Fernando, yet did not her praises please me so much pronounced by him; and therefore began to fear and suspect him, because he let no moment overslip us without making some mention of Lucinda, and would still himself begin the discourse, were the occasion never so far-fetched: a thing which roused in me I cannot tell what jealousy; not that I did fear any traverse in Lucinda's loyalty, but yet, for all, my fates made me the very thing which they most assured me. And Don Fernando procured to read all the papers I sent to Lucinda, or she to me, under pretext that he took extraordinary delight to note the witty conceits of us both. It therefore fell out, that Lucinda, having demanded of me a book of chivalry to read, wherein she took marvellous delight, and was that of Amadis de Gaul'—

Scarce had Don Quixote well heard him make mention of books of knighthood when he replied to him: 'If you had, good sir, but once told me at the beginning of your historical narration that your Lady Lucinda was affected to the reading of knightly adventures, you needed not to have used any amplification to endear or make plain unto me the eminency of her wit, which certainly could not in any wise be so excellent and perspicuous as you have figured it, if she wanted the propension and feeling you have rehearsed to the perusing of so pleasing discourses; so that henceforth, with me, you need not spend any more words to explain and manifest the height of her beauty, worth, and understanding; for by this only notice I have received of her devotion to books of knighthood, I do confirm her for the most fair and accomplished woman for all perfection in the world; and I would to God, good sir, that you had also sent her, together with Amadis, the histories of the good Don Rugel of Grecia; for I am certain the Lady Lucinda would have taken great delight in Darayda and Garaya, and in the witty conceits of the shepherd Darinel, and in those admirable verses of his Bucolics, sung and rehearsed by him with such grace, discretion, and liberty. But a time may come wherein this fault may be recompensed, if it shall please you to come with me to my village; for there I may give you three hundred books, which are my soul's greatest contentment, and the entertainment of my life,—although I do now verily believe that none of them are left, thanks be to the malice of evil and envious enchanters. And I beseech you to pardon me this transgression of our agreement at the first promised, not to interrupt your discourses; for when I hear any motion made of chivalry or knights-errant, it is no more in my power to omit to speak of them than in the sunbeams to leave off warming, or in the moon to render things humid. And therefore I entreat pardon, and that you will prosecute your history, as that which most imports us.'

Whilst Don Quixote spoke those words, Cardenio hung his head on his breast, giving manifest tokens that he was exceeding sad. And although Don Quixote requested him twice to follow on with his discourse, yet neither did he lift up his head or answer a word, till at last, after he had stood a good while musing, he held up his head and said: 'It cannot be taken out of my mind, nor is there any one in the world can deprive me of the conceit, or make me believe the contrary, and he were a bottlehead that would think or believe otherwise, than that the great villain, Master Elisabat the barber, kept Queen Madasima as his leman.'

'That is not so, I vow by such and such!' quoth Don Quixote, in great choler (and as he was wont, rapped out three or four round oaths); 'it is great malice, or rather villany, to say such a thing; for Queen Madasima was a very noble lady, and it ought not to be presumed that so high a princess would fall in love with a quack-salver; and whosoever thinks the contrary lies like an errant villain, as I will make him understand, a-horseback or afoot, armed or disarmed, by night or by day, or as he best liketh.' Cardenio stood beholding him very earnestly as he spoke these words, whom the accident of his madness had by this possessed, and was not in plight to prosecute his history; nor would Don Quixote give ear to it, he was so mightily disgusted to hear Queen Madasima detracted.

A marvellous accident! for he took her defence as earnestly as if she were verily his true and natural princess, his wicked books had so much distracted him. And Cardenio being by this furiously mad, hearing himself answered with the lie, and the denomination of a villain, with other the like outrages, he took the rest in ill part, and, lifting up a stone that was near unto him, gave Don Quixote such a blow therewithal as he overthrew him to the ground on his back. Sancho Panza, seeing his master so roughly handled, set upon the fool with his fist shut; and the ragged man received his assault in such manner, as he likewise overthrew him at his feet with one fist, and, mounting afterward upon him, did work him with his feet like a piece of dough; and the goatherd, who thought to succour him, was like to incur the same danger. And after he had overthrown and beaten them all very well, he departed from them, and entered into the wood very quietly. Sancho arose; and with rage to see himself so belaboured without desert, he ran upon the goatherd to be revenged on him, saying that he was in the fault, who had not premonished them how that man's raving fits did take him so at times; for, had they been advertised thereof, they might have stood all the while on their guard.

The goatherd answered that he had already advised them thereof, and if he had not been attentive thereunto, yet he was therefore nothing the more culpable.

Sancho Panza replied, and the goatherd made a rejoinder thereunto; but their disputation ended at last in the catching hold of one another's beards, and befisting themselves so uncompassionately, as if Don Quixote had not pacified them, they would have torn one another to pieces. Sancho, holding still the goatherd fast, said unto his lord, 'Let me alone, sir Knight of the Ill-favoured Face; for on this man, who is a clown as I am myself, and no dubbed knight, I may safely satisfy myself of the wrong he hath done me, by fighting with him hand to hand, like an honourable man.' 'It is true,' quoth Don Quixote; 'but I know well that he is in no wise culpable of that which hath happened.' And, saying so, appeased them, and turned again to demand of the goatherd whether it were possible to meet again with Cardenio; for he remained possessed with an exceeding desire to know the end of his history.

The goatherd turned again to repeat what he had said at the first, to wit, that he knew not any certain place of his abode; but if he haunted that commark any while, he would some time meet with him, either in his mad or modest humour.

CHAPTER XI

Which Treats of the Strange Adventures That Happened to the Knight of the Mancha in Sierra Morena; and of the Penance He Did There, in Imitation of Beltenebros

DON QUIXOTE took leave of the goatherd, and, mounting once again on Rozinante, he commanded Sancho to follow him, who obeyed but with a very ill will: and thus they travelled by little and little, entering into the thickest and roughest part of all the mountain; and Sancho went almost burst with a desire to reason with his master, and therefore wished in mind that he would once begin, that he might not transgress his commandment of silence imposed on him, but growing at last wholly impotent to contain himself speechless any longer: 'Good sir Don Quixote, I pray you give me your blessing and licence; for I mean to depart from this place, and return to my house, my wife and children, with whom I shall be, at least, admitted to reason and speak my pleasure; for that you would desire to have me keep you company through these deserts night and day, and that I may not speak when I please, is but to bury me alive. Yet, if fortune had so happily disposed our affairs as that beasts could speak, as they did in Guisopete's time, the harm had been less; for then would I discourse a while with Rozinante (seeing my niggardly fortune hath not consented I might do it with mine ass) what I thought good, and in this sort would I waive my mishaps; for it is a stubborn thing, and that cannot be borne with patience, to travel all the days of our life, and not to encounter any other thing than tramplings under feet, tossings in coverlets, blows of stones and buffets, and be besides all this forced to sew up our mouths, a man daring not to break his mind, but to stand mute like a post.' 'Sancho, I understand thee now,' quoth Don Quixote; 'thou diest with longing to speak that which I have forbidden thee to speak; account, therefore, that commandment revoked, and say what thou pleasest, on condition that this revocation be only available and of force whilst we dwell in these mountains, and no longer.'

'So be it,' quoth Sancho; 'let me speak now, for what may after befall, God only knows.' And then, beginning to take the benefit of his licence, he said, 'I pray you, tell me what benefit could you reap by taking Queen Madasima's part? or what was it to the purpose that that abbot was her friend or no? For, if you had let it slip, seeing you were not his judge, I verily believe that the fool had prosecuted his tale, and we should have escaped the blow of the stone, the trampling under feet, and spurnings; yea, and more than five or six good buffets.' 'In faith, Sancho,' quoth Don Quixote, 'if thou knewest as well as I did how honourable and principal a lady was Queen Madasima, thou wouldst rather say that I had great patience, seeing I did not strike him on the mouth out of which such blasphemies issued; for it is a very great dishonour to aver or think that any queen would fall in love with a barber. For the truth of the history is, that Master Elisabat, of whom the madman spoke, was very prudent, and a man of a sound judgment, and served the queen as her tutor and physician; but to think that she was his leman is a madness worthy the severest punishment; and to the end thou mayst see that Cardenio knew not what he said, thou must understand that when he spoke it he then was wholly beside himself.'

'That's it which I say,' quoth Sancho, 'that you ought not to make account of words spoken by a fool; for if fortune had not assisted you, but addressed the stone to your head, as it did to your breast, we should have remained in good plight, for having turned so earnestly in that my lady's defence, whom God confound. And think you that Cardenio would not escape the dangers of the law, by reason of his madness?' 'Any knight-errant,' answered Don Quixote, 'is bound to turn for the honour of women, of what quality soever, against mad or unmad men; how much more for queens of so high degree and worth as was Queen Madasima, to whom I bear particular affections for her good parts? For, besides her being marvellous beautiful, she was, moreover, very prudent and patient in her calamities, which were very many; and the company and counsels of Master Elisabat proved very beneficial and necessary, to induce her to bear her mishaps with prudence and patience: and hence the ignorant and ill-meaning vulgar took occasion to suspect and affirm that she was his friend. But I say again they lie, and all those that do either think or say it, do lie a thousand times.'

'Why,' quoth Sancho, 'I neither say it nor think it. Let those affirm any such thing, eat that lie and swallow it with their bread; and if they of whom you speak lived lightly, they have given account to God thereof by this. I come from my vineyard; I know nothing. I am not afraid to know other men's lives; for he that buys and lies shall feel it in his purse. How much more, seeing I was born naked, and am now naked, I can neither win nor lose! A man is but a man, though he have a hose on his head; but howsoever, what is that to me? And many think there is a sheep where there is no fleece. But who shall bridle a man's understanding, when men are profane?' 'Good God!' quoth Don Quixote, 'how many follies hast thou inserted here! and how wide from our purpose are those proverbs which thou hast recited! Honest Sancho, hold thy peace; and from henceforth endeavour to serve thy master, and do not meddle with things which concern thee nothing; and understand, with all thy five senses, that whatsoever I have done, do, or shall do, is wholly guided by reason, and conformable to the rules of knighthood, which I know better than all the other knights that ever professed them in the world.' 'Sir,' quoth Sancho, 'and is it a good rule of chivalry that we go wandering and lost among these mountains in this sort, without path or way, in the search of a madman, to whom peradventure, after he is found, will return a desire to finish what he began, not of his tale, but of your head and my ribs, by endeavouring to break them soundly and thoroughly?'

'Peace, I say, Sancho, once again,' quoth Don Quixote; 'for thou must wit that the desire of finding the madman alone brings me not into these parts so much, as that which I have in my mind to achieve a certain adventure, by which I shall acquire eternal renown and fame throughout the universal face of the earth; and I shall therewithal seal all that which may render a knight-errant complete and famous.' 'And is the adventure very dangerous?' quoth Sancho Panza. 'No,' answered the Knight of the Ill-favoured Face, 'although the die might run in such sort as we might cast a hazard instead of an encounter; but all consists in thy diligence.' 'In mine?' quoth Sancho. 'Yes,' quoth Don Quixote; 'for if thou returnest speedily from the place whereunto I mean to send thee, my pain will also end shortly, and my glory commence very soon after. And because I will not hold thee long suspended, awaiting to hear the effect of my words, I would have thee to know that the famous Amadis de Gaul was one of the most accomplished knights-errant,—I do not say well saying he was one; for he was the only, the first, and prime lord of as many as lived in his age. An evil year and a worse month for Don Belianis, or any other that shall dare presume to compare with him, for I swear that they all are, questionless, deceived. I also say, that when a painter would become rare and excellent in his art, he procures to imitate the patterns of the most singular masters of his science; and this very rule runs current throughout all other trades and exercises of account which serve to adorn a well-disposed commonwealth; and so ought and doth he that means to obtain the name of a prudent and patient man, by imitating Ulysses, in whose person and dangers doth Homer delineate unto us the true portraiture of patience and sufferance; as likewise Virgil demonstrates, under the person of Aeneas, the duty and valour of a pious son, and the sagacity of a hardy and expert captain, not showing them such as indeed they were, but as they should be, to remain as an example of virtue to ensuing posterities. And in this very manner was Amadis the north star and the sun of valorous and amorous knights, whom all we ought to imitate which march under the ensigns of love and chivalry. And this being so manifest as it is, I find, friend Sancho, that the knight-errant who shall imitate him most shall likewise be nearest to attain the perfection of arms. And that wherein this knight bewrayed most his prudence, valour, courage, patience, constancy, and love, was when he retired himself to do penance, being disdained by his lady Oriana, to the Poor Rock, changing his name unto that of Beltenebros: a name certainly most significative and proper for the life which he had at that time willingly chosen. And I may more easily imitate him herein than in cleaving of giants, beheading of serpents, killing of monsters, overthrowing of armies, putting navies to flight, and finishing of enchantments. And seeing that this mountain is so fit for that purpose, there is no reason why I should overslip the occasion, which doth so commodiously proffer me her locks.'

'In effect,' quoth Sancho, 'what is it you mean to do in these remote places?' 'Have not I told thee already,' said Don Quixote, 'that I mean to follow Amadis, by playing here the despaired, wood, and furious man? To imitate likewise the valiant Orlando, where he found the tokens by a fountain that Angelica the fair had abused herself with Medozo; for grief whereof he ran mad, and plucked up trees by their roots, troubled the waters of clear fountains, slew shepherds, destroyed their flocks, fired the sheepfolds, overthrew houses, trailed mares after him, and committed a hundred thousand other insolences, worthy of eternal fame and memory. And although I mean not to imitate Roldan, or Orlando, or Rowland (for he had all these names), exactly in every mad prank that he played, yet will I do it the best I can in those things which shall seem unto me most essential. And perhaps I may rest contented with the only imitation of Amadis, who, without endamaging, and by his ravings, and only using these of feeling laments, [arrived] to as great fame thereby as anyone whatsoever.'

'I believe,' replied Sancho, 'that the knights which performed the like penances were moved by some reasons to do the like austerities and follies; but, good sir, what occasion hath been offered unto you to become mad? What lady hath disdained you? Or what arguments have you found that the Lady Dulcinea of Toboso hath ever dallied with Moor or Christian?' 'There is the point,' answered our knight, 'and therein consists the perfection of mine affairs; for that a knight-errant do run mad upon any just occasion deserves neither praise nor thanks; the wit is in waxing mad without cause, whereby my mistress may understand, that if dry I could do this, what would I have done being watered? How much more, seeing I have a just motive, through the prolix absence that I have made from my ever supremest Lady Dulcinea of Toboso? For, as thou mightest have heard read in Marias Ambrosio his Shepherd,—

"To him that absent is,
All things succeed amiss."

So that, friend Sancho, I would not have thee lavish time longer in advising to let slip so rare, so happy, and singular an imitation. I am mad, and will be mad, until thou return again with answer upon a letter, which I mean to send with thee to my Lady Dulcinea; and if it be such as my loyalty deserves, my madness and penance shall end; but if the contrary, I shall run mad in good earnest, and be in that state that I shall apprehend nor feel anything. So that, howsoever I be answered, I shall issue out of the conflict and pain wherein thou leavest me, by joying the good thou shalt bring me, as wise; or not feeling the evil thou shalt denounce, as mad. But tell me, Sancho, keepest thou charily yet the helmet of Mambrino, which I saw thee take up from the ground the other day, when that ungrateful fellow thought to have broken it into pieces, but could not, by which may be collected the excellent temper thereof?'

Sancho answered to this demand, saying, 'I cannot suffer or bear longer, sir Knight of the Ill-favoured Face, nor take patiently many things which you say; and I begin to suspect, by your words, that all that which you have said to me of chivalry, and of gaining kingdoms and empires, of bestowing islands and other gifts and great things, as knights-errant are wont, are all matters of air and lies, all cozenage or cozening, or how else you please to term it; for he that shall hear you name a barber's basin Mambrino's helmet, and that you will not abandon that error in more than four days, what other can he think but that he who affirms such a thing doth want wit and discretion? I carry the basin in my bag, all battered and bored, and will have it mended, and dress my beard in it at home, if God shall do me the favour that I may one day see my wife and bairns.'

'Behold, Sancho,' quoth Don Quixote, 'I do likewise swear that thou hast the shallowest pate that ever any squire had or hath in the world. Is it possible that, in all the time thou hast gone with me, thou couldst not perceive that all the adventures of knights-errant do appear chimeras, follies, and desperate things, being quite contrary? Not that they are indeed such; but rather, by reason that we are still haunted by a crew of enchanters, which change and transform our acts, making them seem what they please, according as they like to favour or annoy us; and so this, which seems to thee a barber's basin, is in my conceit Mambrino his helmet, and to another will appear in some other shape. And it is doubtlessly done by the profound science of the wise man my friend, to make that seem a basin which, really and truly, is Mambrino's helmet; because that, in being so precious a jewel, all the world would pursue me to deprive me of it; but now, seeing that it is so like a barber's basin, they endeavour not to gain it, as was clearly showed in him that thought to break it the other day, and would not carry it with him, but left it lying behind him on the ground; for, in faith, he had never left it did he know the worthiness thereof. Keep it, friend; for I need it not at this present, wherein I must rather disarm myself of the arms I wear, and remain as naked as I was at the hour of my birth, if I shall take the humour rather to imitate Orlando in doing of my penance than Amadis.'

Whilst thus he discoursed, he arrived to the foot of a lofty mountain, which stood like a hewn rock divided from all the rest, by the skirt whereof glided a smooth river, hemmed in on every side by a green and flourishing meadow, whose verdure did marvellously delight the greedy beholding eye; there were in it also many wild trees, and some plants and flowers, which rendered the place much more pleasing. The Knight of the Ill-favoured Face made choice of this place to accomplish therein his penance; and therefore, as soon as he had viewed it, he began to say, with a loud voice, like a distracted man, these words ensuing: 'This is the place where the humour of mine eyes shall increase the liquid veins of this crystal current, and my continual and deep sighs shall give perpetual motion to the leaves of these mountainy trees, in testimony of the pain which my oppressed heart doth suffer. O you, whosoever you be, rustical gods! which have your mansion in this inhabitable place, give ear to the plaints of this unfortunate lover, whom a long absence and a few imagined suspicions have conducted to deplore his state among these deserts, and make him exclaim on the rough condition of that ingrate and fair, who is the top, the sun, the period, term, and end of all human beauty. O ye Napeas and Dryads! which do wontedly inhabit the thickets and groves, so may the nimble and lascivious satyrs, by whom (although in vain) you are beloved, never have power to interrupt your sweet rest, as you shall assist me to lament my disasters, or at least attend them, whilst I dolefully breathe them. O Dulcinea of Toboso! the day of my night, the glory of my pain, north of my travels, and star of my fortunes; so Heaven enrich thee with the highest, whensoever thou shalt demand it, as thou wilt consider the place and pass unto which thine absence hath conducted me, and answer my faith and desires in compassionate and gracious manner. O solitary trees (which shall from henceforward keep company with my solitude), give tokens, with the soft motion of your boughs, that my presence doth not dislike you. O thou my squire, and grateful companion in all prosperous and adverse successes! bear well away what thou shalt see me do here, to the end that thou mayst after promptly recount it as the total cause of my ruin.' And, saying so, he alighted from Rozinante, and, taking off in a trice his bridle and saddle, he struck him on the buttock, saying, 'He gives thee liberty that wants it himself, O horse! as famous for thy works as thou art unfortunate by thy fates. Go where thou pleasest; for thou bearest written in thy forehead, how that neither the Hippogriff of Astolpho, nor the renowned Frontino, which cost Bradamante so dearly, could compare with thee for swiftness.'

When Sancho had viewed and heard his lord speak thus, he likewise said, 'Good betide him that freed us from the pains of unpannelling the grey ass; for if he were here, in faith, he should also have two or three claps on the buttocks, and a short oration in his praise. Yet if he were here, I would not permit any other to unpannel him, seeing there was no occasion why; for he, good beast, was nothing subject to the passions of love or despair, no more than I, who was his master when it pleased God. And, in good sooth, sir Knight of the Ill-favoured Face, if my departure and your madness be in good earnest, it will be needful to saddle Rozinante again, that he may supply the want of mine ass; for it will shorten the time of my departure and return again. And if I make my voyage afoot, I know not when I shall arrive there, or return here back unto you; for, in good earnest, I am a very ill footman.'

'Let it be as thou likest,' quoth Don Quixote; 'for thy design displeaseth me nothing; and therefore I resolve that thou shalt depart from hence after three days; for in the mean space thou shalt behold what I will do and say for my lady's sake, to the end thou mayst tell it to her.' 'Why,' quoth Sancho, 'what more can I view than that which I have seen already?' 'Thou art altogether wide of the matter,' answered Don Quixote; 'for I must yet tear mine apparel, throw away mine armour, and beat my head about these rocks, with many other things of that kind that will strike thee into admiration.' 'Let me beseech you,' quoth Sancho, 'see well how you give yourself those knocks about the rocks; for you might happen upon some one so ungracious a rock, as at the first rap would dissolve all the whole *machina* of your adventures and penance; and, therefore, I would be of opinion, seeing that you do hold it necessary that some knocks be given with the head, and that this enterprise cannot be accomplished without them, that you content yourself, seeing that all is but feigned, counterfeited, and a jest,—that you should, I say, content yourself with striking it on the water, or on some other soft thing, as cotton or wool, and leave to my charge the exaggeration thereof; for I will tell to my lady that you strike your head against the point of a rock which was harder than a diamond.'

'I thank thee, Sancho, for thy good will,' quoth Don Quixote; 'but I can assure thee that all these things which I do are no jests, but very serious earnests; for otherwise we should transgress the statutes of chivalry, which command us not to avouch any untruth, on pain of relapse; and to do one thing for another is as much as to lie. So that my head-knocks must be true, firm, and sound ones, without any sophistical or fantastical shadow: and it will be requisite that you leave me some lint to cure me, seeing that fortune hath deprived us of the balsam which we lost.' 'It was worse to have lost the ass,' quoth Sancho, 'seeing that at once, with him, we have lost our lint and all our other provision; and I entreat you most earnestly not to name again that accursed drink; for in only hearing it mentioned, you not only turn my guts in me, but also my soul. And I request you, moreover, to make account that the term of three days is already expired, wherein you would have me take notice of your follies; for I declare them already for seen, and will tell wonders to my lady: wherefore, go write your letter, and despatch me with all haste; for I long already to return, and take you out of this purgatory wherein I leave you.'

'Dost thou call it a purgatory, Sancho?' quoth Don Quixote. 'Thou hadst done better hadst thou called it hell; or rather worse, if there be anything worse than that.' 'I call it so,' quoth Sancho; '"*Quia in inferno nulla est retentio,*" as I have heard say.'

'I understand not,' said Don Quixote, 'what *retentio* meaneth.' '*Retentio,*' quoth Sancho, 'is that, whosoever is in hell, never comes, nor can come, out of it. Which shall fall out contrary in your person, or my feet shall go ill, if I may carry spurs to quicken Rozinante, and that I may safely arrive before my Lady Dulcinea in Toboso; for I will recount unto her such strange things of your follies and madness (for they be all one) that you have, and do daily, as I will make her as soft as a glove, although I found her at the first harder than a cork-tree; with whose sweet and honey answer I will return in the air as speedily as a witch, and take you out of this purgatory, which is no hell, although it seems one, seeing there is hope to escape from it; which, as I have said, they want which are in hell; and I believe you will not contradict me herein.'

'Thou hast reason,' answered the Knight of the Ill-favoured Face; 'but how shall I write the letter?' 'And the warrant for the receipt of the colts also?' added Sancho. 'All shall be inserted together,' quoth Don Quixote; 'and seeing we have no paper, we may do well, imitating the ancient men of times past, to write our mind in the leaves of trees or wax; yet wax is as hard to be found here as paper. But, now that I remember myself, I know where we may write our mind well, and more than well, to wit, in Cardenio's tablets, and thou shalt have care to cause the letters to be written out again fairly, in the first village wherein thou shalt find a schoolmaster; or, if such a one be wanting, by the clerk of the church; and beware in any sort that thou give it not to a notary or court-clerk to be copied, for they write such an entangling, confounded process letter, as Satan himself would scarce be able to read it.' 'And how shall we do for want of your name and subscription?' quoth Sancho. 'Why,' answered Don Quixote, 'Amadis was never wont to subscribe to his letters.' 'Ay, but the warrant to receive the three asses must forcibly be subsigned; and if it should afterward be copied, they would say the former is false, and so I shall rest without my colts.' 'The warrant shall be written and firmed with my hand in the tablets, which, as soon as my niece shall see, she shall make no difficulty to deliver thee them. And as concerning the love-letter, thou shalt put this subscription to it, "Yours until death, the Knight of the Ill-favoured Face." And it makes no matter though it be written by any stranger; forasmuch as I can remember Dulcinea can neither write nor read, nor hath she seen any letter, no, not so much as a character of my writing all the days of her life; for my love and hers have been ever Platonical, never extending themselves further than to an honest regard and view the one of the other, and even this same so rarely, as I dare boldly swear, that in these dozen years which I love her more dearly than the light of these mine eyes, which the earth shall one day devour, I have not seen her four times, and perhaps of those same four times she hath scarce perceived once that I beheld her—such is the care and closeness wherewithal her parents, Lorenzo Corcuelo and her mother Aldonza Nogales, have brought her up.' 'Ta, ta,' quoth Sancho, 'that the Lady Dulcinea of Toboso is Lorenzo Corcuelo his daughter, called by another name Aldonza Lorenzo?' 'The same is she,' quoth Don Quixote, 'and it is she that merits to be empress of the vast universe.' 'I know her very well,' replied Sancho, 'and I dare say that she can throw an iron bar as well as any the strongest lad in our parish. I vow, by the giver, that 'tis a wench of the mark, tall and stout, and so sturdy withal, that she will bring her chin out of the mire, in despite of any knight-errant, or that shall err, that shall honour her as his lady. Out upon her! what a strength and voice she hath! I saw her on a day stand on the top of the church-steeple, to call certain servants of her father's, that laboured in a fallow field; and although they were half a league from thence, they heard her as well as if they were at the foot of the steeple. And the best that is in her is that she is nothing coy; for she hath a very great smack of courtship, and plays with every one, and gibes and jests at them all. And now I affirm, sir Knight of the Ill-favoured Face, that not only you may and ought to commit raving follies for her sake, but eke you may, with just title, also despair and hang yourself; for none shall hear thereof but will say you did very well, although the devil carried you away. And fain would I be gone, if it were for nothing else but to see her; for it is many a day since I saw her, and I am sure she is changed by this; for women's beauty is much impaired by going always to the field, exposed to the sun and weather. And I will now, sir Don Quixote, confess a truth unto you, that I have lived until now in a marvellous error, thinking well and faithfully that the Lady Dulcinea was some great princess, on whom you were enamoured, or such a person as merited those rich presents which you bestowed on her, as well of the Biscaine as of the slaves, and many others, that ought to be, as I suppose, correspondent to the many victories which you have gained, both now and in the time that I was not your squire. But, pondering well the matter, I cannot conceive why the Lady Aldonza Lorenzo—I mean the Lady Dulcinea of Toboso, of these should care whether these vanquished men which you send, or shall send, do go and kneel before her; for it may befall that she, at the very time of their arrival, be combing of flax or threshing in the barn, whereat they would be ashamed, and she likewise laugh, and be somewhat displeased at the present.'

'I have oft told thee, Sancho, many times, that thou art too great a prattler,' quoth Don Quixote, 'and although thou hast but a gross wit, yet now and then thy frumps nip; but, to the end thou mayst perceive the faultiness of thy brain, and my discretion, I will tell thee a short history, which is this: There was once a widow, fair, young, free, rich, and withal very pleasant and jocund, that fell in love with a certain round and well-set servant of a college. His regent came to understand it, and therefore said on a day to the widow, by the way of fraternal correction, "Mistress, I do greatly marvel, and not without occasion, that a woman so principal, so beautiful, so rich, and specially so witty, could make so ill a choice, as to wax enamoured on so foul, so base, and foolish a man as such a one, we having in this house so many masters of art, graduates, and divines, amongst whom you might have made choice as among pears, saying, I will take this, and I will not have that." But she answered him thus, with a very pleasant and good grace: "You are, sir, greatly deceived, if you deem that I have made an ill choice in such a one, let him seem never so great a fool; for, to the purpose that I mean to use him, he knows as much or rather more philosophy than Aristotle." And so, Sancho, is likewise Dulcinea of Toboso as much worth as the highest princess of the world, for the effect I mean to use her. For all the poets which celebrate certain ladies at pleasure, thinkest thou that they all had mistresses? No. Dost thou believe that the Amaryllises, the Phyllises, Silvias, Dianas, Galateas, Alcidas, and others such like, wherewithal the books, ditties, barbers' shops, and theatres are filled, were truly ladies of flesh and bones, and their mistresses which have and do celebrate them thus? No, certainly; but were for the greater part feigned, to serve as a subject of their verses, to the end the authors might be accounted amorous, and men of courage enough to be such. And thus it is also sufficient for me to believe and think that the good Aldonza Lorenzo is fair and honest. As for her parentage, it matters but little; for none will send to take information thereof, to give her an habit; and I make account of her as of the greatest princess in the world. For thou oughtest to know, Sancho, if thou knowest it not already, that two things alone incite men to love more than all things else, and those be, surpassing beauty and a good name. And both these things are found in Dulcinea in her prime; for none can equal her in fairness, and few come near her for a good report. And, for a final conclusion, I imagine that all that which I say is really so, without adding or taking aught away. And I do imagine her, in my fantasy, to be such as I could wish her as well in beauty as principality, and neither can Helen approach, nor Lucrece come near her; no, nor any of those other famous women, Greek, Barbarous, or Latin, of foregoing ages. And let every one say what he pleaseth; for though I should be reprehended for this by the ignorant, yet shall I not, therefore, be chastised by the more observant and rigorous sort of men.'

'I avouch,' quoth Sancho, 'that you have great reason in all that you say, and that I am myself a very ass—but, alas! why do I name an ass with my mouth, seeing one should not mention a rope in one's house that was hanged? But give me the letter, and farewell; for I will change.' With that, Don Quixote drew out his tablets, and, going aside, began to indite his letter with great gravity; which ended, he called Sancho to read it to him, to the end he might bear it away in memory, lest by chance he did lose the tablets on the way; for such were his cross fortunes, as made him fear every event. To which Sancho answered, saying, 'Write it there twice or thrice in the book, and give me it after; for I will carry it safely, by God's grace. For to think that I will be able ever to take it by rote is a great folly; for my memory is so short as I do many times forget mine own name. But yet, for all that, read it to me, good sir; for I would be glad to hear it, as a thing which I suppose to be as excellent as if it were cast in a mould.' 'Hear it, then,' said Don Quixote; 'for thus it says:

'THE LETTER OF DON QUIXOTE TO DULCINEA OF TOBOSO

'SOVEREIGN LADY,—The wounded by the point of absence, and the hurt by the darts of thy heart, sweetest Dulcinea of Toboso! doth send thee that health which he wanteth himself. If thy beauty disdain me, if thy valour turn not to my benefit, if thy disdains convert themselves to my harm, maugre all my patience, I shall be ill able to sustain this care; which, besides that it is violent, is also too durable. My good squire Sancho will give thee certain relation, O beautiful ingrate, and my dearest beloved enemy! of the state wherein I remain for thy sake. If thou please to favour me, I am thine; and if not, do what thou likest: for, by ending of my life, I shall both satisfy thy cruelty and my desires.—Thine until death,

'THE KNIGHT OF THE ILL-FAVOURED FACE.'

'By my father's life,' quoth Sancho, when he heard the letter, 'it is the highest thing that ever I heard. Good God! how well do you say everything in it! and how excellently have you applied the subscription of "The Knight of the Ill-favoured Face!" I say again, in good earnest, that you are the devil himself, and there's nothing but you know it.' 'All is necessary,' answered Don Quixote, 'for the office that I profess.' 'Put, then,' quote Sancho, 'in the other side of that leaf, the warrant of three colts, and firm it with a legible letter that they may know it at the first sight.' 'I am pleased,' said Don Quixote. And so, writing it, he read it after to Sancho; and it said thus:

'You shall please, good niece, for this first of colts, to deliver unto my squire Sancho Panza, three of the five that I left at home, and are in your charge; the which three colts I command to be delivered to him, for as many others counted and received here; for with this, and his acquittance, they shall be justly delivered. Given in the bowels of Sierra Morena, the two-and-twentieth of August, of this present year——.'

'It goes very well,' quoth Sancho; 'subsign it, therefore, I pray you.' 'It needs no seal,' quoth Don Quixote, 'but only my rubric, which is as valuable as if it were subscribed not only for three asses, but also for three hundred.' 'My trust is in you,' answered Sancho; 'permit me, for I will go saddle Rozinante, and prepare yourself to give me your blessing; for I purpose presently to depart, before I see any mad prank of yours; for I will say that I saw you play so many, as no more can be desired.' 'I will have thee stay, Sancho (and that because it is requisite), at least to see me stark naked, playing a dozen or two of raving tricks; for I will despatch them in less than half an hour; because that thou, having viewed them with thine own eyes, mayst safely swear all the rest that thou pleasest to add; and I assure thee that thou canst not tell so many as I mean to perform.' 'Let me entreat you, good sir, that I may not see you naked; for it will turn my stomach, and I shall not be able to keep myself from weeping; and my head is yet so sore since yesternight, through my lamentations for the loss of the grey beast, as I am not strong enough yet to endure new plaints. But, if your pleasure be such as I must necessarily see some follies, do them, in Jove's name, in your clothes briefly, and such as are most necessary; chiefly, seeing none of these things are requisite for me. And, as I have said, we might excuse time (that shall now be lavished in these trifles) to return speedily with the news you desire and deserve so much. And if not, let the Lady Dulcinea provide herself well; for if she answer not according to reason, I make a solemn vow to him that I may, that I'll make her disgorge out of her stomach a good answer, with very kicks and fists; for how can it be suffered that so famous a knight-errant as yourself should thus run out of his wits, without, nor for what, for one——Let not the gentlewoman constrain me to say the rest; for I will out with it, and venture all upon twelve, although it never were sold.'

'In good faith, Sancho,' quoth Don Quixote, 'I think thou art grown as mad as myself,' 'I am not so mad,' replied Sancho, 'but I am more choleric. But, setting that aside, say, what will you eat until my return? Do you mean to do as Cardenio, and take by the highway's side perforce from the shepherds?' 'Care thou not for that,' replied Don Quixote; 'for although I had it, yet would I not eat any other thing than the herbs and fruits that this field and trees do yield; for the perfection of mine affair consists in fasting, and the exercise of other castigations.' To this Sancho replied: 'Do you know what I fear? that I shall not find the way to you again here where I leave you, it is so difficult and obscure.' 'Take well the marks, and I will endeavour to keep here about,' quoth Don Quixote, 'until thou come back again; and will, moreover, about the time of thy return, mount to the tops of these high rocks, to see whether thou appearest. But thou shouldst do best of all, to the end thou mayst not stay and miss me, to cut down here and there certain boughs, and strew them on the way as thou goest, until thou beest out in the plains, and those may after serve thee as bounds and marks, by which thou mayst again find me when thou returnest, in imitation of the clue of Theseus's labyrinth.'

'I will do so,' quoth Sancho; and then, cutting down certain boughs, he demanded his lord's blessing, and departed, not without tears on both sides. And, mounting upon Rozinante, whom Don Quixote commended very seriously to his care, that he should tend him as he would his own person, he made on towards the plains, strewing here and there on the way his branches, as his master had advised him; and with that departed, although his lord importuned him to behold two or three follies ere he went away. But scarce had he gone a hundred paces, when he returned and said, 'I say, sir, that you said well that, to the end I might swear with a safe conscience that I have seen you play these mad tricks, it were necessary that at least I see you do one, although that of your abode here is one great enough.'

'Did not I tell thee so?' quoth Don Quixote. 'Stay Sancho, for I will do it in the space of a creed.' And, taking off with all haste his hose, he remained the half of him naked, and did instantly give two or three jerks in the air, and two tumbles over and over on the ground, with his head downward, and his legs aloft, where he discovered such things, as Sancho, because he would not see them again, turned the bridle and rode away, resting contented and satisfied that he might swear that his lord was mad. And so we will leave him travelling on his way, until his return, which was very soon after.

CHAPTER XII

Wherein Are Prosecuted the Pranks Played by Don Quixote in His Amorous Humours in the Mountains of Sierra Morena

AND, turning to recount what the knight of the ill-favoured face did when he was all alone, the history says that, after Don Quixote had ended his frisks and leaps, naked from the girdle downward, and from that upward apparelled, seeing that his squire Sancho was gone, and would behold no more of his mad pranks, he ascended to the top of a high rock, and began there to think on that whereon he had thought oftentimes before, without ever making a full resolution therein, to wit, whether were it better to imitate Orlando in his unmeasurable furies, than Amadis in his melancholy moods: and, speaking to himself, would say, 'If Orlando was so valorous and good a knight as men say, what wonder, seeing in fine he was enchanted, and could not be slain, if it were not by clapping a pin to the sole of his foot, and therefore did wear shoes still that had seven folds of iron in the soles? although these his draughts stood him in no stead at Roncesvalles against Bernardo del Carpio, which, understanding them, pressed him to death between his arms. But, leaving his valour apart, let us come to the losing of his wits, which it is certain he lost through the signs he found in the forest, and by the news that the shepherd gave unto him, that Angelica had slept more than two noontides with the little Moor, Medoro of the curled locks, him that was page to King Argamante. And if he understood this, and knew his lady had played beside the cushion, what wonder was it that he should run mad. But how can I imitate him in his furies, if I cannot imitate him in their occasion? for I dare swear for my Dulcinea of Toboso, that all the days of her life she hath not seen one Moor, even in his own attire as he is, and she is now right as her mother bore her; and I should do her a manifest wrong, if, upon any false suspicion, I should turn mad of that kind of folly that did distract furious Orlando. On the other side, I see that Amadis de Gaul, without losing his wits, or using any other raving trick, gained as great fame of being amorous as any one else whatsoever. For that which his history recites was none other than that, seeing himself disdained by his lady Oriana, who had commanded him to withdraw himself from her presence, and not appear again in it until she pleased, he retired himself, in the company of a certain hermit, to the Poor Rock, and there crammed himself with weeping, until that Heaven assisted him in the midst of his greatest cares and necessity. And this being true, as it is, why should I take now the pains to strip myself all naked, and offend these trees, which never yet did me any harm? Nor have I any reason to trouble the clear waters of these brooks, which must give me drink when I am thirsty. Let the remembrance of Amadis live, and be imitated in everything as much as may be, by Don Quixote of the Mancha; of whom may be said what was said of the other, that though he achieved not great things, yet did he die in their pursuit. And though I am not contemned or disdained by my Dulcinea, yet it is sufficient, as I have said already, that I be absent from her; therefore, hands to your task; and, ye famous actions of Amadis, occur to my remembrance, and instruct me where I may best begin to imitate you. Yet I know already, that the greatest thing he did use was prayer, and so will I.' And, saying so, he made him a pair of beads of great galls, and was very much vexed in mind for want of an Eremite, who might hear his confession and comfort him in his afflictions; and therefore did entertain himself walking up and down the little green field, writing and graving in the rinds of trees, and on the smooth sands, many verses, all accommodated to his sadness, and some of them in the praise of Dulcinea; but those that were found thoroughly finished, and were legible after his own finding again in that place, were only these ensuing:

'O ye plants, ye herbs, and ye trees,
  That flourish in this pleasant site,
In lofty and verdant degrees,
  If my harms do you not delight,
Hear my holy plaints, which are these,
And let not my grief you molest,

Though it ever so feelingly went,
Since here for to pay your rest,
Don Quixote his tears hath addrest,
Dulcinea's want to lament
Of Toboso.

'In this very place was first spied
The loyallest lover and true,
Who himseif from his lady did hide;
But yet felt his sorrows anew,
Not knowing whence they might proceed.
Love doth him cruelly wrest
With a passion of evil descent
Which robb'd Don Quixote of rest,
Till a pipe with tears was full prest,
Dulcinea's want to lament
Of Toboso.

'He, searching adventures, blind,
Among these dearn woods and rocks.
Still curseth on pitiless mind;
For a wretch amidst bushy locks
And crags may misfortunes find.
Love with his whip, wounded his breast,
And not with soft hands him pent,
And when he his noddle had prest,
Don Quixote his tears did forth wrest,
Dulcinea's want to lament
Of Toboso.'

The addition of Toboso to the name of Dulcinea did not cause small laughter in those which found the verses recited; because they imagined that Don Quixote conceived that if, in the naming of Dulcinea, he did not also add that of Toboso, the rime could not be understood; and in truth it was so, as he himself did afterward confess. He composed many others; but, as we have related, none could be well copied or found entire, but these three stanzas. In this, and in sighing, and invoking the fauns and sylvans of these woods, and the nymphs of the adjoining streams, with the dolorous and hollow echo, that it would answer and they comfort and listen unto him, and in the search of some herbs to sustain his languishing forces, he entertained himself all the time of Sancho his absence;

who, had he stayed three weeks away, as he did but three days, the Knight of the Ill-favoured Face should have remained so disfigured as the very mother that bore him would not have known him.

But now it is congruent that, leaving him swallowed in the gulfs of sorrow and versifying, we turn and recount what happened to Sancho Panza in his embassage; which was that, issuing out to the highway, he presently took that which led towards Toboso, and arrived the next day following to the inn where the disgrace of the coverlet befel him; and scarce had he well espied it, but presently he imagined that he was once again flying in the air; and therefore would not enter into it, although his arrival was at such an hour as he both might and ought to have stayed, being dinner-time, and he himself likewise possessed with a marvellous longing to taste some warm meat—for many days past he had fed altogether on cold viands. This desire enforced him to approach to the inn, remaining still doubtful, notwithstanding, whether he should enter into it or no. And as he stood thus suspended, there issued out of the inn two persons which presently knew him, and the one said to the other, 'Tell me, master licentiate, is not that horseman that rides there Sancho Panza, he whom our adventurer's old woman said departed with her master for his squire?' 'It is,' quoth the licentiate, 'and that is our Don Quixote his horse.' And they knew him so well, as those that were the curate and barber of his own village, and were those that made the search and formal process against the books of chivalry; and therefore, as soon as they had taken full notice of Sancho Panza and Rozinante, desirous to learn news of Don Quixote, they drew near unto him; and the curate called him by his name, saying, 'Friend Sancho Panza, where is your master?' Sancho Panza knew them instantly, and, desirous to conceal the place and manner wherein his lord remained, did answer them, that his master was in a certain place, withheld by affairs for a few days, that were of great consequence, and concerned him very much, and that he durst not, for both his eyes, discover the place to them. 'No, no,' quoth the barber, 'Sancho Panza, if thou dost not tell us where he sojourneth, we must imagine (as we do already) that thou hast robbed and slain him, specially seeing thou comest thus on his horse; and therefore thou must, in good faith, get us the horse's owner, or else stand to thine answer.' 'Your threats fear me nothing,' quoth Sancho; 'for I am not a man that robs or murders any one. Every man is slain by his destiny, or by God that made him. My lord remains doing of penance in the midst of this mountain, with very great pleasure.' And then he presently recounted unto them, from the beginning to the end, the fashion wherein he had left him, the adventures which had befallen, and how he carried a letter to the Lady Dulcinea of Toboso, who was Lorenzo Corcuelo his daughter, of whom his lord was enamoured up to the livers.

Both of them stood greatly admired at Sancho's relation; and although they knew Don Quixote's madness already, and the kind thereof, yet as often as they heard speak thereof, they rested newly amazed. They requested Sancho to show them the letter that he carried to the Lady Dulcinea of Toboso. He told them that it was written in tablets, and that he had express order from his lord to have it fairly copied out in paper, at the first village whereunto he should arrive. To which the curate answered, bidding show it unto him, and he would write out the copy very fairly.

Then Sancho thrust his hand into his bosom, and searched the little book, but could not find it, nor should not, though he had searched till Doomsday; for it was in Don Quixote's power, who gave it not to him, nor did he ever remember to demand it. When Sancho perceived that the book was lost, he waxed as wan and pale as a dead man, and, turning again very speedily to feel all the parts of his body, he saw clearly that it could not be found; and therefore, without making any more ado, he laid hold on his own beard with both his fists, and drew almost the one half of the hair away, and afterward bestowed on his face and nose, in a memento, half a dozen such cuffs as he bathed them all in blood; which the curate and barber beholding, they asked him what had befallen him, that he entreated himself so ill. 'What should befall me,' answered Sancho, 'but that I have lost at one hand, and in an instant, three colts, whereof the least was like a castle?' 'How so,' quoth the barber. 'Marry,' said Sancho, 'I have lost the tablets wherein were written Dulcinea's letter, and a schedule of my lord's, addressed to his niece, wherein he commanded her to deliver unto me three colts, of four or five that remained in his house.' And, saying so, he recounted the loss of his grey ass. The curate comforted him, and said that, as soon as his lord were found, he would deal with him to renew his grant, and write it in paper, according to the common use and practice, forasmuch as those which were written in tablets were of no value, and would never be accepted nor accomplished.

With this Sancho took courage, and said, if that was so, he cared not much for the loss of Dulcinea's letter; for he knew it almost all by rote. 'Say it, then, Sancho,' quoth the barber, 'and we will after write it.' Then Sancho stood still and began to scratch his head, to call the letter to memory; and now would he stand upon one leg, and now upon another. Sometimes he looked on the earth, other whiles upon heaven; and after he had gnawed off almost the half of one of his nails, and held them all the while suspended, expecting his recital thereof, he said, after a long pause: 'On my soul, master licentiate, I give to the devil anything that I can remember of that letter, although the beginning was this: "High and unsavoury lady."' 'I warrant you,' quoth the barber, 'he said not but "super-human" or "sovereign lady."'

'It is so,' quoth Sancho, 'and presently followed, if I well remember: "He that is wounded and wants sleep, and the hurt man doth kiss your worship's hands, ingrate and very scornful fair"; and thus he went roving until he ended in, "Yours until death, the Knight of the Ill-favoured Face."' Both of them took great delight to see Sancho's good memory, and praised it to him very much, and requested him to repeat the letter once or twice more to them, that they might also bear it in memory, to write it at the due season. Sancho turned to recite it again and again, and at every repetition said other three thousand errors. And after this he told other things of his lord, but spoke not a word of his own tossing in a coverlet, which had befallen him in that inn into which he refused to enter. He added besides, how his lord, in bringing him a good despatch from his Lady Dulcinea of Toboso, would forthwith set out to endeavour how he might become an emperor, or at the least a monarch; for they had so agreed between themselves both, and it was a very easy matter for him to become one, such was the valour of his person and strength of his arm; and that when he were one, he would procure him a good marriage; for by that time he should be a widower at the least; and he would wive him one of the emperor's ladies to wife, that were an inheritrix of some great and rich state on the firm land, for now he would have no more islands. And all this was related so seriously by Sancho, and so in his perfect sense, he scratching his nose ever and anon as he spoke, so as the two were stricken into a new amazement, pondering the vehemence of Don Quixote's frenzy, which carried quite away with it in that sort the judgment of that poor man, but would not labour to dispossess him of that error, because it seemed to them that, since it did not hurt his conscience it was better to leave him in it, that the recital of his follies might turn to their greater recreation: and therefore exhorted him to pray for the health of his lord; for it was a very possible and contingent thing to arrive in the process of time to the dignity of an emperor, as he said, or at least to that of an archbishop, or other calling equivalent to it.

Then Sancho demanded of them, 'Sirs, if fortune should turn our affairs to another course, in such sort as my lord, abandoning the purpose to purchase an empire, would take in his head that of becoming a cardinal, I would fain learn of you here, what cardinals-errant are wont to give to their squires?' 'They are wont to give them,' quoth the curate, 'some simple benefice, or some parsonage, or to make them clerks or sextons, or vergers of some church, whose living amounts to a good penny-rent, beside the profit of the altar, which is ofttimes as much more.' 'For that it is requisite,' quoth Sancho, 'that the squire be not married, and that he know how to help mass at least; and if that be so, unfortunate I! that both am married, and knows not besides the first letter of the A B C, what will then become of me, if my master take the humour to be an archbishop, and not an emperor, as is the custom and use of knights-errant?' 'Do not afflict thy mind for that, friend Sancho,' quoth the barber; 'for we will deal with thy lord here, and we will counsel him, yea, we will urge it to him as a matter of conscience, that he become an emperor, and not an archbishop; for it will be more easy for him to be such a one, by reason that he is more valorous than learned.'

'So methinks,' quoth Sancho, 'although I know he hath ability enough for all. That which I mean to do for my part is, I will pray unto our Lord to conduct him to that place wherein he may serve Him best, and give me greatest rewards.' 'Thou speakest like a discreet man,' quoth the curate, 'and thou shalt do therein the duty of a good Christian. But that which we must endeavour now is, to devise how we may win thy lord from prosecuting that unprofitable penance he hath in hand, as thou sayst; and to the end we may think on the manner how, and eat our dinner withal, seeing it is time, let us all enter into the inn.' Sancho bade them go in, and he would stay for them at the door, and that he would after tell them the reason why he had no mind to enter, neither was it in any sort convenient that he should; but he entreated them to bring him somewhat forth to eat that were warm, and some provand for Rozinante. With that they departed into the lodging, and within a while after the barber brought forth unto him some meat. And the curate and the barber, after having pondered well with themselves what course they were to take to attain their design, the curate fell on a device very fit both for Don Quixote's humour, and also to bring their purpose to pass; and was, as he told the barber, that he had bethought him to apparel himself like a lady adventuress, and that he therefore should do the best that he could to fit himself like a squire, and that they would go in that habit to the place where Don Quixote sojourned, feigning that he was an afflicted and distressed damsel, and would demand a boon of him, which he, as a valorous knight-errant, would in no wise deny her, and that the gift which he meant to desire, was to entreat him to follow her where she would carry him, to right a wrong which a naughty knight had done unto her; and that she would besides pray him not to command her to unmask herself, or inquire anything of her estate, until he had done her right against that bad knight. And by this means he certainly hoped that Don Quixote would grant all that he requested in this manner. And in this sort they would fetch him from thence and bring him to his village, where they would labour with all their power to see whether his extravagant frenzy could be recovered by any remedy.

CHAPTER XIII

How the Curate and the Barber Put Their Design in Practice, with Many Other Things Worthy to Be Recorded in This Famous History

THE curate's invention disliked not the barber, but rather pleased him so well as they presently put it in execution. They borrowed, therefore, of the innkeeper's wife a gown and a kerchief, leaving her in pawn thereof a fair new cassock of the curate's. The barber made him a great beard of a pied ox's tail, wherein the innkeeper was wont to hang his horse's comb. The hostess demanded of them the occasion why they would use these things. The curate recounted in brief, reasons of Don Quixote's madness, and how that disguisement was requisite to bring him away from the mountain wherein at that present he made his abode.

Presently the innkeeper and his wife remembered themselves how he had been their guest, and of his balsam, and was the tossed squire's lord; and then they rehearsed again to the curate all that had passed between him and them in that inn, without omitting the accident that had befallen Sancho himself; and in conclusion the hostess tricked up the curate so handsomely as there could be no more desired; for she attired him in a gown of broadcloth, laid over with guards of black velvet, each being a span breadth, full of gashes and cuts; the bodice and sleeves of green velvet, welted with white satin; which gown and doublet, as I suspect, were both made in the time of King Bamba. The curate would not permit them to veil and bekerchief him, but set on his head a white quilted linen nightcap, which he carried for the night, and girded his forehead with a black taffeta garter, and with the other he masked his face, wherewithal he covered his beard and visage very neatly; then did he encasque his pate in his hat, which was so broad, as it might serve him excellently for a *quitasol;* and lapping himself up handsomely in his long cloak, he went to horse, and rode as women use.

Then mounted the barber likewise on his mule, with his beard hanging down to the girdle, half red and half white, as that which, as we have said, was made of the tail of a pied-coloured ox; then taking leave of them all, and of the good Maritornes, who promised (although a sinner) to say a rosary to their intention, to the end that God might give them good success in so Christian and difficult an adventure as that which they undertook. But scarce were they gone out of the inn, when the curate began to dread a little that he had done ill in apparelling himself in that wise, accounting it a very indecent thing that a priest should dight himself so, although the matter concerned him never so much. And acquainting the barber with his surmise, he entreated him that they might change attires, seeing it was much more just that he, because a layman, should feign the oppressed lady, and himself would become his squire, for so his dignity would be less profaned; to which, if he would not condescend, he resolved to pass on no farther, although the devil should carry therefore Don Quixote away. Sancho came over to them about this season, and seeing them in that habit, he could not contain his laughter. The barber (to be brief) did all that which the curate pleased, and making thus an exchange of inventions, the curate instructed him how he should behave himself, and what words he should use to Don Quixote to press and move him to come away with him, and forsake the propension and love of that place which he had chosen to perform his vain penance.

The barber answered, that he would set everything in his due point and perfection, though he had never lessoned him, but would not set on the array until they came near to the place where Don Quixote abode; and therefore folded up his clothes, and master parson his beard, and forthwith went on their way; Sancho Panza playing the guide, who recounted at large to them all that had happened with the madman whom they found in the mountain; concealing, notwithstanding, the booty of the malet, with the other things found therein; for, although otherwise most simple, yet was our young man an ordinary vice of fools, and had a spice of covetousness.

They arrived the next day following to the place where Sancho had left the tokens of boughs, to find that wherein his master sojourned; and having taken notice thereof, he said unto them that that was the entry, and therefore they might do well to apparel themselves, if by change that might be a mean to procure his lord's liberty; for they had told him already, that on their going and apparelling in that manner consisted wholly the hope of freeing his lord out of that wretched life he had chosen; and therefore did charge him, on his life, not to reveal to his lord in any case what they were, nor seem in any sort to know them; and that if he demanded (as they were sure he would) whether he had delivered his letter to Dulcinea, he should say he did, and that by reason she could not read, she answered him by word of mouth, saying that she commanded, under pain of her indignation, that presently abandoning so austere a life, he would come and see her; for this was most requisite, to the end that moved therewithal, and by what they meant likewise to say unto him, they made certain account to reduce him to a better life, and would besides persuade him to that course instantly, which might set him in the way to become an emperor or monarch; for as concerning the being an archbishop, he needed not to fear it at all.

Sancho listened to all the talk and instruction, and bore them away well in memory, and gave them great thanks for the intention they had to counsel his lord to become an emperor, and not an archbishop; for, as he said, he imagined in his simple judgment, that an emperor was of more ability to reward his squire than an archbishop-errant. He likewise added, that he thought it were necessary he went somewhat before them to search him, and deliver his lady's answer; for perhaps it alone would be sufficient to fetch him out of that place, without putting them to any further pains. They liked of Sancho Panza's device, and therefore determined to expect him until his return with the news of finding his master. With that Sancho entered in by the clefts of the rocks (leaving them both behind together), by which ran a little smooth stream, to which other rocks, and some trees that grew near unto it, made a fresh and pleasing shadow. The heats, and the day wherein they arrived there, was one of those of the month of August, when in those places the heat is intolerable; the hour, about three in the afternoon: all which did render the place more grateful, and invited them to remain therein until Sancho's return. Both, therefore, resting there quietly under the shadow, there arrived to their hearing the sound of a voice, which, without being accompanied by any instrument, did resound so sweet and melodiously, as they remained greatly admired, because they esteemed not that to be a place wherein any so good a musician might make his abode; for, although it is usually said that in the woods and fields are found shepherds of excellent voices, yet is this rather a poetical endearment than an approved truth; and most of all when they perceived that the verses they heard him singing were not of rustic composition, but rather of delicate and courtly invention. The truth whereof is confirmed by the verses, which were these:

'Who doth my weal diminish thus and stain?
    Disdain.
And say by whom my woes augmented be?
    By jealousy.
And who my patience doth by trial wrong?
    An absence long.
If that be so, then for my grievous wrong,
No remedy at all I may obtain,
Since my best hopes I cruelly find slain
By disdain, jealousy, and absence long.

'Who in my mind those dolors still doth move?
    Dire love.
And who my glory's ebb doth most importune?
    Fortune.
And to my plaints by whom increase is giv'n?
    By Heav'n.
If that be so, then my mistrust jumps ev'n,
That of my wondrous evil I needs must die;
Since in my harm join'd and united be,
Love, wavering fortune, and a rigorous Heaven.

'Who better hap can unto me bequeath?
    Death.
From whom his favours doth not love estrange?
    From change.
And his too serious harms, who cureth wholly?
    Folly.
If that be so, it is no wisdom truly,

To think by human means to cure that care,
Where the only antidotes and med'cines are
Desired death, light change, and endless folly.'

The hour, the time, the solitariness of the place, voice, and art of him that sung, struck wonder and delight in the hearers' minds, which remained still quiet, listening whether they might hear anything else; but, perceiving that the silence continued a pretty while, they agreed to issue and seek out the musician that sung so harmoniously; and being ready to put their resolution in practice, they were again arrested by the same voice, the which touched their ears anew with this sonnet:

A SONNET.

'Holy amity! which, with nimble wings,
Thy semblance leaving here on earth behind,
Among the blessed souls of heaven, up-flings,
To those imperial rooms to cheer thy mind:
And thence to us, is (when thou lik'st) assign'd
Just Peace, whom shady veil so covered brings;
As oft, instead of her, Deceit we find
Clad in weeds of good and virtuous things.
Leave heaven, O amity! do not permit
Foul Fraud thus openly thy robes to invest;
With which, sincere intents destroy does it:
For if thy likeness from it thou dost not wrest,
The world will turn to the first conflict soon,
Of discord, chaos, and confusion.'

The song was concluded with a profound sigh, and both the others lent attentive ear to hear if he would sing any more; but perceiving that the music was converted into throbs and doleful plaints, they resolved to go and learn who was the wretch, as excellent for his voice as dolorous in his sighs. And after they had gone a little, at the doubling of the point of a crag, they perceived one of the very same form and fashion that Sancho had painted unto them when he told them the history of Cardenio; which man espying them likewise, showed no semblance of fear, but stood still with his head hanging on his breast like a malcontent, not once lifting up his eyes to behold them from the first time when they unexpectedly arrived.

The curate, who was a man very well spoken (as one that had already intelligence of his misfortune; for he knew him by his signs), drew nearer to him, and prayed and persuaded him, with short but very forcible reasons, to forsake that miserable life, lest he should there eternally lose it, which of all miseries would prove the most miserable. Cardenio at this season was in his right sense, free from the furious accident that distracted him so often; and therefore, viewing them both attired in so strange and unusual a fashion from that which was used among those deserts, he rested somewhat admired, but chiefly hearing them speak in his affair, as in a matter known (for so much he gathered out of the curate's speeches); and therefore answered in this manner: 'I perceive well, good sirs (whosoever you be), that Heaven, which hath always care to succour good men; yea, even, and the wicked many times, hath, without any desert, addressed unto me by these deserts and places so remote from the vulgar haunt, persons which, laying before mine eyes with quick and pregnant reasons the little I have to lead this kind of life, do labour to remove me from this place to a better; and by reason they know not as much as I do, and that after escaping this harm I shall fall into a far greater, they account me perhaps for a man of weak discourse, and what is worse, for one wholly devoid of judgment. And were it so, yet is it no marvel; for it seems to me that the force of the imagination of my disasters is so bent and powerful in my destruction, that I, without being able to make it any resistance, do become like a stone, void of all good feeling and knowledge. And I come to know the certainty of this truth when some men do recount and show unto me tokens of the things I have done whilst this terrible accident overrules me; and after I can do no more than be grieved, though in vain, and curse, without benefit, my too froward fortune, and render as an excuse of my madness the relation of the cause thereof to as many as please to hear it; for wise men perceiving the cause will not wonder at the effects, and though they give me no remedy, yet at least will not condemn me; for it will convert the anger they conceive at my misrules into compassion for my disgraces. And, sirs, if by chance it be so that you come with the same intention that others did, I request you, ere you enlarge further your discreet persuasions, that you will give ear awhile to the relation of my mishaps; for perhaps, when you have understood it, you may save the labour that you would take, comforting an evil wholly incapable of consolation.'

Both of them, which desired nothing so much [as] to understand from his own mouth the occasion of his harms, did entreat him to relate it, promising to do nothing else in his remedy or comfort but what himself pleased. And with this the sorrowful gentleman began his doleful history, with the very same words almost that he had rehearsed it to Don Quixote and the goatherd a few days past, when, by occasion of Master Elisabat and Don Quixote's curiosity in observing the decorum of chivalry, the tale remained imperfect, as our history left it above. But now good fortune so disposed things, that his foolish fit came not upon him, but gave him leisure to continue his story to the end; and so arriving to the passage that spoke of the letter Don Fernando found in the book of Amadis de Gaul, Cardenio said that he had it very well in memory, and the sense was this:

' "LUCINDA TO CARDENIO.

' "I discover daily in thee worths that oblige and enforce me to hold thee dear; and therefore, if thou desirest to have me discharge this debt, without serving a writ on my honour, thou mayst easily do it. I have a father that knows thee, and loves me likewise well, who, without forcing my will, will accomplish that which justly thou oughtest to have, if it be so that thou esteemest me as much as thou sayst, and I do believe."

'This letter moved me to demand Lucinda of her father for my wife, as I have already recounted; and by it also Lucinda remained in Don Fernando's opinion crowned for one of the most discreet women of her time. And this billet letter was that which first put him in mind to destroy me ere I could effect my desires. I told to Don Fernando wherein consisted all the difficulty of her father's protracting of the marriage, to wit, in that my father should first demand her; the which I dared not to mention unto him, fearing lest he would not willingly consent thereunto; not for that the quality, bounty, virtue, and beauty of Lucinda were to him unknown, or that she had not parts in her able to ennoble and adorn any other lineage of Spain whatsoever, but because I understood by him, that he desired not to marry me until he had seen what Duke Ricardo would do for me. Finally, I told him that I dared not reveal it to my father, as well for that inconvenience, as for many others that made me so afraid, without knowing what they were, as methought my desires would never take effect.

'To all this Don Fernando made me answer, that he would take upon him to speak to my father, and persuade him to treat of that affair also with Lucinda's. O ambitious Marius! O cruel Catiline! O facinorous Sylla! O treacherous Galalon! O traitorous Vellido! O revengeful Julian! O covetous Judas! Traitor, cruel, revengeful, and cozening, what indeserts did this wench commit, who with such plaints discovered to thee the secrets and delights of her heart? What offence committed I against thee? What words did I speak, or counsel did I give, that were not all addressed to the increasing of thine honour and profit? But on what do I (the worst of all wretches!) complain? seeing that when the current of the stars doth bring with it mishaps, by reason they come down precipitately from above, there is no earthly force can withhold, or human industry prevent or evacuate them. Who would have imagined that Don Fernando, a noble gentleman, discreet, obliged by my deserts, and powerful to obtain whatsoever the amorous desire would exact of him, where and whensoever it seized on his heart, would (as they say) become so corrupt as to deprive me of one only sheep, which yet I did not possess? But let these considerations be laid apart as unprofitable, that we may knit up again the broken thread of my unfortunate history. And therefore I say that, Don Fernando believing that my presence was a hindrance to put his treacherous and wicked design in execution, he resolved to send me to his eldest brother, under pretext to get some money of him for to buy six great horses, that he had of purpose, and only to the end I might absent myself, bought the very same day that he offered to speak himself to my father, and would have me go for the money, because he might bring his treacherous intent the better to pass. Could I prevent this treason? Or could I perhaps but once imagine it? No, truly; but rather, glad for the good merchandise he had made, did make proffer of myself to depart for the money very willingly. I spoke that night to Lucinda, and acquainted her with the agreement passed between me and Don Fernando, bidding her to hope firmly that our good just desires would sort a wished and happy end. She answered me again (as little suspecting Don Fernando's treason as myself), bidding me to return with all speed, because she believed that the conclusion of our affections should be no longer deferred than my father deferred to speak unto hers. And what was the cause I know not, but as soon as she had said this unto me, her eyes were filled with tears, and somewhat thwarting her throat, hindered her from saying many other things, which methought she strived to speak.

'I rested admired at this new accident, until that time never seen in her; for always, as many times as my good fortune and diligence granted it, we conversed with all sport and delight, without ever intermeddling in our discourses any tears, sighs, complaints, suspicions, or fears. All my speech was to advance my fortune for having received her from Heaven as my lady and mistress; then would I amplify her beauty, admire her worth, and praise her discretion. She, on the other side, would return me the exchange, extolling in me what she, as one enamoured, accounted worthy of laud and commendation. After this we would recount a hundred thousand toys and chances befallen our neighbours and acquaintance; and that to which my presumption dared furthest to extend itself, was sometimes to take her beautiful and ivory hands perforce, and kiss them as well as I might, through the rigorous strictness of a niggardly iron grate which divided us. But the precedent night to the day of my sad departure, she wept, sobbed, and sighed, and departed, leaving me full of confusion and inward assaults, amazed to behold such new and doleful tokens of sorrow and feeling in Lucinda. But because I would not murder my hopes, I did attribute all these things to the force of her affection towards me, and to the grief which absence is wont to stir in those that love one another dearly. To be brief, I departed from thence sorrowful and pensive, my soul being full of imaginations and suspicions, and yet knew not what I suspected or imagined: clear tokens, foretelling the sad success and misfortune which attended me. I arrived to the place where I was sent, and delivered my letter to Don Fernando's brother, and was well entertained, but not well despatched; for he commanded me to expect (a thing to me most displeasing) eight days, and that out of the duke his father's presence, because his brother had written unto him to send him certain moneys unknown to his father. And all this was but false Don Fernando's invention; for his brother wanted not money wherewithal to have despatched me presently, had not he written the contrary.

'This was so displeasing a commandment and order, as almost it brought me to terms of disobeying it, because it seemed to me a thing most impossible to sustain my life so many days in the absence of my Lucinda, and specially having left her so sorrowful as I have recounted; yet, notwithstanding, I did obey like a good servant, although I knew it would be with the cost of my health. But on the fourth day after I had arrived, there came a man in my search with a letter, which he delivered unto me, and by the endorsement I knew it to be Lucinda's; for the hand was like hers. I opened it (not without fear and assailment of my senses), knowing that it must have been some serious occasion which could move her to write unto me, being absent, seeing she did it so rarely even when I was present. I demanded of the bearer, before I read, who had delivered it to him, and what time he had spent in the way. He answered me, "that passing by chance at midday through a street of the city, a very beautiful lady did call him from a certain window. Her eyes were all beblubbered with tears, and said unto him very hastily, 'Brother, if thou beest a Christian, as thou appearest to be one, I pray thee, for God's sake, that thou do forthwith address this letter to the place and person that the superscription assigneth (for they be well known), and therein thou shalt do our Lord great service; and because thou mayst not want means to do it, take what thou shalt find wrapped in that handkerchief.' And, saying so, she threw out of the window a handkerchief, wherein were lapped up a hundred reals, this ring of gold which I carry here, and that letter which I delivered unto you; and presently, without expecting mine answer, she departed, but first saw me take up the handkerchief and letter, and then I made her signs that I would accomplish herein her command. And after, perceiving the pains I might take in bringing you it so well considered, and seeing by the endorsement that you were the man to whom it was addressed,—for, sir, I know you very well,—and also obliged to do it by the tears of that beautiful lady, I determined not to trust any other with it, but to come and bring it you myself in person; and in sixteen hours since it was given unto me, I have travelled the journey you know, which is at least eighteen leagues long." Whilst the thankful new messenger spake thus unto me, I remained in a manner hanging on his words, and my thighs did tremble in such manner as I could very hardly sustain myself on foot; yet, taking courage, at last I opened the letter, whereof these were the contents:

'"The word that Don Fernando hath passed unto you to speak to your father, that he might speak to mine, he hath accomplished more to his own pleasure than to your profit. For, sir, you shall understand that he hath demanded me for his wife; and my father (borne away by the advantage of worths which he supposes to be in Don Fernando more than in you) hath agreed to his demand in so good earnest, as the espousals shall be celebrated within these two days, and that so secretly and alone as only the heavens and some folk of the house shall be witnesses. How I remain, imagine, and whether it be convenient you should return, you may consider; and the success of this affair shall let you to perceive whether I love you well or no. I beseech Almighty God that this may arrive unto your hands before mine shall be in danger to join itself with his, which keepeth his promised faith so ill."

'These were, in sum, the contents of the letter, and the motives that persuaded me presently to depart, without attending any other answer or other moneys; for then I conceived clearly that it was not the buyal of the horses, but that of his delights, which had moved Don Fernando to send me to his brother. The rage which I conceived against him, joined with the fear to lose the jewel which I had gained by so many years' service and desires, did set wings on me, for I arrived as I had flown next day at mine own city, in the hour and moment fit to go speak to Lucinda. I entered secretly, and left my mule whereon I rode in the honest man's house that had brought me the letter, and my fortune purposing then to be favourable to me, disposed so mine affairs, that I found Lucinda sitting at that iron grate which was the sole witness of our loves. Lucinda knew me straight and I her, but not as we ought to know one another. But who is he in the world that can truly vaunt that he hath penetrated and thoroughly exhausted the confused thoughts and mutable nature of women? Truly none. I say, then, to proceed with my tale, that as soon as Lucinda perceived me, she said, "Cardenio, I am attired with my wedding garments, and in the hall doth wait for me the traitor Don Fernando, and my covetous father, with other witnesses, which shall rather be such of my death than of mine espousals. Be not troubled, dear friend, but procure to be present at this sacrifice, the which if I cannot hinder by my persuasions and reasons, I carry hidden about me a poniard secretly, which may hinder more resolute forces by giving end to my life, and a beginning to thee, to know certain the affection which I have ever borne and do bear unto thee." I answered her troubled and hastily, fearing I should not have the leisure to reply unto her, saying, "Sweet lady, let thy works verify thy words; for if thou carriest a poniard to defend thy credit, I do here likewise bear a sword wherewithal I will defend thee, or kill myself, if fortune prove adverse and contrary." I believe that she could not hear all my words, by reason she was called hastily away, as I perceived, for that the bridegroom expected her coming. By this the night of my sorrows did thoroughly fall, and the sun of my gladness was set, and I remained without light in mine eyes or discourse in my understanding. I could not find the way into her house, nor could I move myself to any part; yet, considering at last how important my presence was for that which might befall in that adventure, I animated myself the best I could, and entered into the house; and as one that knew very well all the entries and passages thereof, and specially by reason of the trouble and business that was then in hand, I went in unperceived of any. And thus, without being seen, I had the opportunity to place myself in the hollow room of a window of the same hall, which was covered by the ends of two encountering pieces of tapestry, from whence I could see all that was done in the hall, remaining myself unviewed of any. Who could now describe the assaults and surprisals of my heart while I there abode? the thoughts which encountered my mind? the considerations which I had? which were so many and such, as they can neither be said, nor is it reason they should. Let it suffice you to know that the bridegroom entered into the hall without any ornament, wearing the ordinary array he was wont, and was accompanied by a cousin-german of Lucinda's, and in all the hall there was no stranger present, nor any other than the household servants. Within a while after, Lucinda came out of the parlour, accompanied by her mother and two waiting-maids of her own, as richly attired and decked as her calling and beauty deserved, and the perfection of courtly pomp and bravery could afford. My distraction and trouble of mind lent me no time to note particularly the apparel she wore, and therefore did only mark the colours, which were carnation and white; and the splendour which the precious stones and jewels of her tires and all the rest of her garments yielded; yet did the singular beauty of her fair and golden tresses surpass them so much, as being in competency with the precious stones, and flame of four links that lighted in the hall, yet did the splendour thereof seem far more bright and glorious to mine eyes. O memory! the mortal enemy of mine ease, to what end serves it now to represent unto me the incomparable beauty of that my adored enemy? Were it not better, cruel memory! to remember and represent that which she did then, that, being moved by so manifest a wrong, I may at least endeavour to lose my life, since I cannot procure a revenge? Tire not, good sirs, to hear the digressions I make; for my grief is not of that kind that may be rehearsed succinctly and speedily, seeing that in mine opinion every passage of it is worthy of a large discourse.'

To this the curate answered, that not only they were not tired or wearied hearing of him, but rather they received marvellous delight to hear him recount each minuity and circumstance, because they were such as deserved not to be passed over in silence, but rather merited as much attention as the principal parts of the history.

'You shall then wit,' quoth Cardenio, 'that as they thus stood in the hall, the curate of the parish entered, and, taking them both by the hand to do that which in such an act is required at the saying of, "Will you, Lady Lucinda, take the Lord Don Fernando, who is here present, for your lawful spouse, according as our holy mother of the Church commands?" I thrust out all my head and neck out of the tapestry, and, with most attentive ears and a troubled mind, settled myself to hear what Lucinda answered, expecting by it the sentence of my death or the confirmation of my life. Oh, if one had dared to sally out at that time, and cry with a loud voice, "O Lucinda! Lucinda! see well what thou doest; consider withal what thou owest me! Behold how thou art mine, and that thou canst not be any other's; Note that thy saying of Yea and the end of my life shall be both in one instant. O traitor, Don Fernando, robber of my glory! death of my life! what is this thou pretendest? what wilt thou do? Consider that thou canst not, Christian-like, achieve thine intention, seeing Lucinda is my spouse, and I am her husband." O foolish man! now that I am absent, and far from the danger, I say what I should have done, and not what I did. Now, after that I have permitted my dear jewel to be robbed, I exclaim on the thief, on whom I might have revenged myself, had I had as much heart to do it as I have to complain. In fine, since I was then a coward and a fool, it is no matter though I now die ashamed, sorry, and frantic. The curate stood expecting Lucinda's answer a good while ere she gave it; and in the end, when I hoped that she would take out the poniard to stab herself, or would unloose her tongue to say some truth, or use some reason or persuasion that might redound to my benefit, I heard her instead thereof answer, with a dismayed and languishing voice, the word "I will." And then Don Fernando said the same; and, giving her the ring, they remained tied with an indissoluble knot. Then the bridegroom coming to kiss his spouse, she set her hand upon her heart, and fell in a trance between her mother's arms.

'Now only remains untold the case wherein I was, seeing in that Yea, which I had heard, my hopes deluded, Lucinda's words and promises falsified, and myself wholly disabled to recover in any time the good which I lost in that instant. I rested void of counsel, abandoned (in mine opinion) by Heaven, proclaimed an enemy to the earth which upheld me, the air denying breath enough for my sighs, and the water humour sufficient to mine eyes; only the fire increased in such manner as I burned thoroughlv with rage and jealousy. All the house was in a tumult for this sudden amazement of Lucinda; and as her mother unclasped her bosom to give her the air, there appeared in it a paper, folded up, which Don Fernando presently seized on, and went aside to read it by the light of a torch; and after he had read it, he sat down in a chair, laying his hands on his cheek, with manifest signs of melancholy discontent, without bethinking himself of the remedies that were applied to his spouse to bring her again to herself. I, seeing all the folk of the house thus in an uproar, did adventure myself to issue, not weighing much whether I were seen or no, bearing withal a resolution (if I were perceived) to play such a rash part, as all the world should understand the just indignation of my breast, by the revenge I would take on false Don Fernando and the mutable and dismayed traitress. But my destiny, which hath reserved me for greater evils (if possibly there be any greater than mine own), ordained that instant my wit should abound, whereof ever since I have so great want; and therefore, without will to take revenge of my greatest enemies (of whom I might have taken it with all facility, by reason they suspected so little my being there), I determined to take it on myself, and execute in myself the pain which they deserved, and that perhaps with more rigour than I would have used toward them if I had slain them at that time, seeing that the sudden death finisheth presently the pain; but that which doth lingeringly torment, kills always, without ending the life.

'To be short, I went out of the house, and came to the other where I had left my mule, which I caused to be saddled; and, without bidding mine host adieu, I mounted on her, and rode out of the city, without daring, like another Lot, to turn back and behold it; and then, seeing myself alone in the fields, and that the darkness of the night did cover me, and the silence thereof invite me to complain, without respect or fear to be heard or known, I did let slip my voice, and untied my tongue with so many curses of Lucinda and Don Fernando, as if thereby I might satisfy the wrong they had done me. I gave her the title of cruel, ungrateful, false, and scornful, but especially of covetous, seeing the riches of mine enemy had shut up the eyes of her affection, to deprive me thereof, and render it to him with whom fortune had dealt more frankly and liberally; and in the midst of this tune of maledictions and scorns, I did excuse her, saying, That it was no marvel that a maiden kept close in her parents' house, made and accustomed always to obey them, should at last condescend to their will, specially seeing they bestowed upon her for husband so noble, so rich, and proper a gentleman, as to refuse him would be reputed in her to proceed either from want of judgment, or from having bestowed her affections elsewhere, which things must of force greatly prejudice her good opinion and renown. Presently would I turn again to say, that though she had told them that I was her spouse, they might easily perceive that in choosing me she had not made so ill an election that she might not be excused, seeing that before Don Fernando offered himself, they themselves could not happen to desire, if their wishes were guided by reason, so fit a match for their daughter as myself; and she might easily have said, before she put herself in that last and forcible pass of giving her hand, that I had already given her mine, which I would come out to confess, and confirm all that she could any way feign in this case; and concluded in the end, that little love, less judgment, much ambition, and desire of greatness caused her to forget the words wherewithal she had deceived, entertained, and sustained me in my firm hopes and honest desires.

'Using these words, and feeling this unquietness in my breast, I travelled all the rest of the night, and struck about dawn into one of the entries of these mountains, through which I travelled three days at random, without following or finding any path or way, until I arrived at last to certain meadows and fields, that lie I know not in which part of these mountains; and finding there certain herds, I demanded of them which way lay the most craggy and inaccessible places of these rocks, and they directed me hither; and presently I travelled towards it, with purpose here to end my life; and, entering in among those deserts, my mule, through weariness and hunger, fell dead under me, or rather, as I may better suppose, to disburden himself of so vile and unprofitable a burden as he carried of me. I remained afoot, overcome by nature, and pierced through and through by hunger, without having any help, or knowing who might succour me, and remained after that manner I know not how long, prostrate on the ground, and then I rose again without any hunger, and I found near unto me certain goatherds, who were those doubtlessly that fed me in my hunger; for they told me in what manner they found me, and how I spake so many foolish and mad words as gave certain argument that I was devoid of judgment; and I have felt in myself since that time that I enjoy not my wits perfectly, but rather perceive them to be so weakened and impaired, as I commit a hundred follies, tearing mine apparel, crying loudly through these deserts, cursing my fates, and idly repeating the abhorred name of mine enemy, without having any other intent or discourse at that time than to endeavour to finish my life ere long; and when I turn to myself, I am so broken and tired as I am scarce able to stir me. My most ordinary mansion-place is in the hollowness of a cork-tree, sufficiently able to cover this wretched carcase. The cowherds and the goatherds that feed their cattle here in these mountains, moved by charity, gave me sustenance, leaving meat for me by the ways and on the rocks which they suppose I frequent, and where they think I may find it; and so, although I do then want the use of reason, yet doth natural necessity induce me to know my meat, and stirreth my appetite to covet, and my will to take it. They tell me, when they meet me in my wits, that I do other times come out to the highways and take it from them violently, even when they themselves do offer it unto me willingly. After this manner do I pass my miserable life, until Heaven shall be pleased to conduct it to the last period, or so change my memory as I may no more remember the beauty and treachery of Lucinda or the injury done by Don Fernando; for, if it do me this favour, without depriving my life, then will I convert my thoughts to better discourses; if not, there is no other remedy but to pray God to receive my soul into His mercy, for I neither find valour nor strength in myself to rid my body out of the straits wherein for my pleasure I did at first willingly intrude it.

'This is, sirs, the bitter relation of my disasters; wherefore judge if it be such as may be celebrated with less feeling and compassion than that which you may by this time have perceived in myself; and do not in vain labour to persuade or counsel me that which reason should afford you may be good for my remedy, for it will work no other effect in me than a medicine prescribed by a skilful physician to a patient that will in no sort receive it. I will have no health without Lucinda; and since she pleaseth to alienate herself, being or seeing she ought to be mine, so do I also take delight to be of the retinue of mishap, although I might be a retainer to good fortune. She hath ordained that her changing shall establish my perdition; and I will labour, by procuring mine own loss, to please and satisfy her will. And it shall be an example to ensuing ages, that I alone wanted that wherewith all other wretches abounded, to whom the impossibility of receiving comfort proved sometimes a cure; but in me it is an occasion of greater feeling and harm, because I am persuaded that my harms cannot end even with very death itself.'

Here Cardenio finished his large discourse and unfortunate and amorous history; and just about the time that the curate was bethinking himself of some comfortable reasons to answer and persuade him, he was suspended by a voice arrived to his hearing, which with pitiful accents said what shall be recounted in the Fourth Part of this narration; for in this very point the wise and most absolute historiographer, Cid Hamet Benengeli, finished the Third Book of this history.

THE FOURTH BOOK

CHAPTER I

Wherein is Discoursed the New and Pleasant Adventure That Happened to the Curate and the Barber in Sierra Morena

MOST happy and fortunate were those times wherein the thrice audacious and bold knight, Don Quixote of the Mancha, was bestowed on the world, by whose most honourable resolution to revive and renew in it the already worn-out and well-nigh deceased exercise of arms, we joy in this our so niggard and scant an age of all pastimes, not only the sweetness of his true history, but also of the other tales and digressions contained therein, which are in some respects no less pleasing, artificial, and true than the very history itself; the which, prosecuting the carded, spun, and self-twined thread of the relation, says that, as the curate began to bethink himself upon some answer that might both comfort and animate Cardenio, he was hindered by a voice which came to his hearing, said very dolefully the words ensuing:

'O God! is it possible that I have yet found out the place which may serve for a hidden sepulchre to the load of this loathsome body that I unwillingly bear so long? Yes, it may be, if the solitariness of these rocks do not illude me. Ah, unfortunate that I am! how much more grateful companions will these crags and thickets prove to my designs, by affording me leisure to communicate my mishaps to Heaven with plaints, than that of any mortal man living, since there is none upon earth from whom may be expected counsel in doubts, ease in complaints, or in harms remedy?' The curate and his companions heard and understood all the words clearly, and forasmuch as they conjectured (as indeed it was) that those plaints were delivered very near unto them, they did all arise to search out the plaintiff; and, having gone some twenty steps thence, they beheld a young youth behind a rock, sitting under an ash-tree, and attired like a country swain, whom, by reason his face was inclined, as he sat washing of his feet in the clear stream that glided that way, they could not perfectly discern, and therefore approached towards him with so great silence, as they were not descried by him, who only attended to the washing of his feet, which were so white, as they properly resembled two pieces of clear crystal that grew among the other stones of the stream. The whiteness and beauty of the feet amazed them, being not made, as they well conjectured, to tread clods, or measure the steps of lazy oxen, and holding the plough, as the youth's apparel would persuade them; and therefore the curate, who went before the rest, seeing they were not yet spied, made signs to the other two that they should divert a little out of the way, or hide themselves behind some broken cliffs that were near the place, which they did all of them, noting what the youth did with very great attention. He wore a little brown capouch girt very near to his body with a white towel, also a pair of breeches and gamashoes of the same coloured cloth, and on his head a clay-coloured cap; his gamashoes were lifted up half the leg, which verily seemed to be white alabaster. Finally, having washed his feet, taking out a linen kerchief from under his cap, he dried them therewithal, and at the taking out of the kerchief he held up his face, and then those which stood gazing on him had leisure to discern an unmatchable beauty, so surpassing great, as Cardenio, rounding the curate in the ear, said, 'This body, since it is not Lucinda, can be no human creature, but a divine.' The youth took off his cap at last, and, shaking his head to the one and other part, did dishevel and discover such beautiful hairs as those of Phoebus might justly emulate them; and thereby they knew the supposed swain to be a delicate woman; yea, and the fairest that ever the first two had seen in their lives, or Cardenio himself, the lovely Lucinda excepted; for, as he after affirmed, no feature save Lucinda's could contend with hers. The long and golden hairs did not only cover her shoulders, but did also hide her round about in such sort as (her feet excepted) no other part of her body appeared, they were so near and long. At this time her hands served her for a comb, which, as her feet seemed pieces of crystal in the water, so did they appear among her hairs like pieces of driven snow. All which circumstances did possess the three which stood gazing at her with great admiration and desire to know what she was, and therefore resolved to show themselves; and with the noise which they made when they arose, the beautiful maiden held up her head, and, removing her hairs from before her eyes with both hands, she espied those that had made it; and presently arising, full of fear and trouble, she laid hand on a packet that was by her, which seemed to be of apparel and thought to fly away without staying to pull on her shoes, or to gather up her hair. But scarce had she gone six paces when her delicate and tender feet, unable to abide the rough encounter of the stones, made her to fall to the earth; which the three perceiving, they came out to her, and the curate arriving first of all, said to her, 'Lady, whatsoever you be, stay and fear nothing; for we which you behold here come only with intention to do you service, and therefore you need not pretend so impertinent a flight, which neither your feet can endure, nor would we permit.'

The poor girl remained so amazed and confounded as she answered not a word; wherefore, the curate and the rest drawing nearer, they took her by the hand, and then he prosecuted his speech, saying, 'What your habit concealed from us, lady, your hairs have bewrayed, being manifest arguments that the causes were of no small moment which have thus bemasked your singular beauty under so unworthy array, and conducted you to this all-abandoned desert, wherein it was a wonderful chance to have met you, if not to remedy your harms, yet at least to give you some comfort, seeing no evil can afflict and vex one so much, and plunge him in so deep extremes (whilst it deprives not the life), that will wholly abhor from listening to the advice that is offered with a good and sincere intention; so that, fair lady, or lord, or what else you shall please to be termed, shake off your affrightment, and rehearse unto us your good or ill fortune; for you shall find in us jointly, or in every one part, companions to help you to deplore your disasters.'

Whilst the curate made this speech, the disguised woman stood as one half asleep, now beholding the one, now the other, without once moving her lip or saying a word; just like a rustical clown, when rare and unseen things to him before are unexpectedly presented to his view.

But the curate insisting, and using other persuasive reasons addressed to that effect, won her at last to make a breach on her tedious silence, and, with a profound sigh, blow open her coral gates, saying somewhat to this effect: 'Since the solitariness of these rocks hath not been potent to conceal me, nor the dishevelling of my disordered hairs licensed my tongue to belie my sex, it were in vain for me to feign that anew which, if you believed it, would be more for courtesy's sake than any other respect. Which presupposed, I say, good sirs, that I do gratify you highly for the liberal offers you have made me, which are such as have bound me to satisfy your demand as near as I may, although I fear the relation which I must make to you of my mishaps will breed sorrow at once with compassion in you, by reason you shall not be able to find any salve that may cure, comfort, or beguile them; yet, notwithstanding, to the end my reputation may not hover longer suspended in your opinions, seeing you know me to be a woman, and view me young, alone, and thus attired, being things all of them able, either joined or parted, to overthrow the best credit, I must be enforced to unfold what I could otherwise most willingly conceal.'

All this she, that appeared so comely, spoke without stop or staggering, with so ready delivery, and so sweet a voice, as her discretion admired them no less than her beauty; and, renewing again their compliments and entreaties to her to accomplish speedily her promise, she, setting all coyness apart, drawing on her shoes very modestly, and winding up her hair, sat her down on a stone, and the other three about her, where she used no little violence to smother certain rebellious tears that strove to break forth without her permission, and then, with a reposed and clear voice, she began the history of her life in this manner:

'In this province of Andalusia there is a certain town from whence a duke derives his denomination, which makes him one of those in Spain are called grandees. He hath two sons—the elder is heir of his states, and likewise, as may be presumed, of his virtues; the younger is heir I know not of what, if he be not of Vellido, his treacheries or Galalon's frauds. My parents are this nobleman's vassals, of humble and low calling, but so rich as, if the goods of nature had equalled those of their fortunes, then should they have had nothing else to desire, nor I feared to see myself in the misfortunes wherein I now am plunged, for perhaps my mishaps proceed from that of theirs, in not being nobly descended. True it is that they are not so base as they should therefore shame their calling, nor so high as may check my conceit, which persuades me that my disasters proceed from their lowness. In conclusion, they are but farmers and plain people, but without any touch or spot of bad blood, and, as we usually say, old, rusty Christians, yet so rusty and ancient as yet their riches and magnificent port gain them, by little and little, the title of gentility, yea, and of worship also; although the treasure and nobility whereof they made most price and account was to have had me for their daughter; and therefore, as well by reason that they had none other heir than myself, as also because, as affectionate parents, they held me most dear, I was one of the most made of and cherished daughters that ever father brought up. I was the mirror wherein they beheld themselves, the staff of their old age, and the subject to which they addressed all their desires, from which, because they were most virtuous, mine did not stray an inch; and even in the same manner that I was lady of their minds, so was I also of their goods. By me were servants admitted or dismissed; the notice and account of what was sowed or reaped passed through my hands; of the oil-mills, the wine-presses, the number of great and little cattle, the bee-hives—in fine, of all that so rich a farmer as my father was, had, or could have, I kept the account, and was the steward thereof and mistress, with such care of my side, and pleasure of theirs, as I cannot possibly endear it enough. The times of leisure that I had in the day, after I had given what was necessary to the head servants and other labourers, I did entertain in those exercises which were both commendable and requisite for maidens, to wit, in sewing, making of bone lace, and many times handling the distaff; and if sometimes I left those exercises to recreate my mind a little, I would then take some godly book in hand, or play on the harp; for experience had taught me that music ordereth disordered minds, and doth lighten the passions that afflict the spirit.

'This was the life which I led in my father's house, the recounting whereof so particularly hath not been done for ostentation, nor to give you to understand that I am rich, but to the end you may note how much, without mine own fault, have I fallen from that happy state I have said, unto the unhappy plight into which I am now reduced. The history, therefore, is this, that passing my life in so many occupations, and that with such recollection as might be compared to a religious life, unseen, as I thought, by any other person than those of our house; for when I went to mass it was commonly so early, and so accompanied by my mother and other maid-servants, and I myself so covered and watchful as mine eyes did scarce see the earth whereon I trod; and yet, notwithstanding, those of love, or, as I may better term them, of idleness, to which lynx eyes may not be compared, did represent me to Don Fernando's affection and care; for this is the name of the duke's younger son of whom I spake before.'

Scarce had she named Don Fernando, when Cardenio changed colour, and began to sweat, with such alteration of body and countenance, as the curate and barber which beheld it, feared that the accident of frenzy did assault him, which was wont (as they had heard) to possess him at times. But Cardenio did nothing else than sweat, and stood still, beholding now and then the country girl, imagining straight what she was; who, without taking notice of his alteration, followed on her discourse in this manner:

'And scarce had he seen me, when (as he himself after confessed) he abode greatly surprised by my love, as his actions did after give evident demonstration. But to conclude soon the relation of those misfortunes which have no conclusion, I will overslip in silence the diligences and practices of Don Fernando, used to declare unto me his affection. He suborned all the folk of the house; he bestowed gifts and favours on my parents. Every day was a holiday and a day of sports in the streets where I dwelt; at night no man could sleep for music. The letters were innumerable that came to my hands, without knowing who brought them, farsed too full of amorous conceits and offers, and containing more promises and protestations than characters. All which not only could not mollify my mind, but rather hardened it so much as if he were my mortal enemy; and therefore did construe all the endeavours he used to gain my goodwill to be practised to a contrary end: which I did not as accounting Don Fernando ungentle, or that I esteemed him too importunate; for I took a kind of delight to see myself so highly esteemed and beloved of so noble a gentleman; nor was I anything offended to see his papers written in my praise; for, if I be not deceived in this point, be we women ever so foul, we love to hear men call us beautiful. But mine honesty was that which opposed itself unto all these things, and the continual admonitions of my parents, which had by this plainly perceived Don Fernando's pretence, as one that cared not all the world should know it. They would often say unto me that they had deposited their honours and reputation in my virtue alone and discretion, and bade me consider the inequality that was between Don Fernando and me, and that I might collect by it how his thoughts (did he ever so much affirm the contrary) were more addressed to compass his pleasures than my profit; and that if I feared any inconvenience might befall, to the end they might cross it, and cause him to abandon his so unjust a pursuit, they would match me where I most liked, either to the best of that town or any other town adjoining, saying, they might easily compass it, both by reason of their great wealth and my good report. I fortified my resolution and integrity with these certain promises and the known truth which they told me, and therefore would never answer to Don Fernando any word that might ever so far off argue the least hope of condescending to his desires. All which cautions of mine, which I think he deemed to be disdains, did inflame more his lascivious appetite (for this is the name wherewithal I entitle his affection towards me), which, had it been such as it ought, you had not known it now, for then the cause of revealing it had not befallen me. Finally, Don Fernando, understanding how my parents meant to marry me, to the end they might make void his hope of ever possessing me, or at least set more guards to preserve mine honour, and this news or surmise was an occasion that he did what you shall presently hear.

'For, one night as I sat in my chamber, only attended by a young maiden that served me, I having shut the doors very safe, for fear lest, through my negligence, my honesty might incur any danger, without knowing or imagining how it might happen, notwithstanding all my diligences used and preventions, and amidst the solitude of this silence and recollection, he stood before me in my chamber. At his presence I was so troubled as I lost both sight and speech, and by reason thereof could not cry, nor I think he would not, though I had attempted it, permit me; for he presently ran over to me, and, taking me between his arms (for, as I have said, I was so amazed as I had no power to defend myself), he spake such things to me as I know not how it is possible that so many lies should have ability to feign things resembling in show so much the truth; and the traitor caused tears to give credit to his words, and sighs to give countenance to his intention.

'I, poor soul, being alone amidst my friends, and weakly practised in such affairs, began, I know not how, to account his leasings for verities, but not in such sort as his tears or sighs might any wise move me to any compassion that were not commendable. And so, the first trouble and amazement of mind being past, I began again to recover my defective spirits, and then said to him, with more courage than I thought I should have had, "If, as I am, my lord, between your arms, I were between the paws of a fierce lion, and that I were made certain of my liberty on condition to do or say anything prejudicial to mine honour, it would prove as impossible for me to accept it as for that which once hath been to leave off his essence and being. Wherefore, even as you have engirt my middle with your arms, so likewise have I tied fast my mind with virtuous and forcible desires that are wholly different from yours, as you shall perceive, if, seeking to force me, you presume to pass further with your inordinate design. I am your vassal, but not your slave; nor hath the nobility of your blood power, nor ought it to harden, to dishonour, stain, or hold in little account the humility of mine; and I do esteem myself, though a country wench and farmer's daughter, as much as you can yourself, though a nobleman and a lord. With me your violence shall not prevail, your riches gain any grace, your words have power to deceive, or your sighs and tears be able to move; yet, if I shall find any of these properties mentioned in him whom my parent shall please to bestow on me for my spouse, I will presently subject my will to his, nor shall it ever vary from his mind a jot; so that, if I might remain with honour, although I rested void of delights, yet would I willingly bestow on you that which you presently labour so much to obtain: all which I do say to divert your straying thought from ever thinking that any one may obtain of me aught who is not my lawful spouse." "If the let only consists therein, most beautiful Dorothea" (for so I am called), answered the disloyal lord, "behold, I give thee here my hand to be thine alone; and let the heavens, from which nothing is concealed, and this image of Our Lady, which thou hast here present, be witnesses of this truth!"'

When Cardenio heard her say that she was called Dorothea, he fell again into his former suspicion, and in the end confirmed his first opinion to be true, but would not interrupt her speech, being desirous to know the success, which he knew wholly almost before, and therefore said only, 'Lady, is it possible that you are named Dorothea? I have heard report of another of that name, which perhaps hath run the like course of your misfortune; but I request you to continue your relation, for a time may come wherein I may recount unto you things of the same kind, which will breed no small admiration.' Dorothea noted Cardenio's words and his uncouth and disastrous attire, and then entreated him very instantly if he knew anything of her affairs he would acquaint her therewithal; for if fortune had left her any good, it was only the courage which she had to bear patiently any disaster that might befall her, being certain in her opinion that no new one could arrive which might increase a whit those she had already.

'Lady, I would not let slip the occasion,' quoth Cardenio, 'to tell you what I think, if that which I imagine were true; and yet there is no commodity left to do it, nor can it avail you much to know it.' 'Let it be what it list,' said Dorothea; 'but that which after befel of my relation was this: That Don Fernando took an image that was in my chamber for witness of our contract, and added withal most forcible words and unusual oaths, promising unto me to become my husband; although I warned him, before he had ended his speech, to see well what he did, and to weigh the wrath of his father when he should see him married to one so base and his vassal, and that therefore he should take heed that my beauty (such as it was) should not blind him, seeing he should not find therein a sufficient excuse for his error, and that if he meant to do me any good, I conjured him, by the love that he bore unto me, to licence my fortunes to rule in their own sphere, according as my quality reached; for such unequal matches do never please long, nor persevere with that delight wherewithal they began.

'All the reasons here rehearsed I said unto him, and many more which now are fallen out of mind, but yet proved of no efficacy to wean him from his obstinate purpose; even like unto one that goeth to buy, with intention never to pay for what he takes, and therefore never considers the price, worth, or defect of the stuff he takes to credit. I at this season made a brief discourse, and said thus to myself, "I may do this, for I am not the first which by matrimony hath ascended from a low degree to a high estate; nor shall Don Fernando be the first whom beauty or blind affection (for that is the most certain) hath induced to make choice of a consort unequal to his greatness. Then, since herein I create no new world nor custom, what error can be committed by embracing the honour wherewithal fortune crowns me, although it so befel that his affection to me endured no longer than till he accomplished his will? for before God I certes shall still remain his wife. And if I should disdainfully give him the repulse, I see him now in such terms as, perhaps forgetting the duty of a nobleman, he may use violence, and then shall I remain for ever dishonoured, and also without excuse of the imputations of the ignorant, which knew not how much without any fault I have fallen into this inevitable danger; for what reasons may be sufficiently forcible to persuade my father and others that this nobleman did enter into my chamber without my consent?" All these demands and answers did I, in an instant, revolve in mine imagination, and found myself chiefly forced (how I cannot tell) to assent to his petition by the witnesses he invoked the tears he shed, and finally by his sweet disposition and comely feature, which, accompanied with so many arguments of unfeigned affection, were able to conquer and enthrall any other heart, though it were as free and wary as mine own. Then called I for my waiting-maid, that she might on earth accompany the celestial witnesses.

'And then Don Fernando turned again to reiterate and confirm his oaths, and added to his former other new saints as witnesses, and wished a thousand succeeding maledictions to light on him if he did not accomplish his promise to me. His eyes again waxed moist, his sighs increased, and himself enwreathed me more straitly between his arms, from which he had never once loosed me; and with this, and my maiden's departure, I left to be a maiden, and he began to be a traitor and a disloyal man. The day that succeeded to the night of my mishaps came not, I think, so soon as Don Fernando desired it; for, after a man hath satisfied that which the appetite covets, the greatest delight it can take after is to apart itself from the place where the desire was accomplished. I say this, because Don Fernando did hasten his departure from me: by my maid's industry, who was the very same that had brought him into my chamber, he was got in the street before dawning. And at his departure from me he said (although not with so great show of affection and vehemency as he had used at his coming) that I might be secure of his faith, and that his oaths were firm and most true; and for a more confirmation of his word, he took a rich ring off his finger and put it on mine. In fine, he departed, and I remained behind, I cannot well say whether joyful or sad; but this much I know, that I rested confused and pensive, and almost beside myself for the late mischance; yet either I had not the heart, or else I forgot to chide my maid for her treachery committed by shutting up Don Fernando in my chamber; for as yet I could not determine whether that which had befallen me was a good or an evil.

'I said to Don Fernando, at his departure, that he might see me other nights when he pleased, by the same means he had come that night, seeing I was his own, and would rest so, until it pleased him to let the world know that I was his wife. But he never returned again but the next night following, nor could I see him after, for the space of a month, either in the street or church, so as I did but spend time in vain to expect him; although I understood that he was still in town, and rode every other day a-hunting, an exercise to which he was much addicted.

'Those days were, I know, unfortunate and accursed to me, and those hours sorrowful; for in them I began to doubt, nay, rather wholly to discredit Don Fernando's faith; and my maid did then hear loudly the checks I gave unto her for her presumption, ever until then dissembled; and I was, moreover, constrained to watch and keep guard on my tears and countenance, lest I should give occasion to my parents to demand of me the cause of my discontents, and thereby engage me to use ambages or untruths to cover them. But all this ended in an instant, one moment arriving whereon all these respects stumbled, all honourable discourses ended, patience was lost, and my most hidden secrets issued in public; which was, when there was spread a certain rumour throughout the town, within a few days after, that Don Fernando had married, in a city near adjoining, a damsel of surpassing beauty, and of very noble birth, although not so rich as could deserve, by her preferment or dowry, so worthy a husband; it was also said that she was named Lucinda, with many other things that happened at their espousals worthy of admiration.' Cardenio hearing Lucinda named did nothing else but lift up his shoulders, bite his lip, bend his brows, and after a little while shed from his eyes two floods of tears. But yet for all that Dorothea did not interrupt the file of her history, saying, 'This doleful news came to my hearing; and my heart, instead of freezing thereat, was so inflamed with choler and rage, as I had well-nigh run out to the streets, and with outcries published the deceit and treason that was done to me; but my fury was presently assuaged by the resolution which I made to do what I put in execution the very same night, and then I put on this habit which you see, being given unto me by one of those that among us country-folk are called swains, who was my father's servant; to whom I disclosed all my misfortunes, and requested him to accompany me to the city where I understood my enemy sojourned. He, after he had reprehended my boldness, perceiving me to have an inflexible resolution, made offer to attend on me, as he said, unto the end of the world; and presently after I trussed up in a pillow-bear a woman's attire, some money, and jewels, to prevent necessities that might befal; and in the silence of night, without acquainting my treacherous maid with my purpose, I issued out of my house, accompanied by my servant and many imaginations, and in that manner set on towards the city, and though I went on foot, was yet borne away flying by my desires, to come, if not in time enough to hinder that which was past, yet at least to demand of Don Fernando that he would tell me with what conscience of soul he had done it. I arrived where I wished within two days and a half; and at the entry of the city I demanded where

Lucinda her father dwelt; and he of whom I first demanded the question answered me more than I desired to hear. He showed me the house, and recounted to me all that befel at the daughter's marriage, being a thing so public and known in the city, as men made meetings of purpose to discourse thereof.

'He said to me that the very night wherein Don Fernando was espoused to Lucinda, after she had given her consent to be his wife, she was instantly assailed by a terrible accident that struck her into a trance, and her spouse approaching to unclasp her bosom that she might take the air, found a paper folded in it, written with Lucinda's own hand, wherein she said and declared that she could not be Don Fernando's wife, because she was already Cardenio's, who was, as the man told me, a very principal gentleman of the same city; and that if she had given her consent to Don Fernando, it was only done because she would not disobey her parents. In conclusion, he told me that the paper made also mention how she had a resolution to kill herself presently after the marriage, and did also lay down therein the motives she had to do it; all which, as they say, was confirmed by a poniard that was found hidden about her in her apparel. Which Don Fernando perceiving, presuming that Lucinda did flout him, and hold him in little account, he set upon her ere she was come to herself, and attempted to kill her with the very same poniard, and had done it, if her father and other friends which were present had not opposed themselves and hindered his determination. Moreover, they reported that presently after Don Fernando absented himself from the city, and that Lucinda turned not out of her agony until the next day, and then recounted to her parents how she was verily spouse to that Cardenio of whom we spake even now. I learned besides that Cardenio, as it is rumoured, was present at the marriage, and that as soon as he saw her married, being a thing he would never have credited, departed out of the city in a desperate mood, but first left behind him a letter, wherein he showed at large the wrong Lucinda had done to him, and that he himself meant to go to some place where people should never after hear of him. All this was notorious, and publicly bruited throughout the city, and every one spoke thereof, but most of all having very soon after understood that Lucinda was missing from her parents' house and the city, for she could not be found in neither of both; for which her parents were almost beside themselves, not knowing what means to use to find her.

'These news reduced my hopes again to their ranks, and I esteemed it better to find Don Fernando unmarried than married, presuming that yet the gates of my remedy were not wholly shut, I giving myself to understand that Heaven had peradventure set that impediment on the second marriage to make him understand what he ought to the first, and to remember how he was a Christian, and that he was more obliged to his soul than to human respects. I revolved all these things in my mind, and comfortless did yet comfort myself, by feigning large yet languishing hopes, to sustain that life which I now do so much abhor. And whilst I stayed thus in the city, ignorant what I might do, seeing I found not Don Fernando, I heard a crier go about publicly, promising great rewards to any one that could find me out, giving signs of the very age and apparel I wore; and I likewise heard it was bruited abroad that the youth which came with me had carried me away from my father's house —a thing that touched my soul very nearly, to view my credit so greatly wrecked, seeing that it was not sufficient to have lost it by my coming away, without the addition [of] him with whom I departed, being a subject so base and unworthy of my loftier thoughts. Having heard this cry, I departed out of the city with my servant, who even then began to give tokens that he faltered in the fidelity he had promised to me; and both of us together entered the very same night into the most hidden parts of this mountain, fearing lest we might be found. But, as it is commonly said that one evil calls on another, and that the end of one disaster is the beginning of a greater, so proved it with me; for my good servant, until then faithful and trusty, rather incited by his villany than my beauty, thought to have taken the benefit of the opportunity which these inhabitable places offered, and solicited me of love, with little shame and less fear of God, or respect of myself; and now seeing that I answered his impudences with severe and reprehensive words, leaving the entreaties aside wherewithal he thought first to have compassed his will, he began to use his force; but just Heaven, which seldom or never neglects the just man's assistance, did so favour my proceedings, as with my weak forces, and very little labour, I threw him down a steep rock, and there I left him, I know not whether alive or dead; and presently I entered in among these mountains with more swiftness than my fear and weariness required, having therein no other project or design than to hide myself in them, and shun my father and others, which by his entreaty and means sought for me everywhere.

'Some months are past since my first coming here, where I found a herdman, who carried me to a village seated in the midst of these rocks, wherein he dwelt, and entertained me, whom I have served as a shepherd ever since, procuring as much as lay in me to abide still in the field, to cover these hairs which have now so unexpectedly betrayed me; yet all my care and industry availed not, seeing my master came at last to the notice that I was no man, but a woman, which was an occasion that the like evil thought sprung in him as before in my servant; and as fortune gives not always remedy for the difficulties which occur, I found neither rock nor downfall to cool and cure my master's infirmity, as I had done for my man, and therefore I accounted it a less inconvenience to depart thence, and hide myself again among these deserts, than to adventure the trial of my strength or reason with him; therefore, as I say, I turned to imbosk myself, and search out some place where, without any encumbrance, I might entreat Heaven, with my sighs and tears, to have compassion on my mishap, and lend me industry and favour, either to issue fortunately out of it, or else to die amidst these solitudes, not leaving any memory of a wretch, who hath ministered matter, although not through her own default, that men may speak and murmur of her, both in her own and in other countries.'

CHAPTER II

Which Treats of the Discretion of the Beautiful Dorothea, and the Artificial Manner Used to Dissuade the Amorous Knight from Continuing His Penance; and How He Was Gotten Away; With Many Other Delightful and Pleasant Occurrences

THIS is, sirs, the true relation of my tragedy; see therefore, now, and judge, whether the sighs you heard, the words to which you listened, and the tears that gushed out at mine eyes, have not had sufficient occasion to appear in greater abundance; and, having considered the quality of my disgrace, you shall perceive all comfort to be vain, seeing the remedy thereof is impossible. Only I will request at your hands one favour, which you ought and may easily grant, and is, that you will address me unto some place where I may live secure from the fear and suspicion I have to be found by those which I know do daily travel in my pursuit; for although I am sure that my parents' great affection toward me doth warrant me to be kindly received and entertained by them, yet the shame is so great that possesseth me, only to think that I shall not return to their presence in that state which they expect, as I account it far better to banish myself from their sight for ever, than once to behold their face with the least suspicion that they again would behold mine, divorced from that honesty which whilom my modest behaviour promised.' Here she ended, and her face, suddenly overrun by a lovely scarlet, perspicuously denoted the feeling and bashfulness of her soul.

The audients of her sad story felt great motions both of pity and admiration for her misfortunes; and although the curate thought to comfort and counsel her forthwith, yet was he prevented by Cardenio, who, taking her first by the hand, said at last, 'Lady, thou art the beautiful Dorothea, daughter unto rich Clenardo.' Dorothea rested admired when she heard her father's name, and saw of how little value he seemed who had named him, for we have already recounted how raggedly Cardenio was clothed; and therefore she said unto him, 'And who art thou, friend, that knowest so well my father's name? for until this hour (if I have not forgotten myself) I did not once name him throughout the whole discourse of my unfortunate tale.'

'I am,' answered Cardenio, 'the unlucky knight whom Lucinda (as thou saidst) affirmed to be her husband. I am the disastrous Cardenio, whom the wicked proceeding of him that hath also brought thee to those terms wherein thou art, hath conducted me to the state in which I am, and thou mayst behold—ragged, naked, abandoned by all human comfort, and, what is worse, void of sense, seeing I only enjoy it but at some few short times, and that when Heaven pleaseth to lend it me. I am he, Dorothea, that was present at Don Fernando's unreasonable wedding, and that heard the consent which Lucinda gave him to be his wife. I was he that had not the courage to stay and see the end of her trance, or what became of the paper found in her bosom; for my soul had not power or sufferance to behold so many misfortunes at once, and therefore abandoned the place and my patience together, and only left a letter with mine host, whom I entreated to deliver it into Lucinda her own hands, and then came into these deserts, with resolution to end in them my miserable life, which, since that hour, I have hated as my most mortal enemy; but fortune hath not pleased to deprive me of it, thinking it sufficient to have impaired my wit, perhaps reserving me for the good success befallen me now in finding of yourself; for, that being true (as I believe it is) which you have here discoursed, peradventure it may have reserved yet better hap for us both in our disasters than we expect.

'For, presupposing that Lucinda cannot marry with Don Fernando, because she is mine, nor Don Fernando with her, because yours, and that she hath declared so manifestly the same, we may well hope that Heaven hath means to restore to every one that which is his own, seeing it yet consists in being not made away or annihilated. And seeing this comfort remains, not sprung from any very remote hope, nor founded on idle surmises, I request thee, fair lady, to take another resolution in thine honourable thought, seeing

I mean to do it in mine, and let us accommodate ourselves to expect better success; for I do vow unto thee, by the faith of a gentleman and Christian, not to forsake thee until I see thee in Don Fernando's possession; and when I shall not, by reasons, be able to induce him to acknowledge how far he rests indebted to thee, then will I use the liberty granted to me as a gentleman, and with just title challenge him to the field in respect of the wrong he hath done unto thee, forgetting wholly mine own injuries, whose revenge I will leave to Heaven, that I may be able to right yours on earth.'

Dorothea rested wonderfully admired, having known and heard Cardenio, and, ignoring what competent thanks she might return him in satisfaction of his large offers, she cast herself down at his feet to have kissed them, which Cardenio would not permit; and the licentiate answered for both, praising greatly Cardenio's discourse, and chiefly entreated, prayed, and counselled them, that they would go with him to his village, where they might fit themselves with such things as they wanted, and also take order how to search out Don Fernando, or carry Dorothea to her father's house, or do else what they deemed most convenient. Cardenio and Dorothea gratified his courtesies, and accepted the favour he preferred. The barber also, who had stood all the while silent and suspended, made them a pretty discourse, with as friendly an offer of himself and his service as master curate, and likewise did briefly relate the occasion of their coming thither with the extravagant kind of madness which Don Quixote had, and how they expected now his squire's return, whom they had sent to search for him. Cardenio having heard him named, remembered presently, as in a dream, the conflict passed between them both, and recounted it unto them, but could not in any wise call to mind the occasion thereof.

By this time they heard one call for them, and knew by the voice that it was Sancho Panza's, who, because he found them not in the place where he had left them, cried out for them as loudly as he might. They went to meet him, and demanding for Don Quixote, he answered that he found him all naked to his shirt, lean, yellow, almost dead for hunger, and sighing for his Lady Dulcinea; and, although he had told him how she commanded him to repair presently to Toboso, where she expected him, yet, notwithstanding, he answered that he was determined never to appear before her beauty until he had done feats that should make him worthy of her gracious favour. And then the squire affirmed, if that humour passed on any further, he feared his lord would be in danger never to become an emperor, as he was bound in honour, no, nor a cardinal, which was the least that could be expected of him.

The licentiate bid him be of good cheer, for they would bring him from thence whether he would or no; and recounted to Cardenio and Dorothea what they had bethought for Don Quixote's remedy, or, at least, for the carrying him home to his house. To that Dorothea answered that she would counterfeit the distressed lady better than the barber, and chiefly seeing she had apparel wherewithal to act it most naturally, and therefore desired them to leave to her charge the representing of all that which should be needful for the achieving of their design; for she had read many books of knighthood, and knew well the style that distressed damsels used when they requested any favour of knights-adventurers. 'And then need we nothing else,' quoth the curate, 'but only to put our purpose presently in execution; for, questionless, good success turns on our side, seeing it hath so unexpectedly begun already to open the gates of your remedy, and hath also facilitated for us that whereof we had most necessity in this exigent.' Dorothea took forthwith out of her pillow-bear a whole gown of very rich stuff, and a short mantle of another green stuff, and a collar, and many other rich jewels out of a box, wherewithal she adorned herself in a trice so gorgeously as she seemed a very rich and goodly lady. All which, and much more, she had brought with her, as she said, from her house, to prevent what might happen, but never had any use of them until then. Her grace, gesture, and beauty liked them all extremely, and made them account Don Fernando to be a man of little understanding, seeing he contemned such feature. But he which was most of all admired was Sancho Panza, because, as he thought (and it was so indeed), that he had not in all the days of his life before seen so fair a creature; and he requested the curate, very seriously, to tell him who that beautiful lady was, and what she sought among those thoroughfares. 'This fair lady, friend Sancho,' answered the curate, 'is (as if a man said nothing she is so great) heir-apparent, by direct line, of the mighty kingdom of Micomicon, and comes in the search of your lord, to demand a boon of him, which is, that he will destroy and undo a great wrong done unto her by a wicked giant; and, through the great fame which is spread over all Guinea of your lord's prowess, this princess is come to find him out.' 'A happy searcher, and a fortunate finding!' quoth Sancho; 'and chiefly, if my master be so happy as to right that injury and redress that wrong by killing that, O! the mighty lubber of a giant whom you say. Yes, he will kill him, I am very certain, if he can once but meet him, and if he be not a spirit; for my master hath no kind of power over spirits. But I must request one favour of you among others most earnestly, good master licentiate, and it is, that to the end my lord may not take an humour of becoming a cardinal (which is the thing I fear most in this world), that you will give him counsel to marry this princess presently, and by that means he shall remain incapable of the dignity of a cardinal, and will come very easily by his empire, and I to the end of my desires; for I have thought well of the matter, and have found that it is in no wise expedient that my lord should become a cardinal; for I am wholly unfit for any ecclesiastical dignity, seeing I am a married man, and therefore, to trouble myself now with seeking of dispensations to enjoy church livings, having, as I have, both wife and children, were never to end. 'So that all my good consists in that my lord do marry this princess instantly, whose name yet I know not, and therefore I have not said it.' 'She is hight,' quoth the curate, 'the Princess Micomicona; for her kingdom being called Micomicon, it is evident she must be termed so.'

'That is questionless,' quoth Sancho; 'for I have known many to take their denomination and surname from the place of their birth, calling themselves Peter of Alcala, John of Ubeda, and James of Valladolid; and perhaps in Guinea princes and queens use the same custom, and call themselves by the names of their provinces.'

'So I think,' quoth the curate; 'and as touching your master's marriage with her, I will labour therein as much as lies in my power.' Wherewithal Sancho remained as well satisfied as the curate admired at his simplicity, and to see how firmly he had fixed in his fantasy the very ravings of his master, seeing he did believe without doubt that his lord should become an emperor. Dorothea in this space had gotten upon the curate's mule, and the barber had somewhat better fitted the beard which he made of the ox's tail on his face, and did after entreat Sancho to guide them to the place where Don Quixote was, and advertised him withal that he should in no wise take any notice of the curate or barber, or confess in any sort that he knew them, for therein consisted all the means of bringing Don Quixote to the mind to become an emperor. Yet Cardenio would not go with them, fearing lest thereby Don Quixote might call to mind their contention; and the curate, thinking also that his presence was not expedient, remained with him, letting the others go before, and these followed afar off fair and softly on foot; and ere they departed, the curate instructed Dorothea anew what she should say, who bid him to fear nothing, for she would discharge her part to his satisfaction, and as books of chivalry required and laid down.

They travelled about three-quarters of a league, as they espied the knight, and at last they discovered him among a number of intricate rocks, all apparelled, but not armed; and as soon as Dorothea beheld him, she struck her palfrey, her well-bearded barber following her; and as they approached Don Quixote, the barber leaped lightly down from his mule and ran towards Dorothea to take her down between his arms, who, alighting, went with a very good grace towards Don Quixote, and kneeled before him. And although he strived to make her arise, yet she, remaining still on her knees, spake to him in this manner: 'I will not arise from hence, thrice valorous and approved knight, until your bounty and courtesy shall grant unto me one boon, which shall much redound unto your honour and prize of your person, and to the profit of the most disconsolate and wronged damsel that the sun hath ever seen. And if it be so that the valour of your invincible arm be correspondent to the bruit of your immortal fame, you are obliged to succour this comfortless wight that comes from lands so remote, to the sound of your famous name, searching you for to remedy her mishaps.'

'I will not answer you a word, fair lady,' quoth Don Quixote, 'nor hear a jot of your affair, until you arise from the ground.'

'I will not get up from hence, my lord,' quoth the afflicted lady, 'if first, of your wonted bounty, you do not grant to my request.' 'I do give and grant it,' said Don Quixote, 'so that it be not a thing that may turn to the damage or hindrance of my king, my country, or of her that keeps the key of my heart and liberty.' 'It shall not turn to the damage or hindrance of those you have said, good sir,' replied the dolorous damsel; and, as she was saying this, Sancho Panza rounded his lord in the ear, saying softly to him, 'Sir, you may very well grant the request she asketh, for it is a matter of nothing; it is only to kill a monstrous giant, and she that demands it is the mighty Princess Micomicona, queen of the great kingdom of Micomicon in Ethiopia.' 'Let her be what she will,' quoth Don Quixote, 'for I will accomplish what I am bound, and my conscience shall inform me conformable to the state I have professed.' And then, turning to the damsel, he said, 'Let your great beauty arise; for I grant to you any boon which you shall please to ask of me.' 'Why, then,' quoth the damsel, 'that which I demand is that your magnanimous person come presently away with me to the place where I shall carry you, and do likewise make me a promise not to undertake any other adventure or demand until you revenge me upon a traitor who hath, against all laws, both divine and human, usurped my kingdom.' 'I say that I grant you all that,' quoth Don Quixote; 'and therefore, lady, you may cast away from this day forward all the melancholy that troubles you, and labour that your languishing and dismayed hopes may recover again new strength and courage; for, by the help of God, and that of mine arm, you shall see yourself shortly restored to your kingdom, and enthroned in the chair of your ancient and great estate, in despite and maugre the traitors that shall dare gainsay it: and therefore, hands, to the work; for they say that danger always follows delay.' The distressed damsel strove with much ado to kiss his hand, but Don Quixote, who was a most accomplished knight for courtesy, would never condescend thereunto; but, making her arise, he embraced her with great kindness and respect, and commanded Sancho to saddle Rozinante, and help him to arm himself.

Sancho took down the arms forthwith, which hung on a tree like trophies, and, searching the girths, armed his lord in a moment, who, seeing himself armed, said, 'Let us, in God's name, depart from hence to assist this great lady.' The barber kneeled all this while, and could with much ado dissemble his laughter, or keep on his beard that threatened still to fall off, with whose fall, perhaps, they should all have remained without bringing their good purpose to pass. And seeing that the boon was granted, and noted the diligence wherewithal Don Quixote made himself ready to depart and accomplish the same, he arose and took his lady by the hand, and both of them together holp her upon her mule; and presently after Don Quixote leaped on Rozinante, and the barber got on his beast, Sancho only remaining afoot, where he afresh renewed the memory of the loss of his grey ass, with the want procured to him thereby; but all this he bore with very great patience, because he supposed that his lord was now in the way and next degree to be an emperor; for he made an infallible account that he would marry that princess, and at least be king of Micomicon. But yet it grieved him to think how that kingdom was in the country of black Moors, and that therefore the nation which should be given to him for his vassals should be all black, for which difficulty his imagination coined presently a good remedy, and he discoursed with himself in this manner: 'Why should I care though my subjects be all black Moors? Is there any more to be done than to load them in a ship and bring them into Spain, where I may sell them, and receive the price of them in ready money? And with that money may I buy some title or office, wherein I may after live at mine ease all the days of my life. No! but sleep, and have no wit or ability to dispose of things; and to sell thirty or ten thousands vassals in the space that one would say, Give me those straws. I will despatch them all; they shall fly, the little with the great, or as I can best contrive the matter; and be they ever so black, I will transform them into white or yellow ones. Come near, and see whether I cannot suck well my fingers' ends.' And thus he travelled, so solicitous and glad as he quite forgot his pain of travelling afoot. Cardenio and the curate stood in the meantime beholding all that passed from behind some brambles where they lay lurking, and were in doubt what means to use to issue and join in company with them. But the curate, who was an ingenious and prompt plotter, devised instantly what was to be done that they might attain their desire. Thus, he took out of his case a pair of shears, and cut off Cardenio's beard therewithal in a trice, and then gave unto him to wear a riding capouch which he himself had on, and a black cloak, and himself walked in a doublet and hose. Cardenio, thus attired, looked so unlike that he was before, as he would not have known himself in a looking-glass. This being finished, and the others gone on before whilst they disguised themselves, they sallied out with facility to the highway before Don Quixote or his company; for the rocks and many other bad passages did not permit those that were a-horseback to make so speedy an end of their journey as they. And having thoroughly passed the mountain, they expected at the foot thereof for the knight and his company, who when he appeared, the curate looked on him very earnestly for a great space, with inkling that he began to know him. And after he had a good while beheld him, he ran towards him with his arms spread abroad, saying, 'In a good hour be the mirror of all knighthood found, and my noble countryman, Don Quixote of the Mancha! the flower and cream of gentility, the shadow and remedy of the afflicted, and the quintessence of knights-errant!' and, saying this, he held Don Quixote his left thigh embraced; who, admiring at that which he heard that man to say and do, did also review him with attention, and finally knew him, and, all amazed to see him, made much ado to alight; but the curate would not permit him. Wherefore Don Quixote said, 'Good master licentiate, permit me to alight; for it is in no sort decent that I be a-horseback, and so reverend a person as you go on foot.' 'I will never consent thereunto,' quoth the curate; 'your highness must needs stay on horseback, seeing that thereon you are accustomed to achieve the greatest feats of chivalry and adventures which were ever seen in our age. For it shall suffice me, who am an unworthy priest, to get up behind some one of these other gentlemen that ride in your company, if they will not take it in bad part; yea, and I will make account that I ride on Pegasus, or the zebra of the famous Moor Muzaraque, who lies yet enchanted in the steep rock of Zulema, near unto Alcala of Henares.'

'Truly, I did not think upon it, good master licentiate,' answered Don Quixote; 'yet, I presume, my lady the princess will be well apaid, for my sake, to command her squire to lend you the use of his saddle, and to get up himself on the crupper, if so it be that the beast will bear double.' 'Yes, that it will,' said the princess, 'for aught I know; and likewise, I am sure, it will not be necessary to command my squire to alight, for he is of himself so courteous and courtly as he will in no wise condescend that an ecclesiastical man should go on foot when he may help him to a horse.'

'That is most certain,' quoth the barber; and, saying so, he alighted, and entreated the curate to take the saddle, to which courtesy he did easily condescend. But, by evil fortune, as the barber thought to leap up behind him, the mule, which was in effect a hired one, and that is sufficient to say it was unhappy, did lift a little her hinder quarters, and bestowed two or three flings on the air, which had they hit on Master Nicholas his breast or pate, he would have bequeathed the quest of Don Quixote upon the devil. But, notwithstanding, the barber was so affrighted as he fell on the ground, with so little heed of his beard as it fell quite off and lay spread upon the ground; and, perceiving himself without it, he had no other shift but to cover his face with both his hands, and complain that all his cheek teeth were strucken out. Don Quixote, beholding such a great sheaf of a beard fallen away, without jaw or blood, from the face, he said, 'I vow this is one of the greatest miracles that ever I saw in my life; it hath taken and plucked away his beard as smoothly as if it were done of purpose.' The curate beholding the danger which their invention was like to incur if it were detected, went forthwith, and, taking up the beard, came to Master Nicholas, that lay still a-playing, and, with one push, bringing his head towards his own breast, he set it on again, murmuring the while over him certain words, which he said were a certain prayer appropriated to the setting on of fallen beards, as they should soon perceive; and so, having set it on handsomely, the squire remained as well bearded and whole as ever he was in his life. Whereat Don Quixote rested marvellously admired, and requested the curate to teach him that prayer when they were at leisure; for he supposed that the virtue thereof extended itself further than to the fastening on of beards, since it was manifest that the place whence the beard was torn must have remained without flesh, wounded, and ill dight, and, seeing it cured all, it must of force serve for more than the beard. 'It is true,' replied master curate; and then promised to instruct him with the secret with the first opportunity that was presented.

Then they agreed that the curate should ride first on the mule, and after him the other two, each one by turns, until they arrived to the inn, which was about some two leagues thence. Three being thus mounted (to wit, Don Quixote, the princess, and curate), and the other three on foot (Cardenio, the barber, and Sancho Panza), Don Quixote said to the damsel, 'Madam, let me entreat your highness to lead me the way that most pleaseth you.' And before she could answer, the licentiate said, 'Towards what kingdom would you travel? Is it, by fortune, towards that of Micomicon? I suppose it should be thitherwards, or else I know but little of kingdoms.' She, who knew very well the curate's meaning, and was herself no babe, answered, saying, 'Yes, sir, my way lies towards that kingdom.' 'If it be so,' quoth the curate, 'you must pass through the village where I dwell, and from thence direct your course towards Carthagena, where you may luckily embark yourselves. And if you have a prosperous wind, and a quiet and calm sea, you may come within the space of nine years to the sight of the Lake Meona, I mean Meolidas, which stands on this side of your highness's kingdom some hundred days' journey, or more.' 'I take you to be deceived, good sir,' quoth she, 'for it is not yet fully two years since I departed from thence, and, truly, I never almost had any fair weather, and yet, notwithstanding, I have arrived, and come to see that which I so much longed for, to wit, the presence of the worthy Don Quixote of the Mancha, whose renown came to my notice as soon as I touched the earth of Spain with my foot, and moved me to search for him, to commend myself to his courtesy, and commit the justice of my cause to the valour of his invincible arm.'

'No more,' quoth Don Quixote; 'I cannot abide to hear myself praised, for I am a sworn enemy of all adulation; and although this be not such, yet notwithstanding the like discourses do offend my chaste ears. What I can say to you, fair princess, is that whether I have valour or not, that which I have, or have not, shall be employed in your service, even to the very loss of my life. And so, omitting that till this time, let me entreat good master licentiate to tell me the occasion which hath brought him here to these quarters, so alone, without attendants, and so slightly attired, as it strikes me in no little admiration?' 'To this I will answer with brevity,' quoth the curate. 'You shall understand that Master Nicholas the barber, our very good friend, and myself, travelled towards Seville to recover certain sums of money which a kinsman of mine, who hath dwelt these many years in the Indies, hath sent unto me. The sum is not a little one, for it surmounted seventy thousand reals of eight, all of good weight—see if it was not a rich gift. And passing yesterday through this way, we were set upon by four robbers, which despoiled us of all, even to our very beards, and that in such sort as the barber was forced to set on a counterfeit one; and this young man that goeth here with us' (meaning Cardenio) 'was transformed by them anew. And the best of it is that it is publicly bruited about all this commark that those which surprised us were galley-slaves who were set at liberty, as is reported, much about this same place, by so valiant a knight as, in despite of the commissary and the guard, he freed them all. And, questionless, he either was wood, or else as great a knave as themselves, or some one that wanted both soul and conscience, seeing he let slip the wolves amidst the sheep, the fox among the hens, and flies hard by honey, and did frustrate justice, rebel against his natural lord and king; for he did so by oppugning his just commandments; and hath deprived the galleys of their feet, and set all the holy brotherhood in an uproar, which hath reposed these many years past; and finally, would do an act by which he should lose his soul, and yet not gain his body.' Sancho had rehearsed to the curate and barber the adventure of the slaves, which his lord had accomplished with such glory; and therefore the curate did use this vehemence as he repeated it, to see what Don Quixote would say or do, whose colour changed at every word, and durst not confess that he was himself the deliverer of that good people. 'And these,' quoth the curate, 'were they that have robbed us. And God, of His infinite mercy, pardon him who hindered their going to receive the punishment they had so well deserved!'

CHAPTER III

Of Many Pleasant Discourses Passed Between Don Quixote and Those of His Company, After He Had Abandoned the Rigorous Place of His Penance

SCARCE had the curate finished his speech thoroughly, when Sancho said, 'By my faith, master licentiate, he that did that feat was my lord, and that not for want of warning, for I told him beforehand, and advised him that he should see well what he did, and that it was a sin to deliver them, because they were all sent to the galleys for very great villanies they had played.'

'You bottlehead,' replied Don Quixote, hearing him speak, 'it concerneth not knights-errant to examine whether the afflicted, the enchained, and oppressed, which they encounter by the way, be carried in that fashion, or are plunged in that distress, through their own default or disgrace, but only are obliged to assist them as needy and oppressed, setting their eyes upon their pains, and not on their crimes. I met with a rosary or beads of inserted people, sorrowful and unfortunate, and I did for them that which my religion exacts; as for the rest, let them verify it elsewhere: and to whosoever else, the holy dignity and honourable person of master licentiate excepted, it shall seem evil, I say he knows but slightly what belongs to chivalry, and he lies like a whoreson and a villain born, and this will I make him know with the broad side of my sword.' These words he said, settling himself in his stirrups, and addressing his morion (for the barber's basin, which he accounted to be Mambrino's helmet, he carried hanging at the pommel of his saddle, until he might have it repaired of the crazings the galley-slave had wrought in it). Dorothea, who was very discreet and pleasant, and that was by this well acquainted with Don Quixote's faulty humour, and saw all the rest make a jest of him, Sancho Panza excepted, would also show her conceit to be as good as some others, and therefore said unto him, 'Sir knight, remember yourself of the boon you have promised unto me, whereunto conforming yourself, you cannot intermeddle in any other adventure, be it ever so urgent. Therefore, assuage your stomach; for if master licentiate had known that the galley-slaves were delivered by your invincible arm, he would rather have given unto himself three blows on the mouth, and also bit his tongue thrice, than have spoken any word whence might result your indignation.' 'That I dare swear,' quoth the curate; 'yea, and besides torn away one of my moustaches.'

'Madam,' said Don Quixote, 'I will hold my peace, and suppress the just choler already enkindled in my breast, and will ride quietly and peaceably, until I have accomplished the thing I have promised; and I request you, in recompense of this my good desire, if it be not displeasing to you, to tell me your grievance, and how many, which, and what the persons be, of whom I must take due, sufficient, and entire revenge.' 'I will promptly perform your will herein,' answered Dorothea, 'if it will not be irksome to you to listen to disasters.' 'In no sort, good madam,' said Don Quixote. To which Dorothea answered thus: 'Be then attentive to my relation.' Scarce had she said so, when Cardenio and the barber came by her side, desirous to hear how the discreet Dorothea would feign her tale; and the same did Sancho, which was so much deceived in her person as his lord Don Quixote. And she, after dressing herself well in the saddle, bethought and provided herself whilst she coughed and used other gestures, and then began to speak on this manner:

'First of all, good sirs, I would have you note that I am called'— And here she stood suspended a while, by reason she had forgotten the name that the curate had given unto her. But he presently occurred to her succour, understanding the cause, and said, 'It is no wonder, great lady, that you be troubled and stagger whilst you recount your misfortunes, seeing it is the ordinary custom of disasters to deprive those whom they torment and distract their memory in such sort as they cannot remember themselves even of their own very names, as now it proves done in your highness, which forgets itself that you are called the Princess Micomicona, lawful inheritrix of the great kingdom of Micomicon. And with this note, you may easily reduce into your doleful memory all that which you shall please to rehearse.'

'It is very true,' quoth the damsel, 'and from henceforth I think it will not be needful to prompt me any more, for I will arrive into a safe port with the narration of my authentic history; which is, that my father, who was called the wise Tinacrio, was very expert in that which was called art magic, and he knew by his science that my mother, who was called Queen Xaramilla, should die before he deceased, and that he should also pass from this life within a while after, and leave me an orphan; but he was wont to say how that did not afflict his mind so much, as that he was very certain that a huge giant, lord of a great island near unto my kingdom, called Pandafilando of the Dusky Sight (because, although his eyes stood in their right places, yet do they still look asquint, which he doth to terrify the beholders), I say that my father knew that this giant, when he should hear of his death, would pass with a main power into my land, and deprive me thereof, not leaving me the least village wherein I might hide my head; yet might all this be excused if I would marry with him. But, as he found out by his science, he knew I would never condescend thereunto, or incline mine affection to so unequal a marriage; and herein he said nothing but truth, for it never passed once my thought to espouse that giant, nor with any other, were he ever so unreasonable, and great, and mighty. My father likewise added then, that after his death I should see Pandafilando usurp my kingdom, and that I should in no wise stand to my defence, for that would prove my destruction; but, leaving to him the kingdom freely without troubles, if I meant to excuse mine own death, and the total ruin of my good and loyal subjects (for it would be impossible to defend myself from the devilish force of the giant), I should presently direct my course towards Spain, where I should find a redress of my harms by encountering with a knight-errant whose fame should extend itself much about that time throughout that kingdom, and his name should be, if I forgot not myself, Don Azote or Don Gigote.'

'Lady, you would say Don Quixote,' quoth Sancho Panza, 'or, as he is called by another name, the Knight of the Ill-favoured Face.' 'You have reason,' replied Dorothea. 'He said, moreover, that he should be high of stature, have a withered face, and that on the right side, a little under the left shoulder, or thereabouts, he should have a tawny spot with certain hairs like to bristles.' Don Quixote, hearing this, said to his squire, 'Hold my horse here, son Sancho, and help me to take off mine apparel; for I will see whether I be the knight of whom the wise king hath prophesied.' 'Why would you now put off your clothes?' quoth Dorothea. 'To see whether I have that spot which your father mentioned,' answered Don Quixote. 'You need not undo your apparel for that purpose,' said Sancho, 'for I know already that you have a spot with the tokens she named on the very ridges of your back, and argues you to be a very strong man.' 'That is sufficient,' quoth Dorothea; 'for we must not look too near, or be over-curious in our friends' affairs; and whether it be on the shoulder, or ridge of the back, it imports but little, for the substance consists only in having such a mark, and not wheresoever it shall be, seeing all is one and the self-same flesh; and, doubtlessly, my good father did aim well at all, and I likewise in commending myself to Don Quixote; for surely he is the man of whom my father spoke, seeing the signs of his face agree with those of the great renown that is spread abroad of this knight, not only in Spain, but also in Ethiopia; for I had no sooner landed in Osuna, when I heard so many of his prowesses recounted, as my mind gave me presently that he was the man in whose search I travelled.' 'But how did you land in Osuna, good madam,' quoth Don Quixote, 'seeing it is no sea town?' 'Marry, sir,' quoth the curate, anticipating Dorothea's answer, 'the princess would say that after she had landed in Malaga, but the first place wherein she heard tidings of you was at Osuna.' 'So I would have said,' quoth Dorothea. 'And it may be very well,' quoth the curate; 'and I desire your majesty to continue your discourse.' 'There needs no further continuation,' quoth Dorothea, 'but that, finally, my fortune hath been so favourable in finding of Don Quixote, as I do already hold and account myself for queen and lady of all mine estate, seeing that he, of his wonted bounty and magnificence, hath promised me the boon to accompany me wheresoever I shall guide him, which shall be to none other place than to set him before Pandafilando of the dusky sight, to the end you may slay him, and restore me to that which he hath so wrongfully usurped; for all will succeed in the twinkling of an eye, as the wise Tinacrio, my good father, hath already foretold, who said moreover, and also left it written in Chaldaical or Greek characters (for I cannot read them), that if the knight of the prophecy, after having beheaded the giant, would take me to wife, that I should in no sort refuse him, but instantly admitting him for my spouse, make him at once possessor of myself and my kingdom.'

'What thinkest thou of this, friend Sancho?' quoth Don Quixote then, when he heard her say so. 'How likest thou this point? Did not I tell thee thus much before? See now, whether we have not a kingdom to command, and a queen whom we may marry.' 'I swear as much,' quoth Sancho. 'A pox on the knave that will not marry as soon as Master Pandahilado his windpipes are cut! Mount, then, and see whether the queen be ill or no. I would to God all the fleas of my bed were turned to be such!' And, saying so, he gave two or three friskles in the air, with very great signs of contentment, and presently went to Dorothea, and, taking her mule by the bridle, he withheld it, and, laying himself down on his knees before her, requested her very submissively to give him her hands to kiss them, in sign that he received her for his queen and lady. Which of the beholders could abstain from laughter, perceiving the master's madness and the servant's simplicity? To be brief, Dorothea must needs give them unto him, and promised to make him a great lord in her kingdom, when Heaven became so propitious to her as to let her once recover and possess it peaceably. And Sancho returned her thanks with such words as made them all laugh anew.

'This is my history, noble sirs,' quoth Dorothea, 'whereof only rests untold that none of all the train which I brought out of my kingdom to attend on me is now extant but this well-bearded squire; for all of them were drowned in a great storm that overtook us in the very sight of the harbour, whence he and I escaped, and came to land by the help of two planks, on which we laid hold, almost by miracle; as also the whole discourse and mystery of my life seems none other than a miracle, as you might have noted. And if in any part of the relation I have exceeded, or not observed a due decorum, you must impute it to that which master licentiate said to the first of my history, that continual pains and afflictions of mind deprives them that suffer the like of their memory.' 'That shall not hinder me, O high and valorous lady!' quoth Don Quixote, 'from enduring as many as I shall suffer in your service, be they never so great or difficult; and therefore I do anew ratify and confirm the promise I have made, and do swear to go with you to the end of the world, until I find out your fierce enemy, whose proud head I mean to slice off, by the help of God and my valorous arm, with the edge of this (I will not say a good) sword, thanks be to Gines of Passamonte, which took away mine own.' This he said murmuring to himself, and then prosecuted, saying, 'And after I have cut it off, and left you peaceably in the possession of your state, it shall rest in your own will to dispose of your person as you like best; for as long as I shall have my memory possessed, and my will captivated, and my understanding yielded to her——I will say no more; it is not possible that ever I may induce myself to marry any other, although she were a Phoenix.'

That which Don Quixote had said last of all, of not marrying, disliked Sancho so much, as, lifting his voice with great anger, he said, 'I vow and swear by myself that you are not in your right wits, Sir Don Quixote; for how is it possible that you can call the matter of contracting so high a princess as this is in doubt? Do you think that fortune will offer you, at every corner's end, the like hap of this which is now proffered? Is my Lady Dulcinea, perhaps, more beautiful? No, certainly, nor half so fair; nay, I am rather about to say that she comes not to her shoe that is here present. In an ill hour shall I arrive to possess that unfortunate earldom which I expect, if you go thus seeking for mushrubs in the bottom of the sea. Marry, marry yourself presently, the devil take you for me, and take that kingdom comes into your hands, and being a king, make me presently a marquis or admiral, and instantly after let the devil take all if he pleaseth.'

Don Quixote, who heard such blasphemies spoken against his Lady Dulcinea, could not bear them any longer; and therefore, lifting up his javelin, without speaking any word to Sancho, gave him therewithal two such blows as he overthrew him to the earth; and had not Dorothea cried to him to hold his hand, he had doubtlessly slain him in the place.

'Thinkest thou,' quoth he after a while, 'base peasant! that I shall have always leisure and disposition to thrust my hand into my pouch, and that there be nothing else but thou still erring and I pardoning? And dost not thou think of it, excommunicated rascal! for certainly thou art excommunicated, seeing thou hast talked so broadly of the peerless Dulcinea! And dost not thou know, base slave! vagabond! that if it were not for the valour she infuseth into mine arm, that I should not have sufficient forces to kill a flea? Say, scoffer with the viper's tongue! who dost thou think hath gained this kingdom, and cut the head off this giant, and made thee a marquis (for I give all this for done already, and for a matter ended and judged), but the worths and valour of Dulcinea, using mine arm as the instrument of her act? She fights under my person, and overcomes in me; and I live and breathe in her, and from her I hold my life and being. O whoreson villain! how ungrateful art thou, that seest thyself exalted out from the dust of the earth to be a nobleman, and yet dost repay so great a benefit with detracting the person that bestowed it on thee!'

Sancho was not so sore hurt but that he could hear all his master's reasons very well; wherefore, arising somewhat hastily, he ran behind Dorothea her palfrey, and from thence said to his lord, 'Tell me, sir, if you be not determined to marry with this princess, it is most clear that the kingdom shall not be yours; and if it be not, what favours can you be able to do to me? It is of this that I complain me. Marry yourself one for one with this princess, now that we have her here as it were rained to us down from heaven, and you may after turn to my Lady Dulcinea; for I think there be kings in the world that keep lemans. As for beauty, I will not intermeddle; for, if I must say the truth, each of both is very fair, although I have never seen the Lady Dulcinea.' 'How! hast thou not seen her, blasphemous traitor?' quoth Don Quixote, 'As if thou didst but even now bring me a message from her!' 'I say,' quoth Sancho, 'I have not seen her so leisurely as I might particularly note her beauty and good parts one by one, but yet in a clap, as I saw them, they liked me very well.' 'I do excuse thee now,' said Don Quixote, 'and pardon me the displeasure which I have given unto thee, for the first motions are not in our hands.' 'I see that well,' quoth Sancho, 'and that is the reason why talk is in me of one of those first motions, and I cannot omit to speak once, at least, that which comes to my tongue.' 'For all that, Sancho,' replied Don Quixote, 'see well what thou speakest; for "the earthen pitcher goes so oft to the water"—I will say no more.'

'Well, then,' answered Sancho, 'God is in heaven, who seeth all these guiles, and shall be one day judge of him that sins most—of me in not speaking well, or of you by not doing well.' 'Let there be no more,' quoth Dorothea, 'but run, Sancho, and kiss your lord's hand, and ask him forgiveness, and from henceforth take more heed how you praise or dispraise anybody, and speak no ill of that Lady Toboso, whom I do not know otherwise than to do her service; and have confidence in God, for thou shalt not want a lordship wherein thou mayst live like a king.' Sancho went with his head hanging downward, and demanded his lord's hand, which he gave unto him with a grave countenance; and after he had kissed it, he gave him his blessing, and said to him that he had somewhat to say unto him, and therefore bade him to come somewhat forward, that he might speak unto him. Sancho obeyed; and both of them going a little aside, Don Quixote said unto him, 'I have not had leisure after thy coming to demand of thee in particular concerning the ambassage that thou carriedst, and the answer that thou broughtst back; and therefore, now fortune lends us some opportunity and leisure, do not deny me the happiness which thou mayst give me by thy good news.'

'Demand what you please,' quoth Sancho, 'and I will answer you; and I request you, good my lord, that you be not from henceforth so wrathful.' 'Why dost thou say so, Sancho?' quoth Don Quixote. 'I say it,' replied Sancho, 'because that these blows which you bestowed now, were rather given in revenge of the dissension which the devil stirred between us two the other night, than for anything I said against my Lady Dulcinea, whom I do honour and reverence as a relique, although she be none, only because she is yours.' 'I pray thee, good Sancho,' said Don Quixote, 'fall not again into those discourses, for they offend me. I did pardon thee then, and thou knowest that a new offence must have a new penance.'

As they talked thus, they espied a gallant coming towards them, riding on an ass, and when he drew near he seemed to be an

Egyptian; but Sancho Panza, who, whensoever he met any asses, followed them with his eyes and his heart, as one that thought still on his own, had scarce eyed him when he knew that it was Gines of Passamonte, and, by the look of the Egyptian, found out the fleece of his ass, as in truth it was; for Gines came riding on his grey ass, who, to the end he might not be known, and also have commodity to sell his beast, attired himself like an Egyptian, whose language and many others he could speak as well as if they were his mother tongue. Sancho saw him and knew him; and scarce had he seen and taken notice of him, when he cried out aloud, 'Ah! thief, Ginesillo! leave my goods behind thee, set my life loose, and do not intermeddle with my ease! Leave mine ass, leave my comfort! Fly, villain! absent thyself, thief! and abandon that which is none of thine!' He needed not to have used so many words and frumps, for Gines leaped down at the very first, and beginning a trot, that seemed rather to be a gallop, he absented himself, and fled far enough from them in a moment. Sancho went then to his ass, and, embracing him, said, 'How hast thou done hitherto, my darling and treasure, grey ass of mine eyes, and my dearest companion?' and with that stroked and kissed him as if it were a reasonable creature. The ass held his peace, and permitted Sancho to kiss and cherish him, without answering a word. All the rest arrived, and congratulated with Sancho for the finding of his ass, but chiefly Don Quixote, who said unto him that notwithstanding that he found his ass, yet would not he therefore annul his warrant for the three colts; for which Sancho returned him very great thanks.

Whilst they two travelled together discoursing thus, the curate said to Dorothea that she had very discreetly discharged herself, as well in the history as in her brevity and imitation thereof to the phrase and conceits of books of knighthood. She answered that she did ofttimes read books of that subject, but that she knew not where the provinces lay, nor seaports, and therefore did only say at random that she had landed in Osuna. 'I knew it was so,' quoth the curate, 'and therefore I said what you heard, wherewithal the matter was soldered. But is it not a marvellous thing to see with what facility the unfortunate gentleman believes all these inventions and lies, only because they bear the style and manner of the follies laid down in his books?' 'It is,' quoth Cardenio, 'and that so rare and beyond all conceit, as I believe, if the like were to be invented, scarce could the sharpest wits devise such another.'

'There is yet,' quoth the curate, 'as marvellous a matter as that; for, leaving apart the simplicities which this good gentleman speaks concerning his frenzy, if you will commune with him of any other subject whatsoever, he will discourse on it with an excellent method, and show himself to have a clear and pleasing understanding; so that, if he be not touched by matters of chivalry, there is no man but will deem him to be of a sound and excellent judgment.'

Don Quixote on the other side prosecuted his conversing with his squire whilst the others talked together, and said to Sancho, 'Let us two, friend Panza, forget old injuries, and say unto me now, without any rancour or anger, where, how, and when didst thou find my Lady Dulcinea? What did she when thou camest? What saidst thou to her? What answered she? What countenance showed she as she read my letter? And who writ it out fairly for thee? And every other thing that thou shalt think worthy of notice in this affair to be demanded or answered, without either addition or lying, or soothing adulation; and on the other side do not abbreviate it, lest thou shouldst defraud me thereby of expected delight.' 'Sir,' answered Sancho, 'if I must say the truth, none copied out the letter for me; for I carried no letter at all.'

'Thou sayst true,' quoth Don Quixote; 'for I found the tablets wherein it was written with myself two days after thy departure, which did grieve me exceedingly, because I knew not what thou wouldst do when thou didst perceive the want of the letter, and I always made full account that thou wouldst return again from the place where thou shouldst first miss it.' 'I had done so,' quoth Sancho, 'if I had not borne it away in memory, when you read it to me, in such sort as I said to a clerk of a vestry, who did copy it out of my understanding so point by point, as he said that he never in all the days of his life, although he had read many a letter of excommunication, read or seen so fine a letter as it was.' 'And dost thou hold it yet in memory, Sancho?' quoth Don Quixote.

'No, sir,' said Sancho; 'for after I gave it, seeing it served for none other purpose, I did willingly forget it; and if I remember anything, it is that of the "mouldy"—I would say "sovereign lady"; and the end, "yours until death, the Knight of the Ill-favoured Face"; and I put between these two things in the letter three hundred souls, and lives, and sweet eyes.'

CHAPTER IV

Of the Pleasant Discourses Continued Between Don Quixote and His Squire Sancho Panza, with Other Adventures

'ALL this liketh me well,' said Don Quixote; 'therefore say on. Thou arrivedst, and what was that queen of beauty doing then? I daresay that thou foundest her threading of pearls, or embroidering some curious device with Venice gold, for me her captive knight.' 'No, that I did not,' quoth Sancho; 'but winnowing two bushels of wheat in the yard of her house.'

'Why, then,' said Don Quixote, 'thou mayst make account that each corn of that wheat was a grain of pearl, seeing they were touched by her delicate hand. And, friend, didst thou note well what the wheat was, whether of the best or ordinary?' 'It was not, but red,' said Sancho. 'Well, then, I assure thee,' answered Don Quixote, 'that being sifted by her hands, it must needs make very fair bread and white. But pass forward. When thou didst deliver my letter, did she kiss it? Did she set it on her head? Did she use any ceremony worthy of such a letter? Or what did she?' 'When I went to give it unto her,' said Sancho, 'she was holding up of her arms with a good quantity of wheat that she had in her sieve, and therefore said unto me, "Friend, lay down that letter there on the sack, for I cannot read it until I have winnowed all that is here."' 'O discreet lady,' quoth Don Quixote; 'she surely did that because she might read it at leisure, and recreate herself therewithal. Forward, Sancho. And as long as she was thus busied, what discourses passed she with thee? What did she demand of thee concerning me? And thou, what didst thou answer? Say all, good Sancho, say all; recount to me every particularity, and let not the least [minuity] remain in the inkhorn.'

'She demanded nothing of me,' quoth Sancho; 'but I recounted unto her the state I had left you in for her sake, doing of penance, all naked from the girdle upward, among these rocks, like a brute beast, sleeping on the ground, and eating your bread without tablecloths, and that you never combed your beard, but was weeping and cursing your fortune.' 'There thou saidst ill,' quoth Don Quixote; 'for I do not curse my fortune, but rather bless it, and will bless it as long as I shall live, seeing it hath made me worthy to merit the love of so high a lady as Dulcinea of Toboso.' 'She is in good faith so high,' answered Sancho, 'as she surpasseth me almost by a whole cubit.' 'Why, how now, Sancho?' said the knight; 'hast thou measured thyself with her?' 'I did measure myself with her in this manner,' replied Sancho, 'that coming over to help her to lift up a sack of wheat on an ass, we joined so near as I well perceived that she was more than a great span higher than myself.' 'That is true,' quoth Don Quixote; 'but thinkest thou not that the tallness of her extended stature is adorned with a thousand millions of graces and endowments of the soul? But, Sancho, thou canst not deny me one thing: when thou didst thus approach her, didst thou not feel a most odoriferous smell, an aromatical fragrancy, an—I cannot tell what, so pleasing as I know not how to term it—I say such a scent as if thou wert in some curious perfumer's shop?' 'That which I know,' quoth Sancho, 'is that I felt a little unsavoury scent, somewhat rammish and man-like, and I think the reason was because she had sweat a little doing of that exercise.' 'It was not so,' quoth Don Quixote, 'but either thou hadst the mur, or else did smell thyself; for I know very well how that rose among thorns dost scent, that lily of the field, and that chosen amber.' 'It may well be,' said Sancho, 'as you have said, for I have had many times such a smell as methought the Lady Dulcinea had then; and though she smelled too it were no marvel, for one devil is like another.'

'And well,' quoth Don Quixote, 'see here, she hath sifted her corn, and sent it to the mill; what did she after she had read the letter?' 'The letter?' said Sancho. 'She read it not, for she said she could neither read nor write; and therefore she tore it into small pieces, and would have no man to read it, lest those of the village should know her secrets, and [said] that what I had told her by word of mouth of your love and extraordinary penance, which you remained doing for her sake, was sufficient; and, finally, she concluded, commanding me to say unto you that she had her commended unto you, and that she remained with greater desire to see you than to write unto you, and therefore she requested and willed you, as you tendered her affection, that presently upon sight hereof you should abandon these shrubby groves, leave off your frenzy, and take presently the way of Toboso, if some matter of greater importance did not occur, for she had very great desire to see and talk with you. She laughed heartily when I told her that you named yourself "the Knight of the Ill-favoured Face." I demanded of her whether the beaten Biscaine came there, and she answered that he did, and affirmed withal that he was a very honest man. I asked also for the galley-slaves, but she told me that she had seen none of them as yet.'

'All goes well till this,' said Don Quixote; 'but tell me, I pray thee, what jewel did she bestow on thee at thy departure, for reward of the news thou carriedst unto her of me? For it is an usual and ancient custom among knights and ladies errant, to bestow on squires, damsels, or dwarfs, which bring them any good tidings of their ladies, or servants, some rich jewel, as a reward and thanks of their welcome news.'

'It may well be,' quoth Sancho, 'and I hold it for a very laudable custom; but I think it was only used in times past, for I think the manner of this our age is only to give a piece of bread and cheese; for this was all that my lady Dulcinea bestowed on me, and that over the yard walls, when I took my leave with her, and in sign thereof (well fare all good tokens) the cheese was made of sheep's milk.' 'She is marvellous liberal,' quoth Don Quixote; 'and if she gave thee not a jewel of gold, it was, without doubt, because she had none then about her. But it is not lost that comes at last; I will see her, and then all things shall be amended. Knowest thou, Sancho, whereat I wonder? It is at this sudden return; for it seems to me thou wast gone and hast come back again in the air; for thou hast been away but a little more than three days, Toboso being more than thirty leagues from hence; and therefore I do believe that the wise enchanter who takes care of mine affairs, and is my friend (for there is such a one of force, and there must be, under pain that I else should not be a good knight-errant),—I say I verily think that wise man holp thee to trample unawares of thyself; for there are wise men of that condition which will take a knight-errant sleeping in his bed, and without knowing how or in what manner, he will wake the next day a thousand leagues from that place where he fell asleep; and were it not for this, knights-errant could not succour one another in their most dangerous exigents, as they do now at every step. For it ofttimes befals that a knight is fighting in the mountains of Armenia, with some devilish fauno, some dreadful shadow, or fierce knight, where he is like to have the worst, and in this point of death, when he least expects it, there appears there, on the top of a cloud or riding in a chariot of fire, another knight his friend, who was but even then in England, and helps him, and delivers him from death; and returns again that night to his own lodging, where he sups with a very good appetite; and yet, for all that, is there wont to be two or three thousand leagues from the one to the other country. All which is compassed by the industry and wisdom of those skilful enchanters that take care of the said valorous knights. So that, friend Sancho, I am not hard of belief in giving thee credit that thou hast gone and returned in so short a time from this place to Toboso, seeing, as I have said, some wise man my friend hath (belike) transported thee thither by stealth, and unaware of thyself.'

'I easily think it,' replied Sancho; 'for Rozinante travelled, in good faith, as lustily as if he were an Egyptian's ass, with quicksilver in his ears.' 'And thinkest thou not,' quoth Don Quixote, 'that he had not quicksilver in his ears? yes, and a legion of devils also to help it? who are folk that do travel and make others go as much as they list without any weariness. But, leaving all this apart, what is thine opinion that I should do now concerning my lady's commandment to go and see her? For, although I know that I am bound to obey her behests, yet do I find myself disabled at this time to accomplish them by reason of the grant I have made the princess that comes with us; and the law of arms doth compel me to accomplish my word rather than my will. On the one side, I am assaulted and urged by a desire to go and see my lady; on the other, my promised faith, and the glory I shall win in this enterprise, do incite and call me away. But that which I resolve to do is to travel with all speed, that I may quickly arrive to the place where that giant is, and will cut off his head at my coming; and when I have peaceably installed the princess in her kingdom, will presently return to see the light that doth lighten my senses; to whom I will yield such forcible reasons of my so long absence, as she shall easily condescend to excuse my stay, seeing all doth redound to her glory and fame; for all that I have gained, do win, or shall hereafter achieve, by force of arms in this life, proceeds wholly from the gracious favour she pleaseth to bestow upon me, and my being hers.'

'O God!' quoth Sancho, 'I perceive that you are greatly diseased in the pate. I pray you, sir, tell me whether you mean to go this long voyage for nought, and let slip and lose so rich and so noble a preferment as this, where the dowry is a kingdom, which is in good faith, as I have heard say, twenty thousand leagues in compass, and most plentifully stored with all things necessary for the sustaining of human life, and that it is greater than Portugal and Castile joined together? Peace, for God's love, and blush at your own words, and take my counsel, and marry presently in the first village that hath a parish priest; and if you will not do it there, can you wish a better commodity than to have our own master licentiate, who will do it most excellently? And note that I am old enough to give counsel, and that this which I now deliver is as fit for you as if it were expressly cast for you in a mould; for a sparrow in the fist is worth more than a flying bittor.

' "For he that can have good and evil doth choose,
For ill that betides him, must not patience lose" '

'Why, Sancho,' quoth Don Quixote, 'if thou givest me counsel to marry to the end I may become a king, after I have slain the giant, and have commodity thereby to promote thee, and give thee what I have promised, I let thee to understand that I may do all that most easily without marrying myself; for, before I enter into the battle, I will make this condition, that when I come away victor, although I marry not the princess, yet shall a part of the kingdom be at my disposition to bestow upon whom I please; and when I receive it, upon whom wouldst thou have me bestow it but on thyself?' 'That is manifest,' said Sancho; 'but I pray you, sir, have care to choose that part you would reserve towards the seaside, to the end that if the living do not please me, I may embark my black vassals, and make the benefit of them which I have said. And likewise I pray you not to trouble your mind thinking to go and see my Lady Dulcinea at this time, but travel towards the place where the giant is, and kill him, and conclude that business first; for I swear unto you that I am of opinion it will prove an adventure of very great honour and profit.' 'I assure thee, Sancho,' quoth Don Quixote, 'thou art in the right, and I will follow thy counsel in rather going first with the princess to visit Dulcinea. And I warn thee not to speak a word to anybody, no, not to those that ride with us, of that which we have here spoken and discoursed together; for, since Dulcinea is so wary and secret as she would not have her thoughts discovered, it is no reason that I, either by myself or any other, should detect them.'

'If that be so,' quoth Sancho, 'why, then, do you send all those which you vanquish by virtue of your arm to present themselves to my Lady Dulcinea, seeing this is as good as subsignation of your handwriting, that you wish her well, and are enamoured on her? And seeing that those which go to her must forcibly lay them down on their knees before her presence, and say that they come from you to do her homage, how then can the thoughts of you both be hidden and concealed?' 'Oh, how great a fool art thou, and how simple!' quoth Don Quixote. 'Dost not thou perceive, Sancho, how all this results to her greater glory? For thou oughtest to wit that, in our knightly proceedings, it is great honour that one lady alone have many knights-errant for her servitors, without extending their thoughts any further than to serve her only for her high worths, without attending any other reward of their many and good desires, than that she will deign to accept them as her servants and knights.' 'I have heard preach,' said Sancho, 'that men should love our Saviour with that kind of love only for His own sake, without being moved thereunto either by the hope of glory or the fear of pain; although, for my part, I would love and serve Him for what He is able to do.' 'The devil take thee for a clown!' quoth Don Quixote; 'how sharp and pertinently dost thou speak now and then, able to make a man imagine that thou hast studied!' 'Now, by mine honesty,' quoth Sancho, 'I can neither read nor write.'

Master Nicholas perceiving them drowned thus in their discourses, cried out to them to stay and drink of a little fountain that was by the way. Don Quixote rested, to Sancho's very great contentment, who was already tired with telling him so many lies, and was afraid his master would entrap him in his own words; for, although he knew Dulcinea to be of Toboso, yet had he never seen her in his life. And Cardenio had by this time put on the apparel Dorothea wore when they found her in the mountains, which, though they were not very good, yet exceeded with great advantage those which he had himself before. And, alighting hard by the fountain, they satisfied with the provision the curate had brought with him from the inn, although it were but little, the great hunger that pressed them. And whilst they took their ease there, a certain young stripling that travelled past by, who, looking very earnestly on all those which sat about the fountain, he ran presently after to Don Quixote, and, embracing his legs, he said, weeping downright, 'Oh, my lord, do not you know me? Look well upon me; for I am the youth Andrew whom you unloosed from the oak whereunto I was tied.' Don Quixote presently knew him, and, taking him by the hands, he turned to those that were present and said, 'Because you may see of how great importance it is that there be knights-errant in the world, to undo wrongs and injuries that are committed in it by the insolent and bad men which live therein, thou shall wit that a few days past, as I rode through a wood, I heard certain lamentable screeches and cries, as of some needful and afflicted person. I forthwith occurred, borne away by my profession, towards the place from whence the lamentable voice sounded, and I found tied to an oaken tree this boy whom you see here in our presence, for which I am marvellous glad, because if I shall not say the truth he may check me. I say that he was tied to the oak, stark naked from the middle upward, and a certain clown was opening his flesh with cruel blows that he gave him with the reins of a bridle, which clown, as I after understood, was his master. And so, as soon as I saw him, I demanded the cause of those cruel stripes. The rude fellow answered that he beat him because he was his servant, and that certain negligences of his proceeded rather from being a thief than of simplicity. To which this child answered, "Sir, he whips me for no other cause but by reason that I demand my wages of him." His master replied I know not now what speeches and excuses, the which although I heard, yet were they not by me admitted. In resolution, I caused him to be loosed, and took the clown's oath that he would take him home, and pay him there his wages, one real upon another—ay, and those also perfumed. Is it not true, son Andrew? Didst thou not note with what a domineering countenance I commanded it, and with what humility he promised to accomplish all that I imposed, commanded, and desired? Answer me; be not ashamed, nor stagger at all, but tell what passed to these gentlemen, to the end it may be manifestly seen how necessary it is, as I have said, to have knights-errant up and down the highways.'

'All that which you have said,' quoth the boy, 'is very true; but the end of the matter succeeded altogether contrary to that which you imagined.' 'How contrary?' quoth Don Quixote. 'Why, hath not the peasant paid thee?' 'He not only hath not paid me,' answered the boy, 'but rather, as soon as you were past the wood, and that we remained both alone, he turned again and tied me to the same tree, and gave me afresh so many blows, as I remained another St. Bartholomew, all flayed; and at every blow he said some jest or other in derision of you; so that, if I had not felt the pain of the stripes so much as I did, I could have found it in my heart to have laughed very heartily. In fine, he left me in such pitiful case as I have been ever since curing myself in an hospital of the evil which the wicked peasant did then unto me. And you are in the fault of all this, for if you had ridden on your way, and not come to the place where you were not sought for, nor intermeddled yourself in other men's affairs, perhaps my master had contented himself with giving me a dozen or two of strokes, and would presently after have loosed me and paid me my wages. But by reason you dishonoured him so much without cause, and said to him so many villains, his choler was inflamed, and, seeing he could not revenge it on you, finding himself alone, he disburdened the shower on me so heavily as I greatly fear that I shall never again be mine own man.' 'The hurt consisted in my departure,' quoth Don Quixote, 'for I should not have gone from thence until I had seen thee paid; for I might have very well known, by many experiences, that there is no clown that will keep his word, if he see the keeping of it can turn any way to his damage. But yet, Andrew, thou dost remember how I swore that if he paid thee not, I would return and seek him out, and likewise find him, although he conveyed himself into a whale's belly.' 'That's true,' quoth Andrew; 'but all avails not.' 'Thou shalt see whether it avails or no presently,' quoth Don Quixote; and, saying so, got up very hastily, and commanded Sancho to bridle Rozinante, who was feeding whilst they did eat. Dorothea demanded of him what he meant to do. He answered that he would go and find out the villain, and punish him for using such bad proceedings, and cause Andrew to be paid the last denier, in despite of as many peasants as lived in the world. To which she answered, entreating him to remember that he could not deal with any other adventure, according to his promise, until hers were achieved; and seeing that he himself knew it to be true better than any other, that he should pacify himself until his return from her kingdom.

'You have reason,' said Don Quixote, 'and therefore Andrew must have patience perforce until my return, as you have said, madam; and, when I shall turn again, I do swear unto him, and likewise renew my promise, never to rest until he be satisfied and paid.' 'I believe not in such oaths,' quoth Andrew, 'but would have as much money as might carry me to Seville, rather than all the revenges in the world. Give me some meat to eat, and carry away with me, and God be with you and all other knights-errant; and I pray God that they may prove as erring to themselves as they have been to me!'

Sancho took out of his bag a piece of bread and cheese, and, giving it to the youth, said, 'Hold, brother Andrew, for every one hath his part of your misfortune.' 'I pray you what part thereof have you?' said Andrew. 'This piece of bread and cheese that I bestow on thee,' quoth Sancho; 'for, God only knows whether I shall have need of it again or no; for thou must wit, friend, that we the squires of knights-errant are very subject to great hunger and evil luck; yea, and to other things, which are better felt than told.' Andrew laid hold on his bread and cheese, and, seeing that nobody gave him any other thing, he bowed his head, and went on his way. True it is that he said to Don Quixote at his departure, 'For God's love, good sir knight-errant, if you shall ever meet me again in the plight you have done, although you should see me torn in pieces, yet do not succour or help me, but leave me in my disgrace; for it cannot be so great but that a greater will result from your help, upon whom, and all the other knights-errant that are born in the world, I pray God His curse may alight!' Don Quixote thought to arise to chastise him, but he ran away so swiftly as no man durst follow him; and our knight remained marvellously ashamed at Andrew's tale; wherefore the rest with much ado suppressed their desire to laugh, lest they should thoroughly confound him.

CHAPTER V

Treating of That Which Befel All Don Quixote His Train in the Inn

THE dinner being ended, they saddled and went to horse presently, and travelled all that day and the next without encountering any adventure of price, until they arrived at the only bug and scarecrow of Sancho Panza, and though he would full fain have excused his entry into it, yet could he in no wise avoid it. The innkeeper, the hostess, her daughter, and Maritornes, seeing Don Quixote and Sancho return, went out to receive them with tokens of great love and joy, and he entertained them with grave countenance and applause, and bade them to make him ready a better bed than the other which they had given unto him the time before. 'Sir,' quoth the hostess, 'if you would pay us better than the last time, we would give you one for a prince.' Don Quixote answered that he would. They prepared a reasonable good bed for him in the same wide room where he lay before; and he went presently to bed, by reason that he arrived much tired, and void of wit. And scarce was he gotten into his chamber, when the hostess leaping suddenly on the barber, and taking him by the beard, said, 'Now, by myself blessed, thou shalt use my tail no more for a beard, and thou shalt turn me my tail; for my husband's comb goes thrown up and down the floor, that it is a shame to see it. I mean the comb that I was wont to hang up in my good tail.' The barber would not give it unto her for all her drawing, until the licentiate bade him to restore it, that they had now no more use thereof, but that he might now very well discover himself, and appear in his own shape, and [say] to Don Quixote that after the galley-slaves had robbed him he fled to that inn; and if Don Quixote demanded by chance for the princess her squire, that they should tell him how she had sent him before to her kingdom, to give intelligence to her subjects that she returned, bringing with her him that should free and give them all liberty. With this the barber surrendered the tail willingly to the hostess, and likewise all the other borrowed wares which she had lent for Don Quixote's delivery. All those of the inn rested wonderful amazed at Dorothea's beauty, and also at the comeliness of the shepherd Cardenio. Then the curate gave order to make ready for them such meat as the inn could afford; and the innkeeper, in hope of better payment, did dress very speedily for them a reasonable good dinner. Don Quixote slept all this while, and they were of opinion to let him take his rest, seeing sleep was more requisite for his disease than meat. At the table they discoursed (the innkeeper, his wife, daughter, and Maritornes, and all the other travellers being present) of Don Quixote's strange frenzy, and of the manner wherein they found him. The hostess, eftsoons, recounted what had happened there, between him and the carrier; and looking to see whether Sancho were present, perceiving that he was away, she told likewise all the story of his canvassing, whereat they conceived no little content and pastime. And, as the curate said that the original cause of Don Quixote's madness proceeded from the reading of books of knighthood, the innkeeper answered,—

'I cannot conceive how that can be, for, as I believe, there is no reading so delightful in this world, and I myself have two or three books of that kind with other papers, which do verily keep me alive, and not only me, but many other. For in the reaping times, many of the reapers repair to this place in the heats of mid-day, and there is evermore some one or other among them that can read, who takes one of these books in hand, and then some thirty or more of us do compass him about, and do listen to him with such pleasure, as it hinders a thousand hoary hairs; for I dare say, at least of myself, that when I hear tell of those furious and terrible blows that knights-errant give, it inflames me with a desire to become such a one myself, and could find in my heart to be hearing of them day and night.' 'I am just of the same mind, no more, nor no less,' said the hostess, 'for I never have any quiet hour in my house, but when thou art hearing those books whereon thou art so besotted, as then thou dost only forget to chide, which is thy ordinary exercise at other times.' 'That is very true,' said Maritornes; 'and I in good sooth do take great delight to hear those things, for they are very fine, and especially when they tell how such a lady lies embraced by her knight under an orange tree, and that a certain damsel keepeth watch all the while, ready to burst for envy that she hath not likewise her sweetheart, and very much afraid. I say that all those things are as sweet as honey to me.' 'And you,' quoth the curate to the innkeeper's daughter, 'what do you think?' 'I know not in good sooth, sir,' quoth she; 'but I do likewise give ear, and in truth, although I understand it not, yet do I take some pleasure to hear them; but I mislike greatly those blows which please my father so much, and only delight in the lamentations that knights make being absent from their ladies; which in sooth do now and then make me weep through the compassion I take of them.' 'Well, then,' quoth Dorothea, 'belike, fair maiden, you would remedy them, if such plaints were breathed for your own sake?' 'I know not what I would do,' answered the girl, 'only this I know, that there are some of those ladies so cruel, as their knights call them tigers and lions, and a thousand other wild beasts. And, good Jesus, I know not what unsouled folk they be, and so without conscience, that because they will not once behold an honourable man, they suffer him either to die or run mad. And I know not to what end serves all that coyness. For if they do it for honesty's sake, let them marry with them, for the knights desire nothing more.' 'Peace, child,' quoth the hostess; 'for it seems that thou knowest too much of those matters, and it is not decent that maidens should know or speak so much.' 'I speak,' quoth she, 'by reason that this good sir made me the demand; and I could not in courtesy omit to answer him.' 'Well,' said the curate, 'let me entreat you, good mine host, to bring us here those books, for I would fain see them.'

'I am pleased,' said the innkeeper; and then entering into his chamber, he brought forth a little old malet shut up with a chain; and, opening thereof, he took out three great books and certain papers written with a very fair letter. The first book he opened was that of *Don Cirongilio of Thracia,* the other, *Felixmarte of Hircania,* and the third, *The History of the Great Captain, Gonzalo Hernandez of Cordova,* with the life of *Diego Garcia Paredes* adjoined. As soon as the curate had read the titles of the two books, he said to the barber, 'We have now great want of our friends, the old woman and niece.' 'Not so much as you think,' quoth the barber; 'for I know also the way to the yard or the chimney, and, in good sooth, there is a fire in it good enough for that purpose.' 'Would you then,' quoth the host, 'burn my books?' 'No more of them,' quoth the curate; 'but these first two of *Don Cirongilio* and *Felixmarte.*' 'Are my books perhaps,' quoth the innkeeper, 'heretical or phlegmatical, that you would thus roughly handle them?' 'Schismatical, thou shouldst have said,' quoth the barber, 'and not phlegmatical.' 'It is so,' said the innkeeper; 'but if you will needs burn any, I pray you, rather let it be that of the *Great Captain,* and of that *Diego Garcia;* for I would rather suffer one of my sons to be burned than any one of those other two.' 'Good friend, these two books are lying, and full of follies and vanities; but that of the *Great Captain* is true, and containeth the acts of Gonzalo Hernandez of Cordova, who for his sundry and noble acts merited to be termed by all the world the Great Captain, a name famous, illustrious, and only deserved by himself, and this other, Diego Garcia of Paredes, was a noble gentleman, born in the city of Truxillo in Estremadura, and was a most valorous soldier, and of so surpassing force, as he would detain a mill-wheel with one hand from turning in the midst of the speediest motion: and standing once at the end of a bridge, with a two-handed sword, defended the passage against a mighty army that attempted to pass over it; and did so many other things, that if another who were a stranger and unpassionate had written them, as he did himself who was the relater and historiographer of his own acts, and therefore recounted them with the modesty of a gentleman and proper chronicler, they would have drowned all the Hectors, Achilleses, and Rolands in oblivion.'

'There is a jest,' quoth the innkeeper. 'Deal with my father, I pray you see at what you wonder. A wise tale at the withholding of the wheel of a mill. I swear you ought to read that which is read in *Felixmarte of Hircania,* who with one thwart blow cut five mighty giants in halves, as if they were of beans, like to the little friars that children make of bean-cods; and set another time upon a great and most powerful army of more than a million and six hundred thousand soldiers, and overthrew and scattered them all like a flock of sheep. What, then, can you say to me of the good Cirongilio of

Thracia, who was so animous and valiant, as may be seen in his book; wherein is laid down, that, as he sailed along a river, there issued out of the midst of the water a serpent of fire, and he, as soon as he perceived it, leaped upon her, and hanging by her scaly shoulders, he wrung her throat so straitly between both his arms, that the serpent, perceiving herself to be well-nigh strangled, had no other way to save herself but by diving down into the deeps, carrying the knight away with her, who would never let go his grip, and when they came to the bottom he found himself by a palace in such fair and pleasant gardens, as it was a wonder; and presently the serpent turned into an old man, which said to him such things as there is no more to be desired. Two figs for the Great Captain and that Diego Garcia of whom you speak.'

Dorothea, hearing him speak thus, said to Cardenio, 'Methinks our host wants but little to make up a second part of Don Quixote.' 'So it seems to me likewise,' replied Cardenio; 'for, as we may conjecture by his words, he certainly believes that everything written in those books passed just as it is laid down, and barefooted friars would be scarce able to persuade him the contrary.' 'Know, friend,' quoth the curate to the innkeeper, 'that there was never any such a man as Felixmarte of Hircania, or Don Cirongilio of Thracia, nor other such knights as books of chivalry recount; for all is but a device and fiction of idle wits that composed them, to the end that thou sayst, to pass over the time, as your readers do in reading of them. For I sincerely swear unto thee, that there were never such knights in the world, nor such adventures and ravings happened in it.' 'Cast that bone to another dog,' quoth the innkeeper, 'as though I knew not how many numbers are five, and where the shoe wrests me now. I pray you, sir, go not about to give me pap, for by the Lord I am not so white. Is it not a good sport that you labour to persuade me, that all that which these good books say are but ravings and fables, they being printed by grace and favour of the Lords of the Privy Council; as if they were folk that would permit so many lies to be printed at once, and so many battles and enchantments, as are able to make a man run out of his wits.' 'I have told thee already, friend,' said the curate, 'that this is done for the recreation of our idle thoughts, and so even as, in well-governed commonwealths, the plays at chess, tennis, and trucks are tolerated for the pastime of some men which have none other occupation, and either ought not or cannot work, even so such books are permitted to be printed; presuming (as in truth they ought, that no man would be found so simple and ignorant as to hold any of these books for a true history. And if my leisure permitted, and that it were a thing requisite for this auditory, I could say many things concerning the subject of books of knighthood, to the end that they should be well contrived, and also be pleasant and profitable to the readers; but I hope sometime to have the commodity to communicate my conceit with those that may redress it. And in the meanwhile, you may believe, good mine host, what I have said, and take to you your books, and agree with their truths or leasings as you please, and much good may it do you; and I pray God that you halt not in time on the foot that your guest Don Quixote halteth.' 'Not so,' quoth the innkeeper, 'for I will never be so wood as to become a knight-errant, for I see well that what was used in the times of these famous knights is now in no use nor request.'

Sancho came in about the midst of this discourse, and rested much confounded and pensative of that which he heard them say, that knights-errant were now in no request, and that the books of chivalry only contained follies and lies, and purposed with himself to see the end of that voyage of his lord's, and that if it sorted not the wished success which he expected, he resolved to leave him and return home to his wife and children and accustomed labour. The innkeeper thought to take away his books and budget, but the curate withheld him, saying, 'Stay a while, for I would see what papers are those which are written in so fair a character.' The host took them out and gave them to him to read, being in number some eight sheets, with a title written in text letters, which said, *The History of the Curious-Impertinent*. The curate read two or three lines softly to himself, and said after, 'Truly the title of this history doth not mislike me, and therefore I am about to read it through.' The innkeeper hearing him, said, 'Your reverence may very well do it, for I assure you that some guests which have read it here, as they travelled, did commend it exceedingly, and have begged it of me as earnestly, but I would never bestow it, hoping some day to restore it to the owner of this malet, who forgot it here behind him with these books and papers, for it may be that he will sometime return, and although I know that I shall have great want of the books, yet will I make to him restitution, for although I am an innkeeper, yet God be thanked I am a Christian therewithal.' 'You have great reason, my friend,' quoth the curate; 'but yet notwithstanding, if the taste like me, thou must give me leave to take a copy thereof.' 'With all my heart,' replied the host. And as they two talked, Cardenio, taking the book, began to read a little of it, and, it pleasing him as much as it had done the curate, he requested him to read it in such sort as they might all hear him. 'That I would willingly do,' said the curate, 'if the time were not now more fit for sleeping than reading.' 'It were sufficient repose for me,' said Dorothea, 'to pass away the time listening to some tale or other, for my spirit is not yet so well quieted as to afford me licence to sleep, even then when nature exacteth it.' 'If that be so,' quoth the curate, 'I will read it, if it were but for curiosity; perhaps it containeth some delightful matter.' Master Nicholas and Sancho entreated the same. The curate, seeing and knowing that he should therein do them all a pleasure, and he himself likewise receive as great, said, 'Seeing you will needs hear it, be all of you attentive, for the history beginneth in this manner.'

CHAPTER VI

Wherein Is Rehearsed the History of the Curious-Impertinent

'IN Florence, a rich and famous city of Italy, in the province called Tuscany, there dwelt two rich and principal gentlemen called Anselmo and Lothario, which two were so great friends, as they were named for excellency, and by *antonomasia,* by all those that knew them, the Two Friends. They were both bachelors, and much of one age and manners; all which was of force to make them answer one another with reciprocal amity. True it is that Anselmo was somewhat more inclined to amorous dalliance than Lothario, who was altogether addicted to hunting. But when occasion exacted it, Anselmo would omit his own pleasures, to satisfy his friend's; and Lothario likewise his, to please Anselmo. And by this means both their wills were so correspondent, as no clock could be better ordered than were their desires. Anselmo being at last deeply enamoured of a principal and beautiful young lady of the same city, called Camilla, being so worthily descended, and she herself of such merit therewithal, as he resolved (by the consent of his friend Lothario, without whom he did nothing) to demand her of her parents for wife; and did put his purpose in execution; and Lothario himself was the messenger, and concluded the matter so to his friend's satisfaction, as he was shortly after put in possession of his desires; and Camilla so contented to have gotten Anselmo, as she ceased not to render Heaven and Lothario thanks, by whose means she had obtained so great a match. The first days, as all marriage days are wont to be merry, Lothario frequented, according to the custom, his friend Anselmo's house, endeavouring to honour, feast, and recreate him all the ways he might possibly. But after the nuptials were finished, and the concourse of strangers, visitations, and congratulations somewhat ceased, Lothario also began to be somewhat more slack than he wonted in going to Anselmo his house, deeming it (as it is reason that all discreet men should) not so convenient to visit or haunt so often the house of his friend after marriage as he would, had he still remained a bachelor. For although true amity neither should nor ought to admit the least suspicion, yet notwithstanding a married man's honour is so delicate and tender a thing, as it seems it may be sometimes impaired, even by very brethren; and how much more by friends? Anselmo noted the remission of Lothario, and did grievously complain thereof, saying that, if he had wist by marriage he should thus be deprived of his dear conversation, he would never have married; and that since through the uniform correspondency of them both being free, they had deserved the sweet title of the Two Friends, that he should not now permit (because he would be noted circumspect without any other occasion) that so famous and pleasing a name should be lost; and therefore he requested him (if it were lawful to use such a term between them two) to return and be master of his house, and come and go as he had done before his marriage, assuring him that his spouse Camilla had no other pleasure and will, than that which himself pleased she should have; and that she, after having known how great was both their friendships, was not a little amazed to see him become so strange.

'To all these and many other reasons alleged by Anselmo, to persuade Lothario to frequent his house, he answered with so great prudence, discretion, and wariness, as Anselmo remained satisfied of his friend's good intention herein; and they made an agreement between them two, that Lothario should dine at his house twice a week, and the holy days besides. And although this agreement had passed between them, yet Lothario purposed to do that only which he should find most expedient for his friend's honour, whose reputation he tendered much more dearly than he did his own; and was wont to say very discreetly, that the married man, unto whom Heaven had given a beautiful wife, ought to have as much heed of his friends which he brought to his house, as he should of the women friends that visited his wife; for that which is not done nor agreed upon in the church or market, nor in public feasts or stations (being places that a man cannot lawfully hinder his wife from frequenting sometimes at least) are ofttimes facilitated and contrived in a friend's or kinswoman's house, whom perhaps we never suspected. Anselmo on the other side affirmed, that therefore married men ought every one of them to have some friend who might advertise them of the faults escaped in their manner of proceeding; for it befalls many times, that through the great love which the husband bears to his wife, either he doth not take notice, or else he doth not advertise her, because he would not offend her to do or omit to do certain things, the doing or omitting whereof might turn to his honour or obloquy; to which things, being advertised by his friend, he might easily apply some remedy. But where might a man find a friend so discreet, loyal, and trusty as Anselmo demands? I know not truly, if not Lothario: for he it was that with all solicitude and care regarded the honour of his friend; and therefore endeavoured to clip and diminish the number of the days promised, lest he should give occasion to the idle vulgar, or to the eyes of vagabonds and malicious men to judge any sinister thing, viewing so rich, comely, noble, and qualified a young man as he was, to have so free access into the house of a woman so beautiful as Camilla. For though his virtues and modest carriage were sufficiently able to set a bridle to any malignant tongue, yet notwithstanding he would not have his credit, nor that of his friends, called into any question; and therefore would spend most of the days that he had agreed to visit his friend, in other places and exercises; yet feigning excuses so plausible, as his friend admitted them for very reasonable. And thus the time passed on in challenges of unkindness of the one side, and lawful excuses of the other.

'It so fell out, that, as both the friends walked on a day together in a field without the city, Anselmo said to Lothario these words ensuing: "I know very well, friend Lothario, that among all the favours which God of His bounty hath bestowed upon me by making me the son of such parents, and giving to me with so liberal a hand, both the goods of nature and fortune; yet as I cannot answer Him with sufficient gratitude for the benefits already received, so do I find myself most highly bound unto Him above all others, for having given me such a friend as thou art, and so beautiful a wife as Camilla, being both of you such pawns, as if I esteem you not in the degree which I ought, yet do I hold you as dear as I may. And yet, possessing all those things which are wont to be the all and some that are wont and may make a man happy, I live notwithstanding the most sullen and discontented life of the world, being troubled, I know not since when, and inwardly wrested with so strange a desire, and extravagant, from the common use of others, as I marvel at myself, and do condemn and rebuke myself when I am alone, and do labour to conceal and cover mine own desires; all which hath served me to as little effect, as if I had proclaimed mine own errors purposely to the world. And seeing that it must finally break out, my will is, that it be only communicated to the treasury of thy secret; hoping by it and mine own industry, which, as my true friend, thou wilt use to help me, I shall be quickly freed from the anguish it causeth, and by thy means my joy and contentment shall arrive to the pass that my discontents have brought me through mine own folly."

'Lothario stood suspended at Anselmo's speech, as one that could not imagine to what so prolix a prevention and preamble tended; and although he revolved and imagined sundry things in his mind which he deemed might afflict his friend, yet did he ever shoot wide from the mark which in truth it was; and that he might quickly escape that agony, wherein the suspension held him, he said, that his friend did notable injury to their amity, in searching out wreathings and ambages in the discovery of his most hidden thoughts to him, seeing he might assure himself certainly, either to receive counsels of him how to entertain, or else remedy and means how to accomplish them.

'"It is very true," answered Anselmo, "and with that confidence I let thee to understand, friend Lothario, that the desire which vexeth me is a longing to know whether my wife Camilla be as good and perfect as I do account her, and I cannot wholly rest satisfied of this truth, but by making trial of her, in such sort as it may give manifest argument of the degree of her goodness, as the fire doth show the value of gold; for I am of opinion, O friend, that a woman is of no more worth or virtue than that which is in her, after she hath been solicited; and that she alone is strong who cannot be bowed by the promises, gifts, tears, and continual importunities of importunate lovers. For what thanks is it," quoth he, "for a woman to be good, if nobody say or teach her ill? What wonder that she be retired and timorous, if no occasion be ministered to her of dissolution, and chiefly she that knows she hath a husband ready to kill her for the least argument of lightness? So that she which is only good for fear or want of occasion, will I never hold in that estimation, that I would the other solicited and pursued, who, notwithstanding, comes away crowned with the victory. And therefore, being moved as well by these reasons as by many other which I could tell you, which accredit and fortify mine opinion, I desire that my wife Camilla do also pass through the pikes of those proofs and difficulties, and purify and refine herself in the fire of being requested, solicited, and pursued, and that by one whose worths and valour may deserve acceptance in her opinion; and if she bear away the palm of the victory, as I believe she will, I shall account my fortune matchless, and may brag that my desires are in their height, and will say that a strong woman hath fallen to my lot, of whom the wise man saith, 'Who shall find her?' And when it shall succeed contrary to mine expectation, I shall, with the pleasure that I will conceive to see how rightly it jumps with mine opinion, bear very indifferent[ly] the grief which in all reason this so costly a trial must stir in me. And presupposing that nothing which thou shalt say to me shall be available to hinder my design, or dissuade me from putting my purpose in execution, I would have thyself, dear friend Lothario, to provide thee to be the instrument that shall labour this work of my liking, and I will give thee opportunity enough to perform the same, without omitting anything that may further thee in the solicitation of an honest, noble, wary, retired, and passionless woman.

'"And I am chiefly moved to commit this so hard an enterprise to thy trust, because I know that, if Camilla be vanquished by thee, yet shall not the victory arrive to the last push and upshot, but only to that of accounting a thing to be done, which shall not be done for many good respects. So shall I remain nothing offended, and mine injury concealed in the virtue of thy silence; for I know thy care to be such in matters concerning me, as it shall be eternal, like that of death. And therefore if thou desirest that I may lead a life deserving that name, thou must forthwith provide thyself to enter into this amorous conflict, and that not languishing or slothfully, but with that courage and diligence which my desire expecteth, and the confidence I have in our amity assureth me."

'These were the reasons used by Anselmo to Lothario, to all which he was so attentive, as, until he ended, he did not once unfold his lips to speak a word save those which we have above related; and seeing that he spoke no more, after he had beheld him a good while, as a thing that he had never before, and did therefore strike him into admiration and amazement, he said, "Friend Anselmo, I cannot persuade myself that the words you have spoken be other than jests, for, had I thought that thou wert in earnest, I would not have suffered thee to pass on so far, and by lending thee no ear would have excused this tedious oration. I do verily imagine that either thou dost not know me, or I thee; but not so, for I know thee to be Anselmo, and thou that I am Lothario. The damage is, that I think thou art not the Anselmo thou was wont to be, and perhaps thou deemest me not to be the accustomed Lothario that I ought to be; for the things which thou hast spoken are not of that Anselmo my friend, nor those which thou seekest ought to be demanded of that Lothario, of whom thou hast notice. For true friends ought to prove and use their friends, as the poet said, *usque ad aras,* that is, that they should in no sort employ them or implore their assistance in things offensive unto God; and if a Gentile was of this opinion in matters of friendship, how much greater reason is it that a Christian should have that feeling, specially knowing that the celestial amity is not to be lost for any human friendship whatsoever. And when the friend should throw the bars so wide, as to set heavenly respects apart, for to compliment with his friend, it must not be done on light grounds, or for things of small moment, but rather for those whereon his friend's life and honour wholly depend. Then tell me now, Anselmo, in which of these two things art thou in danger, that I may adventure my person to do thee a pleasure, and attempt so detestable a thing as thou dost demand? None of them truly, but rather dost demand, as I may conjecture, that I do industriously labour to deprive thee of thine honour and life together, and, in doing so, I likewise deprive myself of them both. For if I must labour to take away thy credit, it is most evident that I despoil thee of life, for a man without reputation is worse than a dead man, and I being the instrument, as thou desirest that I should be, of so great harm unto thee, do not I become likewise thereby dishonoured, and by the same consequence also without life? Hear me, friend Anselmo, and have patience not to answer me until I have said all that I think, concerning that which thy mind exacteth of thee; for we shall have after leisure enough, wherein thou mayst reply, and I have patience to listen unto thy reasons."

'"I am pleased," quoth Anselmo; "say what thou likest." And Lothario prosecuted his speech in this manner: "Methinks, Anselmo, that thou art now of the Moors' humours, which can by no means be made to understand the error of their sect, neither by citations of the Holy Scripture, nor by reasons which consist in speculations of the understanding, or that are founded in the Articles of the Faith, but must be won by palpable examples, and those easy, intelligible, demonstrative, and doubtless, by mathematical demonstrations, which cannot be denied. Even as when we say, 'If from two equal parts we take away two parts equal, the parts that remain are also equal.' And when they cannot understand this, as in truth they do not, we must demonstrate it to them with our hands, and lay it before their eyes, and yet for all this nought can avail to win them in the end to give credit to the verities of our religion; which very terms and manner of proceeding I must use with thee, by reason that the desire which is sprung in thee doth so wander and stray from all that which bears the shadow only of reason, as I doubt much that I shall spend my time in vain, which I shall bestow, to make thee understand thine own simplicity, for I will give it no other name at this present; and, in good earnest, I was almost persuaded to leave thee in thine humour, in punishment of thine inordinate and unreasonable desire, but that the love which I bear towards thee doth not consent I use to thee such rigour, or leave thee in so manifest a danger of thine own perdition. And, that thou mayst clearly see it, tell me, Anselmo, hast not thou said unto me, that I must solicit one that stands upon her reputation; persuade an honest woman; make proffers to one that is not passionate or engaged; and serve a discreet woman? Yes, thou hast said all this. Well, then, if thou knowest already that thou hast a retired, honest, unpassionate, and prudent wife. what seekest thou more? And, if thou thinkest that she will rest victorious, after all mine assaults, as doubtless she will, what better titles wouldst thou after bestow upon her, than those she possesseth already? Either it proceeds, because thou dost not think of her as thou sayst, or else because thou knowest not what thou demandest. If thou dost not account her such as thou praisest her, to what end wouldst thou prove her? But rather, as an evil person, use her as thou likest best. But, if she be as good as thou believest, it were an impertinent thing to make trial of truth itself. For, after it is made, yet it will still rest only with the same reputation it had before. Wherefore, it is a concluding reason, that, to attempt things, whence rather harm may after result unto us than good, is the part of rash and discourseless brains; and principally when they deal with those things whereunto they are not compelled or driven, and that they see even afar off, how the attempting the like is manifest folly. Difficult things are undertaken for God, or the world, or both. Those that are done for God are the works of the saints, endeavouring to lead angels' lives, in frail and mortal bodies. Those of the world are the travels and toils of such as cross such immense seas, travel through so adverse regions, and converse with so many nations, to acquire that which we call the goods of fortune. And the things acted for God and the world together are the worthy exploits of resolute and valorous martial men, which scarce perceive so great a breach in the adversary wall, as the cannon bullet is wont to make; when, leaving all fear apart, without making any discourse, or taking notice of the manifest danger that threatens them, borne away, by the wings of desire and honour, to serve God, their nation and prince, do throw themselves boldly into the throat of a thousand menacing deaths which expect them.

'"These are things wont to be practised; and it is honour, glory, and profit to attempt them, be they never so full of inconveniences and danger; but that which thou sayst thou will try and put in practice shall never gain thee God's glory, the goods of fortune, or renown among men; for, suppose that thou bringest it to pass according to thine own fantasy, thou shalt remain nothing more contented, rich, or honourable than thou art already; and, if thou dost not, then shalt thou see thyself in the greatest misery of any wretch living; for it will little avail thee then to think that no man knows the disgrace befallen thee, it being sufficient both to afflict and dissolve thee that thou knowest it thyself. And, for greater confirmation of this truth, I will repeat unto thee a stanza of the famous poet Luigi Tansillo, in the end of his first part of *St. Peter's Tears,* which is:

> " 'The grief increaseth, and withal the shame
> In Peter when the day itself did show:
> And though he no man sees, yet doth he blame
> Himself because he had offended so.
> For breasts magnanimous, not only tame,
> When that of others they are seen, they know;
> But of themselves ashamed they often be,
> Though none but Heaven and earth their error see.'

So that thou canst not excuse thy grief with secrecy, be it never so great, but rather shall have continual occasion to weep, if not watery tears from thine eyes, at least tears of blood from thy heart, such as that simple doctor wept, of whom our poet makes mention, who made trial of the vessel, which the prudent Reynaldos, upon maturer discourse, refused to deal withal. And, although it be but a poetical fiction, yet doth it contain many hidden morals, worthy to be noted, understood, and imitated; how much more, seeing that by what I mean to say now, I hope thou shalt begin to conceive the great error which thou wouldest wittingly commit.

' "Tell me, Anselmo, if Heaven or thy fortunes had made thee lord and lawful possessor of a most precious diamond, of whose goodness and quality all the lapidaries that had viewed the same would rest satisfied, and that all of them would jointly and uniformly affirm that it arrived in quality, goodness, and fineness to all that to which the nature of such a stone might extend itself, and that thou thyself didst believe the same without witting anything to the contrary; would it be just that thou shouldest take an humour to set that diamond between an anvil and a hammer, and to try there by very force of blows whether it be so hard and so fine as they say? And further: when thou didst put thy design in execution, put the case that the stone made resistance to thy foolish trial, yet wouldest thou add thereby no new value or esteem to it. And if it did break, as it might befall, were not then all lost? Yes, certainly, and that leaving the owner, in all men's opinion, for a very poor ignorant person. Then, friend Anselmo, make account that Camilla is a most precious diamond as well in thine as in other men's estimation; and it is no reason to put her in contingent danger of breaking, seeing that, although she remain in her integrity, she cannot mount to more worth than she hath at the present; and if she faltered, or did not resist, consider even at this present what state you would be in then, and how justly thou mightest then complain of thyself for being cause of her perdition and thine own. See how there is no jewel in the world comparable to the modest and chaste woman, and that all women's honour consists in the good opinion that's had of them; and seeing that of thy spouse is so great, as it arrives to that sum of perfection which thou knowest, why wouldest thou call this verity in question? Know, friend, that a woman is an imperfect creature, and should therefore have nothing cast in her way to make her stumble and fall, but rather to clear and do all encumbrances away out of it, to the end she may without impeachment run with a swift course to obtain the perfection she wants, which only consists in being virtuous.

'"The naturalists recount that the ermine is a little beast that hath a most white skin; and that, when the hunters would chase him, they use this art to take him. As soon as they find out his haunt, and places where he hath recourse, they thwart them with mire and dirt, and after when they descry the little beast, they pursue him towards those places which are defiled; and the ermine, espying the mire, stands still, and permits himself to be taken and captived in exchange of not passing through the mire, or staining of his whiteness, which it esteems more than either liberty or life. The honest and chaste woman is an ermine, and the virtue of chastity is whiter and purer than snow; and he that would not lose it, but rather desires to keep and preserve it, must proceed with a different style from that of the ermine. For they must not propose and lay before her the mire of the passions, flatteries, and services of importunate lovers; for perhaps she shall not have the natural impulse and force, which commonly through proper debility is wont to stumble, to pass over those encumbrances safely; and therefore it is requisite to free the passage and take them away, and lay before her the clearness of virtue and the beauty comprised in good fame. The good woman is also like unto a bright and clear mirror of crystal, and therefore is subject to be stained and dimmed by every breath that toucheth it. The honest woman is to be used as relics of saints, to wit, she must be honoured but not touched. The good woman is to be kept and prized like a fair garden full of sweet flowers and roses, that is held in estimation, whose owner permits no man to enter and trample or touch his flowers, but holds it to be sufficient that they, standing afar off, without the rails, may joy at the delightful sight and fragrance thereof. Finally I will repeat certain verses unto thee that have now come to my memory, the which were repeated of late in a new play, and seem to me very fit for the purpose of which we treat. A prudent old man did give a neighbour of his that had a daughter counsel to keep and shut her up; and among many other reasons he used these:

" 'Truly woman is of glass;
Therefore no man ought to try
If she broke or not might be,
Seeing all might come to pass.
Yet to break her 'tis more easy;
And it is no wit to venture
A thing of so brittle temper,
That to solder is so queasy.
And I would have all men dwell
In this truth and reason's ground,
That if Danaes may be found,
Golden showers are found as well.'

'"All that which I have said to thee, Anselmo, until this instant, hath been for that which may touch thyself; and it is now high time that somewhat be heard concerning me. And if by chance I shall be somewhat prolix, I pray thee to pardon me; for the labyrinth wherein thou hast entered, and out of which thou wouldest have me to free thee, requires no less. Thou holdest me to be thy friend, and yet goest about to despoil me of mine honour, being a thing contrary to all amity; and dost not only pretend this, but dost likewise endeavour that I should rob thee of the same. That thou wouldest deprive me of mine is evident; for when Camilla shall perceive that I solicit her as thou demandest, it is certain that she will esteem of me as of one quite devoid of wit and discretion, seeing I intend and do a thing so repugnant to that which the being that him I am, and thine amity do bind me unto. That thou wouldest have me rob thee thereof is as manifest, for Camilla, seeing me thus to court her, must imagine that I have noted some lightness in her which lent me boldness thus to discover unto her my depraved desires, and she holding herself to be thereby injured and dishonoured, her disgrace must also concern thee as a principal part of her. And hence springs that which is commonly said, That the husband of the adulterous wife, although he know nothing of her lewdness, nor hath given any occasion to her to do what she ought not, nor was able any way to hinder by diligence, care, or other means, his disgrace, yet is entitled with a vituperous name, and is in a manner beheld by those that know his wife's malice with the eyes of contempt; whereas they should indeed regard him rather with those of compassion, seeing that he falls into that misfortune not so much through his own default, as through the light fantasy of his wicked consort. But I will show thee the reason why a bad woman's husband is justly dishonoured and contemned, although he be ignorant and guiltless thereof, and cannot prevent, nor hath given to it any occasion. And be not grieved to hear me, seeing the benefit of the discourse shall redound unto thyself.

'"When God created our first parent in the terrestrial paradise, the Holy Scripture saith, That God infused sleep into Adam, and that, being asleep, He took out a rib out of his left side, of which He formed our mother Eve; and as soon as Adam awaked and beheld her, he said, 'This is flesh of my flesh, and bone of my bones.' And God said, 'For this cause shall a man leave his father and his mother, and they shall be two in one flesh.' And then was the divine ordinance of matrimony first instituted, with such indissoluble knots as only may be by death dissolved. And this marvellous ordinance is of such efficacy and force, as it makes two different persons to be one very flesh; and yet operates further in good married folk; for, although they have two souls, yet it makes them to have but one will. And hence it proceeds, that by reason the wife's flesh is one and the very same with her husband's, the blemishes or defects that taint it do also redound into the husband's, although he, as we have said, have ministered no occasion, to receive that damage. For as all the whole body feels any pain of the foot, head, or any other member, because it is all one flesh, and the head smarts at the grief of the ankle, although it hath not caused it; so is the husband participant of his wife's dishonour, because he is one and the selfsame with her. And by reason that all the honours and dishonours of the world are, and spring from flesh and blood, and those of the bad woman be of this kind, it is forcible, that part of them fall to the husband's share, and that he be accounted dishonourable, although he wholly be ignorant of it. See then, Anselmo, to what peril thou dost thrust thyself by seeking to disturb the quietness and repose wherein thy wife lives, and for how vain and impertinent curiosity thou wouldest stir up the humours which are now quiet in thy chaste spouse's breast. Note how the things thou dost adventure to gain are of small moment; but that which thou shalt lose so great, that I must leave it in his point, having no words sufficiently able to endear it. But if all that I have said be not able to move thee from thy bad purpose, thou mayst well seek out for some other instrument of thy dishonour and mishaps; for I mean not to be one, although I should therefore lose thine amity, which is the greatest loss that might any way befall me."

'Here the prudent Lothario held his peace, and Anselmo remained so confounded and melancholy, as he could not answer a word to him for a very great while. But in the end he said, "I have listened, friend Lothario, to all that which thou hast said unto me, with the attention which thou hast noted, and have perceived in thy reasons, examples, and similitudes the great discretion wherewithal thou art endowed, and the perfection of amity that thou hast attained; and do also confess and see, that, if I follow not thine advice, but should lean unto mine own, I do but shun the good, and pursue the evil. Yet oughtest thou likewise to consider, how herein I suffer the disease which some women are wont to have, that long to eat earth, lime, coals, and other far worse and loathsome things even to the very sight, and much more to the taste; so that it is behooveful to use some art by which I may be cured; and this might be easily done by beginning only to solicit Camilla, although you did it but weak and feignedly; for I know she will not be so soft and pliable as to dash her honesty about the ground at the first encounters, and I will rest satisfied with this commencement alone; and thou shalt herein accomplish the obligation thou owest to our friendship, by not only restoring me to life, but also by persuading me not to despoil myself of mine honour. And thou art bound to do this, for one reason that I shall allege, to wit, that I being resolved, as indeed I am, to make this experience, thou oughtest not to permit, being my friend, that I should bewray my defect herein to a stranger, whereby I might very much endanger my reputation, which thou labourest so much to preserve; and though thy credit may lose some degrees in Camilla's opinion whilst thou dost solicit her, it matters not very much, or rather nothing; for very shortly, when we shall espy in her the integrity that we expect, thou mayst open unto her sincerely the drift of our practice, by which thou shalt again recover thine impaired reputation. Therefore seeing the adventure is little, and the pleasure thou shalt do me by the enterprising thereof so, too great, I pray thee do it, though ever so many encumbrances represent themselves to thee, for, as I have promised, with only thy beginning, I will rest satisfied and account the cause concluded."

'Lothario perceiving the firm resolution of Anselmo, and nothing else occurring forcibly dissuasive, not knowing what other reasons to use that might hinder this his precipitate resolution, and noting withal how he threatened to break the matter of this his indiscreet desires to a stranger, he determined, to avoid greater inconvenience, to give him satisfaction, and perform his demand, with purpose and resolution to guide the matter so discreetly, as, without troubling Camilla's thoughts, Anselmo should rest contented; and therefore entreated him not to open his mind to any other, for he himself would undertake that enterprise, and begin it whensoever he pleased. Anselmo embraced him very tender and lovingly, and gratified him as much for that promise as if he had done him some very great favour, and there they accorded between them that he should begin the work the very next day ensuing; for he would give him place and leisure to speak alone with Camilla, and would likewise provide him of money, jewels, and other things to present unto her.

He did also admonish him to bring music under her windows by night, and write verses in her praise, and if he would not take the pains to make them, he himself would compose them for him. Lothario promised to perform all himself, yet with an intention far wide from Anselmo's; and with this agreement they returned to Anselmo's house, where they found Camilla somewhat sad and careful, expecting her husband's return, who had stayed longer abroad that day than his custom. Lothario, leaving him at his house, returned to his own, as pensive as he had left Anselmo contented, and knew not what plot to lay, to issue out of that impertinent affair with prosperous success. But that night he bethought himself of a manner how to deceive Anselmo without offending Camilla; and so the next day ensuing he came to his friend's house to dinner, where Camilla, knowing the great good-will her husband bore towards him, did receive and entertain him very kindly with the like. Dinner being ended, and the table taken up, Anselmo requested Lothario to keep Camilla company until his return, for he must needs go about an affair that concerned him greatly, but would return again within an hour and a half. Camilla entreated her husband to stay, and Lothario proffered to go and keep him company; but nothing could prevail with Anselmo, but rather he importuned his friend Lothario to remain and abide there till his return, because he must go to treat of a matter of much consequence. He also commanded Camilla not to leave Lothario alone until he came back. And so he departed, leaving Camilla and Lothario together at the table, by reason that all the attendants and servants were gone to dinner.

'Here Lothario saw that he was entered into the lists which his friend so much desired, with his adversary before him, who was with her beauty able to overcome a whole squadron of armed knights; see then if Lothario had not reason to fear himself; but that which he did at the first onset was to lay his elbow on the arm of his chair and his hand on his cheek, and, desiring Camilla to bear with his respectlessness therein, he said he would repose a little whilst he attended Anselmo's coming. Camilla answered that she thought he might take his ease better on the cushions of state; and therefore prayed him he would enter into the parlour and lie on them. But he excused himself, and so remained asleep in the same place until Anselmo's return, who, coming in, and finding his wife in her chamber and Lothario asleep, made full account that, by reason of his long stay, they had time enough both to talk and repose; and therefore expected very greedily the hour wherein his friend should awake, to go out with him and learn what success he had. All succeeded as he wished; for Lothario arose, and both of them went abroad; and then he demanded of him what he desired. And Lothario answered that it seemed not to him so good to discover all his meaning at the first; and therefore had done no other thing at that time than speak a little of her beauty and discretion; for it seemed to him that this was the best preamble he could use to gain by little and little some interest and possession in her acceptance, to dispose her thereby the better to give ear again to his words more willingly, imitating therein the devil's craft when he means to deceive any one that is vigilant and careful; for then he translates himself into an angel of light, being one of darkness, and laying before him apparent good, discovers what he is in the end, and brings his intention to pass, if his guiles be not at the beginning detected. All this did greatly like Anselmo, who said that he would afford him every day as much leisure, although he did not go abroad; for he would spend the time so at home as Camilla should never be able to suspect his drift.

'It therefore befel that many days passed which Lothario did willingly overslip, and said nothing to Camilla; yet did he ever soothe Anselmo, and told him that he had spoken to her, but could never win her to give the least argument of flexibility, or make way for the feeblest hope that might be; but rather affirmed that she threatened him that, if he did not repel his impertinent desires, she would detect his indirect proceedings to her husband. "It is well," quoth Anselmo. "Hitherto Camilla hath resisted words; it is therefore requisite to try what resistance she will make against works. I will give thee to-morrow four thousand crowns in gold, to the end thou mayst offer, and also bestow them on her; and thou shalt have as many more to buy jewels wherewithal to bait her; for women are naturally inclined, and specially if they be fair (be they ever so chaste), to go brave and gorgeously attired; and if she can overcome this temptation, I will remain pleased, and put thee to no more trouble." Lothario answered, that, seeing he had begun, he would bear his enterprise on to an end, although he made full account that he should depart from the conflict both tired and vanquished. He received the four thousand crowns the next day, and at once with them four thousand perplexities, for he knew not what to invent to lie anew; but concluded finally to tell his friend how Camilla was as inflexible at gifts and promises as at words; and therefore it would be in vain to travail any more in her pursuit, seeing he should do nothing else but spend the time in vain.

'But fortune, which guided these affairs in another manner, so disposed, that Anselmo, having left Lothario and Camilla alone, as he was wont, entered secretly into a chamber, and through the crannies and chinks did listen and see what they would do; where he perceived that Lothario, in the space of half-an-hour, spoke not a word to Camilla, nor yet would he have spoken, though he had remained there a whole age, and thereupon surmised straight that all that which his friend had told him of Camilla's answers and his own speech were but fictions and untruths; and that he might the more confirm himself, and see whether it were so, he came forth, and, calling Lothario apart, he demanded of him what Camilla had said, and in what humour she was at the present? Lothario answered, that he meant not ever any more to sound her in that matter; for she replied unto him so untowardly and sharply, as he durst not attempt any more to speak unto her of such things.

'"Oh," quoth Anselmo, "Lothario, Lothario! how evil dost thou answer to the affection thou owest me, or to the confidence I did repose in thee? I have stood beholding thee all this while through the hole of that lock, and saw how thou never spokest one word to her. Whereby I do also collect that thou hast not yet once accosted her; and if it be so, as doubtlessly it is, say, why dost thou deceive me? or why goest thou about fraudulently to deprive me of those means whereby I may obtain my desires?" Anselmo said no more, yet what he said was sufficient to make Lothario confused and ashamed, who, taking it to be a blemish to his reputation to be found in a lie, swore to Anselmo that he would from thenceforward so endeavour to please his mind, and tell him no more leasings, as he himself might perceive the success thereof, if he did again curiously lie in watch for him; a thing which he might well excuse, because his most serious labour to satisfy his desire should remove all shadow of suspicion. Anselmo believed him, and that he might give him the greater commodity, and less occasion of fear, he resolved to absent himself from his house some eight days, and go to visit a friend of his that dwelt in a village not far from the city; and therefore dealt with his friend, that he should send a messenger to call for him very earnestly, that, under that pretext, he might find an excuse to Camilla for his departure.

'O unfortunate and inconsiderate Anselmo! what is that which thou dost? what dost thou contrive? or what is that thou goest about? Behold, thou workest thine own ruin, laying plots of thine own dishonour, and giving order to thy proper perdition. Thy wife Camilla is good; thou dost possess her in quiet and peaceable manner; no man surpriseth thy delights, her thoughts transgress not the limits of her house. Thou art her heaven on earth, and the goal to which her desires aspire. Thou art the accomplishment and sum of her delectation. Thou art the square by which she measureth and directeth her will, adjusting wholly with thine and with that of Heaven. Since then the mines of her honour, beauty, modesty, and recollection bountifully afford thee, without any toil, all the treasures contained in them, or thou canst desire, why wouldst thou dig the earth and seek out new veins and ne'er-seen treasures, exposing thyself to the danger that thy labours may turn to wreck, seeing, in fine, that they are only sustained by the weak supporters of her frail nature? Remember how he that seeks the impossible may justly be refused of that which is possible, according to that which the poet saith:

" 'In death for life I seek,
Health in infirmity;
For issue in a dungeon deep,
In jails for liberty,
And in a treachour loyalty.

" 'But envious fate, which still
Conspires to work mine ill,
With heaven hath thus decreed,
That easy things should be to me denied
'Cause I crave the impossible.' "

'Anselmo departed the next day following to the village, telling Camilla, at his departure, that, whilst he was absent, his friend Lothario would come and see to the affairs of his house, and to eat with her, and desired her therefore to make as much of him as she would do of his own person. Camilla, like a discreet and modest woman, was grieved at the order her husband did give to her, and requested him to render how indecent it was that any one should possess the chair of his table, he being absent, and if he did it as doubting her sufficiency to manage his household affairs, that at least he should make trial of her that one time, and should clearly perceive how she was able to discharge matters of far greater consequence. Anselmo replied, that what he commanded was his pleasure, and therefore she had nothing else to do but hold down the head and obey it. Camilla answered, that she would do so, although it was very much against her will. In fine, her husband departed, and Lothario came the next day following to the house, where he was entertained by Camilla very friendly, but would never treat with Lothario alone, but evermore was compassed by her servants and waiting maidens, but chiefly by one called Leonela, whom she loved dearly, as one that had been brought up with her in her father's house, even from their infancy, and when she did marry Anselmo she brought her from thence in her company.

'The first three days Lothario spoke not a word, although he might, when the tables were taken up, and that the folk of the house went hastily to dinner, for so Camilla had commanded, and did give Leonela order besides to dine before herself, and that she should still keep by her side; but the girl, who had her fancy otherwise employed in things more pleasing her humour, and needed those hours and times for the accomplishing of them, did not always accomplish so punctually her lady's command, but now and then would leave her alone, as if that were her lady's behest. But the honest presence of Camilla, the gravity of her face, and the modesty of her carriage, was such, that it served as a bridle to restrain Lothario's tongue. But the benefit of Camilla's many virtues, setting silence to Lothario's speech, resulted afterward to both their harms; for though the tongue spoke not, yet did his thoughts discourse, and had leisure afforded them to contemplate, part by part, all the extremes of worth and beauty that were cumulated in Camilla, potent to inflame a statue of frozen marble, how much more a heart of flesh! Lothario did only behold her in the time and space he should speak unto her, and did then consider how worthy she was to be loved. And this consideration did by little and little give assaults to the respects which he ought to have borne towards his friend Anselmo; a thousand times did he determine to absent himself from the city, and go where Anselmo should never see him, nor he Camilla; but the delight he took in beholding her did again withhold and hinder his resolutions. When he was alone, he would condemn himself of his mad design, and term himself a bad friend and worse Christian; he made discourses and comparisons between himself and Anselmo, all which did finish in this point, that Anselmo's foolhardiness and madness were greater than his own infidelity, and that, if he might be as easily excused before God, for that he meant to do, as he would be before men, he needed not to fear any punishment should be inflicted on him for the crime. Finally, Camilla's beauty and worth, assisted by the occasion which the ignorant husband had thrust into his fists, did wholly ruin and overthrow Lothario his loyalty; and therefore, without regarding any other thing than that to which his pleasure conducted him, about three days after Anselmo's departure (which time he had spent in a continual battle and resistance of his contending thoughts), he began to solicit Camilla with such trouble of the spirits and so amorous words, as she was strucken almost beside herself with wonder, and made him no other answer, but, arising from the table, flung away in a fury into her chamber. But yet, for all this dryness, Lothario his hope (which is wont evermore to be born at once with love) was nothing dismayed, but rather accounted the more of Camilla, who, perceiving that in Lothario which she never durst before to imagine, knew not what she might do; but, it seeming unto her to be a thing neither secure nor honest, to give him occasion or leisure to speak unto him again, determined to send one unto her husband Anselmo the very same night, as indeed she did, with a letter to recall him home to her house. The subject of her letter was this.

CHAPTER VII

Wherein Is Prosecuted the History of the Curious-Impertinent

'"EVEN as it is commonly said, that an army seems not well without a general, or a castle without a constable, so do I affirm, that it is much more indecent to see a young married woman without her husband, when he is not justly detained away by necessary affairs. I find myself so ill disposed in your absence, and so impatient and impotent to endure it longer, as, if you do not speedily return, I shall be constrained to return back unto my father, although I should leave your house without any keeping; for the guard you appointed for me, if it be so that he may deserve that title, looks more, I believe, to his own pleasure, than to that which concerns you. Therefore, seeing you have wit enough, I will say no more; nor ought I say more in reason."

'Anselmo received the letter, and by it understood that Lothario had begun the enterprise, and that Camilla had answered to him according as he had hoped. And, marvellous glad at the news, he answered his wife by word of mouth, that she should not remove in any wise from her house; for he would return with all speed. Camilla was greatly admired at his answer, which struck her into a greater perplexity than she was at the first, being afraid to stay at home, and also to go to her father. For by staying she endangers her honesty; by going she would transgress her husband's command. At last she resolved to do that which was worst, which was to remain at home, and not to shun Lothario's presence, lest she should give her servants occasion of suspicion. And now she was grieved to have written what she did to her husband, fearful lest he should think that Lothario had noted in her some token of lightness, which might have moved him to lose the respect which otherwise was due unto her. But, confident in her innocency, she cast her hopes in God and her good thoughts, wherewithal she thought to resist all Lothario's words, and by holding her silent without making him any answer, without giving any further account of the matter to her husband, lest thereby she might plunge him in new difficulties and contention with his friend, and did therefore bethink her how she might excuse Lothario to Anselmo, when he should demand the occasion that moved her to write unto him that letter.

'With these more honest than profitable or discreet resolutions, she gave ear the second day to Lothario, who charged her with such resolution, as her constancy began to stagger, and her honesty had enough to do recurring to her eyes to contain them, lest they should give any demonstration of the amorous compassion which Lothario's words and tears had stirred in her breast. Lothario noted all this, and it inflamed him the more. Finally, he thought that it was requisite [to] the time and leisure which Anselmo's absence afforded him, to lay closer siege to that fortress; and so he assaulted her presumptuously, with the praises of her beauty, for there is nothing which with such facility doth rend and raze to the ground the proudly-crested turrets of women's vanity, than the same vanity being dilated on by the tongue of adulation and flattery. To be brief, he did with all diligence undermine the rock of her integrity with so warlike engines, as although Camilla were made of brass, yet would she be overthrown, for Lothario wept, entreated, promised, flattered, persisted and feigned so feelingly, and with such tokens of truth, as, traversing Camilla's care of her honour, he came in the end to triumph over that which was least suspected, and he most desired; for she rendered herself—even Camilla rendered herself. But what wonder if Lothario's amity could not stand on foot? A clear example, plainly demonstrating that the amorous passion is only vanquished by shunning it, and that nobody ought to adventure to wrestle with so strong an adversary; for heavenly forces are necessary for him that would confront the violence of that passion, although human. None but Leonela knew the weakness of her lady, for from her the two bad friends and new lovers could not conceal the matter; nor yet would Lothario discover to Camilla her husband's pretence, or that he had given him wittingly the opportunity whereby he arrived to that pass, because she should not imagine that he had gotten her lightly, and by chance, and did not purposely solicit her.

'A few days after, Anselmo arrived to his house, and did not perceive what wanted therein, to wit, that which it had lost, and he most esteemed. From thence he went to see his friend Lothario, whom he found at home, and, embracing one another, he demanded of him the news of his life or of his death. "The news which I can give thee, friend Anselmo," quoth Lothario, "are, that thou has a wife who may deservedly be the example and garland of all good women. The words that I spoke unto her were spent on the air, my proffers contemned, and my gifts repulsed, and besides, she hath mocked me notably for certain feigned tears that I did shed. In resolution, even as Camilla is the pattern of all beauty, so is she a treasury wherein modesty resides, courtesy and wariness dwell, and all the other virtues that may beautify an honourable woman, or make her fortunate. Therefore, friend, take back thy money, for here it is ready, and I never had occasion to employ it; for Camilla's integrity cannot be subdued with so base things as are gifts and promises. And, Anselmo, content thyself now with the proofs made already, without attempting to make any further trial. And seeing thou hast passed over the sea of difficulties and suspicions with a dry foot, which may and are wont to be had of women, do not eftsoons enter into the profound depths of new inconveniences, nor take thou any other pilot to make experience of the goodness and strength of the vessel that Heaven hath allotted to thee, to pass therein through the seas of this world; but make account that thou art harboured in a safe haven, and there hold thyself fast with the anchor of good consideration, and so rest thee until death come to demand his debt, from the payment whereof no nobility or privilege whatsoever can exempt us." Anselmo rested singularly satisfied at Lothario's discourse, and did believe it as firmly as if it were delivered by an oracle; but did entreat him notwithstanding to prosecute his attempt, although it were only done for curiosity, and to pass away the time; yet not to use so efficacious means as he hitherto practised; and that he only desired him to write some verses in her praise under the name of Chloris, for he would make Camilla believe that he was enamoured on a certain lady, to whom he did appropriate that name, that he might celebrate her praises with the respect due to her honour; and that if he would not take the pains to invent them, then he himself would willingly compose them. "That is not needful," quoth Lothario, "for the Muses are not so alienated from me, but that they visit me sometimes in the year. Tell you unto Camilla what you have divined of my loves, and as for the verses, I will make them myself; if not so well as the subject deserves, yet at the least as artificially as I may devise them." The impertinent-curious man and his treacherous friend having thus agreed, and Anselmo returned to his house, he demanded of Camilla that which she marvelled he had not asked before, that she should tell unto him the occasion why she sent unto him the letter? Camilla made answer, because it seemed unto her that Lothario beheld her somewhat more immodestly than when he was at home; but that now she did again dissuade herself, and believed that it was but a light surmise, without any ground, because that she perceived Lothario to loathe her presence, or [to] be by any means alone with her. Anselmo told her that she might very well live secure for him, for that he knew Lothario's affections were bestowed elsewhere, and that upon one of the noblest damsels of the city, whose praises he solemnized under the name of Chloris, and that although he were not, yet was there no cause to doubt of Lothario's virtue, or the amity that was between them both. Here, if Camilla had not been premonished by Lothario that the love of Chloris was but feigned, and that he himself had told it to Anselmo to blind him, that he might with less difficulty celebrate her own praises under the name of Chloris, she had without doubt fallen into the desperate toils of jealousy; but being already advertised, she posted over that assault lightly. The day following, they three sitting together at dinner, Anselmo requested Lothario to repeat some one of the verses that he had made to his beloved Chloris; for, seeing that Camilla knew her not, he might boldly say what he pleased. "Although she knew her," quoth Lothario, "yet would I not therefore suppress any part of her praises. For when any lover praiseth his lady for her beauty, and doth withal tax her of cruelty, her credit incurs no danger. But befall what it list, I composed yesterday a sonnet of the ingratitude of Chloris, and is this ensuing:

" 'A SONNET.

" 'Amidst the silence of the darkest night,
When sweetest sleep invadeth mortal eyes;
I poor account, to Heaven and Chloris bright,
Give of the richest harms, which ever rise.
And at the time we Phoebus may devise,
Shine through the roseal gates of the Orient bright,
With deep accents and sighs, in wonted guise,
I do my plaints renew, with main and might.
And when the sun, down from his starry seat,
Directest rays toward the earth doth send,
My sighs I double and my sad regreet;
And night returns; but of my woes no end.
For I find always, in my mortal strife,
Heaven without ears, and Chloris likewise deaf.' "

'Camilla liked the sonnet very well, but Anselmo best of all; for he praised it, and said, that the lady must be very cruel that would not answer such perspicuous truths with reciprocal affection. But then Camilla answered, "Why, then, belike, all that which enamoured poets say is true?" "Inasmuch as poets," quoth Lothario, "they say not truth; but as they are enamoured, they remain as short as they are true." "That is questionless," quoth Anselmo, all to underprop and give Lothario more credit with Camilla, who was as careless of the cause (her husband said so) as she was enamoured of Lothario; and therefore with the delight she took in his compositions, but chiefly knowing that his desires and labours were addressed to herself, who was the true Chloris, she entreated him to repeat some other sonnet or ditty, if he remembered any. "Yes, that I do," quoth Lothario; "but I believe that it is not so good as the first, as you may well judge; for it is this:

" 'A SONNET.

" 'I die, and if I cannot be believed,
My death's most certain, as it is most sure
To see me, at thy feet, of life deprived;
Rather than grieve, this thraldom to endure.
Well may I (in oblivious shades obscure)

Of glory, life, and favour be denied.
  And yet even there, shall in my bosom pure,
The shape of thy fair face, engraved, be eyed.
  For that's a relic, which I do reserve
For the last trances my contentions threaten,
  Which 'midst thy rigour doth itself preserve.
O woe's the wight, that is by tempests beaten
  By night, in unknown seas, in danger rife
  For want of North, or haven, to lose his life.' "

'Anselmo commended also this second sonnet as he had done the first, and added by that means one link to another in the chain wherewith he entangled himself, and forged his own dishonour; seeing, when Lothario dishonoured him most of all, he said unto him then that he honoured him most. And herewithal Camilla made all the links, that verily served only to abase her down to the centre of contempt, seem to mount her in her husband's opinion up to the height of virtue and good fame.

'It befel soon after, that Camilla, finding herself alone with her maiden, said to her, "I am ashamed, friend Leonela, to see how little I knew to value myself, seeing that I made not Lothario spend some time at least in the purchasing the whole possession of me, which I, with a prompt will, bestowed upon him so speedily. I fear me that he will impute my hastiness to lightness, without considering the force he used towards me, which wholly hindered and disabled my resistance." "Let not that afflict you, madam," quoth Leonela; "for it is no sufficient cause to diminish estimation, that that be given quickly which is to be given, if that in effect be good that is given, and be in itself worthy of estimation; for it is an old proverb, 'that he that gives quickly, gives twice.'" "It is also said as well," quoth Camilla, " 'that that which costeth little is less esteemed.'" "That reason hath no place in you," quoth Leonela, "forasmuch as love, according as some have said of it, doth sometimes fly, other times it goes; it runs with this man, and goes leisurely with the other; it makes some key-cold, and inflames others; some it wounds, and some it kills; it begins the career of his desires in an instant, and in the very same it concludes it likewise. It is wont to lay siege to the fortress in the morning, and at night it makes it to yield, for there's no force able to resist it; which being so, what do you wonder? or what is it that you fear, if the same hath befallen Lothario, seeing that love made of my lord's absence an instrument to vanquish us? And it was forcible, that in it we should conclude on it which love had before determined, without giving time itself any time to lead Anselmo that he might return, and with his presence leave the work imperfect. For love hath none so officious or better a minister to execute his desires than is occasion. It serves itself of occasion in all his act, but most of all at the beginning. And all this that I have said I know rather by experience than hearsay, as I will some day let you to understand; for, madam, I am likewise made of flesh and lusty young blood. And as for you, Lady Camilla, you did not give up and yield yourself presently, but stayed until you had first seen in Lothario's eyes, his sighs, in his discourses, in his promises, and gifts, all his soul, in which, and in his perfections, you might read how worthy he is to be loved. And seeing this is so, let not these scruples and nice thoughts assault or further disturb your mind, but persuade yourself that Lothario esteems you as much as you do him, and lives with content and satisfaction, seeing that it was your fortune to fall into the amorous snare, that it was his good luck to catch you with his valour and deserts; who not only hath the four S's which they say every good lover ought to have, but also the whole A B C, which if you will not credit, do but listen to me a while, and I will repeat it to you by rote. He is, as it seems, and as far as I can judge, Amiable, Bountiful, Courteous, Dutiful, Enamoured, Firm, Gallant, Honourable, Illustrious, Loyal, Mild, Noble, Honest, Prudent, Quiet, Rich, and the S's which they say; and besides True, Valorous. The X doth not quader well with him, because it sounds harshly. Y he is Young, and the Z he is Zealous of thine honour." Camilla laughed at her maiden's A B C, and accounted her to be more practised in love-matters than she herself had confessed, as indeed she was; for then she revealed to her mistress how she and a certain young man, well-born, of the city, did treat of love one with another. Hereat her mistress was not a little troubled in mind, fearing that her honour might be greatly endangered by that means; she demanded whether her affection had passed further than words? And the maid answered very shamelessly and freely that they did; for it is most certain, that this kind of reccheless mistress do also make their maidens careless and impudent; who, when they perceive their ladies to falter, are commonly wont to halt likewise themselves, and care not that the world do know it.

'Camilla, seeing that error past remedy, could do no more but entreat Leonela not to reveal anything of their affairs to him she said was her sweetheart, and that she should handle her matters discreetly and secretly, lest they might come to Anselmo or Lothario's notice. Leonela promised to perform her will, but did accomplish her promise in such sort, as she did confirm Camilla's fears that she should lose her credit by her means. For the dishonest and bold girl, after she had perceived that her mistress's proceedings were not such as they were wont, grew so hardy, as she gave entrance and brought her lover into her master's house, presuming that, although her lady knew it, yet would she not dare to discover it. For this among other harms follows the sins of mistresses, that it makes them slaves to their own servants, and doth oblige them to conceal their dishonest and base proceedings, as it fell out in Camilla, who, although she espied Leonela, not once only, but sundry times together, with her lover in a certain chamber of the house, she not only dared not to rebuke her for it, but rather gave her opportunity to hide him, and would remove all occasion out of her husband's way, whereby he might suspect any such thing.

'But all could not hinder Lothario from espying him once, as he departed out of the house at the break of the day; who, not knowing him, thought at the first it was a spirit, but when he saw him post away, and cast his cloak over his face, lest he should be known, he, abandoning his simple surmise, fell into a new suspicion which had overthrown them all, were it not that Camilla did remedy it. For Lothario thought that he whom he had seen issue out of Anselmo's house at so unseasonable an hour, had not entered into it for Leonela's sake, nor did he remember then that there was such a one as Leonela in the world, but only thought that, as Camilla was lightly gotten by him, so belike she was won by some other. For the wickedness of a bad woman bringeth usually all these additions, that she loseth her reputation even with him, to whom prayed and persuaded she yieldeth herself; and he believeth that she will as easily, or with more facility, consent to others, and doth infallibly credit the least suspicion which thereof may be offered.

'And it seems that Lothario in this instant was wholly deprived of all reasonable discourse, and quite despoiled of his understanding; for, without pondering of the matter, impatient and kindled by the jealous rage that inwardly gnawed his bowels, fretting with desire to be revenged on Camilla, who had never offended him, he came to Anselmo before he was up, and said to him, "Know, Anselmo, that I have had these many days a civil conflict within myself whether I should speak or no, and I have used as much violence as I might to myself, not to discover a thing unto you, which now it is neither just nor reasonable I should conceal. Know that Camilla's fortress is rendered, and subject to all that I please to command; and if I have been somewhat slow to inform thee this of truth, it was because I would first see whether it proceeded of some light appetite in her, or whether she did it to try me, and see whether that love was still constantly continued, which I first began to make unto her by thy order and licence. I did also believe that if she had been such as she ought to be, and her that we both esteemed her, she would have by this time acquainted you with my importunacy; but seeing that she lingers therein, I presume that her promises made unto me are true, that when you did again absent yourself out of town, she would speak with me in the wardrobe" (and it was true, for there Camilla was accustomed to talk with him), "yet would not I have thee run rashly to take revenge, seeing the sin is not yet otherwise committed than in thought, and perhaps between this and the opportunity she might hope to put it in execution, her mind would be changed, and she repent herself of her folly. And therefore seeing thou hast ever followed mine advice partly or wholly, follow and keep one counsel that I will give unto thee now, to the end that thou mayst after, with careful assurance and without fraud, satisfy thine own will as thou likest best. Feign thyself to be absent two or three days as thou art wont, and then convey thyself cunningly into the wardrobe, where thou mayst very well hide thyself behind the tapestry, and then thou shalt see with thine own eyes, and I with mine, what Camilla will do; and if it be that wickedness which rather ought to be feared than hoped for, thou mayst, with wisdom, silence, and discretion, be the proper executioner of so injurious a wrong."

'Anselmo remained amazed, and almost besides himself, hearing his friend Lothario so unexpectedly to acquaint him with those things in a time wherein he least expected them; for now he esteemed Camilla to have escaped victress from the forged assaults of Lothario, and did himself triumph for glory of her victory. Suspended thus and troubled, he stood silent a great while looking on the earth, without once removing his eyes from it; and finally, turning towards his friend, he said, "Lothario, thou hast done all that which I could expect from so entire amity, and I do therefore mean to follow thine advice in all things precisely. Do therefore what thou pleasest, and keep that secret which is requisite in so weighty and unexpected an event." "All that I do promise," quoth Lothario; and so departed, wholly repented for that he had told to Anselmo, seeing how foolishly he had proceeded, since he might have revenged himself on Camilla very well, without taking a way so cruel and dishonourable. There did he curse his little wit, and abased his light resolution, and knew not what means to use to destroy what he had done, or give it some reasonable and contrary issue. In the end he resolved to acquaint Camilla with the whole matter, and by reason that he never missed of opportunity to speak unto her, he found her alone the very same day; and she, seeing likewise that she had fit time to speak unto him, said, "Know, friend Lothario, that a certain thing doth pinch my heart in such manner, as it seems ready to burst in my breast, as doubtlessly I fear me that in time it will, if we cannot set a remedy to it. For such is the immodesty of Leonela, as she shuts up a lover of hers every night in this house, and remains with him until daylight, which so much concerns my credit, as it leaves open a spacious field to him that sees the other go out of my house at so unseasonable times, to judge of me what he pleaseth; and that which most grieves me is, that I dare not punish or rebuke her for it. For she being privy to our proceedings, sets a bridle on me, and constrains me to conceal hers; and hence I fear will bad success befall us." Lothario at the first suspected that Camilla did speak thus to make him believe that the man whom he had espied was Leonela's friend, and none of hers; but seeing her to weep indeed, and be greatly afflicted in mind, he began at last to give credit unto the truth, and, believing it, was greatly confounded and grieved for that he had done. And yet, notwithstanding, he answered Camilla that she should not trouble or vex herself any more; for he would take such order, as Leonela's impudence should be easily crossed and suppressed; and then did recount unto her all that he had said to Anselmo, spurred on by the furious rage of jealous indignation, and how her husband had agreed to hide himself behind the tapestry of the wardrobe, that he might from thence clearly perceive the little loyalty she kept towards him; and demanded pardon of her for that folly, and counsel to redress it, and come safely out of the intricate labyrinth whereinto his weak-eyed discourse had conducted him.

'Camilla, having heard Lothario's discourse, was afraid and amazed, and with great anger and many and discreet reasons did rebuke him, reviling the baseness of his thoughts, and the simple and little consideration that he had. But as women have naturally a sudden wit for good or bad, much more prompt than men, although when indeed they would make discourses, it proves defective; so Camilla found in an instant a remedy for an affair in appearance so irremediable and helpless, and therefore bade Lothario to induce his friend Anselmo to hide himself the next day ensuing, for she hoped to take commodity out of his being there for them both to enjoy one another with more security than ever they had before; and without wholly manifesting her proverb to him, she only advertised him to have care that, after Anselmo were hidden, he should presently come when Leonela called for him, and that he should answer her as directly to every question she proposed, as if Anselmo were not in place. Lothario did urge her importunately to declare her design unto him, to the end he might with more security and advice obscure all that was necessary. "I say," quoth Camilla, "there is no other observance to be had, than only to answer me directly to what I shall demand." For she would not give him account beforehand of her determination, fearful that he would not conform himself to her opinion, which she took to be so good, or else lest he would follow or seek any other, that would not prove after so well. Thus departed Lothario; and Anselmo, under pretext that he would visit his friend out of town, departed, and returned covertly back again to hide himself, which he could do the more commodiously, because Camilla and Leonela did purposely afford him opportunity. Anselmo having hidden himself with the grief that may be imagined one would conceive, who did expect to see with his own eyes an anatomy made of the bowels of his honour, and was in danger to lose the highest felicity that he accounted himself to possess in his beloved Camilla; Camilla and Leonela, being certain that he was hidden within the wardrobe, entered into it, wherein scarce had Camilla set her foot, when, breathing forth of a deep sigh, she spoke in this manner:

'"Ah, friend Leonela! were it not better that, before I put in execution that which I would not have thee to know, lest thou shouldest endeavour to hinder it, that thou takest Anselmo's poniard that I have sought of thee, and pass this infamous breast of mine through and through? but do it not, for it is no reason that I should suffer for other men's faults. I will know, first of all, what the bold and dishonest eyes of Lothario noted in me, that should stir in him the presumption to discover unto me so unlawful a desire as that which he hath revealed, so much in contempt of his friend, and to my dishonour. Stand at that window, Leonela, and call him to me, for I do infallibly believe that he stands in the street awaiting to effect his wicked purpose. But first my cruel yet honourable mind shall be performed." "Alas, dear madam," quoth the wise and crafty Leonela, "what is it that you mean to do with that poniard? Mean you perhaps to deprive either your own or Lothario's life therewithal? for whichsoever of these things you do, shall redound to the loss of your credit and fame. It is much better that you dissemble your wrong, and give no occasion to the bad man now to enter into this house, and find us here in it alone. Consider, good madam, how we are but weak women, and he is a man, and one resolute, and by reason that he comes blinded by his bad and passionate intent, he may peradventure, before you be able to put yours in execution, do somewhat that would be worse for you than to deprive you of your life. Evil befall my master Anselmo, that ministers so great occasion to Impudency thus to discover her visage in our house. And if you should kill him by chance, madam, as I suspect you mean to do, what shall we do after with the dead carcase?" What said Camilla? "We would leave him here that Anselmo might bury him; for it is only just that he should have the agreeable task of interring his own infamy. Make an end, then, and call him, for methinks that all the time which I spend untaking due revenge for my wrong, turns to the prejudice of the loyalty which I owe unto my spouse."

'Anselmo listened very attentively all the while, and at every word that Camilla said, his thoughts changed. But when he understood that she was resolved to kill Lothario, he was about to come out and discover himself, to the end that such a thing should not be done; but the desire that he had to see wherein so brave and honest a resolution would end, withheld him, determining then to sally out when his presence should be needful to hinder it. Camilla about this time began to be very weak and dismayed, and casting herself, as if she had fallen into a trance, upon a bed that was in the room, Leonela began to lament very bitterly, and to say, "Alas! wretch that I am, how unfortunate should I be, if the flower of the world's honesty, the crown of good women, and the pattern of chastity should die here between my hands!" Those and such other things she said so dolefully, as no one could hear her that would not deem her to be one of the most esteemed and loyal damsels of the world, and take her lady for another new and persecuted Penelope. Soon after Camilla returned to herself, and said presently, "Why goest thou not, Leonela, to call the most disloyal friend of a friend that ever the sun beheld, or the night concealed? Make an end, run, make haste, and let not the fire of my choler be through thy stay consumed and spent, nor the just revenge, which I hope to take, pass over in threats or maledictions." "I go to call him, madam," quoth Leonela; "but, first of all, you must give me that poniard, lest you should do with it in mine absence somewhat that would minister occasion to us, your friends, to deplore you all the days of our lives." "Go away boldly, friend Leonela," said Camilla, "for I shall do nothing in thine absence; for although I be in thine opinion both simple and bold enough to turn for mine honour, yet mean I not to be so much as the celebrated Lucretia, of whom it is recorded that she slew herself, without having committed any error, or slain him first who was the principal cause of her disgrace. I will die, if I must needs die, but I will be satisfied and revenged on him that hath given me occasion to come into this place to lament his boldness, sprung without my default."

'Leonela could scarce be entreated to go and call Lothario, but at last she went out, and in the meantime Camilla remained, speaking to herself these words: "Good God! had not it been more discretion to have dismissed Lothario, as I did many times before, than thus to possess him, as I have done, with an opinion that I am an evil and dishonest woman, at least all the while that passeth, until mine acts shall undeceive him, and teach him the contrary? It had been doubtlessly better; but then should not I be revenged, nor my husband's honour satisfied, if he were permitted to bear away so clearly his malignity, or escape out of the snare wherein his wicked thoughts involved him. Let the traitor pay with his life's defrayment that which he attempted with so lascivious a desire. Let the world know (if it by chance shall come to know it) that Camilla did not only conserve the loyalty due to her lord, but also took revenge of the intended spoil thereof. But yet I believe that it were best to give Anselmo first notice thereof; but I did already touch it to him in the letter which I wrote to him to the village, and I believe his not concurring to take order in this so manifest an abuse, proceeds of his too sincere and good meaning, which would not, nor cannot believe that the like kind of thought could ever find entertainment in the breast of so firm a friend, tending so much to his dishonour. And what marvel if I myself could not credit it for a great many days together? Nor would I ever have thought it, if his insolency had not arrived to that pass, which the manifest gifts, large promises, and continual tears he shed do give testimony. But why do I make now these discourses? Hath a gallant resolution perhaps any need of advice? No, verily; therefore avaunt treacherous thoughts, here we must use revenge. Let the false man come in, arrive, die, and end, and let after befall what can befall. I entered pure and untouched to his possession, whom Heaven bestowed on me for mine, and I will depart from him purely. And if the worst befall, I shall only be defiled by mine own chaste blood, and the impure gore of the falsest friend that ever amity saw in this world." And saying of this, she pranced up and down the room with the poniard naked in her hand, with such long and unmeasurable strides, and making withal such gestures, as she rather seemed defective of wit, and a desperate ruffian than a delicate woman.

'All this Anselmo perceived very well from behind the arras that covered him, which did not a little admire him, and he thought that what he had seen and heard was a sufficient satisfaction of far greater suspicions than he had, and could have wished with all his heart that the trial of Lothario's coming might be excused, fearing greatly some sudden bad success. And as he was ready to manifest himself, and to come out and embrace and dissuade his wife, he withdrew himself, because he saw Leonela return, bringing Lotharia in by the hand. And as soon as Camilla beheld him, she drew a great stroke with the point of the poniard athwart the wardrobe, saying, "Lothario, note well what I mean to say unto thee, for if by chance thou beest so hardy as to pass over this line which thou seest, ere I come as far as it, I will in the very same instant stab myself into the heart with this poniard which I hold in my hand. And before thou dost speak or answer me any word, I would first have thee to listen to a few of mine; for after, thou mayest say what thou pleasest.

'"First of all, I would have thee, O Lothario! to say whether thou knowest my husband, Anselmo, and what opinion thou hast of him? And next I would have thee to tell me if thou knowest myself? Answer to this without delay, nor do stand long thinking on what thou art to answer, seeing they are no deep questions which I propose unto thee." Lothario was not so ignorant, but that from the very beginning, when Camilla requested him to persuade her husband to hide himself behind the tapestry, he had not fallen on the drift of her invention; and therefore did answer her intention so aptly and discreetly, as they made that untruth pass between them for a more than manifest verity; and so he answered to Camilla in this form: "I did never conjecture, beautiful Camilla, that thou wouldest have called me here to demand of me things so wide from the purpose for which I come. If thou dost it to defer yet the promised favour, thou mightest have entertained it yet further off, for the good desired afflicteth so much the more, by how much the hope to possess it is near. But because thou mayest not accuse me for not answering to thy demands, I say that I know thy husband Anselmo, and both of us know one another even from our tender infancy, and I will not omit to say that which thou also knowest of our amity, to make me thereby a witness against myself of the wrong which love compels me to do unto him, yet love is a sufficient excuse and excuser of greater errors than are mine. Thee do I likewise know and hold in the same possession that he doth; for were it not so, I should never have been won by less perfections than thine, to transgress so much that which I owe to myself and to the holy laws of true amity, now broken and violated by the tyranny of so powerful an adversary as love hath proved." "If thou dost acknowledge that," replied Camilla, "O mortal enemy of all that which justly deserveth love! with what face darest thou then appear before that which thou knowest to be the mirror wherein he looks, in whom thou also oughtest to behold thyself, to the end thou mightest perceive upon how little occasion thou dost wrong him? But, unfortunate that I am, I fall now in the reason which hath moved thee to make so little account of thine own duty, which was perhaps some negligent or light behaviour of mine, which I will not call dishonesty, seeing that, as I presume, it hath not proceeded from me deliberately, but rather through the carelessness that women which think they are not noted do sometimes unwittingly commit. If not, say, traitor, when did I ever answer thy prayers with any word or token that might awake in thee the least shadow of hope to accomplish thine infamous desires? When were not thine amorous entreaties reprehended and dispersed by the roughness and rigour of mine answers? When were thy many promises and larger gifts ever believed or admitted? But forasmuch as I am persuaded that no man can persevere long time in the amorous contention, who hath not been sustained by some hope, I will attribute the fault of thine impertinence to myself; for doubtlessly some carelessness of mine hath hitherto sustained thy care, and therefore I will chastise and give to myself the punishment which thy fault deserveth. And because thou mightest see that I, being so inhuman towards myself, could not possibly be other than cruel to thee, I thought fit to call thee to be a witness of the sacrifice which I mean to make to the offended honour of my most honourable husband, tainted by thee with the blackest note that thy malice could devise, and by me, through the negligence that I used, to shun the occasion, if I gave thee any, thus to nourish and canonise thy wicked intentions. I say again, that the suspicion I have, that my little regard hath engendered in thee these distracted thoughts, is that which afflicteth me most, and that which I mean to chastise most with mine own hands; for if another executioner punished me, then should my crime become more notorious. But before I do this, I, dying, will kill, and carry him away with me, that shall end and satisfy the greedy desire of revenge which I hope for, and I have; seeing before mine eyes, wheresoever I shall go, the punishment which disengaged justice shall inflict, it still remaining unbowed or suborned by him, who hath brought me to so desperate terms."

'And having said these words, she flew upon Lothario with incredible force and lightness, and her poniard naked, giving such arguments and tokens that she meant to stab him, as he himself was in doubt whether her demonstrations were false or true; wherefore he was driven to help himself by his wit and strength, for to hinder Camilla from striking of him, who did so lively act her strange guile and fiction, as to give it colour, she would give it a blush of her own blood: for perceiving, or else feigning that she could not hurt Lothario, she said, "Seeing that adverse fortune will not satisfy thoroughly my just desires, yet at least it shall not be potent wholly to cross my designs." And then striving to free the dagger hand, which Lothario held fast, she snatched it away, and directing the point to some place of her body, which might hurt her, but not very grievously, she stabbed herself, and hid it in her apparel near unto the left shoulder, and fell forthwith to the ground, as if she were in a trance. Lothario and Leonela stood amazed at the unexpected event, and still rested doubtful of the truth of the matter, seeing Camilla to lie on the ground bathed in her blood. Lothario ran, all wan and pale, very hastily to her, to take out the poniard, and seeing how little blood followed, he lost the fear that he had conceived of her greater hurt, and began anew to admire the cunning wit and discretion of the beautiful Camilla; but yet that he might play the part of a friend, he began a long and doleful lamentation over Camilla's body, even as she were dead, and began to breathe forth many curses and execrations not only against himself, but also against him that had employed him in that unfortunate affair. And knowing that his friend Anselmo did listen unto him, he said such things as would move a man to take more compassion of him than of Camilla herself, although they accounted her dead. Leonela took her up between her arms, and laid her on the bed, and entreated Lothario to go out, and find some one that would undertake to cure her secretly. She also demanded of him his advice, touching the excuse they might make to Anselmo concerning her mistress her wound, if he came to town before it were fully cured.

'He answered, that they might say what they pleased, for he was not in a humour of giving any counsel worth the following; and only said this, that she should labour to stanch her lady's blood; for he meant to go there whence they should hear no news of him ever after. And so departed out of the house with very great tokens of grief and feeling; and when he was alone in a place where nobody perceived him, he blest himself a thousand times to think of Camilla's art, and the gestures, so proper and accommodated to the purpose, used by her maid Leonela. He considered how assured Anselmo would remain that he had a second Portia to wife, and desired to meet him, that they might celebrate together the fiction, and the best dissembed truth that could be ever imagined. Leonela, as is said, stanched her lady's blood, which was just as much as might serve to colour her invention and no more; and, washing the wound with some wine, she tied it up the best that she could, saying such words whilst she cured her as were able, though nothing had been done before, to make Anselmo believe that he had an image of honesty in Camilla. To the plaints of Leonela, Camilla added others, terming herself a coward of base spirit, since she wanted time (being a thing so necessary) to deprive her life which she hated so mortally; she demanded counsel of her maiden, whether she would tell or conceal all that success to her beloved spouse. And she answered, that it was best to conceal it, lest she should engage her husband to be revenged on Lothario, which would not be done without his very great peril, and that every good wife was bound, not to give occasion to her husband of quarrelling, but rather to remove from him as many as was possible. Camilla answered, that she allowed of her opinion, and would follow it; and that in any sort they must study some device to cloak the occasion of her hurt from Anselmo, who could not choose but espy it. To this Leonela answered, that she herself knew not how to lie, no, not in very jest itself. "Well, friend," quoth Camilla, "and I, what do I know? for I dare not to forge or report an untruth if my life lay on it. And if we know not how to give it a better issue, it will be better to report the naked truth than to be overtaken in a leasing." "Do not trouble yourself, madam," quoth Leonela; "for I will bethink myself of somewhat between this and to-morrow morning, and perhaps the wound may be concealed from him, by reason that it is in the place where it is; and Heaven perhaps may be pleased to favour our so just and honourable thoughts. Be quiet, good madam, and labour to appease your alteration of mind, that my lord at his return may not find you perplexed; and leave all the rest to God's and my charge, who doth always assist the just."

'With highest attention stood Anselmo listening and beholding the tragedy of his dying honours, which the personages thereof had acted with so strange and forcible effects, as it verily seemed that they were transformed into the opposite truth of their well-contrived fiction. He longed greatly for the night and leisure to get out of his house, that he might go and congratulate with his good friend Lothario, for the precious jewel that he had found in this last trial of his wife. The mistress and maiden had as great care to give him the opportunity to depart; and he, fearing to lose it, issued out in a trice, and went presently to find Lothario, who being found, it is not possible to recount the embracements he gave unto him, the secrets of his contentment that he revealed, or the attributes and praises that he gave to Camilla. All which Lothario heard, without giving the least argument of love; having represented to his mind at that very time, how greatly deceived his friend lived, and how unjustly he himself injured him. And although that Anselmo noted that Lothario took no delight at his relation, yet did he believe that the cause of his sorrow proceeded from having left Camilla wounded, and he himself given the occasion thereof; and therefore, among many other words, said unto him, that there was no occasion to grieve at Camilla's hurt, it doubtlessly being but light, seeing she and her maid had agreed to hide it from him; and that according unto this there was no great cause of fear, but that from thenceforward he should live merrily and contentedly with him, seeing that by his industry and means he found himself raised to the highest felicity that might be desired; and therefore would from thenceforth spend his idle times in writing of verses in Camilla's praise, that he might eternise her name, and make it famous in ensuing ages. Lothario commended his resolution therein, and said that he for his part would also help to raise up so noble an edifice; and herewithal Anselmo rested the most soothingly and contentedly deceived that could be found in the world. And then himself took by the hand to his house, believing that he bore the instrument of his glory, the utter perdition of his fame. Camilla entertained him with a frowning countenance, but a cheerful mind. The fraud rested unknown a while, until, at the end of certain months, fortune turned the wheel, and the wickedness that was so artificially cloaked, issued to the public notice of the world; and Anselmo his impertinent curiosity cost him his life.'

CHAPTER VIII

Wherein Is Ended the History of the Curious-Impertinent: And Likewise Recounted the Rough Encounter and Conflict Passed Between Don Quixote and Certain Bags of Red Wine

A LITTLE more of the novel did rest unread, when Sancho Panza, all perplexed, ran out of the chamber where his lord reposed, crying as loud as he could, 'Come, good sirs, speedily, and assist my lord, who is engaged in one of the most terrible battles that ever mine eyes have seen. I swear that he hath given such a blow to the giant, my lady the Princess Micomicona her enemy, as he hath cut his head quite off as round as a turnip.'

'What sayst thou, friend?' quoth the curate (leaving off at that word to prosecute the reading of his novel). 'Art thou in thy wits, Sancho? What a devil, man, how can that be, seeing the giant dwells at least two thousand leagues from hence?' By this they heard a marvellous great noise within the chamber, and that Don Quixote cried out aloud, 'Stay, false thief! robber, stay! for since thou art here, thy scimitar shall but little avail thee.' And therewithal it seemed that he struck a number of mighty blows on the walls. And Sancho said, 'There is no need to stand thus listening abroad, but rather that you go in and part the fray, or else assist my lord; although I think it be not very necessary, for the giant is questionless dead by this, and giving account for the ill life he led; for I saw his blood run all about the house, and his head cut off, which is as great as a great wine bag.' 'I am content to be hewn in pieces,' quoth the innkeeper, hearing of this, 'if Don Quixote or Don devil have not given some blow to one of the wine-bags that stood filled at his bed's head, and the shed wine must needs be that which seems blood to this good man.' And saying so, he entered into the room, and all the rest followed him, where they found Don Quixote in the strangest guise that may be imagined. He was in his shirt, the which was not long enough before to cover his thighs, and it was six fingers shorter behind. His legs were very long and lean, full of hair, and horribly dirty. He wore on his head a little red but very greasy nightcap, which belonged to the innkeeper. He had wreathed on his left arm the coverlet of his bed; on which Sancho looked very often and angrily, as one that knew well the cause of his own malice to it: and in his right hand he gripped his naked sword, wherewithal he laid round about him many a thwack; and withal spake as if he were in battle with some giant. And the best of all was, that he held not his eyes open; for he was indeed asleep, and dreaming that he was in fight with the giant. For the imagination of the adventure which he had undertaken to finish, was so bent upon it, as it made him to dream that he was already arrived at the kingdom of Micomicon, and that he was then in combat with his enemy, and he had given so many blows on the wine-bags, supposing them to be giants, as all the whole chamber flowed with wine. Which being perceived by the host, all inflamed with rage, he set upon Don Quixote with dry fists, and gave unto him so many blows that if Cardenio and the curate had not taken him away, he would doubtlessly have finished the war of the giant; and yet with all this did not the poor knight awake, until the barber brought in a great kettle full of cold water from the well, and threw it all at a clap upon him, and therewithal Don Quixote awaked, but not in such sort as he perceived the manner wherein he was. Dorothea, seeing how short and how thin her champion was arrayed, would not go in to see the conflict of her combatant and his adversary.

Sancho went up and down the floor searching for the giant's head, and seeing that he could not find it he said, 'Now I do see very well that all the things of this house are enchantments, for the last time that I was here, in this very same room, I got many blows and buffets, and knew not who did strike me, nor could I see any body; and now the head appears not, which I saw cut off with mine own eyes, and yet the blood ran as swiftly from the body as water would from a fountain.' 'What blood, or what fountain dost thou tattle of here, thou enemy of God and His saints?' quoth the innkeeper. 'Thou thief, dost thou not see that the blood and the fountain is no other thing than these wine-bags which are slashed here, and the wine red that swims up and down this chamber? And I wish that I may see his soul swimming in hell which did bore them!' 'I know nothing,' replied Sancho, 'but this, that if I cannot find the giant's head, I shall become so unfortunate, as mine earldom will dissolve like salt cast into water.' And certes, Sancho awake was in worse case than his master sleeping, so much had his lord's promises distracted him. The innkeeper, on the other side, was at his wits' end, to see the humour of the squire and unhappiness of his lord, and swore that it should not succeed with them now as it had done the other time, when they went away without payment; and that now the privileges of chivalry should not any whit avail him, but he should surely pay both the one and the other—yea, even for the very patches that were to be set on the bored wine-bags.

The curate held fast Don Quixote by the hands, who believing that he had achieved the adventure, and was after it come into the Princess Micomicona her presence, he laid himself on his knees before the curate, saying, 'Well may your greatness, high and famous lady, live from henceforth secure from any danger that this unfortunate wretch may do unto you; and I am also freed from this day forward from the promise that I made unto you, seeing I have, by the assistance of the heavens, and through her favour by whom I live and breathe, so happily accomplished it.' 'Did not I say so?' quoth Sancho, hearing of his master. 'Yea, I was not drunk. See if my master hath not powdered the giant by this? The matter is questionless, and the earldom is mine own.' Who would not laugh at these raving fits of the master and man? All of them laughed save the innkeeper, who gave himself for anger to the devil more than a hundred times. And the barber, Cardenio, and the curate, got Don Quixote to bed again, not without much ado, who presently fell asleep with tokens of marvellous weariness. They left him sleeping, and went out to comfort Sancho Panza for the grief he had, because he could not find the giant's head; but yet had more ado to pacify the innkeeper, who was almost out of his wits for the unexpected and sudden death of his wine-bags.

The hostess, on the other side, went up and down whining and saying, 'In an ill season and an unlucky hour did this knight-errant enter into my house, alas! and I would that mine eyes had never seen him, seeing he costs me so dear. The last time that he was here, he went away scot free for his supper, bed, straw, and barley, both for himself and his man, his horse and his ass, saying that he was a knight-adventurer (and God give to him ill venture, and to all the other adventurers of the world!) and was not therefore bound to pay anything, for so it was written in the statutes of chivalry. And now for his cause came the other gentleman, and took away my good tail, and hath returned it me back with two quarters of damage; for all the hair is fallen off, and it cannot stand my husband any more in stead for the purpose he had it; and for an end and conclusion of all, to break my wine-bags and shed my wine: I wish I may see as much of his blood shed. And do not think otherwise; for, by my father's old bones and the life of my mother, they shall pay me every doit, one quart upon another, or else I will never be called as I am, nor be mine own father's daughter.'

These and such like words spake the innkeeper's wife with very great fury, and was seconded by her good servant Maritornes. The daughter held her peace, and would now and then smile a little. But master parson did quiet and pacify all, by promising to satisfy them for the damages as well as he might, as well for the wine as for the bags, but chiefly for her tail, the which was so much accounted of and valued so highly. Dorothea did comfort Sancho, saying to him, that whensoever it should be verified that his lord had slain the giant, and established her quietly in her kingdom, she would bestow upon him the best earldom thereof. With this he took courage, and assured the princess that he himself had seen the giant's head cut off; and for a more certain token thereof, he said that he had a beard that reached him down to his girdle; and that if the head could not now be found, it was by reason that all the affairs of that house were guided by enchantment, as he had made experience to his cost the last time that he was lodged therein. Dorothea replied that she was of the same opinion, and bade him to be of good cheer, for all would be well ended to his heart's desire. All parties being quiet, the curate resolved to finish the end of his novel, because he perceived that there rested but a little unread thereof. Cardenio, Dorothea, and all the rest entreated him earnestly to finish it. And he desiring to delight them all herein and recreate himself, did prosecute the tale in this manner:

'It after befel that Anselmo grew so satisfied of his wife's honesty as he led a most contented and secure life. And Camilla did for the nonce look sourly upon Lothario, to the end Anselmo might construe her mind amiss. And for a greater confirmation thereof, Lothario requested Anselmo to excuse his coming any more to his house, seeing that he clearly perceived how Camilla could neither brook his company nor presence. But the hoodwinked Anselmo answered him that he would in no wise consent thereunto; and in this manner did weave his own dishonour a thousand ways, thinking to work his contentment. In this season, such was the delight that Leonela took also in her affections, as she suffered herself to be borne away by them headlongly, without any care or regard, confident because her lady did cover it, yea, and sometimes instructed her how she might put her desires in practice, without any fear or danger. But finally, Anselmo heard on a night somebody walk in Leonela's chamber, and, being desirous to know who it was, as he thought to enter, he felt the door to be held fast against him, which gave him a greater desire to open it; and therefore he struggled so long and used such violence, as he threw open the door, and entered just at the time that another leaped out at the window; and therefore he ran out to overtake him, or see wherein he might know him, but could neither compass the one nor the other, by reason that Leonela, embracing him hardly, withheld him and said, "Pacify yourself, good sir, and be not troubled, nor follow him that was here; for he is one that belongs to me, and that so much, as he is my spouse." Anselmo would not believe her, but rather, blind with rage, he drew out his poniard and would have wounded her, saying, that she should presently tell him the truth, or else he would kill her. She, distracted with fear, said, without noting her own words, "Kill me not, sir, and I will acquaint you with things which concern you more than you can imagine." "Say quickly, then," quoth Anselmo, "or else thou shalt die." "It will be impossible," replied Leonela, "for me to speak anything now, I am so affrighted; but give respite till morning, and I will recount unto you things that will marvellously astonish you; and in the meantime rest secure, that he which leaped out of the window is a young man of this city betwixt whom and me hath passed a promise of marriage." Anselmo was somewhat satisfied by these words, and therefore resolved to expect the term which she had demanded to open her mind; for he did not suspect that he should hear anything of Camilla, by reason he was already so assured of her virtue. And so, departing out of the chamber, and shutting up Leonela therein, threatening her withal that she should never depart thence until she had said all that she promised to reveal unto him, he went presently to Camilla, to tell unto her all that which his maiden had said, and the promise she had passed, to disclose greater and more important things. Whether Camilla, hearing this, were perplexed or no, I leave to the discreet reader's judgment; for such was the fear which she conceived, believing certainly (as it was to be doubted) that Leonela would tell to Anselmo all that she knew of her disloyalty, as she had not the courage to expect and see whether her surmise would become false or no. But the very same night, as soon as she perceived Anselmo to be asleep, gathering together her best jewels and some money, she departed out of her house unperceived of any, and went to Lothario's lodging, to whom she recounted all that had passed, and requested him either to leave her in some safe place, or both of them to depart to some place where they might live secure out of Anselmo's reach. The confusion that Camilla struck into Lothario was such as he knew not what to say, and much less how to resolve himself what he might do. But at last he determined to carry Camilla to a monastery wherein his sister was prioress; to which she easily condescended: and therefore Lothario departed, and left her there with all the speed that the case required, and did also absent himself presently from the city, without acquainting anybody with his departure.

'Anselmo, as soon as it was day, without heeding the absence of his wife, arose and went to the place where he had shut up Leonela, with desire to know of her what she had promised to acquaint him withal. He opened the chamber door, and entered, but could find nobody therein, but some certain sheets knit together and tied to the window, as a certain sign how Leonela had made an escape by that way. Wherefore he returned very sad to tell to Camilla the adventure; but when he could neither find her at bed nor in the whole house, he remained astonied, and demanded for her of his servants, but none of them could tell him anything. And as he searched for her, he happened to see her coffers lie open and most of her jewels wanting; and herewithal fell into the true account of his disgrace, and that Leonela was not the cause of his misfortune, and so departed out of his house sad and pensive, even as he was, half ready and unapparelled, to his friend Lothario, to recount unto him his disaster: but when he found him to be likewise absented, and that the servants told him how their master was departed the very same night, and had borne away with him all his money, he was ready to run out of his wits. And to conclude, he returned to his own house again, wherein he found no creature, man or woman, for all his folk were departed, and had left the house alone and desert. He knew not what he might think, say, or do; and then his judgment began to fail him. There he did contemplate and behold himself in an instant, without a wife, a friend, and servants; abandoned (to his seeming) of Heaven that covered him, and chiefly without honour; for he clearly noted his own perdition in Camilla's crime. In the end he resolved, after he had bethought himself a great while, to go to his friend's village, wherein he had been all the while that he afforded the leisure to contrive that disaster. And so, shutting up his house, he mounted a-horseback, and rode away in languishing and doleful wise. And scarce had he ridden the half-way, when he was so fiercely assaulted by his thoughts, as he was constrained to alight, and, tying his horse to a tree, he leaned himself to the trunk thereof, and breathed out a thousand pitiful and dolorous sighs; and there he abode until it was almost night, about which hour he espied a man to come from the city a-horseback by the same way, and, having saluted him, he demanded of him what news he brought from Florence. The citizen replied, "The strangest that had happened there many a day; for it is there reported publicly that Lothario, the great friend of the rich man, hath carried away the said Anselmo's wife Camilla this night, for she is also missing: all which a waiting-maid of Camilla's hath confessed, whom the governor apprehended yesternight as she slipped down at a window by a pair of sheets out of the said Anselmo's house.

I know not particularly the truth of the affair, but well I wot that all the city is amazed at the accident; for such a fact would not be as much as surmised from the great and familiar amity of them two, which was so much as they were called, 'The Two Friends.'" "Is it perhaps yet known," replied Anselmo, "which way Lothario and Camilla have taken?" "In no wise!" quoth the citizen, "although the governor hath used all possible diligence to find them out." "Farewell, then, good sir," said Anselmo. "And with you, sir," said the traveller. And so departed.

'With these so unfortunate news poor Anselmo arrived, not only to terms of losing his wits, but also well-nigh of losing his life; and therefore, arising as well as he might, he came to his friend's house, who had heard nothing yet of his disgrace; but perceiving him to arrive so wan, pined, and dried up, he presently conjectured that some grievous evil afflicted him. Anselmo requested him presently that he might be carried to his chamber, and provided of paper and ink to write withal. All was done, and he left in bed, and alone, for so he desired them; and also that the door should be fast locked. And being alone, the imagination of his misfortune gave him such a terrible charge, as he clearly perceived that his life would shortly fail him, and therefore resolved to leave notice of the cause of his sudden and unexpected death; and therefore he began to write it; but before he could set an end to his discourse, his breath failed, and he yielded up his life into the hands of sorrow, which his impertinent curiosity had stirred up in him. The gentleman of the house, seeing that it grew late, and that Anselmo had not called, determined to enter, and know whether his indisposition passed forward, and he found him lying on his face, with half of his body in the bed, and the other half leaning on the table whereon he lay, with a written paper unfolded, and held the pen also yet in his hand. His host drew near unto him and, first of all, having called him, he took him by the hand; and seeing that he answered not, and that it was cold, he knew that he was dead; and greatly perplexed and grieved thereat, he called in his people, that they might also be witnesses of the disastrous success of Anselmo; and after all, he took the paper and read it, which he knew to be written with his own hand, the substance whereof was this:

'"A foolish and impertinent desire hath despoiled me of life. If the news of my death shall arrive to Camilla, let her also know that I do pardon her, for she was not bound to work miracles; nor had I any need to desire that she should work them. And seeing I was the builder and contriver of mine own dishonour, there is no reason"—

'Hitherunto did Anselmo write, by which it appeared that his life ended in that point, ere he could set an end to the reason he was to give. The next day ensuing, the gentleman his friend acquainted Anselmo's kinsfolk with his death; the which had already knowledge of his misfortune, and also of the monastery wherein Camilla had retired herself, being almost in terms to accompany her husband in that forcible voyage; nor for the news of his death, but for grief of others which she had received of her absent friend. It is said that although she was a widow, yet would she neither depart out of the monastery, nor become a religious woman, until she had received within a few days after news how Lothario was slain in a battle given by Monsieur de Lautrec, to the great Captain Gonzalo Fernandez of Cordova, in the kingdom of Naples; and that was the end of the late repentant friend, the which being known to Camilla, she made a profession, and shortly after deceased between the rigorous hands of sorrow and melancholy: and this was the end of them all, sprung from a rash and inconsiderate beginning.'

'This novel,' quoth the curate, having read it, 'is a pretty one; but yet I cannot persuade myself that it is true, and if it be a fiction, the author erred therein; for it cannot be imagined that any husband would be so foolish as to make so costly an experience as did Anselmo; but if this accident had been devised betwixt a gentleman and his love, then were it possible; but being between man and wife, it contains somewhat that is impossible and unlikely, but yet I can take no exception against the manner of recounting thereof.'

CHAPTER IX

Which Treats of Many Rare Successes Befallen in the Inn

WHILST they discoursed thus, the innkeeper, who stood all the while at the door, said, 'Here comes a fair troop of guests, and if they will here alight we may sing Gaudeamus.' 'What folk is it?' quoth Cardenio. 'Four men on horseback,' quoth the host, 'and ride jennet-wise, with lances and targets, and masks on their faces; and with them comes likewise a woman apparelled in white, in a side-saddle, and her face also masked, and two lackeys that run with them a-foot.' 'Are they near?' quoth the curate. 'So near,' replied the innkeeper, 'as they do now arrive.' Dorothea hearing him say so, covered her face, and Cardenio entered into Don Quixote's chamber; and scarce had they leisure to do it, when the others of whom the host spake, entered into the inn, and the four horsemen alighting, which were all of very comely and gallant disposition, they went to help down the lady that rode in the side-saddle, and one of them taking her down in his arms, did seat her in a chair that stood at the chamber door, into which Cardenio had entered: and all this while neither she nor they took off their masks, or spake a word, only the gentlewoman, at her sitting down in the chair, breathed forth a very deep sigh, and let fall her arms like a sick and dismayed person. The lackeys carried away their horses to the stable. Master curate seeing and noting all this, and curious to know what they were that came to the inn in so unwonted an attire, and kept such profound silence therein, went to the lackeys and demanded of one of them that which he desired to know, who answered, 'In good faith, sir, I cannot tell you what folk this is: only this I know, that they seem to be very noble, but chiefly he that went and took down the lady in his arms that you see there; and this I say, because all the others do respect him very much, and nothing is done but what he ordains and commands.' 'And the lady, what is she?' quoth the curate.

'I can as hardly inform you,' quoth the lackey, 'for I have not once seen her face in all this journey; yet I have heard her often groan and breathe out so profound sighs, as it seems she would give up the ghost at every one of them. And it is no marvel that we should know no more than we have said, for my companion and myself have been in their company but two days; for they encountered us on the way, and prayed and persuaded us to go with them unto Andalusia, promising that they would recompense our pains largely.' 'And hast thou heard them name one another?' said the curate. 'No, truly,' answered the lackey; 'for they all travel with such silence, as it is a wonder; for you shall not hear a word among, but the sighs and throbs of the poor lady, which do move in us very great compassion. And we do questionless persuade ourselves that she is forced wheresoever she goes: and as it may be collected by her attire, she is a nun, or, as is most probable, goes to be one; and perhaps she goeth so sorrowful as it seems because she hath no desire to become religious.' 'It may very well be so,' quoth the curate. And so leaving them, he returned to the place where he had left Dorothea; who, hearing the disguised lady to sigh so often, moved by the native compassion of that sex, drew near her and said, 'What ails you, good madam? I pray you think if it be any of those inconveniences to which woman be subject, and whereof they may have use and experience to cure them, I do offer unto you my service, assistance, and good-will to help you, as much as lies in my power.' To all those compliments the doleful lady answered nothing; and although Dorothea made her again larger offers of her service, yet stood she, ever silent, until the bemasked gentleman (whom the lackey said the rest did obey) came over and said to Dorothea, 'Lady, do not trouble yourself to offer anything to that woman, for she is of a most ungrateful nature, and is never wont to gratify any courtesy, nor do you seek her to answer unto your demands, if you would not hear some lie from her mouth.' 'I never said any,' quoth the silent lady, 'but rather because I am so true and sincere, without guiles, I am now drowned here in those misfortunes; and of this I would have thyself bear witness, seeing my pure truth makes thee to be so false and disloyal.'

Cardenio overheard those words very clear and distinctly, as one that stood so near unto her that said them, as only Don Quixote's chamber door stood between them. And instantly when he heard them, he said with a very loud voice, 'Good God! what is this that I hear? What voice is this that hath touched mine ear?' The lady, moved with a sudden passion, turned her head at those outcries, and seeing she could not perceive him that gave them, she got up, and would have entered into the room, which the gentleman espying, withheld her, and would not let her stir out of the place: and with the alteration and sudden motion the mask fell off her face, and she discovered an incomparable beauty, and an angelical countenance, although it was somewhat wan and pale, and turned here and there with her eyes to every place so earnestly as she seemed to be distracted; which motions, without knowing the reason why they were made, struck Dorothea and the rest that beheld her into very great compassion. The gentleman holding her very strongly fast by the shoulders, the mask he wore on his own face was falling; and he being so busied could not hold it up, but in the end [it] fell wholly. Dorothea, who had likewise embraced the lady, lifting up her eyes by chance, saw that he which did also embrace the lady was her spouse Don Fernando; and scarce had she known him, when, breathing out a long and most pitiful 'Alas!' from the bottom of her heart, she fell backward in a trance; and if the barber had not been by good hap at hand, she would have fallen on the ground with all the weight of her body. The curate presently repaired to take off the veil of her face and cast water thereon: and as soon as he did discover it, Don Fernando, who was he indeed that held fast the other, knew her, and looked like a dead man as soon as he viewed her, but did not all this while let go Lucinda, who was the other whom he held so fast, and that laboured so much to escape out of his hands. Cardenio likewise heard the 'Alas!' that Dorothea said when she fell into a trance, and, believing that it was his Lucinda, issued out of the chamber greatly altered, and the first he espied was Don Fernando, which held Lucinda fast, who forthwith knew him. And all the three—Lucinda, Cardenio, and Dorothea—stood dumb and amazed, as folk that knew not what had befallen unto them. All of them held their peace, and beheld one another; Dorothea looked on Don Fernando, Don Fernando on Cardenio, Cardenio on Lucinda, and Lucinda again on Cardenio; but Lucinda was the first that broke silence, speaking to Don Fernando in this manner: 'Leave me off, Lord Fernando, I conjure thee, by that thou shouldst be; for that which thou art, if thou wilt not do it for any other respect; let me cleave to the wall whose ivy I am; to the supporter from whom neither thy importunity nor threats, promises or gifts, could once deflect me. Note how Heaven, by unusual, unfrequented, and from us concealed ways, hath set my true spouse before mine eyes; and thou dost know well, by a thousand costly experiences, that only death is potent to blot forth his remembrance out of my memory. Let, then, so manifest truths be of power (if thou must do none other) to convert thine affliction into rage, and thy good-will into despite, and therewithal end my life; for if I may render up the ghost in the presence of my dear spouse, I shall account it fortunately lost. Perhaps by my death he will remain satisfied of the faith which I have kept sincere towards him until the last period of my life.' By this time Dorothea was come to herself, and listened to most of Lucinda's reasons, and by them came to the knowledge of herself. But seeing Don Fernando did not yet let her depart from between his arms, nor answer anything to her words, encouraging herself the best that she might, she arose, and, kneeling at his feet, and shedding a number of crystal and penetrating tears, she spoke to him thus:

'If it be not so, my lord, that the beams of that sun which thou holdest eclipsed between thine arms do darken and deprive those of thine eyes, thou mightest have by this perceived how she that is prostrated at thy feet is the unfortunate (until thou shalt please) and the disastrous Dorothea. I am that poor humble countrywoman whom thou, either through thy bounty, or for thy pleasure, didst deign to raise to that height that she might call thee her own. I am she which, some time immured within the limits of honesty, did lead a most contented life, until it opened the gates of her recollection and wariness to thine importunity, and seeming just and amorous requests, and rendered up to thee the keys of her liberty; a gift by thee so ill recompensed, as the finding myself in so remote a place as this wherein you have met with me, and I seen you, may clearly testify; but yet for all this, I would not have you to imagine that I come here guided by dishonourable steps, being only hitherto conducted by the tracts of dolour and feeling, to see myself thus forgotten by thee. It was thy will that I should be thine own, and thou didst desire it in such a manner, as although now thou wouldst not have it so, yet canst not thou possibly leave off to be mine. Know, my dear lord, that the matchless affections that I do bear towards thee may recompense and be equivalent to her beauty and nobility for whom thou dost abandon me.

'Thou canst not be the beautiful Lucinda's, because thou art mine; nor she thine, forasmuch as she belongs to Cardenio; and it will be more easy, if you will note it well, to reduce thy will to love her that adores thee, than to address hers, that hates thee, to bear thee affection. Thou didst solicit my recchelessness, thou prayedst to mine integrity, and wast not ignorant of my quality; thou knowest also very well upon what terms I subjected myself to thy will, so as there remains no place nor colour to term it a fraud or deceit; and all this being so, as in verity it is, and that thou beest as Christian as thou art noble, why dost thou with these so many untoward wreathings dilate the making of mine end happy, whose commencement thou didst illustrate so much? And if thou wilt not have me for what I am, who am thy true and lawful spouse, yet at least take and admit me for thy slave, for so that I may be in thy possession I will account myself happy and fortunate. Do not permit that by leaving and abandoning me, meetings may be made to discourse of my dishonour. Do not vex thus the declining years of my parents, seeing that the loyal services which they ever have done as vassals to thine deserve not so [dis]honest a recompense. And if thou esteemest that thy blood by meddling with mine shall be stained or embased, consider how few noble houses, or rather none at all, are there in the world which have not run the same way, and that the woman's side is not essentially requisite for the illustrating of noble descents. How much more, seeing that true nobility consists in virtue, which if it shall want in thee, by refusing that which thou owest me so justly, I shall remain with many more degrees of nobility than thou shalt. And in conclusion, that which I will lastly say is, that whether thou wilt or no, I am thy wife; the witnesses are thine own words, which neither should nor ought to lie, if thou dost esteem thyself to have that for the want of which thou despisest me. Witness shall also be thine own handwriting. Witness Heaven, which thou didst invoke to bear witness of that which thou didst promise unto me: and when all this shall fail, thy very conscience shall never fail from using clamours, being silent in thy mirth and turning, for this truth which I have said to thee now shall trouble the greatest pleasure and delight.'

These and many other like reasons did the sweetly grieved Dorothea use with such feeling, as all those that were present, as well such as accompanied Don Fernando, and all the others that did accompany her, shed abundance of tears. Don Fernando listened unto her without replying a word, until she had ended her speech, and given beginning to so many sighs and sobs, as the heart that could endure to behold them without moving were harder than brass. Lucinda did also regard her, no less compassionate of her sorrow than admired at her discretion and beauty, and although she would have approached to her, and used some consolatory words, yet was she hindered by Don Fernando's arms, which held her still embraced, who, full of confusion and marvel, after he had stood very attentively beholding Dorothea a good while, opening his arms, and leaving Lucinda free, said, 'Thou hast vanquished, O beautiful Dorothea! thou hast vanquished me; for it is not possible to resist or deny so many united truths.' Lucinda, through her former trance and weakness, as Don Fernando left her, was like to fall, if Cardenio, who stood behind Don Fernando all the while lest he should be known, shaking off all fear and endangering his person, had not started forward to stay her from falling; and, clasping her sweetly between his arms, he said, 'If pitiful Heaven be pleased, and would have thee now at last take some ease, my loyal, constant, and beautiful lady, I presume that thou canst not possess it more securely than between these arms which do now receive thee, as whilom they did when fortune was pleased that I might call thee mine own.' And then Lucinda, first severing her eyelids, beheld Cardenio, and having first taken notice of him by his voice, and confirmed it again by her sight, like one quite distracted, without further regarding modest respects, she cast both her arms about his neck, and, joining her face to his, said, 'Yea, thou indeed art my lord; thou, the true owner of this poor captive, howsoever adverse fortune shall thwart it, or this life, which is only sustained and lives by thine, be ever so much threatened.' This was a marvellous spectacle to Don Fernando, and all the rest of the beholders, which did universally admire at this so unexpected an event. And Dorothea, perceiving Don Fernando to change colour, as one resolving to take revenge on Cardenio, for he had set hand to his sword, which she conjecturing, did with marvellous expedition kneel, and, catching hold on his legs, kissing them, she strained them with so loving embracements as he could not stir out of the place, and then, with her eyes overflown with tears, said unto him, 'What meanest thou to do, my only refuge in this unexpected trance? Thou hast here thine own spouse at thy feet, and her whom thou wouldst fain possess is between her own husband's arms. Judge, then, whether it become thee, or is a thing possible, to dissolve that which Heaven hath knit, or whether it be anywise laudable to endeavour to raise and equal to thyself her who, contemning all dangers and inconveniences, and confirmed in faith and constancy, doth in thy presence bathe her eyes with amorous liquor of her true love's face and bosom. I desire thee for God's sake, and by thine own worths I request thee, that this so notorious a verity may not only assuage thy choler, but also diminish it in such sort, as thou mayst quietly and peaceably permit those two lovers to enjoy their desires without any encumbrance all the time that Heaven shall grant it to them; and herein thou shalt show the generosity of thy magnanimous and noble breast, and give the world to understand how reason prevaileth in thee, and domineereth over passion.' All the time that Dorothea spoke thus to Don Fernando, although Cardenio held Lucinda between his arms, yet did he never take his eyes off Don Fernando, with resolution that if he did see him once stir in his prejudice, he would labour both to defend himself and offend his adversary and all those who should join with him to do him any harm, as much as he could, although it were with the rest of his life. But Don Fernando's friends, the curate and barber, that were present and saw all that was passed, repaired in the mean season, without omitting the good Sancho Panza, and all of them together compassed Don Fernando, entreating him to have regard of the beautiful Dorothea's tears, and it being true (as they believed it was) that she had said, he should not permit her to remain defrauded of her so just and lawful hopes, assuring him that it was not by chance, but rather by the particular providence and disposition of the heavens, that they had all met together so unexpectedly; and that he should remember, as master curate said very well, that only death could sever Lucinda from her Cardenio; and that although the edge of a sword might divide and part them asunder, yet in that case they would account their death most happy; and that, in irremediless events, it was highest prudence, by straining and overcoming himself, to show a generous mind, and that he might conquer his own will, by permitting these two to enjoy that good which Heaven had already granted to them; and that he should turn his eyes to behold the beauty of Dorothea, and he should see that few or none could for feature paragon with her, and much less excel her; and that he should confer her humility and extreme love which she bore to him with her other endowments: and principally, that if he gloried in the titles of nobility or Christianity, he could not do any other than accomplish the promise that he had passed to her; and that by fulfilling it he should please God and satisfy discreet persons, which know very well how it is a special prerogative of beauty, though it be in an humble and mean subject, if it be consorted with modesty and virtue, to exalt and equal itself to any dignity, without disparagement of him which doth help to raise or unite it to himself. And when the strong laws of delight are accomplished (so that there intercur no sin in the acting thereof), he is not to be condemned which doth follow them. Finally, they added to these reasons others so many and forcible, that the valorous breast of Don Fernando (as commonly all those that are warmed and nourished by noble blood are wont) was mollified, and permitted itself to be vanquished by that truth which he could not deny though he would. And the token that he gave of his being overcome, was to stoop down and embrace Dorothea, saying unto her, 'Arise, lady; for it is not just that she be prostrate at my feet whose image I have erected in my mind. And if I have not hitherto given demonstrations of what I now aver, it hath perhaps befallen through the disposition of Heaven, to the end I might, by noting the constancy and faith wherewithal thou dost affect me, know after how to value and esteem thee according unto thy merits. And that which in recompense thereof I do entreat of thee is, that thou wilt excuse in me mine ill manner of proceeding and exceeding carelessness in repaying thy good-will; for the very occasion and violent passions that made me to accept thee as mine, the very same did also impel me again not to be thine; and for the more verifying of mine assertion, do but once behold the eyes of the now contented Lucinda, and thou mayst read in them a thousand excuses for mine error; and seeing she hath found and obtained her heart's desire, and I have in thee also gotten what is most convenient—for I wish she may live securely and joyfully many and happy years with her Cardenio: for I will pray the same, that it will license me to enjoy my beloved Dorothea.' And saying so, he embraced her again, and joined his face to hers with so lovely motion, as it constrained him to hold watch over his tears, lest violently bursting forth, they should give doubtless arguments of his fervent love and remorse.

Cardenio, Lucinda, and almost all the rest could not do so, for the greater number of them shed so many tears, some for their private contentments, and others for their friends, as it seemed that some grievous and heavy misfortune had betided them all; even very Sancho Panza wept, although he excused it afterward, saying that he wept only because that he saw that Dorothea was not the Queen Micomicona, as he had imagined, of whom he hoped to have received so great gifts and favours. The admiration and tears joined, endured in them all for a pretty space; and presently after, Cardenio and Lucinda went and kneeled to Don Fernando, yielding him thanks for the favour that he had done to them, with so courteous compliments as he knew not what to answer, and therefore lifted them up, and embraced them with very great affection and kindness, and presently after he demanded of Dorothea how she came to that place, so far from her own dwelling. And she recounted unto him all that she had told to Cardenio; whereat Don Fernando and those which came with him took so great delight, as they could have wished that her story had continued a longer time in the telling than it did—so great was Dorothea's grace in setting out her misfortunes. And as soon as she had ended, Don Fernando told all that had befallen him in the city, after that he had found the scroll in Lucinda's bosom, wherein she declared Cardenio to be her husband, and that he therefore could not marry her; and also how he attempted to kill her, and would have done it, were it not that her parents hindered him; and that he therefore departed out of the house, full of shame and despite, with resolution to revenge himself more commodiously; and how he understood the next day following, how Lucinda was secretly departed from her father's house, and gone nobody knew where, but that he finally learned within a few months after, that she had entered into a certain monastery, with intention to remain there all the days of her life, if she could not pass them with Cardenio; and that as soon as he had learned that, choosing those three gentlemen for his associates, he came to the place where she was, but would not speak to her, fearing lest that, as soon as they knew of his being there, they would increase the guards of the monastery; and therefore expected until he found on a day the gates of the monastery open, and leaving two of his fellows to keep the door, he with the other entered into the abbey in Lucinda's search, whom they found talking with a nun in the cloister; and, snatching her away ere she could retire herself, they brought her to a certain village, where they disguised themselves in that sort they were; for so it was requisite for to bring her away: all which they did with the more facility, that the monastery was seated abroad in the fields, a good way from any village. He likewise told that, as soon as Lucinda saw herself in his power, she fell into a swoon; and that, after she had returned to herself, she never did any other thing but weep and sigh, without speaking a word; and that in that manner, accompanied with silence and tears, they had arrived to that inn, which was to him as grateful as an arrival to heaven, wherein all earthly mishaps are concluded and finished.

CHAPTER X

Wherein Is Prosecuted the History of the Famous Princess Micomicona, with Other Delightful Adventures

SANCHO gave ear to all this with no small grief of mind, seeing that all the hopes of his lordship vanished away like smoke, and that the fair Princess Micomicona was turned into Dorothea, and the giant into Don Fernando, and that his master slept so soundly, and careless of all that had happened. Dorothea could not yet assure herself whether the happiness that she possessed was a dream or no. Cardenio was in the very same taking, and also Lucinda's thoughts ran the same race.

Don Fernando yielded many thanks to Heaven for having dealt with him so propitiously, and unwinding him out of the intricate labyrinth, wherein straying, he was at the point to have at once lost his soul and credit. And finally, as many as were in the inn were very glad and joyful of the success of so thwart, intricate, and desperate affairs. The curate compounded and ordered all things through his discretion, and congratulated every one of the good he obtained. But she that kept greatest jubilee and joy was the hostess, for the promise that Cardenio and the curate had made, to pay her the damages and harms committed by Don Quixote; only Sancho, as we have said, was afflicted, unfortunate, and sorrowful. And thus he entered with melancholy semblance to his lord, who did but then awake, and said unto him,—

'Well and securely may you sleep, sir knight of the heavy countenance, as long as it shall please yourself, without troubling yourself with any care of killing any giant, or of restoring the queen to her kingdom; for all is concluded and done already.' 'I believe thee very easily,' replied Don Quixote; 'for I have had the monstrousest and most terrible battle with that giant that ever I think to have all the days of my life with any; and yet with one thwart blow, thwack I overthrew his head to the ground, and there issued so much blood as the streams thereof ran along the earth as if they were of water.' 'As if they were of red wine, you might better have said,' replied Sancho Panza; 'for I would let you to understand, if you know it not already, that the dead giant is a bored wine-bag, and the blood six-and-thirty gallons of red wine, which it contained in its belly. The head that was slashed off so neatly is the whore my mother; and let the devil take all away for me!' 'And what is this thou sayst, madman?' quoth Don Quixote. 'Art thou in thy right wits?' 'Get up, sir,' quoth Sancho, 'and you yourself shall see the fair stuff you have made, and what we have to pay; and you shall behold the queen transformed into a particular lady, called Dorothea, with other successes, which if you may once conceive them aright will strike you into admiration.' 'I would marvel at nothing,' quoth Don Quixote; 'for if thou beest well remembered, I told thee the other time that we were here, how all that succeeded in this place was done by enchantment. And what wonder, then, if now the like should eftsoons befall?' 'I could easily be induced to believe all,' replied Sancho, 'if my canvassing in the coverlet were of that nature. But indeed it was not, but most real and certain. And I saw well how the innkeeper that is here yet this very day alive, held one end of the coverlet, and did toss me up towards heaven with very good grace and strength, no less merrily than lightly. And where the notice of parties intercurs, I do believe, although I am a simple man and a sinner, that there is no kind of enchantment, but rather much trouble, bruising, and misfortune.' 'Well, God will remedy all,' said Don Quixote. 'And give me mine apparel; for I will get up and go forth, and see those successes and transformations which thou speakest of.' Sancho gave him his clothes; and whilst he was a-making of him ready, the curate recounted to Don Fernando and to the rest Don Quixote's mad pranks, and the guile he had used to bring him away out of the Poor Rock, wherein he imagined that he lived exiled through the disdain of his lady. He told them, moreover, all the other adventures which Sancho had discovered, whereat they did laugh not a little, and wonder withal, because it seemed to them all to be one of the extravagantest kinds of madness that ever befel a distracted brain. The curate also added, that seeing the good success of the Lady

Dorothea did impeach the further prosecuting of their design, that it was requisite to invent and find some other way how to carry him home to his own village. Cardenio offered himself to prosecute the adventure, and Lucinda should represent Dorothea's person. 'No,' quoth Don Fernando, 'it shall not be so; for I will have Dorothea to prosecute her own invention: for so that the village of this good gentleman be not very far off from hence, I will be very glad to procure his remedy.' 'It is no more than two days' journey from hence,' said the curate. 'Well, though it were more,' replied Don Fernando, 'I would be pleased to travel them, in exchange of doing so good a work.' Don Quixote sallied out at this time completely armed with Mambrino's helmet (although with a great hole in it) on his head, his target on his arm, and leaned on his trunk or javelin. His strange countenance and gait amazed Don Fernando and his companions very much, seeing his ill-favoured visage so withered and yellow, the inequality and unsuitability of his arms, and his grave manner of proceeding; and stood all silent to see what he would; who, casting his eyes on the beautiful Dorothea, with very great gravity and staidness, said,—

'I am informed, beautiful lady, by this my squire, that your greatness is annihilated, and your being destroyed; for of a queen and mighty princess which you were wont to be, you are now become a particular damsel; which if it hath been done by particular order of the magical king your father, dreading that I would not be able to give you the necessary and requisite help for your restitution, I say that he neither knew nor doth know the one half of the enterprise, and that he was very little acquainted with histories of chivalry; for if he had read them, or passed them over with so great attention and leisure as I have done, and read them, he should have found at every other step, how other knights of a great deal less fame than myself have ended more desperate adventures, seeing it is not so great a matter to kill a giant, be he ever so arrogant; for it is not many hours since I myself fought with one, and what ensued I will not say, lest they should tell me that I do lie; but time, the detector of all things, will disclose it, when we do least think thereof.'

'Thou foughtest with two wine-bags, and not with a giant,' quoth the host at this season. But Don Fernando commanded him to be silent and not interrupt Don Quixote in any wise, who prosecuted his speech, saying, 'In fine, I say, high and disinherited lady, that if your father hath made this metamorphosis in your person for the causes related, give him no credit; for there is no peril so great on earth but my sword shall open a way through it, wherewithal I, overthrowing your enemy's head to the ground, will set your crown on your own head within a few days.' Here Don Quixote held his peace, and awaited the princess her answer, who, knowing Don Fernando's determination and will that she should continue the commenced guile until Don Quixote were carried home again, answered, with a very good grace and countenance, in this manner: 'Whosoever informed you, valorous Knight of the Ill-favoured Face, that I have altered and changed my being, hath not told you the truth, for I am the very same to-day that I was yesterday; true it is, that some unexpected yet fortunate successes have wrought some alteration in me, by bestowing on me better hap than I hoped for, or could wish myself; but yet for all that I have not left off to be that which [I was] before, or to have the very same thoughts which I ever had, to help myself by the valour of your most valorous and invincible arm. And therefore I request you, good my lord, of your accustomed bounty, to return my father his honour again, and account of him as of a very discreet and prudent man, seeing that he found by this skill so easy and so infallible a way to redress my disgraces; for I do certainly believe, that if it had not been by your means, I should never have happened to attain to the good fortune which now I possess, as all those noblemen present may witness; what therefore rests is, that to-morrow morning we do set forward, for to-day is now already so overgone as we should not be able to travel very far from hence. As for the conclusion of the good success that I do hourly expect, I refer that to God and the valour of your invincible arm.'

Thus much the discreet Dorothea said; and Don Quixote having heard her, he turned him to Sancho, with very manifest tokens of indignation, and said, 'Now I say unto thee, little Sancho, that thou art the veriest rascal that is in all Spain. Tell me, thief and vagabond didst not thou but even very now say unto me that this princess was turned into a damsel, and that called Dorothea? and that the head which I thought I had slashed from a giant's shoulders was the whore that bore thee? with a thousand other follies, which did plunge me into the greatest confusion that ever I was in my life? I vow' (and then he looked upon heaven, and did crash his teeth together) 'that I am about to make such a wreck on thee, as shall beat wit into the pates of all the lying squires that shall ever hereafter serve knights-errant in this world.' 'I pray you have patience, good my lord,' answered Sancho, 'for it may very well befall me to be deceived in that which toucheth the transmutation of the lady and Princess Micomicona; but in that which concerneth the giant's head, or at least the boring of the wine-bags, and that the blood was but red wine I am not deceived, I swear; for the bags lie yet wounded there within at your own bed's head, and the red wine hath made a lake in the chamber; and if it be not so, it shall be perceived at the frying of the eggs, I mean that you shall see it when master innkeeper's worship, who is here present, shall demand the loss and damage.' 'I say thee, Sancho,' quoth Don Quixote, 'that thou art a madcap; pardon me, and so it is enough.' 'It is enough indeed,' quoth Don Fernando, 'and therefore let me entreat you to say no more of this, and seeing my lady the princess says she will go away to-morrow, seeing it is now too late to depart to-day, let it be so agreed on, and we will spend this night in pleasant discourses, until the approach of the ensuing day, wherein we will all accompany and attend on the worthy knight Sir Don Quixote, because we would be eye-witnesses of the valorous and unmatchable feats of arms which he shall do in the pursuit of this weighty enterprise which he hath taken upon him.' 'I am he that will serve and accompany you, good my lord,' replied Don Quixote; 'and I do highly gratify the honour that is done me, and the good opinion that is held of me, the which I will endeavour to verify and approve, or it shall cost me my life, or more, if more it might cost me.'

Many other words of compliment and gratification passed between Don Quixote and Don Fernando, but a certain passenger imposed silence to them all, by his arrival to the inn in that very season, who by his attire showed that he was a Christian newly returned from among the Moors, for he was apparelled with a short-skirted cassock of blue cloth, sleeves reaching down half the arm, and without a collar; his breeches were likewise of blue linen, and he wore a bonnet of the same colour, a pair of date-coloured buskins, and a Turkish scimitar hanging at his neck in a scarf, which went athwart his breast. There entered after him, riding on an ass, a woman clad like a Moor, and her face covered with a piece of the veil of her head; she wore on her head a little cap of cloth of gold, and was covered with a little Turkish mantle from the shoulders down to the feet. The man was of strong and comely making, of the age of forty years or thereabouts; his face was somewhat tanned, he had long mustachios and a very handsome beard; to conclude, his making was such as, if he were well attired, men would take him to be a person of quality and good birth. He demanded a chamber as soon as he had entered, and being answered that there was no one vacant in the inn, he seemed to be grieved, and coming to her which in her attire denoted herself to be a Moor, he took her down from her ass. Lucinda, Dorothea, the hostess, her daughter and Maritornes, allured to behold the new and strange attire of the Moor, compassed her about; and Dorothea, who was always most gracious, courteous, and discreet, deeming that both she and he that had brought her were discontented for the want of a lodging, she said, 'Lady, be not grieved for the trouble you are here like to endure for want of means to refresh yourself, seeing it is an universal vice of all inns to be defective herein; yet notwithstanding, if it shall please you to pass away the time among us' (pointing to Lucinda), 'perhaps you have met in the discourse of your travels other worse places of entertainment than this shall prove.' The disguised lady made none answer, nor other thing than arising from the place wherein she sat, and setting both her arms across on her bosom, she inclined her head and bowed her body, in sign that she rendered them thanks; by her silence they doubtlessly conjectured her to be a Moor, and that she could not speak the Castilian tongue. On this the Captive arrived, who was otherwise employed until then, and, seeing that they all had environed her that came with him, and that she made no answer to their speech, he said, 'Ladies, this maiden scarce understands my tongue yet, nor doth she know any other than that of her own country, and therefore she hath not, nor can make any answer to your demands.' 'We demand nothing of her,' quoth Lucinda, 'but only do make her an offer of our companies for this night, and part of the room where we ourselves are to be accommodated, where she shall be cherished up as much as the commodity of this place, and the obligation wherein we be tied to show courtesies to strangers that may want it, do bind us; especially she being a woman to whom we may do this service.' 'Sweet lady, I kiss your hands both for her and myself,' replied the Captive; 'and I do highly prize, as it deserveth, the favour you have proffered, which in such an occasion, and offered by such persons as you seem to be, doth very plainly show how great it is.' 'Tell me, good sir,' quoth Dorothea, 'whether is this lady a Christian or a Moor? for by her attire and silence she makes us suspect that she is that we would not wish she were.' 'A Moor she is in attire and body,' answered the Captive; 'but in mind she is a very fervent Christian, for she hath very expressly desired to become one.' 'Then she is not yet baptised?' said Lucinda. 'There hath been no opportunity offered to us,' quoth the Captive, 'to christen her, since she departed from Algiers, which is her town and country; and since that time she was not in any so eminent a danger of death as might oblige her to be baptised before she were first instructed in all the ceremonies which our holy mother, the Church, commandeth; but I hope shortly (if it shall please God) to see her baptised with that decency which her quality and calling deserves, which is greater than her attire or mine makes show of.'

These words inflamed all the hearers with a great desire to know who the Moor and her captive were, yet none of them would at that time entreat him to satisfy their longing, because the season rather invited them to take some order how they might rest after their travels, than to demand of them the discourse of their lives. Dorothea, then, taking her by the hand, caused her to sit down by herself, and prayed her to take off the veil from her face. She instantly beheld the Captive, as if she demanded of him what they said, and he in the Arabical language told her how they desired her to discover her face, and bade her to do it; which presently she did, and discovered so beautiful a visage as Dorothea esteemed her to be fairer than Lucinda, and Lucinda prized her to excel Dorothea; and all the beholders perceived that if any one could surpass them both in beauty, it was the Moor; and there were some that thought she excelled them both in some respects. And as beauty hath evermore the prerogative and grace to reconcile men's minds and attract their wills to it, so all of them forthwith dedicated their desires to serve, and make much of the lovely Moor. Don Fernando demanded of the Captive how she was called, and he answered that her name was Lela Zoraida; and as soon as she heard him, and understood what they had demanded, she suddenly answered with anguish, but yet with a very good grace, 'No, not Zoraida, but Maria,' giving them to understand that she was called Maria, and not Zoraida.

These words, and the great effect and vehemency wherewithal the Moor delivered them, extorted more than one tear from the hearers, especially from the women, who are naturally tender-hearted and compassive. Lucinda embraced her then with great love, and said, 'Ay, ay, Maria, Maria.' To which she answered, 'Ay, ay, Maria, Zoraida mancange;' that is, 'and not Zoraida.' By this it was grown some four of the clock in the afternoon; and by order of those which were Don Fernando's companions, the innkeeper had provided for them as good a beaver as the inn could in any wise afford unto them. Therefore, it being the hour, they sat down altogether at a long table (for there was never a square or round one in all the house), and they gave the first and principal end (although he refused it as much as he could) to Don Quixote, who commanded that the Lady Micomicona should sit at his elbow, seeing he was her champion. Presently were placed Lucinda and Zoraida, and Don Fernando and Cardenio right over against them, and after the Captive and other gentlemen, and on the other side the curate and barber. And thus they made their drinking with very great recreation, which was the more augmented to see Don Quixote leaving of his meat, and, moved by the like spirit of that which had made him once before talk so much to the goatherds, begin to offer them an occasion of speech in this manner:

'Truly, good sirs, if it be well considered, those which profess the order of knighthood do see many great and unexpected things.

If it be not so, say what mortal man alive is there that, entering in at this castle gate, and seeing of us all in the manner we be now present here, can judge or believe that we are those which we be? Who is it that can say that this lady which sits here at my sleeve is the great queen that we all know her to be, and that I am that Knight of the Heavy Countenance that am so much blabbed of abroad by the mouth of fame? therefore it cannot be now doubted, but that this art and exercise excelleth all the others which ever human wit, the underminer of nature, invented; and it is the more to be prized, by how much it exposeth itself, more than other trades, to dangers and inconveniences. Away with those that shall affirm learning to surpass arms; for I will say unto them, be they what they list, that they know not what they say; for the reason which such men do most urge, and to which they do most rely, is, that the travails of the spirit do far exceed those of the body; and that the use of arms are only exercised by the body, as if it were an office fit for porters, for which nothing were requisite but bodily forces; or as if in that which we that profess it do call arms, were not included the acts of fortitude which require deep understanding to execute them; or as if the warrior's mind did not labour as well as his body, who had a great army to lead and command, or the defence of a besieged city. If not, see if he can arrive by his corporal strength to know or sound the intent of his enemy, the designs, stratagems, and difficulties, how to prevent imminent dangers, all these being operations of the understanding wherein the body hath no meddling at all. It being therefore so, that the exercise of arms requires spirit as well as those of learning, let us now examine which of the two spirits, that of the scholar or soldier, do take most pains; and this may be best understood by the end to which both of them are addressed; for that intention is most to be esteemed which hath for object the most noble end. The end and conclusion of learning is—I speak not now of divinity, whose scope is to lead and address souls to heaven; for to an end so much without end as this, no other may be compared—I mean of human sciences or arts, to maintain distributive justice in his perfection, and give to every one that which is his own; to endeavour and cause good laws to be religiously observed—an end most certainly generous, high, and worthy of great praise, but not of so much as that to which the exercise of arms is annexed, which hath for his object and end peace, which is the greatest good men can desire in this life. And therefore the first good news that ever the world had or men received, were those which the angels brought on that night which was our day, when they sang in the skies, "Glory be in the heights, and peace on earth to men of good minds." And the salutation which the best Master that ever was on earth or in heaven taught to His disciples and favourites was, that when they entered into any house they should say, "Peace be to this house"; and many other times He said, "I give unto you My peace; I leave My peace unto you; peace be amongst you." It is a good, as precious as a jewel, and a gift given, and left by such a hand; a jewel, without which neither on earth nor in heaven can there be any perfect good. This peace is the true end of war; for arms and war are one and the selfsame things. This truth being therefore presupposed, that the end of war is peace, and that herein it doth excel the end of learning, let us descend to the corporal labours of the scholar, and to those of him which professeth arms, and consider which of them are more toilsome.'

Don Quixote did prosecute his discourse in such sort, and with so pleasing terms, as he had almost induced his audience to esteem him to be, at that time at least, exempt from his frenzy; and therefore, by reason that the greater number of them were gentlemen, to whom the use of arms is in a manner essential and proper, they did willingly listen to him; and therefore he continued on with his discourse in this manner:

'I say, then, that the pains of the student are commonly these: principally poverty (not that I would maintain that all students are poor, but that I may put the case in greatest extremity it can have), and by saying that he may be poor, methinks there may be no greater aggravation of his misery; for he that is poor is destitute of every good thing; and this poverty is suffered by him sundry ways, sometimes by hunger, other times by cold or nakedness, and many times by all of them together; yet it is never so extreme but that he doth eat, although it be somewhat later than the custom, or of the scraps and reversion of the rich man; and the greatest misery of the student is that which they term to live by sops and pottage: and though they want fire of their own, yet may they have recourse to their neighbour's chimney, which if it do not warm, yet will it weaken the cold: and finally, they sleep at night under a roof. I will not descend to other trifles—to wit, the want of shirts and shoes, the bareness of their clothes, or the overloading of their stomachs with meat when good fortune lends them as good a meal—for by this way, which I have deciphered so rough and difficult, stumbling here, falling there; getting up again on the other side, and refalling on this, they attain the degree which they have desired so much; which many having compassed, as we have seen, which having passed through these difficulties, and sailed by Scylla and Charybdis (borne away flying, in a manner, by favourable fortune), they command and govern all the world from a chair, turning their hunger into satiety, their nakedness into pomp, and their sleeping on a mat into a sweet repose among hollands and damask—a reward justly merited by their virtue. But their labours, confronted and compared to those of the militant soldier, remai very far behind, as I will presently declare.'

CHAPTER XI

Treating of the Curious Discourse Made by Don Quixote Upon the Exercises of Arms and Letters

DON QUIXOTE, continuing his discourse, said, 'Seeing we begin in the student with poverty and her parts, let us examine whether the soldier be richer? Certainly we shall find that no man can exceed the soldier in poverty itself; for he is tied to his wretched pay, which comes either late or never; or else to his own shifts, with notable danger of his life and conscience. And his nakedness is ofttimes so much, as many times a leather jerkin gashed serves him at once for a shirt and ornament. And in the midst of winter he hath sundry times no other defence or help to resist the inclemencies of the air in the midst of the open fields than the breath of his mouth, which I verily believe doth against nature come out cold, by reason it sallies from an empty place; expect there till the night fall, that he may repair all these discommodities by the easiness of his bed, the which, if it be not through his own default, shall never offend in narrowness; for he may measure out for it on the earth as many foot as he pleaseth, and tumble himself up and down it without endangering the wrinkling of his sheets. Let after all this the day and hour arrive wherein he is to receive the degree of his profession—let, I say, a day of battle arrive; for there they will set on his head the cap of his dignity, made of lint to cure the wound of some bullet that hath passed through and through his temples, or hath maimed an arm or a leg. And when this doth not befall, but that Heaven doth piously keep and preserve him whole and sound, he shall perhaps abide still in the same poverty wherein he was at the first; and that it be requisite that one and another battle do succeed, and he come off ever a victor, to the end that he may prosper and be at the last advanced. But such miracles are but few times wrought; and say, good sirs, if you have noted it, how few are those which the wars reward, in respect of the others that it hath destroyed? You must answer, without question, that there can be no comparison made between them, nor can the dead be reduced to any number; but all the living, and such as are advanced, may be counted easily with three arithmetical figures: all which falls out contrary in learned men, for all of them have wherewithal to entertain and maintain themselves by skirts—I will say nothing of sleeves. So that although the soldier's labour is greater, yet is his reward much less. But to this may be answered, that it is easier to reward two hundred thousand learned men than thirty thousand soldiers; for they may be advanced by giving unto them offices, which must of necessity be bestowed on men of their profession; but soldiers cannot be recompensed otherwise than by the lord's substance and wealth whom they serve. And yet this objection and impossibility doth fortify much more my assertion.

'But leaving this apart, which is a labyrinth of very difficult issue, let us return to the pre-eminency of arms over learning, which is a matter hitherto depending, so many are the reasons that everyone allegeth for himself; and among those which I myself have repeated, then learning doth argue thus for itself, that arms without it cannot be long maintained, forasmuch as the war hath also laws, and is subject to them, and that the laws are contained under the title of learning, and belong to learned men.

'To this objection arms do make answer: that the laws cannot be sustained without them, for commonwealths are defended by arms, and kingdoms preserved, cities fenced, highways made safe, the seas freed from pirates; and, to be brief, if it were not for them, commonwealths, kingdoms, monarchies, cities, and ways by sea and land, would be subject to the rigour and confusion which attendeth on the war all the time that it endureth, and is licensed to practice his prerogatives and violence; and it is a known truth, that it which cost most, is or ought to be most accounted of. That one may become eminent in learning, it costs him time, watchings, hunger, nakedness, headaches, rawness of stomach, and other such inconveniences as I have partly mentioned already; but that one may arrive by true terms to be a good soldier, it costs him all that it costs the student, in so exceeding a degree as admits no comparison, for he is at every step in jeopardy to lose his life. And what fear of necessity or poverty may befall or molest a student so fiercely as it doth a soldier, who, seeing himself at the siege of some impregnable place, and standing sentinel in some ravelin or half-moon, feels the enemies undermining near to the place where he is, and yet dares not to depart or abandon his stand, upon any occasion whatsoever, or shun the danger which so nearly threatens him? but that which he only may do, is to advise his captain of that which passeth, to the end he may remedy it by some countermine, whilst he must stand still, fearing and expecting when he shall suddenly fly up to the clouds without wings, and after descend to the depths against his will. And if this appear to be but a small danger, let us weigh whether the grappling of two galleys, the one with the other in the midst of the spacious main, may be compared, or do surpass it, the which nailed and grappled fast the one to the other, the soldier hath no more room in them than two foot broad of a plank in the battlings, and notwithstanding, although he clearly see laid before him so many ministers of death, for all the pieces of artillery that are planted on the adverse side do threaten him, and are not distant from his body the length of a lance; and seeing that if he slipped ever so little aside, he should fall into the deeps, doth yet nevertheless, with undaunted heart, borne away on the wings of honour, which spurreth him onward, oppose himself as a mark to all their shot, and strives to pass by that so narrow a way into the enemy's vessel. And what is most to be admired is to behold how scarce is one fallen into that place, from whence he shall never after arise until the world's end, when another takes possession of the same place; and if he do likewise tumble into the sea, which gapes like an enemy for him also, another and another will succeed unto him, without giving any respite to the times of their death, valour, and boldness, which is the greatest that may be found among all the trances of warfare. Those blessed ages were fortunate which wanted the dreadful fury of the devilish and murdering pieces of ordnance, to whose inventor I am verily persuaded that they render in hell an eternal guerdon for his diabolical invention, by which he hath given power to an infamous, base, vile, and dastardly arm to bereave the most valorous knight of life; and that, without knowing how or from whence, in the midst of the stomach and courage that inflames and animates valorous minds, there arrives a wandering bullet (shot off, perhaps, by him that was afraid, and fled at the very blaze of the powder, as he discharged the accursed engine), and cuts off and finisheth in a moment the thoughts and life of him who merited to enjoy it many ages.

'And whilst I consider this, I am about to say that it grieves me to have ever undertaken the exercise of a knight-errant in this our detestable age; for although no danger can affright me, yet notwithstanding I live in jealousy to think how powder and lead might deprive me of the power to make myself famous and renowned by the strength of mine arm and the edge of my sword throughout the face of the earth. But let Heaven dispose as it pleaseth; for so much the more shall I be esteemed, if I can compass my pretensions, by how much the dangers were greater to which I opposed myself, than those achieved in foregoing times by knights-adventurous.'

Don Quixote made all this prolix speech whilst the rest of his company did eat, wholly forgetting to taste one bit, although Sancho Panza did now and then put him in remembrance of his victuals, saying that he should have leisure enough after to speak as much as he could desire. In those that heard was again renewed a kind of compassion, to see a man of so good a wit as he seemed to be, and of so good discourse in all the other matters which he took in hand, to remain so clearly devoid of it when any occasion of speech were offered treating of his accursed chivalry. The curate applauded his discourse, affirming that he produced very good reasons for all that he had spoken in the favour of arms; and that he himself (although he was learned and graduated) was likewise of his opinion.

The beaver being ended, and the table-cloths taken away, whilst Maritornes did help her mistress and her daughter to make ready the room where Don Quixote had slept for the gentlewomen, wherein they alone might retire themselves that night, Don Fernando entreated the Captive to recount unto them the history of his life, forasmuch as he suspected that it must have been rare and delightful, as he gathered by the tokens he gave by coming in the lovely Zoraida's company. To which the Captive replied, that he would accomplish his desire with a very good will, and that only he feared that the discourse would not prove so savoury as they expected; but yet for all that he would tell it, because he would not disobey him. The curate and all the rest thanked him for his promise, and turned to request him again to begin his discourse; and he perceiving so many to solicit him, said that prayers were not requisite when commandments were of such force. 'And therefore I desire you,' quoth he, 'to be attentive, and you shall hear a true discourse, to which perhaps no feigned invention may be compared for variety or delight.' The rest, animated by these his words, did accommodate themselves with very great silence; and he, beholding their silence and expectation of his history, with a modest and pleasing voice, began in this manner.

CHAPTER XII

Wherein the Captive Recounteth His Life, and Other Accidents

IN a certain village of the mountains of Leon my lineage had beginning, wherewithal nature dealt much more liberally than fortune, although my father had the opinion, amidst the penury and poverty of that people, to be a rich man, as indeed he might have been, had he but used as much care to hoard up his wealth as prodigality to spend it. And this his liberal disposition proceeded from his being a soldier in his youthful years; for war is the school wherein the miser is made frank, and the frank man prodigal. And if among soldiers we find some wretches and niggards, they are accounted monsters which are seldom seen. My father passed the bounds of liberality, and touched very nearly the confines of prodigality; a thing nothing profitable for a married man, who had children that should succeed him in his name and being. My father had three sons, all men, and of years sufficient to make an election of the state of life they meant to lead; wherefore he perceiving, as he himself was wont to say, that he could not bridle his nature in that condition of spending, he resolved to deprive himself of the instrument and cause which made him such a spender and so liberal, to wit, of his goods; without which Alexander the Great himself would be accounted a miser; and therefore, calling us all three together on a day into his chamber, he used these or such like reasons to us:

'"Sons, to affirm that I love you well may be presumed, seeing I term you my sons; and yet it may be suspected that I hate you, seeing I do not govern myself so well as I might in the husbanding and increasing of your stock. But to the end that you may henceforth perceive that I do affect you with a fatherly love, and that I mean not to overthrow you like a step-father, I will do one thing to you which I have pondered, and with mature deliberation purposed these many days. You are all of age to accept an estate, or at least to make choice of some such exercise as may turn to your honour and profit at riper years; and therefore, that which I have thought upon, is to divide my goods into four parts; the three I will bestow upon you, to every one that which appertains to him, without exceeding a jot; and I myself will reserve the fourth to live and maintain me with as long as it shall please Heaven to lend me breath. Yet I do greatly desire that after every one of you is possessed of his portion, he would take one of the courses which I mean to propose. There is an old proverb in this our Spain, in mine own opinion very true (as ordinarily all proverbs are, being certain brief sentences collected out of long and discreet experiences), and it is this, 'The Church, the Sea, or the Court.' The meaning is, that whosoever would become wealthy, or worthy, must either follow the Church, haunt the seas by exercising the trade of merchandises, or get him a place of service and entertainment in the king's house; for men say that 'A king's crumb is more worth than a lord's loaf.' This I say because I desire, and it is my will, that one of you do follow his book, another merchandise, and the third the war, seeing that the service of his own house is a difficult thing to compass; and although the war is not wont to enrich a man, yet it adds unto him great worth and renown. Within these eight days I do mean to give you all your portions in money, without defrauding you of a mite, as you shall see in effect. Therefore, tell me now whether you mean to follow mine opinion and device in this which I have proposed?" And then he commanded me, by reason that I was the eldest, to make him an answer.

'I, after I had entreated him not to make away his goods, but to spend and dispose of them as he listed, seeing we were both young and able enough to gain more, at last I concluded that I would accomplish his will, and that mine was to follow the wars, therein serving God and my king together. The second brother made the same offer, and, employing his portion in commodities, would venture it to the Indies. The youngest, and as I deem the discreetest, said that either he would follow the Church, or go at the least to

Salamanca to finish his already commenced studies. And as soon as we had ended the agreement and election of our vocations, my father embraced us all, and afterwards performed unto us, in as short a time as he had mentioned, all that he promised; giving unto each of us a portion, amounting, if I do well remember, to three thousand ducats apiece in money; for an uncle of ours bought all the goods, and paid ready money, because he would not have them made away from our own family and lineage. We all took our leave of our good father in one day; and in that instant, it seeming to me a great inhumanity to leave my father so old and with so little means, I dealt so with him as I constrained him to take back again two thousand ducats of the three he had given me, forasmuch as the rest was sufficient to furnish me in very good sort with all things requisite for a soldier. My brothers, moved by mine example, did each of them give him a thousand crowns; so that my father remained with four thousand crowns in money, and three in goods, as they were valued, which goods he would not sell, but keep them still in stock. Finally, we bade him (and our said uncle) farewell, not without much feeling and many tears on both sides; and they charged us that we would from time to time acquaint them with our successes, whether prosperous or adverse. We promised to perform it; and then, embracing us, and giving us his blessing, one departed towards Salamanca, another to Seville, and myself to Alicant.

'I arrived prosperously at Genoa, and from thence went to Milan, where I did accommodate myself with arms and other braveries used by soldiers, and departed from thence to settle myself in Piedmont; and being in my way towards the city of Alexandria de la Paglia, I heard news that the great Duke of Alva did pass towards Flanders; wherefore, changing my purpose, I went with him, and served him in all the expeditions he made. I was present at the beheading of the Earls of Egmont and Hornes, and obtained at last to be ensign to a famous captain of Guadalajara, called Diego de Urbina. Within a while after mine arrival to Flanders, the news were divulged of the league that Pius V., the pope of famous memory, had made with the Venetians and the King of Spain, against our common enemy the Turk, who had gained by force the famous island of Cyprus much about the same time, which island belonged to the state of Venice, and was an unfortunate and lamentable loss. It was also certainly known that the most noble Don John of Austria, our good King Don Philip's natural brother, did come down for general of this league, and the great provision that was made for the war was published everywhere.

'All this did incite and stir on my mind and desire to be present at the expedition so much expected; and therefore, although I had conjectures, and half promises to be made a captain in the first occasion that should be offered, yet I resolved to leave all those hopes, and to go into Italy, as in effect I did. And my good fortune so disposed, as the lord Don John of Austria arrived just at the same time at Genoa, and went towards Naples, to join himself with the Venetian navy, as he did after at Messina. In this most fortunate journey I was present, being by this made a captain of foot, to which honourable charge I was mounted rather by my good fortune than by my deserts. And that very day which was so fortunate to all Christendom; for therein the whole world was undeceived, and all the nations thereof freed of all the error they held, and belief they had, that the Turk was invincible at sea: in that very day I say, wherein the swelling stomach and Ottomanical pride was broken among so many happy men as were there (for the Christians that were slain were much more happy than those which they left victorious alive), I alone was unfortunate, seeing that in exchange of some naval crown which I might expect had I lived in the times of the ancient Romans, I found myself the night ensuing that so famous a day with my legs chained and my hands manacled, which befel in this manner, that Uchali, king of Algiers, a bold and venturous pirate, having invested and distressed the admiral of Malta (for only three knights remained alive, and those very sore wounded), John Andrea's chief galley came to her succour, wherein I went with my company; and doing what was requisite in such an occasion, I leapt into the enemy's vessel, the which falling off from that which had assaulted her, hindered my soldiers from following me; by which means I saw myself alone amidst mine enemies, against whom I could make no long resistance, they were so many. In fine, I was taken, full of wounds. Now, as you may have heard, Uchali saved himself and all his squadron, whereby

I became captive in his power, and only remained sorrowful among so many joyful, and captive among so many freed; for that day fifteen thousand Christians, which came slaves and enchained in the Turkish galleys, recovered their desired liberty. I was carried to Constantinople, where the Great Turk, Selim, made my lord General of the Sea, by reason that he had so well performed his duty in the battle, having brought away, for a witness of his valour, the standard of the Order of Malta. I was the year ensuing of 1572 in Navarino, rowing in the Admiral of the *Three Lanterns,* and saw and noted there the opportunity that was lost, of taking all the Turkish navy within the haven; for all the janizaries and other soldiers that were in it made full account that they should be set upon, even within the very port, and therefore trussed up all their baggage, and made ready their shoes, to fly away presently to the land, being in no wise minded to expect the assault, our navy did strike such terror into them. But God disposed otherwise of the matter, not through the fault or negligence of the general that governed our men, but for the sins of Christendom, and because God permits and wills that we have always some executioners to chastise us. In sum, Uchali got into Modon, which is an island near to Navarino, and, landing his men there, he fortified the mouth of the haven, and there remained until Don John departed. In this voyage was taken the galley called *Presa,* whereof the famous pirate Barbarossa his son was captain; it was surprised by the captain-galley of Naples, called the *She-Wolf,* that was commanded by the thunderbolt of war, the father of soldiers—that fortunate and never overthrown Don Alvaro de Baçan, the Marquis of Santa Cruz. And here I will not forget to recount what befel at the taking of the *Presa.* This son of Barbarossa's was so cruel, and used his slaves so ill, that as soon as they that were rowing perceived the *She-Wolf* to approach them, and that she had overtaken them, they cast away their oars all at one time, and laying hands on their captain that stood on the poop, crying to them to row with more speed, and passing him from one bank to another, from the poop to the prow, they took so many bits out of him, as he had scarce passed beyond the mast when his soul was already wasted to hell; such was the cruelty wherewithal he entreated them, and so great the hate they also bore towards him. We returned the next year after to Constantinople, being that of seventy and three, and there we learned how Don John had gained Tunis, and, taking that kingdom away from the Turks, had, by installing Muley Hamet therein, cut away all Muley Hameda's hopes to reign again there, who was the most cruel and valiant Moor that ever lived.

'The Great Turk was very much grieved for this loss; and therefore, using the sagacity wherewithal all his race wise endued, he made peace with the Venetians, which wished for it much more than he did himself. And the year after of seventy-and-four, he assaulted the fortress of Goleta, and the other fortress that Don John had raised near unto Tunis. And in all these occasions I was present, tied to the oar without any hope of liberty, at leastwise by ransom, being resolved never to signify by letter my misfortunes to my father. The Goleta was lost, in fine, and also the fortress, before which two places lay in siege seventy-five thousand Turks, and more than four hundred thousand Moors, and other Saracens of all the other parts of Africa, being furnished with such abundance of munition and warlike engines, and so many pioneers as were able to cover Goleta and the fortress, if every one did cast but his handful of earth upon them. Thus was Goleta, accounted until then impregnable, first lost, the which did not happen through default of valour in the defendants, who in defence thereof did all they could or ought to have done, but because experience showed the facility wherewithal trenches might be raised in that desert sand; for though water had been found in it within two spans' depth, the Turks could not find it in the depth of two yards; and therefore, filling many sacks full of sand, they raised their trenches so high as they did surmount the walls of the sconce, and did so gall the defendants from them with their shot as no one could stand to make any defence. It was a common report that our men would not immure themselves within Goleta, but expect the enemy in the champaign at their disembarking; but those that gave this out spake widely, as men very little acquainted with the like affairs; for if in Goleta and the fortress there were scarce seven thousand soldiers, how could so few a number, were they ever so resolute, make a sally, and remain in the forts against so great a number of enemies? or how is it possible that the forces which are not seconded and supplied should not be overcome, specially being besieged by many and obstinate enemies, and those in their own country? But many others esteemed, and so did I likewise among the rest, that Almighty God did a particular grace and favour unto Spain in that manner, permitting to be destroyed the stop and cloak of all wickedness, and the sponge and moth of innumerable sums of money spent there unprofitably, without serving to any other end than to preserve the memory of being gained by the Emperor Charles the Fifth, as if it had been requisite for the keeping of it eternal (as it is, and shall be ever) that those stones should sustain it. The fortress was also won; but the Turks were constrained to gain it span by span, for the soldiers which defended it fought so manfully and resolutely, as the number of the enemies slain in two-and-twenty general assaults which they gave unto it, did pass five-and-twenty thousand. Never a one was taken prisoner but three hundred which survived their fellows—a certain and manifest token of their valour and strength, and how well they had defended themselves and kept their fortresses with great magnanimity. A little fort or turret that stood in the midst of the place, under the command of Don John Zanoguera, a Valencian gentleman and famous soldier, was yielded upon composition; and Don Pedro de Puerto Carrero, general of Goleta, was taken prisoner, who omitted no diligence possible to defend the place, but yet was so grieved to have lost it as he died for very grief on the way towards Constantinople, whither they carried him captive. The general likewise of the fort, called Gabriel Cerbellon, being a gentleman of Milan, and a great engineer, and most resolute soldier, was taken; and there died; in both the places many persons of worth, among which Pagan de Oria was one, a knight of the Order of Saint John, of a most noble disposition, as the exceeding liberality which he used towards his brother, the famous John Andrea de Oria, clearly demonstrates; and that which rendered his death more deplorable was, that he was slain by certain Saracens (which he trusted, perceiving how the fort was lost), who had offered to convey him thence in the habit of a Moor to Tabarca, which is a little haven or creek possessed by the Genoese that fish for coral in that coast. These Saracens cut off his head and brought it to the general of the Turkish army, who did accomplish in them the Spanish proverb, "That although the treason pleaseth, yet is the traitor hated," and so it is reported that he commanded those to be hanged that had brought him the present, because they had not brought it alive.

'Among the Christians that were lost in the fort there was one, called Don Pedro de Aguilar, born in Andalusia, in some town whose name I have forgotten; he had been Ancient in the fortress, and was a soldier of great account, and of a rare understanding, and specially had a particular grace in poetry. This I say because his fortune brought him to be slave to my patron, even into the very same galley and bench whereon I sat. This gentleman made two sonnets in form of epitaphs, the one for the Goleta, the other for the fort; and I will repeat them, because I remember them very well, and do believe that they will be rather grateful than anything disgustful to the audience.'

As soon as ever the Captive named Don Pedro de Aguilar, Don Fernando beheld his camaradas, and they all three did smile. And when he began to talk of the sonnets, one of them said, 'Before your pass further, I beseech you, good sir, let me entreat you to tell me what became of that Don Pedro de Aguilar whom you have named.'

'That which I know of that affair,' answered the Captive, 'is that, after he had been two years in Constantinople, he fled away in the attire of an Armenian with a Greek spy, and I cannot tell whether he recovered his liberty or no, although I suppose he did, for within a year after I saw the Greek in Constantinople, but I had not the opportunity to demand of him the success of that voyage.'

'He came then into Spain,' quoth the gentleman; 'for that same Don Pedro is my brother, and dwells now at home in our own town, very well, rich married, and a father of three sons.'

'God be thanked,' quoth the Captive, 'for the infinite favour He hath showed unto him; for in mine opinion there is not on earth any contentment able to be compared to that of recovering a man's lost liberty.'

'I do moreover,' said the gentleman, 'know the sonnets which my brother composed.'

'I pray you then, good sir,' quoth the Captive, 'repeat them; for perhaps you can say them better than I.'

'With a very good will,' answered the gentleman; 'and that of the Goleta is thus.'

CHAPTER XIII

Wherein Is Prosecuted the History of the Captive

'"A SONNET

'"O happy souls, which from this mortal vale
Freed and exempted, through the good you wrought,
Safe from the harms that here did you assail,
By your deserts to highest heaven were brought,
Which here inflamed by wrath, and noble thought,
Showed how much your forces did avail:
When both your own and foreign bloods you taught,
From sandy shores, into the deeps to trail.
Your lives before your valour's end deceased
In your tired arms, which, though they were a-dying
And vanquish'd, yet on victory have seized.
And this your life, from servile thraldom flying,
Ending, acquires, between the sword and wall,
Heaven's glory there, fame here on earth, for all."'

'I have it even in the very same manner,' quoth the Captive.

'Well, then,' said the gentleman, 'that of the fort is thus, if I do not forget it:

'"A SONNET

'"From midst the barren earth, here overthrown,
In these sad clods, which on the ground do lie,
Three thousand soldiers' holy souls are flown,
And to a happier mansion gone on high:
Here, when they did in vain the vigour try
Of their strong arms, to cost of many a one,
After the most, through extreme toil, did die,
The cruel sword a few did light upon.
And this same plot eternally hath been,
With thousand doleful memories replete,
As well this age, as in foregoing time.
But from his cruel bosom Heaven ne'er yet
Received sincerer souls than were the last,
Nor earth so valiant bodies aye possess'd."'

The sonnets were not misliked; and the Captive was greatly recreated with the news which he received of his companion, and, prosecuting his history, he said:

'The Goleta and the fort being rendered, the Turks gave order to dismantle Goleta; for the fort was left in such sort as there remained nothing up that might be overthrown: and to do it with more brevity and less labour, they undermined it in three places, but that which seemed least strong could not be blown up by any of them, which was the old walls; but all that which had remained afoot of the new fortifications and works of Fratin, fell down to the ground with great facility. And this being ended, the navy returned triumphant and victorious to Constantinople, where, within a few months afterward, my lord Uchali died, whom they called Uchali Fartax, which signifies in the Turkish language, the Scald or Scurvy Runagate, for he was such. And it is a custom among the Turks to give one another nicknames, either of the defects or perfections and virtues which they have; and the reason hereof is, that among them all they have but four lineages that have surnames, and these do contend with that of Ottoman's, for nobility of blood; and all the rest, as I have said, do take denomination sometime from the blemishes of the body, and sometime from the virtues of the mind. And this scurvy fellow did row fourteen years, being the Great Turk's slave, and did renounce his faith, being four-and-thirty years old, for despite, and because he might be revenged on a Turk that gave him a cuff on the face as he rowed; and his valour was so great, as without ascending by the dishonourable means and ways usually taken by the greatest minions about the Great Turk, he came first to be King of Algiers, and after to be General of the Sea, which is the third most noble charge and dignity of all the Turkish empire. He was born in Calabria, and was a good moral man, and used with great humanity his slaves, whereof he had above three thousand, which were after his death divided, as he had left in his testament, between the Great Turk (who is ever an inheritor to every dead man, and hath a portion among the deceased his children) and his runagates. I fell to the lot of a Venetian runagate, who being a ship-boy in a certain vessel. was taken by Uchali, who loved him so tenderly as he was one of the dearest youths he had, and he became after the most cruel runagate that ever lived. He was called Azanaga, and came to be very rich, and King of Algiers. With him I came from Constantinople somewhat contented in mind, because I should be nearer unto Spain; not for that I meant to write unto any one of my unfortunate success, but only to see whether fortune would prove more favourable to me in Algiers than at Constantinople, where I had attempted a thousand ways to escape, but none of them sorted to any good effect. And I thought to search out in Algiers some other means to compass that which I so greedily desired, for the hope of attaining liberty some time had never abandoned me; and when in the contriving I thought, or put my designs in practice, and that the success did not answer mine expectation, presently without forsaking me, it forged and sought out for another hope that might sustain me, although it were debile and weak.

'With this did I pass away my life, shut up in a prison or house, which the Turks call baths, wherein they do enclose the captive Christians, as well those that belong to the king as other particular men's, and those which they call of the Almazen, which is as much to say, as slaves of the council, who are deputed to serve the city in the public works and other affairs thereof; and these of all other captives do with most difficulty attain to liberty; for, by reason they belong to the commonalty, and have no particular master, there is none with whom a man may treat of their redemption, although they should have the price of their ransom. To these baths, as I have said, some particular men carry their captives to be kept, chiefly if they be to be ransomed; for there they have them at their ease and secure, until they be redeemed. The king's captives of ransom, also, do not go forth to labour with the other poor crew, if it be not when the paying of their ransom is deferred; for then, to the end they may make them write for money more earnestly, they make them labour and go to fetch wood with the rest, which is no small toil and trouble. I then was one of those of ransom; for as soon as it was known how I was a captain, notwithstanding that I told them of my little possibility and want of means, all could not prevail to dissuade them from consorting me with the multitude of gentlemen, and those of ransom. They put on me then a chain, rather to be a token that I was there for my ransom than to keep me the better with it. And so I passed away my time there with many other gentlemen and men of mark, held and kept in there for their ransom. And although both hunger and nakedness did vex us now and then, or rather evermore, yet nothing did afflict us so much as to hear and see every moment the cruelties that my master used towards Christians. Every day he hanged up one; he set this man on a stake, and would cut off the other's ears, and that for so little occasion, or wholly without it, as the very Turks themselves perceived that he did it not for any other cause but because he had a will to do it, and that it was his natural inclination to be a homicide of all human kind. Only one Spanish soldier, called such a one of Saavedra, was in his good grace, who although he did sundry things that will remain in the memory of that nation for many years, and all to the end to get his liberty, yet he never struck him, nor commanded him to be stricken, nor said as much as an evil word unto him; and yet we all feared that he should be broached on a stake for the least of many things which he did, and himself did also dread it more than once; and if it were not that time denieth me leisure to do it, I would recount unto you things done by this soldier, which might both entertain and astonish you much more than the relation of my life.

'There were over the square court of our prison certain windows that looked into it, and belonged to a certain rich and principal Moor; the which windows (as ordinarily are all the Moors' windows) rather seemed to be holes than windows, and even these were also very closely covered and shut fast with linen coverings. It therefore befel that, standing one day upon the battlements of our prison with other three companions, trying which of us could leap best in his shackles to pass away the time, and being alone (for all the other Christians were gone abroad to labour), I lifted up by chance mine eyes, and I saw thrust out at one of those so close shut windows a cane, and a linen tied at the end thereof, and the cane was moved and wagged up and down, as if it had made signs that we should come and take it. We looked upon it, and one of my companions went under the cane, to see whether they would let it fall, or what they would do else; but as soon as he approached it, the cane was lifted up, and did stir it to either side, as if they had said (with wagging of the head), "No." The Christian returned to us; and the cane being eftsoons let fall, and beginning to move as it had done before, another of my fellows went, and the same succeeded unto him that did to the first.

'Finally, the third approached it, with no better success than the former two; which I perceiving, would not omit to try my fortitude: and as soon as I came near to stand under the cane, it was let slip, and fell within the baths, just at my feet. I forthwith went to untie the linen which was knotted, wherein I found ten zianiys, which are certain pieces of base gold used among the Moors, and worth, each of them, ten reals of our money. I leave to your discretion to think if I was not glad of my booty; certes, my joy and admiration was much, to think whence that good might come unto us, but specially to myself, since the signs of refusal to let it fall to the other did confirm clearly that the favour was only addressed to myself. I took my welcome money, broke the cane, and returned to the battlements, and viewed the window earnestly, and perceived a very beautiful hand issue out thereat, which did open and shut it again very speedily. By which imagining and thinking that some woman that dwelled in that house had done us the charity and benefit, in token of our thankful minds, we made our courtesies after the Moorish fashion, by inclining of our heads, bending of the body, and pressing our hands to our breasts. Within a while after, there appeared out of the same window a little cross made of canes, which presently was taken in again. This sign did confirm us in the opinion that there was some Christian woman captive in that place, and that it was she which did to us the courtesy; but the whiteness of her hand, and her rich bracelets, destroyed this presumption: although we did, notwithstanding, conjecture that it was some runagate Christian, whom their masters there do very ordinarily take to wives, yea, and account very good hap to light on one of them, for they are much more accounted of than the women of the nation itself.

'Yet in all these discourses we strayed very far from the truth of the accident; and so, from thenceforward, all our passing of the time was employed in beholding that window as our north, wherein had appeared the star of the cane. But fifteen days passed over, or we could descry either it or the hand again, or any other sign. And although in the meantime we endeavoured all that we might to know who dwelled in that house, or whether there were any runagate Christian therein, yet never a one could tell us any other things but that it belonged to a very rich and noble Moor, called Aguimorato, who had been constable of the Pata—a dignity among them of very great quality.

'But when we thought least that it would rain any more zianiys by that way, we saw the cane suddenly to appear and another linen hanging on it, whose bulk was much greater. And this befel when the bath was freed of concourse, and void, as the other time before. We made the accustomed trial, every one approaching it before me, but without effect until I came; for presently, as I approached it, it was permitted to fall. I untied the knot, and found enwreathed in it forty ducats of Spanish gold, with a letter written in the Arabian tongue, and at the end thereof was drawn a very great cross. I kissed the cross, took up the money, and returned again to the battlements, and we all together made our receivers. The hand also appeared. I made signs that I would read the paper, and the window was shut incontinently. All of us were marvellously astonished, yet joyful at that which had befallen us; and by reason that none of us understood the Arabian tongue, the desire that we had to understand the contents of the letter was surpassing great, but greater the difficulty to find out some trusty persons that might read it. In the end I resolved to trust in this affair a runagate of Murcia, who did profess himself to be my very great friend, and having, by my liberality and other good turns done secretly, obliged him to be secret in the affair wherein I would use him—for some runagates are accustomed, when they have an intention to return into the Christian countries, to bring with them testimonies of the most principal captives, wherein they inform, and in the amplest manner they may, how the bearer is an honest man, and that he hath ever done many good turns to the Christians, and that he hath himself a desire to escape by the first commodity. Some runagates there are which procure those testimonies sincerely, and with a good intention; others take the benefit of them either by chance or industry, who, intending to go and rob into the countries of Christians, if by chance they be astray or taken, bring forth their testimonies, and say that by those papers may be collected the purpose wherewithal they came, that is, to remain in Christian countries, and that therefore they came abroad a-pirating with the other Turks; and by this means they escape that first brunt, and are reconciled again to the Church, without receiving any harm at all; and when they espy their time, do return again into Barbary, to be such as they were before. Others there are which procure those writings with a pure intention, and do after stay in Christian countries. Well, this my friend was a runagate of this last kind, who had the testimonies of all my companions, wherein we did commend him as amply as we could devise. And certainly if the Moors had found those papers about him, they would have burnt him for it. I understand how he could speak the Arabian tongue very perfectly, and not only that alone, but also write it withal; yet before I would wholly break my mind to him, I requested him to read me that scroll which I had found by chance in a hole of my cabin. He opened it, and stood a good while beholding and construing thereof, murmuring somewhat between his teeth. I demanded therefore of him whether he understood it. And he answered that he did very well, and that if I desired to have it translated verbatim I should bring unto him pen and ink, to the end he might do it more completely. We presently gave unto him that which he asked, and he did translate it by little and little; and having finished it, he said, "All that is here in Spanish, is punctually, without omitting a letter, the contents of the Moorish paper. And here you must note that where it says Lela Marien, it means our Lady the blessed Virgin Mary." We read the paper, whereof the contents were these which ensue:

'"When I was a child, my father had a certain Christian woman captive, that taught me in mine own tongue all the Christian religion, and told me many things of Lela Marien. The Christian died, and I know she went not to the fire, but to Allah; for she appeared to me twice after her death, and bade me go to the Christian country to see Lela Marien, who loved me much. I know not how I may go. I have seen many Christians through this window, and none of them hath seemed to me a gentleman but thyself. I am very beautiful and young, and I have a great deal of riches to carry with me. See thou whether thou canst contrive the way how we may depart, and thou shalt there be my husband, if thou pleasest; and if thou wilt not, I do not greatly care, for Lela Marien will provide me of a husband. I wrote myself the billet; be therefore wary whom thou trustest to read it. Do not trust any Moor; for they are all of them deceitful traitors. It is this that grieves me most of all; for I would not have thee, if it were possible, to disclose the matter to any living body; for if my father did know it, he would throw me down into a well, and oppress me in it with stones. I will hang a thread to the end of the cane, and therein thou mayst tie thine answer. And if thou canst not write the Arabian, tell me thy mind by signs, for Lela Marien will make me to understand it, who, with Allah, preserve thee, and this cross, which I do many times kiss; for so the captive commanded me to do."

'See, good sir, if it was not great reason, that the reasons comprehended in this letter should recreate and astonish us. And certainly the one and the other was so great, as the runagate perceived well that the paper was not found by chance, but was really addressed unto some one of us; and therefore desired us earnestly, that if that were true which he suspected, that we would trust and tell it unto him, and he would adventure his life to procure our liberties. And saying this, he took out of his bosom a crucifix of metal, and protested, with very many tears, by the God which that image represented, in whom he, although a sinner and wicked man, did most firmly believe, that he would be most loyal and secret to us in all that which we would discover unto him; for it seemed to him, and he almost divined, that both himself and we all should recover our liberties by her means that did write the letter; and he should then also see himself in the state which he most desired, to wit, in the bosom of his mother the holy Catholic Church; from which, through his ignorance and sin, he was departed and divided as an unprofitable and corrupt member. The runagate said this with so many tears, and with such evident tokens of repentance, as all of us consented to open our minds unto him, and declare the truth of the matter; and so we recounted unto him the whole discourse, without concealing any circumstance, and showed unto him the window by which the cane was wont to appear; and he marked the house from thence, and rested with special charge to inform himself well of those that dwelled therein. We thought also that it was requisite to answer the Moorish lady's letter; and therefore, having him present that could so well perform that task, we caused the runagate to draw out an answer presently as I did dilate it to him, which was punctually such as I will recount; for of all the most substantial points that befel me in that affair, no one is fallen out of my memory, nor shall ever as long as I have breath. In effect that which I answered to the Moor was this:

'"The true Allah preserve you, dear lady, and that blessed Marien who is the true mother of God, and is she that hath put in your mind the desire to go into the Christian countries, because she doth love you well. Pray unto her that she will vouchsafe to instruct you how you may bring the matter to pass which she commandeth you to do; for she is so good as she will easily condescend to do it. As for my part, I do promise, as well for myself as for these other Christians that are with me, to do for you all that we are able to do until death. Do not omit to write unto me, and acquaint me with your purposes, and I will answer you every time; for great Allah hath given us a captive Christian that can write and read your language well, as you may perceive by this paper; so that you may securely, and without any dread, advise us of all that you shall think good. And as concerning that which you say, that you will become my wife after we arrive to the Christian countries, I do promise you the same, as I am a good Christian; and you shall understand that the Christians do accomplish their words far better than do the Moors. Allah and Marien his mother preserve you, my dearest lady!"

'The letter being written and enclosed, I expected two days, that the baths might be free of concourse, as it was wont, which as soon as it befel, I went up to my accustomed place of the battlements, to see whether the cane appeared; which was presently after thrust out at the window. And as soon as I perceived it, although I could not note who it was that set it, I showed my paper, to give them warning to set on the thread; but it was already hanging thereon; to the which I tied the letter, and within a while after began to appear our star, with the white flag of peace, and the knotted linen; which they let fall, and I took up: and I found therein, in divers sorts of money and gold, more than fifty ducats, which redoubled our joys more than fifty times, and confirmed the hope we conceived of attaining liberty. The very same night our runagate returned to us, and told how he had learned that the very same Moor which we were informed of before, called Aguimorato, dwelt there, and was excessive rich, and had one only daughter, the heir of all his goods; of whom the common opinion throughout the city was, that she was the fairest woman of all Barbary; and that many of the viceroys that came there had demanded her to wife, but she would never condescend to any notion of marriage; and that he likewise had understood that she had sometimes a Christian captive, which now was deceased: all which agreed with the contents of the letter. We presently entered in council with the runagate about the means we were to use to fetch away the Moor, and come all of us to Christian lands; and in the end we concluded to attend, for that time, the second advice of Zoraida (for so was she then called, who now means to name herself Maria), forasmuch as we clearly perceived that it was she, and none other, that could minister to us the means to remove all these difficulties. After we had rested on this resolution, the runagate bid us be of good courage, for he would engage his life, or set us at liberty. Four days after, the baths were troubled with people, which was an occasion that the cane appeared not all that while; but that impediment being removed, and the accustomed solitude returned, the cane did again appear, with a linen hanging thereat so grossly impregned as it promised to be delivered of a most happy burden. Both cane and linen bent themselves to me, and in them I found another paper, and a hundred ducats in gold, besides other small money. The runagate was present, and we gave him the letter to read, the effect whereof was this:

'"I know not, good sir, what order to give for our going into Spain, nor hath Lela Marien told me anything concerning it, although I have demanded her counsel. That which at present I conceive may be done is, that I will through this window give unto you great store of money, wherewith you may redeem yourself and your friends. And let one of you go into the Christian's country and buy a barque, and after return for his fellows, and he shall find me in my father's garden, which is at the gate of Babazon, near to the sea-coast, where I mean to stay all the summer, with my father and my servants; from whence you may take me out boldly by night, and carry me to the barque. And see well that thou wilt be my husband; for if thou wilt not, I will demand of Marien to chastise thee: and if thou darest trust nobody to go for the vessel, redeem thyself and go, for I know thou wilt rather return than another, seeing thou art a gentleman and a Christian. Learn out the garden, and when I see thee walk there where thou now art, I will make account that the bath is empty, and will give thee great store of money. Allah preserve thee, my dear friend!"

'These were the contents of the second letter, which being heard by us all, every one offered to be himself the ransomed person, and promised to go and return with all punctuality, and among the rest I also made a proffer of myself; to all which resolutions the runagate opposed himself, saying that he would consent in no wise that any one of us should be freed until we were all together delivered; for experience had taught him how evil ransomed men were wont to keep those promises which they passed in the times of their thraldom; for many times certain principal captives had made that kind of trial, redeeming of some one or other that should go to Valencia or Majorca, with money to freight a barque or frigate, and return for him that had ransomed them, and did never return again; for the recovered liberty, and the fear of adventuring to lose it again concurring, did blot out of their memory all the other obligations of the world. And to confirm the truth which he averred, he briefly recounted unto us an accident which befel much about the same time to certain Christian gentlemen, the strangest as I suppose that ever happened in those quarters, wherein do succeed every other day events full of wonder and admiration; and therefore concluded that what ought and might be done was, that they would give unto him to buy a barque such money as they meant to employ in the ransom of a captive, and he would buy it there in Algiers, under pretext of becoming a merchant and sailor in Tetuan and that coast. And being once owner of a barque, he would easily devise how to have them out of the baths and embark them all: how much more, if the Moorish lady did as she promised, give them money enough to ransom them all, was it a most easy thing, they being free, to embark themselves at midday. But the greatest difficulty in this affair was, that the Moors use not to permit any runagate to buy any barque or other small vessel, but only great vessels of war; for they suspect that he that buys a barque, specially if he be a Spaniard, does it for no other end but to run away to Christian countries. And yet he knew how to facilitate that inconvenience, by inducing a Tangerine Moor to become his partner of the barque and the gains that should be gotten by the commodities thereof, and with this colour he would become lord of it himself, and therewithal accounted the matter ended. And although that myself and my comrades held it the better course to send unto Mallorca for one, as the Moorish lady said, yet durst we not contradict him, fearful that if we did not what he would have us to do he would discover us and endanger our lives, if he did once detect Zoraida's practices, for the safeguard of whose life we would all of us most willingly adventure our own; and therefore we determined to put ourselves into God's and the runagate's hands. And so we answered at the same instant to Zoraida, telling her that we would accomplish all that she had admonished us, because she had advertised us as well as if Lela Marien had told her what she should say, and that the dilating or shortening of the affair did consist only in herself. I did offer myself anew to become her husband; and with this the day ensuing wherein the bath was also free, she sent me down at divers times by the cane two thousand ducats and a letter, wherein she said that she would go to her father's garden the next Juma, that is, the Friday following, and that before she went away she would give us more money; and that if it were not enough, we should advise her, and she would give unto us as much as we would demand; for her father had so much treasure as he would never perceive it; how much more, seeing she had and kept the keys of all. We gave five hundred crowns presently to the runagate to buy a barque, and with eight hundred I redeemed myself, giving the money to a Valencian merchant which was at that season in Algiers, who did ransom me of the king, taking me forth on his word, which he passed to pay my ransom at the arrival of the first ship that should come from Valencia; for if he had delivered the money instantly, it would have given occasion to the king to suspect that my ransom was many days before in Algiers, and that the merchant had kept it silently to make his benefit thereof. Finally, my master was so cavillous as I durst not in any wise pay him presently.

'The Thursday before the Friday of the beautiful Zoraida's departure towards the garden, she gave unto us other two thousand ducats, and did likewise advise us of her going away, entreating me, that as soon as I had ransomed myself, I should learn the way to the garden, and take occasion howsoever to go to it, and see her. I answered her briefly that I would do so, and prayed her that she would carefully commend our proceedings to Lela Marien with those prayers which the captive had taught her. This being done, order was also given for the ransoming of my three companions to facilitate our issue out of the baths, and also that they seeing me free, and themselves undelivered, might not be troubled or persuaded by the devil to do anything in prejudice of Zoraida; for although that they, being the men of that quality they were, might assure me from this fear, I would not, for all that, adventure the matter; and therefore I caused them to be ransomed by the same means that I was redeemed myself, giving all the money to the merchant, that he might with the more security pass his word for us; to whom yet we never did discover our practice and secret, by reason of the eminent danger of the discovery thereof.'

CHAPTER XIV

Wherein the Captive Prosecuteth the Pleasant Narration of His Life

FIFTEEN days were not fully expired when the runagate had bought him a very good barque, able to hold thirty persons or more; and for the better colour and assurance of his business; he made a voyage to a place called Sargel, which is thirty leagues distant from Algiers towards the side of Oran, and is a great place of traffic for dry figs. He made this voyage twice or thrice in company with the Tagarine of whom we made mention; and the name of Tagarino is in Barbary given to the Moors of Aragon, Granada, and Mudajares. And in the kingdom of Fez those Mudajares are called Elches, and are the nation which that king doth most employ in warlike affairs. You shall therefore understand that every time he passed by with his barque, he did cast anchor in a little creek, twice the shot of a crossbow from the garden wherein Zoraida attended; and there the runagate would, in very good earnest, exercise himself with the Moors that rowed, either to fly, or else to assault one another in jest, as he meant to do after in good earnest; and would now and then go to Zoraida's garden and demand fruits, which her father would bestow upon him, without knowing what he was; and although he desired to have spoken with Zoraida, as he told me afterward himself, and have informed her how it was he that was to carry her away, by my direction, into the land of Christians, and that she should therefore live cheerful and secure, yet was it never possible, forasmuch as the women of that nation do not suffer themselves to be viewed by any Moor or Turk, if he be not their husband, or that their parents command them, yet do they haunt and communicate themselves to Christian captives freely, and that sometimes more than is convenient. And truly it would have grieved me that he should have spoken to her, for perhaps it would have perplexed her extraordinarily, to see her affair committed to the trust of a runagate;

but God, who did otherwise dispose it, did not concur with this good desire of our runagate, who, seeing how safely he went and returned from Sargel, and that he sounded when and where he pleased, and that the Tagarino, his partner, did only what he liked, and that I was ransomed, and nothing else wanting but to find out some Christian that would row, he bade me bethink myself what men I would bring away with me beside those that I had ransomed, and that I should warn them to be ready against the next Friday, wherein he was resolved that we should depart.

'Seeing this, I spake to twelve Spaniards, very lusty rowers, and those that could with most liberty get out of the city; and it was not a little matter to find so many there at that time, for there were twenty galleys abroad a-robbing, which had carried all the other rowers with them, and these were left behind, because their master did keep at home that summer to finish a galley that was on the stocks a-making. To these I said nothing else, but only warned them that the Friday ensuing, in the evening, they should closely steal out by one and one, and go towards Aguimorato's garden, and there expect me until I came unto them. I gave this advice to every one of them apart, with order also, that although they saw any other Christian there, they should tell them nothing else but that I had commanded them to expect me in that place.

'This diligence being used, yet wanted there another, which was the most expedient of all, to wit, to advise Zoraida of the terms wherein our affairs did stand, to the end she might be likewise ready and prepared, and not affrighted, though we did assault her before the time that she could imagine the barque of the Christians to be come to fetch her; and therefore I resolved to go myself into the garden, and see whether I might speak with her. And taking the occasion to go and gather some herbs, I went unto it the day before our departure, and the first person with whom I encountered was her father, who demanded of me, in a language which in all Barbary and Constantinople is usually spoken by the Moors to their captives, and is neither Arabian, Spanish, nor of any other nation, but rather a mixture of all languages, wherewith all of us understand one another: he, I say, in that kind of speech, demanded of me what I sought for in that his garden, and to whom I did belong.

I answered that I was one Arnaute Mami his slave (and this because I was very certainly informed that he was his entire friend), and that I came thither to gather of all sorts of herbs to make a salad. He consequently asked of me whether I was a man of ransom or no, and how much my master demanded for me. And being in those questions and demands, the beautiful Zoraida descended from the house into the garden, who had espied me a good while before. And as the Moorish women do not greatly estrange themselves from the sights of Christians, nor are in their behaviour or conversation with them anything squeamish, as we have said already, she did not greatly fear to approach the place where her father talked with me, but rather her father perceiving that she came on slowly, did call, and commanded her to draw near.

'It were a thing impossible for me to recount the great beauty and gallant disposition, or the bravery and riches of attire wherein my beloved Zoraida then showed herself to mine eyes. I will only say this, that there hung more pearls at her ears, superlative fair neck, and hair, than she hath hairs on her head; about the wrists of her legs, which were naked, after the manner of her country, she wore two carcaxes (for so the manacles or bracelets of the feet are called in the Moresco tongue) of the finest gold, wherein were enchased so many diamonds, that, as she told me after, her father valued them at twenty thousand crowns; and those about the wrists of her hands were of equal esteem. Her pearls were many, and those most orient; for all the chief bravery and ornament of the Moorish ladies consists in the adorning of themselves with pearls and pearl-seed, by reason whereof there is more pearls and pearl-seed to be found among the Moors than among all other nations of the world. And Zoraida's father had the fame to have many, and those the very best that were in Algiers; and also above two hundred thousand ducats of Spanish gold, of all which was she the lady who now is mine. And if with all this ornament she could then seem fair, by the relics that have remained unto her among so many labours, may be easily guessed what she would have been in the time of prosperity; for all of us do know that the beauty of some women hath limited days and seasons, and requireth certain accidents either to diminish or increase it; and it is a thing natural to the passions of the mind, either to raise or abase it, but most commonly they wholly destroy it. To be brief, I say that she arrived to the place where we discoursed at that time, most richly attired, and beautiful beyond measure, or I at least deemed her the fairest that I had ever beheld until then; and herewithal, remembering the obligation wherein she had tied me, thought that some deity had presented itself to my view, being come from heaven to the earth for my recreation and relief.

'As soon as she was arrived, her father told her in her own language how I was his friend Arnaute Mami his captive, and that I came there to gather a salad; then she, taking the speech, demanded in that medley of tongues of which I have spoken, whether I was a gentleman, and what the reason was why I redeemed not myself. I made answer that I was already ransomed, and by the ransom might be conjectured in how much my master valued me, seeing he had for my liberty a thousand and five hundred coltamis. To this she answered, "In good sooth, if thou wert my father's, I would cause him not to give thee for twice as much more; for you Christians are great liars, and do make every one of yourselves poor men, to defraud the Moors of their due ransom." "It may well be so, madam," quoth I; "but I have, for my part, used all truth in this affair with my master, and do, and will use truth with as many persons as I shall ever have occasion to treat with in this world."

'"And when dost thou go away?" quoth Zoraida. "To-morrow, as I believe," quoth I; "for there is a French vessel here which sets forth to-morrow, and I mean to depart in her." "Were it not better," replied Zoraida, "to expect until vessels come out of Spain, and go away with them, than with those of France, which are not your friends?" "No," quoth I; "although if it were true, as the news runs, that there comes a vessel from Spain, I would attend it; but yet it is more certain that I shall depart to-morrow; for the desire I have to see myself at home in my country, and with those persons whom I love, is so great as it will not permit me to expect any other commodity that foreslows itself, be it never so good." "Thou art doubtlessly married in thy country," said Zoraida, "and therefore desirest to go see thy wife?" "I am not married," quoth I; "but I have passed my word to marry as soon as I am there safely arrived." "And is she beautiful to whom thou hast passed it?" quoth Zoraida.

"So beautiful," said I, "as, to endear it and tell you the truth, she is very like unto yourself." Hereat her father laughed very heartily, and said, "In good earnest, Christian, she must be very fair that may compare with my daughter, who is the most beautiful of all this kingdom; and if thou wilt not believe me, look on her well, and thou shalt see that I tell thee but the truth." He himself, as most perfect in the tongue, did serve for the interpreter of most of our speeches: for although she could speak that illegitimate language which is there in use, yet did she manifest her mind more by signs than by words.

'Whilst thus we reasoned of many matters, there came running towards us a certain Moor, and told his master how four Turks had leaped over the garden walls, and were gathering the fruits, although they were not yet ripe. The old man and his daughter Zoraida started hereat; for it is an universal and natural defect in the Moors to fear the Turks, but specially the soldiers of that nation, who are commonly so insolent, and have such command over the Moors that are their subjects, as they do use them worse than if they were their slaves. Therefore Zoraida's father said unto her, "Daughter, retire thyself into the house, and keep thyself in, whilst I go speak to those dogs. And thou, Christian, go and seek out thine herbs, and depart in a good hour; and I pray Allah to conduct thee safely to thy country." I inclined myself to him, and he departed to search out the Turks, leaving me alone with Zoraida, who began to make ado as if she went whither her father had commanded her. But scarce was he covered among the trees of the garden, when she returned to me, with her eyes full of tears, and said, "Amexi, Christiano? amexi?" that is, "Goest thou away, Christian? Goest thou away?" I answered, "Yes, lady, that I do; but I will never depart without thee. Expect me the next Friday, and be not affrighted when thou shalt see us; for we will go to the Christian country then without all doubt." This I said to her in such sort as she understood all my words very well; and, casting her arm over my neck, she began to travel with languishing steps towards the house; and fortune would (which might have been very ill, if Heaven had not rectified it) that as we walked together in that manner and form, her father (who did by this return. after he had caused the Turks to depart) espied us; and we saw also very well how he had perceived us; wherefore Zoraida, who is very discreet, would not take away her arm from my neck, but rather drew nearer unto me, and laid her head on my breast, and bowed her knees a little, with evident token that she swooned; and I likewise made as though I did sustain her up by force. Her father came running over towards us, and, seeing his daughter in that state, demanded the cause of her; but seeing she made no answer, he himself said, "She doubtlessly is dismayed by the sudden affright she took at the entrance of those dogs"; and, taking her away from me, he bowed her to his own breast; and she, breathing out a sigh, with her eyes yet full of tears, said again, "Amexi, Christiano, amexi,"—"Go away, Christian; go away." To which her father replied, "There is no cause, daughter, why the Christian should go away; for he hath done thee no harm, and the Turks are already departed." "Sir, they have affrighted her," quoth I, "as you have said; but yet since she hath commanded me to go away, I will not offend her; therefore, rest in peace; for I will return, if it please you to give me leave, for herbs to this garden when it is needful; for my master says none better are to be found for salads in any garden than you have in this." "Come as oft as thou wilt," said Aguimorato; "for my daughter says not this in respect that thou or any other Christian hath offended her, but that, meaning to say that the Turks should go away, she bade thee to depart, or else she spake it because it is time for thee to gather thine herbs."

'With this I took leave of both, and she seemed at the instant of my departure to have had her heart torn away from her as she departed with her father; and I, under colour of seeking herbs, went about all the garden at my leisure, and viewed all the sallies and the entrances thereof, the strength of the house, and the commodities that might be offered to facilitate our enterprise. This being done, I came home, and made a relation to the runagate and my other fellows of all that had passed, and did long infinitely to see the hour wherein I might, without any affright or danger, possess that happiness which fortune, in the fair and lovely Zoraida, offered unto me. In fine, the time passed over, and the so much desired day and term arrived; and, every one of us following the order which, with mature consideration and long discourse, we had agreed on, we found the good success we desired; for the very Friday following the day wherein I had spoken with Zoraida in the garden, Morenago (for so was the runagate called) near night cast anchor almost right before the place wherein the beautiful Zoraida remained. The Christians, also, that were to row were ready, and hidden in sundry places thereabouts. All were suspended, and resolutely expected my coming, desirous to set upon the barque that was before their face; for they knew not of the agreement that was between me and the runagate, but rather made full account that they were to gain their liberty by force of arms, and killing the Moors that came in that vessel.

'It therefore befel that, as soon as I and my fellows appeared, all the rest that were hidden, espied us, made forthwith over towards us. This was at an hour when the city gates were shut, and never a body abroad among all those fields. And when we were all together, we were in doubt whether it would be best first to go and fetch Zoraida, or to imprison and stone the Taragin Moors that rowed in the frigate. And being in this doubt, the runagate came to us, asking upon what we stayed, for it was now high time to be going away, and all his Moors were reccheless, and the greater number of them asleep. We told him then the cause of our stay. And he answered that it was of most importance first to subject the vessel, which might be done with very great facility, and without any peril; and that we might go after for Zoraida. His opinion liked us all very well; and therefore, without lingering any longer, he leading the way, we came to the vessel, and he himself leaping in first of all, set hand to his falchion, and said in Moresco, "Let none of you that is here stir himself, if he loves his life." And saying so, all the rest of the Christians entered. The Moors, which were of little spirit, hearing their master say so, were marvellously amazed, and, without daring any one of them to set hand to their arms, which were but a few at all, they suffered themselves very quietly to be taken and bound by the Christians, which did it very dexterously, threatening them that if they did let slip the least outcry, they should presently be all put to the sword. This being finished, and the half of our people remaining in their guard, we that were left conducted also by the runagate, went towards Aguimorato's garden. The door thereof did, by very good hap, open with as little noise as if it had had no lock at all; whereupon we went with great quietness and silence towards the house, unseen or espied of any.

'The beautiful Zoraida was the while expecting us at a window, and as soon as she saw people approach, demanded, with a low voice, whether we were Nazarenes, as if she would say or ask whether we were Christians. I answered that we were, and willed her to come down. As soon as she knew me, she stayed not a minute, but without answering any word came down in an instant, and, opening the door, showed herself to us all, more beautiful and richly attired than I am able in any sort to express. As soon as I saw her, I took her by the hand and kissed it; the same did the runagate, and my two comrades; and all the rest, which knew not the matter, did as they had seen us do before them; for it seemed that we did no more but give her thanks, and acknowledge her the auctress of all our liberties. The runagate demanded of her, in her own language, whether her father were in the garden or no. She answered that he was, and that he slept. "Then will it be requisite," quoth the runagate, "to rouse him, and bear him and all the other things of worth in this garden away with us." "That shall not be so," quoth she; "for I will have no man to touch my father; and in this house there is nothing of value, but that which I mean to carry away with myself, which is so much as will be sufficient to cheer and enrich you all; as, if you will stay but a while, you shall perceive."

'And saying so, she entered again into the house, promising to return to us speedily, and bade us stand still without making any noise. I demanded of the runagate what speech had passed between them, and he told me all she had said; and I answered him again, that I would not have Zoraida's will transgressed in any sort. By this time she returned laden with a little casket full of gold, so that she was scarce able to bear it. And her father, in the mean season, by bad fortune, awaked, and heard the noise that was beneath in his garden; and, looking out at a window, he perceived that they were all Christians that were in it, and therefore cried out, in a loud and unmeasurable manner, in the Arabian tongue, "Christians, Christians! thieves, thieves!" by which cries we were all of us strucken into very great fear and confusion. But the runagate, seeing the peril wherein we were, and how nearly it concerned him to come off from that enterprise before he were discovered, ran up very speedily to the place where Aguimorato stood, and some of our fellows accompanied him (for I durst not abandon Zoraida, who had fallen between mine arms all amazed); and in conclusion, those which had mounted, behaved themselves so well, as they brought Aguimorato down in a trice, having tied his hands, and set a gag in his mouth, which hindered his speech, threatening him that if he did speak but a word it should cost him his life.

'When his daughter saw him she covered her eyes, because she would not behold him; and he marvelled, wholly ignoring with how good a will she came away with us. But then, considering that nothing was so requisite as our legs, we did with all velocity and diligence get into the frigate; for our companions did perplexedly expect our return, half afraid that some disgrace had befallen us. Scarce were two hours of the night overrun, when we were all embarked; and then we unmanacled Zoraida's father's hands, and took the cloth out of his mouth. But the runagate did again admonish him that, as he tendered his life, he should not speak one word. He, beholding his daughter likewise there, began to sigh very feelingly, but chiefly perceiving me to hold her so straitly embraced, and that she made no resistance, nor did complain or seem coy, but stood quiet; but yet for all that he kept silence, fearing lest they should put the runagate's menaces in execution. Zoraida, seeing herself now safe within the barque, and that we were ready to row away, looking on her father and the other Moors that were tied therein, she entreated the runagate to tell me how she desired me to do her the favour to set those Moors and her father at liberty; for she would rather cast herself into the sea than see her father, who had loved her so dearly, carried away captive before her eyes, and that also by her occasion. The runagate told me her mind, and I answered how I was very well pleased it should be so. But he replied that it was in no sort expedient, by reason that if they were landed there, they would presently raise the country and put the whole city into a tumult, and cause certain light frigates to be manned and sent out in our pursuit, and lay both sea and land for us in such sort as it would be impossible for us to escape; but what was at the present possible to be done, was to give them liberty at the first Christian country whereat we happened to arrive.

'All of us agreed to this opinion; and Zoraida also (to whom reason was given of the motives we had, not to free them forthwith, and accomplish her will therein) remained satisfied; and therefore presently, with joyful silence and cheerful diligence, every one of our lusty rowers seizing upon his oar, we began, after we had commended ourselves unto Almighty God, to launch forth, and address our course towards the isles of Mallorca, which is the nearest Christian country; but by reason that the wind blew somewhat from the mountains, and that the sea began to be rough, it was not possible to continue that course, and so we were forced to approach the shore, and go by little and little towards Oran, not without great grief and anguish, for fear to be espied by the town of Sargel, which is on that coast, and falls some seventy leagues beyond Algiers. And we did likewise fear to meet in that passage some galliot of those which come ordinarily with merchandise from Tetuan, although every one of us for himself, and for all together, did presume that if we encountered a galliot of merchandise, so it were not a pirate, that not only we would not be lost, but rather would take the vessel, that therein we might with more security finish our voyage. Zoraida, whilst thus we sailed, went with her head between my hands, because she would not look on her father; and I felt her, how she was still invoking of Lela Marien to assist us. And having sailed about some thirty leagues, the morning overtook us about some three musket-shot from land, in a place that seemed to be desert, and free from all access of those that might discover us; and yet for all that, we got by might and main somewhat farther into the seas that now was become a little calmer; and having entered some two leagues into the main, order was given that they should row by turns, whilst they did refresh themselves, and take a little sustenance, for the barque was very well furnished with victuals, although those which did row refused the offer, saying that then it was no time to repose, and that they should set those that did not row to dinner, for they would not yet in any sort let go their oars. It being done as they had said, the wind did rise so much as it made us, abandoning our oars, to set sail, and direct our boat towards Oran, being unable to take any other course. All was done with very great speed; and so we made by the sail more than eight miles an hour, free from all other fear than that of encountering some vessel of war. We gave the Moors, our prisoners, their dinner, and the runagate comforted them, saying that they went not as prisoners, for they should receive their liberty upon the first commodity that were proffered. The same was likewise said of Zoraida's father, who returned them this answer: "I would easily expect and believe any other thing, O Christians, of your liberality and honourable manner of proceeding; but do not think that I am so simple as once to imagine that you will give me my liberty, for you did never expose yourself to the danger of despoiling me thereof with intention to return it me so prodigally again, especially knowing, as you do, who I am, and the profit you may reap by giving me it again, to which profit, if you will put a name, and tell me how much would you demand, I do even from hence offer unto you all that which you will seek for me, and for that unfortunate daughter of mine; or if you will not deliver me, I will give you it for her alone, who is the greatest and the best part of my soul." And saying so, he began to weep so bitterly as he moved us all to compassion, and forced Zoraida to look upon him, who, seeing him weep, was so strangely moved as, arising from my feet, she went and embraced her father; and, laying her face upon his, they began together so tender a lamentation as many of us that were in the barque were forced to keep them company. But when her father noted her to be so richly adorned, and with so many jewels on, he asked her in his own language, "How haps this, daughter, that yesternight late, before this terrible disaster befel us wherein we are plunged, I saw thee attired in thine ordinary household array, and that now, without having had any leisure to apparel thyself, or having given thee any glad tidings, for whose solemnising thou oughtest to adorn and publish thyself, I do view thee thus clad in the richest attire which I could bestow upon thee when our fortune was most favourable? Answer me to this, for thou hast suspended and astonished me more than the very disgrace itself wherein I am."

'All that the Moor said to his daughter the runagate declared unto us; and she did not answer a word to him. But when he saw the little coffer lie at one side of the barque, wherein she was wont to keep her jewels, and that he knew very well he had left at Algiers, and not brought to the garden, he was much more amazed, and demanded of her how that coffer was come into our possession, and what things she had there within it. To which the runagate, without attending that Zoraida should answer him, said, "Sir, do not trouble yourself by demanding so many things of your daughter Zoraida, for with one that I will say I shall satisfy them all; and therefore you shall understand that she is a Christian, and hath been the file that cut off our chains, and is the liberty itself of our captivity; and she goeth along with us of her own free will, as content (if mine imagination do not wrong me) to see herself in this state, as he is that cometh out of darkness to the light, from death unto life, and out of pain into glory." "Is it true, daughter, which this man says?" quoth the Moor. "It is," answered Zoraida. "That thou in effect art a Christian," replied the old man, "and she that hath put her father into his enemy's hands?" To which Zoraida answered, "I am she that is a Christian, but not she that hath brought thee to this pass; for my desire did never so estrange itself from thee as to abandon or harm thee, but only endeavoured to do myself good." "And what good hast thou done thyself, daughter?" "Demand that," said she, "of Lela Marien, for she can therein inform thee better than I can."

'Scarce had the Moor heard her say so, when, with incredible haste, he threw himself headlong into the sea, wherein he had been questionlessly drowned, if the long apparel he wore on had not kept him up a while above the water. Zoraida cried out to us to save him; and so we all presently ran, and, laying hold on a part of his Turkish robe, drew him up half drowned, and wholly devoid of feeling; whereat Zoraida was so grieved, that she lamented him as dolefully as if he had been dead. There we laid him with his mouth downward, and he avoided a great quantity of water, and after the space of two hours returned to himself again. And in the meantime, the wind also turning, it did drive us towards the coast, so that we were constrained to keep ourselves by very force of arms from striking upon it; and our good fortune directing us, we arrived to a little creek at the side of a certain cape or promontory, called by the Moors the Cape of the Cava Rumia, which in our language signifies "the ill Christian woman." And the Moors hold it for a tradition, that in the very same place was the Cava buried, for whom Spain was lost, and conquered by the Moors; for Cava in their language signifies an ill woman, and Rumia a Christian. Yea, and they hold it for a sign of misfortune to arrive or cast anchor there, when mere necessity drives them thither, without which they never approach it: yet did it not prove to us the shelter of an ill woman, but the secure haven of our safety. We sent our sentinels ashore, and never let the oars slip out of our hands. We did likewise eat of the runagate's provision, and heartily besought Almighty God and Our Lady to assist and favour us with a happy end to so lucky a beginning. And we agreed, upon Zoraida's entreaty, to set her father and the other Moors that we had tied a-land in that place; for she was of so tender and compassionate a mind as she could in no wise brook to see her father tied in her presence, or her countrymen borne away captives. Wherefore we made her a promise that we would, at our departure, let them all go away, seeing we incurred no danger by leaving them in so desolate a region. Our prayers were not so vain but that they found gentle acceptance in Heaven, which presently changed the wind and appeased the sea, inviting us cheerfully to return to it again, and prosecute our commenced voyage.

'Seeing that the weather was favourable, we loosed the Moors, and set them all a-land one by one; and coming to disembark Zoraida's father, who was by that time wholly come to himself, he said, "For what do you conjecture, Christians, that this bad woman is glad that you give me liberty? Do you think that she doth it for pity that she takes of me? No, truly; but she doth it only to remove the hindrance my presence gave her when she would execute her unlawful desires. Nor ought you to believe that she is moved to change religion by reason that she understands yours to be better than her own, but only because she knows licentiousness to be more publicly and freely practised in your country than among us." And then, turning to Zoraida, whom I and another Christian held fast by both the arms, lest she should do some desperate fact, he said,

"O infamous girl, and ill-advised maiden! where dost thou run thus blinded and distracted, in the power of those dogs, our natural enemies? Cursed be the hour wherein I engendered thee! and cursed the delights and pleasures wherein thou wast nousled!" I perceiving that he was not like to make an end of his execrations so soon as I could wish, had him set on shore, and thence he prosecuted his maledictions and plaints, praying unto Mahomet that he would intercede with Allah that we might be all destroyed, confounded, and cast away. And when we could hear his words no longer, by reason that we set sail, we perceived his works, that were, to pluck his beard, tear his hair, and cast himself on the ground; but once he did lift up his voice so high, as that we heard him say, "Return, beloved daughter, return to the land; for I do pardon thee all that thou hast done: and deliver that money to those men, for it is now their own; and return thou to comfort thy sad and desolate father, who will forsake his life on these desolate sands, if thou dost abandon him."

'Zoraida heard him say all this, and lamented thereat, but knew not how to speak, or answer him any other thing but this: "Father mine, I pray Allah that Lela Marien, who hath been the cause of my becoming a Christian, may likewise comfort thee in thy sorrow. Allah knows well that I could do none other than I did, and that these Christians do owe me nothing for my good-will, seeing that though I had not come away with them, but remained at my house, yet had it been impossible (such was the haste wherewithal my soul pressed me) not to have executed this my purpose, which seems to me to be as good as thou, O beloved father, dost account it wicked." She said this in a time that neither her father could hear her, nor we behold him; and therefore, after I had comforted Zoraida, we did thenceforth only attend our voyage, which was so much holpen by the favourable wind as we made full account to be the next day on the coast of Spain. But as good very seldom, or rather never, betides a man thoroughly and wholly, without being accompanied or followed by some evil which troubles and assaults it, our fortune would, or rather the maledictions of the Moor poured on his daughter (for the curses of any father whatsoever are to be feared), that being engulfed three hours within night, and going before the wind with a full sail, and our oars set up, because the prosperous wind had rid us of the labour of rowing, we saw near unto us, by the light of the moon that shined very clearly, a round vessel which, with all her sails spread, did cross before us into the sea, and that so nearly, as we were fain to strike down our sail, that we might avoid the shock she was like to give us; and those that were in her had on the other side laboured also what they might to turn her out of our way, standing all of them on the hatches to demand of us what we were, from whence we came, and whither we did sail. But by reason that they spake French, the runagate bade us not to speak a word, saying, "Let none answer; for these are French pirates, which make their booty of everybody." For this cause none of us answered; and, being passed a little forward, and that the ship remained in the lee of us, they suddenly shot off two pieces of artillery, and as I think, both of them had chain bullets, for with the one they cut our mast asunder, and overthrew it and the sail into the sea, and instantly after they discharged another. The bullet alighting in our barque, did pierce it through and through, without doing any other hurt; but we, seeing that our vessel began to sink, began all to cry out, and request them to succour us, and prayed them that they would take us into their vessel, for we were a-drowning. Then they came amain, and, casting out their cock-boat, there entered into it as good as a dozen Frenchmen, well appointed, with their arquebuses and matches lighted, and so approached unto us; and, perceiving how few we were, and that the barque did sink, they received us into their boat, saying, that because we had used the discourtesy of not making them answer, that misfortune had befallen us. Our runagate about this time took the coffer wherein Zoraida's treasures were kept, and threw it into the sea, unperceived of any.

'In conclusion, we went all of us into the great vessel with the Frenchmen, who, after they had informed themselves of all that which they desired to know, as if they were our capital enemies, they afterwards despoiled us of all that ever we had about us; and of Zoraida they took all, even unto her very bracelets that she wore on her ankles. But the wrong they did to Zoraida did not afflict me so much as the fear I conceived that, after they had taken away from her her most rich and precious jewels, they would also deprive her of the jewel of most prize, and which she valued most. But the desires of that nation extend themselves no further than to the gain of money; and their avarice in this is never thoroughly satisfied, and at that time was so great, as they would have taken from us the very habits of slaves that we brought from Barbary, if they had found them to have been worth anything. And some there were of opinion among them, that we should be all enwreathed in a sail and thrown into the sea, because they had intention to traffic into some havens of Spain, under the name of Britons, and that if they carried us alive, they should be punished, their robbery being detected; but the captain, who was he that had pilled my beloved Zoraida, said that he was so contented with his booty, as he meant not to touch any part of Spain, but would pass the Straits of Gibraltar by night, or as he might, and so return again to Rochelle, from whence he was come: and thereupon they all agreed to give us their cock-boat, and all that was necessary for our short voyage; as, indeed, they performed the day ensuing, when we were in the view of Spain; with the sight whereof all our griefs and poverties were as quite forgotten as if we never had felt any, so great is the delight a man takes to recover his liberty. It was about mid-day when they put us into the cock, giving unto us two barrels of water and some biscuit; and the captain, moved with some compassion, as the beautiful Zoraida embarked herself, bestowed on her about forty crowns in gold; nor would he permit his soldiers to despoil her of these very garments which then and now she doth wear.

'We entered into the cock-boat, and, giving them thanks for the good they did, and showing at our departure more tokens of thankfulness than of discontent, they sailed presently away from us, towards the Straits; and we, without looking on any other north or star than the land itself, which appeared before us, did row towards it so lustily, that at sunset we were so near as we made full account to arrive before the night was far spent. But by reason that the moon did not shine, and the night was very dark, and that we knew not where we were, we did not hold it the best course to approach the shore too near; yet others there were that thought it convenient and good, desiring that we should make to it, although we ran the boat on the rocks, and far from any dwelling; for, by doing so, we should free ourselves from the fear, which we ought of reason to have, lest there should be up and down on that coast any frigates of the pirates of Tetuan, which are wont to leave Barbary overnight, and be on the coast of Spain ere morning, and ordinarily make their booty, and turn to their supper again to Barbary, the night following; but, of the contrary opinions, that which was followed was, that we should draw near the land by little and little, and that if the quietness of the sea would permit it, we should take land where we might best and most commodiously do it. This was done; and a little before midnight we arrived to the foot of a high and monstrous mountain, which was not altogether so near to the sea but that it did grant a little patch of ground whereon we might commodiously disembark; wherefore we ran ourselves on the sands, and came all a-land, and kissed the earth, and, with tears of most joyful content and delight, gave thanks unto our Lord God for the incomparable favours which He had done us in our voyage. Then took we out our victuals from the boat, and drew itself up on the shore, and ascended a great part of the mountain; for although we were in that place, yet durst we not assure ourselves, nor did thoroughly believe, that it was a Christian country whereon we did tread.

'The day breaking somewhat slower than I could have wished it, we ascended the mountain wholly, to see whether we might discover any dwelling or sheepfolds from thence; but although we extended our sight into every quarter, yet could we neither decry dwelling, person, path, nor highway; yet did we resolve, notwithstanding, to enter into the land, seeing that we could not choose but discover ere long somebody who might give us notice of the place where we were. And that which afflicted me most of all was to see Zoraida go afoot through those rugged places; for although I did sometimes carry her on my shoulders, yet did the toil I took more weary her than the repose she got could ease her, and therefore would never after the first time suffer me to take that pains again, and so she went ever after afoot with great patience and tokens of joy, I holding her still by the hand. And having travelled little less than a quarter of a league, we heard the noise of a little bell, an infallible argument that near at hand there was some cattle; whereupon, all of us looking very wistly to see whether anybody appeared, perceived under a cork tree a young shepherd, who very quietly and carelessly was carving of a stick with a knife. We called to him, and he leaped up lightly on foot, and, as we afterwards learned, the first that he got sight of were the runagate and Zoraida; whom he seeing apparelled in the Moresco habit, thought that all the people of Barbary had been at his heels; and therefore, running very swiftly into the wood, he cried all along, with marvellous loudness, "Moors! Moors are in the land! Moors! Moors! Arm! arm!" These outcries struck us anew into a great perplexity, and scarce did we know what we should do; but considering how the shepherd's alarm would cause all the country to rise up, and that the horsemen that kept the coast would presently come to see what it was, we all agreed that the runagate should put off his Turkish attire, and put on a captive's cassock, which one of the company gave unto him forthwith, although the giver remained after in his shirt. And thus committing the affair unto Almighty God, we followed on by the same way which we saw the shepherd had taken, always expecting when the horsemen of the coast would fall upon us. And we were not deceived in our expectation, for within two hours after, having issued out of those woods into a plain, we discovered about some fifty horsemen, which came running towards us as swiftly as their horses could drive; and, having perceived them, we stood still, and stayed until they came to us, and saw instead of the Moors they sought for, so many poor Christians, and remained somewhat ashamed thereat; and one of them demanded whether we were the occasion that a shepherd had given the alarm. "Yes," quoth I; and as I was about to inform what I was, and of all our adventure, and from whence we came, one of the Christians that came with us did take notice of the horseman who had spoken unto us; and so, interrupting my speech, he said, "Sirs, let God be praised which hath brought us to so good a place as this is; for, if I be not deceived the earth which we tread is of Velez-Malaga; and, if the years of my captivity have not confounded my memory, you likewise, sir, that demand what we be, are Peter of Bostamente, mine uncle." As soon as ever the Christian Captive had spoken those words, the horse man, leaping off his horse, ran and embraced him, saying, "O nephew, as dear to me as my soul and life! now I do know thee very well, and many a day since have I wept for thee, thinking thou wast dead; and so hath my sister, thy mother, and all the rest of thy friends which do live yet! and God hath been pleased to preserve their lives, that they may enjoy the pleasure to behold thee once again. We know very well that thou wert in Algiers; and, by the signs and tokens of my clothes, and that of all the rest here of thy companions, I surmise that your escape hath been miraculous?" "Indeed it was so," replied the Captive; "and we shall have time, I hope, to recount unto you the manner."

'As soon as the horsemen had understood that we were Christian captives, they alighted off their horses, and every one of them invited us to mount upon his own, to carry us to the city of Velez-Malaga, which was yet a league and a half from that place; and some of them went to the place where we had left the boat, to bring it to the city; whom we informed first of the place where it lay: others did mount us up on horseback behind themselves, and Zoraida rode behind the Captive's uncle. All the people issued to receive us, being premonished of our arrival by some one that had ridden before. They did not wonder to see captives freed, nor Moors captived there, being an ordinary thing in those parts; but that whereat they wondered was the surpassing beauty of Zoraida, which at that season and instant was in her prime, as well through the warmth she had gotten by her travel, as also through the joy she conceived to see herself in Christian lands, secure from all fear of being surprised or lost; and these things called out to her face such colours as, if it be not that affection might then have deceived me, I durst aver that a more beautiful than she was the world could not afford, at least among those which I had ever beheld.

'We went directly to the church to give thanks unto Almighty God for the benefit received; and as soon as Zoraida entered into it, she said there were faces in it that resembled very much that of Lela Marien. We told her that they were her images; and the runagate, as well as the brevity of the time permitted, instructed her what they signified, to the end she should do them reverence, as if every one of them were truly that same Lela Marien which had spoken unto her. She, who had a very good understanding and an easy and clear conceit, comprehended presently all that was told unto her concerning images. From thence they carried us, and divided us among different houses of the city; but the Christian that came with us carried the runagate, Zoraida, and me to the house of his parents, which were indifferently accommodated and stored with the goods of fortune, and did entertain me with as great love and kindness as if I were their own son. We remained six days in Velez, in which time the runagate, having made an information of all that which might concern him, he went to the city of Granada, to be reconciled, by the holy Inquisition's means, to the bosom of our holy mother the Church. The rest of the freed captives took every one the way that he pleased; and Zoraida and I remained behind, with those ducats only which the Frenchman's courtesy was pleased to bestow on Zoraida; and with part of that sum I bought her this beast whereon she rides; I myself serving her hitherto as her father and her squire, and not as her spouse. We travel with intention to see if my father be yet living, or any of my brothers have had more prosperous hap than myself; although, seeing Heaven hath made me Zoraida's consort, methinks no other good fortune could arrive, were it never so great, that I would hold in so high estimation. The patience wherewithal she bears the incommodities usually annexed unto poverty, and the desires she shows to become a Christian, is such and so great, as it strikes me into an admiration, and doth move me to serve her all the days of my life; although that the delight which I take to see myself hers, and she mine, is ofttimes interrupted, and almost dissolved, by the fear which I have that I shall not find in mine own country some little corner wherein I may entertain her, and that time and death have wrought such alteration in the goods and lives of my father and brothers, as I shall scarce find any one at home that knows me. I have no more, good sirs, to tell you of my life's history, than which, whether it be pleasing and rare, or no, your clear conceits are to judge. As for myself, I daresay that, if it had been possible, I would have told it with more brevity; fearing it might be tedious unto you, I purposely omitted many delightful circumstances thereof.'

CHAPTER XV

Which Speaks of That Which After Befel in the Inn, and of Sundry Other Things Worthy To Be Known

THE Captive having said this, held his peace; and Don Fernando replied to him thus: 'Truly, captain, the manner wherewithal you have recounted this marvellous success hath been such as it may be paragoned to the novelty and strangeness of the event itself. And so great is the delight we have taken in the hearing thereof, as I do believe that although we had spent the time from hence till to-morrow in listening to it, yet should we be glad to hear it told over once again.'

And saying so, Cardenio and all the rest did offer themselves and their means to his service, as much as lay in them, with so cordial and friendly words as the Captive remained thoroughly satisfied with their good wits; but specially Don Fernando offered, that if he would return with him, he would cause the marquis his brother to be Zoraida her godfather in baptism; and that he, for his part, would so accommodate him with all things necessary, as he might enter into the town with the decency and authority due to his person. The Captive did gratify his large offers very courteously, but would not accept any of them at that time. By this the night drew on, and about the fall thereof there arrived at the inn a coach, with some men a-horseback, and asked for lodging; to whom the hostess answered that in all the inn there was not a span free, the number of her guests was already so many. 'Well, although that be so,' quoth one of the horsemen that had entered, 'yet must there be a place found for Master Justice who comes in this coach.' At this name the hostess was afraid, and said, 'Sir, the misfortune is that I have no beds; but if Master Justice brings one with him, as it is probable he doth, let him enter in boldly, and I and my husband will leave our own chamber to accommodate his worship.' 'So be it,' quoth the squire; and by this time alighted out of the coach a man whose attire did presently denote his dignity and office, for his long gown and his great and large sleeves did show that he was a judge, as the serving-men affirmed. He led a young maiden by the hand, of about some sixteen years old, apparelled in riding attire; but she was therewithal of so disposed, beautiful, and cheerful a countenance, as her presence did strike them all into admiration; so as if they had not seen Dorothea, Lucinda, and Zoraida, which were then in the inn, they would hardly have believed that this damsel's beauty might anywhere have been matched.

Don Quixote was present at the judge's and the gentlewoman's entry; and so, as soon as he had seen him, he said, 'Sir, you may boldly enter and take your ease in this castle, which although it be but little and ill accommodated, yet there is no narrowness nor discommodity in the world but makes place for arms and learning, and specially if the arms and letters bring beauty for their guide and leader, as your learning doth, conducted by this lovely damsel, to whom ought not only castles to open and manifest themselves, but also rocks to part and divide their cliffs, and mountains to bow their ambitious crests, to give and make her a lodging. Enter, therefore, I say, worshipful sir, into this paradise, wherein you shall find stars and suns to accompany this sky which you bring along with you. Here shall you find arms in their height, and beauty in her prime.' The judge marvelled greatly at Don Quixote's speech, whom he began to behold very earnestly, and wondered no less at his shape than at his words; and knowing not what answer he might return him, he was diverted, on the other side, by the sudden approach of the three ladies, Lucinda, Dorothea, and Zoraida, which stood before him; for, having heard of the arrival of new guests, and also being informed by the hostess of the young lady's beauty, they were come forth to see and entertain her. But Don Fernando, Cardenio, and the curate did give him more complete and courtly entertainment than the rusty knight. In effect, the judge was marvellously amazed at that which he saw and heard in that inn: and the fair guests thereof bade the beautiful maiden welcome. The judge perceived very well that the guests of the inn were all men of account; but Don Quixote's feature, visage, and behaviour did set him out of all bias, being not able to conjecture what he might be.

And after some court-like intercourses passed, and the commodities of the inn examined, they all agreed again, as they had done before, that all the women should enter into Don Quixote's room, and the men remain without in their guard: and so the judge was content that the damsel, who was his daughter, should also go with those ladies, which she did with a very good will; and, with a part of the innkeeper's narrow bed, and half of that which the judge had brought with him, they made shift to pass over that night the best they could.

The Captive, who from the instant that he had first seen the judge, did greatly suspect that he was his brother, and demanded of one of his servants how he was called, and where he was born. The other answered how he was called the licentiate, John Perez of Viedma, and, as he had heard, he was born in a village of the mountains of Leon. With this relation, and the rest that he had noted, he finally confirmed his opinion that it was the brother who, following his father's advice, had dedicated himself to his studies; and, full of joy and contentment, calling aside Don Fernando, Cardenio, and the curate, he certified them of all that had passed, and that the judge was his brother. The serving-man told him likewise how he went towards the Indies, where he had his place and office in the courts of Mexico; and also that the young gentlewoman was his daughter, of whose birth her mother had died, and he ever after remained a widower, and very rich by her dowry and portion that she had left to her daughter. He demanded of them advice how he might discover himself to his brother, or first know whether, after he had detected himself, he would receive him with a good countenance and affection, and not be ashamed to acknowledge him for his brother, seeing him in so poor an estate. 'Leave the trial of that experience to me,' quoth the curate, 'and the rather because there is no occasion why you, sir captain, should not be kindly entertained by him; for the prudence, worths, and good countenance of your brother give manifest tokens that he is nothing arrogant.' 'For all that,' said the captain, 'I would not make myself known on the sudden, but would use some pretty ambages to bring him acquainted with me.' 'I say unto you,' quoth the curate, 'that I will trace the matter in such sort as we will all rest satisfied.'

Supper was by this made ready, and all of them sat down to the table, the Captive excepted and ladies, which supped together within the room; and about the midst of supper the curate said, 'Master Justice, I have had in times past a comrade of your very surname in Constantinople, where I was sometime captive, who was one of the most valiant soldiers and captains that might be found among all the Spanish foot; but he was as unfortunate as he was valorous and resolute.' 'And how was that captain called, good sir?' quoth the judge. 'His name was,' replied master curate, 'Ruy Perez of Viedma, and he was born in a village of the mountains of Leon; and he recounted unto me an occurrence happened between his father, him, and his other brethren, which, if I had not been told by a man of such credit and reputation as he was, I would have esteemed for one of these fables which old wives are wont to rehearse by the fireside in winter; for he said to me that his father had divided his goods among his three sons, and gave them withal certain precepts, better than those of Cato; and I know well that the choice which he made to follow the war had such happy success, as within a few years, through his forwardness and valour, without the help of any other arm, he was advanced to a company of foot, and made a captain, and was in the way and course of becoming one day a colonel; but fortune was contrary to him, for even there where he was most to expect her favour, he lost it, with the loss of his liberty, in that most happy journey wherein so many recovered it, to wit, in the battle of Lepanto. I lost mine in Goleta; and after, by different success, we became companions in Constantinople, from whence we went to Algiers, where did befall him one of the most notable adventures that ever happened in the world'; and there the curate, with sufficient brevity, recounted all that had happened between the captain and Zoraida; to all which the judge was so attentive, as in all his life he never listened to any cause so attentively as then. And the curate only arrived to the point wherein the Frenchmen spoiled the Christians that came in the barque, and the necessity wherein his companion and the beautiful Zoraida remained; of whom he had not learned anything after, nor knew not what became of them, or whether they came into Spain, or were carried away by the Frenchmen into France.

The captain stood listening somewhat aloof off to all the curate's words, and noted the while the motions and gestures of his brother; who, seeing that the curate had now made an end of his speech, breathing forth a great sigh, and his eyes being filled with tears, he said, 'Oh, sir, if you had known the news which you have told me, and how nearly they touch me in some points, whereby I am constrained to manifest these tears, which violently break forth in despite of my discretion and calling, you would hold me excused for this excess. That captain of whom you spoke is my eldest brother, who, as one stronger and of more noble thoughts than I or my younger brother, made election of the honourable military calling, one of the three estates which our father proposed to us, even as your comrade informed, when, as you thought, he related a fable. I followed my book, by which God and my diligence raised me to the state you see. My younger brother is in Peru, and with that which he hath sent to my father and myself, hath bountifully recompensed the portion he carried, and given to him sufficient to satisfy his liberal disposition, and to me wherewithal to continue my studies with the decency and authority needful to advance me to the rank which now I possess. My father lives yet, but dying through desire to learn somewhat of his eldest son, and doth daily importune God with incessant prayers that death may not shut his eyes until he may once again see him alive. I only marvel not a little, considering his discretion, that among all his labours, afflictions, or prosperous successes, he hath been so careless in giving his father notice of his proceedings; for if either he or any one of us had known of his captivity, he should not have needed to expect the miracle of the cane for his ransom. But that which troubles me most of all is to think whether these Frenchmen have restored him again to liberty, or else slain him, that they might conceal their robbery the better; all which will be an occasion to me to prosecute my voyage, not with the joy wherewithal I began it, but rather with melancholy and sorrow. Oh, dear brother, I would I might know now where thou art, that I myself might go and search thee out, and free thee from thy pains, although it were with the hazard of mine own. Oh, who is he that could carry news to our old father that thou wert alive, although thou wert hidden in the most abstruse dungeons of Barbary? for his riches, my brother's, and mine, would fetch thee from thence. O beautiful and bountiful Zoraida! who might be able to recompense thee for the good thou hast done to my brother? How happy were he that might be present at thy spiritual birth and baptism, and at thy nuptials, which would be so grateful to us all.' These and many other such words did the judge deliver, so full of compassion for the news that he had received of his brother, as all that heard him kept him company in showing signs of compassion for his sorrow.

The curate therefore, perceiving the happy success whereto his design and the captain's desire had sorted, would hold the company sad no longer; and therefore, arising from the table, and entering into the room wherein Zoraida was, he took her by the hand, and after her followed Lucinda, Dorothea, and the judge his daughter. The captain stood still to see what the curate would do, who, taking him fast by the other hand, marched over with them both towards the judge and the other gentlemen, and saying, 'Suppress your tears, Master Justice, and glut your desire with all that good which it may desire, seeing you have here before you your good brother and your loving sister-in-law. This man whom you view here is the Captain Viedma, and this the beautiful Moor which hath done so much for him. The Frenchmen which I told you of have reduced them to the poverty you see, to the end that you may show the liberality of your noble breast.'

Then did the captain draw near to embrace his brother; but he held him off a while with his arms, to note whether it was he or no; but when he once knew him, he embraced him so lovingly, and with such abundance of tears, as did attract the like from all the beholders. The words that the brothers spoke one to another, or the feeling affection which they showed, can hardly be conceived, and therefore much less written by any one whatsoever. There they did briefly recount the one to the other their successes; there did they show the true love and affection of brothers in his prime; there did the judge embrace Zoraida; there he made her an offer of all that was his; there did he also cause his daughter to embrace her; there the beautiful Christian and the most beautiful Moor renewed the tears of them all; there Don Quixote was attentive, without speaking a word, pondering of these rare occurrences, and attributing them to the chimeras which he imagined to be incident to chivalry; and there they agreed that the captain and Zoraida should return with their brother to Seville, and thence advise their father of his finding and liberty, that he, as well as he might, should come to Seville to the baptism and marriage of Zoraida, because the judge could not possibly return, or discontinue his journey, in respect that the Indian fleet was to depart within a month from Seville towards New Spain.

Every one, in conclusion, was joyful and glad at the Captive's good success; and two parts of the night being well-nigh spent, they all agreed to repose themselves a while. Don Quixote offered himself to watch and guard the castle whilst they slept, lest they should be assaulted by some giant or other miscreant, desirous to rob the great treasure of beauty that was therein immured and kept. Those that knew him rendered unto him infinite thanks, and withal informed the judge of his extravagant humour, whereat he was not a little recreated; only Sancho Panza did fret, because they went so slowly to sleep, and he alone was best accommodated of them all, by lying down on his beast's furniture, which cost him dearly, as shall be after recounted. The ladies being withdrawn into their chamber, and every one laying himself down where best he might, Don Quixote sallied out of the inn, to be sentinel of the castle, as he had promised. And a little before day it happened that so sweet and tuneable a voice touched the ladies' ears, as it obliged them all to listen unto it very attentively, but chiefly Dorothea, who first awaked, and by whose side the young gentlewoman, Donna Clara of Viedma (for so the judge's daughter was called), slept. None of them could imagine who it was that sung so well without the help of any instrument. Sometimes it seemed that he sung in the yard, others that it was in the stable. And being thus in suspense, Cardenio came to the chamber door, and said, "Whosoever is not asleep, let them give ear, and they shall hear the voice of a lackey that so chants as it likewise enchants.' 'Sir,' quoth Dorothea, 'we hear him very well.' With this Cardenio departed; and Dorothea, using all the attention possible, heard that his song was this following.

CHAPTER XVI

Wherein Is Recounted the History of the Lackey, with Other Strange Adventures Befallen in the Inn

'I am a mariner to love,
Which in his depths profound
Still sails, and yet no hope can prove
Of coming aye to th' ground.

'I following go a glist'ring star,
Which I aloof descry,
Much more resplendent than those are
That Palinure did spy.

'I know not where my course to bend,
And so confusedly,
To see it only I pretend
Careful and carelessly.

'Her too impertinent regard,
And too much modesty,
The clouds are which mine eyes have barred
From their deserved fee.

'O clear and soul-reviving star!
Whose sight doth try my trust,
If thou thy light from me debar,
Instantly die I must.'

The singer arriving to this point of his song, Dorothea imagined that it would not be amiss to let Donna Clara hear so excellent a voice, and therefore she jogged her a little on the one and other side, until she had awaked her, and then said, 'Pardon me, child, for thus interrupting your sweet repose, seeing I do it to the end you may joy, by hearing one of the best voices that perhaps you ever heard in your life.' Clara awaked at the first drowsily, and did not well understand what Dorothea said, and therefore demanding of her what she said, she told it her again; whereupon Donna Clara was also attentive; but scarce had she heard two verses repeated by the early musician, when a marvellous trembling invaded her, even as if she had then suffered the grievous fit of a quartan ague. Wherefore, embracing Dorothea very straitly, she said, 'Alas, dear lady! why did you awake me, seeing the greatest hap that fortune could in this instant have given me, was to have mine eyes and ears so shut as I might neither see nor hear that unfortunate musician.' 'What is that you say, child?' quoth Dorothea. 'Did you not hear one say that the musician is but a horse-boy?' 'He is no horse-boy,' quoth Clara, 'but a lord of many towns, and he that hath such firm possession of my soul, as if he himself will not reject it, he shall never be deprived of the dominion thereof.' Dorothea greatly wondered at the passionate words of the young girl, whereby it seemed to her that she far surpassed the discretion which so tender years did promise, and therefore she replied to her, saying, 'You speak so obscurely, Lady Clara, as I cannot understand you; expound yourself more clearly, and tell me what is that you say of souls and towns, and of this musician whose voice hath altered you so much. But do not say anything to me now, for I would not lose, by listening to your disgusts, the pleasure I take to hear him sing; for methinks he resumes his music with new verses, and in another tune.' 'In a good hour,' quoth Donna Clara; and then, because she herself would not hear him, she stopped her ears with her fingers: whereat Dorothea did also marvel, but being attentive to the music, she heard the lackey prosecute his song in this manner:

'O sweet and constant hope,
That break'st impossibilities and briers,
And firmly runn'st the scope
Which thou thyself dost forge to thy desires!
Be not dismay'd to see
At ev'ry step thyself nigh death to be.

'Sluggards do not deserve
The glory of triumphs or victory;
Good hap doth never serve
Those which resist not fortune manfully,
But weakly fall to ground,
And in soft sloth their senses all confound.

'That love his glories hold
At a high rate, it reason is and just;
No precious stones nor gold
May be at all compared with love's gust;
And 'tis a thing most clear,
Nothing is worth esteem that cost not dear.

'An amorous persistence
Obtaineth ofttimes things impossible;
And so though I resistance
Find of my soul's desires, in her stern will,
I hope time shall be given,
When I from earth may reach her glorious heaven.'

Here the voice ended, and Donna Clara's sighs began; all which inflamed Dorothea's desire to know the cause of so sweet a song and so sad a plaint; and therefore she eftsoons required her to tell her now what she was about to have said before. Then Clara, timorous lest Lucinda should overhear her, embracing Dorothea very nearly, laid her mouth so closely to Dorothea's ear, as she might speak securely without being understood by any other, and said, 'He that sings is, dear lady, a gentleman's son of the kingdom of Aragon, whose father is lord of two towns, and dwelled right before my father's house at the court; and although the windows of our house were in winter covered with cere-cloth, and in summer with lattice, I know not how it happened, but this gentleman, who went to the school, espied me; and whether it was at the church, or elsewhere, I am not certain. Finally, he fell in love with me, and did acquaint me with his affection from his own windows, that were opposite to mine, with so many tokens and such abundance of tears, as I most forcibly believed, and also affected him, without knowing how much he loved me. Among the signs that he would make me, one was, to join the one hand to the other, giving me thereby to understand that he would marry me; and although I would be very glad that it might be so, yet as one alone, and without a mother, I knew not to whom I might communicate the affair, and did therefore let it rest without affording him any other favour, unless it were, when my father and his were gone abroad, by lifting up the lattice or cere-cloth only a little, and permitting him to behold me; for which favour he would show such signs of joy as a man would deem him to be reft of his wits.

'The time of my father's departure arriving, and he hearing of it, but not from me (for I could never tell it to him), he fell sick, as far as I could understand, for grief; and therefore I could never see him all the day of our departure, to bid him farewell at least with mine eyes; but after we had travelled two days, just as we entered into an inn in a village, a day's journey from hence, I saw him at the lodging door, apparelled so properly like a lackey, as if I had not borne about me his portraiture in my soul, it had been impossible to know him. I knew him, and wondered, and was glad withal; and he beheld me, unwitting my father, from whose presence he still hides himself when he crosses the ways before me as I travel, or after we arrive at any inn. And because that I know what he is, and do consider the pains he takes by coming thus afoot for my sake, and that with so great toil, I die for sorrow; and where he puts his feet, I also put mine eyes. I know not with what intention he comes, nor how he could possibly thus escape from his father, who loves him beyond measure, both because he hath none other heir, and because the young gentleman also deserves it, as you will perceive when you see him; and I dare affirm besides, that all that which he says he composes extempore, and without any study; for I have heard that he is a fine student, and a great poet; and every time that I see him, or do hear him sing, I start and tremble like an aspen leaf, for fear that my father should know him, and thereby come to have notice of our mutual affections. I have never spoken one word to him in my life, and yet I do nevertheless love him so much, as without him I shall not be able to live. And this is all, dear lady, that I am able to say unto you of the musician whose voice hath pleased you so well, as by it alone you might conjecture that he is not a horse-boy, as you said, but rather a lord of souls and towns, as I affirmed.'

'Speak no more, Lady Clara,' quoth Dorothea at that season, kissing her a thousand times; 'speak no more, I say, but have patience until it be daylight; for I hope in God so to direct your affairs, as that they shall have the fortunate success that so honest beginning deserves.' 'Alas, madam!' quoth Donna Clara, 'what end may be expected, seeing his father is so noble and rich, as he would scarce deem me worthy to be his son's servant, how much less his spouse? And for me to marry myself unknown to my father, I would not do it for all the world. I desire no other thing but that the young gentleman would return home again and leave me alone; perhaps by not seeing him, and the great distance of the way which we are to travel, my pain, which now so much presseth me, will be somewhat allayed; although I daresay that this remedy, which now I have imagined, would avail me but little; for I know not whence with the vengeance, or by what way this affection which I bear him got into me, seeing both I and he are so young as we be, for I believe we are much of an age, and I am not yet full sixteen, nor shall be, as my father says, until Michaelmas next.' Dorothea could not contain her laughter, hearing how childishly Donna Clara spoke; to whom she said, 'Lady, let us repose again, and sleep that little part of the night which remains; and when God sends daylight, we will prosper, or my hands shall fail me.' With this they held their peace, and all the inn was drowned in profound silence; only the innkeeper's daughter and Maritornes were not asleep, but knowing very well Don Quixote's peccant humour, and that he was armed and on horseback without the inn keeping guard, both of them consorted together, and agreed to be someway merry with him, or at least to pass over some time in hearing him speak ravingly.

It is therefore to be understood that there was not in all the inn any window which looked out into the field, but one hole in a barn, out of which they were wont to cast their straw. To this hole came the two demi-damsels, and saw Don Quixote mounted and leaning on his javelin, and breathing forth ever and anon so doleful and deep sighs, as it seemed his soul was plucked away by every one of them; and they noted besides how he said, with a soft and amorous voice, 'O my lady Dulcinea of Toboso! the sun of all beauty, the end and quintessence of discretion, the treasury of sweet countenance and carriage, the storehouse of honesty, and finally, the idea of all that which is profitable, modest, or delightful in the world! and what might thy ladyship be doing at this present? Hast thou perhaps thy mind now upon thy captive knight, that most wittingly exposeth himself to so many dangers for thy sake? Give unto me tidings of her, O thou luminary of the three faces! Peradventure thou dost now with envy enough behold her, either walking through some gallery of her sumptuous palaces, or leaning on some bay-window, and thinking how (saving her honour and greatness) she shall mitigate and assuage the torture which this mine oppressed heart endures for her love, what glory she shall give for my pains, what quiet to my cares, what life to my death, and what guerdon to my services. And thou, sun, which art, as I believe, by this time saddling of thy horses to get away early and go out to see my mistress, I request thee, as soon as thou shalt see her, to salute her in my behalf; but beware that when thou lookest on her and dost greet her, that thou do not kiss her on the face; for if thou dost, I become more jealous of thee than ever thou wast of the swift ingrate which made thee to run and sweat so much through the plains of Thessaly or the brinks of Peneus; for I have forgotten through which of them thou rannest so jealous and enamoured.'

To this point arrived Don Quixote, when the innkeeper's daughter began to call him softly unto her, and say, 'Sir knight, approach a little hitherward, if you please'; at which voice Don Quixote turned his head, and saw by the light of the moon which shined then very clearly, that he was called to from the hole, which he accounted to be a fair window full of iron bars, and those costly gilded with gold, well befitting so rich a castle as he imagined that inn to be; and presently in a moment he forged to his own fancy, that once again, as [s]he had done before, the beautiful damsel, daughter to the lady of that castle, overcome by his love, did return to solicit him; and with this thought, because he would not show himself discourteous and ungrateful, he turned Rozinante about and came over to the hole; and then, having beheld the two wenches, he said, 'I take pity on you, beautiful lady, that you have placed your amorous thoughts in a place whence it is not possible to have any correspondence answerable to the desert of your high worth and beauty, whereof you are in no sort to condemn this miserable knight-errant, whom love hath wholly disabled to surrender his will to be any other than to her whom at the first sight he made absolute mistress of his soul. Pardon me therefore, good lady, and retire yourself to your chamber, and make me not, by any further insinuation of your desires, more unthankful and discourteous than I would be; and if, through the love that you bear me, you find in me any other thing wherewithal I may serve and pleasure you, so that it be not love itself, demand it boldly; for I do swear unto you by mine absen[t], yet sweetest enemy, to bestow it upon you incontinently, yea, though it be a lock of Medusa's hairs, which are all of snakes, or the very sunbeams enclosed in a vial of glass.'

'My lady needs none of those things, sir knight,' answered Maritornes. 'What doth she then want, discreet matron?' quoth Don Quixote. 'Only one of your fair hands,' said Maritornes, 'that therewithal she may disburden herself of some part of those violent desires which compelled her to come to this window, with so great danger of her honour; for if her lord and father knew of her coming, the least slice he would take off her should be at the least an ear.' 'I would fain once see that,' quoth Don Quixote; 'but I am sure he will beware how he do it, if he have no list to make the most disastrous end that ever father made in this world, for having laid violent hands on the delicate limbs of his amorous daughter.' Maritornes verily persuaded herself that Don Quixote would give up his hand as he was requested, and having already contrived in her mind what she would do, descended with all haste from the hole, and, going into the stable, fetched out Sancho Panza his ass's halter, and returned again with very great speed, just as Don Quixote (standing up on Rozinante's saddle, that he might the better reach the barred windows, whereat he imagined the wounded damsel remained) did, stretching up his hand, say unto her, 'Hold, lady, the hand, or as I may better say, the executioner of earthly miscreants; hold, I say, that hand, which no other woman ever touched before, not even she herself that hath entire possession of my whole body, nor do I give it to you to the end you should kiss it, but that you may behold the contexture of the sinews, the knitting of the muscles, and the spaciosity and breadth of the veins, whereby you may collect how great ought the force of that arm to be whereunto such a hand is knit.' 'We shall see that presently,' quoth Maritornes; and then, making a running knot on the halter, she cast it on the wrist of his hand, and then descending from the hole, she tied the other end of the halter very fast to the lock of the barn door. Don

Quixote, feeling the roughness of the halter about his wrist, said, 'It rather seems that you grate my hand than that you cherish it; but yet I pray you not to handle it so roughly, seeing it is no fault of the evil which my will doth unto you; nor is it comely that you should revenge or disburden the whole bulk of your indignation on so small a part: remember that those which love well do not take so cruel revenge.' But nobody gave ear to these words of Don Quixote's; for as soon as Maritornes had tied him, she and the other, almost burst for laughter, ran away, and left him tied in such manner as it was impossible for him to loose himself.

He stood, as we have recounted, on Rozinante his saddle, having all his arm thrust in at the hole, and fastened by the wrist to the lock, and was in very great doubt and fear that if Rozinante budged never so little on any side he should fall and hang by the arm; and therefore he durst not once use the least motion of the world, although he might well have expected, from Rozinante's patience and mild spirit, that if he were suffered, he would stand still a whole age without stirring himself. In fine, Don Quixote seeing himself tied, and that the ladies were departed, began straight to imagine that all had been done by way of enchantment, as the last time, when in the very same castle the enchanted Moor (the carrier) had so fairly belaboured him; and then to himself did he execrate his own want of discretion and discourse, seeing that having escaped out of that castle so evil dight the first time, he would after adventure to enter into it the second; for it was generally observed by knights-errant that when they had once tried an adventure, and could not finish it, it was a token that it was not reserved for them, but for some other; and therefore would never prove it again. Yet for all this he drew forward his arm to see if he might deliver himself; but he was so well bound as all his endeavours proved vain. It is true that he drew it very warily, lest Rozinante should stir; and although he would fain have sat and settled himself in the saddle, yet could he do no other but stand, or leave the arm behind. There was many a wish for Amadis his sword, against which no enchantment whatsoever could prevail; there succeeded the malediction of his fates; there the exaggerating of the want that the world should have of his presence all the while he abode enchanted (as he infallibly believed he was) in that place; there he anew remembered his beloved Lady Dulcinea of Toboso; there did he call oft enough on his good squire Sancho Panza, who, entombed in the bowels of sleep, and stretched along on the pannel of his ass, did dream at that instant but little of the mother that bore him; there he invoked the wise men Lirgandeo and Alquife to help him. And finally, the morning did also there overtake him so full of despair and confusion, as he roared like a bull; for he had no hope that by daylight any cure could be found for his care, which he deemed would be everlasting, because he fully accounted himself enchanted; and was the more induced to think so, because he saw that Rozinante did not move little nor much; and therefore he supposed that both he and his horse should abide in that state without eating, drinking, or sleeping, until that either the malignant influence of the stars were past, or some greater enchanter had disenchanted him.

But he deceived himself much in his belief; for scarce did the day begin to peep, when there arrived four horsemen to the inn-door, very well appointed, and having snap-hances hanging at the pommel of their saddles. They called at the inn-door (which yet stood shut), and knocked very hard, which being perceived by Don Quixote, from the place where he stood sentinel, he said, with a very loud and arrogant voice, 'Knights, or squires, or whatsoever else ye be, you are not to knock any more at the gates of that castle, seeing it is evident, that at such hours as this, either they which are within do repose them, or else are not wont to open fortresses until Phoebus hath spread his beams over the earth; therefore stand back, and expect till it be clear day, and then we will see whether it be just or no that they open their gates unto you.' 'What a devil, what castle or fortress is this,' quoth one of them, 'that it should bind us to use all those circumstances? If thou beest the innkeeper, command that the door be opened; for we are travellers that will tarry no longer than to bait our horses and away, for we ride in post haste.' 'Doth it seem to you, gentlemen,' quoth Don Quixote, 'that I look like an innkeeper?' 'I know not what thou lookest like,' answered the other, 'but well I know that thou speakest madly, in calling this inn a castle.' 'It is a castle,' replied Don Quixote, 'yea, and that one of the best in this province, and it hath people within it which have had a sceptre in hand, and a crown on their head.' 'It were better said quite contrary,' replied the traveller, 'the sceptre on the head, and the crown in the hand; but perhaps (and so it may well be) there is some company of players within, who do very usually hold the sceptres and wear those crowns whereof thou talkest; for in such a paltry inn as this is, and where I hear so little noise, I cannot believe any one to be lodged worthy to wear a crown or bear a sceptre.' 'Thou knowest but little of the world,' replied Don Quixote, 'seeing thou dost so much ignore the chances that are wont to befall in chivalry.' The fellows of him that entertained this prolix dialogue with Don Quixote waxed weary to hear them speak idly so long together, and therefore turned again to knock with great fury at the door, and that in such sort as they not only waked the innkeeper, but also all the guests, and so he arose to demand their pleasure.

In the meanwhile it happened that one of the horses whereon they rode drew near to smell Rozinante, that, melancholy and sadly, with his ears cast down, did sustain without moving his outstretched lord; and he being indeed of flesh and blood, although he resembled a block of wood, could not choose but feel it, and turn to smell him again who had thus come to cherish and entertain him; and scarce had he stirred but a thought from thence, when Don Quixote's feet, that were joined, slipt asunder, and, tumbling from the saddle, had doubtlessly fallen to the ground, had he not remained hanging by the arm; a thing that caused him to endure so much pain, as he verily believed that either his wrist was a-cutting, or his arm a-tearing off from his body; and he hung so near to the ground as he touched it with the tops of his toes, all which turned to his prejudice; for, having felt the little which he wanted to the setting of his feet wholly on the earth, he laboured and drew all that he might to reach it; much like unto those that get the strappado, with the condition to touch or not to touch, who are themselves a cause to increase their own torture, by the earnestness wherewith they stretch themselves, deceived by the hope they have to touch the ground if they can stretch themselves but a little farther.

CHAPTER XVII

Wherein Are Prosecuted the Wonderful Adventures of the Inn

SO many were the outcries which Don Quixote made, as the innkeeper opened the door very hastily and affrighted, to see who it was that so roared; and those that stood without did also the same. Maritornes, whom the cries had also awakened, imagining straight what it might be, went into the barn, and, unperceived of any, loosed the halter that sustained Don Quixote, and forthwith he fell to the ground in the presence of the innkeeper and the travellers, who, coming towards him, demanded the occasion why he did so unmeasurably roar. He, without making any answer, took off the halter from his wrist, and, getting up, he leaped upon Rozinante, embraced his target, set his lance into the rest, and, wheeling about a good part of the field, returned with a half-gallop, saying, 'Whosoever shall dare to affirm that I have not been with just title enchanted, if my lady the Princess Micomicona will give me leave to do it, I say that he lies, and I do presently challenge him to combat.' The new travellers were amazed at Don Quixote's words; but the host removed that wonder by informing them what he was, and that they should make no account of his words, for the man was bereft of his wits. Then they demanded of the innkeeper if there had arrived to his inn a young stripling of some fifteen years old or thereabouts, apparelled like a horse-boy, and having such and such marks and tokens; and then gave the very signs of Donna Clara's lover. The host made answer, that there were so many people in his inn as he had taken no notice of him for whom they demanded. But one of them having seen the coach wherein the judge came, said, 'Questionlessly he must be here; for this is the coach that they say he hath followed. Let, therefore, one of us remain at the door, and the rest enter to seek him out; yea, and it will not be from the purpose if one of us ride about without the inn, lest he should make an escape from us by the walls of the yard.' 'We will do so,' said another of them. And thus two of them entered into the house, one stayed at the door, and the other did compass the inn about. The innkeeper beheld all, but could never judge aright the reason why they used all this diligence, although he easily believed that they sought for the youth whose marks they had told unto him.

By this the day was grown clear, and as well by reason thereof, as through the outcries of Don Quixote, all the strangers were awake, and did get up, especially both the ladies, Clara and Dorothea; for the one through fear to have her lover so near, and the other with desire to see him, could sleep but very little all that night. Don Quixote perceiving that none of the four travellers made any account of him, or answered his challenge, was ready to burst with wrath and despite; and if he could any wise have found that it was tolerated by the statutes of chivalry that a knight-errant might have lawfully undertaken any enterprise, having plight his word and faith not to attempt any until he had finished that which he had first promised, he would have assailed them all, and made them maugre their teeth to have answered him. But because it seemed to him not so expedient nor honourable to begin any new adventure until he had installed Micomicona in her kingdom, he was forced to be quiet, expecting to see whereunto the endeavours and diligence of those four travellers tended: the one whereof found out the youth, that he searched, asleep by another lackey, little dreaming that anybody did look for him, and much less would find him out thus. The man drew him by the arm, and said, 'Truly, Don Louis, the habit that you wear answers very well your calling; and the bed whereon you lie the care and tenderness wherewith your mother did nurse you.' The youth hereat rubbed his drowsy eyes, and beheld very leisurely him that did hold him fast, and knew him forthwith to be one of his father's servants, whereat he was so amazed as he could not speak a word for a great while. And the serving-man continuing his speech, said, 'Here is nothing else to be done, Lord Louis, but that you be patient and depart again with us towards home, if you be not pleased to have your father and my lord depart out of this world to the other; for no less may be expected from the woe wherein he rests for your absence.' 'Why, how did my father know,' said Don Louis, 'that I came this way, and in this habit?' 'A student,' answered the other, 'to whom you betrayed your intention, did discover it, moved through the compassion he took to hear your father's lamentations when he found you missing. And so he despatched four of his men in your search; and we are all at your service, more joyful than may be imagined for the good despatch wherewithal we shall return, and carry you to his sight which doth love you so much.' 'That shall be as I please or Heaven will dispose,' said Don Louis. 'What would you please, or what should Heaven dispose of, other than that you agree to return? For certainly you shall not do the contrary, nor is it possible you should.' All these reasons that passed between them both did the lackey that lay by Don Louis hear; and, arising from thence, he went and told all that passed to Don Fernando, Cardenio, and all the rest that were gotten up; to whom he told how the man gave the title of Don to the boy, and recounted the speech he used, and how he would have him return to his father's house, which the youth refused to do. Whereupon, and knowing already what a good voice the heavens had given him, they greatly desired to be more particularly informed what he was, and intended also to help him, if any violence were offered unto him, and therefore went unto the place where he was, and stood contending with his servant.

Dorothea issued by this out of her chamber, and in her company Donna Clara, all perplexed. Dorothea, calling Cardenio aside, told unto him succinctly all the history of the musician and Donna Clara. And he rehearsed to her again all that passed of the serving-men's arrival that came in his pursuit, which he did not speak so low but that Donna Clara overheard him, whereat she endured such alteration as she had fallen to the ground, if Dorothea, running towards her, had not held her up. Cardenio entreated Dorothea to return with the other to her chamber, and he would endeavour to bring the matter to some good pass, which they presently performed. The four that were come in Don Louis his search were by this all of them entered into the inn, and had compassed him about, persuading him that he would, cutting off all delays, return to comfort his father. He answered that he could not do it in any sort until he had finished an adventure, which imported him no less than his life, his honour, and his soul. The servants urged him then, saying, that they would in no sort go back without him, and therefore would carry him home, whether he would or no. 'That shall not you do,' quoth Don Louis, 'if it be not that you carry me home dead.' And in this season all the other gentlemen were come into the contention, but chiefly Cardenio, Don Fernando, and his comrades, the judge, the curate, and the barber, and Don Quixote; for now it seemed to him needless to guard the castle any more. Cardenio, who knew already the history of the youth, demanded of those that would carry him away, what reason did move them to seek to take that lad away against his will. 'We are moved unto it,' answered one of them, 'by this reason, that we shall thereby save his father's life, who for his absence is like to lose it.' To this said Don Louis, 'It is to no end to make relation of mine affairs here. I am free, and will return if I please; and if not, no one shall constrain me to do it perforce.' 'Reason shall constrain you, good sir, to do it,' quoth the man; 'and when that cannot prevail with you, it shall with us, to put that in execution for which we be come and are bound to do.' 'Let us know this affair from the beginning,' said the judge to those men. 'Sir,' quoth one of them, who knew him very well, as his master's next neighbour, 'Master Justice, doth not your worship know this gentleman who is your neighbour's son, and hath absented himself from his father's house, in an habit so undecent and discrepant from his calling, as you may perceive?' The judge beheld him then somewhat more attentively, knew him, and embracing him, said, 'What toys are these, Don Louis; or what cause hath been of efficacy sufficient to move you to come away in this manner and attire, which answers your calling so ill?' The tears stuck then in the young gentleman's eye, and he could not answer a word to the judge, who bade the four serving-men appease themselves, for all things should be done to their satisfaction; and then, taking Don Louis apart, he entreated him to tell him the occasion of that his departure.

And whilst he made this and other demands to the gentleman, they heard a great noise at the inn-door; the cause whereof was, that two guests which had lain there that night, seeing all the people busied to learn the cause of the four horsemen's coming, had thought to have made an escape scot-free, without defraying their expenses; but the innkeeper, who attended his own affairs with more diligence than other men's, did stay them at their going forth, and demanded his money, upbraiding their dishonest resolution with such words as moved them to return him an answer with their fists, which they did so roundly as the poor host was compelled to raise the cry and demand succour. The hostess and her daughter could see no man so free from occupation as Don Quixote; to whom the daughter said, 'I request you, sir knight, by the virtue that God hath given you, to succour my poor father, whom two bad men are grinding like corn.' To this Don Quixote answered very leisurely, and with great gravity, 'Beautiful damsel, your petition cannot prevail at this time, forasmuch as I am hindered from undertaking any other adventure until I have finished one wherein my promise hath engaged me, and all that I can now do in your service is, that which I shall say now unto you: run unto your father, and bid him continue and maintain his conflict manfully, the best that he may, until I demand license of the Princess Micomicona to help him out of his distress; for if she will give it unto me, you may make full account that he is delivered.' 'Sinner that I am,' quoth Maritornes, who was by, and heard what he said, 'before you shall be able to obtain that license of which you speak, my master will be departed to the other world.' 'Work you so, lady,' quoth Don Quixote, 'that I may have the license; for so that I may have it, it will make no great matter whether he be in the other world or no, even from thence would I bring him back again, in despite of the other world itself, if it durst contradict me; or at least I will take such a revenge of those that do send him to the other world, as you shall remain more than contented.' And so, without replying any more, he went and fell on his knees before Dorothea, demanding of her, in knightly and errant phrases, that she would deign to license him to go and succour the constable of that castle, who was then plunged in a deep distress. The princess did grant him leave very willingly; and he presently, buckling on his target, and laying hold on his sword, ran to the inn-door, where yet the two guests stood handsomely tugging the innkeeper. But as soon as he arrived, he stopped and stood still, although Maritornes and the hostess demanded of him twice or thrice the cause of his restiness in not assisting her lord and husband. 'I stay,' quoth Don Quixote, 'because, according to the laws of arms, it is not permitted to me to lay hand to my sword against squire-like men that are not dubbed knights. But call to me here my squire Sancho, for this defence and revenge concerns him as his duty.' This passed at the inn-door, where fists and blows were interchangeably given and taken in the best sort, although to the innkeeper's cost, and to the rage and grief of Maritornes, the hostess, and her daughter, who were like to run wood, beholding Don Quixote's cowardice, and the mischief their master, husband, and father endured. But here let us leave them; for there shall not want one to succour him; or if not, let him suffer, and all those that wittingly undertake things beyond their power and force; and let us turn backward to hear that which Don Louis answered the judge, whom we left somewhat apart with him, demanding the cause of his coming afoot, and in so base array; to which the youth, wringing him hard by the hands, as an argument that some extraordinary grief pinched his heart, and shedding many tears, answered in this manner:

'I know not what else I may tell you, dear sir, but that from this instant that Heaven made us neighbours, and that I saw Donna Clara, your daughter and my lady, I made her commandress of my will; and if yours, my true lord and father, do not hinder it, she shall be my spouse this very day. For her sake have I abandoned my father's house, and for her I donned this attire, to follow her wheresoever she went, as the arrow doth the mark, or the mariner the north star. She is as yet no further acquainted with my desires, than as much as she might understand sometimes by the tears which she saw mine eyes distil afar off. Now, sir, you know the riches and nobility of my descent, and how I am my father's sole heir, and if it seem unto you that these be conditions whereupon you may venture to make me thoroughly happy, accept of me presently for your son-in-law; for if my father, borne away by other his designs, shall not like so well of this good which I have sought out for myself, yet time hath more force to undo and change the affairs than men's will.' Here the amorous gentleman held his peace, and the judge remained astonied as well at the grace and discretion wherewith Don Louis had discovered his affections unto him, as also to see himself in such a pass, that as he knew not what course he might best take in so sudden and unexpected a matter; and therefore he answered no other thing at that time, but only bade him to settle his mind, and entertain the time with his servants, and deal with them to expect that day, because he might have leisure to consider what might be most convenient for all. Don Louis did kiss his hands perforce, and did bathe them with tears, a thing able to move a heart of marble, and much more the judge's, who (as a wise man) did presently perceive how beneficial and honourable was that preferment for his daughter; although he could have wished, if it had been possible, to effect it with the consent of Don Louis his father, who he knew did purpose to have his son made a nobleman of title.

By this time the innkeeper and his guests had agreed, having paid him all that they owed, more by Don Quixote's persuasion and good reasons than by any menaces; and Don Louis his servants expected the end of the judge, his discourse, and his resolution; when the devil (who never sleeps) would have it, at that very time entered into the inn the barber from whom Don Quixote took away the helmet of Mambrino, and Sancho Panza the furniture of the ass, whereof he made an exchange for his own; which barber, leading his beast to the stable, saw Sancho Panza, who was mending some part of the pannel; and as soon as he had eyed him, he knew him, and presently set upon Sancho, saying, 'Ah, sir thief, have I found you here, with all the furniture whereof you robbed me?' Sancho, that saw himself thus assaulted unexpectedly, and had heard the disgraceful terms which the other used, laying fast hold on the pannel with the one hand, gave the barber such a buffet with the other, as he bathed all his teeth in blood. But yet, for all that, the barber held fast his grip of the pannel, and therewithal cried out so loud, as all those that were in the house came to the noise and conflict; and he said, 'I call for the king and justice, for this thief and robber by the highways goeth about to kill me, because I seek to recover mine own goods.' 'Thou liest,' quoth Sancho, 'for I am not a robber by the highways; for my lord Don Quixote won those spoils in a good war.' By this time Don Quixote himself was come thither, not a little proud to see how well his squire defended himself, and offended his adversary; and therefore he accounted him from thenceforth to be a man of valour, and purposed in his mind to dub him knight on the first occasion that should be offered, because he thought that the order of knighthood would be well employed by him.

Among other things that the barber said in the discourse of his contention, this was one: 'Sirs, this pannel is as certainly mine as the death which I owe unto God, and I know it as well as if I had bred it; and there is my ass in the stable, who will not permit me to tell a lie; or otherwise, do but try the pannel on him, and if it fit him not justly I am content to remain infamous. And I can say more, that the very day wherein they took my pannel from me, they robbed me likewise of a new brazen basin, which was never used, and cost me a crown.' Here Don Quixote could no longer contain himself from speaking; and so, thrusting himself between them two, and putting them asunder, and causing the pannel to be laid publicly on the ground until the truth were decided, he said, 'To the end that you may perceive the clear and manifest error wherein this good squire lives, see how he calls that a basin which is, was, and shall be, the helmet of Mambrino, which I took away perforce from him in fair war, and made myself lord thereof in a lawful and warlike manner. About the pannel I will not contend; for that which I can say therein is, that my squire Sancho demanded leave of me to take away the furniture of this vanquished coward's horse, that he might adorn his own withal. I gave him authority to do it, and he took them. And for his converting thereof from a horse's furniture into a pannel, I can give none other reason than the ordinary one, to wit, that such transformations are usually seen in the successes of chivalry; for confirmation whereof, friend Sancho, run speedily and bring me out the helmet which this good man avoucheth to be a basin.' 'By my faith, sir,' quoth Sancho, 'if we have no better proof of our intention than that which you say, I say that the helmet of Mambrino is as arrant a basin as this good man's furniture is a pannel.' 'Do what I command,' said Don Quixote: 'I cannot believe that all the things in this castle will be guided by enchantment.' Sancho went for the basin, and brought it: and as soon as Don Quixote saw it, he took it in his hands, and said, 'See, sirs, with what face can this impudent squire affirm that this is a basin, and not the helmet that I have mentioned? and I swear to you all, by the order of knighthood which I profess, that this is the very same helmet which I won from him, without having added or taken anything from it.' 'That it is, questionless,' quoth Sancho; 'for since the time that my lord won it until now, he never fought but one battle with it, when he delivered the unlucky chained men; and but for this basin-helmet, he had not escaped so free as he did, so thick a shower of stones rained all the time of that conflict.'

CHAPTER XVIII

Wherein Are Decided the Controversies of the Helmet of Mambrino and of the Pannel, with Other Strange and Most True Adventures

'GOOD sirs,' quoth the barber, 'what do you think of that which is affirmed by these gentlemen, who yet contend that this is not a basin, but a helmet?' 'He that denies it,' quoth Don Quixote, 'I will make him know that he lies, if he be a knight; and if he be but a squire, that he lies and lies again a thousand times.' Our barber, who was also present, as one that knew Don Quixote's humour very well, would fortify his folly and make the jest pass yet a little further, to the end that they all might laugh; and therefore, speaking to the other barber, he said, 'Sir barber, or what else you please, know that I am also of your occupation, and have had my writ of examination and approbation in that trade more than these thirty years, and am one that knows very well all the instruments of barbery whatsoever; and have been besides, in my youthful days, a soldier; and do therefore likewise know what is a helmet, and what a morion, and what a close castle, and other things touching warfare—I mean all the kind of arms that a soldier ought to have; and therefore I say (still submitting myself to the better opinion) that this piece which is laid here before us, and which this good knight holds in his hand, not only is not a barber's basin, but also is so far from being one as is white from black, or verity from untruth; yet do I withal affirm that although it is an helmet, yet it is not a complete helmet.' 'No, truly,' quoth Don Quixote, 'for it wants the half, to wit, the nether part and the beaver.' 'It is very true,' quoth the curate, who very well understood his friend the barber his intention; and the same did Cardenio, Don Fernando, and the rest of his fellows confirm; yea, and even the judge himself, had not Don Louis his affair perplexed his thoughts, would, for his part, have holpen the jest well forward; but the earnestness of that affair held his mind so busied, as he little or nothing attended the pastime. 'Lord have mercy upon me!' quoth the other barber, then half beside himself; 'and is it possible that so many honourable men should say that this is no basin, but a helmet? This is a thing able to strike admiration into a whole university, how discreet soever it were. It is enough; if this basin must needs be a helmet, the pannel must also be a horse's furniture, as this gentleman says.' 'To me it seems a pannel,' quoth Don Quixote; 'but, as I have said, I will not meddle with it, nor determine whether it be a pannel or the caparison of a horse.'

'Therein is nothing else to be done,' said the curate, 'but that Sir Don Quixote say at once; for in these matters of chivalry, all these noblemen and myself do give unto him the prick and the prize.' 'I swear unto you by Jove, good sirs,' quoth Don Quixote, 'that so many and so strange are the things which have befallen me in this castle, these two times that I have lodged therein, as I dare avouch nothing affirmatively of anything that shall be demanded of me concerning the things contained in it; for I do infallibly imagine that all the adventures which pass in it are guided by enchantment. The first time, I was very much vexed by an enchanted Moor that was in it, and Sancho himself sped not very well with the Moors' followers and yesternight I stood hanging almost two hours' space by this arm, without knowing how, or how that disgrace befel me; so that for me to meddle now in so confused and difficult a matter, as to deliver mine opinion, were to pass a rash judgment. So that they which say that this is a basin and no helmet, I have already made answer; but whether this be a pannel or furniture, I dare pronounce no definitive sentence, but only remit it to your discreet opinions: perhaps because you are not dubbed knights as I am, the enchantments of this place will have no power over you, and your understanding shall be freed and able to judge of the things in this castle really and truly, and not as they seem unto me.' 'Doubtless,' quoth Don Fernando, 'Don Quixote says very well that the definition of this case belongs unto us; and therefore, and because we may proceed in it upon the better and more solid grounds, I will secretly take the suffrages of all those gentlemen, and afterwards make a clear and full relation of what shall come of them.'

To those that knew Don Quixote his humour, this was a matter of marvellous laughter and sport; but to such as were not acquainted therewithal, it seemed the greatest folly of the world, especially to Don Louis and his four servants, and with other three passengers that had arrived by chance to the inn, and seemed to be troopers of the holy brotherhood, as indeed they were. But he that was most of all beside himself for wrath was the barber whose basin they had transformed before his own face into the helmet of Mambrino, and whose pannel he made full account should likewise be turned into the rich furniture and equipage of a great horse. All of them laughed heartily to see Don Fernando go up and down, taking the suffrages of this man and that, and rounding every one of them in the ear, that they might declare in secret whether that was a pannel or a furniture for which such deadly contention had passed. After that he had taken the suffrages of so many as knew Don Quixote, he said very loudly, 'The truth is, good fellow, that I grow weary of demanding so many opinions; for I can no sooner demand of any man what I desire to know, but they forthwith answer me, how it is mere madness to affirm that this is the pannel of an ass, but rather the furniture of a horse, yea, and of a chief horse of service; and therefore you must have patience; for in despite both of you and of your ass, and notwithstanding your weak allegations and worse proofs, it is, and will continue, the furniture of a great horse.' 'Let me never enjoy a place in heaven,' quoth the barber, 'if you all be not deceived; and so may my soul appear before God, as it appears to me to be a pannel, and no horse furniture. But the law carries it away, and so farewell it. And yet surely I am not drunk; for unless it be by sinning, my fast hath not been broken this day.'

The follies which the barber uttered stirred no less laughter among them than did the roarings of Don Quixote, who then spoke in this manner: 'Here is now no more to be done, but that every man take up his own goods, and to whom God hath given them, let St. Peter give his blessing.' Then said one of the four serving-men, 'If this were not a jest premeditated, and made of purpose, I could not persuade myself that men of so good understanding as all these are, or seem to be, should dare to say and affirm that this is not a basin, nor that a pannel; but seeing that they aver it so constantly, I have cause to suspect that it cannot be without mystery, to affirm a thing so contrary to that which very truth itself, and experience, demonstrates unto us; for I do vow' (and, saying so, he rapped out a round oath or two) 'that as many as are in the world should never make me believe that this is no basin, nor that no pannel of a he-ass.' 'It might as well be of a she-ass,' quoth the curate. 'That comes all but to one,' replied the other; 'for the question consists not therein, but whether it be a pannel or not, as you do avouch.' Then one of the troopers of the Holy Brotherhood, who had listened to their disputation, and was grown full of choler to hear such an error maintained, said, 'It is as very a pannel, as my father is my father; and he that hath said, or shall say the contrary, is, I believe, turned into a grape.' 'Thou liest like a clownish knave!' quoth Don Quixote; and, lifting up his javelin, which he always held in his hand, he discharged such a blow at the trooper's pate, as if he had not avoided, it would have thrown him to the ground. The javelin was broken by the force of the fall into splinters; and the other troopers, seeing their fellow misused, cried out for help and assistance for that Holy Brotherhood. The innkeeper, who also was one of the same fraternity, ran in for his rod of justice and his sword, and then stood by his fellows. Don Louis's four servants compassed him about, lest he should attempt to escape whilst the tumult endured. The barber, seeing all the house turned upside down, laid hand again upon his pannel, and the same did Sancho.

Don Quixote set hand to his sword, and assaulted the troopers. Don Louis cried to his serving-men that they should leave him, and go to help Don Quixote, Cardenio, and Don Fernando; for all of them took Don Quixote's part. The curate cried out, the hostess shrieked, her daughter squeaked, Maritornes howled, Dorothea stood confused, Lucinda amazed, and Donna Clara dismayed; the barber battered Sancho, and Sancho pounded him again. Don Louis, on whom one of his serving-men had presumed to lay hands, and hold him by the arm, gave him such a pash on the mouth as he broke his teeth, and then the judge took him into his own protection. Don Fernando had gotten one of the troopers under his feet, where he stood belabouring him at pleasure. The innkeeper renewed his outcry, and reinforced his voice, demanding aid for the Holy Brotherhood. So that all the inn seemed nothing else but plaints, cries, screeches, confusions, fears, dreads, disgraces, slashes, buffets, blows, spurnings, and effusion of blood.

In the midst of the chaos and labyrinth of things, Don Quixote began to imagine and fancy to himself that he was at that very time plunged up to the ears in the discord and conflict of King Agramante his camp; and therefore he said, with a voice that made all the inn to tremble, 'All of you, hold your hands; all of you, put up your swords; all of you, be quiet and listen to me, if any of you desire to continue alive.' That great and monstrous voice made them all stand still; thereupon he thus proceeded: 'Did not I tell you, sirs, that this castle was enchanted, and that some legion of devils did inhabit it? In confirmation whereof, I would have you but to note with your own eyes how the very discord of King Agramante's camp is transferred hither, and passed over among us. Look how there they fight for the sword, here for the horse, yonder for the eagle, beyond for the helmet; and all of us fight, and none of us know for what. Come therefore, you Master Justice, and you master curate, and let the one represent King Agramante, and the other King Sobrino, and make peace and atonement among us; for I swear by almighty Jove, that it is great wrong and pity that so many noblemen as we are here should be slain for so slight causes.'

The troopers, which did not understand Don Quixote's manner of speech, and saw themselves very ill-handled by Don Fernando and Cardenio, would in no wise be pacified. But the barber was content, by reason that in the conflict both his beard and his pannel had been torn in pieces. Sancho to his master's voice was quickly obedient, as became a dutiful servant. Don Louis his four serving-men stood also quiet, seeing how little was gained in being other; only the innkeeper persisted as before, affirming that punishment was due unto the insolences of that madman, who every foot confounded and disquieted his inn. Finally, the rumour was pacified for that time; the pannel remained for a horse furniture until the day of judgment, the basin for a helmet, and the inn for a castle—in Don Quixote's imagination.

All the broils being now appeased, and all men accorded by the judge's and curate's persuasions, then began Don Louis his servants again to urge him to depart with them, and whilst he and they debated the matter, the judge communicated the whole to Don Fernando, Cardenio, and the curate, desiring to know their opinions concerning that affair, and telling them all that Don Louis had said to him; whereupon they agreed that Don Fernando should tell the serving-men what he himself was, and how it was his pleasure that Don Louis should go with him to Andalusia, where he should be cherished and accounted of by the marquis his brother, according unto his calling and deserts; for he knew well Don Louis his resolution to be such, as he would not return into his father's presence at that time, although they tore him into pieces. Don Fernando his quality and Don Louis his intention being understood by the four, they agreed among themselves that three of them should go back to bear the tidings of all that had passed to his father, and the other should abide there to attend on him, and never to leave him until they returned to fetch him home, or knew what else his father would command: and in this sort was that monstrous bulk of division and contention reduced to some form by the authority of Agramante and the wisdom of King Sobrino.

But the enemy of concord and the adversary of peace finding his projects to be thus illuded and condemned, and seeing the little fruit he had gotten by setting them all by the ears, resolved once again to try his wits, and stir up new discords and troubles, which befel in this manner. The troopers were quieted, having understood the calling of those with whom they had contended, and retired themselves from the brawl, knowing that howsoever the cause succeeded, they themselves should have still the worst end of the staff. But one of them, who was the very same whom Don Fernando had buffeted so well, remembered how among many other warrants that he had to apprehend malefactors, he had one for Don Quixote, whom the Holy Brotherhood had commanded to be apprehended for freeing of the galley slaves (a disaster which Sancho had beforehand with very great reason feared). As soon as he remembered it, he would needs try whether the signs that were given him of Don Quixote did agree with his person; and so, taking out of his bosom a scroll of parchment wherein they were written, he presently found out that which he looked for; and, reading it a while very leisurely, as one that was himself no great clerk, at every other word he looked on Don Quixote, and confronted the marks of his warrant with those of Don Quixote's face, and found that he was infallibly the man that was therein mentioned. And scarce was he persuaded that it was he, when, folding up his parchment, and holding the warrant in his left hand, he laid hold on Don Quixote's collar with the right, so strongly as he could hardly breathe, and cried out aloud, saying, 'Aid for the Holy Brotherhood! and that you may perceive how I am in good earnest, read that warrant, wherein you shall find that this robber by the highway side is to be apprehended.' The curate took the warrant, and perceived very well that the trooper said true, and that the marks agreed very near with Don Quixote's; who, seeing himself so abused by that base rascal, as he accounted him, his choler being mounted to her height, and all the bones of his body crashing for wrath, he seized as well as he could with both his hands on the trooper's throat, and that in such sort as if he had not been speedily succoured by his fellows, he had there left his life ere Don Quixote would have abandoned his grip.

The innkeeper, who of force was to assist his fellow in office, forthwith repaired unto his aid. The hostess, seeing her husband re-enter into contentions and brabbles, raised a new cry, whose burden was borne by her daughter and Maritornes, asking succour of Heaven and those that were present. Sancho, seeing all that passed, said, 'By the Lord, all that my master hath said of the enchantments of this castle is true; for it is not possible for a man to live quietly in it one hour together.'

Don Fernando parted the trooper and Don Quixote, and with the goodwill of both, unfastened their holds. But yet the troopers for all this desisted not to require their prisoner, and withal, that they should help to get him tied and absolutely rendered unto their wills; for so it was requisite for the King and the Holy Brotherhood, in whose name they did again demand their help and assistance for the arresting of that public robber and spoiler of people in common paths and highways.

Don Quixote laughed to hear them speak so idly, as he imagined, and said, with very great gravity, 'Come hither, you filthy, base extractions of the dunghill! dare you term the loosening of the enchained, the freeing of prisoners, the assisting of the wretched, the raising of such as are fallen, and the supplying of those that are in want,—dare you, I say, term these things robbing on the highway? O infamous brood! worthy, for your base and vile conceit, that Heaven should never communicate with you the valour included in the exercise of chivalry, we give you to understand the sin and error wherein you are, by not adoring the very shadow, how much more the assistance of a knight-errant? Come hither, O you that be no troopers, but thieves in troop, and robbers of highways by permission of the Holy Brotherhood! come hither, I say, and tell me, who was that jolt-head that did subscribe or ratify a warrant for the attaching of such a knight as I am? Who was he that knows not how knights-errant are exempted from all tribunals? and how that their sword is the law, their valour the bench, and their wills the statutes of their courts? I say again, what madman was he that knows not how that no privilege of gentry enjoys so many pre-eminences, immunities, and exemptions as that which a knight-errant acquires the day wherein he is dubbed and undertakes the rigorous exercise of arms? What knight-errant did ever pay tribute, subsidy, tallage, carriage, or passage over water? What tailor ever had money for making his clothes? What constable ever lodged him in castle, that made him after to pay for the shot? What king hath not placed him at his own table? What damsel hath not fallen in love with him, and permitted him to use her as he liked? And finally, what knight-errant was there ever, is, or ever shall be in the world, which hath not the courage himself alone to give four hundred blows with a cudgel to four hundred troopers that shall presume to stand before him in hostile manner?'

CHAPTER XIX

In Which Is Finished the Notable Adventure of the Troopers, and the Great Ferocity of Our Knight, Don Quixote, and How He Was Enchanted

WHILST Don Quixote said this, the curate laboured to persuade the troopers how the knight was distracted, as they themselves might collect by his works and words, and therefore it would be to no end to prosecute their design any further, seeing that although they did apprehend and carry him away he would be presently delivered again as a madman. To this, he that had the warrant made answer, that it concerned him not to determine whether he was mad or no, but only to obey and execute his superior's command; and that being once prisoner, they might deliver him three hundred times and if it were their good pleasure. 'For all that,' quoth the curate, 'you may not carry him with you at this time; nor, as I suppose, will he suffer himself to be taken.' To be brief, the curate said so much, and Don Quixote played so many mad pranks, as the troopers themselves would have proved greater fools than he if they had not manifestly discerned his defect of judgment; and therefore they held it to be the best course to let him alone, yea, and be compounders of peace and amity between Sancho Panza and the barber, which still continued their most rancorous and deadly contention. Finally, they, as the officers of justice, did mediate the cause, and were arbiters thereof in such sort, as both the parties remained, though not wholly contented, yet in some sort satisfied, for they only made them exchange their pannels, but not their girths or headstalls.

As touching Mambrino's helmet, the curate did unawares to Don Quixote give to the barber eight reals by it, and the barber gave back unto him an acquittance of the receipt thereof, an everlasting release of all actions concerning it. These two discords, which were the most principal and of most consequence, being thus accorded, it only rested that three of Don Louis his serving-men would be content to return home, and leave the fourth to accompany his master whither Don Fernando pleased to carry him. And as good hap and better fortune had already begun to break lances, and facilitate difficulties, in the favour of the lovers and worthy persons of the inn, so did it resolve to proceed forward, and give a prosperous success unto all; for the serving-men were content to do whatsoever their master would have them: whereat Donna Clara was so cheerful, as no one beheld her face in that season but might read therein the inward contentment of her mind. Zoraida, although she did not very well understand all the successes of the things she had seen, yet was she interchangeably grieved and cheered according to the shows made by the rest, but chiefly by her Spaniard, on whom her eyes were always fixed, and all the affects of her mind depended. The innkeeper, who did not forget the recompense made by the curate to the barber, demanded of him Don Quixote's expenses, and satisfaction for the damage he had done to his wine-bags, and the loss of his wine, swearing that neither Rozinante nor Sancho his ass should depart out of the inn until he were paid the very last farthing. All was quietly ended by the curate; and Don Fernando paid the whole sum, although the judge had also most liberally offered to do it; and all of them remained afterwards in such quietness and peace, as the inn did no longer resemble the discorded camp of Agramante, as Don Quixote termed it, but rather enjoyed the very peace and tranquillity of the Emperor Octavian's time; for all which the common opinion was, that thanks were justly due to the sincere proceeding and great eloquence of master curate, and to the incomparable liberality and goodness of Don Fernando. Don Quixote, perceiving himself free, and delivered from so many difficulties and brabbles wherewithal as well he as his esquire had been perplexed, held it high time to prosecute his commenced voyage, and bring to an end the great adventure unto which he was called and chosen. Therefore, with resolute determination to depart, he went and cast himself on his knees before Dorothea, who, not permitting him to speak until he arose, he to obey her stood up, and said, 'It is a common proverb, beautiful lady, that "diligence is the mother of good hap"; and in many and grave affairs experience hath showed that the solicitude and sore of the suitor oft brings a doubtful matter to a certain and happy end; but this truth appears in nothing more clearly than in matters of war, wherein celerity and expedition prevent the enemy's designs, and obtain the victory before an adversary can put himself in defence. All this I say, high and worthy lady, because it seems to me that our abode in this castle is nothing profitable, and may therewithal turn so far to our hindrance as we may palpably feel it one day; for who knows but that your enemy, the giant, hath learned by spies, or other secret intelligence and means, how I mean to come and destroy him, and (opportunity favouring his designs) that he may have fortified himself in some inexpugnable castle or fortress, against the strength whereof neither mine industry nor the force of mine invincible arm can much prevail. Wherefore, dear lady, let us prevent, as I have said, by our diligence, and let us presently depart unto the place whereunto we are called by our good fortune, which shall be deferred no longer than I am absent from your highness's foe.' Here he held his peace, and did expect, with great gravity, the beautiful princess's answer, who, with *débonnaire* countenance, and a style accommodated unto Don Quixote, returned him this answer: 'I do gratify and thank, sir knight, the desire you show to assist me in this my great need, which denotes very clearly the great care you have to favour orphans and distressed wights; and I beseech God that your good desires and mine may be accomplished, to the end that you may see how there are some thankful women on earth. As touching my departure, let it be forthwith, for I have none other will than that which is yours; therefore you may dispose of me at your own pleasure; for she that hath once committed the defence of her person unto you, and hath put into your hands the restitution of her estate, ought not to seek to do any other thing than that which your wisdom shall ordain.' 'In the name of God,' quoth Don Quixote, 'seeing that your highness doth so humble yourself unto me, I will not lose the occasion of exalting it, and installing it again in the throne of your inheritance. Let our departure be incontinent; for my desires, and the way, and that which they call the danger that is in delay, do spur me on. And seeing that Heaven never created, nor hell ever beheld, any man that could affright me or make a coward of me, go therefore, Sancho, and saddle Rozinante, and empannel thine ass, and make ready the queen's palfrey, and let us take leave of the constable and those other lords, and depart away from hence instantly.'

Then Sancho, who was present at all this, wagging of his head, said, 'O my lord, my lord! how much more knavery (be it spoken with the pardon of all honest kerchiefs) is there in the little village than is talked of!' 'What ill can there be in any village, or in all the cities of the world, able to impair my credit, thou villain?' 'If thou be angry,' quoth Sancho, 'I will hold my tongue, and omit to say that which, by the duty of a good squire and of an honest servant, I am bound to tell you.' 'Say what thou wilt,' quoth Don Quixote, 'so thy words be not addressed to make me afraid; for if thou beest frighted, thou dost only like thyself; and if I be devoid of terror, I also do that which I ought.' 'It is not that which I mean,' quoth Sancho, 'but that I do hold, for most sure and certain, that this lady which calls herself queen of the great kingdom of Micomicon, is no more a queen than my mother; for if she were what she says, she would not, at every corner and at every turning of a hand, be billing as she is with one that is in this good company.' Dorothea blushed at Sancho's words; for it was true, indeed, that her spouse, Don Fernando, would now and then privately steal from her lips some part of the reward which his desires did merit (which Sancho espying, it seemed to him that that kind of wanton familiarity was more proper to courtesans than becoming the queen of so great a kingdom), and yet she neither could nor would reply unto him, but let him continue his speech, as followeth: 'This I do say, good my lord,' quoth he, 'to this end: that if, after we have run many ways and courses, and endured bad nights and worse days, he that is in this inn sporting himself, shall come to gather the fruit of our labours, there is no reason to hasten me thus to saddle Rozinante, or empannel the ass, or make ready the palfrey, seeing it would be better that we stayed still, and that every whore spun, and we fell to our victuals.'

O God! how great was the fury that inflamed Don Quixote when he heard his squire speak so respectlessly! I say it was so great that, with a shaking voice, a faltering tongue, and the fire sparkling out of his eyes, he said, 'O villanous peasant! rash, unmannerly, ignorant, rude, blasphemous, bold murmurer and detractor! hast thou presumed to speak such words in my presence, and in that of these noble ladies? and hast thou dared to entertain such rash and dishonest surmises into thy confused imagination? Depart out of my sight, thou monster of nature, storehouse of untruths, armoury of falsehood, sink of roguery, inventor of villany, publisher of ravings, and the enemy of that decency which is to be used towards royal persons! Away, villain! and never appear before me, under pain of mine indignation!' And, saying so, he bended his brows, filled up his cheeks, looked about him on every side, and struck a great blow with his right foot on the ground—all manifest tokens of the rage which inwardly fretted him. At which words and furious gestures, poor Sancho remained so greatly affrighted, as he could have wished in that instant that the earth, opening under his feet, would swallow him up, and knew not what to do, but turn his back, and get him out of his lord's most furious presence. But the discreet Dorothea, who was now so well schooled in Don Quixote's humour, to mitigate his ire, said unto him, 'Be not offended, good Sir Knight of the Sad Face, at the idle words which your good squire hath spoken; for perhaps he hath not said them without some ground; nor of his good understanding and Christian mind can it be suspected that he would wittingly slander or accuse anybody falsely; and therefore we must believe, without all doubt, that as in this castle, as you yourself have said, sir knight, all things are represented, and succeed by manner of enchantment; I say it might befall that Sancho may have seen, by diabolical illusion, that which he says he beheld, so much to the prejudice of my reputation.'

'I vow by the omnipotent Jove,' quoth Don Quixote, 'that your highness hath hit the very prick, and that some wicked vision appeared to this sinner, my man Sancho, that made him to see that which otherwise were impossible to be seen by any other way than that of enchantment; for I know very well the great goodness and simplicity of that poor wretch is such as he knows not how to invent a lie on anybody living.' 'It is even so, and so it shall be,' quoth Don Fernando; 'and therefore, good sir Don

Quixote, you must pardon him, and reduce him again to the bosom of your good grace, *sicut erat in principio,* and before the like visions did distract his sense.' Don Quixote answered that he did willingly pardon him. And therefore the curate went for Sancho, who returned very humbly, and, kneeling down on his knees, demanded his lord's hand, which he gave unto him; and after that he had permitted him to kiss it, he gave him his blessing, saying, 'Now thou shalt finally know, Sancho, that which I have told thee divers times, how that all the things of this castle are made by way of enchantment.' 'So do I verily believe,' said Sancho, 'except that of the canvassing in the blanket, which really succeeded by an ordinary and natural way.' 'Do not believe that,' said Don Quixote; 'for if it were so, I would both then, and also now, have taken a dire revenge; but neither then nor now could I ever see any on whom I might revenge that thine injury.' All of them desired greatly to know what that accident of the blanket was; and then the innkeeper recounted it, point by point, the flights that Sancho Panza made, whereat they all did laugh not a little; and Sancho would have been ashamed no less, if his lord had not anew persuaded him that it was a mere enchantment. And yet Sancho's madness was never so great as to believe that it was not a real truth verily befallen him, without any colour or mixture of fraud or illusion, but that he was tossed by persons of flesh, blood, and bone, and not by dreamed and imagined shadows or spirits, as his lord believed, and so constantly affirmed.

Two days were now expired when all that noble company had sojourned in the inn; and then, it seeming unto them high time to depart, they devised how, without putting Dorothea and Don Fernando to the pains to turn back with Don Quixote to his village, under pretence of restoring the Queen Micomicona, the curate and barber might carry him back as they desired, and endeavour to have him cured of his folly in his own house. And their invention was this: they agreed with one, who by chance passed by that way with a team of oxen, to carry him in this order following: They made a thing like a cage, of timber, so big as that Don Quixote might sit or lie in it at his ease; and presently after, Don Fernando and his fellows, with Don Louis his servants, the troopers, and the innkeeper, did all of them, by master curate's direction, cover their faces, and disguise themselves, every one as he might best, so that they might seem to Don Quixote other people than such as he had seen in the castle. And this being done, they entered with very great silence into the place where he slept, and took his rest after the related conflicts; and, approaching him who slept securely, not fearing any such accident, and laying hold on him very strongly, they tied his hands and his feet very strongly, so that when he started out of his sleep he could not stir himself, nor do any other thing than admire and wonder at those strange shapes that he saw standing before him; and presently he fell into the conceit which his continual and distracted imagination had already suggested unto him, believing that all those strange figures were the spirits and shadows of that enchanted castle, and that he himself was now without doubt enchanted, seeing he could neither move nor defend himself. All this succeeded just as the curate, who plotted the jest, made full account it would. Only Sancho, among all those that were present, was in his right sense and shape; and although he wanted but little to be sick of his lord's disease, yet for all that he knew all those counterfeit ghosts; but he would not once unfold his lips, until he might see the end of that surprisal and imprisonment of his master; who likewise spoke never a word, but only looked to see what would be the period of his disgrace; which was that, bringing him to the cage, they shut him within, and afterwards nailed the bars thereof so well as they could not be easily broken. They presently mounted him upon their shoulders; and as he issued out at the chamber door, they heard as dreadful a voice as the barber could devise (not he of the pannel, but the other), which said, 'O Knight of the Sad Countenance! be not grieved at the imprisonment whereinto thou art led; for so it must be, that thereby the adventure, into which thy great force and valour hath thrust thee, may be the more speedily ended; and ended it will be when the furious Manchegan lion and the white Tobosian dove shall be united in one; and after they have humbled their lofty crest unto the soft yoke of wedlock, from whose wonderful comfort shall issue to the light of the orb fierce whelps, which shall imitate the raunching paws of their valorous father. And this shall be before the pursuer of the fugitive nymph do, with his swift and natural course, make two turns in visitation of the glittering images. And thou, O the most noble and obedient squire that ever had sword at a girdle, beard on a face, or dent in a nose! let it not dismay or discontent thee to see carried away before thy eyes the flower of all chivalry-errant; for very speedily, if it please the Framer of the world, thou shalt see thyself so exalted and ennobled as thou shalt scarce know thyself. Nor shalt thou be defrauded of the promises made unto thee by thy noble lord; and I do assure thee, from the wise Mentironiana, that thy wages shall be paid thee, as thou shalt quickly see in effect. And therefore follow the steps of the valorous and enchanted knight; for it is necessary that thou go to the place where you both shall stay. And because I am not permitted to say more, farewell; for I do return, I well know whither.' Towards the end of this prophecy he lifted up his voice, and afterwards lessened it, with so slender an accent that even those which were acquainted with the jest almost believed what they had heard.

Don Quixote was very much comforted by the prophecy; for he presently apprehended the whole sense thereof, and perceived how he was promised in marriage his beloved Dulcinea of Toboso, from whose happy womb should sally the whelps, which were his sons, to the eternal glory of the Mancha. And, believing all this most firmly, he elevated his voice, and, breathing forth a great sigh, thus said: 'O thou, whatsoever thou beest, which hath prognosticated so great good to me, I desire thee to request, in my name, the wise man who hath charge to record mine acts, that he permit me not to perish in this prison, to which they now do carry me, before the accomplishment of so joyful and incomparable promises as now have been made unto me; for, so that this may befall, I will account the pains of my prison a glory, and the chains that environ me an ease; and will not esteem this bed whereon I am laid a hard field of battle, but a soft tick and a most fortunate lodging. And, as concerning the consolation of my squire Sancho Panza, I trust in his goodness and honest proceeding, that he will not abandon me in good or bad fortune; for though it should fall out, through his or my hard hap, that I shall not be able to bestow on him an island, or other equivalent thing, as I have promised, his wages at least cannot be lost; for in my testament, which is made already, I have set down what he is to have, though not conformably to his many good services, yet according to my possibility.' Sancho Panza bowed his head with great reverence, and kissed both his hands, for one alone he could not, by reason they were bound together; and presently those visions did lift up the cage and accommodate it on the team of oxen.

CHAPTER XX

Wherein Is Prosecuted the Manner of Don Quixote's Enchantment, with Other Famous Occurrences

WHEN Don Quixote saw himself to be encaged after that manner, and placed in the cart, he said, 'I have read many and very grave histories of knights-errant, but I never read, saw, nor heard that they were wont to carry knights-errant enchanted after this manner, and with the leisure that those slothful and heavy beasts do threaten; for they were ever accustomed to be carried in the air with wonderful speed, shut in some dusky and obscure cloud, or in some fiery chariot, or on some hippogriff, or some other such like beast; but that they carry me now on a team of oxen, I protest it drives me into a great amazement; but perhaps both chivalry, and the enchantments of these our times, do follow a course different from those of former ages; and peradventure it may also be, that as I am a new knight in the world, and the first that hath again revived the now neglected and forgotten exercise of arms, so have they also newly invented other kinds of enchantments, and other manners of carrying away enchanted knights. What dost thou think of this, son Sancho?' 'I know not,' quoth Sancho, 'what to think, because I am not so well seen in scriptures-errant as you are; but for all this I durst affirm and swear, that these visions which go up and down in this place are not altogether catholic.' 'Catholics! my father!' quoth Don Quixote; 'how can they be catholics, when they be all devils, which have assumed phantastical bodies to come and put me into this state? And if thou wilt prove the truth hereof, do but touch and feel them, and thou shalt find them to have no bodies but of air, and that they consist of nothing but an outward appearance.' 'Now, by my faith, sir,' quoth Sancho, 'I have already touched them, and find this devil that goeth there so busily up and down, both plump and soft-fleshed; and that he hath besides another property very different from that which I have heard say devils have; for it is said that they smell all of brimstone and other filthy things, but one may feel, at least half a league off, the amber that this devil smells of.' Sancho spoke this of Don Fernando, who belike, as lords of his rank are wont, had his attire perfumed with amber.

'Marvel not thereat, friend Sancho,' quoth Don Quixote; 'for the devils are very crafty, and although they bring smells or perfumes about them, yet they themselves smell nothing, because they are spirits; or if they do smell aught, it is not good, but evil and stinking savours: the reason is, for that as they do always bear, wheresoever they be, their hell about them, and can receive no kind of ease of their torments, and good smells be things that delight and please, it is not possible that they can smell any good thing; and if it seem to thee that that devil whom thou dost mention smells of amber, either thou art deceived, or he would deceive thee, by making thee to think that he is no devil.' All these discourses passed between the master and the man, the whilst Don Fernando and Cardenio, fearing lest Sancho should find out the deceit whereto he was already come very near, resolved to hasten the knight's departure; and therefore, calling the innkeeper aside, they commanded him to saddle Rozinante, and empannel Sancho's beast, which he did with all expedition. And the curate agreed with the troopers for so much a day, to accompany him unto his village. Cardenio hanged, at the pommel of Rozinante's saddle, the target on the one side, and on the other the basin; and by signs he commanded Sancho to get up on his ass, and to lead Rozinante along by the bridle, and afterwards placed on either side of the cart two troopers, with their firelocks.

But before the cart departed, the hostess, her daughter, and Maritornes came out to bid Don Quixote farewell, feigning that they wept for sorrow of his disaster; to whom Don Quixote said, 'My good ladies, do not weep; for all these mischances are incident to those which profess that which I do, and if these calamities had not befallen me, I would never have accounted myself for a famous knight-errant; for the like chances never happen to knights of little name or renown, because there [is] none in the world that makes any mention of them; but they often befall to the valorous, who have emulators of their virtue and valour, both many princes and many other knights, that strive by indirect means to destroy them. But for all that, virtue is so potent, as by herself alone, in spite of all the necromancy that ever the first inventor thereof, Zoroaster, knew, she will come off victorious from every danger, and will shine in the world as the sun doth in heaven. Pardon me, fair ladies, if by any carelessness I have done you any displeasure, for with my will and knowledge I never wronged any. And pray unto God for me, that he will please to deliver me out of this prison, whereinto some ill-meaning enchanter hath thrust me; for if I once may see myself at liberty again, I will never forget the favours which you have done me in this castle, but greatly acknowledge and recompense them as they deserve.' Whilst the ladies of the castle were thus entertained by Don Quixote, the curate and barber took leave of Don Fernando and his companions, of the captain and his brother, and of all the contented ladies, especially of Dorothea and Lucinda. All of them embraced, and promised to acquaint one another with their succeeding fortunes; Don Fernando entreating the curate to write unto him what became of Don Quixote, assuring him that no affair he could inform him of should please him better than that, and that he would, in lieu thereof, acquaint him with all occurrences which he thought would delight him, either concerning his own marriage or Zoraida's baptism, or the success of Don Louis, and Lucinda's return into her house.

The curate offered willingly to accomplish to a hair all that he had commanded him; and so they returned once again to embrace one another, and to renew their mutual and complimentary offers. The innkeeper came also to the curate, and gave him certain papers, saying that he had found them within one of the linings of the wallet wherein the Tale of the Curious-Impertinent was had, and that, since the owner did not return to fetch it, he bade him take them all with him; for, seeing he could not read, he would keep them no longer. Master curate yielded him many thanks; and then, opening them, found in the beginning thereof these words, The Tale of Riconete and Cortadillo, by which he understood that it was some history, and collected that it must be a good one, seeing that of the Curious-Impertinent, contrived perhaps by the same author, had proved so well; and therefore he laid it up, with an intention to read it as soon as he had opportunity. Then he mounted on horseback with his friend the barber; and both of them, putting on their masks, that they might not quickly be known by Don Quixote, they travelled after the team, which held on in this order: first went the cart, guided by the carter; on both sides thereof the troopers rode, with their firelocks; then followed Sancho upon his ass, leading Rozinante by the bridle; and last of all came the curate and barber, upon their mighty mules, and with their faces covered; all in a grave posture, and with an alderman-like pace, and travelling no faster than the slow steps of the heavy oxen permitted them. Don Quixote sat with his hands tied, his legs stretched out, and leaning against the bar of the cage, with such a silence and patience as he rather seemed a statue than a man. In this quiet and leisurely manner they travelled for the space of two leagues, when, arriving to a valley, it seemed to their conductor a fit place to repose and bait his oxen; and, acquainting the curate with his purpose, the barber was of opinion that they should yet go on a little farther, because he knew that there lay behind a little mountain, which was within their view, a certain vale, much better furnished with grass than that wherein he meant to abide. The barber's opinion was allowed; and therefore they continued on their travel: when the curate, looking by chance behind him, saw coming after them six or seven men on horseback, and very well appointed, who quickly got ground of them; for they came not the lazy and phlegmatic pace of oxen, but as men that were mounted on canons' mules, and pricked forward with a desire to pass over the heat of the day in their inn, which was not much more than a league from thence. Finally, those diligent travellers overtook our slothful ones, and saluted them courteously; and one of them, that was a canon of Toledo and master of the rest, noting the orderly procession of the cart, troopers, Sancho, Rozinante, the curate and barber, but chiefly the encaged Don Quixote, he could not forbear to demand what meant the carriage of that man in so strange a manner, although he did already conjecture, by observation of the troopers, that he was some notable robber, or other delinquent, the punishment of whom belonged to the Holy Brotherhood. One of the troopers, to whom the demand was made, did answer in this manner: 'Sir, we know not wherefore this knight is carried in this form; and therefore let he himself, who best may, tell you the reason thereof.'

Don Quixote had overheard their discourse, and said, 'If, gentlemen, you be conversant and skilful in matters of chivalry, I will communicate my misfortunes with you; but if you be not, I have no reason to trouble myself to recount them.' The curate and barber, seeing the travellers in talk with Don Quixote, drew near to make answer for him in such sort that their invention might not be discovered; the whilst the canon replied to the knight, and said, 'Truly, brother, I am better acquainted with books of knighthood than with Villalpando's Logic; and therefore, if all the difficulty rest only in that, you may safely communicate whatsoever you will with me.' 'A God's name be it,' quoth Don Quixote; 'you shall therefore understand, sir knight, that I am carried away enchanted in this cage, through the envy and fraud of wicked magicians; for virtue is much more persecuted of the wicked than honoured of the good. I am a knight-errant; but none of those whose names are not recorded in the books of fame, but one of those who, in despite of envy itself, and of all the magicians of Persia, the Brahmins of India, or of the Gymnosophists of Ethiopia, shall hang his name in the temple of eternity, that it may serve as a model and pattern to ensuing ages, wherein knights-errant may view the steps which they are to follow, if they mean to aspire to the top and honourable height of arms.' 'The knight Sir Don Quixote saith true,' quoth the curate, speaking to the travellers, 'that he is carried away in this chariot enchanted, not through his own default or sins, but through the malignant treachery of those to whom virtue is loathsome and valour odious. This is, good sir, the Knight of the Sad Countenance (if you have at any time heard speak of him), whose valorous acts shall remain ensculped in stubborn brass and time-surviving marble, though envy and malice do labour never so much to obscure them.'

When the canon heard the imprisoned man and the three speak thus in one tenor, he was about to bless himself for wonder, and could not conjecture what had befallen him; and into no less admiration were they brought that came with him. But Sancho Panza having in the meantime approached to hear their speech, to plaster up the matter, added: 'Now, sirs, whether you will love me well or ill for what I shall say, the very truth of the matter is, that my lord, Don Quixote, is as much enchanted as my mother, and no more; for his judgment is yet whole and sound—he eats and drinks, and doth his necessities as other men do, and as he himself did yesterday and other days before they encaged him: all which being so, how can you make me believe that he goeth enchanted? for I have heard many persons avouch that enchanted persons neither eat, nor drink, nor speak; and yet, my lord, if he be not thwarted, will talk more than twenty barristers.' And then, turning towards the curate, he said, 'O master curate, master curate do you think that I do not know you? And think you that I do not suppose, yea, and presage whereto these new enchantments are addressed? Well, know then that I know you well, although you cover your face never so much, and that I understand your meaning, how deeply soever you smother your drifts. But in fine, where emulation and envy reign, virtue cannot live; where pinching sways, liberality goes by. A pox take the devil! for, but for your reverence, my lord had e'er this time been wedded to the Princess Micomicona, and I myself had been created an earl at least; for no less might be expected either from the bounty of my lord or the greatness of my deserts. But now I perceive that to be true which is commonly said, "that the wheel of fortune turns about more swiftly than that of a mill," and that they which were yesterday on the top thereof, lie to-day all along on the ground. I am chiefly grieved for my wife and children; for whereas they ought and might hope to see their father come in at his gates made a governor or viceroy of some isle or kingdom, they shall now see him return unto them no better than a poor horse-boy. All which I have urged so much, master curate, only to intimate to your paternity how you ought to have remorse, and make a scruple of conscience, of treating my dear lord as you do; and look to it well, that God do not one day demand at your hands, in the other life, amends for the prison whereinto you carry him, and that you be not answerable for all the succours and good deeds which he would have afforded the world in this time of his captivity.'

'Snuff me those candles,' quoth the barber, hearing him speak so.

'What, Sancho! art thou also of thy master's fraternity? I swear by the Lord, I begin to see that thou art very like to keep him company in the cage, and that thou shalt be as deeply enchanted as he, for the portion which thou hast of humour and chivalry. Thou wast in an ill hour begotten with child by his promises, and in a worse did the isle, which thou so greatly longest for, sink into thy pate.' 'I am not with child by anybody,' said Sancho; 'nor am I a man of humour, to let anybody get me with child, no, though it were the king himself; and although I be poor, yet am I a Christian, and owe nothing to any one; and if I desire islands, others there are that desire worse things, and every one is the son of his own works; and under the name of a man I may become pope, how much more the governor of an island, and chiefly seeing my lord may gain so many as he may want men to bestow them on? And therefore, master barber, you should take heed how you speak; for all consists not in trimming of beards; and there is some difference between Peter and Peter. I say it, because all of us know one another, and no man shall unperceived put a false dye upon me. As concerning my lord's enchantment, God knows the truth; and therefore let it rest as it is, seeing it is the worse for the stirring in.' The barber would not reply unto Sancho, lest that, with his simplicities, he should discover what the curate and himself did labour so much to conceal. And the curate, doubting the same, had entreated the canon to prick on a little forward, and he would unfold to him the mystery of the encaged knight, with other matters of delight. The canon did so, and, taking his men along with them, was very attentive to all that he rehearsed of the condition, life, madness, and fashion of Don Quixote. There did he briefly acquaint him with the original cause of his distraction, and all the progress of his adventures, until his shutting up in that cage; and their own design in carrying him home to his country, to try whether they might by any means find out a remedy for his frenzy. The canon and his men again admired to hear so strange a history as that of Don Quixote; and as soon as the curate had ended his relation, the canon said:

'Verily, master curate, I do find by experience that those books which are instituted of chivalry or knighthood are very prejudicial to well-governed commonwealths; and although, borne away by an idle and curious desire, I have read the beginning of almost as many as are imprinted of that subject, yet could I never endure myself to finish and read any one of them through; for methinks that somewhat, more or less, they all import one thing, and this hath no more than that, nor the other more than his fellow. And in mine opinion, this kind of writing and invention falls within the compass of the fables called *Milesiae,* which are wandering and idle tales, whose only scope is delight, and not instruction; quite contrary to the project of those called *Fabulae Apologae,* which delight and instruct together. And though that the principal end of such books be recreation, yet cannot I perceive how they can yield it, seeing they be forced with so many and so proportionless untruths; for the delight that the mind conceives must proceed from the beauty and conformity which it sees or contemplates in such things as the sight or imagination represents unto it, and all things that are deformed and discordant must produce the contrary effect. Now, then, what beauty can there be, or what proportion between the parts and the whole, or the whole and the parts, in a book or fable wherein a youth of sixteen years of age gives a blow to a giant as great as a tower, and with that blow divides him in two as easily as if he were a pellet of sugar? And when they describe a battle, after that they have told us how there were at least a million of men on the adverse side, yet if the knight of the book be against them, we must of force, and whether we will or no, understand that the said knight obtained the victory through the invincible strength of his arm. What, then, shall we say of the facility wherewithal the inheritrix of a kingdom or empire falls between the arms of those errant and unknown knights? What understanding, if it be not altogether barren or barbarous, can delight itself, reading how a great tower full of knights doth pass through the sea as fast as a ship with the most prosperous wind? and that going to bed a man is in Lombardy, and the next morning finds himself in Prester John's country, among the Indians, or in some other region which never was discovered by Ptolemy, nor seen by Marco Polo? And if I should be answered, that the inventors of such books do write them as fables, and therefore are not bound unto any respect of circumstances or observation of truth, I would reply, that an untruth is so much the more pleasing by how much the nearer it resembles a truth, and so much the more grateful by how much the more it is doubtful and possible; for lying fables must be suited unto the reader's understanding, and so written as that, facilitating impossible things, levelling untrue things, and holding the mind in suspense, they may ravish a more delight, and entertain such manners, as pleasure and wonder may step by step walk together: all which things he that writes not likelihoods shall never be able to perform. And as touching imitation (wherein consists the perfection of that which is written), I have not seen in any books of knighthood an entire bulk of a fable so proportioned in all the members thereof, as that the middle may answer the beginning, and the end the beginning and middle; but rather they have composed them of so many members, as it more probably seems that the authors intended to frame chimeras or monsters than to deliver proportionate figures, most harsh in their style, incredible in exploits, impudent in love matters, absurd in compliments, prolix in battles, fond in discourses, uncertain and senseless in voyages; and finally, devoid of all discretion, art, and ingenious disposition: and therefore they deserve, as most idle and frivolous things, to be banished out of all Christian commonwealths.'

Master curate did listen to the canon with very great attention; and he seemed unto him to be a man of good understanding, and that he had great reason for what he had alleged; and therefore said that, in respect they did concur in opinions, and that he had an old grudge to the vanity of such books, he had likewise fired all Don Quixote's library, consisting of many books of that subject. And then he recounted to him the search and inquisition he had made of them; and which he had condemned, and which reserved: whereat the canon laughed heartily, and said that, 'notwithstanding all the evil he had spoken of such books, yet did he find one good in them, to wit, the subject they offered a good wit to work upon and show itself in them; for they displayed a large and open plain, through which the pen might run without let or encumbrances, describing of shipwrecks, tempests, encounters, and battles; delineating a valorous captain with all the properties required in him—as wisdom to frustrate the designs of his enemy, eloquence to persuade or dissuade his soldiers, ripeness in advice, promptness in execution, as much valour in attending as in assaulting of an enemy; deciphering now a lamentable and tragical success, then a joyful and unexpected event; there a most beautiful, honest, and discreet lady, here a valiant, courteous, and Christian knight; there an unmeasurable, barbarous braggart, here a gentle, valorous, and wise prince; representing the goodness and loyalty of subjects, the magnificence and bounty of lords. Sometimes he may show himself an astrologer, sometimes a cosmographer, sometimes a musician, sometimes a statist, and sometimes, if he please, he may have occasion to show himself a necromancer. There may he demonstrate the subtlety of Ulysses, the piety of Aeneas, the valour of Achilles, the misfortunes of Hector, the treachery of Sinon, the amity of Euryalus, the liberality of Alexander, the resolution of Caesar, the clemency and truth of Trajan, the fidelity of Zopyrus, the prudence of Cato, and finally, all those parts that make a worthy man perfect; one whiles by placing them all in one subject, another by distributing them among many; and this being done, and set out in a pleasing style and a witty fashion, that approacheth as near as is possible unto the truth, will questionless remain a work of many fair drafts, which being accomplished will represent such beauty and perfection as shall fully attain to the best end aimed at in all writing; that is, as I have said, jointly to instruct and delight: for the irregularity and liberality of those books give[s] to the author the means to show himself an epic, lyric, tragedian, and comedian, with all other things which the most graceful and pleasant sciences of poetry and oratory include in themselves; for epics may be as well written in prose as in verse.'

CHAPTER XXI

Wherein the Canon Prosecutes His Discourse Upon Books of Chivalry, and Many Other Things Worthy of His Wit

'SIR, you say very true,' quoth the curate; 'and for this very reason are they which have hitherto invented such books the more worthy of reprehension, because they neither heeded the good discourse, the art, nor the rules by which they might have guided themselves, and by that means have grown as famous for their prose as be the two princes of the Greek and Latin poetry for their verse.' 'I have, for my part,' quoth the canon, 'at least attempted to write a book of chivalry, observing therein all the points by me mentioned; and in truth I have written above a hundred sheets thereof; and to the end that I might try whether they were correspondent to my estimation, I did communicate them both with certain skilful and wise men, that are marvellously affected to that subject, and with some ignorant persons that only delight to hear fanatical inventions, and I have found in them all a great approbation of my labours; yet would I not for all that prosecute the work, as well because it seemed unfit for my profession, as also because I find the number of the ignorant to exceed that of the judicious; and though more good come to a man by the praise of a few wise men, than hurt by the scoffs of a number of fools, yet would I not willingly subject myself to the confused judgment of the senseless vulgar, who commonly give themselves most unto the reading of such books. But that which most of all rid my hands, yea, and my memory, of all desire to end it, was this argument, drawn from our modern comedies, and thus made to myself: If those (as well the fictions as historical ones) are all, or the most part of them, notorious fopperies, and things without either head or foot, and yet are by the vulgar heard with such delight, and held and approved for good; and both the authors that compose them, and actors that represent them, say that they must be such as they be for to please the people's humours, and not more conformable to reason or truth; and that because those wherein decorum is observed, and the fable followed according to the rules of art, serve only for three or four discreet men (if so many may be found at a play) which do attend unto them, and all the rest of the auditors remain fasting, by reason they cannot conceive the artificial contexture thereof; therefore it is better for them to gain good money and means by many than bare opinion or applause by a few. The very same would be the end of my book, after I had used all possible industry to observe the aforesaid precept; and I should remain only for a need, and as the tailor that dwells in a corner, without trade or estimation.

'And although I have sundry times endeavoured to persuade the players that their opinion was erroneous herein, and that they would attract more people and acquire greater fame by acting artificial comedies than those irregular and methodical plays then used, yet are they so wedded to their opinion, as no reason can woo nor demonstration win them from it. I remember how, dealing upon a day with one of those obstinate fellows, I said unto him, "Do not you remember how a few years ago were represented in Spain three tragedies, written by a famous poet of our kingdom, which were such as delighted, yea, and amazed all the auditors, as well the learned as the simple, the exact as the slight ones, and that the players got more by those three alone than by thirty of the best that were penned or acted since that time," "You mean, without question," quoth the actor, answering me, "*Isabella, Phyllis,* and *Alexandra.*" "The very same," quoth I; "and note whether in them were not rightly observed all the rules and precepts of art; and yet thereby they neither wanted any part of their dignity nor the approbation of all the world; so that I infer the fault not to be in the vulgar that covet idle toys, but rather in those which know not how to pen or act any other thing; for no such fond stuff was in the comedy of *Ingratitude Revenged,* nor found in *Numantia,* nor perceived in that of *The Amorous Merchant,* and much less in *The Favourable Enemy,* nor in some others made by judicious poets, which both redounded to their infinite fame and renown, and yielded unto these actors abundant gain." To these I added other reasons, wherewith I left him, in mine opinion, somewhat perplexed, but not satisfied, or desirous to forego his erroneous opinion.'

'Truly, master canon,' quoth the curate, 'you have touched a matter that hath roused an ancient rancour and heart-burning of mine against the comedies now in request, the which is equal to the grudge that I bear to books of knighthood; for, seeing the comedy, as Tully affirms, ought to be a mirror of man's life, a pattern of manners, and an image of truth, those that are now exhibited are mirrors of vanity, patterns of folly, and images of voluptuousness. For what greater absurdity can be in such a subject, than to see a child come out in the first scene of the first act in his swaddling clouts, and issue in the second already grown a man, yea, a bearded man? And what greater vanity than to present before us a valiant old man and a young coward? a layman become a divine? a page a councillor? a king a scoundrel? a princess a scour-kettle? What should I say of the little care had of the due observation of time for the succeeding of that they represent, other than that I myself have seen comedies whose first act began in Europe, the second in Asia, and the third ended in Africa; and truly, if there had been a fourth, it would questionless have finished in America, and by consequence, we should have seen a round walk about the four parts of the world. And feigning an exploit performed in the time of King Pepin or of Charlemagne, they make the principal actors thereof either Heraclius the emperor that entered into Jerusalem bearing of the holy cross, or Godfrey of Bouillon that recovered the Holy Land; many years, yea, and ages having occurred between the times of the one and the other: yea, and the comedy being grounded on a fiction, to attribute unto it the verities of a history, and mingle it and patch it up with pieces of others having relation to different persons and times; and this with no plausible invention, or draft resembling the truth, but rather with palpable, gross, and inexcusable errors. And which is worse, some gulls are found to affirm that all perfection consists herein, and that they are too dainty that look for any other.

'Now, if we would pass further, to examine the divine comedies that treat of God, or the lives of saints, what a multitude of false miracles do the composers devise! what a bulk of matters apocryphal and ill-understood, attributing to one saint the miracles done by another; yea, and in human comedies they presume to do miracles (without further respect or consideration but that such a miracle or show, as they term it, would do well in such a place), to the end that the ignorant folk may admire them, and come the more willingly to them: all which doth prejudice truth, discredit histories, and turn to the disgrace of our Spanish wits; for strangers which do with much punctuality observe the method of comedies, hold us to be rude and ignorant, when they see such follies and absurdities escape us; and it will be no sufficient excuse for this error to say that the principal end of well-governed commonwealths, in the permitting of comedies, is only to entertain the commonalty with some honest pastime, and thereby divert the exorbitant and vicious humours which idleness is wont to engender; and seeing that this end is attained to by whatsoever comedies, good or bad, it were to no purpose to appoint any laws or limits unto them, or to tie the composers to frame, or actors to play them, as they should do: for hereunto I answer, that this end would, without all comparison, be compassed better by good comedies than by evil ones; for the auditor having heard an artificial and well-ordered comedy, would come away delighted with the jests and instructed by the truths thereof, wondering at the successes, grow discreeter by the reasons, warned by the deceits, become wise by others' example, incensed against vice, and enamoured of virtue: all which affects a good comedy should stir up in the hearer's mind, were he never so gross or clownish. And it is of all impossibilities the most impossible, that a comedy consisting of all these parts should not entertain, delight, satisfy, and content the mind much more than another that should be defective in any of them, as most of our nowaday comedies be. Nor are the poets that pen them chiefly to be blamed for this abuse; for some of them know very well where the error lurks, and know also as well how to redress it; but because that comedies are become a vendible merchandise, they affirm, and therein tell the plain truth, that the players would not buy them if they were of any other than the accustomed kind; and therefore the poet endeavours to accommodate himself to the humour of the player who is to pay him for his labour. And that this is the truth may be gathered by an infinite number of comedies, which a most happy wit of this kingdom hath composed with such delicacy, so many good jests, so elegant a verse, so excellent reasons, so grave sentences, and finally, with so much eloquence and such a loftiness of style, as he hath filled the world with his fame; and yet by reason that he was forced to accommodate himself to the actors, all of them have not arrived to the height of perfection which art requires. Others there are that write without any judgment, and with so little heed of what they do, as after their works have been once acted, the players are constrained to run away and hide themselves, fearing to be punished, as often they have been for acting things obnoxious to the prince, or scandalous to some families.

'All which inconveniences might be redressed if there were some understanding and discreet person ordained at the court to examine all comedies before they were acted, and that not only such as were played at the court itself, but also all others that were to be acted throughout Spain, without whose allowance, under his hand and seal, the magistrate of no town should permit any comedy to be played; by which means the players would diligently send their plays to the court, and might boldly afterwards act them, and the composers would, with more care and study, examine their labours, knowing that they should pass the strict censure of him that could understand them; and by this means would good comedies be written, and the thing intended by them most easily attained to, viz. entertainment of the people, the good opinion of Spanish wits, the profit and security of the players, and the saving of the care that is now employed in chastising their rashness. And if the same charge were given to this man, or to some other, to examine the books of knighthood which should be made hereafter, some of them doubtless would be put forth adorned with that perfection whereof you spoke but now, enriching our language with the pleasing and precious treasure of eloquence, and being an occasion that the old books would become obscure in the bright presence of those new ones published, for the honest recreation not only of the idler sort, but also of those that have more serious occupations; for it is not possible for the bow to continue still bent, nor can our human and frail nature sustain itself long without some help of lawful recreation.'

The canon and curate had arrived to this point of their discourse, when the barber, spurring on and overtaking them, said to the curate, 'This is the place I lately told you was fit to pass over the heat of the day in, while the oxen baited amidst the fresh and abundant pastures.' 'It likes me very well,' quoth the curate; and telling the canon what he meant to do, he also was pleased to remain with them, as well invited by the prospect of a beautiful valley which offered itself to their view, as also to enjoy the curate's conversation, towards whom he began to bear a marvellous affection; and lastly, with the desires he had to be thoroughly acquainted with Don Quixote's adventures. Therefore he gave order to some of his men that they should ride to the inn, which was hard by, and bring from thence what meat they could find, sufficient to satisfy them all, because he meant likewise to pass the hot time of the day in that place. To which one of his men did answer, that their sumpter mule was by that time, as he thought, in the inn, so copiously furnished with provision of meat, that, as he supposed, they needed not buy anything there but barley for their mules. 'If it be so,' quoth the canon, 'let our mules be carried thither, and the sumpter one returned hither.'

Whilst this passed, Sancho, being free from the continual presence of the curate and barber, whom he held as suspected persons, thought it a fit time to speak with his lord, and therefore drew near to the cage wherein he sat, and said to him in this manner: 'Sir, that I may discharge my conscience, I will reveal unto you all that hath passed in this affair of your enchantment, which briefly is, that those two which ride with their faces covered, are the curate of our village and the barber, and as I imagine they both are the plotters of this your kind of carrying away, for mere emulation that they see you surpass them both in achieving of famous acts: this truth being presupposed, it follows that you are not enchanted, but beguiled and made a fool; for the proof whereof I will but demand of you one question, and if you do answer me according to my expectation, as I believe you will, you shall feel the deceit with your own hands, and perceive how you are not enchanted, but rather have your wits turned upside-down.'

'Son Sancho, demand what thou wilt,' quoth Don Quixote, 'and I will satisfy thee, and answer directly to thy desire; but as touching thy averment that those which go along with us be the curate and barber, our gossips and old acquaintance, it may well befall that they seem to be such, but that they are so really, and in effect, I would not have thee believe in any manner; for that which thou art to believe and shouldst understand in this matter is, that if they be like those our friends, as thou sayst, it must needs be that those which have enchanted me have assumed their semblance and likeness (for it is an easy thing for magicians to put on any shape they please) thereby to give thee occasion to think that which thou dost, to drive thee into such a labyrinth of imaginations as thou shalt not afterwards know how to sally out, although thou hadst the assistance of Theseus' clue; and withal to make me waver in mine understanding, to the end I may not conjecture from whence this charm is derived unto me; for if thou on the one side dost affirm that the barber and curate of our village do accompany me, and I on the other side find myself encaged, and am so assured of mine own force that no human strength, be it not supernatural, is able thus to encage me, what wouldst thou have me to say or think, but that the manner of mine enchantment exceeds as many as ever I read throughout all the histories entreating of knights-errant which have been enchanted? Wherefore thou mayst very well appease and quiet thyself in that point of believing them to be those thou sayst; for they are those as much as I am a Turk; and, as touching thy desire to demand somewhat of me, speak; for I will answer thee, although thou puttest me questions until to-morrow morning.'

'Our Lady assist me!' quoth Sancho, as loud as he could, 'and is it possible that you are so brain-sick and hard-headed as you cannot perceive that I affirm the very pure truth, and that malice hath a greater stroke in this your disgrace and employment than any enchantments? But seeing it is so, I will prove evidently that you are not enchanted; if not, tell me, as God shall deliver you out of this tempest, and as you shall see yourself, when you least think of it, in my Lady Dulcinea's arms—' 'Make an end of conjuring me,' said Don Quixote, 'and ask me what question thou wilt; for I have already told thee that I will answer with all punctuality.' 'That is it I demand,' quoth Sancho; 'and the thing I would know is, that you tell me, without adding or diminishing aught, but with all truth used or looked for of all those which profess the exercise of arms as you do, under the title of knights-errant.' 'I say,' answered Don Quixote, 'that I will not lie a jot; make therefore a beginning or an end of these demands, for in good sooth thou dost weary me with so many salutations, petitions, and preventions.' Sancho replied, 'I say that I am secure of the bounty and truth of my lord; and therefore, because it makes to the purpose in our affair, I do, with all respect, demand whether your worship, since your encagement and, as you imagine, enchantment in that coop, have not had a desire to make greater or less water, as men are wont to say?' 'I do not understand, good Sancho, that phrase of making water; and therefore explicate thyself, if thou wouldst have me to answer thee directly.' 'And is it possible,' replied he, 'that your worship understands not what it is to make great or little waters? then go to some school and learn it of the boys, and know that I would say, "Have you had a desire to do that which cannot be undone?"' 'Oh, now, now I understand thee, Sancho. Yes, very many times; yea, and even now I have. Wherefore, I pray thee, deliver me from the extremity thereof; for I promise thee I am not altogether so clean as I would be.'

CHAPTER XXII

Wherein the Discreet Discourse That Passed Between Sancho Panza and His Lord Don Quixote Is Expressed

'HA,' quoth Sancho, 'have I caught you at last? This is that which I desired to know, as much as my soul or life. Come now, sir, and tell me, can you deny that which is wont to be said, when a body is ill-disposed, "I know not what ails such a one; for he neither eats nor drinks nor sleeps, nor answers directly to that which is demanded him, so as it seems that he is enchanted"? By which may be collected, that such as neither eat, drink, sleep, nor do the other natural things you wot of, are enchanted; but not those which have a desire as you have, and eat meat when they get it, and drink drink when it is given them, and answer to all that is propounded unto them.' 'Thou sayst true, Sancho,' quoth Don Quixote; 'but I have told thee already that there are divers sorts of enchantments, and perhaps they change with the times from one kind into another, and that now the enchanted use to do all that which I do, although they did not so in times past; and therefore there is no disputing or drawing of conclusions against the customs of the time. I know, and do verily persuade myself, that I am enchanted, and that is sufficient for the discharge of my conscience, which would be greatly burdened if I thought that I were not enchanted, and yet permitted myself to be borne away in this cage idly, and like a coward withholding the succour I might give to many distressed and needy persons, which even at this hour be like enough to have extreme want of mine aid and assistance.' 'Yet say I, notwithstanding,' replied Sancho, 'that for more abundant satisfaction, your worship might do well to attempt the getting out of this prison, the which I do oblige myself with all my power to facilitate, yea, and to get out, and then you may recount eftsoons on the good Rozinante, who also seems enchanted, so sad and melancholy he goes. And this being done, we may again essay the fortune of seeking adventures, which, if it have no good success, we have time enough to return to our cage; wherein I promise, by the faith of a good and loyal squire, to shut up myself together with you, if you shall prove so unfortunate, or I so foolish, as not to bring our designs to a good issue.' 'I am content to do what thou sayst, brother Sancho,' replied Don Quixote; 'and when thou seest opportunity offered to free me, I will be ruled by thee in everything; but yet thou shalt see how far thou art over-wrought in the knowledge thou wilt seem to have of my disgrace.'

The knight-errant and the ill-errant squire beguiled the time in those discourses, until they arrived to the place where the canon, curate, and barber expected them. And then, Sancho alighting, and helping to take down the cage, the wainman unyoked his oxen, permitting them to take the benefit of pasture in that green and pleasant valley, whose verdure invited not such to enjoy it as were enchanted like Don Quixote, but rather such heedful and discreet persons as was his man, who entreated the curate to license his lord to come out but a little while, for otherwise the prison would not be so cleanly as the presence of so worthy a knight as his lord was required. The curate understood his meaning, and answered that he would satisfy his requests very willingly, but that he feared when he saw himself at liberty, he would play them some prank or other, and go whither nobody should ever set eye on him after. 'I will be his surety that he shall not fly away,' quoth Sancho. 'And I also, quoth the canon, 'if he will but promise me, as he is a knight, that he will not depart from us without our consent.' 'I give my word that I will not,' quoth Don Quixote, who heard all that they had said, 'and the rather because that enchanted bodies have not free will to dispose of themselves as they list; for he that enchanted them may make them unable to stir from one place in three days; and if they make an escape, he can compel them to return flying; and therefore, since it was so, they might securely set him at liberty, especially seeing it would redound so much to all their benefits; for if they did not free him, or get farther off, he protested that he could not forbear to offend their noses.' The canon took his hand (although it were bound), and [Don Quixote promised by] his faith and word that he would not depart, and then they gave him liberty; whereat he infinitely rejoiced, especially seeing himself out of the cage. The first thing that he did after was to stretch all his body, and then he went towards Rozinante, and, striking him twice or thrice on the buttocks, he said, 'I hope yet in God and His blessed mother, O flower and mirror of horses! that we two shall see ourselves very soon in that state which our hearts desire; thou with thy lord on thy back, and I mounted on thee, and exercising the function for which God sent me into this world.' And, saying so, Don Quixote with his squire Sancho retired himself somewhat from the company, and came back soon after a little more lightened, but greatly desiring to execute his squire's designs.

The canon beheld him very earnestly, and with admiration, wondering to see the strangeness of his fond humour, and how that he showed, in whatsoever he uttered, a very good understanding, and only left the stirrups (as is said before) when any mention was made of chivalry; and therefore, moved to compassion, after they were all laid down along upon the grass, expecting their dinner, he said unto him, 'Gentleman, is it possible that the idle and unsavoury lecture of books of knighthood hath so much distracted your wit as thus to believe that you are carried away enchanted, with other things of that kind, as much wide from truth as untruths can be from verity itself? Or how is it possible that any human understanding can frame itself to believe that in this world there have been such an infinity of Amadises, such a crew of famous knights, so many emperors of Trapisonda, such a number of Felixmartes of Hircania; so many palfreys, damsels-errant, serpents, robbers, giants, battles, unheard-of adventures, sundry kinds of enchantments, such immeasureable encounters, such bravery of apparel, such a multitude of enamoured and valiant princesses, so many squires, earls, witty dwarfs, viragoes, love-letters, amorous dalliances; and finally, so many, so unreasonable and impossible adventures as are contained in the books of knighthood?

'Thus much I dare avouch of myself, that when I read them, as long as I do not think that they are all but toys and untruths, they delight me; but when I ponder seriously what they are, I throw the very best of them against the walls, yea, and would throw them into the fire if they were near me, or in my hands, having well deserved that severity, as false impostors and seducers of common sense, as broachers of new sects and of uncouth courses of life, as those that give occasion to the ignorant vulgar to believe in such exorbitant untruths as are contained in them; yea, and are withal so presumptuous, as to dare to confound the wits of the most discreet and best descended gentlemen; as we may clearly perceive by that they have done to yourself, whom they have brought to such terms as it is necessary to shut you up in a cage and carry you on a team of oxen, even as one carries a lion or tiger from place to place, to gain a living by the showing of him. Therefore, good Sir Don Quixote, take compassion of yourself, and return into the bosom of discretion, and learn to employ the most happy talent of understanding and abundance of wit, wherewith bountiful Heaven hath enriched you, to some other course of study, which may redound to the profit of your soul; and advancement of your credit and estate. And if, borne away by your natural disposition, you will yet persist in the reading of warlike and knightly discourses, read in the Holy Scripture the Acts of Judges, for there you shall find surpassing feats and deeds, as true as valorous. Portugal had a Viriathus; Rome a Caesar; Carthage a Hannibal; Greece an Alexander; Castile an Earl Fernan Gonzalez; Valencia a Cid; Andalusia a Gonzalo Hernandez; Estremadura a Diego Garcia de Paredes; Xerez a Garcia Perez de Vargas; Toledo a Garcilaso de la Vega; Seville a Don Manuel de Leon: the discourses of whose valorous acts may entertain, teach, delight, and make to wonder the most sublime wit that shall read them. Yea, this were indeed a study fit for your sharp understanding, my dear Sir Don Quixote, for by this you should become learned in histories, enamoured of virtue, instructed in goodness, bettered in manners, valiant without rashness, bold without cowardice; and all this to God's honour, your own profit, and renown of the Mancha, from whence, as I have learned, you deduce your beginning and progeny.'

Don Quixote listened with all attention unto the canon's admonition, and perceiving that he was come to an end of them, after he had looked upon him a good while he said, 'Methinks, gentleman, that the scope of your discourse hath been addressed to persuade me that there never were any knights-errant in the world, and that all the books of chivalry are false, lying, hurtful, and unprofitable to the commonwealth, and that I have done ill to read them, worse to believe in them, and worst of all to follow them, by having thus taken on me the most austere profession of wandering knighthood, whereof they entreat; denying, moreover, that there were ever any Amadises, either of Gaul or Greece; or any of all the other knights wherewith such books are stuffed.'

'All is just as you have said,' quoth the canon: whereto Don Quixote replied thus, 'You also added, that such books had done me much hurt, seeing they had turned my judgment, and immured me up in this cage, and that it were better for me to make some amendment, and alter my study, reading other that are more authentic, and delight and instruct much better.'

'It is very true,' answered the canon.

'Why, then,' quoth Don Quixote, 'I find, by mine accounts, that the enchanted and senseless man is yourself, seeing you have bent yourself to speak so many blasphemies against a thing so true, so current, and of such request in the world, as he that should deny it, as you do, merits the same punishment which as you say you give to those books when the reading thereof offends you; for to go about to make men believe that Amadis never lived, nor any other of those knights wherewith histories are fully replenished, would be none other than to persuade them that the sun lightens not, the earth sustains not, nor the ice makes anything cold. See what wit is there in the world so profound, that can induce another to believe that the history of Guy of Burgundy and the Princes Floripes was not true? Nor that of Fierabras, with the Bridge of Mantible, which befel in Charlemagne's time, and is, I swear, as true as that it is day at this instant? And if it be a lie, so must it be also that ever there was an Hector, Achilles, or the war of Troy; the Twelve Peers of France; or King Arthur of Britain, who goes yet about the world in the shape of a crow, and is every foot expected in his kingdom. And they will as well presume to say that the History of Guarino Mezquino and of the quest of the Holy San Greal be lies; and that for the love between Sir Tristram and La Bella Ysoude, and between Queen Guenevor and Sir Lancelot Dulake, we have no sufficient authority; and yet there be certain persons alive which almost remember that they have seen the Lady Queintanonina, who was one of the best skinkers of wine that ever Great Britain had; and this is so certain, as I remember that one of my grandmothers of my father's side was wont to say unto me, when she saw my matron, with a long and reverend kerchief or veil, "My boy, that woman resembles very much Lady Queintanonina." From which I argue, that either she knew her herself, or at the least had seen some portraiture of hers. Who can, moreover, deny the certainty of the history of Peter of Provence and the beautiful Magalona, seeing that, until this very day, one may behold, in the king's armoury, the pin wherewith he guided and turned anyway he listed the horse of wood whereupon he rode through the air, which pin is a little bigger than the thill of a cart; and near unto it is also seen Babieca his saddle; and in Roncesvalles there yet hangs Orlando's horn, which is as big as a very great joist, whence is inferred that there were Twelve Peers, that there was a Pierres of Provence, that also there were Cids, and other such knights as those which the world terms adventurers. If not, let them also tell me, that the valiant Lusitanian, John de Melo, was no knight-errant, who went to Burgundy, and in the city of Ras fought with the famous lord of Charni, called Mosen Pierres, and after with Mosen Henry of Ramestan, in the city of Basilea, and bore away the victory in both the conflicts, to his eternal fame; and that there was no such curres as the adventures and single combats begun and ended in Burgundy by the valiant Spaniards, Pedro Garba and Guttierre Quixada (from whom I myself am lineally descended), who overcame the Earl of Saint Paul's sons. They may also aver unto me that Don Fernando de Guevarra went not to seek adventures in Germany, where he fought with Micer George, a knight of the Duke of Austria his house. Let them likewise affirm that Suero de Quinonnes of the Pass his jousts were but jests; as also the enterprise of Mosen Louis de Falses against Don Gonzalo de Guzman, a gentleman of Castile, with many other renowned acts, done as well by Christian knights of this kingdom as of other foreign lands, which are all so authentic and true, as that I am compelled to reiterate what I said before, which is, that whosoever denies them is defective of reason and good discourse.'

Full of admiration remained the good canon to hear the composition and medley that Don Quixote made of truths and fictions together, and at the great notice he had of all things that might anyway concern his knighthood-errant; and therefore he shaped him this answer: 'I cannot deny, Sir Don Quixote, but that some part of that which you have said is true, especially touching those Spanish adventurers of whom you have spoken, and will likewise grant you that there were Twelve Peers of France, but I will not believe that they have accomplished all that which the Archbishop Turpin hath left written of them; for the bare truth of the affair is, that they were certain noblemen chosen out by the kings of France, whom they called peers, because they were all equal in valour, quality, and worth; or if they were not, it was at least presumed that they were; and they were not much unlike the military orders of Saint James or Calatrava, were in request, wherein is presupposed that such as are of the profession are, or ought to be, valourous and well-descended gentlemen: and as now they say a knight of Saint John or Alcantara, so in those times they said a knight of the Twelve Peers, because they were twelve equals, chosen to be of that military order. That there was a Cid and a Bernard of Carpio is also doubtless; that they have done the acts recounted of them I believe there is very great cause to doubt. As touching the pin of the good Earl Pierres, and that it is by Babieca his saddle in the king's armoury, I confess that my sin hath made me so ignorant, or blind, that although I have viewed the saddle very well, yet could I never get a sight of that pin, how great soever you affirm it to be.'

'Well, it is there without question,' quoth Don Quixote; 'and for the greater confirmation thereof, they say it is laid up in a case of neat's leather to keep it from rusting.' 'That may very well so be,' said the canon; 'yet by the orders that I have received, I do not remember that ever I saw it: and although I should grant it to be there, yet do I not therefore oblige myself to believe the histories of all the Amadises, nor those of the other rabblement of knights which books do mention unto us; nor is it reason that so honourable a man, adorned with so many good parts and endowed with such a wit as you are, should believe that so many and so strange follies as are written in the raving books of chivalry can be true.'

CHAPTER XXIII

Of the Discreet Contention Between Don Quixote and the Canon, With Other Accidents

'THAT were a jest indeed,' quoth Don Quixote, 'that books which are printed with the king's licence and approbation of those to whom their examination was committed, and that are read with universal delight and acceptance, and celebrated by great and little, rich and poor, learned and ignorant, plebeians and gentlemen, and finally, by all kind of persons of what state or condition soever, should be so lying and fabulous, specially seeing they have such probability of truth, seeing they describe unto us the father, mother, country, kinsfolk, age, town, and acts of such a knight or knights, and that so exactly, point by point, and day by day. Hold your peace, and never speak again such a blasphemy, and believe me; for I do sincerely counsel you, what you, as a discreet man, ought to do herein; and if not, read them but once, and you shall see what delight you shall receive thereby: if not, tell me, what greater pleasure can there be than to behold, as one would say, even here and before our eyes, a great lake of pitch boiling hot, and many serpents, snakes, lizards, and other kinds of cruel and dreadful beasts swimming athwart it, and in every part of it, and that there issues out of the lake a most lamentable voice, saying, "O thou knight, whatsoever thou art, which dost behold the fearful lake, if thou desirest to obtain the good concealed under these horrid and black waters, show the valour of thy strong breast, and throw thyself into the midst of this sable and inflamed liquor; for if thou dost not so, thou shalt not be worthy to discover the great wonders hidden in the seven castles of the seven fates, which are seated under these gloomy waves": and that scarce hath the knight heard the fearful voice, when, without entering into any new discourses, or once considering the danger whereinto he thrusts himself, yea, or easing himself of the weight of his ponderous armour, but only commending himself unto God and his lady mistress, he plunges into the midst of that burning puddle, and when he neither cares nor knows what may befall him, he finds himself in the midst of flourishing fields, with which the very Elysian plains can in no sort be compared. There it seems to him that the element is more transparent, and that the sun shines with a clearer light than in our orb; there offers itself to his greedy and curious eye a most pleasing forest, replenished with so green and wellspread trees as the verdure thereof both joys and quickens the sight, whilst the ears are entertained by the harmonious though artless songs of infinite and enamelled birds, which traverse the intricate boughs of that shady habitation; here he discovers a small stream, whose fresh waters, resembling liquid crystal, slide over the small sands and white little stones, resembling sifted gold wherein oriental pearls are enchased; there he discerns an artificial fountain, wrought of motley jasper and smooth marble; and hard by it another, rudely and negligently framed, wherein the sundry cockleshells, with the wreathed white and yellow houses of the periwinkle and snail intermingled, and placed after a disorderly manner (having now and then pieces of clear crystal and counterfeit emeralds mingled among them), do make a work of so graceful variety as art imitating nature doth herein seem to surpass her.

'Suddenly he discovers a strong castle or goodly palace, whose walls are of beaten gold, the pinnacles of diamonds, the gates of jacinths; finally, it is of so exquisite workmanship, as although the materials whereof it is built are no worse than diamonds, carbuncles, rubies, emeralds, pearls, and gold, yet is the architecture thereof of more estimation and value than they; and is there any more to be seen, after the seeing hereof, than to see sally out at the castle gates a goodly troop of lovely damsels, whose brave and costly attire, if I should attempt to describe, as it is laid down in histories, we should never make an end? And she that seems the chiefest of all, to take presently our bold knight, that threw himself into the boiling lake, by the hand, and carry him into the rich castle or palace without speaking a word, and cause him to strip himself as naked as he was when his mother bore him and bathe him in very temperate waters, and afterwards anoint him all over with precious ointments, and put on him a shirt of most fine, odoriferous, and perfumed sendall; and then another damsel to come suddenly, and cast on his back a rich mantle, which they say is wont to be worth, at the very least, a rich city, yea, and more. Then what a sport it is, when they tell us after, that after this he is carried into another hall, where he finds the tables covered so orderly as he rests amazed! what, to see cast on his hands water distilled all of amber, and most fragrant flowers! what, to see him seated in a chair of ivory! what, to see him served by all the damsels with marvellous silence! what, the setting before him such variety of acates, and those so excellently dressed, as his appetite knows not to which of them it shall first address his hand! what, to hear the music which sounds whilst he is at dinner, without knowing who makes it, or whence it comes! And after that dinner is ended, and the tables taken away, the knight to remain leaning on a chair, and perhaps picking of his teeth, as the custom is, and on a sudden to enter at the hall door another much more beautiful damsel than any of the former, and to sit by his side, and begin to recount unto him what castle that is, and how she is enchanted therein, with many other things that amazed the knight and amazed the readers. I will not enlarge myself any more in this matter, seeing that you may collect out of that which I have said, that any part that is read of any book of a knight-errant will delight and astonish him that shall peruse it with attention. And therefore, I pray you, believe me, and, as I have said already, read those kind of books, and you shall find that they will exile all the melancholy that shall trouble you, and rectify your disposition, if by fortune it be depraved. For I dare affirm of myself, that since I am became a knight-errant, I am valiant, courteous, liberal, well-mannered, generous, gentle, bold, mild, patient, and an endurer of labours, imprisonments, and enchantments. And although it be but so little a while since I was shut up in a cage like a madman, yet do I hope, by the valour of mine arm (Heaven concurring, and fortune not crossing me), to see myself within a few days the king of some kingdoms, wherein I may show the bounty and liberality included within my breast; for in good truth, sir, a poor man is made unable to manifest the virtue of liberality toward any other, although he virtually possess it himself in a most eminent degree;

and the will to gratify which, only consisting of will, is a dead thing, as faith without works. For which cause I do wish that fortune would quickly present me some occasion whereby I might make myself an emperor, that I may discover the desire I have to do good unto my friends, but especially to this my poor squire Sancho Panza, who is one of the honestest men in the world, on whom I would fain bestow the earldom which I promised him many days past, but that I fear me he will not be able to govern his estate.'

Sancho, overhearing those last words of his master's, said, 'Labour you, Sir Don Quixote, to get me that earldom as often promised by you, as much longed for by me; and I promise you that I will not want sufficiency to govern it; and though I should, yet have I heard say that there are men in the world who take lordships to farm, paying the lord so much by the year, and undertaking the care of the government thereof, whilst the lord himself, with outstretched legs, doth live at his ease, enjoying the rents they bring him, and caring for nothing else; and so will I do, and will not stand racking it to the utmost, but presently desist from all administration, and live merrily upon my rent, like a young duke, and so let the world wag and go how it will.' 'That, friend Sancho, is to be understood,' quoth the canon, 'of enjoying the revenues; but as concerning the administration of justice, the lord of the seigniory is bound to look to it: in that is required a sufficiency and ability to govern, and above all a good intention to deal justly and determine rightly; for if this be wanting when we begin, our means and ends will always be subject to error; and therefore is God wont as well to further the good designs of the simple, as to disfavour the bad ones of those that be wittily wicked.'

'I understand not those philosophies,' quoth Sancho Panza; 'but this I know well, that I would I had as speedily the earldom as I could tell how to govern it; for I have as much soul as another, and as much body as he that hath most; and I would be as absolute a king in my estate as any one would be in his; and being such, I would do what I liked; and doing what I liked, I would take my pleasure, and taking my pleasure, I would be content; and when one is content, he hath no more to desire; and having no more to desire, the matter were ended: and then, come the estate when it will, or farewell it, and let us behold ourselves, as one blind man said to another.' 'They are no bad philosophies which thou comest out with, kind Sancho,' quoth the canon; 'but yet for all that, there is much to be said concerning this matter of earldoms.' To that Don Quixote replied, 'I know not what more may be said, only I govern myself by the example of Amadis de Gaul, who made his squire earl of the Firm Island, and therefore I may without scruple of conscience make Sancho Panza an earl; for he is one of the best squires that ever knight-errant had.' The canon abode amazed at the well-compacted and orderly ravings of Don Quixote; at the manner wherewith he had deciphered the adventure of the Knight of the Lake; at the impression which his lying books had made into him; and finally, he wondered at the simplicity of Sancho Panza, who so earnestly desired to be made earl of the county his lord had promised him.

By this time the canon's serving-men, which had gone to the inn for the sumpter mule, were returned; and, making their table of a carpet and of the green grass of that meadow, they sat down under the shadow of the trees, and did eat there, to the end that the wain-man might not lose the commodity of the pasture, as we have said before. And as they sat at dinner, they suddenly heard the sound of a little bell issuing from among the briers and brambles that were at hand; and instantly after they saw come out of the thicket a very fair she-goat, whose hide was powdered all over with black, white, and brown spots: after her followed a goatherd, crying unto her, and in his language bidding her stay or return to the fold; but the fugitive goat, all affrighted and fearful, ran towards the company, and, as it were, seeking in her dumb manner to be protected, strayed near unto them. Then did the goatherd arrive; and, laying hold of her horns (as if she had been capable of his reprehension), said unto her, 'O ye wanton ape, ye spotted elf! how come ye to halt with me of late days? What wolves do scare you, daughter? Will you not tell me, fair, what the matter is? But what can it be other than that you are a female, and therefore can never be quiet? A foul evil take your conditions, and all theirs whom you so much resemble! Turn back, love, turn back; and though you be not so content withal, yet shall you at least be more safe in your own fold, and among the rest of your fellows; for if you that should guide and direct them go thus distracted and wandering, what then must they do? What will become of them?'

The goatherd's words did not a little delight the hearers, but principally the canon, who said unto him, 'I pray thee, good fellow, take thy rest here a while, and do not hasten that goat so much to her fold; for, seeing she is a female, as thou sayst, she will follow her natural instinct, how much soever thou opposest thyself unto it. Take therefore that bit, and drink a draught wherewithal thou mayst temper thy choler, and the goat will rest her the whilst.' And, saying so, he gave him the hinder quarter of a cold rabbit; which he receiving, rendered him many thanks, and, drinking a draught of wine, did pacify himself, and said presently after, 'I would not have you, my masters, account me simple, although I spoke to this beast in so earnest a fashion; for in truth the words which I used unto her were not without some mystery. I am indeed rustic, and yet not so much but that I know how to converse with men and with beasts.' 'I believe that easily,' quoth the curate; 'for I know already, by experience, that the woods breed learned men, and sheepcotes contain philosophers.' 'At the least, sir,' replied the goatherd, 'they have among them experienced men; and that you may give the more credit to this truth, and, as it were, touch it with your own hands (although, till I be bidden, I may seem to invite myself), I will, if you please to hear me but a while, relate unto you a very true accident, which shall make good what this gentleman' (pointing to the curate) 'and myself have affirmed.' To this Don Quixote answered, 'Because the case doth seem to have in it some shadow of knightly adventures I will, for my part, listen unto thee with a very good will: and I presume that all these gentlemen will do the like, so great is their discretion and desire to know any curious novelty which amaze, delight, and entertain the senses, as I do certainly believe thy history will. Therefore begin it, friend, and all of us will lend our ears unto it.' 'I except mine,' quoth Sancho; 'for I will go with this pasty unto that little stream, where I mean to fill myself for three days; for I have heard my lord Don Quixote say that a knight-errant's squire must eat when he can, and always as much as he can, because that oftentimes they enter by chance into some wood so intricate as they cannot get out of it again in five or six days, and if a man's paunch be not then well stuffed, or his wallet well stored, he may there remain, and be turned, as many times it happens, into mummy.'

'Thou art in the right of it, Sancho,' quoth Don Quixote; 'go, therefore, where thou wilt, and eat what thou mayst; for I am already satisfied, and only want refection for my mind, which now I will give it by listening to this good fellow.' 'The same will we also give unto ours,' quoth the canon, who therewithal entreated the goatherd to keep promise, and begin his tale. Then he, stroking once or twice his pretty goat (which he yet held fast by the horns), said thus, 'Lie down, pied fool, by me; for we shall have time enough to return home again.' It seemed that the goat understood him; for as soon as her master sat down, she quietly stretched herself along by him, and, looking him in the face, did give to understand that she was attentive to what he was saying; and then he began his history in this manner.

CHAPTER XXIV

Relating That Which the Goatherd Told to Those That Carried Away Don Quixote

'THERE is a village distant some three leagues from this valley, which, albeit it be little, is one of the richest of this commark: therein some time did dwell a wealthy farmer of good respect, and so good, as although reputation and riches are commonly joined together, yet that which he had was rather got him by his virtue than by any wealth he possessed; but that which did most accumulate his happiness (as he himself was wont to say) was, that he had a daughter of so accomplished beauty, so rare discretion, comeliness, and virtue, that as many as knew and beheld her admired to see the passing endowments wherewith Heaven and nature had enriched her. Being a child she was fair; and, increasing daily in feature, she was at the age of sixteen most beautiful: the fame whereof extended itself over all the bordering villages. But why say I the bordering villages alone, if it spread itself over the furthest cities, yea, and entered into the king's palace, and into the ears of all kind of people, so that they came from all parts to behold her, as a rare thing and pattern of miracles? Her father did carefully keep her, and she likewise heeded herself; for there is neither guard, lock, nor bolt able to keep a maiden better than is her own wariness and care. The wealth of the father and worth of the daughter moved divers, as well of his own village as strangers, to demand her to wife; but he (as one whom the disposal of so rich a jewel most nearly concerned) was much perplexed, and unable to determine on whom, among such an infinite number of importunate wooers, he might bestow her. Among others that bore this goodwill towards her, I myself was one to whom they gave many and very great hopes of good success; the knowledge that her father had of me, my birth in the same village, my descent honest, and blood untainted, flourishing in years, very rich in goods, and no less in gifts of the mind. Another of the same village and qualities was also a suitor unto her; which was an occasion to hold her in suspense, and put his will in the balance, deeming, as he did, that she might be bestowed on either of us two. And that he might be rid of that doubt, he resolved to tell it to Leandra (for so do they call the rich maid which hath brought me to extreme misery), noting discreetly that, seeing we both were equals, it would not be amiss to leave in his dear daughter's power the making choice of whether she liked best: a thing worthy to be noted by all those parents that would have their children marry; wherein my meaning is not that they should permit them to make a bad or a base choice, but that they propound certain good ones, and refer to their liking which of them they will take. I know not what was the liking of Leandra, but only know this that the father posted us off, by alleging the over-green years of his daughter, and using general terms, which neither obliged him nor discharged us. My rival was called Anselmo, and myself Eugenio, that you may also have some knowledge of the persons which were actors in this tragedy, whose conclusion is yet depending, but threatens much future disaster.

About the very same time there arrived to our village one Vincent de la Rosa, son to a poor labourer of the same place, which Vincent returned as then from Italy and divers other countries, wherein he had been a soldier; for, being of some twelve years of age, a certain captain, that with his company passed along by our village, did carry him away with him; and the youth, after a dozen years more, came back again attired like a soldier, and painted with a hundred colours, full of a thousand devices of crystal [and with] five steel chains. To-day he would put on some gay thing, the next day some other, but all of them slight, painted, and of little weight, less worth. The clownish people, which are naturally malicious, and if they have but ever so little idleness or leisure become malice itself, did note and reckon up all his braveries and jewels, and found that he had but three suits of apparel of different colours, with garters and stockings answerable to them; but he used so many disguisements, varieties, transformations, and inventions, which they, as if they had not counted them all, some one would have sworn that he had made show of more than ten suits of apparel, and more than twenty plumes of feathers; and let not that which I tell you of the apparel be counted impertinent, or from the matter, for it makes a principal part in the history. He would sit on a bench that stood under a great poplar-tree in the midst of the market-place, and there would hold us all with gaping mouths, listening to the gallant adventures and resolute acts he recounted unto us. There was no land in all the world whose soil he had not trodden on, no battle wherein he had not been present; he had slain more Moors than the kingdoms of Morocco and Tunis contained, and undertaken more single combats, as he said, than ever did either Gante, Luna, or Diego Garcia de Paredes, and a thousand others whom he named; and yet he still came away with the victory, without having ever left one drop of blood. On the other side, he would show us signs of wounds, which, although they could not be discerned, yet would he persuade us that they were the marks of bullets which he received in divers skirmishes and wars. Finally, he would "thou" his equals, and those which knew him very well, with marvellous arrogancy; and said that his arm was his father, his works his lineage, and that beside his being a soldier he owed not a whit to the king. To these his arrogancies was annexed some superficial skill in music, for he could scratch a little on a gitern, and some would say that he made it speak; but his many graces made not a stop there, for he had likewise some shadows of poetry, and so would make a ballad of a league and a-half long upon every toy that happened in the village.

'This soldier, therefore, whom I have deciphered, this Vincent of the Rose, this braggart, this musician, this poet, eyed and beheld many times by Leandra, from a certain window of her house that looked into the market-place; and the golden show of his attire enamoured her, and his ditties enchanted her; for he would give twenty copies of every one he composed. The report of his worthy acts, beautified by himself, came also unto her ears; and finally (for so it is likely the devil had ordered the matter) she became in love with him, before he presumed to think once of soliciting her. And, as in love-adventures no one is accomplished with more facility than that which is favoured by the woman's desire, Leandra and Vincent made a short and easy agreement; and ere any one of her suitors could once suspect her desires, she had fully satisfied them, abandoned her dear and loving father's house (for her mother lives not), and running away from the village with the soldier, who departed with more triumph from that enterprise than from all the others which he had arrogated to himself. The accident amazed all the town; yea, and all those to whom the rumour thereof arrived were astonished, Anselmo amazed, her father sorrowful, her kinsfolk ashamed, the ministers of justice careful, and the troopers ready to make pursuit. All the ways were laid, and the woods and every other place nearly searched; and at the end of three days they found the lustful Leandra hidden in a cave within a wood, naked in her smock, and despoiled of a great sum of money and many precious jewels which she had brought away with her. They returned her to her doleful father's presence, where, asking how she became so despoiled, she presently confessed that Vincent de la Rosa had deceived her; for, having passed his word to make her his wife, he persuaded her to leave her father's house, and made her believe that he would carry her to the richest and most delightful city of the world, which was Naples; and that she, through indiscretion and his fraud, had given credit to his words, and, robbing her father, stole away with him the very same night that she was missed; and that he carried her to a very rough thicket, and shut her up in that cave wherein they found her. She also recounted how the soldier, without touching her honour, had robbed her of all that she carried, and, leaving her in that cave, was fled away; which success struck us into greater admiration than all the rest, for we could hardly be induced to believe the young gallant's continency; but she did so earnestly protest it as it did not a little comfort her comfortless father, who made no reckoning of the riches he had lost, seeing his daughter had yet reserved that jewel which, being once gone, could never again be recovered. The same day that Leandra appeared, she also vanished out of our sights, being conveyed away by her father, and shut up in a nunnery at a certain town not far off, hoping that time would illiterate some part of the bad opinion already conceived of his daughter's facility. Leandra her youth served to excuse her error, at least with those which gained nothing by her being good or ill; but such as knew her discretion and great wit did not attribute her sin to ignorance, but rather to her too much lightness, and the natural infirmity of that sex, which for the most part is inconsiderate and slippery. Leandra being shut up, Anselmo's eyes lost their light, or at least beheld not anything that could delight them; and mine remained in darkness without light that could address them to any pleasing object, in Leandra's absence. Our griefs increased, our patience diminished; we cursed the soldier's ornaments, and abhorred her father's want of looking to her. To be brief, Anselmo and myself resolved to abandon the village and come to this valley, where, he feeding a great flock of sheep of his own, and I as copious a herd of goats of mine, we pass our lives among these trees, giving vent to our passions, either by singing together the beautiful Leandra's praises or dispraises, or by sighing alone, and alone communicating our quarrelsome complaints with Heaven. Many others of Leandra's suitors have since, by our example, come to these intricate woods, where they use our very exercise; and they are so many as it seems that this place is converted into the pastoral Arcadia; it is full of shepherds and sheepfolds, and there is no one part thereof wherein the name of the beautiful Leandra resoundeth not. There one doth curse her, and termeth her humours inconstant and dishonest; another condemns her of being so facile and light; some one absolves and pardons her; another condemns and despises her, and celebrates her beauty; another execrates her disposition; and finally, all blame, but yet adore her; and the raving distraction of them all doth so far extend itself, as some one complains of disdain that never spoke word unto her, and some one laments and feels the enraged fits of jealousy though she never ministered any occasion thereof; for, as I have said, her sin was known before her desires. There is no cleft of a rock, no bank of a stream, nor shadow of a tree, without some shepherd or other, that breathes out his misfortunes to the silent air. The echo repeats Leandra's name wheresoever it can be formed; the woods resound Leandra; the brooks do murmur Leandra; and Leandra holds us all perplexed and enchanted, hoping without hope, and fearing without knowledge what we fear.

'And among all this flock of frantic men, none shows more or less judgment than my companion, Anselmo, who, having so many other titles under which he might plain him, only complains of absence, and doth to the sound of a rebec (which he handles admirably well) sing certain doleful verses, which fully discover the excellency of his conceit. I follow a more easy and, in mine opinion, a more certain way—to wit, I rail on the lightness of women, on their inconstancy, double-dealing, dead promises, cracked trust, and the small discretion they show in placing of their affections; and this, sir, was the occasion of the words and reasons I lately used to this goat, whom I do esteem but little because she is a female, although she be otherwise the best of all my herd. And this is the history which I promised to tell you, wherein, if I have been prolix, I will be altogether as large in doing you any service; for I have here at hand my cabin, and therein store of fresh milk and savoury cheese, with many sorts of excellent fruit, no less agreeable to the sight than pleasing to the taste.'

CHAPTER XXV

Of the Falling Out of Don Quixote and the Goatherd; with the Adventure of the Disciplinants, to Which the Knight Gave End to His Cost

THE goatherd's tale bred a general delight in all the hearers, but specially in the canon, who did exactly note the manner wherewithal he delivered it, as different from the style or discourse of a rude goatherd, and approaching to the discretion of a perfect courtier; and therefore he said that the curate had spoken very judiciously in affirming that the woods bred learned men. All of them made bountiful tenders of their friendship and service to Eugenio, but he that enlarged himself more than the rest was Don Quixote, who said unto him, 'Certes, friend goatherd, if I were at this time able to undertake any adventure, I would presently set forward, and fall in hand with it to do you a good turn; and I would take Leandra out of the monastery (wherein, without doubt, she is restrained against her will), in despite of the lady abbess, and all those that should take her part; and would put her into your hands, to the end you might dispose of her at your pleasure, yet still observing the laws of knighthood, which command that no man do any wrong and offer violence unto a damsel. Yet I hope in our Lord God, that the skill of a malicious enchanter shall not be of such force, but that the science of a better-meaning wizard shall prevail against him; and whensoever that shall befall, I do promise you my help and favour, as I am bound, by my profession, which chiefly consists in assisting the weak and distressed.'

The goatherd beheld him, and, seeing the knight so ill arrayed, and of so evil-favoured a countenance, he wondered, and questioned the barber, who sat near to him, thus: 'I pray you, sir, who is this man of so strange a figure, and that speaks so oddly?' 'Who else should he be,' answered the barber, 'but the famous Don Quixote of the Mancha, the righter of wrongs, the redresser of injuries, the protector of damsels, the affrighter of giants, and the overcomer of battles?'

'That which you say of this man,' answered the goatherd, 'is very like that which in books of chivalry is written of knights-errant, who did all those things which you apply to this man; and yet I believe that either you jest, or else that this gentleman's head is void of brains.'

'Thou art a great villain,' said Don Quixote, 'and thou art he whose pate wants brains; for mine is fuller than the very, very whore's that bore thee'; and, saying so, and snatching up a loaf of bread that stood by him, he raught the goatherd so furious a blow withal, as it beat his nose flat to his face; but the other, who was not acquainted with such jests, and saw how ill he was handled, without having respect to the carpet, napkins, or those that were eating, he leaped upon Don Quixote, and, taking hold of his collar with both the hands, would certainly have strangled him, if Sancho Panza had not arrived at that very instant, and, taking him fast behind, had not thrown him back on the table, crushing dishes, breaking glasses, and shedding and overthrowing all that did lie upon it. Don Quixote, seeing himself free, returned to get upon the goatherd, who, all besmeared with blood, and trampled to pieces under Sancho's feet, groped here and there, grovelling as he was, for some knife or other, to take a bloody revenge withal, but the canon and curate prevented his purpose; and yet, by the barber's assistance, he got under him Don Quixote, on whom he rained such a shower of buffets, as he poured as much blood from the poor knight's face as had done from his own. The canon and curate were ready to burst for laughter; the troopers danced for sport; every one hissed, as men use to do when dogs fall out, and quarrel together; only Sancho Panza was wood, because he could not get from one of the canon's serving-men, who withheld him from going to help his master. In conclusion, all being very merry save the two buffetants, that tugged one another extremely, they heard the sound of a trumpet, so doleful as it made them turn their faces towards that part from whence it seemed to come. But he that was most troubled at the noise thereof was Don Quixote, who, although he was under the goatherd full sore against his will, and by him exceedingly bruised and battered, yet said unto him, 'Brother devil (for it is impossible that thou canst be any other, seeing that thou hast had valour and strength to subject my forces), I pray thee, let us make truce for one only hour; for the dolorous sound of that trumpet, which toucheth our ears, doth, methinks, invite me to some new adventure.' The goatherd, who was weary of buffeting, and being beaten, left him off incontinently; and Don Quixote stood up, and turned himself towards the place from whence he imagined the noise to proceed; and presently he espied, descending from a certain height, many men apparelled in white, like disciplinants. The matter indeed was, that the clouds had that year denied to bestow their dew on the earth, and therefore they did institute rogations, processions, and disciplines throughout all that country, to desire Almighty God to open the hands of His mercy, and to bestow some rain upon them; and to this effect, the people of a village near unto that place, came in procession to a devout hermitage, built upon one of the hills that environed that valley.

Don Quixote, noting the strange attire of the disciplinants, without any calling to memory how he had often seen the like before, did forthwith imagine that it was some new adventure, and that the trial thereof only appertained to him, as to a knight-errant; and this his presumption was fortified the more, by believing that an image which they carried, all covered over with black, was some principal lady whom those miscreants and discourteous knights did bear away perforce. And as soon as this fell into his brain, he leaped lightly towards Rozinante, that went feeding up and down the plains, and dismounting from his pommel the bridle and his target that hanged thereat he bridled him in a trice; and, taking his sword from Sancho, got instantly upon his horse, and then, embracing his target, said in a loud voice to all those that were present: 'You shall now see, O valorous company, how important a thing it is to have in the world such knights as profess the order of chivalry-errant. Now, I say, you shall discern, by the freeing of that good lady, who is there carried captive away, whether knights-adventurous are to be held in price'; and, saying so, he struck Rozinante with his heels (for spurs he had none), and making him to gallop (for it is not read in any part of this true history that Rozinante did ever pass one formal or full career), he posted to encounter the disciplinants, although the curate, canon, and barber did what they might to withhold him; but all was not possible, and much less could he be detained by these outcries of Sancho, saying, 'Whither do you go, Sir Don Quixote? What devils do ye bear in your breast, that incite you to run thus against the Catholic faith? See, sir, unfortunate that I am! how that is a procession of disciplinants, and that the lady whom they bear is the blessed image of the immaculate Virgin. Look, sir, what you do; for at this time it may well be said that you are not you know what.' But Sancho laboured in vain; for his lord rode with so greedy a desire to encounter the white men, and deliver the mourning lady, as he heard not a word, and although he had, yet would he not then have returned back at the king's commandment. Being come at last near to the procession, and stopping Rozinante (who had already a great desire to rest himself a while), he said, with a troubled and hoarse voice, 'O you that cover your faces, perhaps because you are not good men, give ear and listen to what I shall say.' The first that stood at this alarm were those which carried the image; and one of the four priests which sung the litanies, beholding the strange shape of Don Quixote, the leanness of Rozinante, and other circumstances worthy of laughter, which he noted in our knight, returned him quickly this answer: 'Good sir, if you would say anything to us, say it instantly; for these honest men, as you see, are toiled extremely, and therefore we cannot, nor is it reason we should, stand lingering to hear anything, if it be not so brief as it may be delivered in two words.' 'I will say it in one,' said Don Quixote, 'and it is this: that you do forthwith give liberty to that beautiful lady, whose tears and pitiful semblance clearly denote that you carry her away against her will, and have done her some notable injury; and I, who was born to right such wrongs, will not permit her to pass one step forward, until she be wholly possessed of the freedom she doth so much desire and deserve.' All those that overheard Don Quixote gathered by his words that he was some distracted man, and therefore began to laugh very heartily, which laughing seemed to add gunpowder to his choler; for, laying his hand on his sword, without any more words, he presently assaulted the image-carriers; one whereof, leaving the charge of the burden to his fellows, came out to encounter the knight with a wooden fork (whereon he supported the bier whensoever they made a stand), and receiving upon it a great blow which Don Quixote discharged at him, it parted the fork in two; and yet he with the piece that remained in his hand, returned the knight such a thwack upon the shoulder, on the sword side, as his target not being able to make resistance against that rustic force, poor Don Quixote was overthrown to the ground, and extremely bruised.

Sancho Panza, who had followed him puffing and blowing as fast as he could, seeing him overthrown, cried to his adversary that he should strike no more; for he was a poor enchanted knight, that had never all the days of his life done any man harm; but that which detained the swain was not Sancho's outcries, but to see that Don Quixote stirred neither hand nor foot; and therefore, believing that he had slain him, he tucked up his coat to his girdle as soon as he could, and fled away through the fields like a deer. In the meanwhile Don Quixote's companions did hasten to the place where he lay, when those of the procession seeing them (but principally the troopers of the Holy Brotherhood, with their crossbows) run towards them, did fear some disastrous success; and therefore they gathered together in a troop about the image, and, lifting up their hoods and laying fast hold on their whips, and the priests on their tapers, they awaited the assault, with resolution both to defend themselves, and offend the assailants if they might. But fortune disposed the matter better than they expected; for Sancho did nothing else than throw himself on his lord's body, making over him the most dolorous and ridiculous lamentation of the world, and believing that he was dead. The curate was known by the other curate that came in the procession, and their acquaintance appeased the conceived fear of the two squadrons. The first curate, in two words, told the other what Don Quixote was; and therefore he, and all the crew of the disciplinants, went over to see whether the poor knight were dead or alive; and then might hear Sancho Panza, with the tears in his eyes, bewailing him in this manner: 'O flower of chivalry, who hast with one blow alone ended the career of thy so well bestowed peers! O renown of this lineage, the honour and glory of all the Mancha! yea, and of all the world beside! which, seeing it wanteth thee, shall remain full of miscreants, secure from being punished for their misdeeds! O liberal beyond all Alexanders, seeing thou hast given me only for eight months' service the best island that the sea doth compass or engirt! O humbler of the proud, and stately to the humbled, undertaker of perils, endurer of affronts, enamoured without cause, imitator of good men, whip of the evil, enemy of the wicked, and, in conclusion, knight-errant than which no greater thing may be said!'

Don Quixote was called again to himself by Sancho his outcries, and then the first word that ever he spake was: 'He that lives absented from thee, most sweet Dulcinea, is subject to greater miseries than this! Help me, friend Sancho, to get up into the enchanted chariot again; for I am not in plight to oppress Rozinante's saddle, having this shoulder broken all into pieces.' 'That I will do with a very good will, my dear lord,' replied the squire; 'and let us return to my village with those gentlemen, which desire your welfare so much; and there we will take order for some other voyage, which may be more profitable and famous than this hath been.' 'Thou speakest reasonable, Sancho,' quoth Don Quixote; 'and it will be a great wisdom to let overpass the cross aspect of those planets that reign at this present.' The canon, curate, and barber commended his resolution; and so, having taken delight enough in Sancho Panza's simplicity, they placed Don Quixote, as before, in the team. The processioners returning into their former order, did prosecute their way. The goatherd took leave of them all. The troopers would not ride any farther; and therefore the curate satisfied them for the pains they had taken. The canon entreated the curate to let him understand all that succeeded of Don Quixote, to wit, whether he amended of his frenzy or grew more distracted; and then he took leave to continue his journey. Lastly, all of them departed; the curate, barber, Don Quixote, Sancho Panza, and the good Rozinante only remaining behind. Then the wainman yoked his oxen, and accommodated the knight on a bottle of hay, and afterwards followed on in his wonted [s]low manner, that way which the curate directed. At the end of two days they arrived to Don Quixote's village, into which they entered about noon. This befel on a Sunday, when all the people were in the market-sted, through the middle whereof Don Quixote's cart did pass: all of them drew near to see what came in it, and when they knew their countryman they were marvellously astonished; the whilst a little boy ran home before, to tell the old wife and the knight's niece that their lord and uncle was returned, very lean, pale, disfigured, and stretched all along on a bundle of hay.

It would have moved one to compassion to have heard the lamentations and outcries then raised by the two good women, the blows they gave themselves, and the curses and execrations which they poured out against all books of knighthood; all which was again renewed when they saw Don Quixote himself entered in at their doors. At the news of this his arrival, Sancho Panza's wife repaired also to get some tidings of her goodman; for she had learned that he was gone away with the knight, to serve him as his squire; and as soon as ever she saw her husband, the question she asked him was, whether the ass were in health or no? Sancho answered that he was come in better health than his master. 'God be thanked,' quoth she, 'who hath done me so great a favour; but tell me now, friend, what profit hast thou reaped by this thy squireship? What petticoat hast thou brought me home? What shoes for thy little boys?' 'I bring none of these things, good wife,' quoth Sancho; 'although I bring other things of more moment and estimation.' 'I am very glad of that,' quoth his wife: 'show me those things of more moment and estimation, good friend; for I would fain see them, to the end that this heart of mine may be cheered, which hath been so swollen and sorrowful all the time of thine absence.' 'Thou shalt see them at home,' quoth Sancho, 'and therefore rest satisfied for this time; for and it please God that we travel once again to seek adventures, thou shalt see me shortly after an earl or governor of an island, and that not of every ordinary one neither, but of one of the best in the world.' 'I pray God, husband, it may be so,' replied she, 'for we have very great need of it. But what means that island? for I understand not the word.' 'Honey is not made for the ass's mouth,' quoth Sancho; 'wife, thou shalt know it in good time, yea, and shalt wonder to hear the title of ladyship given thee by all thy vassals.' 'What is that thou speakest, Sancho, of lordships, islands, and vassals?' answered Joan Panza (for so was she called, although her husband and she were not kinsfolk, but by reason that in the Mancha the wives are usually called after their husband's surname). 'Do not busy thyself, Joan,' quoth Sancho, 'to know these things on such a sudden; let it suffice that I tell thee the truth, and therewithal sew up thy mouth. I will only say thus much unto thee, as it were by the way, that there is nothing in the world so pleasant as for an honest man to be the squire of a knight-errant that seeks adventures. It is very true that the greatest number of adventures found out succeeded not to a man's satisfaction so much as he would desire; for of a hundred that are encountered, the ninety-and-nine are wont to be cross and untoward ones. I know it by experience, for I have come away myself out of some of them well canvassed, and out of others well beaten. But yet, for all that, it is a fine thing to expect events, traverse groves, search woods, tread on rocks, visit castles, and lodge in inns at a man's pleasure, without paying the devil a cross.'

All these discourses passed between Sancho Panza and his wife Joan Panza, whilst the old woman and Don Quixote's niece did receive him, put off his clothes, and lay him down in his ancient bed: he looked upon them very earnestly, and could not conjecture where he was. The curate charged the niece to cherish her uncle very carefully, and that they should look well that he made not the third escape, relating at large all the ado that they had to bring him home. Here both the women renewed their exclamations; their execrations of all books of knighthood here came to be reiterated; here they besought Heaven to throw down, into the very centre of the bottomless pit, the authors of so many lies and ravings; finally, they remained perplexed and timorous that they should lose again their master and uncle, as soon as he was anything recovered: and it befel just as they suspected; but the author of this history, although he have with all diligence and curiosity inquired after the acts achieved by Don Quixote in his third sally to seek adventures, yet could he never attain, at least by authentic writings, to any notice of them: only fame hath left in the memories of the Mancha, that Don Quixote after his third escape was at Saragossa, and present at certain famous jousts made in that city, and that therein befel him events most worthy of his valour and good wit; but of his end he could find nothing, nor ever should have known aught, if good fortune had not offered to his view an old physician, who had in his custody a leaden box, which, as he affirmed, was found in the ruins of an old hermitage as it was a-repairing; in which box were certain scrolls of parchment written with Gothical characters, but containing Castilian verses, which comprehended many of his acts, and specified Dulcinea of Toboso her beauty, deciphered Rozinante, and entreated of Sancho Panza's fidelity, as also of Don Quixote's sepulchre, with sundry epitaphs and elogies of his life and manners; and those that could be read and copied out thoroughly were those that are here set down by the faithful author of this new and unmatched relation; which author demands of the readers no other guerdon in regard of his huge travel spent in the search of all the old records of the Mancha, for the bringing thereof unto light, but that they will deign to afford it as much credit as discreet men are wont to give unto books of knighthood, which are of so great reputation now-a-days in the world; for herewith he will rest most fully contented and satisfied, and withal encouraged to publish and seek out for other discourses, if not altogether so true as this, at least of as great both invention and recreation. The first words written in the scroll of parchment, that was found in the leaden box, were these.

THE ACADEMICS OF ARGAMASILLA, A TOWN OF THE MANCHA, ON THE LIFE AND DEATH OF THE VALOROUS DON QUIXOTE OF THE MANCHA: *HOC SCRIPSERUNT*.

An Epitaph of Monicongo, the Academic of Argamasilla, to Don Quixote's Sepulchre.

The clatt'ring thunderbolt that did adorn
  The Mancha, with more spoils than Jason Crete;
The wit, whose weathercock was sharp as thorn,
  When somewhat flatter it to be was meet;
The arm which did his power so much dilate,
  As it Gaeta and Cathay did retch;
The dreadfull'st muse, and eke discreetest, that
  In brazen sheets did praises ever stretch;

He that the Amadises left behind,
And held the Galaors but in small esteem,
Both for his bravery and his loving mind;
He dumb that made Don Belianis to seem;
And he that far on Rozinante err'd,
Under this frozen stone doth lie interr'd.

PANIAGANDO, AN ACADEMIC OF ARGAMASILLA, IN PRAISE OF DULCINEA OF TOBOSO.

SONNET.

She which you view, with triple face and sheen
High-breasted and courageous, like a man,
Is tall Dulcinea, of Toboso queen;
Of great Quixote well-beloved than.
He, for her sake, treads the one and the other side
Of the brown mountain, and the famous fields
Of Montiel and Aranjuez so wide,
On foot, all tired, loaden with spear and shield
(The fault was Rozinante's). O hard star!
That this Manchegan dame and worthy knight,
In tender years, when people strongest are.
She lost by death the glimpse of beauty bright;
And he, although in marble richly done,
Yet love's wrath and deceits she could not shun.

CAPRICHIOSO, THE MOST INGENIOUS ACADEMIC OF ARGAMASILLA, IN PRAISE OF ROZINANTE, DON QUIXOTE HIS STEED.

SONNET.

Into the proud erected diamond stock,
Which Mars with bloody plants so often bored,
Half wood with valour, the Manchegan stuck
His wav'ring standard; and his arms restored:
For them thereon he hung, and his bright sword,
Wherewith he hacks, rents, parts, and overthrows
(New prowesses), to which art must afford
New styles on this new Palatine to gloze.
And if Gaul much her Amadis doth prize,
Whose brave descendants have illustred Greece,
And filled it full of trophies and of fame;
Much more Bellona's court doth solemnise
Quixote. whose like in Gaul or Grecia is;

So honoured none as in Mancha his name.
Let no oblivion his glory stain,
Seeing in swiftness Rozinante his steed
Even Bayard doth, and Briliador exceed.

Burlador, Academic of Argamasilla, to Sancho Panza.

SONNET.

This Sancho Panza is of body little;
But yet, O miracle! in valour great;
The simplest squire, and, sooth to say, least subtle
That in this world, I swear, lived ever yet.
From being an earl, he scarce was a thread's breadth,
Had not at once conspired to cross his guerdon
The malice of the times, and men misled,
Which scarce, an ass encount'ring, would him pardon.
Upon the like he rode: Oh, give me leave
To tell how this meek squire after the horse
Mild Rozinante, and his lord, did drive!
Oh, then, vain hopes of men! what thing is worse?
Which proves us, desired ease to lend,
Yet do at last in smokes our glories end.

Chachidiablo, Academic of Argamasilla, on Don Quixote his Tomb.

AN EPITAPH.

The worthy knight lies there,
Well bruised, but evil-andant,
Who, borne on Rozinante,
Rode ways both far and near.
Sancho, his faithful squire,
Panza yclept also,
Lieth beside him too;
In his trade without peer.

Tiquitoc, Academic of Argamasilla, on Dulcinea of Toboso's Sepulchre.

AN EPITAPH.

Dulcinea here beneath
Lies, though of flesh so round,
To dust and ashes ground
By foul and ugly death.

She was of gentle breath,
And somewhat like a dame,
Being great Quixote's flame,
And her town's glory, eath.

These were the verses that could be read. As for the rest, in respect that they were half consumed and eaten away by time, they were delivered to a scholar, that he might by conjectures declare their meaning; and we have had intelligence that he hath done it, with the cost of many nights' watching and other great pains, and that he means to publish them, and also gives hope of a third sally made by Don Quixote.

GLOSSARY

Abased, lowered.
Aboard, v. *approach,* accost.
Address, direct.
Addressing, straightening.
Admire, astonish.
Admired, in a state of admiration.
Advertised, warned.
Affect, feel affection for.
Affront, encounter.
All and some, total, sum.
Allowed, approved.
Altisonant, high sounding.
Ambages, equivocal courses.
Anatomy, dissection.
Ancient, ensign, standard-bearer.
Animous, spirited.
Answerable, corresponding.
Antic, strange figure.
Antonomasia, the use of an epithet or title instead of a true name.
Apaid, pleased.
Apart, v. *remove.*
Argument, indication.
Arguments, proofs.
Artificial, constructed by rules of art.
Attending, awaiting.
Auctress, authoress.
Authorise (*autorizar*), do credit to, maintain the dignity of.
Aveer (*encaminase*), approach.
Avoided, discharged, emptied.

Bait, v. *attract.*
Beadstones, the larger beads in a rosary.
Beaver, luncheon.
Beaver, lower part of a helmet.
Benefit, profit.
Be-thouing, talking as a superior to an inferior.
Bias, "set out of all bias," disconcert.
Billing, caressing.
Bittor, bittern.
Bombase (*algodones*), a cotton texture.
Brabbles (*pendencias*), quarrels.
Brag, boast.
Break, open, communicate.
Bruit, noise,
Bucking, washing.
Bugles, wild oxen.
Bulks, great bodies.
Burden, chorus, undersong.
Burnished (*flamante*), brilliant, conspicuous.
Buyal, purchase.

Camarades, comrades.
Canvassing, tossing in a blanket.
Capable, able to understand.
Capouch, hood or cape.
Careful, anxious.
Cavillous, apt to raise objections.
Cerecloth, waxed cloth.
Charily, carefully, jealously.
Cheapen, bargain for.
Clew, skein.
Close castle, a kind of helmet.
Cockering, feasting.
Coil, "keep a," make a fuss.
Commark, district.
Commodity, convenience, opportunity, occasion.
Compassive (*compasivo*), sympathetic.
Conclude, finish off, destroy.
Confer, compare.
Confratriety, confraternity.
Cony catching, knavery.
Crackling, talkativeness.
Crowd, fiddle.
Curiosity (*puntualidad*), carefulness.
Curious, painstaking.
Curres, encounters.

Damage, harm, trouble.
Debates, contests.
Debile, feeble.
Delicate, faint, feeble.
Depending, hung up, suspended.
Deputed (*diputo*), set down as, considered.
Detect, reveal.
Dight, array.
Dilate, defer, expound.
Disastrous (*desdichada*), suffering disaster.
Disgrace (*desgracia*), inconvenience, misfortune.
Disgustful, distasteful.

Disgusts, dislikes.
Disventures (*disventuras*), misadventures.
Dodkin (*dos maravedis*), a Dutch farthing.
Doit, a Dutch coin worth about a farthing.
Dolour, grief.
Drafts, designs.
Draughts, devices, tricks.
Drive, hurry on.

Earnest, payment in advance.
Eftsoons, soon after.
Embosk (*emboscasen*), shelter, conceal.
Embushing, concealing.
Empannel, put pannels on an ass.
Emulated, regarded as a rival.
Encask, envelope.
Every foot (*por momentos*), continually.
Exigent, pitch, point demanding action.
Expect, await.
Exprobates, reviles, casts in the teeth.

Facility, looseness.
Facinorous (*facineroso*), evil doing.
Farsed, stuffed.
Fauno, faun, wild creature.
File, thread.
Files (*filos*), edges.
Fluent, stream.
Fond, foolish.
Force, "of force," of necessity.
Forced, stuffed.
Forcible, inevitable.
Foreslows itself, tarries.
Fortitude, luck.
Frequentation, resort, habitation.
Friskles, capers.
Frumps, flouts, insults, slaps.
Fulling mace, hammer for beating clothes clean.

Gallimaufry, hodge-podge, hash.
Gamashoes, leggings.
Gard, trimming.
Gaudeamus, O be joyful.
Gittern, small guitar.
Gratify (*agradecia*), thank for.
Grossly, heavily.
Gusts (*gusto*), pleasures.
Gymnosophists, naked philosophers.
Gypson, gypsy.

Herd, herdsman.
Hight, was called.
Hippogriff, griffin.
His, its.

Ignoring, being ignorant of.
Illiterate, wipe out.
Illude, deceive.
Illuded, frustrated.
Illustrate, render illustrious.
Imbosk, conceal.
Impertinent, unsuitable, inconvenient.
Impregned, burdened.
Imprese (*impresa*), device.
Impudency, unchastity.
Inceasable, incessant.
Incharge, burden.
Ingrateful, ungrateful.
Inhabitable, not habitable.
Intercur, intervene.
Intertexed, interwoven.

Jennet-wise, the stirrups short, the legs trussed up.
Journey, day's fight.

Kenned, knew.
Kennel, dogs.
Key-cold, cold as a key.

Laughsome, ready to laugh.
Leasings, lies.
Lecture, reading.
Let, hindrance.
Links, torches.

Malet, mail, wallet.
Malign (*maligno*), evil spirit.
Marvedi, maravedi, the smallest Spanish coin, half a farthing.
Meddled, intermixed.
Minuity, small matter, detail.
Mochachoes, mustachios.
Mumpsimus, any one who has got hold of a wrong word ("Mumpsimus" instead of "Sumpsimus" in the Mass), an ignorant person.
Murrey, mulberry coloured.
Mushrubs, mushrooms.

Neeze, sneeze.
North, lode-star.
Nousled, nourished, nursed.

Occurred, ran up.
Offend, ward off.
Opinion, reputation.
Oppugning, opposing.

Ordinary, "walked the ordinary" (*habiendo paseado las acostumbradas*), made the rounds, *i. e.*, been exhibited through the streets.

Paragon with, rival.
Particular, in a private station.
Pash, blow.
Pawns, pledges.
Pensative (*pensativo*), pensive.
Period, limit, end.
Pie, magpie.
Pilled, robbed.
Pillow-bere, pillow-case, lady's travelling bag.
Plain, lament.
Plumes, feathers of a bed.
Poor John, a coarse fish.
Portraited, depicted.
Posted off, put off.
Powdering, seasoning.
Presently, immediately.
Prevent, anticipate.
Prevention, prelude.
Price, esteem.
Pricked, rode hastily.
Propension, inclination, affection for.
Prosecuted (*prosiguio*), continued.
Provant, provender, food.
Proverb (*pensamiento*), design.
Publish, show abroad.

Quader, square with, fit in.
Quick, alive.
Quitasoll, parasol.

Raunching, tearing, clawing.
Reasons, arguments.
Rebec, small harp.
Reccheless, thoughtless.
Recchelessness, thoughtlessness.
Receivers, acknowledgments.
Reduce, bring back.
Resolution "in resolution" (*en resolution*), finally.
Respectlessness, absence of respect.
Restiness, obstinacy.
Rounded, whispered.
Rumour, noise, tumult.
Runagates, renegades.

Seconding (*segundar*), repeating.
Securely, without anxiety.
Shot, bill, reckoning.
Sideling, sideways.
Skill, plan, reason.
Skinkers, hard drinkers.
Snaphances, springlocks.
Sort, issue in.
Squamy, scaly.
Staccado, stockade.
Stomach, pride.
Strait, narrow.
Succeeded, befallen, occurred.
Success, event.
Successes, experiences, issues, accidents.
Succory water, chicory-water.

Tables, backgammon.
Tallage, tax.
Terms (*termo*), goal.
Thill, shaft.
Torment, judicial torture.
Tracts, drawing ropes.
Trance, swoon.
Trance (*paso*), plight.
Trances, passages, episodes.
Transversals, side strokes.
Travails, labours.
Treachour, traitor.
Trucks, a kind of billiards.

Umbrills (*quitasoles*), parasols.
Unhappiness, ill-luck, awkwardness.
Unhappy, awkward.
Underprop, support.
Untaxing, without taxing.
Untowardly, crossly.

Vent (*rastrear*), v. *discover*.
Vent (*venta*), tavern.
Viewed, examined.
Virtue, curative quality.

Want, be lacking.
Warder-house, pantry.
Warner, bèadle.
Welted, quilted.
Winches, sharp turns.
Wistly, wistfully.
Wood, mad.
Wreathings, windings.